ABOUT THE AUTHOR

Geoffrey Archer is the former Defence and Diplomatic Correspondent for ITN's *News at Ten*. His work as a frontline broadcaster has provided him with the deep background for his thrillers – the bestselling *Skydancer*, *Shadow Hunter*, *Eagle Trap*, *Scorpion Trail*, *Java Spider*, *Fire Hawk*, *The Lucifer Network* and *The Burma Legacy*. A keen traveller, he now writes full time and lives with his wife and family in Surrey.

By the same author

Eagle Trap
Scorpion Trail
Java Spider
Fire Hawk
The Lucifer Network
The Burma Legacy

SKYDANCER
SHADOW HUNTER

Geoffrey Archer

arrow books

This edition published by Arrow Books in 2005

Arrow Books
The Random House Group Limited
20 Vauxhall Bridge Road, London SW1V 2SA

Random House Australia (Pty) Limited
20 Alfred Street, Milsons Point, Sydney
New South Wales 2061, Australia

Random House New Zealand Limited
18 Poland Road, Glenfield
Auckland 10, New Zealand

Random House (Pty) Limited
Endulini, 5a Jubilee Road, Parktown 2193, South Africa

The Random House Group Limited Reg. No. 954009

www.randomhouse.co.uk

A CIP catalogue record for this book is available from the British Library

Papers used by Random House are natural, recyclable products made from wood grown in sustainable forests. The manufacturing processes conform to the environmental regulations of the country of origin

ISBN 0 09 190729 2

Printed and bound in Great Britain by
Cox & Wyman Ltd, Reading, Berkshire

SKYDANCER

Geoffrey Archer

arrow books

Chapter One

The strengthening south-westerly wind scooped the slate-grey waters of the Gare Loch into small foam-crested peaks. To his right, towards the open sea, the angler watched a stubby naval launch butt its bows into the waves. At the sight of the white ensign streaming from its stern, he turned his head to one side and spat on to the ground in a private ritual. It was still early in the afternoon, but the sky had darkened as if it were dusk. Rain threatened.

The fisherman pulled up the zip of his drab-green waterproof to shut out the early autumn chill, and settled himself on to the canvas seat. His twelve-foot glass-fibre rod reached out from the tree-lined bank, the float cast well out on the water. His tackle box was well stocked, and a small bucket of maggots seethed by his side.

The man seemed curiously inattentive to his float, however, and before casting he had omitted to bait the hook.

'Crawford' was the name the angler used in the seedy drinking places that passed for bars on the Clyde Estuary. He had lived in the area for years, though no one seemed sure of his ancestry. He owned a small motor-boat and sometimes attended lobster-pots – with little enthusiasm.

Crawford found fishing a tough life, and a hard one in which to make money. But he had long since ceased to work at it, apart from for appearance's sake. He had found an easier way to earn the price of a drink – just by watching the comings and goings on the other side of the loch.

The Royal Navy's shore base at Faslane is the home of the 3rd and 10th Submarine Squadrons. To Crawford the vessels that slipped silently to and from the quayside, with its towering cranes, were like iron sharks piloted by silent and secretive men with arrogant eyes.

At first the boats had all looked the same to him, black and sleek with smooth, square fins; but he knew better now, thanks to a man he had met one night in Kath's Bar in Helensburgh. 'Donald' was what he had called himself, but Crawford had not been fooled; the man's accent was foreign.

They had met again the next night and had talked about the sea. Crawford had begun his habitual slander of the men of the Royal Navy, 'toffee-nosed pansies' as he called them. He had loathed them since leaving school, when the Navy had rejected him for service. It had been a bitter blow not to have been accepted; from a young age he had boasted to his classmates that he would be a sailor when he grew up. He had never forgiven the callous indifference of the recruiting officer who had turned him away.

What the foreigner had offered him that second time they met was a chance to get even with the men in dark blue – and an easy way to make money took. 'Donald' had given him pictures of the different submarines that visited Faslane, showing him how to tell them apart. Crawford had agreed to phone London at prearranged times to report what he had seen, and for his trouble 'Donald' came north once a month to hand him an envelope full of banknotes.

The vessel Crawford was studying now, through a small but powerful pair of binoculars focused half-a-mile across the water, was the most deadly submarine of all, a Polaris boat, HMS *Retribution*. Behind the fin, the long blunt-ended casing housing the sixteen nuclear missiles made its identification unmistakeable.

Suddenly he was startled by a noise. He snatched at the bucket of maggots and slipped the glasses under the recess of its base. On the road just twenty yards behind him, a vehicle slowed to a halt, its rattling diesel sounding alarmingly like a police patrol from the dockyard opposite.

Checking that his float was still bobbing freely, he pulled a small square tin from his pocket, and began to roll a cigarette. His heart was pounding, fearing that his trick with the maggot bucket had been spotted. He felt the steely glare of the security men on the back of his neck, and he shivered.

It seemed as if they watched him for a full five minutes. Then he heard the crunch from the gearbox and the judder of the engine as the police van moved on again. When the noise faded he chanced a glance after it, confirming that his identification of the motor had been correct.

The police were ignoring him. He whistled with relief, then drew on his cigarette. The smoke bit sourly into his throat.

There was nothing illegal about fishing in the loch, nor about looking at submarines through binoculars, but if the security men took an interest in him and learned what he did with the information he gathered, he would be in trouble. Crawford did not know exactly who the foreigner was, but he knew damned well where the information went.

He did not consider it *spying*. There was nothing secret about the information 'Donald' wanted. After all, the Navy did not try to hide the comings and goings of their ships. But by ensuring that the 'other side' knew what those self-satisfied submariners were up to, his need for revenge was beginning to be fulfilled.

His brief use of the binoculars was enough for his purposes. He had seen fresh food being taken on board. HMS *Retribution* was making ready for sea. High tide was in two hours; Crawford guessed the submarine planned to sail when it ebbed.

Two days earlier he had watched *Retribution* emerge from the enclosed dock at Coulport, on the other side of the spit of land that separates the Gare Loch from the open sea. He knew it was there that the missiles were stored: the Polaris rockets with their nuclear warheads. 'Donald' had told him the submarines never go to Coulport during normal routine because their missiles are kept on board, sealed beneath deck hatches.

But *Retribution* had gone there, so something was up – something out of the ordinary. 'Donald' had been most interested in that particular news when Crawford had phoned the London number to tell him about it. He had asked him to ring again as soon as the submarine had sailed.

Crawford shivered as the water gusted across the open water. That police patrol was certain to come back again before long. There was only one road around the loch.

He reeled in his line. The hook spun and danced in front of him. He grabbed for it and impaled a pair of maggots on its barb. He would have to be there for a few more hours yet, and the best way to curb the suspicions of the police was to catch some fish.

Two weeks later, in north London, General David Twining, British Army retired, struck out across

Parliament Hill Fields for his early morning constitutional, sucking a throat pastille to counter the effects of the cold, damp air.

The dog at his feet looked ridiculously small to belong to such a tall man. Short-haired and almost legless, the bundle of wiry brown fur darted backwards and forwards across the path, tracing complex and invisible smells.

Mist clung firmly to the ground. It was late October and wet leaves made the path slippery where it passed under the almost bare trees. The sun had only recently risen, and showed no sign yet of burning through the grey.

Twining's bearing was unmistakeably military, his back parade-ground straight. A brown felt hat covered his balding head, and he wore a dark green loden coat, acquired during his days commanding a division of the British Rhine Army. Most mornings he could be seen striding up this path on Parliament Hill, but only by the few who arose as early as he did. Recently his wife had urged him to choose a less lonely route for his morning walk; Hampstead Heath had become a haunt for muggers in the past few months. He had scoffed at her worries, but had to admit to himself that this morning the gaunt branches of the old oaks did look curiously menacing in the fog.

Suddenly his scurrying dog stopped dead in its tracks. Hackles raised like a worn scrubbing brush, the animal began to growl.

'Ollie, you fool! What's the matter?' snapped the retired soldier. He shared some of the dog's alarm, though, and strained to identify the vague noises he could hear above the dull dripping of the wet branches.

His walking stick had a heavy handle carved from bone, and he reversed the cane in his hand, ready to use as a weapon if necessary. The sound was eerie in the gloom – the rustling of paper and the clatter of tin cans. The general's pulse quickened; he was not as young as he once was, and felt unsure whether he could defend himself against determined muggers, whatever blustering assurances he had given his wife.

The dog, still growling, had taken up a position behind his master now, as Twining walked cautiously forward towards the source of the noise. Slowly, through the mist, he began to make out a dark figure rummaging through the contents of a litter bin.

'Huh! It's a bloody tramp!' Twining muttered to himself, slightly ashamed at having allowed himself to fear something worse.

The dog darted forward, hurling a torrent of barks at the figure wearing an oversized black coat, who pulled back in alarm from his investigation of the rubbish. The tramp's face was obscured by upturned lapels and, with a curse and an ill-aimed kick at the dog, he turned and shuffled hurriedly off into the mist.

Ollie made as if to give chase to the departing itinerant, but after a sufficient show of bravery he scurried back to his master, wagging his tail in anticipation of praise.

'Good boy, Ollie! Good boy!' the General murmured, patting the animal as much to steady his own nerves as the dog's.

'Look at this mess!' he exclaimed, as he straightened his back, and stared at the litter bin. In his eagerness to find something of interest, the tramp had strewn its contents all over the path. Twining swore angrily; he loathed litter, and would frequently clear up after untidy tourists on summer evenings here. He bent down and began slowly to collect the rubbish and return it to the bin, taking care there was nothing unsavoury amongst it to foul his pigskin gloves.

Halfway through his task, he suddenly stopped in surprise. In his hand he held something that had been tediously familiar during his military career – a buff-coloured folder with the letters MOD. stamped on it. The initials stood for Ministry of Defence, and the cardboard file looked fresh and clean.

Startled, he opened the folder and took out the single sheet of paper it contained. He had left his reading glasses at home but, holding the document at arm's length, he could still make out the words 'R.V. Separation Mechanism', and the acronym AWRE.

'Good God!' he exclaimed under his breath. 'That's the Atomic Weapons place.'

A small group of protesters had been camping outside the gates of Aldermaston Research Establishment for several years now, on and off. Banners denouncing the evil of nuclear weapons hung on the chain-link fence – next to the camp washing.

Every morning and evening, the protesters' numbers were augmented by a dozen or so local women, who came to wave their placards and to stare in stony reproach at the thousands of Aldermaston employees entering or leaving the establishment. These protesters saw themselves as part of an international sorority struggling to save the world from nuclear destruction. From time to time their activities would feature in the national newspapers, and though the reports were frequently insulting, this only served to strengthen their sense of alienation from the Establishment.

Peter Joyce drove up to the gates of Aldermaston soon after eight o'clock on that particular October morning. He had taken to making an early start in recent months, to cope with the colossal workload that had built up for him. Joyce headed the project to which most of the Aldermaston's extensive facilities were currently devoted – the creation of an advanced new nuclear warhead for the Polaris missiles that Britain had maintained operational for over twenty years.

The design team had been assembled almost overnight two years ago, following a dramatic Government decision to cancel plans for replacing Polaris with the much larger and more sophisticated American Trident missiles. Faced with the danger that new Soviet Ballistic Missile Defences might make the ten-billion-pound Trident obsolete early in the next century, the Government had suddenly decided to save money by modernising Polaris instead.

Peter Joyce was a physicist by training and had developed a knowledge of military electronics that was unequalled in Britain. In his late forties, he looked fit and energetic. His square jaw gave him the appearance of a 1950s cricketer. Several major armaments manufacturers both at home and in the USA had tried to buy his talents over the years, but he had always resisted them. Working for the Government at Aldermaston did little to swell his bank account, but it gave him access to the most advanced technology in the world, the 'cutting edge' of research, with the use of vastly more comprehensive scientific facilities than any commercial arms manufacturer could afford to maintain.

Hundreds of millions of pounds had been spent on buying the most powerful computers in the world, including the massive number-crunching Crays. They had been worked around-the-clock to fulfil the Government's latest requirement: to develop a deception system that would enable the Polaris warheads to penetrate any defences the Soviet Union could devise this century.

It had been no easy task; packing the advanced electronic deception systems into the small nose-cone of a Polaris missile was 'like squeezing a Rolls-Royce engine into a Mini', as Peter muttered to his colleagues whenever the problems seemed insurmountable. But that task had now been nearly completed; unarmed warheads together with their decoy systems were about to be fired off in a Polaris test rocket, for the first time later that week.

Countless times each day, as the test launch drew nearer, Peter ran through his mental checklist, for fear some vital component of the system had been overlooked. To him the development process had been like a chess game, using his brainpower and ingenuity to outwit his Russian opponents. The weapons that he was developing may have the ability to slaughter millions of people, yet for him the exercise of designing them had been almost academic. It was inconceivable, he felt sure, that human beings would ever be mad enough to actually use them.

As he drove in through the gates of Aldermaston, the few dozen placard-waving protesters on the roadside had a rather less optimistic view of human nature. Few of those watching knew the identity or particular importance of the man behind the wheel of the grey Vauxhall. But one woman certainly did – she was his wife.

Sharp at nine o'clock, the Permanent Undersecretary at the Ministry of Defence was at his desk on the sixth floor of the bleak, grey military powerhouse in Whitehall. Sir Marcus Beckett was a punctual man, steeped in the ethic of professionalism and academic excellence by which the British Civil Service likes to think it is characterised.

He was a short man, not quite five feet nine inches in his socks. Self-consciousness at his stature had fuelled his determination to succeed in a career where a height of more than six feet seemed a requisite for rapid promotion.

His last job had been at the Treasury, and he had arrived at the Defence Ministry fired by determination to cut the ever-growing cost of Defence, undaunted by the limited success his predecessors had enjoyed in that same task.

The phone rang just as he was saying 'Good morning' to his secretary. The caller was an anxious clerk in the main reception area downstairs.

'She says there's a retired general called Twining standing at the desk,' the secretary whispered to the PUS, covering the mouthpiece of the phone with her hand. 'He insists on talking to you personally; says it's a matter of national security. She's checked his ID, and he seems genuine.'

Beckett frowned. The country seemed to be full of retired generals, and his own connection with Defence had been too short to give him any memory of a man called Twining.

'Better get him escorted up here,' he muttered eventually, but added sharply, 'Be ready to have him thrown out if he turns out to be a nutter!'

Three minutes later, as General David Twining was ushered into his office, Beckett scrutinised him critically, concluding that the man certainly looked genuine. In two short sentences, the general summarised his military career by way of introduction, then, with a distinct sense of drama, he placed on the civil servant's desk the buff-coloured folder he had found that morning.

'I found this in a rubbish bin on Hampstead Heath.

Parliament Hill to be exact,' he intoned, narrowing his eyes to observe Beckett's reaction.

The civil servant frowned as he opened the folder and stared at the single sheet of paper inside. Suddenly his eyebrows shot upwards in undisguised horror.

'Good Lord!' he exploded. 'In a rubbish bin? Are you sure?'

Twining looked affronted.

'Well of course you're sure. Otherwise you wouldn't be here!'

Beckett swung round sharply to press the switch on his office intercom, asking his secretary to send immediately for the head of security.

'Sit down. Sit down please, General,' he gestured to a chair, while taking a longer and closer look at the document. After a moment he groaned softly. 'This does *not* look good.'

He put the folder down again.

'Anyone else know about this? Was anyone with you when you found it?'

Twining shook his head. 'Only my dog.'

Sir Marcus winced.

There was a respectful tap at the door.

'Come in!' Beckett yelled. 'Ah, Commander Duncan! We've got some work for you, I'm afraid.'

After brief introductions Sir Marcus slipped the buff folder across his desk towards his head of security.

'What, er . . . what do you make of that then?' he asked, after allowing the commander a few moments to study it.

'Well, sir,' Duncan answered grimly, 'I know what it is, and I know which security vault it's come from. What I don't know is what it's doing up here.'

'*He* found it! This morning! Lying around on Hampstead Heath! General Twining here!' Sir Marcus spluttered in his anger and concern. 'How could it have got there, Commander?'

Duncan looked uncomfortable.

'There's clearly been some sort of lapse . . .' he began lamely. 'Clearly a major breach of security. And er . . .' – glancing uneasily towards the retired general – 'I think it's something we should discuss in *private*, if you don't mind, sir.'

'Yes, of course,' Beckett nodded. 'General, would you like to explain to Commander Duncan just exactly what happened this morning, and then we won't need to detain you any further.'

The security man pulled a pad from his pocket and began to take a careful long-hand note of Twining's description of events. Then, with a request that the general keep himself available at home to help investigating officers later, Sir Marcus shook him warmly by the hand and thanked him profusely for his discretion in bringing the document to the Ministry directly.

'Right! Tell me the worst!' Sir Marcus barked as soon as the door had closed behind their elderly visitor.

'It's project Skydancer, sir. Here's the identification code in the bottom right-hand corner. This paper is one of a set of engineering plans – classified "top secret". This is probably a photocopy, but the originals are under the custody of the Strategic Nuclear Secretariat, down on the fifth floor. Must be only a handful of people with access to such a document.'

'Bugger!' Beckett exploded. 'How the hell could this one have got loose?'

Commander Duncan felt a prickling at the back of his neck. By his tone the Permanent Undersecretary almost seemed to be blaming him for it.

'I don't know, sir. Give me a little time and I'll try to find out,' he answered as coolly as he could.

Sir Marcus paced over to the window and stared down at the passing traffic.

'We'd better call a conference, right away,' he decided, turning back towards his desk. 'The key people in Skydancer – I'll get them here, so we can evaluate the seriousness of this business. I mean . . . God Almighty! The whole bloody project might be compromised! It has to be the bloody Russians!'

Peter Joyce squealed the tyres of his car as he turned through the gates of Aldermaston in his hurry to reach the motorway for London. The gaggle of protesters had dispersed by now. The permanent residents of the 'peace camp' were settling down to their morning chores, while the other protesters – including his wife – had gone off to their daily work.

On the insecure telephone line from the Ministry of Defence, Sir Marcus Beckett had been understandably vague about the exact nature of the security breach. But his voice carried an edging of ice which had made that vagueness additionally disturbing.

The road from the atomic weapons plant wound through picturesque villages and over bridges, which were a pleasure to pass on any normal day. But Peter cursed them as he struggled unsuccessfully to overtake a slow-moving lorry. Eventually, with a surge of relief, he swung his car on to the motorway and, pressing his foot to the floor, raced towards the capital. He leaned forward in his seat, concentrating on the road ahead, his dark eyes focusing far in front. Occasionally he lifted a hand briefly to push back the hank of straight brown hair that fell across his forehead.

In less than two hours he had reached the Defence Ministry in Whitehall. In the PUS's office he found himself joined by Alec Anderson, the civil servant at the head of the Strategic Nuclear Secretariat. Unsuspectingly, Anderson had arrived a little late for work that morning, and now looked shocked and confused. He was a policy man, not a technician, and like Sir Marcus Beckett was waiting anxiously for Peter Joyce to reveal whether General Twining's discovery was as significant as they feared.

Several pairs of eyes focused on Joyce's tall figure as he scanned the page of secrets.

'Christ Almighty!' he breathed after the first glance. 'This *is* a page from the Skydancer plans. Shows the re-entry vehicle separation mechanism. The full set describes precisely how the decoy system works, how it can defeat the Soviet defences. This page on its own is sensitive enough, but if someone's given the Russians the full set . . . it'll be a disaster!'

'Well let's not jump the gun,' Beckett countered hurriedly. 'It may not be as serious as that.'

As a personal friend of the Prime Minister, the civil servant was dreading the public outcry and political uproar that could result from a full-blown security leak in his Ministry. The previous government had been brought down by a top-level Soviet infiltration of the security service MI5.

'Commander Duncan,' Beckett turned hopefully to his security chief. 'What have you been able to find out?'

'Well, sir, I checked in the documents register and I've found there are only two sets of these papers in existence, one kept here and the other at Aldermaston. While Mr Joyce was on his way up here, I took the liberty of ringing George Dogson, head of security at AWRE, and got him to check the vaults. Hope you don't mind, Mr Joyce,' he added, looking across.

'Of course not. What did he say?'

'All in order. Nothing missing there. Now, as for the other set, the ones here in MOD, they are kept in a strictly controlled security room, but a room to which dozens of people have access. All of them with top-level clearance, of course. But the nuclear papers are kept in a special filing cabinet there, and the only people with keys to that cabinet are Mr Anderson here and his secretary Miss Maclean.'

'Well.' Alec Anderson felt sweat breaking out on his forehead. 'We'd better go and look, hadn't we?'

Now a deeply unhappy man, he led the commander down to his office, to check the file. Mary Maclean, an attractive dark-haired woman in her late thirties, looked up in surprise at the sight of her principal being escorted into the room by the stern-faced security chief. She blanched when Anderson asked her to collect the Skydancer technical file from the secure room. Closing her eyes momentarily, she seemed to hesitate as if struck by some painful realisation.

The two men watched closely as she slowly opened her desk drawer, took from it a key, then stood up and walked rigidly from the room. Anderson and the commander looked at one another with silent alarm.

'Do you always keep that key in your desk drawer?' the policeman asked her icily when she returned with the file.

'Yes, I do,' Mary Maclean replied defensively. 'But I keep the drawer locked whenever I'm out of the room. And I keep the key to the drawer in my handbag. It's always with me, I can assure you.'

The Commander's heart sank. This simple lapse of security procedures meant that his list of suspects had grown dramatically. Literally dozens of people could have attained access to the vital papers.

He watched intently as Anderson opened the file and checked through the sheaf of papers. The thirty sheets of paper were all numbered – and they were all there.

Duncan then took hold of the file and thumbed through the pages himself, until he found the one that matched the photocopy in the buff folder. Each sheet had been hand-stamped with a Ministry seal. He checked the angle of the imprint on the original and on the copy. They matched perfectly.

'No doubt about that,' he muttered to himself with a certain satisfaction.

'May I . . . may I enquire what this is about?' Mary asked uneasily.

'Someone's got at the file – and copied it,' Duncan responded bluntly.

She gasped. 'And you think it's because . . .' her voice faltered.

'We're not thinking anything yet, Mary,' Anderson interposed as gently as he could.

'Well I should hope not,' she remarked almost indignantly. She had put in long service at the Ministry and was proud of her record. Skydancer had played a significant part in her recent life, and it was not solely because of her professional involvement. In the last three months there had been personal reasons why she found it painful just to hear mention of the project.

From the look on Alec Anderson's face it was beginning to hurt him too.

'Would you mind, Mary?'

Anderson was handing her the file.

'Would you mind putting this back in the vault?'

*

As the two men re-entered the office of the Permanent Undersecretary, Sir Marcus Beckett's face expressed his heartfelt wish that they could have solved the mystery. But the Commander's brooding scowl and Anderson's look of shocked bewilderment soon dashed his hopes.

'How the hell could this have happened?' he demanded when they had told him what they had learned. 'These are about the most sensitive documents in the whole bloody building, for Christ's sake! How on earth could someone make copies without your knowing?'

Anderson made as if to speak, but no words emerged.

'What do you know about this, Anderson?' Sir Marcus continued, looking ready to launch a physical attack on anyone he could hold responsible for the disaster.

'Nothing at all, PUS,' Anderson half stammered in reply. His face was flushed. 'I'm shocked . . . utterly.'

'I'll start a review of procedure immediately, sir,' the security man broke in, eager to press on with a detailed investigation.

'It's a bit bloody late for that!' Beckett snapped. 'The bird seems to have flown!'

He strode across the room to glare angrily out of the window at the Thames Embankment below. Peter Joyce stared at the Undersecretary's hands clasped tightly behind him. The fingers of one hand turned white with the pressure of his grip, and then began to colour again as the sight of the slow-moving river traffic seemed to exert a calming effect.

'All right,' Sir Marcus said eventually, breaking the uneasy silence, 'let's look at the worse case scenario.'

He sat himself at his desk, and drew a blank sheet of paper from a drawer. Then he wrote the figure '1' at the top left-hand corner.

'We have to assume that every page of the document

has been photocopied,' he began. 'There would be little purpose in doing just one, unless someone is simply trying to make a point.' He paused to look round at the expectant faces of the three men opposite.

'Well? Is someone trying to make a point?' he demanded. 'Someone who knew there was a weakness in the security system, and wanted to show it up?'

His enquiry was greeted by murmured denials and frowns.

'What about your secretary, Anderson? Could she be up to something? Any odd behaviour lately? Change of life, that sort of thing?'

'Oh . . . I hardly think so, PUS,' Alec Anderson answered hurriedly. 'She's a bit young for that, and although she's been careless with the keys, I'm sure her loyalty is not in question.'

Anderson cast a furtive glance at Peter Joyce, but the scientist stared back impassively.

Sir Marcus began to write.

'Then we have to assume we are talking about espionage,' he declared. 'The assumption must be that someone had copied the Skydancer plans and is feeding them to the Russians. But why was this single page found in a rubbish bin? Were the Russians meant to pick it up from there? It's damned odd; I mean there must be dozens of safer places to make the handover – why choose a rubbish bin?'

'I've already got someone observing the place, sir,' the Commander interjected, 'in case someone comes looking for the document. But I agree it's an odd place.'

'The big question,' Beckett continued, as if he had not heard what the security man had just said, 'is whether this bungle occurred at the start of the handover process, or whether the Russians already have all or most of the rest of the papers.'

There was no sure answer to that question, but as Peter Joyce had explained, the Skydancer plans were of critical national importance, and if the secrets were already largely in the Russians' hands, several hundred million pounds of taxpayers' money could now have been totally wasted. A political hornet's nest of huge dimensions would be stirred up the moment news of this security leak emerged.

There was a chance, just the slightest chance that the mystery could be solved rapidly, Beckett thought to himself. In which case it might never need to become public knowledge, and the Prime Minister could be spared the damaging publicity and the taunting from the opposition in parliament. He would have to call in the security service immediately, that was clear, but he would hold back from telling his Secretary of State about it in the hope the matter could be quickly resolved, without the politicians' involvement and the inevitable and damaging attention of the media that would follow.

Bringing the meeting to an abrupt end, he instructed his officials to return to their duties, and to discuss the matter with no one other than the men from the security departments. After they left the sixth-floor office, Alec Anderson and Peter Joyce paused in the corridor outside to look at one another uneasily. Each recognised alarm and suspicion on the other's face. Then they nodded at one another and walked off in different directions, without speaking.

Peter Joyce hardly noticed the road as he motored back to Aldermaston. From time to time he touched his forehead to push back those strands of hair that stubbornly refused to grow any way but forwards. His usual air of confidence had largely evaporated that morning.

He was driving back at only half the speed he had maintained on his journey up to London, his mind in turmoil as he began to assess what a devastating blow this security leak was about to deal him. For the moment he was less concerned by the critical national issue of the leakage of nuclear secrets; he was gripped instead by a personal foreboding, a fear that it could emerge that indirectly and unwittingly he himself had been somehow responsible for the leak – and that those closest to him would see this as just retribution on him.

He vividly remembered the day, three months earlier, when he had first taken that set of vital documents up to London. They were to form the core of a top-level briefing of Government ministers who demanded to know in detail what this vast amount of public money had been spent on. He remembered the occasion with painful clarity, because it was the last time he had spent an evening with Mary Maclean – the night on which he had to tell her that their relationship was over.

Their love affair had lasted two years. It had begun almost by accident, and had blossomed freely, without strains and complications, at a period when his marriage to Belinda was proving increasingly stressful. But eventually Mary had begun to make assumptions about their future together, assumptions involving steps he was not prepared to take.

She had been devastated when he had told her their affair must come to an end. It was the night before the ministerial briefing; and he had visited her flat. Guiltily he remembered now that the top secret plans had been in his briefcase all the time. The crazy – but not so crazy – thought now passed through his mind, that she could have copied the papers later and given them to the

Soviets in an act of revenge. 'Hell hath no fury . . .' But no – he could not really believe that.

Peter stamped on the brake pedal and swerved into the left-hand lane, as he realised he was about to overshoot the turning off the motorway. He cut in front of a lorry which hooted loudly.

'Damn!' the scientist hissed. He would end up crashing if he was not more careful. Heading for the country lanes leading back to Aldermaston, he slowed down further, and continued to ponder how events might develop.

His secret affair with Mary Maclean was bound to be uncovered. The security men would question him closely on his care of those secret papers, and be alarmed by what they learned. They would also talk to his wife, and discover she was a confirmed anti-nuclear activist – and an associate of political groupings well to the left of the normal British political spectrum. They might begin to speculate whether it really was only now that those secrets had gone missing, and not months or even years previously.

And what would they say to Belinda? Would the security men ask her how much she knew of her husband's affair with Mary? She had not known anything – Peter was certain of that. But how would she react when she found out? Would she walk out on him? And what of the children, for whose sake he had finally chosen to reject his mistress and preserve his marriage – would he lose them after all?

'What a mess!' he muttered as he finally turned the car through the gates of Aldermaston.

Once back at his desk, he instructed his secretary to discourage telephone callers. Peter Joyce was a methodical man who had spent his working life confronting apparently insoluble problems. Pulling out a thick notepad, he sat back and forced his brain to concentrate. First he had to list and analyse the dangers that both he and the Skydancer project now faced. Then he had to think of ways to counter them, or at least to limit the damage.

Three thousand miles away the surface of the western Atlantic heaved and surged in a long, lazy swell, the aftermath of a depression which had moved off to the east to dump its rain on the soft green hills of Ireland.

Five hundred feet below that surface, the dark, still waters were unaffected by the weather above. It was down there that HMS *Retribution* slipped silently westwards, her 8,400 tons of sleek, black steel propelled by the tireless energy of her nuclear reactor. Longer than a football pitch, the leviathan of the Clyde was in her true element down there, amongst the other weird creatures of the deep that relied on sound, and sound alone, to protect themselves from predators.

And predators there were, in increasing numbers, for these boats and their crews who lived under water for two months at a time. The normal role of ballistic missile submarines like HMS *Retribution* was to lie in wait, lurking in the Atlantic depths far enough from the Russian coast to go undetected, but close enough for the sixteen Polaris missiles on board to stay within range of their targets. To lie in wait in the fervent hope that the very existence of her weapons would deter a war, and that they would never have to fire the rockets that could destroy several Soviet cities and slaughter tens of millions of people.

The predators for HMS *Retribution* were the Russian hunter-killer submarines, whose task was to scour the oceans for Western missile boats. If a war was ever to start, the Russians would try to sink *Retribution* before her deadly missiles could be fired.

The navies of Nato had the reverse task of tracking the Soviet missile boats, and in peacetime the roles of hunter and hunted were constantly rehearsed in a sophisticated game of hide-and-seek.

Evenly placed along the smooth flank of *Retribution*'s hull were small, flat plates, the ears of the submarine which could hear other vessels hundreds of miles away. Trailing behind the boat's fan-like propeller, a cable hundreds of yards long towed an array of hydrophones which could listen for distant sounds, unencumbered by the tiny noises generated by the movement of the submarine itself through the water. This was the most powerful tool of all in the electronic armoury that had enabled the Royal Navy's 'bombers' – as the Polaris boats were called – to stay ahead of the game, to hear the Russians before the Russians heard them, and to remain undetected on their Atlantic patrols.

In the belly of the submarine's massive carcase one hundred and forty-three men lived their lives, apparently oblivious of their great depth under water, the pressure of which was such that, without the protection of the steel hull, it would crush them to death within seconds.

It had been nearly two weeks since they had last seen daylight, and Commander Anthony Carrington, the captain of *Retribution*, was looking forward to smelling fresh air again. He had just announced on the boat's public address system that they were due to dock in Port Canaveral, Florida, the following day. An air of anticipation and readjustment had immediately swept through the boat.

Cut off as they were from the regulating influence of the sun, the crew's time on board was broken into periods of work and periods of rest, rather than of day and night. Men found it easy to lose their sense of time. Now, though, with the prospect of shore leave imminent, they began to adjust their watches from Greenwich Mean Time to the hours observed in the girly-bars of Florida.

Information about the submarine's activities was strictly rationed on board to those few who needed to know. On a normal patrol the majority of the crew would have no knowledge whereabouts they were in the world's oceans. On this voyage, though, the entire company had been informed they were heading for America, and all knew from past experience that meant they were going to use the American Eastern Test Range, and fire a missile. Only a handful of officers and specialist technicians, however, knew that the missile would be carrying the new Skydancer warhead, on which hundreds of millions of pounds of income tax had been spent in recent years.

'What's the latest from the sound room?' Carrington quietly asked the officer of the watch, as he prepared to leave the control room and return to his cabin.

'Plankton are being a bit noisy, sir, but not much else,' the young lieutenant joked. 'Oh, about an hour ago we heard a Benjamin Franklin boat passing us in the other direction. About a hundred miles south of us. Presumably heading for her patrol area over our side of the pond.'

The Benjamin Franklins were American submarines carrying Trident missiles, and the signal-processing computer on board *Retribution* had automatically identified the vessel from a library of acoustic signatures. Analysis by microprocessors meant that almost every vessel could be positively identified from its individual sounds, and all but the very latest Russian submarines had their tell-tale noises recorded.

'All right, OOW., I shall be in my cabin,' Carrington told his junior as he weaved his tall shape past the shiny periscopes which had not been raised from their rests since *Retribution* left the Clyde two weeks earlier.

Moving from one part of this submarine to another was easy compared to the traditional diesel-electric boats with their narrow gangways, claustrophobic hatches, and bunks amongst the torpedo tubes. Being six feet four inches tall, Carrington was grateful to have command of a nuclear-powered vessel which was almost as spacious as a surface ship. His cabin, though, only had room for a small desk apart from his bunk, and he found it cramped for his tall frame.

He sat at that desk and turned the pages of his log, reflecting on a voyage which had been exceptionally full of incident. The problems had started the moment they had left the Clyde. A Russian submarine had been heard nosing around just outside the estuary, clearly hoping to tail the Polaris boat out on to patrol. The Royal Navy still made the proud boast that none of their 'bombers' had ever been successfully tracked by the Russians, and they were prepared to go to extreme lengths to maintain that record.

Another British nuclear-powered submarine – a hunter-killer boat similar in size and sound to the *Retribution*, but carrying torpedoes rather than ballistic missiles – had been called back from patrol near Iceland to act as a decoy. Using the cover of a noisy cargo ship to drown its own propeller sounds, the submarine had slipped unnoticed into the Clyde, and had then immediately turned out to sea again. Pretending to be the *Retribution*, it had led the Russian shadow on a wild-goose chase round the Scottish islands, while the Polaris boat itself had slipped unnoticed into the deep waters of the Atlantic.

Two weeks was much longer than was needed to cross the ocean, but HMS *Retribution* had just been modified and refitted, requiring a long series of tests and sea trials to be undertaken. These had been the cause of Commander Carrington's second major headache.

The *Retribution* was over twenty years old, and so was most of her missile-launching equipment. The grafting of new systems on to old often produced teething problems, and with the vital test launch of the new Skydancer warheads coming up, Carrington had been determined that if the firing failed, it would not be because of inadequate practice with the systems beforehand. During their journey across the Atlantic they had repeatedly run through the complex countdown procedures. On the first four successive runs, four different electronic faults had appeared which could have caused an abort if the launch had been for real. The engineers had sweated and cursed as they grappled with the printed-circuit panels. Eventually they had solved all the problems, but only after four perfect tests did the captain consider they were ready.

'Can I bring you a cuppa tea, sir?' the chief steward poked his head round the cabin door, which had been left half open.

'Ready for the rock shrimps?' the commander asked, when the tea was brought in. They were a speciality around Cape Canaveral.

'Er . . . well, I'm a steak man myself, sir,' the steward answered with a grin of anticipation of his run ashore.

'You should try 'em. They steam them in beer, you know.'

'Yes sir, I know. Some of the lads go for them, but me . . . well, I know what I like.'

*

When Alec Anderson arrived home that evening from one of the most harrowing days he had ever spent at the Ministry of Defence, he had timed his return to the house in North London to coincide with the moment when his wife Janet would be too preoccupied with the children to bother him with questions. He knew he could not disguise his anxiety, and if he had to tell her what had happened that day, she would make matters worse with her worrying.

Anderson was aged thirty-seven and had been doing very well in his career as a civil servant. He had enjoyed a succession of good promotions through a wide variety of departments – just what was needed if he was to succeed in reaching the top of the professional tree, and he was an ambitious man.

The position he now held as head of the Strategic Nuclear Secretariat had been one of the ripest plums on that tree, and he had plucked it eagerly when offered to him some six months earlier.

'Hullo. You're early,' Janet called from upstairs. The sound of running bathwater and the high-pitched chatter of his two small daughters told him that his return had been well timed.

'Had to bring some work home,' he shouted up to her. 'I'll be in the library.'

'Library' was a somewhat pretentious word for the front room of their suburban Edwardian house, but it was the place where he kept his father's old roll-top desk and the few possessions that he really valued. On the shelves of a glass-fronted mahogany cabinet there were rows of leather-bound volumes in varying states of repair, and most of the Latin text-books from his schooldays. On the walls hung his most prized items of all, miniature paintings that he had collected over the past fifteen years – delicate watercolours of lakes and castles painted by Victorian artists making the Grand Tour of Europe.

He rolled open the lid of the desk and switched on the brass lamp that shone down on to the tooled green-leather interior, marked with the ink stains of past decades. From his briefcase he pulled a file, and spread it open before him. His eyes did not focus on the printed pages, though; the file was there only to provide an excuse for the seclusion that he sought.

Anderson had always favoured Britain being a true nuclear power. Having developed the technology in the first place, it would undermine the country's stature to abandon it, he believed. He had always argued his case forcefully in the Ministry with those of his colleagues who considered a British nuclear deterrent redundant alongside the massive American arsenals. His fluent advocacy of the case had clearly played a part in his selection for his present job.

He even used to expound his arguments regularly at the dinner table when they had guests round, much to Janet's annoyance. She hated to think of the horror that would be unleashed if such weapons were ever used, and preferred to shut her mind to the whole issue. To her there were innumerable more pleasant topics of conversation, and secretly she rather regretted that Alec had gained his last promotion.

Nevertheless Janet adored her husband, devoting all her energies to him, their home, and their two girls aged seven and nine. She had never been academic by nature; much of her education had been directed towards learning the social graces. She knew she was in no way an 'intellectual' companion for Alec, and she loathed 'women's-libbers', because they made her feel guilty at being so satisfied with the life she had chosen.

Although content to have an adoring wife – and to an

extent his ego demanded that his female companion should be his intellectual inferior – Anderson occasionally found that the mundane level of their conversation and her clinging lack of independence grated on his nerves. He longed secretly for the mental companionship he had experienced in his boarding-school, something he had never been able to recapture in his adult life. The closest he ever came to that now was his regular escape from domestic claustrophobia on Friday nights, when he would visit the local pub and relax with a group of male friends, drinking draught bitter and playing bar billiards.

Suddenly, however, the world had become threatening. He was under suspicion. Friends were becoming enemies, and the bright future he had envisaged was now clouded by uncertainty. As he stared absently at his father's old gold-plated pen-stand, and fiddled nervously with a bottle of ink, he realised how important to him were those three members of his family splashing the bathwater upstairs. Whatever their inadequacies, they were devoted to him, and he needed that devotion more than anything else.

'I'm sorry, darling. I had to see to the children,' Janet bustled into the room, her sleeves rolled up and her arms still red from their immersion in the hot water. 'Can I get you a drink or something? And how awful that you have to work this evening . . .'

She stopped in mid-flow when she saw his face so drained of colour, and the haunted look in his eyes.

'Alec, you look dreadful,' she exclaimed. 'What on earth's happened?'

For a few seconds he stared at her without answering.

'Oh, it's nothing much,' he answered eventually, trying to smile confidently. 'Just some papers that have gone missing from the office, and I've got to try to figure out how it happened.'

Peter Joyce turned the car gently into the driveway to his house, anxious for the wheels not to scatter gravel on to the lawn, where it would blunt the blades of his mower. Built in the previous century, his home had originally been a small farm, but when Peter had bought the property it had been left with just over an acre of ground. During the years of their occupancy the Joyces had developed the land lovingly.

At the side of the house he had built a double garage, one half of it occupied by a small sailing boat on a trailer, which Peter raced at a nearby lake during the summer months. The other garage space was empty. The Citroën was not there, so Belinda would not be at home to greet him. He parked his own car next to the boat, swung the jacket of his grey herring-bone tweed suit over his shoulder, and walked through the back door of the garage into the large rear garden. In the flower bed to the left, under the partial shade of an oak tree, the buds on the azaleas were setting well, ready for the following spring. He looked beyond them to the half-completed greenhouse at the far end of the lawn, and wondered when he would next find time to continue with its construction.

'Daddy!' A yell of enthusiasm burst through the kitchen doorway as thirteen-year-old Suzanne ran out to greet him.

'Sylvie and I are doing our homework, groan, groan!' She reached up to hug him. 'And Mark is out playing football. But Mummy's late as usual.'

Peter put his arm round her shoulder and they walked back into the house. Suzanne adored her father, whereas at fifteen her elder sister had grown more circumspect – involved with boyfriends of whom her father disapproved and holding rebellious young views about the Establishment which he represented.

'Shall I make you a cup of tea?' the thirteen-year-old suggested.

'No, I think it would be better if I made it myself and you got on with your homework,' Peter replied kindly, patting her gently on the backside. She smiled selfconsciously, pulling her shoulders back so that her developing breasts gave shape to her school blouse, and set off back to her bedroom, grumbling quietly.

Peter found it both pleasing and sad to see the second of his daughters turning from a child into a woman. He wondered how long it would be before she too began to find fault with him, like her elder sister.

He filled the electric kettle at the sink and plugged it into the mains. While waiting for it to boil, he eased himself on to a chair at the kitchen table. A cork pinboard on the wall opposite was plastered with 'Ban the Bomb' posters, and notices announcing the dates of forthcoming protest meetings.

Peter was forty-eight and had been married for nearly twenty years. Staring at those posters which criticised his lifetime's work, he reflected on how much had changed since he had first met Belinda.

Brought up in a middle-class district on Tyneside, he had moved south after graduating, to take up a research post at Imperial College London. Belinda had been working there as a laboratory assistant.

She had undoubtedly been one of the most attractive women in the college; he had first spotted her in the canteen. A frequent focus of attention when students and lecturers gathered for lunch, her face was oval and her chestnut hair shoulder-length. He remembered how her skin had looked so perfectly smooth, without need of make-up, her lips wide and sensual. Her dark brown eyes had seemed to extend an invitation, yet promised a challenge too.

The third time he had seen her there, she was sitting alone at a table. He had stifled his shyness and had carried his tray across the room to join her. She had smiled at him encouragingly, and it had been easy to chat to her. She was sharp and witty, yet with an attractive sense of reserve. In those days he had tended to express himself in bursts of wild enthusiasm, and she had found that exciting.

A relationship had developed quickly. They had become lovers within a few days. It was the 1960s, when the moral climate was newly liberated, and before long they had been sharing a two-roomed flat together.

There was a click as the boiling kettle switched itself off. He stood up, dropped a tea bag into a mug, and extracted a milk bottle from the fridge. Giving the tea a few moments to brew, he looked through the window into the garden. He loved his home; it was peaceful, secure and permanent. Those early days with Belinda seemed like distant history to him now. They had been carefree in some ways, he supposed, but uncertain too. The relationship had begun so quickly that he always suspected it could end just as suddenly.

Life with Belinda had been fun then, and that fun had lasted for a long time. They had lived together for over a year before marrying. The ceremony had been brief and simple, one Saturday morning. They had invited only their closest relatives to the register office, and had not bothered with a honeymoon. They had felt no different after the wedding, which had somehow seemed wrong at the time, and they had spent the next few days fearing the marriage had been a mistake. Before long, though, their relationship had developed a new sense of security. Peter went on to establish his career at Aldermaston, and Belinda decided to become pregnant.

For the next ten years or so she had devoted herself almost exclusively to motherhood, immersing herself in its ethos. Breast-feeding the three babies had come easy to her; she had studied manuals on child-rearing. She also turned her hand to horticulture, and a large corner of the garden had been cultivated to make the family self-sufficient in vegetables. She had baked bread enthusiastically, had woven and knitted. But this total involvement with creation had produced a traumatic and unexpected effect on her relationship with Peter. Originally they had seen eye to eye on most issues, but motherhood had changed Belinda; her concept of morality had grown radically different from her husband's.

The crunch had come five years ago when Belinda had grown bored and dissatisfied by her 'earth-mother' role and decided to find a job.

As he drank his tea, Peter could still sense the surprise he had felt when she had confronted him with this. What a fool he had been for not anticipating it. He had been away for a few days attending a conference, and had returned home to find her in a state of obvious agitation.

'Peter, we've got to talk,' she had announced while he was still hanging up his coat. There was a tremor in her voice.

'Why? What's happened?' he had answered instinctively. He feared some family catastrophe. The children were nowhere to be seen.

'Where are they all?'

'They're staying with friends for the night – I thought it best.'

'What are you on about, love?' he pressed, seizing her by the shoulders and peering anxiously into her hostile eyes.

Belinda had twisted herself from his grip.

'I can't go on like this anymore!' she had burst out theatrically, tears brimming. 'This lie! We're living a lie, don't you see?'

Stunned, he had followed her into the kitchen.

'Don't be so bloody melodramatic! What are you talking about?' He was tired and unready for a confrontation.

'You . . . your work . . . what you're doing at Aldermaston . . . it's wrong, it's criminal. It's immoral! You're planning genocide . . . mass murder. You spend your days working out how to do it. It's evil, don't you see?'

Peter then shook his head in disbelief. His work had never before been an issue between them. They had hardly ever discussed it.

'Don't be daft!' he had countered cautiously. 'You know bloody well that isn't true!'

His wife had clenched her fists in a gesture of controlled fury.

'Don't you tell me what I do or do not know to be true! I'm not one of your damned computers! You haven't programmed me, you know!' She began to shout. 'You've no idea what I think about most things – things that are really important.'

'And that's my fault?' he snapped back.

'Yes! . . . well, partly.'

She had been thrown for a moment, then continued.

'You gave up being interested in my views years ago. And I . . . well, I suppose I just kept them bottled up.'

He had stared at her blankly.

'Oh boy,' he finally breathed. 'What brought all this on? Have you joined CND or something?'

She glared at him defiantly.

'Yes. As a matter of fact I have.'

Then he had begun to pace round the kitchen.

'Okay, okay. Let's talk then. Let's get it over with. Firstly, let me make it clear that there's nothing immoral about my work. Everything I do is aimed at *preventing* people from killing one another – *stopping* them going to war. I . . . I'm not planning genocide, for God's sake!'

'I know that that's what you believe, Peter,' Belinda answered, controlling her voice with difficulty. 'But I am also very, very sure that you are wrong, terribly and fatally wrong. When a weapon gets invented, eventually it gets used. That, sadly, is human nature.'

'Except the nukes! For over forty years the world has had nuclear weapons and never used them!'

'Hiroshima?'

'It's because of Hiroshima that they've never been used since!' he had shouted in exasperation.

Belinda's shoulders slumped. Her eyes had filled with a great sadness.

'You're wrong, Peter.' Her voice trembled. 'One day, perhaps not very far in the future, mankind will prove that you're wrong. Millions will die, and you and people like you will be responsible.'

Her words had felt like a kick in the stomach.

Suddenly, though, her resolve had crumpled. She rushed towards him, flinging her arms around his neck and sobbing against his chest. For several minutes she clung to him, weeping uncontrollably.

Eventually her tears had subsided.

'I didn't want to hurt you, darling,' she stammered, strands of hair sticking to the tear-stains on her cheeks. 'I love you, you see. I love you as much as ever. Which is why it hurts so much to feel what I feel.'

She had begged him to change his job, to take up some other scientific work not involved with weaponry. But he had dismissed her appeal, and instead had sought to change her new-found attitude by reasoning – then by pouring scorn on her ideas.

But soon he realised that to be self-defeating. She was not susceptible to his arguments any more. A deep rift seemed to have opened up between them, and as the ensuing days passed he realised it was permanently to affect their relationship. Worse still, the lack of consensus on this fundamental issue had spawned disagreements on other subjects too.

They had nevertheless tried to be 'adult' about it, assuring one another there was no need for their relationship and their love to change just because of differing viewpoints That had not worked out either. Belinda had already set up for herself a job at a local craft workshop, learning to turn wood on a lathe. She had made friends there with a group of militant feminists deeply involved in radical anti-nuclear protest. The house had begun to fill with posters and books describing the horrors of Hiroshima and Nagasaki, and they had soon begun to argue over the effect this dispute would have on their children.

Peter was brought back to the present by the sound of car tyres on the drive, and the spluttering engine note of Belinda's ancient Citroën 2cv. He walked to the front door and saw that their eleven-year-old son Mark was sitting in the car with her. She must have called in for him at the sports-field on her way home.

'Just look at this creature,' she called to no one in particular as she entered the house, holding the boy at arm's length. 'The school showers have broken down again. Ever seen anything so disgusting?'

Peter could see the broad grin half-hidden by the mud on his son's face, a grin that seemed almost attached to his prominent ears. The blue and white football kit was caked with mire.

'Playing in goal again?' he asked.

''Sright. Only let one through, too,' Mark answered proudly, stripping off his clothes and dropping them on the kitchen floor.

'Straight into the bath with you,' his mother replied, pushing him towards the stairs.

Belinda walked past her husband and headed for a kitchen cupboard.

'Like one?' she asked over her shoulder, holding up a bottle of red wine.

'Why not,' he replied, taking two glasses down from a shelf.

Belinda found some peanuts in the larder and poured them into a bowl which she placed on the table.

'Why the special treats?' he asked with irony.

'Thought you might need them. I have a feeling you've had rather a busy day.'

His arm froze, halfway through lifting the glass to his lips. What did she know, and how did she know it?

'You were seen leaving the base in a very great hurry this morning,' she continued, smiling at his consternation. 'Looking rather anxious, according to witnesses.'

Her insistence in calling the research establishment 'the base' annoyed him intensely. It sounded so military.

'I thought your lot were all washing their smalls at that time of the day,' he countered. She raised an eyebrow warningly. 'I had to go to London at short notice,' he countered, wondering how much to tell her at this stage.

'Trouble at mill?' she asked flippantly.

'You could say that. Security scare. I, er . . . ought to warn you,' he went on hesitantly, 'that we may get some security people coming round here asking questions.'

Belinda stared at him in astonishment, a mouthful of wine unswallowed. She gulped hard, and placed her glass back on the table.

'What sort of security scare,' she questioned.

'Papers,' he answered vaguely. 'Seems as if someone has copied some classified papers and left them lying around.'

Belinda frowned. 'Is that serious? And what do you mean "lying around"? Where exactly?'

Peter hesitated. He was not supposed to discuss the matter.

'In a rubbish bin,' he stated flatly.

Belinda eyed him thoughtfully for a moment, then she began to laugh.

'It's not funny, love,' he growled.

'Oh, yes, it is,' she exploded. 'I've been telling you to put your work there for years!'

He stared at her forlornly. This woman for whom he still had so much affection, despite the distance that had grown between them, had no concept of the seriousness of the situation, no idea of the thunderstorm of unhappiness likely to burst over their heads at any minute. He agonised whether to tell her about Mary Maclean before she learned about his affair from someone else.

Belinda stopped laughing abruptly. Peter's face normally expressed a self-confidence bordering on cockiness, but there was no sign of that now. Instead she recognised an emotion she'd rarely seen there before. Fear.

'Can't you tell me more about it?' she asked with sudden concern.

'Not yet,' he replied firmly.

Anyone observing the MI5 man since he arrived at the Defence Ministry late that morning could have been forgiven for thinking that he did not seem to be reacting very quickly to the disastrous situation confronting the Strategic Nuclear Secretariat. Commander Duncan of the Ministry police had telephoned the Security Service as soon as that morning meeting in the Permanent Undersecretary's office had concluded. John Black had arrived within thirty minutes of the commander's call, and to Duncan's annoyance, had insisted on turning one of the senior secretaries in the police section out of her office so that he could use her desk and telephone.

It was as if Black was setting up camp, Duncan thought to himself as he watched the MI5 man unload the contents of his briefcase, including a plastic sandwich box, a vacuum flask and, most extraordinary of all, an ashtray.

'Can't stand those chipped-glass things the Civil Service provides,' Black explained.

His own had a porcelain base and a chromium-plated lid with a knob which, when pressed, spun the cigarette end out of sight.

'If I conceal the evidence I feel less bad about the amount I smoke,' he joked.

Duncan reckoned Black was in his late forties. He had a square, featureless face, greasy hair cut short at the back, and skin of the grubby grey colour and dead texture that characterises a heavy smoker. His eyes were contemptuous and mocking.

'How much have you uncovered so far, then?' John

Black demanded eventually, his lunch safely stowed away in a drawer.

The Commander was senior in age and rank to the MI5 man, but now felt more like a junior constable as he reported all that he knew of the affair and detailed the investigations he had already set in motion.

John Black was the head of a counter-espionage section at 'C' Branch in the Security Service, dealing with Government ministries. To his colleagues at the Curzon Street headquarters he appeared a bit of a loner and rather antisocial. A good investigator, they would concede, but he seldom drank at the pub after work or partook of the in-fighting that was normal life for MI5.

Recently, Black's reticence and secretiveness had even made him a suspect in an internal investigation at MI5. A defecting 'trade counsellor' from the Soviet Embassy in London had revealed the KGB had a highly placed agent in MI5. Circumstantial evidence had seemed to point to Black after three successive cases that he had been working on were broken by the Russians at an early stage. He had been suspended from duty for several weeks. Eventually Black's name had been cleared, however. A Russian double agent in Moscow had identified Black's own head of department as being in the pay of Moscow for over ten years. The affair had caused such political uproar that first the Home Secretary and then the Prime Minister had resigned.

Early that evening Black sat on his own in his office at the Defence Ministry. Most of the thousands who worked there daily had left for home. He inhaled deeply from a cigarette whose glowing end was nearly burning his fingers, savouring the bitterness of the smoke, and then ground the butt into the ashtray. As he slammed his palm down on the knob, the metal plate spun unevenly; the realisation that the bowl was nearly full caused him to wince.

The pocket notebook open in front of him had its pages half covered with untidy geometric patterns, subconsciously sketched as he had repeatedly pondered the circumstances of this curious case.

There was nothing normal about it; it did not have the 'feel' of a professional espionage operation. Yet for copies of the missile plans to have been made at all, it must have taken organisation and a treacherous intent, he concluded. But a rubbish bin? Why on earth did *one* page of the plans turn up in a rubbish bin? And what about the other pages? Why weren't they all together?

He had not been at all surprised when Duncan informed him that the Ministry policeman watching the spot on Parliament Hill had reported no sign of anyone subsequently searching there for the file. The vital clue that could crack this case did not lie out on the ground – of that Black was certain. It lay in someone's mind.

In a space still left between the angular shapes on his notebook page, John Black wrote the name 'Mary Maclean', and underlined it. The woman had been as white as a sheet when she was summoned into his office for an interview, and desperately contrite. She clearly expected instant dismissal from the Civil Service for her carelessness with the secret file keys. Mary Maclean had given every appearance of wanting to co-operate, he remembered, and yet her answers to his questions had seemed hesitant and incomplete. There was something she was holding back, of that he was certain. The woman had a secret, and he did not care for people with secrets.

Black took another pen from his inside jacket pocket. In ink of a different hue, he drew a frame round the name he had written, and then began to colour the letters, in such a way that the words 'Mary Maclean' cast a red shadow.

For Mary Maclean the click of the door closing firmly behind her in her garden flat in Chiswick was the most comforting sound she had heard all day. She leaned her head against the door in relief at being home, and snapped the lock shut, holding her finger against it for several minutes as if afraid it might slip open again. She swallowed hard and clenched her teeth against the tears she could feel welling up – tears of anger and self-pity.

Then pulling herself together, Mary Maclean headed for the kitchen. She reached up to the cupboard over the sink and took down a bottle of gin and then another of tonic. She was in a state of shock after the day's events, and was finding it hard to think clearly. She had felt like such a criminal to be interrogated first by Commander Duncan and then by that sinister security man, John Black.

Dropping an ice-cube into the full glass, she took it into the living room and collapsed on the small sofa facing the French windows. The leaves of the flowering cherry-tree outside were deep red and gold, and they were beginning to carpet the lawn. She loved her garden and could sit gazing at it for hours. The autumn colours were so beautiful, yet in a way she dreaded seeing them each year; they reminded her that time was passing and that she faced a lonely future.

'How could I have been so stupid?' she murmured bitterly.

Keeping that key in her desk drawer had seemed sensible enough at the time. She had dreaded losing it if she had carried it around with her as she was supposed to do. Carrying the key to the desk instead had seemed a lesser risk somehow. If she lost that, at least the secret papers would still be safe – or so she had reasoned.

The two policemen were clearly unimpressed by this logic, however, and had treated her with scorn and contempt. They had not actually accused her of stealing the documents, but had implied it was primarily her fault that someone else had been able to.

She had mixed her drink with almost as much gin as tonic, and now felt the alcohol spread its comforting relaxation through her limbs.

Mary Maclean was thirty-eight years old and had never married, though there had been a couple of opportunities when she could have done. Each time she had hesitated, unable to make the final commitment. The intensity of feeling she wanted had not been there. She longed for contact with men she could admire, forthright and intellectually dynamic, but those who actually approached her tended to be the opposite, looking to her to inspire and direct their lives.

She had a pleasant face, more attractive for its character than for outright beauty. Her brown hair had a natural wave, and she had concealed recent grey strands by judicious application of henna. Her grey eyes had a look of intelligent intensity which some men found appealing and others unnerving. She wore bright, plain colours and she would not stand out in a crowd, but then she never wanted to.

The beginning of her love affair with Peter Joyce had been totally unexpected. For several years she had known him only on an official basis, whenever he visited the Ministry for meetings. She had assumed he was already married, and had never particularly considered whether or not she found him attractive.

But then, two years ago, Peter was in Whitehall for a routine conference one afternoon when a sudden drivers' strike had paralysed the railways. He had come up to London by train, and in the chaos of the emergency the Ministry had no official car or driver spare to take him home. It was already late, and since he had to be in London again the following day, he had decided to find a cheap hotel for the night. By chance he had asked Mary to help him, and she had successfully found him one among those listed in the yellow pages. He thanked her profusely and was on the point of leaving her office when he turned back on impulse.

'Why don't you join me for dinner this evening?' he had asked hesitantly. 'I hate going to restaurants on my own.'

To her own surprise she had accepted immediately, and then became embarrassed by her eagerness.

They chose a busy little Italian restaurant in Bayswater. Inevitably their conversation had centred on common ground at first, the Ministry and its curious workings. He had been amusingly indiscreet about the way politicians could be manipulated by the technical departments, and she had found her own humour growing waspish as she talked of the odd personalities she encountered in her work. Their conversation had ranged widely after that. They had laughed a lot, and been reflective too. They had compared their upbringings, his in the steely clamour of Tyneside, hers in the quieter comforts of a London suburb. The food had been passable and they had been well into their second bottle of Valpolicella by the time the bill arrived.

It had still been daylight outside, on a fine summer's evening, and they had decided to go for a walk; their second bottle only half consumed, Peter had taken it with him, she remembered. Strolling along the railings by Hyde Park, Mary had burst out giggling.

'Just look at you with that bottle sticking out of your

pocket!' she had exclaimed. 'If you're not careful I'll ring the *Daily Mirror* and get them to come and take a picture of you. It'd look good on the front page with "Britain's Mr H-Bomb" beneath it!'

'But they'd brand you as a Russian spy!' he had countered, smiling.

She had slipped her arm through his, and before long they headed to his hotel to finish the wine. There had been just one glass in his room, so they shared it. It had been years since she had felt so at ease with a man.

'I want to make love to you,' he had said suddenly.

The hotel bedroom was cramped, and had smelled of stale pipe-smoke. She had blinked at him in momentary surprise.

'I . . . I think I'd like that.'

It had seemed as if her voice answered without her brain instructing it. His invitation had been so casual and so natural that it appeared simple, yet quite unlike her to agree so readily.

She had already known he was married – he had talked about his family during dinner – but on that evening such knowledge seemed no barrier. Normally she would never have considered such spontaneous intimacy with a man – particularly a married man. But somehow this had not felt like adultery; simply a natural conclusion to an extraordinarily pleasant evening.

It had not stayed so simple however. Perhaps it might have done if they had merely said goodbye the following morning, and returned to their previous official relationship across the desk in the Defence Ministry, but everything had been too good that evening for them not to want to repeat it.

Peter had arranged to stay in London again a few weeks later, and he contacted Mary discreetly a week in advance. On that second meeting she had asked him more about his wife. She had not intended to at first, but she felt she had to know more.

At first he had joked about his continuing disagreements with Belinda, and the irony of a nuclear weapons specialist being married to an ardent disarmer. Mary had seen behind the humour, though, and realised his marriage was in serious trouble. Instinct had told her to be cautious, but already she was in the grip of a sexual longing the strength of which she had never experienced before.

'Damn you, Peter!' Mary cursed in retrospect, tightly pinching the bridge of her nose to try to hold back the tears now relentlessly filling her eyes. 'It's all your fault!'

She picked up the glass from the coffee table and downed the rest of the gin.

'Oh hell!' she shouted out loud, tempted to hurl the glass across the room.

Three months had passed since he had told her their affair must end, but that still hurt. Feelings of hatred for him alternated with a passionate craving to win him back again. She had been trying to put it all behind her, but now she would not be allowed to. The investigators were starting to pry – and sexual indiscretion would attract them like bees to honey. Her affair with Peter had been so private and secret; now it would become public knowledge.

Mary clasped her arms tightly round her chest and shivered. She stared at the silent telephone, willing it to ring, willing it to be Peter at the other end.

Chapter Two

Following a day of acute anxiety, Sir Marcus Beckett had just fallen into an uneasy sleep at his Buckinghamshire home. The telephone woke him abruptly soon after midnight. His wife groaned and pulled a pillow over her ear.

'Great Middleton 2367,' he mumbled automatically into the mouthpiece.

'Sir Marcus?' came a crisp voice. 'Downing Street here.'

'Oh? Oh yes!' he answered, adrenalin pumping into his veins.

'I have the PM for you, sir. Just a moment,' the telephonist continued smoothly. There was a click and the sound of an extension ringing.

'Marcus? Are you awake?' a familiar voice bellowed into his ear.

'I am now,' he answered quietly, struggling to guess the significance of the call.

'What the hell's going on, Marcus? Have you seen the *Daily Express*?'

'We, er . . . we don't get the papers until morning out here, Prime Minister,' he winced, dreading what was to follow.

'H-bomb secrets in litter bin. Defence Ministry secrets probe! That's what the bloody thing says! First edition. All over the front page!' the head of the Government was yelling down the line.

Beckett guessed that a few whiskies had been consumed that evening before the early copies of the Fleet

Street papers had been delivered to Downing Street.

'Oh, dear God!' Sir Marcus groaned. 'How the hell did that get out?'

'More to the point, why the hell didn't I know about it?'

'I . . . I'd hoped it was a minor matter, a mistake . . . and could be cleared up without bothering you,' he explained lamely.

'Minor?' the PM shrieked even louder. 'Doesn't sound minor to me! Bloody retired general spouting his mouth off to the papers about how he found a diagram for the new missile warheads on Parliament Hill. You call that minor? What's the matter with you, Marcus?'

'General Twining talked to the press? I don't believe it!' Beckett gasped.

'Well, you'd better believe it, Marcus! So get your finger out of Doris's bum, and come over here right away!'

With that, the phone at the other end was slammed down. That man could be disgustingly crude at times, Beckett brooded to himself as he pulled on his clothes.

It was raining hard as he drove himself towards the capital. Normally he would be conveyed by a Ministry chauffeur, but there was no way of getting his driver to come round to collect him in the middle of the night at such short notice. He was driving his wife's rusty old Fiat, which he now realised had a decidedly worn exhaust. He would take some pleasure in driving it straight into Downing Street and parking right outside Number 10, something normally unheard of for private cars. He hoped the racket of the exhaust would wake up the whole of Westminster.

His mind had fully cleared now, and he had determined to counter the PM's anger with aggression. After all, he had been acting in his friend's best interest, trying to keep this business out of the political arena. The man should be grateful instead of downright rude, he thought.

'Good morning, Sir Marcus,' exclaimed the policeman at the Whitehall end of Downing Street, looking uneasily at the car the civil servant was driving. The officer had been warned to expect this late-night visitor, and reluctantly agreed that he could park outside Number 10, but not for too long. He winced at the throaty roar that proceeded on down the street.

In the event, two hours passed before Beckett emerged again, a chastened man. The Prime Minister had been totally unconvinced by the arguments for keeping him in the dark, and he was summoning a full-scale crisis meeting later that morning. It was nearly 4 a.m., and Sir Marcus decided there was no point in returning to his bed. The PM wanted to see all his top officials immediately after breakfast, so Beckett drove across Whitehall to the slab-sided building which controlled Britain's defences. He went straight up to his office on the sixth floor to prepare for the meeting. There were several phone calls he would have to make before long.

By 7.30 a.m. that same newspaper headline had also caused consternation at the Royal Navy's Headquarters at Northwood. Polaris missile submarines are sent their orders from inside a deep concrete bunker there, hidden in the leafy suburban hills north-west of London. The Commander-in-Chief of the Royal Navy Fleet read the *Daily Express* over his toast and marmalade, sitting at breakfast under the carefully restored

Adam ceiling of his elegant official residence a short distance from the command centre.

Scalding his mouth on coffee sipped too eagerly, he hurriedly scanned the rest of the paper, but found no other reference to the story.

The admiral was acutely concerned to know more, remembering that HMS *Retribution* was now approaching the final proving trials of the new Skydancer warheads. Rising from the table, he strode to his study to telephone the First Sea Lord at his official residence in Admiralty Arch overlooking the Mall.

'Good morning, First,' the C-in-C began. 'I hope I'm not disturbing your breakfast.'

'Don't worry,' Admiral Baker replied. 'Had my breakfast ages ago. Been up for hours. Got a morning call from Marcus Beckett at six o'clock. I suppose you're ringing about the same thing.'

'The story in the *Express* – I assume you've seen it?'

'Certainly have!' Admiral Baker confirmed. 'The PM is calling a crisis meeting at 9.30, so it looks serious. Whatever you do, don't let them go ahead with that test until you've found out how bad things are.'

The Royal Navy was extremely proud of its role as keeper of the British Strategic nuclear deterrent. If the weapon's secret new ability to penetrate the strengthened Soviet defences had been lost to the Russians, it could be like cutting off Samson's hair, the two admirals agreed. If that happened, the damaging effect on the Navy's status could be dramatic.

Precisely at half-past nine, eight men sat themselves down at the table in the Cabinet Room at 10 Downing Street. The angriest of them was Michael Hawke, the Secretary of State for Defence, who was clearly furious that his most senior civil servant had failed to inform him of such a monumental security breach. Hawke had entered politics late in life, and was fiercely ambitious. The fact that the Prime Minister had learned of this security leak before he had would not look good on his record.

The most unhappy man at the table was the Permanent Undersecretary himself, whose efforts to keep the politicians out of the investigation had failed so dismally.

They all stood up as the Prime Minister stormed in. It was the sort of formality he expected in his efforts to show that he was as tough and domineering as the woman who had preceded him in office.

Sir Richard Sproat, Director of MI5, was the first to be called on. Conscious of heading an organisation for which he was still struggling to regain public confidence, he looked uncomfortable as he admitted their investigations had made little progress.

'We have learned one thing,' he assured the meeting. 'The *Daily Express* got their story from some anonymous caller with a well-spoken voice. An English voice at that. He rang their defence correspondent. The quotes from General Twining were then elicited by a newspaper reporter posing on the telephone as someone from the Defence Ministry seeking clarification on precisely where the document had been found. The general was most indignant to find himself quoted all over the *Express* this morning, and he is demanding that the Government refer the matter to the Press Council.'

Most of those sitting around the table had felt themselves to be victims of the media at some stage in their careers, and there was a murmur of agreement.

'It's still far from clear what this security leak amounts to,' Sproat continued. 'Some or all of the plans for the new Polaris warheads have apparently been photocopied, and one page has mysteriously found its way in a Defence Ministry folder to a rubbish bin on Hampstead Heath. Now this may well have been a dead-letter box, and the handover to some foreign power may have been aborted by the tramp – we haven't traced him yet, by the way – and by the general taking his morning constitutional. We don't know that for sure – but there could well be some other explanation, too. We're putting out feelers both here and abroad to discover if the Soviets are really behind it, and whether or not they've already received other pages from the blueprint.'

'The point is this,' the Prime Minister broke in, aggravated by the lack of firm information, 'we *have* to assume the Russians have acquired the papers – all of them. It's simply not safe to assume anything else. And we've got to make plans to counter whatever advantage the Soviets might now have over us.'

The PM turned to study the faces of the other men present. The Home Secretary and the Foreign Secretary were there from his Government, joined by the head of MI6, the First Sea Lord, and the Chief of the Defence Staff. None of them, though, was fully qualified to assess exactly what was at risk in this affair.

'It's time to call in that chap we've got waiting outside,' the PM then announced. 'Would you mind, Marcus?'

Beckett crossed the room to the door and called down the corridor, 'Would you come in now, Mr Joyce?'

As he entered the room, Peter Joyce noticed a look combining both expectation and hostility on the faces of the various politicians. He knew they needed him to tell them precisely what was what – since they were ignorant of the technology – but that they resented the power that his knowledge now gave him. He quietly took the spare chair that Beckett gestured him towards.

'Now then, Mr Joyce,' the Prime Minister continued, 'we need your technical expertise so that we can judge the seriousness of this affair. Would you be so good as to explain, in the simplest terms possible, just what the stolen plans revealed. And please remember that most of us in this room are laymen when it comes to the business of ballistic missiles.'

Peter stood up so that he could get a clearer view of the nine other men around the table. He looked from one face to the next, to see who he recognised. Despite what the PM had just said, four of the men were from the Defence Ministry, so had already been briefed on the project. The security men were the only ones unfamiliar to him.

'Well, gentlemen, as you know, the document found on Parliament Hill was part of the secret plans for Skydancer,' he began. 'Perhaps the first thing I should do is remind you why Skydancer was set up to start with. About five years ago, the Soviet Union began to spend a great deal of extra money on Ballistic Missile Defence – literally defences against incoming ballistic missiles. The Americans had already launched their own BMD programme, the Strategic Defence Initiative, the one the media called Star Wars, and, as you will remember, the 1972 ABM treaty between the two countries, which had limited BMD systems, rather fell by the wayside as a result of the technical advances being made.

'We in Britain were faced with a dilemma. We were investing ten billion pounds in the Trident system to replace Polaris, but suddenly faced the danger that the new Soviet Defences might make Trident obsolete early in the next century, only giving us a few years use of it as an invulnerable deterrent. As a nation, Britain cannot really afford defences against Russian missiles, so not only could we not defend ourselves against nuclear attack; we soon wouldn't have been able to deter one either.

'Well, faced with all this, the Government, as you remember, took a crucial three-pronged decision. The first factor was to cancel Trident as being a waste of money. The second was to launch a new investigation into what form of nuclear deterrence might still be feasible in the twenty-first century. And the third – and this is where I came in – was to instruct Aldermaston to make further modifications to the old Polaris missiles to enable them to penetrate Soviet defences for the next decade or so. And to do that as cheaply as possible.'

Michael Hawke glanced at his ministerial colleagues and winced, knowing full well that Skydancer had been anything but cheap. The expenditure of hundreds of millions of pounds on the project had been the source of constant complaint from other ministers in the Cabinet.

'So we set up the Skydancer programme,' Joyce continued firmly, 'to design and build a new front end for the Polaris rockets, which would be clever enough to get through the Russian defences.'

'I think we all know the history bit, Mr Joyce,' the Prime Minister interjected impatiently. 'Perhaps you would get to the point now. What we want to know is how much of the project may have been compromised.'

Peter turned to the PM and nodded. He smoothed back his hair and continued.

'Very well, then. The Russian defences consist of a mixture of technologies, both missiles and high-powered lasers. The key to those defences lies not in the weapons themselves, but in the radar and electro-optical detection systems used to spot the incoming missile warheads, and to track them accurately so that the defending weapons can attack them. Our task with Skydancer was to devise new gadgets that would deceive, blind or mislead those Russian detection systems.'

He paused to scan the faces of his audience, to see if they were still following him.

'Skydancer itself is what we call a "space-bus", something that sits on the front end of the missile and separates from the rocket part after it's been launched from the submarine and gets outside the earth's atmosphere. This "bus" can manoeuvre in space and change course in a way which makes its future path difficult for observers on the ground to predict, hence its name "Skydancer".

'Now, into that "bus" fit the re-entry vehicles, the six objects that will eventually plummet down from space towards the target on the ground. Some of those RVs are warheads with nuclear bombs inside them, but the others carry an assortment of electronic and mechanical devices designed to help make the warheads themselves "invisible" to the scanners on the ground. Once released from the space-bus, those re-entry vehicles are in free fall; they just drop straight down. So, as you can imagine, the accuracy of the weapon depends entirely on the position and attitude of the space-bus when the RVs are ejected from it. And the plans that seem to have been stolen describe with mathematical precision the pattern for the ejection of those RVs.'

He paused there and waited to see if there were any questions.

It was the Home Secretary who was the first to speak. He harboured a deep suspicion of scientists in the defence industries, always suspecting them of inventing new problems in an effort to suck more money out of the public purse for their projects. He half suspected the Aldermaston men of setting up this whole spy scare for their own ends.

'Are you trying to tell us, Mr Joyce,' he whined sarcastically, 'that all these clever inventions of yours have suddenly become worthless – if the Russians have learned how your bus scatters its goodies over the earth?' He glared at the scientist with the icy stare he had perfected during years of withering interrogation of civil servants.

'No, I'm not saying that, Home Secretary,' Peter Joyce replied. 'It's not that easy. The problem is this. Suppose one of our missiles is fired at Moscow; the observers manning the Soviet defences round the city would see four objects falling very rapidly out of the sky towards them. Only there wouldn't be four objects, in fact. There would be six, but two would be invisible, do you follow? So the Russians would most probably attack those four "warheads" and destroy them; but seconds later the two real bombs would have detonated and flattened most of Moscow.'

The Home Secretary's brow knitted in a frown.

'So,' Joyce continued, 'if the Russians know how many objects they should be seeing, and know the exact pattern in which they started their journey downwards from space, they might just be able to do some very clever calculations. With a high-powered computer they could feed in the positions and the trajectories of the objects they *can* see, and calculate the exact positions of the ones they *can't*.'

He could sense that his message had struck home painfully.

'And if they can calculate where the bombs are, they can shoot them down even if they can't actually see them?' the Prime Minister asked incredulously.

Peter Joyce nodded uncomfortably. 'It *is* possible, Prime Minister,' he conceded.

'Good God!' the First Sea Lord muttered under his breath. Admiral Barker had a sudden vision of his prized new weapon, designed to keep the Royal Navy's proudly-held nuclear deterrent viable, being humiliatingly still-born.

'And if the Russians believe they can defeat our nuclear deterrent,' the Prime Minister continued, still thinking through the implications of what he had been told, 'then it won't be a deterrent any more. It won't stop them launching a nuclear attack on us if they feel like it.'

'And it'll be a complete waste of hundreds of millions of pounds of tax-payers' money,' the Home Secretary grunted. The political implications of that would not be lost on the Prime Minister.

'Now, look here,' intervened Field-Marshal Buxton, the Chief of the Defence Staff, annoyed at the panic around the table and the paranoia of his naval subordinate, who appeared to fear most the loss of a role and the consequent diminution of his own service. 'You're assuming one hell of a lot from the Russians, Mr Joyce. If they did decide to develop a counter to Skydancer, it would cost them a packet, wouldn't it?'

'Well, it wouldn't be cheap,' Peter conceded.

'And they're already up to their eyes in financial problems, building the BMD system to defend against the older missiles, so they'd have to be pretty certain they could beat our new warheads before they decided to spend the money on it.'

'You could be right,' the scientist nodded.

'So, what are you saying, Field-Marshal?' the Prime Minister interjected. 'You think we should forget all about it?'

'Certainly not, Prime Minister. What I'm saying is

that the Russians would need to be convinced that the Skydancer plans they have, if they have them at all, are the right ones. Before they pour money into new computer systems, they'd need to be certain that the problem the computer is intended to solve is the right problem, if you get me.'

'In other words,' Peter Joyce chipped in, 'if we could persuade them that they've been sold a pup, that the plans are fakes, then they wouldn't be prepared to waste their money.'

'Precisely. Ivan's so short of the readies at the moment, he's only going to want to bet on certainties,' Buxton concluded with a smile.

'Aah!' the Prime Minister exclaimed, slamming the flat of his palm down on the table. 'Now we have the makings of a plan, I think. How about some counter-intelligence, Dick?'

Sir Richard Sproat stroked his chin uneasily. 'Well, I'm not so sure. It seems a bit early to launch into that sort of game,' he cautioned. 'I mean, at this stage we don't even know if the Russians are involved, let alone whether or not they've actually got hold of the plans.'

'I tend to agree with Dick,' the MI6 chief added. 'But if we do set something up, it should be too difficult to sow doubts about the stolen papers in the appropriate quarters, when the right moment comes along.'

'I've had a thought,' Peter Joyce announced. 'The first test of the Skydancer warheads is due to take place a few days from now. The Russians will be watching that trial shot very closely indeed from their spyships and satellites. If they do have the plans, they'll be trying to check that the re-entry vehicles behave as the blueprint says they should.'

'Ah, yes,' the CDS muttered, guessing at what was about to be suggested.

'Now, it is possible to re-programme the missile, to get the space-bus to do something that utterly contradicts the description in the drawings. It would pretty well invalidate the test for us from a scientific point of view, but it would also certainly confuse them in Moscow,' he concluded with the hint of a smile.

'But how would you ever be able to test the thing properly, without giving the game away?' Michael Hawke demanded.

'That could be a problem,' Peter conceded, thinking hard. 'But if its main purpose is to deter, rather than to be used as a weapon, what matters most is that the Russians should be convinced the missile works properly. So as long as we express confidence and satisfaction with Skydancer, even if it's never fully tested, that might be enough.'

There was a snort of derision from the Home Secretary. 'And a bloody convenient way of avoiding being held to account if the thing's a flop,' he muttered.

'Don't you think we should just wait for a while, until we know if the Russians have got those papers?' Sproat persisted with his caution.

'We may never know that for certain, judging by the past performance of our intelligence operations,' the Prime Minister countered bitterly, remembering how his predecessor in Downing Street had finally lost the post he now held. 'No. We must assume the worst case,' he continued, 'and I suggest that Mr Joyce should make immediate moves to set his deception plan in motion. All agreed?'

The intelligence men shrugged their shoulders. In the face of the concurrence of the politicians with their leader, there was no more they could say.

The Prime Minister then insisted that Joyce's mission should be kept a total secret. No one outside that room should learn about it unless it became absolutely essential.

As the meeting broke up, Peter Joyce took Field-Marshal Buxton to one side.

'Look, I could be ready to move this afternoon if I really work at it,' he confided. 'If you can fix me a plane, I could fly over to Florida and do most of the work during the journey. Should have everything ready by the time I get on board *Retribution*. I'd need to take an assistant with me, and we'd want a power supply for our portable computers.'

'You're on,' Buxton agreed. 'I'll get Brize Norton to provide the flight. The sooner we get this moving, the better.'

Peter hurried out through the front door of Number 10, and into the back seat of the official car that had brought him to London earlier that morning. There was much to do if he was to keep the deadline he had set himself.

As his uniformed driver sped down the motorway towards Aldermaston, Peter began to consider the enormity of the task ahead. He was certain that the deception plan he had described at the meeting was indeed possible, but exactly how to carry it out was another matter.

He closed his eyes to concentrate, and his mind's eye began slowly to focus on a face. The square-jowled features were a composite, belonging to a man whose name he did not know, but a man of whose existence he was certain. He had often focused on this face in the past, whenever he needed some encouragement to overcome seemingly impossible difficulties. He thought of the face simply as 'the Russian'.

The primary motivation behind his work at Aldermaston had been to outfox 'the Russian'. With a combination of information from intelligence sources and guesswork based on an understanding of the way he expected 'the Russian' to think, Peter had calculated what Skydancer would need to be able to overcome the new Soviet defences around Moscow. To him it was an exercise in scientific theory rather than a plan for fighting a war; he well understood the disaster that would ensue if the weapons were ever used in anger, and he was convinced 'the Russian' did too. He likened his work to a game of chess, calculating how to avoid the traps his opponent had set for him. Now, however, he was facing an additional problem. 'The Russian' seemed to be cheating.

He had met several Russians in the flesh at international conferences on such 'non-military' subjects as computer technology. Many of those attending were in fact military scientists looking to learn something from their competitors. Scientists from the West were usually open about the nature of their employment; the Soviets were not, disguising many of their top weapon designers behind academic titles. It gave them a certain advantage.

Peter felt certain that some Soviet scientist he had already met must be the man behind the new batteries of defences round Moscow; and that the man whose skills he believed he had beaten with Skydancer was now seeking to gain an advantage, to achieve by theft what he could not through his own skill. He did not know the Russian's identity, of course, but he was determined not to let him win.

Even though his Ministry was only a few minutes' walk from Downing Street, Michael Hawke climbed into the back seat of his official Jaguar when he left Number 10, and allowed himself to be driven the short distance back to his office across Whitehall. As a vociferous proponent of Britain's nuclear might, the Defence Secretary was a potential target for attack from some of the more violent anti-nuclear groups, and the police insisted he should be driven wherever he went.

Before leaving Downing Street he had secured a quiet word with the Prime Minister, eager to ensure that the blame for failure to inform the PM of this spy scandal the previous day was laid firmly at the feet of his Permanent Undersecretary, Sir Marcus Beckett, and that none of it would stick to him personally. It had been a tricky conversation on two accounts: Beckett was a personal friend of the PM, and he himself was strongly disliked by his chief. It seemed to have gone all right though: he was assured that Sir Marcus had been given a thorough roasting for his misdemeanour.

Back in his sixth-floor office, he stood for a moment behind the antique mahogany desk at which innumerable defence reviews had been planned. Waiting for his attention was a fat folder labelled 'Long-term Costings'. The Ministry had a ten-year rolling plan for expenditure, which was constantly updated and adjusted to cope with the delays and cost-overruns which seemed endemic to weapons production. There were key decisions to be taken over which programmes they should axe to keep within budget, and until that morning this task had seemed likely to absorb all his time for the next few days. This secrets scare would change all that, he reflected.

Behind the thick stone walls of the GRU headquarters in Moscow's Znamesky Street, General Novikov was betraying signs of unease. The normally poker-faced head of the military intelligence-gathering network had just replaced one of his four telephones on its rest – the one that linked him directly with his civilian counterpart, the KGB.

The news from London was alarming. For an operation to appear to have become unstuck, almost before it had begun, was an embarrassment that was hard to conceal. The GRU worked in collaboration with the KGB, but since the intelligence to be gathered in Britain was purely military in nature, the operatives were under his control. There was a long history of rivalry between the two organisations, and the KGB never lost an opportunity to launch sniping criticism at its military counterpart.

The problem for Novikov was that he had heard nothing from his operatives in London. He remained optimistic that the blueprints would soon be in Moscow. But the KGB had been demanding clarification, and he had no idea when he would be able to provide it.

He was well aware how important those British missile plans were. The air defence forces, the PVO, had just spent billions of roubles modernising their rocket systems to defend against ballistic missiles, and wanted reassurance that their money had not been wasted. Also the Department of Military Sciences, which was continually devising measures to counter the enemy's countermeasures, was desperate to learn of the latest twist added to the spiral.

One man in particular had applied acute pressure on the intelligence services to find out what the British were up to – a man whose true role in Soviet life was known to only the most senior personnel in the military and intelligence communities.

*

Across the other side of Moscow, Oleg Kvitzinsky had just arrived home. The small name-plate on the door of his apartment described him as a professor of mathematics, which his neighbours believed him to be. He was a tall, burly man in his late forties, with straight, rather lank hair held in place by a light coating of oil.

'Katrina?' he called out as he headed for the bedroom of his apartment, which was spacious by Moscow standards. His wife had decorated it in styles she had selected from the shops or copied from the magazines of Europe and America.

There was no reply, and he guessed she must be visiting a friend in a neighbouring apartment in their block, which was reserved for the administrative elite of the Communist state. The women always had plenty to talk about; they lived in the small, self-protective circle of privilege at the top of Soviet society, with its own services and shops, where there were no queues and virtually no shortages. At their level, the men were usually free to travel abroad with their wives, and they did so at every opportunity, returning to Moscow laden with possessions that most of their fellow countrymen could never dream of owning.

The large Japanese transistor radio which Kvitzinsky now switched on in the bedroom was one such object. He had obtained it in America as being the most refined and sensitive radio that money could buy. He spun the dial until the needle reached a familiar resting point: the BBC World Service. He looked at his Swiss watch, and smiled at the good fortune of his timing. He had not heard any news that day, and the London bulletin would begin in precisely one minute.

He hummed to himself as the familiar signature tune blared through the apartment – but the news headlines soon wiped the smile from his lips. For the third item mentioned was the discovery of an apparent attempt to steal British nuclear missile secrets.

'It can't be true!' he howled.

Impatiently he paced the room, waiting for the full details to be read out.

'The idiots!' he hissed, when the newsreader had finished. 'They can't have fouled that up so soon!'

Angrily he turned off the radio and marched into the living-room with its fine view over the Moskva River. He poured himself a glass of vodka and drank it quickly. Then, shuddering at the oily warmth of the liquid, he filled the glass again and took it into the kitchen to lace it with ice.

Staring out through the picture window at the city, Kvitzinsky reminded himself of what was at stake. In his hands lay the responsibility for the protection of Moscow if there should be a nuclear war – at least that was more or less how the Military Committee had put it when they appointed him. As chief scientist for the Ballistic Missile Defence modernisation programme, it was his special responsibility to ensure that the technology of their defences could match that of the missiles aimed at them.

Trying to stop any small nuclear warhead hurtling out of the sky at thousands of miles per hour was a brainstorming problem. The idea of defending an area the size of the Soviet Union against such an attack was nonsense. What mattered to the leaders in the Kremlin, however, was that Moscow itself should never be destroyed. Without its capital, the nation would cease to exist, they believed. It was for that reason, when the first Russian anti-ballistic missiles were built in the 1960s, they were concentrated in a ring round the city.

Until a few years ago, those ABMs all carried nuclear warheads. If the city was attacked, these would have been fired into space and detonated in the path of the enemy rockets, hoping to destroy the incoming warheads through blast and radiation, even from a considerable distance. Accuracy had not been so easy to attain in those days; Kvitzinsky had thought of it as trying to crack a nut with a hand-grenade, and feared that much of Moscow could be destroyed by the defences themselves.

New technology had changed all that, though. New radars and infra-red detectors had made it easier to pinpoint and track objects in space, so that new super-accurate missiles and ground-based lasers could destroy attacking warheads individually and with great precision.

But to every measure there was a counter-measure, as Kvitzinsky knew well. The new American approach would be to saturate the defences round Moscow – to fire so many missiles at the city that eventually all the defences would be exhausted. An ever-increasing expansion of the number of defences was the only effective answer to that.

With the British it was a different matter. They could not afford the massive numbers of weapons the Americans possessed, and had resorted to guile to achieve their aims. With a nuclear force of just sixty-four missiles, Kvitzinsky knew that the British had one main target in mind, the capital itself.

The British scientists at Aldermaston had been assiduous in their efforts to ensure their Polaris H-bombs would be able to penetrate Moscow's defensive ring. At the end of the 1970s they had started an improvement programme called 'Chevaline', hardening the Polaris warheads so that they could withstand the blast and radiation effects of Moscow's nuclear-tipped ABMs. Chevaline also involved the firing of several missiles in rapid succession so that their warheads and decoys would arrive over the target at the same time, causing the maximum of confusion and difficulty for the Soviet defences.

At the end of the 1980s, Chevaline's potential effectiveness had been almost negated by the Soviet introduction of new radars and infra-red detectors, and a massive increase in the number of defensive missiles round Moscow.

Inevitably, the game had not ended there. The British had decided to follow the American lead and go for massive numbers of warheads. The Trident system was to be bought, with eight bombs per missile. Moscow had resigned itself to expanding its defences yet further.

But suddenly, two years ago, the British had changed their minds again. They had cancelled their expensive Trident plans, and resorted to guile once again.

'Skydancer!' Kvitzinsky spat out the English word. He had to know what tricks of technology the British had invented this time, tricks the Military Committee had designated him to counter.

Standing by the window, hands deep in his pockets, he looked across the roofs of Moscow to the onion domes of the Kremlin in the distance. There had been snow flurries earlier in the day, and he saw that it was now beginning to rain.

It would be raining in London, too, he guessed. He had visited the British capital several times and liked his stays there. It was an unprotected city, though, he mused: if there was a nuclear war, London would have no means of stopping Soviet missiles raining down to destroy it. Curious, he thought: the British talked with vague optimism about surviving a nuclear war, yet they made no effort to protect their centre of power.

'Perhaps they are right,' he murmured. 'Perhaps protection is indeed a waste of time.'

He tossed back the remains of the vodka. This would not do: those were negative thoughts. His orders were to keep Moscow safe. The trouble was that to learn how to do it, he needed those people in London to get him the Skydancer plans, and in that they seemed to be failing.

The day in Britain was three hours younger than in Moscow; and in Florida, where the big grey RAF VC10 jet was now heading, it was five hours earlier still. As the aircraft strained upwards into the clouds over the wet grasslands of Oxfordshire, Peter Joyce breathed in deeply, eager for the seat-belt sign to be switched off so that he could press on with his work.

He sat in an executive section of the cabin: two pairs of deeply padded seats facing each other, and a large table top between them. Opposite him sat a young woman with curly blonde hair and brown eyes. Her pretty face was turned towards the window, and she made no effort to conceal her excitement as she peered through the window.

'Ever been to America before, Jill?' Peter asked.

He did not know the girl well but had been assured she was one of the best computer programmers at Aldermaston.

'I've never even flown in an aeroplane before!' she confided, blushing with embarrassment.

'What? Never even been to Majorca?' he joked.

She shook her head. 'I'm an outdoor girl. I prefer hill-climbing to lying on a beach.' Her accent was broad Yorkshire.

'Well, there won't be time for anything like that

where we're going. I'm sorry to say.'

As the aircraft began to level out, Peter looked up and saw the sign was finally off. As he unclipped his seat-belt and stood up, a steward came forward from his place near the rear galley.

'The flight engineer's laid on a power supply for you from a socket in the galley, sir,' the man announced, glancing at the girl and wondering where these scientists were from. He had been told their mission was secret.

'Would you like me to bring the cable along right away?'

'Yes, please,' Joyce replied. 'Then perhaps you could give us a hand with these.' He pointed across the aisle to where the components of two microcomputers had been carefully strapped in to protect them from the jolting of the takeoff.

They lifted the heavy boxes and placed them on the table, plugging in the leads that linked the components together. The flight engineer had reappeared from the cockpit by the time the steward had uncoiled the cable from the galley, and he supervised the final connection of the equipment.

'Do you have everything you need now?' the engineer enquired, standing back and looking with satisfaction at the green glow emanating from the VDUs.

'Yes, thank you,' Joyce replied. He could see curiosity on the RAF men's faces, but he wanted them out of the way. 'We'll press the call button if we want anything.'

The engineer and steward returned to their posts.

Peter drew across the blue curtain which shut off each end of their 'suite' from the rest of the aircraft.

'Right, Jill. Now with luck we won't be disturbed.'

They sat down opposite one another at their

keyboards. Peter fumbled in a jacket pocket for the spectacles he wore for reading, and placed the tortoise-shell half-moon frames on the end of his nose. They gave him a somewhat bookish appearance, slightly at odds with his square features.

'I finalised the parameters in the car on my way to Brize Norton,' he declared, passing a sheet of paper across the table to his junior. 'It's only a compromise. We could have made Skydancer turn cartwheels, and that would really upset Moscow; but we can't be too clever or they'll realise it's an expensive leg-pull. I think I've got it right,' he continued, pointing to the paper which the girl was now studying. 'But if you don't think so, for God's sake say so now. If you can work on the programme for the manoeuvring, I'll get on with the ejection routine.'

The operation of the missile was controlled by computer software; a variety of programmes could be selected, containing subtle differences to enable the warheads to cope with both short and long ranges. Completely changing the character of the missile would require a massive rewriting of the programmes, to be fed into the missile's control system when they went on board the submarine in Florida.

Peter could not help feeling apprehensive about what he was doing. Having spent most of the past two years refining and perfecting a complex electro-mechanical device, he was now about to sabotage its first operational test. Instead of demonstrating to himself and the keepers of the public purse that the money had been well spent, he was about to obfuscate the issue, possibly for ever.

Sitting in that aircraft, with the blinds drawn so the afternoon sun would not reflect from the computer screens, Peter found it difficult to get started. An image of 'the Russian' was firmly fixed in one corner of his brain, as if the man was peering over his shoulder at the keyboard. The face of Mary Maclean filled another corner, provoking in him a deep sense of guilt.

At the end of his second full day of enquiries into the nuclear secrets case, John Black had decided the whole business stank. British agents in Moscow had not been able to detect any KGB or GRU activity over the missile plans; and GCHQ had not intercepted a single communication between the Soviet Embassy and Moscow that seemed to relatc to it. Nothing but routine reporting back to the Kremlin on what the newspapers were saying.

Yet somebody was definitely up to something, that much was clear. It either meant the Russians were being unusually cunning, and exceptionally clever at concealing their activities, or else that all this had nothing to do with Moscow at all. He had a strong suspicion that the missile document had been deliberately dumped in that rubbish bin for the express purpose of being found. Some mysterious person had certainly made sure that the world got to know about it by tipping off the *Daily Express*.

Thanks to the carelessness of Mary Maclean in leaving that vital key in her desk drawer, up to about thirty people within the Defence Ministry with access to the secrets room could have 'borrowed' her key to the nuclear weapons filing-cabinet, and copied those papers. If he had to check all thirty of them, it would make his investigation long and tedious, but he somehow felt that would not be necessary. His instinct told him that the culprit was someone who knew precisely what the papers were about – and what a stir it would cause if one of them was found in the wrong place.

On his desk lay the personal security files of three people. The one he had been studying for the past few minutes referred to Mr Peter Joyce. He could see that the scientist had had an impeccable career pattern. The report on his family life looked unremarkable too, except perhaps for a small admission at his last positive vetting, when he volunteered that his wife had become a supporter of the Campaign for Nuclear Disarmament.

On the surface this looked innocent enough: CND was a perfectly legitimate organ of protest, and there was nothing unusual about husbands and wives having differences of opinion over such sensitive issues. But the timing was curious; his admission about the wife's membership of CND had first been made three years ago. John Black had now learned it was just one year later that Peter Joyce had begun an adulterous affair with Mary Maclean. There was no mention of *that* liaison in the security file, and there damn well should have been. The sequence of events intrigued him. First the scientist's wife turns against the work he is doing, then the scientist takes up with another woman - events which could well be the tip of an iceberg of stress, intrigue and blackmailable goings-on that spelled SECURITY RISK in large letters.

The positive vetting system to which all officials in sensitive posts were regularly subjected was something of a joke as far as Black was concerned. Successive governments had been so nervous about 'invasions of privacy' or 'infringing the civil rights of the individual' that a vetting procedure had been allowed to continue whereby individuals were able to nominate their own referees, and security-clearance officers had no power to make inquiries of other people. Over the years the system had allowed the concealment of countless personal weaknesses and misdemeanours which had then been exploited to great effect by KGB blackmail and bribery. In John Black's view, people in high-security positions should be subjected to regular investigation with the same intensity as suspected criminals.

He pushed back his chair, stretched out his arms, and let out a muted belch. The Defence Ministry office which he had occupied for the past two days was beginning to depress him. The walls were a dirty cream colour and seemed designed to induce sleep in the most wakeful of civil servants. He would move back to his own office in Curzon Street the next day, he decided, squeezing the square flabbiness of his chin. He had time for one more cigarette before he set out for his evening visit.

It was Alec Anderson who had tipped him off about Peter Joyce and Mary Maclean. The man had pretended to find it awkward and embarrassing to discuss the subject, but had found it his duty to mention it under the present circumstances. Black had detected a distinctly vicarious flicker in Anderson's eyes; the man must have been quite a sneak at school, he decided.

Anderson's own file had revealed nothing out of the ordinary. He had lived in the same house for seven years, regularly ran up a modest overdraft, but had never defaulted on his debts or been involved with the police except for a parking offence three years earlier. The referees he had nominated during the vetting process had all spoken of him in glowing terms. He seemed a typical civil servant on the way up, well educated, alert and efficient, happily married with a devoted wife and two children in private schools. Yet the man from MI5 was suspicious by nature, always on the look-out for dark secrets behind the facade of normality.

He had given Anderson quite a grilling that afternoon, starting gently by taking him through all he could remember about the secret documents, from the moment they had first arrived in his department for the Ministerial briefing three months earlier. He asked precisely who had been shown the papers since then, and how often they had been removed from safe-keeping to be studied. Anderson claimed he had never looked at the papers since their first arrival, finding the technical details difficult to comprehend.

Then Black had turned to personal matters, questioning the civil servant about his normal routine, who his friends were, how often he went out, what was the state of his marriage, and so on. On those questions he had found Anderson less than satisfactory, but then he had not expected anything else from someone so stereotyped. The man's somewhat chubby features had twisted themselves into an expression of indignation at the intimate nature of these enquiries. His eyes had seemed occasionally to cower behind the lenses of his spectacles, but the trace of perspiration that broke out on his brow could have indicated simple nervousness rather than any effort at concealment.

When the interview had ended, Black continued to watch his subject closely as he stood up to leave the room. Anderson was tall with an unathletic gait. His dark hair was greying at the temples; there was a slight ruddiness to the cheeks and a somewhat bibulous mouth.

Mary Maclean scraped the edge of the record as she aimed the gramophone needle for the groove. The wine she had been drinking since she returned home had unsteadied her hand. Her second attempt was more successful, and within moments the crackling from the loudspeakers had given way to the opening choral blasts of *Carmina Burana.* She wanted the intensity of Carl Orff's work to blow the dark thoughts from her mind like a March wind.

She had just been watching the BBC nine o'clock news with its report on the Prime Minister's statement to Parliament, in which he had insisted there was no evidence yet of any loss of vital secrets following the discovery of the document on Parliament Hill two days earlier. The opposition parties had howled derisively, believing themselves on the scent of a security scandal as had helped unseat the current Prime Minister's predecessor.

Mary's day at the Ministry had been long and painful. Wherever she went in the rectangular labyrinth, she imagined once-friendly eyes staring after her with curiosity and suspicion. No one referred directly to what they had all read in the paper that morning, not wanting her to think they were putting blame on her. But Mary felt accused by their very silence.

The music reverberating round the apartment began to work its usual therapy. Mary felt herself start to unwind.

Suddenly the rapping of the door knocker startled her. From the small sofa she stared fearfully at the door, as if trying to peer through it and see who was there.

It was probably that nosey old bat who lived at the front of the house, Mary thought. Come to complain about the loudness of the music, no doubt. Mary turned down the volume before peeping through the spyhole in the door. But it was not her neighbour; it was John Black. She opened the door on the security-chain.

'I'm sorry to disturb you, Ms Maclean,' he smiled through the narrow gap.

To her the way he used the term 'Ms' always sounded offensive, as if he was mocking her unmarried status.

'I wonder if you would let me in. I have some important new questions to put to you.'

It was more of a demand than a request, and she slipped the chain from its runner and opened the door fully.

'I don't know what more I can tell you, Mr Black,' she began uneasily, leading him in. 'Nothing that's relevant anyway.'

The investigator settled his heavy frame into an armchair and smiled in a manner calculated to be reassuring but which managed instead to be both patronising and belittling. His eyes focused on hers with disconcerting steadiness.

'Do you mind if I call you Mary? It's so much easier, and I'd prefer our conversation to be informal.' He raised his eyebrows inquiringly.

Mary shrugged in reply. She did not consider she had any choice in the matter.

'My first name is John, but you can call me whatever you want,' he continued with a self-deprecating smile. 'Yes. You said *relevant*. That's a very *relative* word, don't you think?' He chuckled at his own attempt at word play.

'I mean, what *you* as an ordinary citizen consider relevant, and what *I* do, as an investigator into a crime which in wartime would be a capital offence, those are of course two completely different things, don't you think so, Mary?' He stopped, with his eyebrows raised again, as if insisting on a reply.

'I, er . . . I'm sure you're right,' she replied, determined not to be seduced into an informality which could lead to her dropping her guard. The man was spinning a web in her path, the threads of which she needed to keep in focus.

'I mean, let's just take an example,' he continued, looking theatrically round the room and then settling his eyes on the glass still clasped in her right hand. 'Well, for example, I happen to notice that you have a half-consumed glass of red wine in your right hand. Now . . .'

'Oh, I'm sorry. Would you like . . .' Mary cut in, but he dismissed her offer with a wave of an arm.

'No, thank you. But take that glass, for example. Now you would say, I feel sure, that it has no relevance to my inquiries at all.'

He leaned forward in his chair, like a school-teacher trying to ensure that his class was following his argument.

'But I have to ask myself, how often does she have a glass of wine? How many glasses a day? What else does she drink? Whisky? Gin?' He paused for a second in his rapid flow.

'Vodka perhaps? And when she drinks, does she start to talk about things to strangers? Secret things, personal things. Does she expose those little skeletons in the cupboard, which when she's sober she keeps firmly locked away? Give away secret documents even?'

'That's preposterous!' she burst out in indignation.

'Of course, it is. Of course, it's preposterous,' Black replied softly, sitting back in the armchair and clasping his hands over his broad stomach. He smiled at her almost benignly. 'But I have to ask these questions. I have to think of outrageous motives for people who are caught up on the fringes of espionage, and see if they just happen to fit. It's not a part of my job that I enjoy,

Mary, and that's why I've come round here tonight to ask for your help. Would you like a cigarette?'

He pulled a packet from his pocket, flipped back the lid and held it out towards her.

She shook her head, allowing a flicker of distaste to cross her face. 'I don't, thank you,' she answered crisply.

'Do you mind if I smoke?'

'Well . . . I,' she hesitated.

'You do mind. I can see that. And of course you're absolutely right. It's a filthy habit.' He put the packet carefully back in his pocket.

'But have I made my point? Have you understood how you can help me?'

Mary was confused. The man had not been specific. She had understood the drift of his argument, but what exactly did he want to know? Most crucial of all, what did he know already? Did he know about her relationship with Peter Joyce?

'You'll have to forgive me . . .' she ventured timidly. 'Sometimes I'm a little obtuse. I'm really not entirely sure what I can tell you that would be of any help.'

The faint smile disappeared from his flabby lips, and his eyes grew cold and expressionless. He stared at her for a few moments before continuing.

'I want to know some personal details, Mary. We've already talked in the office, haven't we, but, as I'm sure you will remember, the only ground we covered there was on things like office procedure, routines, access to documents, and so on. Well, to be frank, that didn't clarify anything very much, so I want to learn a little bit more about your personal life, just so that I can put my suspicious old mind at rest and cross you off my list of people who need investigating.'

'Yes, well, of course, that sounds perfectly reasonable,' Mary replied uneasily.

He smiled briefly, as a reward for her answer, then waited for her to continue.

She looked back at him anxiously, hoping that he would ask her questions and so reveal his hand. He did not however.

'Well, there's not a lot to say,' she began uncomfortably. 'I er . . . I lead a pretty quiet sort of life. I er . . . live here alone, as you can see, but I have lots of good friends whom I see from time to time.'

She stopped and shrugged her shoulders as if there was no more to be said. Black looked at her icily.

'How much do you drink?' The question was hardly audible.

'What?'

'One bottle of wine a day? Two?'

'Oh, nothing like . . .'

'Whisky? Gin?'

'Well, yes. From time to . . .'

'How much? Two glasses a day? Half a bottle?'

'Now, look here . . .'

'Ever had treatment for it? Alcoholism?'

'No!'

'Are you sure? I can easily check.'

She shook her head in disbelief, but found herself putting down the wine glass she had been holding.

'Go to pubs, do you?'

'Sometimes, but . . .'

'On your own? Sitting in a corner hoping someone will come up and talk to you and buy you a drink?'

'No! I . . .'

'Is that how you get your men? Pick them up in the pubs, do you? Tell them they can come home with you if they bring a bottle of scotch?'

'For God's sake! You can't just come round . . .'

'Don't you like men then?'

'What do you mean?'

'Lesbian, are you? A student of Sappho?'

Mary found herself trembling uncontrollably. She was dumbfounded, and felt that at any minute she would be sick. Through the mist of tears clouding her eyes she could no longer clearly see the monster of a man who was taunting her. Part of her wanted to get up and run away, escape from her own home, but the rest of her felt incapable of movement, like a rabbit mesmerised by a stoat.

She was aware that Black had stood up from his chair and was now wandering round the room. She heard the click of a cigarette-lighter behind her, and then smelled the Virginia tobacco smoke that swirled around her head.

'Interesting books you've got, Mary.'

The man's voice was softer now, less aggressive.

'You've done a bit of travelling in your time, judging by the number of guide-books on the shelf here. France, Spain, Morocco. Oh, and here's the Soviet Union.'

Mary was breathing deeply, trying to steady her racing heartbeat and to bring herself back in control of her voice. She knew the interrogation had a long way to go.

'You have been to Russia, have you?' Black asked pointedly.

'Yes, I went to Moscow and Leningrad in 1984. It was a holiday organised by a civil-service travel club. We looked at museums and art galleries.'

She breathed a silent sigh of relief at having given the answer without a quaver in her voice. She heard Black chuckling to himself behind her. Another cloud of smoke swirled past her head. He is doing it deliberately, she thought to herself.

'Interesting titles you've got here, though, Mary.

Marxism Today must make good bedtime reading. *The Spread of Socialism in the 1980s* can't be a bad yarn either. Good heavens, we've got a whole shelf of such treats here. *The Long Road to Freedom, Socialist Progress*, they're all here.'

She heard him take first one book from the shelves and flip through its pages, then, with the occasional chuckle and a whistle through his teeth, he would replace it and take another.

'I'm sure there's something you'd like to tell me about all this, isn't there, Mary?' he asked with amused resignation.

'I've always been interested in political philosophy,' she answered flatly. 'I read PPE at university. And I am a supporter of the Labour Party. I have been for many years. But that will be in your file on me already, I'm sure.'

She heard him breathing heavily. His lungs must be coated with tar, she thought to herself. She found herself praying that he would die from cancer.

He was standing at the end of the sofa now, looking straight down at her.

'It's still the policy of the Labour Party to scrap British nuclear weapons, isn't it?' he asked innocently.

'Yes. But not all members of the party support that policy,' she answered coldly, looking straight ahead. She reached for her glass, and swallowed the remains of her wine.

'Good God!' he exclaimed in disgust. 'It amazes me that we have any secrets left in this country. There you've been for the past God-knows-how-many years, sitting in the nuclear weapons department of the Ministry of Defence, with top-security clearance, and all the time you've been an alcoholic, lesbian, left-wing anti-nuclear activist!'

'Look, you evil pig of a man!' Mary exploded in rage, rising to her feet so that he could not dominate her. 'I've had quite enough of your vile insinuations and lies. I am not a left-wing anti-nuclear activist! I happen to believe in nuclear deterrence, and in Britain keeping the bomb. I couldn't possibly have done the work I do if I didn't believe that. Also, I am not an alcoholic, and above all I am not a lesbian!'

Her voice had risen to a penetrating crescendo, and she was trembling again. This time with anger at the faint expression of amusement discernible on John Black's face.

'Oh,' he nodded amiably. 'Oh well, you should have said that before. Would have saved a lot of trouble.'

With that he turned away from her and studied a watercolour on the wall. Sighing gently he moved on to examine some prints, and stopped by an antique walnut-veneered bureau, on top of which were two photo-frames. One contained a picture of an elderly couple in a country garden. They looked to him as if they could be her parents. Next to it was a more recent colour print of Mary with her arms round two young children.

'Nice-looking kids,' he commented sincerely.

'They're my brother's.'

'Sort of substitute for not having any of your own, are they?'

Mary ignored the remark and bit her lip.

'You've never been married, have you?' he persisted.

'No,' she answered softly.

Suddenly there was a squeak from the hinges of the old bureau.

'You can bloody well keep out of there!' she shouted furiously. 'That's private!'

'I know,' Black murmured without turning round.

'You've got no right to look in there!' she screamed, striding across the room and grabbing him by the arm, to pull him away.

'Rights?' he mocked, swinging round and brushing her hand from his arm. 'Rights? This country's most precious nuclear secrets are being stolen by some self-interested sneak-thief, and you talk about rights!'

His outrage blazed from his eyes.

'What is it you want? A warrant? I can whistle up a search warrant in half an hour, if that's what you want. But along with the warrant will come three of my heaviest-handed men who will not only search this place from top to bottom, they'll slit the very elastic out of your knickers to check that it hasn't got code-words written on it. Those are you rights, Miss Maclean!'

Mary knew that she could not stop her tears anymore. Her privacy was going to be violated, and there was nothing more she could do to prevent it happening. Turning back to the French windows, she pressed her head against the glass and hugged her arms tightly round her chest in an effort to hold herself together.

She heard him rustling through her private papers, which were stuffed inside the cubby-holes of the burcau. Suddenly the rustling stopped, and she assumed he had found what he was looking for. Inside a tattered brown envelope were the snapshots she had taken during her two-year affair with Peter Joyce, together with the three letters that he had written to her during their relationship.

She flinched as she felt John Black's hand on her shoulder.

'Don't you think the time has now come, Mary, for you to tell me about Peter Joyce?'

*

It was after midnight when John Black eventually left the garden flat in Chiswick. The air smelt of fog, and the street lamps looked like orange-headed sentinels glaring sullenly down through the mist. Black sniffed at the air, finding it curiously refreshing after the despair-laden atmosphere he had just left.

He was not proud of the methods he had used to make her tell him what he wanted to hear, but he knew no other way. He shivered in the cold air, hurriedly climbed into his car, started the engine, and set off for home. He failed to notice the large Mercedes parked on the other side of the road.

Chapter Three

Midnight in London was seven o'clock in the evening Florida time. The sun was low in the sky and painted the endless beaches with a wash of golden orange, as the RAF VC10 banked for its final turn over the coast and settled smoothly down towards the runway of Patrick Air Force Base. Beyond Patrick, a few miles to the north, the pilot could see the towers and gantries of the Kennedy Space Center pointing challengingly at the stars.

Peter Joyce looked down at the long oblongs of the cars cruising slowly up and down the coastal boulevards. The pilot had sent back a note to say the temperature on the ground was a humid seventy-five degrees. It certainly looked hot down below, and Peter was grateful he had remembered to wear a lightweight suit.

Jill Piper's face was glued to the window, her eyes drinking in their first sight of the USA. Suddenly Peter remembered he had meant to warn her of something. He glanced down to check, and cursed himself. The girl was wearing a skirt.

'Christ, Jill! Have you brought a pair of trousers with you, by any chance?' he enquired, embarrassed.

She turned from the window, a knowing smile on her lips.

'For the submarine, you mean? Don't worry, I was warned! A friend of mine went on one last year in a skirt, and had ten sailors round the bottom of each hatchway looking up at her as she came down the ladder! I'll change as soon as we've landed.'

Peter smiled; the girl was quite sharp. He was very tired, but satisfied that they had managed to complete the writing of the new programmes. It had been a full eight hours' work, but he was as confident as he could be that the deception plan for the missile test would be convincing.

The plane bounced once as it touched the tarmac; then the nose levelled out and the four engines shook and roared as they went into reverse thrust. Peter glanced across the aisle to check that their micro-computers, packed away in their boxes, were still firmly strapped in the seats and cushioned against the force of the landing. When the plane stopped moving, he left Jill on her own in the compartment to change.

As they stepped out on to the steps the warm air enveloped them. The naval officer standing below was wearing a crisply starched white shirt and shorts. He looked up at Peter with recognition.

'Good evening, Mr Joyce, and welcome to the US of A,' he smiled. 'Phil Dunkley. We met last year.' He extended his hand. 'I'm the PSO, the Polaris Systems Officer from *Retribution*.'

Peter was grateful for the reminder, but pretended he did not need it. 'Of course. I remember you well. Nice to see you again.'

The smile on the Lt. Commander's face broadened as he turned to greet the second visitor from Aldermaston.

'Ah, Miss Piper, is it?' With a quick all-over glance he took in her blonde hair and the shapely figure clad in blue cotton blouse and slacks.

'Jill will do!' she smiled back.

The equipment was loaded carefully into a US Navy van. Then they climbed into a large black automobile, with the officer from HMS *Retribution* sitting next to the US Navy driver in the front. During their forty-minute journey up the coast, Dunkley gave them a running commentary on the local attractions of Florida.

Once through the gates of the US Navy Base at Port Canaveral, Peter felt a sense of anticipation and unease. The smooth black hulls of several submarines lined the quayside – in harbour for maintenance, or waiting to conduct missile tests out in the Atlantic. The sight of this most sinister of military hardware brought him down to earth; the hours spent re-writing the missile warhead programmes had been an academic challenge, but the sight of the slim fins and opened missile hatches reminded him of the monstrous destructive potential of the weapons he designed.

At the end of the quay, the White Ensign fluttering limply in the light evening breeze distinguished HMS *Retribution* from her lookalike American counterparts. As the car pulled to a halt, two sailors on her deck snapped to attention, while a third spoke urgently into a microphone connected by cable to the inside of the hull.

Within seconds the tall, bony figure of the submarine's captain had emerged from a hatchway, and he stood at the head of the gangway with his hand outstretched in greeting.

'Nice to see you again, Mr Joyce,' Commander Carrington exclaimed. They had also met the previous year, when the scientist had attended the test firing of early prototypes of the Skydancer warheads.

'Likewise,' Peter answered, smiling politely. 'And this is Jill Piper, my assistant. She knows much more about using that stuff than I do,' he explained, pointing at the computers that were being unloaded from the US Navy van.

Carrington bowed his head respectfully. 'I'm afraid that usually when ladies come aboard we give them tea and show them the wardroom,' he grinned. 'It's a new experience to have a woman tell us how to programme our missiles.'

His words had sounded pompous even to his own ears, and he covered his embarrassment by leading the way down into the bowels of the submarine.

'Now, how much have you been told about all this?' Joyce asked, once he was alone with Carrington and the Polaris Systems Officer. Jill was elsewhere, supervising the stowage of equipment.

'Not much,' Carrington answered. 'They said there was no need for us to know the details.' The injunction to secrecy was a restraint they were well used to, but the two Navy men were clearly burning with curiosity.

'I'm sorry, I can't explain much to you, as secrecy is terribly important in this matter,' Joyce went on, his eyebrows arched in apology. 'And I'm going to need your help, please, in damping down speculation among the crew. Many of them will remember me from my last visit, but if anyone asks, could you simply say I'm here to make minor adjustments to the missiles?'

The two officers nodded.

'Unfortunately what I have to do is not really minor at all. It involves extensive re-programming of the war-heads. Your test launch procedures won't be affected, but the changes will make a big difference to what happens at the other end of the range. And I shouldn't really have told you that much!'

'Don't worry, it'll go no further,' Carrington re-assured him. 'Now when do you want to start work? Tonight?'

'No, I don't think we can do any more today,' Peter sighed, drawing a hand round his chin and feeling the stubble of nearly twenty-four hours. 'I'd rather get some sleep and start fresh in the morning. With any luck we might be finished by lunchtime.'

'Fine,' the Commander replied. 'We've booked a couple of rooms for you in a motel down the road. Nothing very special, I'm afraid, but it's on the beach and you should be more comfortable there than on board. We don't have proper facilities for ladies anyway!'

Peter nodded. He suddenly felt a desperate need to sleep; he had been concentrating solidly for the past sixteen hours.

The equipment they had brought from Britain had now been carried carefully down the metal ladders and into the missile compartment in the heart of the submarine. As the PSO led him down there, Peter was pleased to notice sentries standing in the corridors leading to the chamber. He would want complete privacy the following morning.

He stood for a moment looking along the two rows of missile tubes, sixteen in all. Their white casings, over five feet in diameter, looked clean and clinical, and bore large red identification numbers on their sides. Inside each one was a weapon ten times as destructive as the primitive bomb dropped on Hiroshima in 1945.

On this occasion however one tube did not contain a bomb. The one he would have to work on the following day held the product of his recent efforts, a warhead of dummies and complex electronic creations, the testing of which was of vital concern both to London and to Moscow.

Satisfied that the equipment was safe, Peter escorted Jill up to the black steel outer casing of the submarine, and down the gangway to the shore. The US Navy driver was still waiting there to take them to their hotel.

It was mid-evening Florida time, though three in the morning by Peter's body-clock. Large convertibles cruised lazily up and down the boulevards, and the bars, motels and arcade houses competed for attention in garish neon. The air smelled of seaweed and grilled meat, and it still retained much of the humid warmth of the day.

'It's just like on television, only worse,' Jill commented in surprise. 'Do they *only* eat pizzas and hamburgers?'

'Just about,' Peter sighed.

The Navy car turned into the driveway of the Cocoa-Beach Lodge, and pulled up by the hotel entrance. The two Britons climbed out, carrying their small suitcases, and arranged for the driver to collect them at eight the next morning.

Peter entered the reception uneasily; American motels all looked alike to him, but there was something familiar about this one. It was only after checking in, and after he had bid Jill a weary goodnight, that he remembered. As he let himself into his room, he realised this was where he had stayed on his last visit, a year ago, the visit when Mary Maclean had accompanied him.

He exhaled sharply, cursing the coincidence that was stirring memories he preferred to keep buried. It might even have been the very same room; above the king-sized bed was an identical cheap print of a space-shuttle launching from Cape Canaveral.

Peter took off his sweaty clothes and lay back on the bed, listening to the surf pounding on the sand fifty yards away. His affair with Mary had begun in London, but it had been here in Florida in a room like this that it had become more than a casual flirtation.

He had surprised himself that first evening of the

train strike when Mary had joined him for dinner in London. He had not been looking for an affair, he was certain of that, but suddenly the opportunity was there. At the time, neither of them had expected the relationship to develop, but it had, and his occasional visits to America had given them the chance for a week on their own.

He clearly remembered their first night here. They had both experienced a childlike excitement at being able to walk around together openly, without the constant secretiveness they had learned to practise back home. They had enjoyed shrimp and lobster at a restaurant on a tumbledown jetty, with a view up the coast to the launching towers of the Space Center, and then they strolled down the beach as the sun set. At the first onset of a chilly evening breeze, they had hurried back to the hotel.

Once inside their room, they had looked at one another and hesitated. There was something unsavoury about this motel.

'What's this room smell of to you?' he had asked, frowning. 'They must spray it with something.'

Mary had made much of sniffing the air.

'No. It's the smell of adultery!' she'd proclaimed with a wicked smile. 'Now stifle your conscience and get on with it!'

He had snorted with laughter, and then nudged her attention towards the phallic photo of the space-shuttle above the bed. She had turned the picture to the wall.

That week had changed their relationship irrevocably. Until then, neither of them had defined precisely what their affair meant to them. Peter had considered it little more than a flirtation, a compensation for the erosion of his relationship with Belinda. Not in any way an alternative to his marriage, he was determined it should not affect his family. But Mary had brought a new dimension to his life, and that week in Florida had turned the affair into something much more serious. For the first time Peter had realised he was deeply involved with Mary, and that she was intensely in love with him. But warning bells had soon rung in Peter's mind, and he had known instinctively that the end was already in sight.

On their third evening, Peter remembered, they had revisited the restaurant on the tumbledown jetty, and something he said had caused Mary to giggle uncontrollably. Suddenly she looked twenty years younger. All traces of spinsterishness had vanished. Her face had shed its worry-lines and her eyes shone softly.

Peter knew she had not had many relationships with men; her inexperience was clear to him in the way her body had moved against his with hesitancy and uncertainty when they made love. That evening, however, when they returned to their motel, her reserve had evaporated, and she had given herself to him with a totality that was almost sacrificial.

Suddenly everything had changed. His desire to be with Mary was becoming overwhelming. The possibility of leaving Belinda – separation and divorce – had begun to haunt his thoughts.

In Mary's heart a spark of hope had been lit. She had finally found the love that she had always been seeking, and it seemed to her there was now a chance that it could last for ever. In the months that followed their week in Florida, that spark had grown into a flame, eventually so bright and visible that Peter made his painful but inevitable decision. He could not inflict the misery of a break-up on his children. He had to extinguish the flame for ever.

Now he was back in the very place where his real

love-affair with Mary had begun – and where its end had first been signalled.

Could Mary have taken the Skydancer blueprints in revenge, desperate to hurt him? It would be so unlike her, yet was it really impossible?

Rising, he closed the glass door to the balcony, shutting out the sound of the sea, and began to unpack his suitcase. There was much to do the following day; he had to try to sleep.

In London the following morning, John Black looked at the date on his newspaper to remind himself it was Wednesday. It was the third day of his investigation and he still had no clear leads. He was glad to see that the newspapers were turning cold on the story, with no fresh revelations to keep them going.

His first cigarette of the day came before breakfast, and the second immediately afterwards, while he finished his coffee. That done, he set off for Reading – not far from the Atomic Weapons Research Establishment at Aldermaston. It was easy driving out of London at that time of day. As he sped westwards and saw thousands of commuters jammed on the eastbound carriageway, trying to get in to the capital, he was relieved to be heading the other way.

He drove directly to the main police station in Reading, where he had arranged to meet the local Special Branch man. Tom McQuade was an old mate; Black knew he would get help there. This part of Britain was a focal point for anti-nuclear activists, what with the Aldermaston complex and the Greenham Common cruise missile base as well.

'Well, you old poacher, what are you after this time?' McQuade asked suspiciously as they greeted one another. His voice bore the merest trace of an Ulster accent.

'What, me? On the scrounge? Whatever gave you that idea, Tom?' Black countered with a smirk.

Though good friends, there had always been a certain reserve in their relationship. To some extent MI5 and the Special Branch were rivals as well as collaborators.

With the door of McQuade's cramped office firmly closed, John Black lit up another cigarette and slumped in a chair.

'Got a little problem with Polaris, have we?' McQuade needled.

John Black explained the circumstances of his visit. He wanted information on the activities of one woman in particular. At the mention of her name, McQuade smiled wryly and reached for the drawer of a filing cabinet. Extracting a green folder, he opened it and browsed through the pages it contained.

'Ye . . . es,' he mused, 'we seem to know the name of Belinda Joyce quite well.'

Without letting go of the file, for fear perhaps of losing the power over John Black that its information gave him, the Special Branch officer began to explain.

'Quite a successful little operation this one,' he said, tapping the folder. 'Young woman detective on the force here – quite a star. Jenny Ward – good operator. A few months ago Jenny turned herself into a radical feminist, at my request. She signed up with a women's militant anti-nuclear group locally, and penetrated their organisation pretty thoroughly. Usual set-up; you know the form. Lesbians most of them. Not our Jenny though – I can vouch for that personally!' he concluded with a grin.

'Tch, tch. Man of your age, you ought to know

better!' John Black chuckled indulgently.

'Well now,' McQuade continued, smiling with self-satisfaction, 'our Jenny made a very interesting discovery. The group in question is called ATSA – stands for Action To Stop Annihilation. And one of the leading lights turned out to be none other than the wife of one of Aldermaston's most senior and respected scientists, Belinda Joyce. Quite a prize for ATSA. Make quite a fuss of her, they do.'

'Now then, there's an element in the group that I would call basically anarchist, a bit of a throwback to the 1960s. And one woman who fits into that category is called Helene Venner. Definitely a dyke, she is,' McQuade added, wrinkling his nose in distaste.

'We don't know much about Venner. She doesn't seem to be on record anywhere, but she's certainly one of the prime movers in ATSA. It was she who recruited Belinda Joyce. There's a craft co-operative in one of the villages – trendy-lefty sort of place where they make pots and country furniture. That's where they met. They both work there.

'Well, at one of ATSA's evening meetings which Jenny Ward attended, Helene Venner came up with a plan which was a bit of a stunner. She wanted Belinda Joyce to get hold of some of her old man's secret plans for the new Polaris warheads, and hand them over so that Venner could get them published in some left-wing newspaper. She argued that with the weapon's secrets made public, they'd become useless, and they could successfully campaign for the missiles to be scrapped.'

John Black whistled softly. None of this appeared on Peter Joyce's security file. There had been an appalling failure of communication somewhere within the security services.

The scheme itself, though dangerous, sounded absurdly naive – and rather like putting the paper on Parliament Hill deliberately to be discovered.

'And Mrs Joyce went along with all this?' he asked attentively.

'Apparently not,' McQuade continued. 'She got pretty annoyed at the ATSA meeting when all this was suggested. Obviously those behind the idea were depending on her to get hold of the plans for them, but she insisted it was a ludicrous idea. She claimed her husband never brought secret documents home, and she was in no position to ask him to do so. Apparently she flatly refused to take part in anything illegal.'

'Hmm,' John Black mused, stroking his chin with a nicotine-stained hand. 'This ATSA mob, do they discuss everything at these general meetings, or does the real action get decided by one or two individuals privately? I mean, could your girl Jenny have missed out on what was really being planned?'

'It's possible, although they certainly make a show of being ever-so democratic – you know the sort of thing: insistence on a full-scale debate and then a vote to decide what to do, with the result that they hardly achieve anything in the end. But perhaps that Venner woman continued to work on Belinda Joyce over at their craft workshop.'

'Your undercover girl hasn't tried to get a job there, then,' Black pressed.

'Not exactly arty-crafty, our Jenny. Bit clumsy with her hands, you could say.'

'Clumsy hands, eh?' John Black chuckled. 'You want to watch that – she could do you an injury!'

McQuade smirked.

For nearly two hours the two men continued their conversation, with several other files being taken out of the Special Branch man's cabinet, to be studied at length.

It was nearly half-past eleven by the time Black swung his vehicle into the visitors' car park outside the gates of Aldermaston. In the security office he proffered his pass, which identified him as an official from the Home Office.

'Do you have an appointment with Mr Joyce?' asked the guard, checking through the messages list to see if this visitor was expected.

'No. It's what you might call a surprise visit,' Black answered. 'But if you put me through to him on the phone, I'm sure he'll be happy to see me.'

The guard dialled Peter Joyce's number, and spoke to his secretary. Then he put the phone down and looked up at Black coldly.

'He's not here. Gone away for a few days.'

'That's impossible!' Black was irritated. 'Put me through to Mr Dogson, the head of security.'

Dogson was a man he had dealt with frequently in the past, and whom he had consulted when he was first assigned to this case. Reluctantly the guard dialled the new number, and then passed the phone across.

'John Black here. Just arrived to talk to your Mr Joyce, only to be told that he's away for a few days. Know anything about it?'

Dogson did, and expressed astonishment that John Black did *not*. Peter Joyce's visit to America had been sanctioned at the highest level, he said, and that must have involved MI5, surely?

Black felt a hot flush colour his face, and he turned away from the guard so as not to be overheard.

'But I'm in the middle of the investigation, for

God's sake,' he hissed into the phone. 'How the hell can he be allowed to go swanning off to America for a few days?'

'It's not – unrelated, shall we say?' Dogson answered mysteriously.

Black climbed back into his car and slammed the door angrily. He felt humiliated, and he hated that feeling more than anything else in life. It reminded him painfully of commencing his National Service, aged eighteen. He had been fat and breathless as a teenager, and had been thoroughly victimised during the start of his two years in the army.

He picked up the receiver of his radio-telephone, with its built-in encryption device that prevented his words from being deciphered if the call was intercepted. On the keypad he punched out the secret direct-line code to the office of the MI5 director, Dick Sproat. When a secretary answered, Black identified himself and insisted that he talk urgently to his boss.

'Yes, John, what is it?' Sproat's voice crackled in his ear.

'I'm sorry to bother you, sir, but I'm down here at Aldermaston and have just been told that Peter Joyce has left the country for a few days. Seems a bit odd when he's a central figure in my investigation. I gather you know something about it, sir.'

'Oh,' Sproat grunted. 'He, er . . . he'll be back in a day or two. You can talk to him then.'

'But, with respect, sir,' Black continued, his voice rising, 'don't you think that as investigating officer I should have known about this?'

'Normally, yes,' Sproat snapped back, 'but this is not a normal case. Its secrecy classification is so high there are some things you don't need to know, and this is one of them.'

The line clicked, and a dialling tone returned. Sproat had hung up on him.

'Bloody ridiculous!' Black exploded, as he snapped the receiver back into its rest. 'It's like trying to fight a gorilla with one hand tied behind your back!'

To console himself while deciding his next move, he sought a pub for some lunch. He did not have far to drive, and pulled into the crowded car-park of a half-timbered roadhouse advertising bar food.

Following a couple of pints of bitter and a steak pie and chips, he felt reasonably more comforted. He had even positioned himself on a stool close to two young technicians from Aldermaston, so he could eavesdrop casually on their ill-informed speculation about the stolen nuclear secrets.

After relieving his bladder of most of the beer, he then returned to his car and took out his road atlas.

It took him some time to find the Joyces' house, which stood on the very edge of their village. Black stopped his car in the road a few yards from the gateway on to the drive, and he studied the building. It was an attractive red-brick house with a slate roof. A golden-yellow climbing rose covered a side wall, still bearing a few late blooms. In the garden stood a magnificent oak tree that had shed most of its leaves for the coming winter. The tree and the house might well be about the same age, he speculated; early nineteenth century perhaps.

'Must be worth a bit,' he pondered suspiciously.

This part of Berkshire was prime commuter country. Could a government scientist afford to live here without earning a bit extra on the side? Of course, if they had bought the place some time ago, the price might have been more reasonable, he conceded.

Tom McQuade had said Belinda Joyce worked at a craft co-operative, but he did not know whether that was just part-time. Black locked the car door and set off up the gravel drive to check if she was at home. An old, rusting Citroën 2cv stood outside the large garage, and some of the ground-floor windows were open. Through one of them he could hear the rumble of a washing-machine, and he saw the figure of a woman working in the kitchen.

Belinda Joyce looked startled when he introduced himself, but Black was used to that.

'I'm enquiring into some problems to do with your husband's work, Mrs Joyce. It's a matter of national security. I'd like to come in and ask you some questions, if you don't mind.'

The woman was exactly as he had pictured her, dressed in faded grey jeans and an oversized hand-knitted sweater of an indeterminate 'country' colour. Her oval face was framed by straight hair hanging down to her shoulders, brown hair that was streaked with grey and needed a wash. Her dark eyes showed an intelligent intensity, but radiated hostility when he asked to come inside. He had seen a thousand other women who looked like Belinda Joyce, middle-aged and losing their looks, women who had committed themselves fervently to a cause late in life and were now determined to change the world. He knew the way their minds worked and he did not like them much.

Lieutenant Robert Simpson was the supply officer on board HMS *Retribution*. He found it odd walking through the empty passageways of the submarine when half the crew were on shore leave. The lower-ratings' recreation area was almost deserted, and whole compartments of bunks had not been slept in that night. It reminded him uncomfortably of one summer during his childhood, when he had had to spend the half-term holiday on his own at his boarding-school because his family had been abroad.

Today would be busy for Simpson; he had to complete his inventory of foodstocks and other supplies, and place orders for the rest of their voyage, allowing a generous reserve for emergencies. Known in naval jargon as the 'Pusser' or Purser, his job was more like that of an hotel manager than a sailor.

In the galley the leading chef handed over his list of the most urgently needed food items, and asked Simpson how many of the officers would be at lunch that day. Simpson told him that six were on shore leave, but there would be two visitors on board.

As he headed back towards the middle of the submarine, where lay the control room and the officers' accommodation, he began to wonder about those visitors. At breakfast in the wardroom that morning, the captain had refused to be drawn on the purpose of their visit. Simpson had resented the look of cold dismissal in Carrington's eyes when he had asked. It was as if the captain did not consider him a real officer, and certainly not one who could be trusted with secrets.

The visitors were due aboard soon after 8 am, and Simpson was loitering close to the forward hatch then. For Robert Simpson was not just the ship's 'Pusser'; he had a personal mission of his own to carry out, one that he had been planning and dreaming of for a full five years.

He had been a member of *Retribution*'s crew for less than a year, so did not recognise Peter Joyce as he climbed down the ladder. One of the petty officers did, however, and remarked within Simpson's hearing that the stranger was 'that bloke from Aldermaston' who had been on board the previous autumn.

Simpson followed, as casually as he could, while the visitors were escorted by Lt. Commander Phil Dunkley towards the stern. But, in the passage leading to the missile chamber, he saw his way would be blocked by the unusual presence of an armed sentry, and so he turned back.

'Curious!' he muttered to himself. 'Never seen that before.'

The submarine crew had been told they were to perform a routine missile test within the next few days, but Simpson knew from hints dropped in the wardroom that the test was to be far from routine – the missile in question being the first to be fitted with the new Skydancer warhead system. He had also read the news summary from Britain which came through to the submarine by telex, and which included a report on the missing Polaris papers in London. With the sudden clandestine arrival of the scientists on board, he began to divine a connection here.

Peter Joyce was not feeling his best after a night of little sleep. He removed the jacket of his light-grey suit and hung it on a hook next to the launcher control panel, whose lights and dials would reveal whether the missile gyros and arming mechanisms were operational when the weapons were fired. Hanging from the same hook was an old baseball bat, to be used as a cudgel by the missile technicians in case any member of the ship's company suffering from mental derangement or troubled conscience should ever try to interfere with the countdown.

'Let's check those boxes, Jill,' Joyce said, looking to see that the seals had not been broken overnight. His assistant ticked off the contents against an inventory.

As Peter turned to the Polaris Systems Officer to explain what they had to do, he spoke directly, aware that Dunkley was one of the few members of the crew of HMS *Retribution* who had been trained in the workings of the new warheads.

'I'll need my assistant with me for this,' Dunkley said soberly after Peter had described the task ahead. 'We operate a two-man rule when doing anything to the missiles. It's in the regulations. It avoids mistakes as well as keeping the security people happy.'

Peter nodded. On the side of each of the sixteen launch tubes was a circular access hatch about two feet in diameter, secured tightly to withstand the colossal pressure inside from the gas used to eject the missiles at thc start of thc launching process. With his assistant watching his every move, Dunkley wrenched at the two-handed brass key that released the securing bolts, and swung the hatch open. The curved skin of the missile with its matt-grey radar-absorbing paint could be seen inside.

'Have you got the tray there?' Dunkley asked. They had to take great care when the hatch was open so as not to drop anything down between the missile and the side of the tube. The assistant PSO passed him a tray which bridged the gap precisely.

The task which Peter had outlined was complex. After opening the launch tube, the PSO had to unscrew a second panel on the missile itself, uncovering the rotating 'bus' on which the warheads were mounted. Each re-entry vehicle in turn would have to be rotated in line with the opening, so that a printed-circuit memory board could be withdrawn from its internal computer for reprogramming. The components would then need to be replaced with the greatest care.

It was half an hour later before the engineer handed over the first board of microchips to the scientists. The magnetic bubble memories on the card looked like miniature tablets of Swiss chocolate. Jill Piper slotted the board into a test socket mounted on a programmer, which in turn was connected to one of the micro-computers they had brought with them from Aldermaston. Her fingers flew expertly across the keyboard, and row upon row of data rolled across the screen, signifying that the circuitry was functioning correctly. With a few more deft key-strokes, she ordered the equipment to erase the data in the memories and replace it with the programme written on the flight over from Britain.

After comparing a printout of the new data with the original, Peter Joyce was satisfied, and returned the board to the engineer for fitting back into the warhead. Six times this process was repeated before the scientists could make their final check. They connected a lead to a test socket on the 'bus', fed in electronic instructions, and read on the computer screen the responses from the individual warheads.

'I do believe we've done it!' exclaimed Peter, grinning in triumph. He reached across and firmly shook the hands of the two submariners in turn.

'I wish I knew exactly what it was I've just done!' Dunkley joked modestly. 'All I know is I'm damned glad I don't have to tinker with the thing every time we launch a missile!'

Peter observed the look of expectant curiosity on the officers' faces. 'Look, I'd love to tell you what this is all about, but I just can't. It's extremely secret.'

'Something to do with that spy business in London?' Dunkley ventured casually.

'You really mustn't press me. I am sure you'll make your own assumptions anyway. But it really would be best if you didn't speculate too much, particularly not in front of any of your colleagues,' Peter added.

'Point taken. Now, how about a spot of lunch?'

Dunkley answered, putting an end to the conversation.

As they entered the wardroom, Lieutenant Bob Simpson slipped past them.

'I'll tell the captain you're here, Mr Joyce,' he announced.

'Would you like a drink? I'm certainly in need of a pint.' The PSO headed for a small cupboard in a corner and opened it to reveal a barrel of beer.

'Excellent idea!' Peter exclaimed, beginning to relax.

'We don't drink much when we're at sea, but in harbour . . . well, that's a different matter,' Dunkley chuckled, handing out the brimming glasses.

'Ah, Jill, did they find somewhere suitable for you?' he inquired as Peter's assistant was escorted into the wardroom.

'Yes, fine thanks,' she breezed. 'I can't remember having a guard when I've been to the loo before!'

'Well, we couldn't have any of our young sailors bursting in on you, could we?' Dunkley snorted. 'Drink?'

'Just an orange juice, thanks.'

The young supply officer re-entered the wardroom.

'The captain wonders if you could spare him a few minutes in his cabin, Mr Joyce,' Simpson ventured. 'He would like a quiet word before lunch.'

'Yes, of course,' Peter replied, placing his pint mug on the wardroom table.

When he had left the room, Simpson turned his attention to Jill.

'We don't often have the pleasure of having ladies visit the *Retribution*,' he began awkwardly. He had a shy nature. 'Been doing something special have you?'

For a moment her face froze at his outright enquiry.

'Oh no, just checking the sparking plugs,' she answered sweetly.

*

'Just wanted to ask how things have gone this morning,' Carrington questioned when they were alone, keen to know more but not wishing to pry beyond the areas of information he was entitled to know.

'Yes, of course. Well, we've completed our work successfully, thanks to your excellent systems officers,' Peter answered formally. 'The warheads on the test missile have now been reprogrammed, and within a few days you will probably get your orders to launch.'

He paused, and studied the unsatisfied look on the captain's face. He would have to tell him more.

'In absolute confidence, I suppose I shall have to confirm what you are all guessing: this sudden crisis with the test missile *is* connected with that secret document found in a rubbish basket on Hampstead Heath.'

'It did seem the most likely reason for your visit, I must say,' Carrington's thin face creased into a fleeting smile.

Peter puffed out his cheeks, then let out a long steady breath as he lowered his heavy frame into a small armchair covered with the yellow and green floral print that was standard issue for Royal Naval officers' quarters.

'It's a weird business,' he ventured in a half-whisper.

'It's serious, is it? We couldn't tell from the news reports,' Carrington responded in the same hushed tone. 'The Russians presumably?'

Peter shrugged and shook his head.

'That's just the trouble; no one seems to be sure. At least they weren't when I left England yesterday. But we're having to assume the Soviets have got hold of some very sensitive information. Hence all these last-minute changes.'

For several minutes more they talked around the subject, with Peter increasingly careful not to reveal any details of the alterations to the missile warheads, nor of the precise purpose behind them. When Carrington stood up and suggested they return to the wardroom for lunch, he had realised he would learn no more.

The normal Royal Naval routine is for the captain to take his meals in his own cabin, but the tradition is different on a submarine, where there is a certain levelling of the ranks due to the lack of space and a dependence on the reliability of every individual for their joint survival under water.

Over lunch, a naval version of chop suey described on the menu as 'Chinky Nosh', Carrington led the conversation on to the harmless subject of the perils and pleasures of shore leave in Florida. Peter Joyce hardly noticed how the young lieutenant at the end of the table was staring at him with ill-concealed curiosity.

The conversation had not progressed far, however, when a signaller knocked at the wardroom door and handed in an urgent telex from London. It was addressed to Peter Joyce, and an awkward silence descended on the table as the naval men surreptitiously watched the scientist's expression for some hint of what the message contained.

'They want me back in London as soon as possible,' he announced, frowning.

The rest of the meal was hurried and confused, as messages were sent to Patrick Air Force Base to alert the crew of his RAF plane that he must return to Britain that same afternoon.

Two thousand miles south of Cape Canaveral, in the steamy heat of mid-Atlantic, the 21,000-ton Soviet ship *Akademik Sergey Korolev* dropped her speed from the seventeen knots at which she had been steaming for most of her journey from the Black Sea. She had reached her 'station' now, and would simply have to wait and watch, training her massive radar and telemetry antennae on the segment of the upper atmosphere used by the US Navy's Eastern test range.

It had taken two weeks to sail from Sevastopol in the Crimea, down through the NATO-controlled narrows of the Bosporus and Gibraltar and out into the Atlantic. It was a journey the ship had undertaken many times in the past, with her alternate missions of observing and listening in to the latest Western missile tests or of acting as a tracking station and data relay terminal for her own country's extensive activities in space.

Her departure from her home port had been very rushed this time, though, triggered by a message that had originated in Scotland.

At the moment when the *Retribution* had submerged beneath the waters of the Clyde, heading out for the Atlantic, and had escaped the attentions of a Soviet submarine, the *Korolev* had been steaming slowly past the Golden Horn of Istanbul. Her passage had been reported by Turkish naval officers to NATO's Southern naval intelligence headquarters to Gaeta in Italy, and the information had been fed into the central files of Alliance intelligence data, to which the British Royal Navy had access.

A few days later, as the *Korolev* was passing under the eyes of British observers on the Rock of Gibraltar, she had received a coded signal from Moscow reporting the dates that HMS *Retribution* had been allocated on the American missile range off Florida. This had given her little time in which to reach the area of the Atlantic where the missile warheads would splash down into the sea, and where she would be able to observe them with accuracy.

Kapitan Karpov sat in his cabin with his feet up, smoking a cigar. He was happy to have arrived on station on time, and not to have missed the 'party', but the ship's maintenance reports that he was studying did not please him. Most of the air-conditioning plant was unserviceable, and what was left of it had to be used to keep the temperature down in the massive racks of electronics that powered the gigantic dish aerials on the upper deck. He hoped desperately that the British would get a move on with their missile test, so he could steam north again to a climate that was not so uncomfortably hot and humid.

As the pale grey RAC VC10 sped back across the Atlantic carrying its two passengers, Peter Joyce stared absently out of the window at the streaks of cloud below, tinted by the setting sun.

The world was such a miraculous creation, still able to withhold many of its secrets. How strange, he thought, that people should devise two totally opposing concepts of how to prevent it from being destroyed. Particularly strange since both concepts claimed to base themselves on an understanding of human nature.

He had argued this issue so often with Belinda – until the time had come when they could no longer discuss the subject because of the stress it placed on their relationship.

Though Peter admired the eloquence with which Belinda made her own anti-nuclear case, he still could not accept it. There was a logic to both their arguments, but he was convinced his was the stronger. To his mind there was only one nation that posed any real threat to Britain's survival, and that was the Soviet Union armed with tens of thousands of nuclear weapons. But he was not a 'hawk' and did not believe, like so many of those he met in Western military circles, that Russia was hell-bent on world domination. He did consider, however, that the Soviet Union was led by opportunists who would seize anything to their advantage given the chance. So the Western possession of nuclear weapons should prevent the *big* chance from ever arising.

As the VC10 headed east, away from the sun, the sky darkened rapidly, and Peter began to adjust his mind forward five hours, trying to attune to the fact that it was late evening in Britain.

He had lost track of the days, and had to do some thinking to work out it was Wednesday. He swore quietly when he remembered he was due to attend a parent-teacher meeting at the children's school that very evening. He was active on the fund-raising committee, but he hoped Belinda would have gone in his place.

It was odd this being called back to Britain at such short notice and with no explanation. Something else must have happened, some further development in the investigation. It could not be anything very positive, though, or they would have commented about his work on the missile and whether it was still necessary.

He thought again of Mary Maclean, and could not dismiss from his mind the fear that she could somehow be responsible for this crisis. The memory of the last time he had really talked to her still caused pangs of remorse. He felt he had handled it badly, but he knew of no easy way to end a love affair.

Soon afterwards he had taken his family on holiday to the Lake District, where they had sailed and gone walking on the fells. For Peter it had been like a period of rehabilitation; he'd concentrated wholeheartedly on getting closer again to Belinda and his children. He had found extraordinary pleasure simply being in their company, and he had achieved a certain peace of mind that week, an acceptance of how things must be from then on. But now that peace had been shattered by a dread suspicion which verged on paranoia.

Both women had the motive and the means to betray him. Peter winced at the realisation of how careless he had been.

Three months earlier when he had been to London to explain the Skydancer project to the ministers, he had carried the blueprints with him to Mary's flat on the night he had ended their affair, then taken them to the Ministry, and then to his own home afterwards. Two major security lapses in forty-eight hours.

He told himself he had to stop the drift of his thoughts and try to concentrate on sleep. They would be landing back in England in the small hours of the morning. He looked across to the seat opposite where Jill Piper was dozing. The girl had been disappointed at the brevity of her first visit to America, but was oblivious to the complex reasons behind it.

Lieutenant Robert Simpson was now dressed in pale-blue cotton slacks and a striped shirt with short sleeves. He had just taken a shower and washed his hair. Looking at himself in the tiny mirror in his cabin, he decided he was in a fit state to go ashore. The captain had given him a twenty-four-hour pass, and he felt he had deserved it. HMS *Retribution* was as well stocked for the rest of her voyage as she would ever be.

He leaned through the door of the wardroom to see if his fellow lieutenant was ready, the Assistant Polaris Systems Officer, George Grundy. They had decided to sample some of the bars and discotheques together.

'Come on, George, let's get at it before all the talent's snapped up!'

As they hurried down the gangway on to the quayside, they welcomed the warm freshness of unconditioned air. George had hired them a car for the evening, and it was parked near the main gate.

'You looked pretty busy this morning,' Bob Simpson ventured as they drove down the long straight road through a succession of beach resorts. 'Who were the visitors in the wardroom at lunchtime? The girl was rather fanciable.'

'Oh, they were from Aldermaston. You remember the tall guy from last year, surely?' George answered cautiously. 'Oh no, you weren't on board then, were you?'

'From Aldermaston?' Simpson answered, feigning surprise. 'What were they doing here?

'Adjusting things, I suppose you could say.'

'What, on the new warheads, you mean?'

George tightened his grip on the wheel.

'I can't talk about that, as you bloody well know, Bob!'

'Sorry. Just curious.'

They motored on in silence for a few moments.

'Must have been important, though,' Bob muttered, half to himself.

'Oh, yes.' George turned the car into the enormous parking lot flanking a complex of bars and restaurants. 'You could certainly say it was important.'

He switched off the engine and they stared at the bright neon signs in front of them.

'Well, this is the place the lads came to last night. Two of them got their legs over, so it can't be bad!' George proclaimed.

Simpson laughed uneasily. 'Well, let's get at it then!'

He opened the door and stepped on to the tarmac.

The name 'Millies' in green neon surmounted the doorway which they entered. Inside the air was warm, and sweet with smoke and perfume sprays. Bob Simpson spotted a telephone in the foyer.

'George, must make a quick phone call. Buy me a gin would you, and I'll see you at the bar in a minute. Leave the best one for me!'

His mate gave a V-sign and pushed his way towards the counter.

Simpson took a handful of quarters from his pocket and dialled the operator. Within seconds the number in England was ringing.

The voice which answered sounded extremely sleepy; it was the early hours of the morning over there. But the drowsiness vanished quickly enough when she heard what Simpson had to say.

The VC10 touched down at RAF Brize Norton just after three in the morning. Peter had only managed two hours' sleep on the flight and felt crumpled and unwashed as he stepped carefully down the steps, blinking in the glare of the floodlights.

He had expected an official car to meet him, but not to see the rear seat already half occupied by a large man with a somewhat featureless face that he did not recognise. A door was opened towards him from inside, and a cloud of warm cigarette smoke wafted out into the chilly English air.

'Mr Joyce?' The man's voice sounded tired. 'My name is John Black. I'm from MI5.'

As Peter slid into the free rear-seat he could see even in the pale glow from the courtesy light that the stranger was regarding him with some curiosity. As he closed the door behind him, he immediately found the foul air stifling; and wound down his window.

'MI5?' Peter answered weakly, sensing reluctantly that he was about to be told something deeply shocking. 'It's kind of you to meet me . . .'

'It's not kindness that brings me here, Mr Joyce,' Black answered sombrely.

The driver slammed the car boot. John Black waited until they were outside the air-base and on the road towards London before he spoke again.

'I have some news for you . . . and some of it you will find distressing,' he announced, staring straight ahead. 'The good news is that we seem to have identified who has been playing around with your secret papers.'

'Oh?' Peter turned to look at him in surprise.

'But the bad news *is* bad, I'm afraid.' Black paused and chewed his lip.

Peter felt his heart beat faster.

'The bad news is that Mary Maclean has killed herself.'

'What?' Peter gasped, clutching at the seat in front of him. 'Oh, God!'

'Cut her wrists,' Black continued softly.

'Oh, Jesus.' Peter's voice caught in his throat. His head spun and, as the car lurched round a double bend, he pressed a hand to his stomach.

'Shall I stop the car for a few minutes?' Black asked with sudden concern.

'I . . . I think you'd better,' Peter whispered.

Black tapped the driver on the shoulder and ordered him to pull over. The car slowed to a halt, bumping on the soft earth at the edge of the road. Peter struggled with the handle and pushed the door open. He swung his legs out and stood up, supporting himself against the side of the car, drawing great gulps of cold air into his lungs to try to stem the nausea rising from his stomach.

He struggled to comprehend the trauma and despair that could have been great enough to drive Mary to such a thing. To cut her own wrists! Giddiness overcoming him, he slumped on to the edge of the car seat, leaning out into the air, his head in his hands.

Suddenly it dawned on him what Black had really just told him. Carefully he lifted his legs back into the car and turned to face the man from MI5.

'You said you knew who took the Skydancer plans?' he began with a sense of resignation.

Black nodded, knowing that Peter had understood.

'She wrote you a note admitting it,' he stated flatly. 'It was addressed to you, but I'm afraid we opened it.'

'I can't believe it,' Peter answered. His worst suspicions seemed confirmed.

'She felt herself to be a woman scorned,' Black remarked pointedly.

For a few minutes they sat in silence, Peter shaking his head from time to time in disbelief.

'Are you ready for us to move on now, Mr Joyce?'

'Yes, I think I'm all right now.'

'Perhaps you would take the corners more slowly, driver,' Black called. He slipped his hand into the inside pocket of his jacket and pulled out an envelope.

Peter stared at it silently for a moment, not realising what it was, and not taking hold of it.

'There's a light behind you, if you want to read it,' Black urged him. 'That little white button.'

Peter found the flexible silver tube with a lamp at the end, designed for government officials to study documents while being driven to their appointments.

The envelope was blank, but he pulled from it a folded photocopy of a typewritten letter. He held it in the light and began to read.

Dear Peter,

I've been such a fool. I'm so sorry. I didn't mean to cause all this trouble.

But you hurt me very deep, you know, and I wanted so badly to hurt you back. Causing a fuss over your precious Skydancer seemed the only way to get at you.

It was me who copied a page from your plans and left it on Parliament Hill, just for someone to find it and make a fuss, to get you into trouble. I feel so ashamed now. It was so silly of me and so selfish.

There never were any spies involved, no Russians, plotting against you. Just me.

But I see now what a mess I've made, and I can't go on. I know you can't let me live with you, but I can't live without you.

Goodbye.

Love M.

Peter could almost hear her saying it, see her tear-filled eyes pleading with him as on the last time they had been together. He swallowed hard to keep his own eyes from watering.

Every moment of that night came back to him – that night their affair ended, three months ago. He had been a coward. He should have told her all as soon as he arrived at her flat in Chiswick, but he could not find the courage. She had cooked them some salmon and had bought a bottle of Sancerre to go with it. It had felt so right being there with Mary that evening – so right that he had to fight to hang on to his resolve to end it all.

They had slipped into bed together after their meal. He wanted to make love to her for one last time. He remembered the stunned disbelief on her face when he told her, as they lay together afterwards. He had explained that the preservation of his family and the happiness of his children was more important than his personal feelings.

Disbelief had turned to anger at his deceit in making love to her while knowing he was just about to end their relationship, then to despair when she finally realised they would never be together like this again. Her face looked crumpled and ugly as she buried it in her pillow to sob uncontrollably.

So, now this, he thought to himself, staring hazily at the typewritten note. She had killed herself because of him. He had caused someone to die.

'What . . . what happened exactly?' he asked, without turning to the man on his right.

'She didn't turn up for work yesterday,' John Black explained brusquely. 'There'd been no word from her, and there was no reply from her phone, so in the circumstances we decided to break into her flat. Found her dead in the bath with her wrists slashed. It wasn't a pretty sight.'

Peter took a deep breath, but felt unable to speak.

'And that note was on her desk, in an envelope addressed to you. That's a photocopy; we've got the original in the forensic lab. Just routine checks, of course.'

'It couldn't have been anything else?' Peter asked, clutching at any means to reduce his guilt. 'You're sure it was suicide?'

'Oh, I don't think there's much doubt. Besides it fits in with the evidence. We've not really uncovered anything that points to a Soviet intelligence operation. I'd had a feeling the whole business was "personal" right from the very start.'

The car had now passed Oxford and was heading south towards Aldermaston. Peter was being taken home.

'Have you . . . have you talked to my wife about this?' he inquired a few minutes later.

'Yesterday. Saw her yesterday. Before we got worried about Maclean.'

'What did you ask her? What sort of questions?'

'Oh, just things that were relevant to my enquiry,' John Black answered evasively.

'Including presumably whether she knew about Mary and me?'

'Of course. Your affair wasn't exactly insignificant, after all, was it?' His eyebrows arched in self-righteousness.

'And what did she say?' Peter asked sharply, suspecting the MI5 man took pleasure in invading people's privacy.

'Seemed a bit shocked. Apparently she hadn't known anything about it, or at least that's what she claimed. She got rather uppish after that. Refused to answer any more questions, and even started trying to ring some lawyer or other, so I decided to leave. With women like your wife there comes a point where you just can't get any more sense out of them – but then I expect you know that already. I suppose that's why you went off with Maclean?'

Peter turned to glare at the MI5 man.

'If I were you I would keep opinions like that to myself!' he exploded. 'I don't think you could even begin to understand what that affair was about. Are you married, Mr Black?'

The MI5 man chuckled. 'No, not me. I don't really like women that much. They're all right for just one thing, but when they start expressing opinions, that's when trouble starts.' He paused reflectively for a few moments. 'But between you and me, Mr Joyce, it's *people* that I don't really like, people in general. Life could run so smoothly if it wasn't for people fouling it up, don't you think?'

Peter felt further conversation was pointless. Black's remarks were odious and insensitive. So he sat in silence for the rest of the journey, Mary's agonised face filling his thoughts. As they neared his village in the rolling hillocks of Berkshire, he began to dread how he would cope with Belinda.

Black leaned forward to instruct the driver to pull up outside Peter's house.

'I'd be glad if you would call into my office at Curzon Street tomorrow morning around eleven,' John Black said. 'There are still a number of security details that need clearing up. All right?'

'Eleven o'clock? I'll try,' Peter answered coolly.

The driver retrieved his small suitcase from the boot and handed it to him.

'Goodnight, Mr Joyce,' Black called from inside the car.

The car purred away down the road, and Peter was left with the sounds of the night. It had been raining, and moisture dripped from the branches of the oak tree in his garden.

The clouds prevented the moon from illuminating his path, but that did not matter. Light was streaming on to the drive from the bedroom window. His wife was awake and waiting for him.

Chapter Four

Belinda had just reached the foot of the stairs as he opened the front door. She was in her dressing-gown. She gazed at him for less than a second, her face tear-stained and pained; then, without speaking, she turned towards the kitchen and moved away from him.

He deposited his overnight bag on the hall floor, and listened momentarily to the stillness of the house. He could almost sense the presence of his three children upstairs, sleeping in happy ignorance of the conflict about to engulf their parents.

He heard a kettle being filled, and followed his wife into the kitchen, knowing they could not put off the confrontation. Belinda plugged in the kettle and turned to face him with her arms folded.

'Hello,' he greeted her weakly from the doorway, without even attempting to smile.

She did not reply. She was like a primed bomb of tense emotion, her whole body rigid, not daring to speak for fear the last remnants of self-control would slip from her grasp. Peter watched her uncomfortably, terribly aware that he was the cause of her acute distress. Her skin looked pale grey from lack of sleep, and her straight, streaked hair was uncombed.

'I'm sorry . . .' Peter whispered, his voice catching in his throat. Pulling out one of the rickety pine chairs from under the kitchen table, he sat down staring vacantly into the corner of the room.

'It would help . . . if you were to tell me how much

you know, Belinda,' he ventured, hoping to find a way through to her.

'Huh!' she snapped angrily. 'Of course it would bloody well help you! Help you to decide how little you need tell me!'

She found herself shouting but quickly moderated her tone, conscious of the sleeping children upstairs.

'I'll tell you just one thing, Peter, give you just one clue,' she continued, unable to control the trembling in her voice. 'Yesterday I had a visit from a man calling himself John Black. You know him perhaps?'

Peter nodded.

'Well this man Black tried to interrogate me. He accused me of conspiracy, treason and theft . . . and of *sexual deviation*.'

Her voice rose to a pitch of indignation.

'Then he told me tales about you which I refused to believe – until he showed me things to prove it.'

The kettle came to the boil behind her, and she swung round to turn it off, her eyes filling with tears.

'I'm making some tea. I take it you'd like some?' she offered, struggling to steady her voice.

'Yes, please.'

Peter took a deep breath before continuing.

'I expect,' he began carefully, 'that John Black told you I was having an affair with another woman.'

She stirred the tea noisily.

'He showed me a letter you wrote her,' Belinda choked on the words. 'It was full of . . . of love! You cheated, Peter. I trusted you!'

'Did he tell you that I broke it off three months ago?' Peter asked hurriedly. 'Did he? Did he tell you that?'

She placed his mug on the table, her face contorted with her effort not to cry. She shook her head.

'Well, I did. It was all over. I haven't had any contact

with her since then . . . hadn't even heard any news of her until just now.'

His wife leaned back against the dresser, clasping her mug in both hands to keep it steady. She shivered; it was cold in the kitchen. She was not sure she was ready to listen to his pleas of mitigation.

'What do you mean? What news? What have you heard just now?' she asked cautiously.

Peter pushed away the tea; the feeling of nausea was returning.

'John Black just told me,' he said haltingly. 'He told me . . . that she's dead. She killed herself yesterday.' Finally the words spilled out.

'Oh, Peter!' Belinda gasped. She was shocked, yet deep inside she felt an uncomfortable gladness at the news. 'How dreadful!'

The distress on his face would normally have evoked her sympathy, but at that moment she could feel none. His grief was for a woman who had been her rival, someone she could only think of as a thief.

'Why did she kill herself?' Belinda asked after a pause.

Peter stared down at his tea.

'It wasn't because of you . . . because of your breaking up with her, was it?'

He pulled a handkerchief from his pocket and blew his nose.

'Oh God,' she whispered, 'it was, wasn't it?'

She pulled another chair from under the table and sat down opposite him.

Peter drew in a deep breath.

'I met her . . .' he tried to steady his voice. 'I met her two years ago. It began as . . . as nothing really. Just a little flirtation. There was no particular reason for it . . . it just happened.'

Peter spread his arms in a gesture of helplessness. He badly wanted to avoid a probing analysis of his motives.

Belinda turned her mind back two years trying to guess when he had first been unfaithful to her. Surely she should have noticed something? In bed perhaps? How could he have been making love to another woman and not show it?

'Two years! For two years you've been deceiving me,' she burst out.

Why had it all happened? There *had* to be a reason for it.

'It was about two years ago I started campaigning seriously,' she continued more quietly. 'That's when I got involved at the craft co-operative and began campaigning against your work, wasn't it?'

'Well . . . it *was* about that time,' he conceded uncomfortably.

'So this . . . this was you getting your own back, was it?'

'No! It really didn't begin for any reason that I can explain. It was just – an opportunity that suddenly presented itself; a temptation if you like, and . . . I failed to resist it,' he ended feebly.

He knew his explanation would not satisfy his wife. His fingers fumbled with the peppermill on the table.

'We didn't meet very often, and I didn't really take it very seriously at first, but . . . Mary became more involved than I did. And in the end . . . I mean she knew I was married – always knew that . . . But in the end she seemed to expect me to leave you and the children and set up home with her – and I wasn't having it. So I told her I couldn't see her anymore.'

Belinda eyed him suspiciously. He must have encouraged the woman to fall in love with him.

'And now she's dead . . .'

Peter flinched at the accusation in her tone.

'Yes, she's dead.'

He still found it hard to believe.

'There was a note. She left a note,' he continued with an effort. 'In it she said that she was very bitter . . . that she'd wanted to hit back at me in some way. She said she took a page from a secret file at the Defence Ministry, photocopied it and left it on Parliament Hill . . . expecting that it would be found by a passer-by and cause a scandal which would damage my work at Aldermaston.'

'What?' Belinda gasped with astonishment. 'So *she* was at the bottom of this security scandal? You mean *she* was the one who's had you running round in circles the past few days? Well, she's certainly got her own back!' She shook her head with a certain admiration at the panic the woman had been able to cause.

For a few moments neither spoke, as Belinda took in the seriousness of what had happened. It was not just that Peter had been unfaithful to her; he was now at the very centre of a national crisis over Skydancer. It would be he who would take the blame for all that had happened. He faced disgrace in his professional life and his career would be in ruins.

His handsome face looked crumpled and crushed. She began to feel a little sorry for him, despite her anger and resentment at what he had done.

'She must have been really desperate,' Belinda reflected.

'I still can't believe she did it,' her husband murmured. 'However much she may have got to hate me, I just can't believe she'd have done this. She was too . . . too professional. This is so out of character – it really is. I mean, it seemed obvious the Soviets would try to steal the Skydancer plans. They're bound to want to know what we're up to. So when that paper was found on Parliament Hill, it looked exactly like a drop that had gone wrong. That explanation fitted perfectly. But now . . . Mary.'

He frowned as he tried to recall the exact words in the note John Black had given him. There had been something about that note that did not seem quite right, he thought in retrospect. He puzzled about what that was.

'Is there any doubt?' Belinda asked, curious at the implications. 'There is, isn't there? I can see it in your eyes?'

Peter was concentrating hard, trying to remember exactly what the letter had said. It was still in his jacket pocket, but he did not want Belinda to read it.

The more he thought about it now, the stranger it all seemed. Mary had been such a stable person. Would she really have taken such drastic revenge on him, and then killed herself? He somehow could not believe it. Or was he just telling himself that to lessen the guilt pressing down on his shoulders?

'John Black said there was little doubt that she killed herself. It seemed to fit the circumstances,' he murmured.

'John Black?' Belinda spat. 'You believe that *creature*?'

'He *is* conducting the investigation,' Peter answered flatly.

'Well, God help poor old Britain!' she exclaimed. 'He's an evil man! And, anyway, I thought MI5 were discredited these days. Aren't they all supposed to be Russian moles? How do you know Black didn't murder your . . . friend, to cover up some spy operation being run by Moscow?'

Peter looked at Belinda in astonishment.

Whether meant seriously or not, her words further

stirred the growing doubts in his mind. For the past three days the Defence Ministry's guard had been up, trying to counter the loss of the Skydancer plans. But now, conveniently, it seemed there had been no loss of secrets after all, so they could all relax again. It was very comforting – perhaps too comforting.

Belinda was torn between both a need and a reluctance to know more about the secret life her husband had been leading for the past two years.

'You loved her, didn't you?' she asked eventually.

'What?' Peter was jolted back to the present. 'I . . . I don't really know,' he stammered. 'I suppose I was . . . sort of infatuated . . . *in love* with her maybe, but that's not the same thing is it? We got on together,' he continued carelessly. 'There was no conflict between us until . . .'

'Conflict! So that's it! Conflict. Something you didn't have with her, but you did have with me. But what *was* that conflict, Peter. What was it about? How did it happen? Well, I'll tell you, in case you've forgotten. That conflict only arose because, as I got older, I began to understand the meaning of morality, and you didn't. It all makes sense in a way; it explains your mistress. One immorality begat another!'

'Immorality? What the hell are you talking about?' he rounded on her.

'You know perfectly well what I mean,' she persisted. 'Your work – that's the source of our conflict. It is utterly immoral for you to devote your life to designing means of genocide, building weapons of mass murder! And it is the moral duty of every rational human being to oppose your work and demand that it ends!'

'Belinda, please! Let's not go through that all over again!' Peter pleaded.

'Yes. I can see how nice it must have been for you to

find a woman who didn't object to what you did for a living. No wonder you fell in love with your Mary if she never said anything that would make your conscience trouble you! If it wasn't for the bloody bomb, none of this . . .'

She stopped halfway through her sentence, turning towards the door. Peter turned in his chair to follow her gaze.

'I heard a noise and thought it was burglars.' Suzanne stood in the doorway, rubbing the sleep from her eyes. 'Is it morning or what?'

Peter rose from the table and crossed the room. Putting his arm round her shoulders he led her back towards the stairs.

'No, it's still the middle of the night. I've just got back from America, and Mummy and I were – talking,' he explained gently, taking her back up to her bedroom. 'I'm sorry we woke you.'

He tucked her back under her blankets and kissed her on the forehead.

'You were having a row!' said Suzanne, holding on to his arm.

Peter wondered how much she had heard.

'Well, just a small one, but it's over now,' he conceded with a smile. 'Back to sleep with you now.'

When he returned to the kitchen, Belinda was placing their mugs in the sink.

'That girl has ears on stalks,' she complained. 'Do you think she heard much?'

'I don't know,' he answered, grateful for the unexpected interruption to Belinda's tirade.

She turned to face him with a reproachful look in her eyes.

'I'm sorry for what I said, but you've hurt me deeply, you know – very deeply indeed.'

Those words. The same words that stuck in the back of his mind, and yet they were not quite the same. '*You hurt me very deeply, you know*'. Wasn't that what Mary had written? Not quite. He had to look at the letter again.

Belinda came over to him, as if looking for a response.

'I'm desperately sorry, too. I've buggered things up dreadfully,' Peter admitted.

He took her hands in his own. She snatched them away and turned back towards the dresser, folding her arms tightly across her chest.

'It's not as easy as that.' She was choking back a new threat of tears. 'You can't just say sorry and expect everything to be all right.'

'No, it's not that simple. I know that.'

She looked so vulnerable, struggling with her feelings, that he felt an urge to clasp her firmly in his arms, to reassure her that their own relationship could and should survive all that had happened.

'You may not find this easy to believe but, whatever may have happened in the last two years, I've never stopped loving you,' he insisted.

Although sincerely meant, his words sounded hollow.

'Do you think you might forgive me one day?' he asked softly.

His wife stared hard at the floor for a few moments, before looking him coolly in the eye.

'I shall never forget,' she answered finally.

'No. I don't suppose either of us will,' he answered sombrely. 'Well, we can't stay down here all night. You go back to bed, and I'll follow in a minute.'

As soon as she had left the room and he heard the stairs creak under her tread, Peter pulled from his inside pocket the envelope containing the letter Mary had written. He held the page under the light over the kitchen table.

He stared fixedly at those crucial words: '*But you hurt me very deep, you know.*'

'Hurt very deep'? Mary would never have said that. 'Deeply', yes, but not 'deep'. It was ungrammatical, and even under such stress she would have still written correct English, Peter was certain.

Suddenly he looked at the page with suspicion; so much of it now seemed wrong. The whole letter had been typed, including the '*love M.*' at the bottom. Surely she would have signed it? All the letters she had sent him in the past had been hand-written. He knew she had a typewriter in her flat, but used it only for business letters.

He was stirred by a sudden sense of unease. What had first appeared the tragic last words of a distraught woman now began to look totally different – something altogether more alarming and sinister.

With only two hours' sleep that night, Peter felt worse in the morning than if he had not gone to bed at all. At breakfast he was conscious of his younger daughter's silent stare as she searched for clues to the conflict between her parents that had disturbed her night's sleep.

By 8.30 he was at his desk at Aldermaston, struggling to make sense of his aroused suspicions. A note left by his secretary the previous evening reminded him that John Black wanted to see him at eleven in London, and announced that the Chief of the Defence Staff had invited him for lunch at his club.

Peter felt at a loss about what to do next; Mary Maclean now dominated his thoughts completely. He felt certain now that her death was by no means the end of the Skydancer secrets affair, but more likely just its beginning.

Suddenly he knew what he had to do. Absent-mindedly he had been fingering the keys in his pocket, and realised that one belonged to the door of Mary's flat. He had omitted to give it back to her.

The motorway traffic into London was heavy at that time of day, and it was nearly ten o'clock by the time he drew up outside the large Victorian house in Chiswick where Mary have lived in the garden flat.

Looking at the house, he felt overwhelmed by sadness, remembering the pleasure and anticipation he used to feel when visiting her here, though a pleasure tinged with guilt. Mary had adored him, and to come here to see her had been a rejuvenation for him. But now she was dead. For a few minutes he just sat in his car, staring at the house, weighed down with his grief.

Eventually he walked up the drive, with dread in his heart. He had had to come – to discover more about how she had died.

The big house was divided into six apartments and the door to Mary's garden flat was round at the side. He tried the key in the lock. It did not fit. The lock had been changed.

There was a wooden gate leading into the garden, and he tried to open it, thinking he might see something through the French windows, but the gate was bolted from the other side.

'You won't find her, you know. She's gone,' an elderly female voice croaked behind him.

Startled, he spun round to see the old woman who occupied the flat at the front of the house. She had been living there longer than anyone else and saw herself as something of a caretaker. Mary had considered her a busybody.

'Oh, it's you,' she continued, puffing at the cigarette clamped firmly in the corner of her mouth. She recognised him as the man she had often spotted stealing away from Mary's flat in the early mornings.

'Yes,' Peter answered abruptly, annoyed at the way she had crept up on him. 'Yes, I was trying to get into her flat, but the key she gave me doesn't seem to fit anymore.'

'No, it wouldn't.' She stared accusingly into his eyes. 'They changed the lock after they broke the door down. You know what happened to her, I suppose?'

He nodded.

'Yes, well you would,' she sniffed self-righteously.

She was in her late sixties, with curly grey hair, and a pair of glasses sat crookedly on her nose.

'So you're a scientist, are you?'

'How did you know that?' Peter asked in surprise.

'Policeman told me. His name was Black. Asked me all sorts of questions about Miss Maclean and her visitors. Seemed to know all about you. Even had a photo of you in his briefcase.'

'Did he indeed?' Peter answered as casually as possible trying to control his growing annoyance. 'Tell me, do you by any chance have a spare key for the new lock? I seem to remember Miss Maclean saying you used to keep one for her in case she locked herself out.'

'Want to go in there, do you?' She looked at him oddly, her lower lip quivering. 'No one's cleaned up in there, you know. It was a horrible mess the policeman said. Told me I should keep well out of it. He said some relative of hers would come down at the weekend and sort things out.'

'Do you have a key?' Peter repeated abruptly.

'Well, yes. As a matter of fact Mr Black gave me one so as I could let her relatives in when they come.'

'Then may I borrow it, please? Obviously you know I was a close friend of hers,' he insisted.

She hesitated, looking anxious.

'I suppose it's all right,' she muttered, turning back towards her own flat. 'The police did say they'd finished.'

As Peter waited for her, he was dreading what he might find inside.

After a few minutes she returned and handed him a key. As he went in, she hovered by the door, not daring to enter. He closed the door firmly behind him.

In the small entrance hall he stood still for a few moments, conscious of the silence. Mary had always treasured the way she could cut herself off from the world outside simply by closing that front door. None of the noise of passing traffic or aircraft seemed to penetrate in here. Today, though, that silence seemed unreal, as if any moment it might be broken by the sound of her voice calling out to him.

He looked around; splintered wood on the door frame bore witness to the force used by the police to enter the flat. A rough job of carpentry had been done when the new lock was fitted, and wood shavings still littered the floor.

Peter paused by the door to the living-room. Inside it looked much as always, though the cushions were squeezed into the corners of the chairs, where heavy policemen had clearly been sitting on them.

At the end of the hall, two doors stood ajar. One led into the bedroom, but through the other he could see the edge of the bath and the washbasin beyond. He dreaded entering that room, but knew he had to. As he drew nearer he could see streaky red-brown stains on the bathroom carpet.

Fighting to control his nausea, he forced himself to look into the room. Blood streaks were also daubed round the edge of the bath and a concentrated stain round the plughole had been left where the water that had formed Mary's shroud had drained her blood away.

Peter choked at the sight and backed away. Turning into the neighbouring room he sat on the bed, clutching his head in his hands. He could not believe that she had done such a thing to herself. The sight of that blood made him realise just how violent her death had been. But that was the key to it. She was just not capable of such an act of violence. If Mary had ever contemplated suicide, it would have been by some other means. Gas or drugs maybe, but not to slash her own veins with a knife.

'Somebody murdered you!' he said out loud, astonished at the certainty of his conviction.

And, yet, was he deceiving himself? Was there any real evidence of murder – or was it simply what he preferred to believe?

He stood up. There might be something else, some other clue in this flat that would point to the truth of what had happened, something the police had overlooked. Against one wall of the bedroom stood a small writing table, and on it the portable typewriter on which her final letter was apparently written. Its keys were dusty with fingerprint powder. The police had been thorough, at least.

He looked round the bedroom again, but nothing struck him as out of the ordinary. Then he walked down the hall to the living-room. Standing by the sofa, he rested a hand on it to support himself. A trace of Mary's perfume seemed to linger in the air. He cast his eye round the room, looking for anything out of place – something that had not been there before, or something familiar missing from its usual position. He began with the bookcase, running his finger along the volumes which had meant so much to her. Then he moved into the kitchen; an unwashed wine glass stood on the draining-board, its lip and stem coated with the white powder used by the forensic men. Next to the cooker a rack for kitchen knives was fixed to the wall. He stared at it for a moment, conscious that one knife was missing. There should have been five. He had always noticed the perfect symmetry with which they were arranged there, with the largest knife in the middle and blades of decreasing size on each side. It was the smallest one that was missing, the one she had kept particularly sharp for slicing vegetables.

He shuddered as he realised what it might have been used for. Surely she could never have used that knife on herself. She just could not have done that, he was sure of that. But suppose she had been murdered, who would have done it, and why?

Peter returned to the living-room. The thought of finding something which Black's men had overlooked, something that would point towards murder instead of suicide, began to seem impossible. He furrowed his brow in concentration, and tried to direct his gaze systematically at every detail of the room, from one end to the other. After a few minutes he shook his head in despair; it all seemed just as he remembered it.

The antique bureau with its walnut veneer was a fine piece of furniture, he realised. He had never really studied it before, but now crossed the floor to inspect it closely. He ran his hand over the waxed surface which felt almost warm to the touch. He vaguely remembered Mary explaining it had been in her family for generations; it was her continuity with her past. How much had her family really been told of what had happened, he asked himself? Their framed photographs had stood on top of the bureau. There was now only one of her parents here, but surely there had been two before. He remembered the other picture distinctly; Mary with her arms round two children, her niece and nephew.

He turned his head to scan the bookshelf, in case the photograph had been moved there. Then he walked briskly round the room in search of it, before hurrying back to the bedroom. It was nowhere to be seen.

'That's odd.' His voice sounded like an intrusion in the stillness of the flat.

That photograph had always stood on the bureau – from the day he first visited her, of that he was certain. Its position had never changed. Perhaps the police had taken it, but why should they? It was hardly evidence. He hurried back to the bureau and pulled open the lid.

The compartments inside were empty. All her papers were gone. That must have been the police, he assumed; they would have reason to look through her documents. Closing the lid, he opened the drawers below in case the photograph had been put away, but there was still no sign of it.

Suddenly he peered at his watch. He had almost forgotten his appointment with John Black. It was half-past ten, with just thirty minutes for him to get to MI5's headquarters. He would have to leave immediately, and take the underground. It would be quicker than driving and trying to find somewhere to park in Mayfair.

In the hall he lingered for a moment, looking again towards the bathroom.

'Goodbye,' he whispered softly.

'You were in there a long time,' the old woman commented as he emerged. She held out her hand for the key.

'Was I?' Peter answered vaguely. She was staring expectantly at him through her crooked glasses, trying to assess how he was affected by what he had seen inside.

'It's like you said,' Peter answered her unspoken question, 'a horrible mess.'

'Poor soul. Such a nice girl . . .' She turned her head away.

'Tell me,' Peter asked impulsively. 'The night before she was found . . . do you know if she had any visitors?'

'Oh, I wouldn't know. I never see or hear anything. I'm at the front and she's at the back, see,' she insisted hurriedly.

'No, I'm sure you don't,' Peter reassured her gently. 'But try to remember about the night before last, just in case there was something unusual. It could be important.'

The old woman turned away and made as if she was thinking deeply as she walked slowly back towards the front of the house. Just as they reached the front drive, she turned round with a gesture of sudden recollection.

'Now you mention it, I do remember someone leaving her flat, sometime after midnight. I couldn't sleep because of the indigestion. It's been terrible lately, and the doctors are no use with that sort of thing, are they? Well, I heard some feet on the gravel here, and I looked out of the window. It was a man, quite large he was, with a raincoat. He must have had a car, because I heard him slam the door. Inconsiderate, I call it, making such a noise late at night . . .'

'It's dreadful how thoughtless some people can be,'

Peter agreed patiently. 'But that was it? No other noises that night?'

'Well, no. It went on, you see. I was just dropping off, after taking some Milk of Mag., when he came back. Or *someone* did. I heard feet on the gravel again.'

'Same man again, was it? Did he look the same?'

'Oh, I don't know what he looked like. I was under the covers that time. Didn't see him at all.'

'So you didn't hear anything more after that?' Peter persisted earnestly.

'No. No, I slept like a baby. Didn't know any more about it until the police came yesterday evening.'

Thanking her for her help, Peter hurried away down the drive. As he turned on the pavement, he glanced back and noticed that she was still watching him.

He arrived five minutes late at the Curzon Street office of MI5, with its windowless ground floor. John Black looked aggravated by his lack of perfect punctuality as he pointed him to a chair in a sparsely furnished room used for interviews.

'Make yourself comfortable. We've got a lot to talk about,' he gestured impatiently.

'Rcally? I thought the case was solved, as far as you were concerned,' Peter replied with an edge to his voice.

'There are a lot of details, Mr Joyce. If you knew the amount of paperwork I have to do . . .'

'I suppose so.'

As if to make his point, the investigator slapped a fat folder down on the table and lowered his over-weight body on to a swivel-chair behind it. The impact with the seat expelled from the man's lungs a blast of air which carried the smell of stale cigarette smoke across to Peter's nostrils.

'You know, Mr Joyce,' Black continued in a voice that was tired and irritable, 'it seems to me that the way you've been conducting your business during the past few years is totally at variance with the high standards of personal behaviour required in a man of your status, a man entrusted with some of the nation's most sensitive secrets. You wouldn't disagree with that, would you?'

Peter was stunned by the suddenness of the attack; he knew he was bound to face official criticism for what had happened, but did not feel ready to cope with it quite like this.

'I think you had better explain what you mean,' he answered defensively.

'Oh, come now, for heaven's sake! Then let me itemise it for you.'

Counting off his accusations on the fingers of his outstretched hand, Black held the scientist with a gaze that was cold and derisive.

'First: your wife takes issue with your work, and joins a subversive organisation whose purpose is to undermine Britain's nuclear capabilities. You knew about this but failed to report it to your security officer at your last positive vetting.

'Second: you start up an adulterous relationship with Miss Maclean, a relationship which lays both you and her open to the possibility of blackmail – a very real possibility considering the secret material to which you both had access. This affair you also failed to report to your security officer.'

Peter made as if to interrupt, but Black gestured him to silence.

'Third: you have flagrantly disregarded the Defence Ministry rules concerning the safe storage of classified documents. Three months ago you left them lying around in your briefcase at the home of the woman with whom you had been having the adulterous affair, at a time when your termination of that relationship might give Miss Maclean the motive to do something foolish and dangerous with those papers –'

'Did Mary tell you about that? Did she admit to you that she had taken the plans?' Peter burst in, seizing the opportunity to divert the criticism that Black so painfully and accurately aimed at him.

John Black's eyelids seemed to blink for the first time since this conversation had started. He looked almost surprised that he himself should face a question.

'She certainly told me that you had the plans in your case that last night you spent in her flat.'

'But did she actually tell you that she'd done anything with them?'

'No, she didn't admit that to me in person,' Black shifted his position on the chair. 'But we have the letter, don't we?'

'Yes. Well, I'm not happy about that,' Peter answered firmly. 'Let me get it quite clear. What you gave me last night was an exact photocopy of what you found in her flat?'

'Yes, it was.'

'And you're convinced it was she who wrote it?'

'Her fingerprints were all over the letter and the typewriter keys, so unless you –'

'Yes, but she never typed letters to me,' Peter insisted. 'They were always hand-written. And some of the grammar – it just wasn't her.'

The MI5 man permitted himself a wry smile.

'People under sufficient stress to kill themselves don't always behave according to previously established patterns, Mr Joyce,' he countered firmly. 'And what exactly are you suggesting by all this, anyway?'

'I'm suggesting that she was murdered,' Peter ventured.

Black heaved himself upright in the chair and sighed.

'I wouldn't want you to think we hadn't thought of that. It was one of the first possibilities we considered. But we have to deal in *evidence*, and there simply isn't any to suggest that someone else killed her. The knife she used had her prints on, and no one else's. The pathologist's report confirms that death was caused solely by loss of blood, and there's no trace of any pacifying or tranquillising agent in her body. As I said before, her prints were all over the suicide note – and, let's face it, she was sufficiently cut up over the way you dumped her to have the motive to do herself in. The business with the document in the rubbish bin fits too, since there's still no sign from any intelligence source that the Russians have got hold of the secrets.'

At the end of his explanation, Black moistened his lips and there was a glint of triumph in his eyes. He extracted the packet from his pocket, wrenched back the flip-top, tugged out one of the cigarettes and placed it between his lips in one smooth movement. Then, as an afterthought, he extended the packet across the table and enquired with his eyebrows whether the scientist would like one too.

Peter shook his head. From Black's slouching, untidy appearance and off-hand manner, he found it impossible to assess whether the man could be trusted. He was conscious of the persisting widespread suspicion about MI5 following its recent disastrous infiltration by Soviet agents, yet the Security Commission had scoured the organisation afterwards and pronounced it clean.

Peter thought back to his conversation with Mary's elderly neighbour. Black was a large man, and could fit the description she gave of the figure who had visited Mary that fatal night.

'Did you call to see Mary at her home the night she died?' Peter asked.

Black looked up sharply. 'Yes, I did. Why do you ask?'

'I went to her flat this morning,' Peter answered casually. 'The woman next-door told me she had seen someone about your size.'

'Oh? Been playing policeman, have you?' he snapped sarcastically. 'Yes, I interviewed Miss Maclean at her home that evening, but I hope you're not insinuating my visit had any connection with her suicide . . .'

'Did you . . . did you remove anything from her flat at any time?' Peter asked cautiously. 'Any documents or papers, for example?'

Black smiled. 'If you mean the letters you wrote to her, then yes, I have them here. They're quite safe.'

'And what about photographs? She had family photographs in frames on her bureau. Have you taken one of those?'

John Black frowned.

'Describe them to me,' he answered evasively.

'There were two. One showed her mother and father, and that's still there; the missing one was of Mary herself, with her young niece and nephew. I wondered whether you'd taken it.'

'No, I've not got any photographs.'

For a moment he looked uncomfortable, as if the question had caught him out.

'But I think you may be a little out of date with your recollection,' Black added hurriedly. 'When I interviewed her two nights ago, there was only one picture on the bureau – one of her parents. I remember it distinctly because I asked her about it. There was only one, then, Mr Joyce.'

His eyes sparkled with innocence, but Peter felt certain he was lying.

'That's odd,' he persisted. 'Tell me one other thing: was it you the neighbour heard leaving after midnight?'

Black did not at all like being questioned. It was like reversing the natural order of things.

'It probably would have been,' he mumbled irritably.

'And did you return to her flat after that? The neighbour heard footsteps coming back again later.'

'She *has* been talkative,' Black exclaimed angrily. 'Now, if you don't mind, I'll have a turn at asking the questions!' But he still looked thoughtful.

Peter realised he would achieve nothing further, so for the next half hour he submitted to a detailed probing of his work routines, his wife's anti-nuclear involvements, and his own private life. By the time the questioning eventually ended, he felt emotionally and physically drained.

It was about three-quarters of a mile from Curzon Street to St James's Square, and Joyce had a brisk walk to reach the East India Club by one o'clock. The exercise was a help in sorting out his thoughts before he met the Defence Chief.

Field-Marshal Buxton was waiting for him in the panelled bar, clutching a whisky and soda.

'What would you like, Peter? Kind of you to join me today. Hope it wasn't inconvenient.'

'I'll have the same as you,' Peter replied. 'It's not inconvenient at all.'

Buxton was dressed in worn tweeds, and looked more like a country gentleman than the head of the nation's armed forces.

'I use this place when I want to get away from my

military chums,' he confided. 'Unlike in the Army and Navy Club, hardly anyone here knows who I am, so it's ideal for private chats.'

He studied Peter's face thoughtfully, trying to assess his general reaction to the events of the past two days.

'You must be jet-lagged!' he exclaimed suddenly. 'How extremely inconsiderate of me to summon you to lunch when you should be getting your head down.'

'Don't worry, I haven't had time to get jet-lagged, and I've just spent the morning with John Black of MI5.'

'Have you, now?' said Buxton. Looking round at the handful of people in the bar, he took Peter by the arm. 'Tell you what, why don't we take ourselves and our drinks to the dining-room. Then we can sit comfortably and natter privately to our hearts' content.'

Seated at a corner table in the palatial restaurant with its gilded ceiling, they were a comfortable distance from anyone else, and the CDS began to talk freely.

'Bad business about that girl Mary Maclean,' he growled. 'Distressing for you, I imagine.' His face expressed a combination of sympathy and disapproval.

Peter glanced at him uncomfortably. He had not yet accustomed himself to the idea that his affair with Mary had become such public knowledge.

'But it's disturbing, too,' Peter replied carefully.

Just then the waiter came for their order. The field-marshal recommended the Dover sole, and Peter concurred with his suggestion.

'Disturbing? In what way?' Buxton probed, when the waiter was again out of earshot.

Peter then explained at length his doubts about the 'suicide', and described the conversation he had already had with Black.

'Sure you're not imagining things?' Buxton

remarked. 'A woman scorned is pretty unpredictable, you know. Suicide is in itself an irrational act, so I feel you're asking a bit much to expect her to behave in any normal way while carrying it out.'

Buxton could see that Peter was taken aback by this dismissive statement.

'Look, I'm sorry. I don't mean to doubt your word, but let's face it, it sounds a little as if you're trying to make excuses. All this has been a hell of a strain for you, and it's obviously personally embarrassing. There's bound to be a full internal inquiry at the end of it all, and inevitably you aren't going to come out of it very well. There's firstly your affair with that poor girl, and then, from what I've been told, you've been pretty lax about security procedures too.'

Peter looked startled.

'Oh yes. I've heard about it, I'm afraid. The Prime Minister is horrified at what's been going on, and is after your blood. The only thing that's likely to save you from his wrath is his need to sweep the whole thing under the carpet in case it damages his tenuous hold on the reins of government. The press haven't yet heard about Mary Maclean's death, but the PM's planning to feed them something this afternoon. He may make a statement to the House of Commons.'

'Good God!' Peter was aghast. 'This is crazy. Don't you see, blaming the whole thing on a woman's revenge is too tidy – too convenient an end to the business.'

He pushed away his half-finished plate, and swallowed a mouthful of the white Burgundy Buxton had chosen.

'Look, if you were in charge of the new anti-missile system protecting Moscow, and you learned by whatever sources that Britain had developed a new warhead enabling its nuclear bombs to penetrate those defences, wouldn't you do everything you could to acquire the details of those new weapons?'

'Probably,' Buxton replied briefly.

'Now, if you were the head of the KGB department responsible for getting hold of those plans, and your agent in the field made a colossal bungle of the operation, what would *you* do about it? You'd try desperately to cover your tracks. And if you were a KGB chief, wouldn't you be ruthless enough to commit murder if it would succeed in throwing the poor old British off the scent?'

Buxton studied his glass of wine thoughtfully.

'It's not inconceivable,' he conceded.

'So, to go rushing in and blame the whole thing on an emotional woman has to be shortsighted, don't you think? At least get the PM to wait a few days before saying anything to the House.'

'Not sure I can do that,' Buxton mused. 'He thinks he's obliged to tell them something. But I might be able to persuade him to keep the details to a minimum. And anyway, come to think of it, if there is substance to your theory, it wouldn't do any harm for Ivan to think we'd fallen for his little trick. Might make him careless, don't you think?'

The waiter was hovering again.

'More to eat, or just coffee?' Buxton enquired.

'Coffee, thanks.'

'What about John Black?' Peter continued as the waiter moved away. 'He seems to be closing the investigation. He maintains there's no evidence that it was anything but suicide.'

'Hmmm.' Buxton dropped a spoonful of sugar crystals into his coffee.

'I suppose . . .' Peter persisted. 'I suppose they *are* clean now? MI5, I mean. The Soviet infiltration seemed pretty extensive. There was something odd in what John Black said to me.'

'That business with the photograph, you mean?'

'Yes. He insisted that picture wasn't in the flat when he interviewed her – yet there was something odd about the way he said it. I'm sure he was lying.'

'Why should he bother to lie about a thing like that?'

'I don't know,' Peter frowned. 'But let's be fanciful for a moment. Let's pretend that Black is a Soviet agent, and that he murdered Mary and fixed it to look like suicide. Supposing there was some sort of struggle, and the photograph was smashed. He'd have got rid of it, wouldn't he? And of course he'd deny it had ever been there.'

'Well, yes, but that's an awful lot of supposing,' Buxton answered doubtfully. 'The curious thing is there is still no word from any of our agents suggesting the KGB are doing anything at all. Our men are pretty well placed, you know. They would almost certainly have heard some whisper of an operation if one was underway.' The Chief of the Defence Staff paused, frowning. 'And yet that in itself is damned odd, isn't it?' he then continued. 'If I was Ivan, I'd be bloody *sure* to be hatching some plot to learn the secrets of Skydancer.'

'That's exactly my point,' Peter interrupted in relief. 'So perhaps the Soviets are deliberately by-passing all their usual intelligence people. Perhaps there's some special team involved, and the reason we've heard nothing about it is that this team includes undiscovered Soviet moles inside our own security services!'

'Clearly we mustn't draw any conclusions too soon,' Buxton determined. 'We'll have to keep an open mind on the matter for the time being. And that leaves a big question-mark hanging over the test launch of Skydancer. You've just set up a complex deception plan to counter a Soviet espionage operation which may or may not exist. If there's no plot, you could put the original programmes back in the missiles and do a proper test. But we don't know that for sure, so for the time being we'd better just do nothing. I'll send the boat back out into the Atlantic just to confuse the Russians, then we'll just sit tight and see what pops its head up out of the trench. Agreed?'

A waiter approached table. 'Excuse me, sir, your secretary is on the phone,' he told Peter.

Peter made his apologies and followed the waiter out of the room.

The message was a summons to the Defence Secretary's office.

In Moscow snow was swirling in great determined gusts round the city squares and along the broad boulevards. It was still early for such intense snowfall Oleg Kvitzinsky reckoned, as he eased his Mercedes saloon into the parking area behind his apartment block. The tyres crunched tracks in the virgin whiteness as he drew to a halt.

He had just returned from the headquarters of the GRU, and could feel a deep depression settling over him. General Novikov had been abrupt and dismissive at his doubts about the intelligence organisation's competence. Novikov was an old-style soldier, a Party hard-liner who would never willingly accept criticism. The general considered Oleg a mere scientist, not qualified to comment on his methods.

At the lift entrance he gave his customary smile to the old woman who pressed the buttons. Like all those who acted out this menial role in Moscow, she was a KGB freelance who earned money by reporting the comings and goings of citizens, and taking particular note of any visiting foreigners. Oleg found it painful that the organisations which were essential to providing information for his own work should also find it necessary to spy on *him*.

As he opened the door to his apartment he saw Katrina waiting for him. She was standing in their living-room, framed by the light of the picture window, staring out at the view of Moscow – its stylish prerevolutionary architecture contrasting strongly with modern concrete slabs and factory chimneys. She turned to face her husband, and folded her arms. She had a round face and thick black hair expensively set in a bouffant style that was chic for Moscow but which would look cheap and clumsy in the West. The intensity of her dark eyes was further defined by thick mascara. As Oleg crossed the room, he saw her heavily lipsticked mouth was clamped firmly shut in an expression of brooding unhappiness.

'Hello, my little dove,' he began sarcastically, knowing he was in for a further round of niggling criticism.

'The Ivanovs are going to Geneva again tomorrow!' she burst out, unable to contain any longer the source of her unhappiness.

'Are you surprised?' he countered, struggling to remove his heavy overcoat. 'Igor is an adviser on our mission to the United Nations.'

'Well, why can't *you* get a job like that?' she called after him as he returned to the hall to hang up his coat.

'Katrina, don't ask questions to which you already know the answers!' he called back with forced patience.

Until two years ago, Oleg had nothing to do with military affairs, specialising instead in the extension of the use of computers and industrial robots in the Soviet

Union's heavy engineering plants. Such a senior civilian post had given him the right to foreign travel and, much to Katrina's satisfaction, he had taken full advantage of it. Switzerland, West Germany, Japan and the USA had all been frequent destinations on their overseas itineraries.

But all that had ended when he was summoned by the Academy of Military Sciences to take control of the Ballistic Missile Defence modernisation programme, which had found itself in deep trouble because of lack of coordination between the missile makers and the electronics and radar industries. Working for the military had its attractions – funds were almost unlimited, for example – but its great disadvantage was the refusal of the authorities to allow military scientists to travel to the West for fear they could be compromised, kidnapped or seduced away with the secrets they held inside their heads.

His salary had increased dramatically with this military job, and they now had the use of one of the finest apartments in Moscow – but Katrina was increasingly miserable. She had moulded her lifestyle round the acquisition of Western possessions for the home. She had once cultivated friends who had similar tastes and ambitions, but now she felt increasingly like a leper, rejected socially because her access to these foreign pleasures had been cut off.

Having removed his snow-scuffed boots, Oleg slipped his feet into a pair of sheepskin moccasins bought in Canada, and headed for the heavy oak sideboard where the drinks were kept. He pulled out a bottle of Scotch whisky and poured a two fingers' measure into a cut-crystal tumbler. Without turning round, he swallowed it in one gulp. As the spirit burned his throat, he shook his head like a dog that has just emerged from a swim in the river, and refilled his glass.

'Aah!' he sighed. The alcohol was already beginning to numb his nerves, and he turned to face his wife with a tolerant smile on his lips.

Kvitzinsky was forty-six, and had a pleasant face with a long, thin nose and those arched brows and childlike Russian eyes that always looked poised halfway between laughter and tears. His bald scalp was covered by long strands of straight hair combed up from the side and carefully held in position by a light coating of hair-oil.

'Irina showed me a photograph of the dress she's going to buy in Geneva,' Katrina persisted. 'It was in *Vogue* magazine. She's started dieting again to fit into it.'

'Well, at least that's something you won't have to worry about,' Oleg laughed. Katrina had been fighting a losing battle against fat in recent years.

'I could lose weight if I had a good reason to,' she retorted sourly.

'Then do it for *me*,' Oleg whispered half-audibly into his glass.

'I heard that! Even if I looked like a Hollywood film-star it wouldn't make any difference to your capabilities!' she snapped back. Seizing a glossy magazine from the glass-topped coffee table, she dropped angrily into an armchair with her back to him. 'And don't get drunk tonight. We're going to the dacha tomorrow, remember?'

He had forgotten that, but was not going to admit it. The way things were going, he would not be able to leave Moscow that weekend, but he decided to keep that news to himself for the time being.

Peter Joyce. Peter Joyce. He muttered the name of the British scientist over and over again in his head. What had Joyce been doing on board that British submarine the previous day? General Novikov had received a report from Florida that the scientist was seen making last-minute alterations to the test missile. But had he been altering the warheads so that the forthcoming test would be deliberately misleading, or simply making the final adjustments that any complex weapon system demanded? Oleg desperately needed to know.

Kvitzinsky clearly remembered meeting this Peter Joyce three years earlier, at an international scientific symposium in Geneva, on one of his last visits to the West before taking up the military post. The British scientist had impressed him greatly, with his strong determined face and secretive eyes. It would not be easy to get the better of Peter Joyce, he had concluded. The GRU's incompetence at the start of their operation was certain to have put Joyce on his guard. Getting hold of the Skydancer plans would not be simple now.

Kvitzinsky had been bitingly critical of the GRU at the start of his meeting with the general, angrily accusing his agents of incompetence. The intelligence chief had rounded on him harshly for so readily believing what he heard on the BBC. The plan was proceeding steadily, he insisted. What had happened was only a small hitch which had required minor changes to the schedule. Those adjustments had now been carried out, and the complete plans for Skydancer should be in Moscow within a few days, he had assured him.

'I shall believe that when I see it,' Oleg now muttered to himself pessimistically, savouring the whisky growing warm in his grasp.

Through the forgiving haze of the spirit he looked across the room to where Katrina sat, still pointedly ignoring him. Her freshly coiffured hair and cream dress, patterned with large peach-coloured roses, made her look like a woman dressed for a party but with no party to go to. She was a picture of discontent.

It was not just the prohibition on travel to the West which had created her unhappiness, as Oleg knew only too well. The cause was far more basic than that. Katrina was unsatisfied in the most fundamental way a woman can be.

They had been married now for over ten years, but were childless. Their marriage was barren, and in the Soviet Union, where children symbolise the future and the justification for all the struggles and hardships of the present, being childless was not a happy state.

Oleg insisted to his friends that the fault lay with Katrina. In truth, medical examinations had revealed nothing wrong with Katrina at all. She blamed Oleg for their failure to conceive, but he had refused to undergo medical tests himself.

Her nagging suspicions had seriously undermined his libido, and now that age and excess had taken their toll of her once shapely figure, he found it increasingly difficult to produce a useable erection. When he was totally sober the task had become almost impossible. After an invigorating intake of alcohol, he could usually succeed, yet with one glass too many he would slip back into impotence.

But tonight he had no sexual expectations, and no intention of limiting his intake of comforting liquor.

'Oleg?' Katrina had finally put down her magazine and was trying to smile.

'Mmmm?'

'Why don't you take me out to dinner? I feel like going out. What about the Tsentralny? We haven't been there for months.'

It was a trap, and he knew it. He should have realised that as soon as she had started demanding the impossible – a visit to Geneva. It was a game played many times before, but which never failed to take him by surprise. Dutifully he played the counter-move she expected.

'We'll never get in there this evening. They're always full,' he replied wearily.

'I telephoned this morning,' Katrina smiled triumphantly. 'I booked a table. I thought it would make a nice change.'

He shrugged his inevitable consent. He knew what it meant: the evening had been prearranged, and they would be meeting other couples who were Katrina's friends rather than his. The conversation would revolve around Paris and New York, and he would have nothing to say because he had not been anywhere recently apart from Novosibirsk in Siberia – and he could not even mention that, because his work there was top secret.

It was going to be a dreadful evening. He knew he would get very drunk indeed.

In the kitchen of the old farmhouse in Berkshire, Belinda Joyce held open the door of her deep-freeze, trying to decide what to cook her children for supper. It would have to be fish fingers – she could not concentrate enough on anything more elaborate.

Something had transpired that day which gave her a strange creepy feeling: Helene Venner had disappeared.

She had first met the woman three years earlier, when Belinda was already establishing her skills as a lathe-operator at the craft co-operative. Helene had joined as a potter, producing attractive hand-made jugs and bowls which sold well to American tourists in a souvenir shop in Oxford. They had taken an instant liking to one another, sharing the same jaundiced view of the vested interests of big international companies and of the nuclear arms race.

Belinda had quickly recognised that Helene had lesbian tendencies, and knew that Helene found her desirable. To start with she was mentally quite attracted to the idea of sex with another woman, just as an experiment, but in the end her deep-seated disinclination had proved insurmountable. Even so, their friendship remained firm and intimate.

It had been Helene who encouraged her to join ATSA, or Action To Stop Annihilation, Helene who had helped her co-ordinate her loosely gathered anti-nuclear thoughts into a coherent thread, and Helene who tried to persuade her to steal secret papers from her husband so that they could be leaked to a left-wing newspaper.

Yesterday Helene had not turned up for work. Today she was again absent, and there had been still no phone-call to explain. So Belinda had called round at the terraced cottage she rented in the village, but found no one at home. A neighbour who held a key let her in to the house. Every trace of Helene was gone: the cupboards were bare, the bed stripped of linen; even the fridge had been emptied. The place was spotlessly clean, as if it had been scrubbed to remove any sign that she had ever lived there.

Belinda could not make herself believe Helene would just disappear without a word. She would surely have said something if going away of her own choice. So at first she wondered whether her friend had been kidnapped. But then she reflected on the line of questioning John Black had pursued, and began to consider that his talk of subversive left-wing groups plotting to undermine the fabric of the nation might not be entirely fanciful after all. Had Helene Venner been a spy? Surely not. Yet with growing disquiet Belinda remembered how close she had come to being physically seduced by Helene, and began to wonder whether such an act had been designed to achieve her final mental seduction as well.

The sound of a bicycle bell jerked her thoughts back to the present.

'Oh Christ! Back already,' she cursed, pushing the fish fingers under the grill.

By the time she next had a moment to herself, the early evening news was coming on television. The lead story concerned the Prime Minister's statement that afternoon to the House of Commons that 'following the untimely death of a female employee of the Ministry of Defence, the source of the leak of secret documents from the Ministry seems to have been uncovered. There is no evidence of any loss of secret material to a foreign power.'

'He doesn't know about Helene Venner,' Belinda thought. 'Nobody knows about Helene, except me.' Suddenly she longed for Peter to come home.

At that very moment he walked in. Belinda turned towards him anxiously, and the sight of his ashen face and crushed expression brought her to her feet.

'What's the matter, Peter? What's happened now, for God's sake?'

'I've been suspended,' he croaked. 'I've just spent the afternoon being bollocked by the Defence Secretary, Mr Michael bloody Hawke, and he's suspended me from duty until further notice!'

Chapter Five

Just before sunrise a US Navy tug positioned itself to ease the smooth fat shape of the submarine away from the quayside. The grey, pre-dawn light cast no shadow, and the overall-clad dock-hands looked almost faceless to Commander Carrington as he peered down at them from the top of the fin. The anonymous figures unhooked the mooring lines from the bollards and cast them into the water. The seamen on the narrow casing of HMS *Retribution* hauled the sodden ropes from the sea and stowed them securely under a steel hatch.

Once clear of the dockside, the multi-bladed fan-like propeller began to turn, causing the water behind the rudder to bubble and foam. The tow-line from the tug was released and the submarine's foredeck party hurried below, closing the forward hatch tightly behind them.

'Slow ahead!' Carrington almost whispered the command into the microphone he held close to his lips. His voice was hushed in spontaneous reverence at the sight of the crimson curve of the sun rising smoothly over the edge of the world, separating at last the greyness of the sea from that of the sky.

'Take a good look at it!' he told himself. It might be weeks before any of them on board saw the sun again.

The growing intensity of the light caused Carrington to shade his eyes. They were passing through the harbour entrance and he squinted anxiously along the line of buoys that marked the deep-water channel, to ensure there were no other vessels ahead which could hamper his passage. It would be a while yet before the water would be deep enough for them to dive and return to the secret world which had become his most natural environment.

His orders from Northwood had been at the same time specific and vague. He was to make his boat ready to launch the test missile at twelve hours' notice, but no hint had been given as to when that firing might take place. In the meantime he had been instructed to hide his submarine in the eastern Atlantic and to avoid the attention of any Soviet vessels that might try to track him, but the intelligence reports had been less specific than usual as to what Russian ships might be in the area.

Carrington focused his powerful binoculars on the furthest of the channel buoys which he knew, from his earlier study of the chart, to be three miles ahead. A thin haze covered the sea, and he scanned slowly to the left and then to the right, searching for the support ship which was essential to their success in hiding below the waves. The *Retribution*'s most sensitive listening device was her sonar array, the plastic tube towed hundreds of yards astern which contained hydrophones capable of hearing ships and submarines two hundred miles away. The technology had been invented long after *Retribution* had been built, so the array had to be clipped on by a support ship each time she went to sea.

'Any sign of her, sir?' The officer of the watch had joined Carrington on the bridge. He shivered briefly at the coolness of the morning air.

'Not yet. She can't be far away though. Only left harbour about half an hour ahead of us,' the captain replied, lowering his glasses and scanning the horizon with the naked eye.

'Half ahead! Revolutions for eight knots!' he ordered

into the microphone. Within seconds the water at the stern began to splash and froth more strongly, and a creamy wake spread out behind them.

'Give me a shout when you spot her,' Carrington called, as he gripped the handrails of the ladder and disappeared down the tower into the metallic warmth below. Passing through the control room he paused by the chart table.

'Where is the rendezvous point exactly?' he enquired, looking over the navigator's shoulder.

The young officer pointed to a cross on the chart.

'Three miles inside the territorial limit, sir,' he added smartly. 'Shouldn't have anybody watching while we do the deed.'

Carrington nodded and returned to his cabin.

Lieutenant Robert Simpson sat quietly in the tiny ship's office next to the wardroom. In front of him on the small table was the galley stores register, and he was making a pretence at checking it through. But the task that really concerned him was quite different, one of obsessive importance to him, one he was convinced could save millions of lives. It was to prevent HMS *Retribution*'s nuclear missiles from ever being fired in anger. It was a mission inspired by his conscience.

Bob had been educated at a small, select boarding school, where his housemaster had made a lasting impression on almost every pupil who passed through his care. An old-fashioned crusader, seeking to inspire his pupils to fight for morality and justice in whatever areas their careers might take them, Andrew McGregor had created on his own a sort of secret society perpetuated by annual reunions held at the school.

By the time Bob ended his studies there, he had

become the man's devoted disciple. On his last day at school, 'old Greg', as the teacher was known, had warned him as he had warned others before him, that he might need to 'go underground', to work in secret, if he was to strike his eventual blow for morality.

They were words of advice that Simpson took to heart in the years that followed. An only child, he had decided to follow his father into the Royal Navy eventually, but wanted to take a degree course first. During his three years at Exeter University, he had faithfully returned each summer to his school for the weekend reunion with Old Greg. At that time, he had still had no clear idea what the 'great mission' in his life would be, but felt instinctively that the Navy would one day present him with it.

At university he had fallen in love with Susan Parkinson, who was sweetness itself. Yet even when she had become his closest friend as well as his lover, he had not dared confide in her totally his sense of mission. She was different from him – lively and extrovert, forming firm opinions from first impressions. She had joined a Ban the Bomb group and urged him to accompany her on protest rallies, but he never did, preferring to keep his views private until he had developed them fully.

Susan lived near Newbury now, and worked as a schoolteacher. As they grew closer Bob had become more open about Andrew McGregor and his moral crusade, and when he had been posted to HMS *Retribution* she had understood immediately that he had finally found the role he had been looking for.

It had not been easy trying to decide what was right and what was wrong, when it came to warfare. Simpson could understand the moral rectitude of using military means to destroy a man like Adolf Hitler, and could accept the need for nations to be armed to prevent such tyrants from gaining power again. But those armaments were for use against other military forces, not civilians. 'The bomb' was different. Every missile on *Retribution* was aimed at Moscow. Millions of innocents would die if they were ever launched.

'You've got it, boy,' McGregor had said to him at the last school reunion. 'It's that crucial difference which makes the nukes immoral. You know what you have to do. Don't tell me anything about it – I don't want to know the details, but you'll know what to do when the time comes. It's no accident you are where you are, remember that! You're there for a purpose, boy!'

Simpson devoutly hoped it would never come to that – the weapons were intended as a deterrent after all. But the fact that chance, or the Almighty, in the form of a Naval selection board, had chosen *him* to be on board that particular boat made Simpson fear the worst.

It would be no easy task to stop a launch of the Polaris missiles if war broke out, he concluded. The firing procedures on board the submarine were hedged about with safeguards designed to prevent any individual acting on his own, either in firing the missiles or in sabotaging the launch. Simpson had studied those procedures carefully. As a supply officer he was not closely involved in the war-fighting tasks of the boat, but the policy of the Navy was that every one of the thirteen officers on board had a part to play if the missiles were ever launched. It was a way of spreading the responsibility and making it seem less awesome.

Simpson's war role was to verify the navigation data to be fed into the missile-guidance computers, data which told the missiles precisely where they were on the globe at the moment of firing. He had soon realised that a simple refusal to carry out his task would achieve nothing; the data could easily be verified by any of the other officers. The only way to stop the launch would be through deliberate sabotage.

When he had first joined the boat, the captain had talked to him privately in his cabin to ensure that he had no doubts about the rightness of maintaining a nuclear deterrent and of being prepared to use it. 'If you have any doubts, you shouldn't be here,' Carrington had told him. Simpson had kept his thoughts to himself. He believed this was *precisely* where people with doubts should be if the world was to be saved from destruction.

Bob often worried about his girlfriend. It was hard, his being away at sea for months at a time. Susan had always had a lively social life, and he had a fear in the back of his mind that she would get tired of his frequent absences and find another man.

Opposition to nuclear weapons had become the strongest bond between them. Susan was now actively campaigning for the cancellation of the Skydancer project, and needed all the information she could get. His phone-calls to tell her what was happening on board the submarine did not reveal much, but she always seemed grateful for them, and to Simpson they were a lifeline keeping Susan attached to him.

With a steely hiss the main periscope was raised from its housing in the control room deck. Carrington pressed his face against the binocular eyepiece and rotated the sight through a full 360 degrees.

'Officer of the watch, I have control. Come below. Shut the upper lid!'

Carrington's order triggered a routine on board the boat that was so well practised it was automatic.

'Upper lid shut! And clipped!' the voice of a crewman yelled from inside the top of the tower, as the spring-loaded latches completed the hermetic sealing of the hull. Another voice at the base of the ladder relayed the message to the control room.

'Dive the submarine!' Carrington ordered.

'Open one, two and three main vents,' yelled a strong Glasgow accent from the buoyancy control panel. Hands scrabbled at the stopcock switches above, and there was the roar of air escaping from the main tanks as water rushed in to replace it.

'Diving now!' the helmsman shouted, pressing forward on his joystick controls. The hydroplanes cut into the water and pressed the bulbous nose of the vessel down towards the depths. On a gauge above his control stick, the helmsman watched a miniature silhouette of the boat tilt downwards through five, then ten degrees. It was enough to ensure that HMS *Retribution* would slide cleanly and smoothly beneath the waves.

'Keep periscope depth!' Carrington called, raising the scope again for an all-round look. Satisfied that the only vessel in the area was the support ship that had just helped them with their towed sonar, and that they were leaving it well astern, he lowered the periscope and moved over to the chart table. The navigator pointed out a line indicating the edge of the continental shelf, beyond which they would be able to dive into the comforting deep of the Atlantic.

For a while yet they must stay close to the surface, and every few minutes Carrington raised the periscope for a further all-round scan. Small fishing boats with trawl-nets were a hazard that might be visible only seconds before collision or entanglement.

One hour later Carrington ordered the submarine to two hundred feet, and the periscope was lowered into its seating for the last time. No one knew when they would need to raise it again.

The excitement of their shore leave over, the crew of the Polaris submarine slipped quickly back into their routines, almost as if they were a part of the machinery itself. The task of the boat now was to remain undetected and wait for orders. Trailing horizontally from the stern was the sonar array, several hundred yards behind the rudder, listening intently for the tell-tale sounds of other ships and submarines in the area. A second cable also streamed out from the vessel, stretching upwards at an angle of forty-five degrees towards the surface of the ocean. At the end of it was a float which would remain just below the surface throughout their patrol, a buoy which could pick up radio signals from England while staying hidden beneath the waves.

This was the Very Low Frequency radio antenna, able to hear transmissions which could penetrate the surface to a depth of twenty feet. It kept the submarine in permanent contact with Naval Headquarters, ready to receive at any time the order to go to war. The antenna could not easily be detected by surface ships or aircraft, so did not reveal the existence of the 'bomber' in the depths below.

Although *Retribution* could listen thus for her orders, she could not reply to them; the antenna could receive but not transmit. Normally she did not need to, and only in an emergency would come up to periscope depth and transmit back through a satellite aerial pushed above the waves.

The rumbling in his stomach told Carrington it was close to lunchtime. Breakfast had been very early that morning to accommodate their dawn departure from the Cape. He was naturally a very thin man with sunken cheeks and a tall angular frame. It always surprised his wife that he could be such a healthy eater and remain so skinny. As he walked to the wireless room to reassure himself that the communications link was properly established, he tried to calculate what hour of the day it would be in the Hampshire village of West Meon, which was home. His wife Alice would still be asleep there unless the baby had woken her early.

'All hunky-dory, sir,' his executive officer announced. 'Everything bleeping away nicely.'

To confirm that the radio link was established, a coded message was transmitted constantly from three giant aerials situated in remote parts of Britain.

'Very good, Number One,' Carrington smiled. 'I think it's lunchtime, don't you? I'll just check the sound room, then we can eat. Happen to know what's on the menu?'

'"Babies' Heads", I think, sir,' replied Lt. Commander Smith.

Carrington rubbed his hands. He was very fond of the individual steak-and-kidney puddings so named.

Inside the sonar room, the rating at the towed array control panel was clasping his headphones to his ears, and he looked puzzled. In front of him a green cathode-ray tube displayed the oscillating wave patterns of the multitude of sounds the array was detecting. By selecting switches the operator could direct the inbuilt computer to filter out unwanted noises and concentrate its analytical power on one particular frequency, which was what the rating was now trying to do.

'Got a problem?' Carrington asked, tapping the blue-shirted operator on the shoulder.

The man slipped his earphones off and shook his head.

'Don't understand it, sir. Never heard nothing like it before. Don't even know if it's really there, it's so faint.'

The words sent a shiver up the captain's spine, and all thoughts of food disappeared.

'What sort of thing are you talking about?' he asked. 'And where is it?'

'Well, the array says it's dead astern, sir. But what it is, I don't know. There's no cavitation or anything, no propeller noise. Sounds like something moving through the water, but there's no machine noise or reactor bubbling. No propulsion sound at all.'

'Computer doesn't recognise it?'

'No way, sir. Thinks it's just background. Can't pick it out at all.'

'But *you're* sure it's there?' Carrington pressed anxiously.

The rating hesitated before replying: 'I suppose it could be damage to the array, sir. The Yanks might have knocked it about a bit while we were in the Cape. I'll run a test on it. Shouldn't take more than ten minutes.'

Instinctively Carrington felt sure there was nothing wrong with the sonar. He recalled his orders for this voyage, which had been so specific and yet so vague; the extra warning to be on the alert for Soviet shadows, as if Fleet HQ suspected there was something in the area, yet could not identify what sort of vessel.

'No. Stick with it. I'll reduce speed and we'll go silent – see if that helps clarify things.'

Carrington strode back to the control room and seized the microphone that hung from the roof by the main periscope.

'Assume the ultra-quiet state! Ultra-quiet until further notice!'

His voice was relayed throughout the length of the boat on a network of loudspeakers. At his command, conversation stopped, or was reduced to a whisper, and all inessential domestic or mechanical tasks that could make a noise were brought to a halt.

'Reduce speed to one knot,' he ordered quietly.

'One knot it is, sir.'

He could not stop altogether, or the array would start to sink towards the ocean floor.

The executive officer came out of the wireless room, his eyebrows raised inquiringly.

'Sound room's got something, Mike. Something very faint,' Carrington explained.

The two officers returned to the sonar booth, where the operator was working away at his control panel. Impotently they stood behind him, waiting for him to report.

'Coming closer, sir!' he hissed suddenly. 'There's a doppler shift.' Then he forgot himself in his excitement. '*Must* be a fucking sub!'

The frequency of the sound had risen, shifting up the scale, indicating, like the whistle from an approaching train, that the object creating the sounds was moving towards them.

Behind them the spools of a tape-recorder turned continuously, recording the full spectrum of sounds picked up by the array, for further analysis later. If Carrington's suspicion was correct, what they were recording was history, the first sounds ever heard in the West of a new type of Soviet submarine.

Until five years earlier the Russian nuclear-powered boats, operated from the base at Severomorsk inside the Arctic Circle, had been characteristically noisy. Their loudness was due to a lack of sophistication in sound-proofing, and was largely caused by particularly noisy pumps circulating cooling water in the reactors. When they sailed south towards the Atlantic, they passed over a network of listening devices laid on the floor of the ocean by the US Navy. Those sensors reported their passage to NATO ships and aircraft, which could then follow them with comparative ease.

Details of NATO tracking capabilities had been leaked to the Russians by the Walker family spy-ring, early in the 1980s, and the shock of learning how much the Western navies could hear had led the Soviet navy to institute a crash programme of new design.

The first of the latest type of Soviet submarine had recently been photographed by American satellites as it left Severomorsk on patrol, and again three weeks later when it returned, but no sound trace whatever had been found of it during the intervening period. Code-named Akula by NATO assessors, the submarine was a massive eight thousand tons, similar in size to *Retribution*, but instead of ballistic missiles for threatening Western cities, she carried a stock of torpedoes and anti-ship missiles able to destroy boats like HMS *Retribution* before they could fire their weapons at Moscow.

The silent operation of the Akula class boats had made many of NATO's listening techniques obsolete. It was feared the Soviets could now patrol the Atlantic shipping lanes undetected by the West. No one knew how they had achieved such silence, but there were reports that the Akulas had a secret new motor in addition to their nuclear-powered turbines, a motor that used the revolutionary technique of electro-magnetic thrust, producing a speed of ten knots in almost total silence and without leaving any detectable wake.

'Akula!' Carrington exclaimed hoarsely. 'It has to be. Nothing else could be as quiet as that. The bastard must have been waiting for us!'

'He's still closing on us, sir! Doesn't seem to realise we've slowed down,' the rating whispered excitedly. 'I can definitely hear turbulence round his hull. I don't understand it, sir! Why can't I hear his fucking propeller?'

'Because he's not using one,' Carrington answered softly. 'Right, let's see what he can do!'

He leapt to his feet and strode back to the control room.

'Wind in that VLF antenna, or we'll lose it. Then make maximum revs!' he barked. 'Full speed ahead!'

The helmsman turned from his dials and hydroplane controls in astonishment. Polaris missile patrols were normally conducted at a stately three knots. Now the skipper was ordering a speed of thirty!

An even vibration took the submarine in its grip as the control rods were raised in the nuclear reactor core, producing an instant increase in heat and steam for the turbines. The needle on the dial showing the rotational speed of the propeller shaft rose steadily, until it approached the section marked in red. The chief engineer watched it closely.

'Twenty-eight knots!' the executive officer called, peering fixedly at the log.

Carrington prowled round the control room, glaring at the dials one minute and studying the chart the next. He had taken a calculated gamble. If the Soviet submarine which he believed was sitting on his tail was to keep up with the speeding *Retribution*, it would have to abandon its silent electro-magnetic thrust and resort to the greater power of its nuclear reactor and large propeller. That was bound to be noisier, and they would be forcing the Akula to make a sonar fingerprint, allowing a Western navy to record its noise characteristics for the first time.

Carrington grinned to himself; either way he was going to win something. If the Akula stayed on his tail the Soviets would lose some of their secrets. If the boat stayed quiet, it would rapidly drop behind and *Retribution* would give it the slip.

Confident that all was well in the control room, the captain returned to the sonar booth where the rating was urgently pressing switches on his panel. Their high speed through the water was making so much noise on their own sonar systems that he could no longer tell if the Russian was behind them. Suddenly he cocked his head on one side.

'Cavitation, sir!' he exclaimed. 'Dead astern! Suddenly come on. Nothing there before, but I can hear the bubbles on his propeller now.'

'So! We have a huntsman on our tail! A hunting pinko no less!' Carrington looked at Mike Smith for appreciation of the pun. He glanced across at the spools of the tape-recorder, rotating smoothly, and debated how to make the most of the opportunity that faced him.

'We'll keep up this speed until he's firmly hooked, then cut the power and let him come closer,' he decided.

The sonar operator was busy with his controls again, filtering and processing the signals which were now audible not only to the towed array but also to the hydrophones fixed to the side of the hull. By comparing bearings from the two sets of sensors, he could now calculate that the Soviet submarine was fifty feet above them and about half a mile astern.

The captain returned to the control room and bent his tall frame over the chart, talking urgently with his navigator.

Lieutenant Robert Simpson leaned into the control room, eager to know what had caused the submarine's unaccustomed burst of speed.

'George? What's going on?' he whispered to the assistant Polaris systems officer who was standing to one side with his arms folded.

'Hide and Seek! And we're "it"!'

'Who else is playing? A Russian?'

'Well, it's not one of ours, is it?'

Commander Carrington paced past them, scowling.

'Permission to be in the control room, sir?' Simpson asked smartly, knowing he had no automatic right to be there.

'As long as you keep out of the way,' was the brusque reply.

The commander carefully scanned the dials which showed how the propulsion machinery was performing.

'I want you to cut the power and dive to four hundred feet,' he told the marine engineer quietly. 'Then turn hard to port – that'll keep us in the deep water. What I want is to let the bugger go shooting over our heads, so we can get a good listen to all his noise parameters, and then for us to creep back the way we came in an effort to lose him. Think you can make us quiet enough?'

'Can but try, sir,' the engineer answered stolidly. 'After all that speed, the reactor pumps'll keep churning for a bit, even if everything else is quiet.'

'Right away then,' Carrington ordered.

The depth at which the hunt had been pursued up to now was in the middle of a broad band of water of even temperature, allowing free passage of sound waves. Nervously rubbing his jaw, inadequately shaven in his haste that morning, Carrington judged that by diving steeply the *Retribution* would pass through a thermocline, where the water would become sharply colder. The temperature difference should create a sound barrier, below which the *Retribution* could hide. What an extraordinary medium the sea was; its salinity and temperature variations sometimes allowed sound waves to travel for hundreds of miles, and at others made it impossible to hear another craft just a few feet away.

The men in the control room grasped at the pipework as the large vanes either side of the bulbous nose tilted the submarine steeply downwards.

'Oh, shit!' Simpson whispered at the suddenness of the manoeuvre.

The tension on the faces around him had given him a nightmare vision of what it would be like in war, wrestling in the deep with a Russian submarine: a trial of strength which only one of them could win.

He had been taught that when it began, the Soviet boats would make an all-out attack to try to neutralise the Western missile submarines in a pre-emptive strike. For a split-second he imagined it could actually be happening at that very moment: men in a Russian submarine trying to kill them, kill him even though he was committed to saving the lives of those same men's wives and families.

In sudden confusion he thought about the secret role he had been chosen to play, and realised with a jolt that he was far from ready, far from certain what he would do. The meagre preparations he had made were secreted illegally in the drawer beneath his bunk.

He glanced at the captain. There was a look in Carrington's eye that was not just excitement; it was fear too.

To hide his uncertainty, Carrington quickly turned away and went over to the sonar booth. The Soviet boat was faster and quieter than his own, and its sonar equipment probably at least as good. If the contest was purely technical the Russian would win, he felt sure of that. There was another element, though, which could decide this contest – human skill.

He had never faced the test so directly before. The endless simulations he had practised were supposed to have prepared him for this moment, yet now he felt strangely unready. In the past they had tended to take for granted that British equipment and techniques were so superior that the Soviets would never get close enough to challenge the Polaris boats' mastery of the deep.

'Want to listen on these, sir?' the rating asked, passing him a spare set of headphones. Carrington struggled to separate the different sounds that crowded in on his brain. It took him a few moments, but at last he could pick out the cavitation, the turbulence caused by the Akula's propeller biting into the water.

'Getting closer?' Carrington asked anxiously.

The sonar operator nodded. 'And following us down, sir.'

'Shit!'

He snapped the headphones back on to the table, then swung his long body out of the swivel-chair and through the doorway back into the control room, in one continuous movement.

'Hard a-port now!' he yelled at the helmsman. 'We're going to have to shake the bastard off!'

Bob Simpson felt the shirt sticking to his neck. The submarine manoeuvred with unaccustomed violence. It was not just the motion that made him feel queasy; it was also the claustrophobia created by the tension of the men around him.

He thought of Susan. Was she really with him still? Would she care if he died here at sea, buried alive? The uneven motion of the boat began to affect him seriously, and he hurried back to his bunk.

Carrington hovered over the chart table in a pose that was almost predatory. His hair was ruffled where he had nervously run his fingers through it, and his once-crisp white shirt had dark patches under the arms.

The chart itself was scrawled with lines marking the zig-zag course they had followed in their unavailing efforts to lose the Akula.

He was beginning to despair; the readiness of the Russian captain to reveal the capabilities of his new boat suggested that his orders had been very specific: any price was worth paying in order to observe from close quarters the test launch of the missile that would carry Skydancer aloft for the first time.

'Captain!'

The shout had come from the sound room.

'Got something here you might be interested in, sir,' the rating grinned. He turned up the volume on one of the loudspeakers. The heavy rumbling noise was unmistakeable.

'*QE2*, sir. On her way south from New York to the Caribbean!'

A grin spread across Carrington's tired features. The good old *QE2*. It was the answer to a prayer.

'What's her range?' he asked eagerly.

'About thirty miles, sir.'

'Good! Give me the very best bearing you can! We're going to say hello to her!'

By the time Bob Simpson returned to the control room, he was feeling better and had regained his composure. HMS *Retribution* had settled on to a steady course at a speed of twenty knots. High speed would not shake off their adversary; the Akula was faster than they were and was firmly on their tail. What they needed was a sonar 'smoke screen', and there was none bigger than the *QE2*.

He went over to the chart table and rested an elbow on the edge of it.

'What's the latest?' he asked the navigator casually.

'We're on our way to a rendezvous with a big, fat, red herring!' his young colleague answered, grinning.

Simpson raised his eyebrows.

The navigator pointed to the chart and a small cross where two straight lines met.

'This one's us,' he indicated, 'and the other line is the estimated course of the liner *QE2*. We're on track to intercept her in about two hours' time.'

'And this track here?' Simpson asked, pointing to a third line running parallel and very close to their own course, but a short distance astern. 'That's the Russian?'

''Sright. That's Boris, currently playing the part of the cat. A fat cat at that, at eight thousand tons.'

'About the same size as the mouse,' Simpson commented quietly.

'True,' the navigator conceded, 'and in a couple of hours we'll find out which one's more cunning. My money's on the mouse!'

Back on the American mainland, the FBI's electronic surveillance systems had been carrying out their allotted tasks meticulously. With so many sensitive military installations close to Cape Canaveral, every public phone-box within a fifty-mile radius of the missile-launching centre was monitored by a central computer. Every call was listened to electronically; the bugging was by microprocessor rather than by man.

The computer was programmed to analyse speech. Each call made from those hundreds of telephones was recorded digitally. The computer would listen for the use of certain key words stored in its memory, and would check the callers against a 'voice-print' file, in case they were known to the authorities. Each digital recording would be checked through twice, but if the voices were unknown, and if no keywords were present, then it was automatically erased. If it held something of significance, it was transferred to magnetic tape, together with a record of when and from where the call had been made. Twice a day the tapes were studied by FBI agents at a counter-espionage centre in Miami.

The telephone-call which Lieutenant Robert Simpson had made from outside Millies' disco to his girlfriend in England was now on that tape. His English voice had produced no response from the digitised 'rogues' gallery' in the central memory. However, one particular word that he had used had not gone unnoticed. It was one which had never triggered this particular alerting system before; 'Aldermaston' was not an American establishment after all, and had only been included in the list of FBI keywords as a gesture of transatlantic co-operation. But there it was, in the middle of a conversation from a Florida call-box to a number in the home counties of England.

Because it was an unusual word, not related to any American defence project, 'Aldermaston' had caused the computer's priority coding system to work in Bob Simpson's favour for a while. If he had referred to an American defence establishment, his conversation would have received urgent attention from a human agent. 'Aldermaston' did not mean much to the men from the FBI, so for the time being the tape which could reveal that an informer was on board the British nuclear submarine *Retribution* lay on an American intelligence officer's desk marked 'Low Priority'.

Commander Carrington had returned to his cabin to

think, after instructing the officer of the watch to call him when they were within ten minutes of their rendezvous with the *QE2*.

'What a fucking shambles,' he muttered, as the long-term significance of what was happening began to sink in. The Soviet Navy had managed to sail a hunter-killer submarine right through several lines of Western detection barriers in the Norwegian sea, through the Iceland-Faroes gap which NATO considered almost as a Maginot line, and right across the Atlantic to within a few miles of the American coastline, but had remained utterly undetected until it revealed its presence by giving chase to HMS *Retribution*.

With this new Soviet capability, NATO's chances of defending itself against a Russian submarine attack had been dramatically reduced, as Carrington realised with dread. But more than that, the Royal Navy's confidence in being able to successfully hide its Polaris missile submarines could no longer be justified, particularly when the Skydancer warheads were installed. Carrington had been told that the manoeuvring and decoy equipment in the Skydancer nose-cones made the new warheads heavier than the old ones, and the rockets would have a shorter range as a result. Less range meant that the *Retribution* and her sister vessels would have to patrol closer to the Soviet coast than before, and the closer to Russia they came, the easier it would be for the Soviet navy to find them.

Carrington shuddered. He pulled a signal pad from his locker and began to outline the message that he must send back to his HQ as soon as it was safe to poke the transmitter mast above the surface.

'Control room to Captain!' The voice of the officer of the watch squawked from the communications box on the cabin wall.

Carrington pressed a key. 'Captain!' he called back.

'Three miles to target, sir!'

'Right!'

He opened his wall safe and pushed the signal pad inside. He would finish it later. The message was top secret, so he closed the safe door and spun the combination lock to secure it. Then he headed back to the control room.

At the navigator's table he paused briefly to look at the chart. He was pleased to note there was more than a thousand feet of water beneath them, and it was getting deeper all the time as they headed east.

Then he hurried to the sonar room, where he clamped on the second set of headphones. The throbbing cavitation from the giant screws of the Cunard liner seemed to be drowning out everything else. However, the sonar operator pointed to the green cathode ray tube, and indicated a barely-visible but separate line, below the jagged pattern created by the *QE2*.

'That's our Akula, sir,' he explained. 'Still sitting on our tail about half a mile astern, keeping about three cables off our starboard quarter. He'll be nibbling our array if he comes any closer!'

'What's he expect us to do, that's the big question isn't it?' Carrington asked, half to himself.

'Certainly is, sir. Trouble is, this stuff's pretty good but it can't read minds yet,' the operator joked, patting the top of his screen.

'Damned shame, I call it!' Carrington forced a laugh.

Back in the control room the captain was suddenly conscious of the harsh meaning of the words 'the loneliness of command'. Here he was, surrounded by young enthusiasts who would be only too eager to give him their opinions of what to do, were he to ask them. It was the last thing in the world that he needed at that moment, however; to listen to a host of conflicting views could only hinder the already difficult process of deciding on his tactics when they met the *QE2*.

In his mind he had narrowed the options down to two: they could take up position underneath the liner and follow the same course, knowing that all noises from the submarine would be masked for as long as they stayed there, or he could pass right through the 'noise footprint' of the ship and out the other side, hoping the Soviet boat would think he had stayed beneath the liner and would follow the *QE2* towards the Caribbean.

What if their positions were reversed, Carrington thought to himself? What would the Soviet captain do if he was 'driving' *Retribution*? There was an obvious answer to that, based on years of study of Soviet submarine tactics. A Russian captain would hide his vessel under a surface ship for days, if necessary. They did it regularly, particularly when sailing their northern fleet round into the Mediterranean for annual exercises. A submarine would invariably try to make the journey undetected by sailing beneath the keel of an aircraft carrier or a cruiser.

But even if the Soviet captain's own instinct would be to hide himself under the liner, would he expect Carrington to think in the same way? There was no answer to that.

'Rendezvous point now half a mile distant, sir!' the navigator shouted across the control room.

'What speed the Cunarder?' he snapped back.

'Twenty-four knots sir!'

'Chief, give us maximum revs! I want twenty-eight knots on the clock!'

'Aye, aye, sir!'

All round the control room, men stiffened at their

posts. Eyes focused hard on charts and dials, hands hovered over levers, ready to respond instantly to the orders which were about to come thick and fast.

'Where's Boris?' Carrington barked into the intercom linking him with the sound room.

'Still on our starboard quarter, sir!'

'Cunarder's dead ahead, three hundred yards, sir!'

'Course?'

'One-nine-five, sir.'

'Coxswain! Steer one-nine-zero! Maintain one hundred and fifty feet!'

The chief engineer glanced uneasily at the captain. Getting close to a fast-moving liner was a dangerous business. Unexpected suctions and vortices could suddenly drag the two vessels together. The Cunarder would draw about forty feet, so that only gave them about a hundred feet clearance, not much when travelling so fast.

Suddenly, as one man, the control-room crew all looked up to the curved roof. The sound of the *QE2*'s propellers was pounding through the hull. The coxswain wiped the sweat from his brow.

'Cunarder overhead now, sir!' the voice barked from the sound room intercom.

'Steer one-nine-five! Drop back to twenty-four knots! Stay under her!'

They were now on exactly the same course as the massive cruise liner above them, where three thousand passengers and crew continued their afternoon activities, blissfully unaware that two gigantic submarines were playing hide-and-seek in the dark waters beneath them.

'Can you still hear Boris with all this din?' Carrington shouted into the microphone.

'Fallen behind to one mile, sir! Still on the quarter!'

What was he doing, that Soviet captain? What was he thinking? Carrington was sure the Russian was now 'deaf', unable to hear the British submarine any more because of the noise from the liner. The *Retribution* was not quite so 'deaf', however, because her listening array was towing well behind the liner and between herself and the Soviet boat. They could still hear the Akula, but she could no longer hear them. It was the best situation possible.

What the Russian did next would dictate which tactics Carrington would choose.

'Sound room!'

'Captain here!' Carrington came back.

'Burst of speed, sir! He's gone up to thirty knots! Just crossed our track, coming up fast to port!'

At last! He had made his move! Carrington grinned. The Soviet skipper had gambled that the *Retribution* had maintained a speed faster than the liner overhead and was hoping to disappear through the noise screen. The Akula was racing ahead on the port side of the ship, hoping to recapture a trace of *Retribution* as she came out ahead of her.

But the bastard's got it wrong, Carrington chuckled gleefully. He's not going to find us where he's going.

'Coxswain! Hard-a-starboard!'

In the control room, men hung on to tables and supports as the submarine began to heel over and turn sharply to the right. The thudding of the *QE2*'s propellers began to fade away to port, but they were keeping the noise firmly between themselves and the Soviet vessel. Carrington calculated that as the Akula pulled steadily ahead of the liner on the port side, the *Retribution* would fall back further and further to starboard, and the liner's noise shadow would continue to hide them.

'Lost him, sir! Sound room here! The Russian's the other side of the liner. Still making thirty knots at last trace.'

'Reduce speed to ten knots and take her down to five hundred feet, Coxswain,' Carrington ordered quietly. They needed to go deep rapidly, but had to cut their noise dramatically, too. At twenty-four knots the *Retribution* sounded like a steam train, but at ten she was a lot quieter.

'Well, gentlemen? Do you think we've done it?' the captain smiled round the control room.

'I think you may well have done, sir!' the navigator grinned back.

'Better not count the chickens just yet, though,' Carrington continued, hooking his hands together and stretching the tension out of his shoulder muscles. 'I'll be in the sound room.'

Weaving his tall frame round the periscope housings, he headed for the sonar booth.

Two thousand miles south-east of the submarines' position, Kapitan Karpov was finding the almost equatorial heat of the mid-Atlantic increasingly uncomfortable. The giant *Akademik Sergey Korolev* was now steaming slowly in circles, waiting for information from Moscow that would tell her precisely where to position herself to observe the British missile test. The British could launch their Polaris from anywhere within an area of several thousand square kilometres. Where the missile was fired from would dictate the part of the ocean in which it would come down, and it was within fifty kilometres of there that the *Korolev* had to be.

For the time being her massive radar and telemetry dishes were at rest, but when the time came they would be pointing upwards, carefully recording the responses from the Skydancer warheads as they re-entered the earth's atmosphere, trying to crack the code for the data being transmitted to earth, and to learn something from the outlines and reflections recorded by the radar.

'I suppose we do have something following that British submarine,' Karpov grumbled to his first officer. His headquarters had told him no more about the operation than he needed to know. 'We'll probably find our submarine is still in harbour with engine trouble!'

'Perhaps we should ask Comrade Smirnov!' the other said sarcastically. They had managed to escape the overbearing company of the ship's political officer for a few minutes. Colonel Smirnov had his own communications equipment on board which kept him in direct touch with KGB headquarters in Moscow. Hence he was often better informed about the ship's plans than the captain himself.

'To do that, I'd have to like the smell of his arse,' Karpov growled. 'And I don't.'

That morning a Nimrod reconnaissance plane from the Royal Air Force had flown out from Ascension Island to take a look at them. Kapitan Karpov had never expected to be able to hide a ship as large as his, but he was nonetheless annoyed that the British should have pinpointed his location so easily. He felt certain they had had help from their American allies, who could have used an intelligence satellite to fix the Soviet ship's position by detecting one of the political officer's radio transmissions. Even when Soviet naval rules dictated radio silence, the KGB man could not be stopped from calling up his headquarters, much to Karpov's annoyance.

The RAF Nimrod had made several low passes over the ship, taking photographs of all the antennae mounted on the upper deck. Karpov hadn't minded that so much; the most sensitive pieces of equipment were safely covered up.

It was late afternoon; there would be no more activity that day. Karpov looked at his watch. The KGB man was bound to inflict his presence on them again before long, and there was something very important to do before he did. Comrade Smirnov was a very youthful political officer, who had done his KGB training at the height of First Secretary Gorbachev's anti-alcohol campaign. And Comrade Smirnov was not a very understanding man.

The captain pulled open a drawer in his desk and took out a bottle of vodka. With a conspiratorial wink, he passed it to his first officer.

Chapter Six

Peter Joyce had spent much of that Friday pacing round his house in frustration. He was still smarting from the ignominy of being suspended by the Defence Secretary, pending completion of the investigation into the affair of the Skydancer papers.

Shortly before lunchtime an official car had arrived from the Ministry of Defence, and the driver had handed him a letter from Sir Marcus Beckett formally confirming his suspension on full pay. There had been no other communication and, with Belinda working at the craft co-operative and the children at school, he had been left alone with his thoughts all day.

He knew he had been careless, knew he had broken several security regulations, and that the department had every right to dismiss him if they chose to. But he was certain too that the crisis over the Skydancer secrets was not the result of anything he had done, and had nothing to do with his affair with Mary Maclean.

The night before, his wife had told him about Helene Venner's strange disappearance, and her consequent suspicion that the woman might have been something other than she seemed. He had telephoned John Black first thing that morning to inform him about it, but the MI5 man had been almost dismissive.

'You'd be surprised, Mr Joyce,' he had purred, 'but in almost every investigation I've ever run, there's always been at least one unnoticed little predator that has felt the heat and decided to break cover and run. We know about Ms Venner . . . and about her dubious relationship with your wife. But it wasn't she who left your secret documents on Hampstead Heath, I can assure you of that.'

Peter had felt so soiled by that conversation that he had vented his anger on a pile of logs that needed splitting. Later he had taken a walk in the beech woods, unable to shake from his mind the picture of the bloodstains in Mary's flat. Guilt gnawed at his soul; perhaps it had been suicide after all. Perhaps he was just trying to avoid acceptance of his own responsibility for her death – as Black and Field-Marshal Buxton seemed to believe.

'No, dammit!' he thought. 'They're wrong, but how the hell do I prove it?'

Something or somebody was being overlooked in the official investigation, deliberately or otherwise. There seemed no other explanation for MI5's unquestioning acceptance of Mary's death as suicide. Who or what had they missed? One name kept coming back to him; he *knew* it was significant. One name . . .

In his house in Hampstead, Alec Anderson took off his spectacles and put them on his father's old desk. In the last few days it seemed he had spent every waking moment sitting in this library when he was not at work at the Strategic Nuclear Secretariat in the Defence Ministry, with Mary Maclean's unattended desk outside his office door as a constant reminder of his dilemma.

Pressing down on the leather-upholstered arms of the lovingly restored swivel-chair, he lifted himself up and rubbed the small of his back. He took little regular exercise apart from an early-morning walk, and his joints were stiff. His normally ruddy cheeks had grown visibly paler in the last few days, and dark shadows under his eyes reflected his difficulty in sleeping. Every evening when he came home with another worry-line etched into his face, he took shelter in this room in an effort to avoid Janet's mostly unspoken questions.

When Mary's suicide had been reported on the television news – with the Prime Minister's reassurance that the Skydancer leak had not affected national security – Janet could simply not understand why her husband seemed more distressed at the news rather than relieved that the crisis appeared to be over. When she had probed him about it, he had mumbled something about the situation being a 'tragedy', but that it was impossible for him to explain the real reason. How could he tell her that he *wanted* the crisis to continue, wanted the Ministry to keep its guard up, all in the interests of protecting his wife and the children?

He now looked at his watch: nearly time to go down to the Maid's Head pub. Every Friday he would go there to meet a small group of friends for beer and billiards. This particular evening it was the last thing he wanted. But Karl had insisted.

Karl Metzger had first joined their drinking circle one evening about a year ago. He had introduced himself as a West German working in the travel business, with an agency in Hampstead High Street specialising in Rhineland cultural tours. He had stood up patiently to their schoolboy jokes about 'Krauts', and had quickly shown himself a master with the billiards cue. Soon he had become a regular member of the Friday group, and Alec discovered their shared interest in nineteenth-century painting, which led to a more personal friendship between them.

Anderson sat on the edge of the desk and polished his glasses with a handkerchief. The fruits of that year's friendship now hung on the walls of his library: some of the finest works in his collection of Victorian miniatures had been acquired thanks to Karl.

Setting his glasses firmly in place again, he peered at the exquisite craftsmanship contained within these small gilded frames. The intricacy of brushwork depicting Swiss and Italian landscapes was the closest thing to perfection that he knew. Yet now he wished to God that he had never clapped eyes on them. Those exquisite little masterpieces had brought him to this present situation which threatened with destruction both his career and his family's happiness.

Joyce had decided against telephoning before he arrived in Hampstead. He was determined to talk to Alec Anderson that evening, and was worried that Anderson might find some excuse to avoid a meeting. He had never visited the house before, but knew the address from a Christmas card Anderson had sent him the previous year. Belinda had a habit of hoarding old cards which he had never had cause to be thankful for before.

It was nearly ten o'clock as he drove down the quiet side-road, peering at the numbers, till he found the house. A reproduction brass coach-lamp glowed in the porch. Somehow the style of it seemed wrong for Anderson.

The doorbell chimed a melody. Through the bottle-glass panel he could see the outline of a figure moving down the hall towards him, hesitating and leaning to one side as if trying to recognise his shape through the glass.

There was the rattle of the lock and the door opened a few inches, secured by a chain.

'Yes?' came a timid female voice from inside. Peter could see one dark eye blinking at him through the gap.

'Mrs Anderson?' Peter enquired gently.

'Yes?'

'I'm so sorry to trouble you. My name is Joyce, Peter Joyce. I'm a colleague of your husband's from work. Is he . . . is he at home?'

There was silence as Janet pondered what to do next.

'Do you have some identification?' she demanded, talking in a louder voice to project a braveness she did not feel.

For a moment Peter was thrown by the request. It was hardly what he had anticipated.

'Oh, er, yes, of course.'

He fumbled for his wallet, wondering what sort of document would satisfy her.

'If Alec is here, he would . . .'

'He's not,' she replied sharply.

'Well, look, here's my security pass from Aldermaston. That's where I work. The atomic weapons place.'

He slipped the card through the crack in the door and she snatched it from his fingers. She seemed to study it for ages, then suddenly the chain was slipped free and the door swung open.

'I'm terribly sorry, Mr Joyce,' she fluttered. 'You must think me very foolish. It's just that some truly dreadful things have happened in this area to people opening their doors to strangers. And I'm on my own, you see, with two little *girls* upstairs . . .'

The way she stressed the word *girls* conjured a vision of rapists prowling for victims. Perhaps he *should* have telephoned beforehand.

'I quite understand, Mrs Anderson. You're absolutely right to be careful, and I suppose it is rather late for me to turn up on your doorstep. It's just that I need to talk to your husband right away. Do you expect him back soon?'

'Oh yes, I should think so,' she replied resignedly. 'When the pub shuts. It depends on Karl really, and you know what he's like.'

Janet Anderson was one of those women who tend to assume that even complete strangers know all the friends and personalities who feature in their lives.

'I'm sorry, Mrs Anderson, but I don't know Karl,' Peter explained patiently.

'Oh, good heavens! But how silly! Why should you! Well, he's a great friend of Alec's. They meet at the pub every Friday. You see, this is Alec's night for getting away from me and the children!' She laughed awkwardly.

'I have my night off on Mondays, though I don't always take advantage of it. Anyway, Karl rang this evening to check that Alec was going to be drinking. Sounded terribly keen to see him, and Alec went rushing off hot foot. I wish *I* could say something to Alec that would have the same effect!'

She laughed shrilly at her own cattiness. She was a short, bird-like woman, forever touching her hair to ensure it was in place.

'What would you like to do? You could wait for him,' she suggested eagerly. The thought had suddenly occurred to her that if her own husband would not talk to her about that suicide girl, perhaps this man would.

'Well, if he's not going to be very long . . .' Peter answered hesitantly.

'Why don't you come into the library, Mr Joyce?'

She opened the door to the front room and led him in.

'This is Alec's favourite room. All his pictures and things are here.'

Peter was immediately struck by its style. An antique glass-fronted mahogany cabinet was packed with leather-bound volumes, and the floor was covered with a Persian rug. At least a dozen small paintings lined the walls.

'Lovely room,' he began, crossing to the far wall to examine one of the pictures more closely. 'These are nice. Have they been in your family a long time?'

'Oh, no. Alec's bought them all. It's his hobby. They're sweet, aren't they?'

'Mmmm, delightful.'

'Karl knows a dealer who specialises in that type of art, so Alec's bought quite a few of them in the last six months.'

She could have added that there were plenty of other things they needed which he could have spent his money on, but she restrained herself. Instead she was silent for a moment, wondering how to raise the subject that was concerning her.

'Are you . . . are you involved in this secrets business?' she blurted out eventually.

Peter was surprised by the directness of her question.

'Well, yes. I suppose I am.'

'What . . . on the investigating side? Police? Security, that sort of thing?'

'No,' he replied carefully. 'No, I'm not the police. I'm a scientist. I helped design the weapon that all the fuss is about.'

'Oh. Oh, I see.'

Her eyes seemed to lose their concentration and she gazed vaguely into the corner of the room, puzzling whether he might be able to answer her questions.

'Have you been under suspicion, too, then?' she went on. 'I mean Alec, he . . . he's been so nervous lately. As if he was going to get blamed for everything. He said they were investigating *everybody* involved. You . . . you too, I suppose?'

'Oh yes. None of us has escaped the suspicion of MI5,' Peter said bitterly.

'Then I suppose you must have been upset about this woman who killed herself. His secretary, Mary something or other. Alec is devastated. I heard him crying last night, and I've never known him do that before.'

Peter did not want to talk about Mary, but he was startled by what the woman had just said. Why should Anderson have been so affected? Mary Maclean may have been his secretary, but he had never shown any particular interest in her. Why should he be so distressed?

'Did he talk to you about what happened?' he asked cautiously.

'No. He's said nothing. But he was so upset I . . . I began to wonder if there'd been something between them!' The corners of her mouth turned down involuntarily, betraying her unhappiness.

'No, definitely not. I can promise you that,' Peter reassured her. But then what *was* the reason for his grief?

'And then there was something they said on the television news, about the crisis being over. That seemed to upset him even more.'

She looked at him expectantly, hoping that he might explain. But suddenly Peter had the uneasy feeling there was no time to lose: he had to get to Anderson right away.

'I've just had a thought, Mrs Anderson. If the pub is not too far away, I might go and find him there. If I wait here until he gets back, it could make it a rather late night for all of us, don't you think?'

Janet Anderson was disappointed: she had learned

nothing from him. Her face took on a look of resignation.

'Well, you can try,' she conceded, staring at the floor. 'The pub's called the Maid's Head. It's just down the bottom of the road. Turn right out of the house and keep going. You can't miss it.'

'All right, I'll try there. Thank you,' Peter smiled. 'If I don't find him, I'm afraid I'll have to come back and disturb you again. I hope you won't think me a dreadful nuisance.'

'No,' she shrugged, 'I shall be here.'

She stood on the doorstep watching him as he headed down the road.

The pub was crowded and smoky. Amid such a sea of faces he began to doubt whether he would ever spot Anderson. However, being tall and stocky, he managed to ease his way through to the bar, and looked about him uneasily. But what exactly would he say to Anderson if he did find him? He still did not know.

'Yes?' the barman asked.

'Er, a half of bitter, thanks.'

A shout of jubilation caused him to focus on the far corner of the bar-room. A burly youth was waving a billiard-cue in the air.

'That's sixty-five pence.'

Momentarily the barman drew back his attention.

'Thank you.'

He sipped at the glass and peered through the fog of cigarette smoke. The men at the billiard table looked too young to be company for Anderson. He scanned them carefully to be certain, but Alec was not there.

Damn!

Drinkers eager to refill their glasses before closing-time were elbowing him away from the bar. He eased back through the crowd, searching faces, searching looks. Suddenly he stopped.

Alec Anderson was sitting at a small table just six feet away.

He was not alone and he looked like death. Peter backed away so as not to be seen. He found a shelf by the wall where he could rest his glass, and from where he had a clear view.

The man sitting opposite him must be Karl, Peter thought. He had thin, straight hair, a pointed nose, and metal-framed spectacles, and seemed to be issuing instructions. His eyes never left Anderson's face, which was pale and slack-jawed, as if from shock.

Peter sipped his beer, and kept his eye on the two men. It was ten to eleven and the landlord was calling for last orders.

Anderson had an almost full pint in front of him, but was making no effort to drink it. The other man had been drinking spirits, and his glass was empty.

Suddenly Anderson shook his head as if in violent disagreement. The other man eyed him threateningly and reached down to the floor. His hand came up clutching a brown-paper parcel the size of a small book.

Anderson looked thunderstruck as the parcel was pushed across the table. He clearly did not want to take it, but Karl thrust it into his hands.

A group of people sitting at a large table in front of Peter stood up suddenly, and began to pull coats over their shoulders, obscuring his view.

'Hurry up, for God's sake!' he hissed under his breath.

They took their time, though, discussing whose house they would return to for a nightcap. Finally Peter took his glass from the shelf and pushed his way round them, desperate not to lose sight of Anderson. But he saw with annoyance that the two chairs were now empty, Anderson's full glass still standing on the table unconsumed. He looked desperately round the exits and caught sight of the back of Karl's head disappearing through a door into the street.

He dumped his glass and hurried after them, but ran into the group who had been blocking his view. They were still debating where to go as he tried to push through them.

'I'm so sorry. I'm in a terrible rush,' he mumbled.

'Careful!' a woman shouted, as he trod on her foot.

Outside he heard car engines being started in the small car-park. But surely Anderson would have come on foot?

Then he saw them, on the pavement. Anderson was still being forcefully urged to take the parcel. Harsh words were clearly raised between them. Suddenly Karl turned and crossed the road to a large Mercedes. He opened the door, slipped inside, and drove off at speed. Anderson stared after him.

Slowly Anderson turned and began to walk up the hill towards his house. Peter strode briskly after him.

'Alec! I thought it was you. I've been looking for you,' he announced breathlessly as he came up to him.

Anderson swung round, not recognising the voice at first.

'What the hell . . .? Peter? What are you doing here, for God's sake?' he stammered.

'I was looking for you. Wanted to talk to you. Your wife said you might be down at the pub.'

The astonishment on Anderson's face turned rapidly to bewilderment and then to fear as he began to suspect what Peter might have witnessed.

'I was having a drink with someone,' he explained lamely.

'So I saw.'

'What . . . what is it you want?' His voice seemed flat with dread.

'I wanted to talk to you about Mary.'

Anderson's face crumpled. He looked like a schoolboy faced with a caning.

'I don't see there's anything to discuss,' he said abruptly, starting up the road again.

'What is it that man Karl wants from you, Alec?'

Anderson's head spun round like a snake's. His eyes were wild and desperate, searching Peter's face for a clue to what he knew. Joyce sensed he was on the verge of finding out everything he wanted to know.

'You've got a choice,' he needled. 'You can either tell *me* about it or tell John Black. If I call him, he'll be round like a shot.'

'Oh Christ!' Anderson's words came in a strangled gasp. 'Look, why don't you p-piss off! It's none of your business!'

'Yes, it bloody well is!' Peter snapped back. 'Mary was murdered, and you know all about it!'

He peered at the package under Anderson's arm. It had a broad, hard edge, like a frame.

'What *is* in that parcel, Alec? Another picture?'

Anderson seemed paralysed, unable to respond. The brown package clamped under his arm felt like a ticking bomb.

'Oh Jesus!' He said at last, his words hardly audible. 'Look, Peter, I need time to think. That's not too much to ask, is it?' His eyes begged. 'Please? Look . . . I admit I'm in some trouble, but I'm sure I can find a way out if only I have time to think.'

Peter grabbed him by the arm and began to hurry him up the hill.

'I can ring from your house. It's down to MI5 now.'

'Peter, Peter!' Alec croaked. 'I'll get life! Do you understand? *Life!* And for Janet that'll mean death!'

For a moment Peter was silenced.

'Do you mean . . . are you telling me that *you* killed Mary?' he asked aghast.

'No, no! God no! Not me . . . Oh, Christ!'

Anderson had become a pathetic, desolate figure.

'I think you'd better explain, Alec. Then we'll see if there's a way to avoid bringing in the police. Come on, now.'

The brass coach-lamp in the porch had been switched off. Anderson fumbled with his key, still hugging the parcel tightly. He opened the door and led the way inside.

'You can leave your coat round here, Peter.' He indicated a small cloakroom. Peter hung his raincoat on a hanger, next to a remarkably shabby brown overcoat. Anderson must use it for gardening, he guessed.

'Alec?' Janet called from upstairs. 'Oh, I see you found each other,' she continued, as Peter was led across the hall towards the library.

'Yes, it's all right, darling,' Alec reassured her. 'You go to bed. I'll be a little while yet.'

'I was in bed already,' Janet grumbled, before disappearing.

Alec closed the library door firmly behind them. At last he released his grip on the parcel, placing it on the desk. For a while he stood there, staring down at it, without a word. Peter sat in an upright Victorian armchair and waited. Anderson would start talking in his own good time.

Alec expelled a deep sigh, then he pulled out a handkerchief and blew his nose.

'You've seen these, have you?' he asked, indicating the paintings on the walls. 'Janet showed you in here?'

'Yes, she did. They're very fine.'

'Well, they're the reason I'm in this mess!' he began to explain as he lowered himself into the swivel-chair. 'Karl got most of them for me. Karl Metzger, that's what he calls himself. I don't know what his real name is.'

Anderson put his hand to his mouth and tugged at his lower lip. His eyes seemed to beg for Peter's sympathy.

'Karl Metzger is a colonel in the East German intelligence service – the HVA. He's a spy!'

'Good God!' Peter murmured.

He had suspected something like that, but it was still a shock.

Anderson's face showed the helplessness of a child.

'I only learned this two weeks ago. They set me up, Peter. They just set me up; it was the oldest trap in the book, and I fell right into it. But it really wasn't my fault – I . . .' His voice tailed away.

'Go on,' Peter urged grimly.

Alec pushed his fingers underneath the rims of his spectacles and rubbed his eyes.

'I've known Karl for about a year,' he went on awkwardly. 'He joined our Friday group at the pub. Beer, billiards, dirty jokes – you know the sort of thing. All harmless fun and gets us away from our women-folk. Well, I must admit I *liked* the man when he joined us.' He seemed pained at having to make this small confession.

'He was funny – made jokes about the Germans, and there aren't many Krauts who'll do that. He said he was from West Germany, of course. I had no reason to doubt that. He said Hamburg was his home town. He's in the travel business, sells German culture to tourists, or that's what he said. Well, er, he and I became . . . sort of chums. We had plenty to talk about . . . specially the paintings. You see, we shared an interest in Victorian miniatures.'

Anderson shook his head.

'Shared an interest, huh! He was just setting me up, of course. But he was good, oh, he was good! He really knew his stuff. Must have taught himself the lot just to get me on his hook!' He laughed bitterly.

'Well . . . he knew what I collected. I only had three or four of them at that time, but he said he knew a dealer who specialised in them and who would look out for some for me at a reasonable price. They can be pricey, you see. And suddenly, one day in the pub, he appeared with a picture wrapped up in brown paper. That one there.'

He pointed to the small gilded frame nearest to the door.

'The thing was so elaborate – that's what I can't get over. I mean, in my sort of job you're on your guard. Spies and so on. It never occurred to me that they would go to such lengths, just to make me feel everything was all right. That's what the pictures were for – just to lull me into a false sense of security.'

'But what *happened* exactly? I still don't understand,' Peter sighed with exasperation.

'There were photographs,' he whispered.

He seemed reluctant to continue.

'It was one weekend,' he began sheepishly. 'Karl said he and I had been invited to spend a couple of days at a house in Suffolk which belonged to the dealer who'd found the paintings for me. He claimed the man was keen to meet me, and it would be just Karl and me – no wives. It sounded interesting – a weekend talking with a real expert, and no women to be kept occupied.

'And so it was . . . initially. The man said he was from

Eastern Europe originally and had come to this country as a child, just after the war. He lived in a lovely old farmhouse with enormous gardens. The house was *full* of paintings . . .'

Beads of sweat were breaking out on his brow.

'He lived there on his own, but he had a . . . sort of servant. A . . . a young man.'

Anderson's face began to turn grey.

'I . . . I . . .' He shook his head, faltering.

'What *happened*?' Peter could guess the answer.

'It's difficult to explain it . . . *cold* like this,' he stammered, wiping the sweat from his lip.

'I mean . . . I'm not gay, I'm really not. But, it was just one of those occasions when the atmosphere made one think of doing things that one would never normally consider . . .'

'I see.'

'Please . . . *please* try to understand.' Anderson picked up a paper-knife from the desk and fiddled with it.

'It was just the atmosphere. We were all very relaxed. We'd all eaten well and drunk plenty, and it was . . . bohemian, I suppose. The dealer and his servant were obviously homosexuals. It was the atmosphere – they might even have put something in my drink. And . . .'

He was searching for the right words.

'And I suppose there are plenty of normal men who think about having that sort of sex – *think* about it but never *do* it, because of the social conventions. But . . . but there *weren't* any conventions that weekend, and so I . . . I did it!'

He completed the sentence in a rush of acute embarrassment.

'But there was a camera,' he added in a whisper.

'I never saw it, but there was a camera taking pictures of everything that happened.'

He swallowed hard.

'Karl said he would send the photographs to Janet, to the Prime Minister, to the Defence Secretary, to everyone necessary to ruin my career and my personal life. Janet – God! If Janet ever saw them! – it would kill her. She could never understand. She worships me, you know,' he whispered pityingly. 'Karl can destroy me and destroy everything dear to me. He's got me where he wants me.'

'And what exactly does he want?'

'Skydancer! The full technical blueprints for the warheads!'

'And you've given them to him?'

'No!' Anderson shouted defiantly. 'No, I've given him nothing. Nothing at all. Not yet. But . . .'

'Yes?'

'But I did agree to do it! I had to tell him that, Peter, I had no choice, don't you understand?

'I arranged to leave them under some leaves by a tree on Hampstead Heath, where he could collect them. Only I had a plan, you see. A trick so that he wouldn't actually get any of the secrets.'

He leaned forward, eager for Peter to accept his good intentions.

'I reckoned that if I could make the handover go wrong in a very public way, I might be able to persuade him that the sudden security hoo-ha would make it impossible for me to get the stuff for him at that time, and that we should delay everything. That way I thought I could buy time to think. To try to work out a way of saving both the secrets and my own . . . situation.

'So I pretended I had made a mistake about the place where I was to leave the papers, and I put the folder with just one sheet from the Skydancer plans inside a litter bin close to the real dead-letter box. You see, I knew that General Twining walked along that path every morning early, regular as clockwork. I occasionally go for early morning walks myself, and I'd passed the time of day with him there in the past.

'So after I left the folder, I rushed back to some bushes where I'd hidden some old clothes, and dressed up as a tramp . . . wore an old overcoat –'

'The one I saw hanging up in your cloakroom?' Peter interrupted.

'Yes. That one,' Anderson answered, obviously put out that he had not thought to dispose of it.

'Yes. You see, I reckoned that if I got back to the litter bin right away and pretended to be rustling through it I could stop Karl's men collecting the folder, and could also see that it was conspicuous when the general came by. I knew he was a meticulous sort of man and was bound to pick up the mess.'

'My God, Alec! You were taking one hell of a risk, weren't you? Suppose the East Germans had got there first?'

'Well, there was only one page from the set, remember. They wouldn't have learned much from that.'

'Don't be so sure.' Peter frowned.

'Anyway, it worked. The general delivered the folder to the Defence Ministry just as I thought he would, but there was a hitch after that. I desperately needed a great public hue-and-cry to convince Karl that the hullabaloo would make it impossible to get the rest of the plans for the time being. Only, Sir Marcus Beckett decided to try to keep the whole business secret so as not to stir up the politicians. That was a potential disaster for me, so I did the only thing I could think of: I leaked the story to the press.'

'So that was you, was it? But what was your friend Karl's reaction to all this?'

'He went wild, of course. He had copies made of those dreadful photographs, and had the envelopes already addressed to send off. He didn't send them, though. I swore to him that it had all been an honest mistake, and said I would do what he wanted eventually – but that they had to give me more time. Well, that promise kept him quiet for a couple of days, but then . . . it was like a bombshell.

'Mary Maclean was dead! Killed herself, they said, confessing to something she hadn't done! I was terribly upset. I couldn't believe it. But then suddenly I realised what it meant. The hue-and-cry was over. The pressure was off, and Karl could now demand that I get him the papers immediately. My excuse was removed by the death of one carefully selected victim!'

Alec caught Peter's look of anger.

'Yes. Karl Metzger killed Mary. He admitted it this evening. He doped her with some hypnotic drug untraceable by forensic tests, then dumped her in her bath and cut her wrists.'

Peter recoiled at this abrupt summary of her end.

'He gave me this.'

Anderson reached his shaking hand across the desk and lightly touched the brown-paper parcel he had brought back from the pub.

'He said it was to remind me. I don't dare . . . Here, *you* open it, would you?'

Peter shook his head, struggling to control the bitter emotions welling up inside him. He had felt certain that Mary was murdered, but this confirmation was devastating. He felt his whole body begin to tremble. Just a short while ago he had stood within feet of the man who had killed her.

'What the . . .?' Alec started in surprise. He had now opened the parcel himself. It contained a picture, and he passed it across.

It was the photograph of Mary with her nephew and niece, the one that Peter had not been able to find in her flat.

Anderson stood up and crossed to the sideboard. He poured whisky into two glasses.

'Here.' He passed one across, and Peter swallowed a mouthful.

'The bastard!' Peter exploded. 'The evil little bastard! He's got to be caught. Come on! Call the police now! You've no choice! Mary died because of you – you and your efforts to save your own skin!'

'It's not just *my* skin! There are three people upstairs, two of them small children, who matter more than I do. Their lives will be ruined if those photographs get out!'

'Look, if you co-operate fully with John Black, he'll probably be able to grab Karl before he has a chance to do anything,' Peter insisted, knowing he did not sound convincing.

'John Black! You trust that man, do you? Have you ever asked yourself who he's *really* working for?' Anderson leaned forward intensely. 'Karl has got someone in MI5! At the top. An informer,' he whispered.

'What?'

Anderson nodded meaningfully.

'How many people know that you went over to the United States to make alterations to the test missile, Peter? I didn't, and I'm head of the Nuclear Secretariat. It was my business to know, and I didn't – until Karl told me!'

'Christ! Karl told you about that? Bloody hell! That was classified top secret! Only the most senior military men, some ministers and security chiefs, and a handful of blokes at Aldermaston knew about it. Did Karl say his source was in MI5? Was he specific?'

'Well, yes, the hint was pretty heavy.'

Peter's thoughts were racing. If the Soviets knew that he had made changes to the Skydancer warheads, then what was to be done about the test launch? The weapons had been reprogrammed specifically to make the Russians doubt the genuineness of the plans they might have stolen – though it was now clear that they did not have the plans at all. If he turned Anderson in and got Metzger arrested, it still would not be the end of the affair for the Soviets. They would try some other way to get hold of the blueprints, he was sure of that. They would only stop trying once they had obtained what they thought were the real Skydancer plans.

Anderson, he suddenly realised, had a unique value.

'What were Karl's last instructions to you?'

Alec shivered. 'He's given me until midday Monday. I have to phone a number at twelve noon on that day to confirm I have the Skydancer papers, and to arrange a handover point. If I don't do this, he'll put the photographs in the afternoon post.'

'So we have the weekend in which to think,' Peter murmured to himself. 'Alec, if you want me to help you, you've got to do precisely what I ask you. I have the beginnings of an idea which might save you *and* save Skydancer at the same time.'

The snow that had fallen in the past few days in Moscow had melted in a sudden thaw. The winter had receded for a while, and it felt like autumn again. Even the grey clouds that covered the city almost continually at this time of year had parted sufficiently that morning to let rays of watery sunshine cast shadows in the road.

Oleg Kvitzinsky was loading suitcases into his car. He had not expected to be able to leave the city that weekend. The GRU had told him repeatedly that the British missile secrets would be in his hands any day, and he had believed them. Suddenly, however, on the previous afternoon he had decided to ignore General Novikov's unfulfilled promises and try to forget about the problem for a couple of days. The pressure of waiting was making him dangerously irritable.

'Where can we put this? It mustn't get damaged,' Katrina called out, struggling towards him with a large pot-plant.

'What are we taking that for?' he demanded in exasperation.

'For my mother. A present for my mother. It's her anniversary, you know!'

Oleg shrugged, and wedged the pot safely in the corner of the rear seat. His wife's family was aggravatingly conscientious about celebrating. Katrina's father had died four years earlier, but she still insisted on marking the date of her parents' wedding every year.

The traffic flowed steadily on the ring-road as he headed for the turning that would take them north-east towards the town of Zagorsk. Their dacha belonged to Katrina's family, and was a large timber house with enough bedrooms to accommodate her brother's family and her mother as well as themselves. Oleg knew it was going to be a weekend of tears mixed with happiness. It always was when Katrina's family got together.

As they drove away from the city and into the birch-woods, the sun broke through the clouds again, gilding the white bark of the trees. He opened the window to smell the air, and patted the steering-wheel with spontaneous enthusiasm.

'Katya, this was a good idea!' he exclaimed.

She smiled at him and stroked his knee. She wanted him to relax this weekend, to forget the secret work about which he would never talk, and to remember the fun they used to have when he was just a computer specialist in the civilian sector, travelling all over the world. She was determined to persuade him to return to that way of life somehow.

'Bella promised to do lunch,' she commented, 'and I shall cook this evening. Will you be going to see the priest?' There was a certain frost in her voice. She had no time for religion, and it annoyed her that her husband found such solace in communicating with clerics.

'I might,' he stated firmly. 'If there's time.'

But he had every intention of finding time to drive into Zagorsk during the next two days to visit a small house with a hand-decorated doorway, close to the Trinity-Saint Sergei monastery. For the man who lived there was not only a priest in that town celebrated as the spiritual centre of the Russian Orthodox church; he had also been Oleg Kvitzinsky's confidant for many years.

It took them a little over an hour to reach the dacha, seven kilometres outside Zagorsk on the Moscow road.

'Look, Oleg! The children!' Katrina suddenly pointed ahead.

As they neared the dacha, her brother's two daughters could be seen walking by the roadside, carrying baskets full of mushrooms.

Oleg pressed his foot on the brake pedal and smiled. He would give them a lift back to the house.

Peter Joyce looked at his watch for the fifth time in as many minutes. It was after 8 a.m. He would try the number the Chief of Defence Staff had given him; the man was bound to be awake by now.

Lady Buxton answered the phone of their Pimlico townhouse, only to tell him that her husband had gone out for a walk. Peter silently cursed the way military men seemed to be obsessed with early-morning exercise. However, the field-marshal's wife promised to get her husband to call back the moment he returned home.

'Hiya, Dad!'

Peter's eleven-year-old son bounced into the kitchen in his pyjamas.

'You won't forget I'm playing in the first eleven this afternoon, Dad? You will watch, won't you?'

'Oh, Mark,' Peter groaned, smacking himself on the forehead. 'It's not that I've forgotten . . .'

'It's just that it slipped your memory,' Mark cut in sarcastically.

Shoulders stiff with resentment, the boy walked past his father and began to search for some breakfast.

'Look, it's not that. I *will* try to come and see you play, but it just may not be possible in the end, that's all. I'm sorry, old chap. You know what's been going on the last few days,' he explained. 'Well, it's not over yet.'

'But I've never played in the first eleven before,' Mark insisted, sulkily shaking corn-flakes into a bowl.

'I'm sure Mum will come and watch you.'

'Yeah . . .'

'I *do* promise I'll come if I can.'

Belinda was awake and sitting up in bed as he brought in the tray. The strain of the past few days had deepened the lines on her face. Peter thought she suddenly looked old.

'Was that you on the phone?' she asked.

'Yes, I need to get hold of someone urgently.'

She took the mug he offered her and murmured her thanks.

'You were very late last night,' she ventured, sipping

slowly. 'I don't even know what time you got back. Where did you go?'

Peter sat down on the bed.

'I went to see the person who is at the bottom of this whole spying business. I think I know the entire story now.'

'But you're not going to tell me.'

'Not yet. I can't.'

Belinda raised an eyebrow disdainfully, and drank more tea.

'You're still suspended?'

'Yes. That's not changed.'

'Wouldn't this be a good time to resign?' she suggested quietly. 'I mean, they suspended you because they thought it was your fault the secrets went missing. Now if you have evidence that someone else was to blame, your good name will be restored. So you could resign in protest at the way you have been treated, and everybody would support you.'

'God! That's a bit tortuous, isn't it? Why should I want to resign, anyway?'

'So that you could take up a new job that didn't involve building weapons of mass-destruction,' she explained gently, as if addressing someone of lower-than-average intelligence.

Peter snorted with laughter. 'You never give up, do you?'

'Peter, I'm serious!' she pleaded. 'You're a highly qualified electronics specialist. British industry must be crying out for people like you! Why not get out of this nuclear business while you can?'

Her dark eyes implored him to listen.

'And, frankly, all this cloak-and-dagger stuff is frightening the life out of me.'

There was the hint of a tremor in her voice. Peter

reached across to where her knees made a mound in the bedclothes.

'Even if I wanted to change jobs, it's not that easy. My knowledge of electronics has been related to nothing but nuclear weapons for the past fifteen years. It's not the sort of knowledge needed by many companies in Britain.'

'Where there's a will . . .' she murmured wistfully.

Peter turned away from her again. He did not want to have to cope with an argument that morning.

'Look, I expect to be out most of the day. I've got to see the Chief of the Defence Staff, if I can get hold of him . . . It's Mark: his football match this afternoon. I don't think I can get there. I'm going to have to disappoint him. Can you go and watch?'

'Of course. I was going anyway,' she said dismissively.

The telephone rang on the bedside table, and Peter leaned across to answer it.

Field-Marshal Buxton suggested they meet in his office at the Defence Ministry. He had warned security staff on duty that Saturday to expect Peter.

'Not sure this is quite proper, with you being suspended from duty and all that,' the CDS stated with some discomfort when they were alone together. 'Not sure I'm allowed to speak to you officially. Still, if necessary we can pretend this conversation never took place!'

'I don't think you'll have any objections when you've heard what I've got to say.'

As Peter began to describe his visit to Alec Anderson the previous evening, the old soldier's face was fixed in an expression of unyielding concentration. Peter talked for nearly ten minutes.

For a moment Buxton seemed to be searching for words.

'Dammit! That's one of the most appalling stories I've ever heard!' he exclaimed at last. 'But what have you done about it, apart from telling me? You've put the security people on to him, I hope?'

Peter shook his head.

'Why not, for God's sake? The man's a menace, and that East German – he needs to be locked up right away.'

'It's not as simple as that,' Peter urged. 'Anderson is convinced that the East Germans have an agent in MI5! Somehow this man Karl knew that I had been over to Florida to adjust the warheads on HMS *Retribution*!'

'Oh? Buxton looked startled. He well remembered how highly classified that visit had been. 'And Anderson thinks the source was in MI5?'

Peter nodded.

'You had your own suspicions about Mr John Black, didn't you?'

'I'm sure he tried to deliberately conceal the fact that photograph was missing from Mary's flat. Perhaps it was because he knew who'd really got it.'

Buxton looked doubtful. 'But we can't disregard the entire security service just because of a vague suspicion over one individual!' he exploded. 'I mean, for God's sake, these men have got to be apprehended right away, before they can do more damage. They might skip the country any minute. There must be plenty more information inside Anderson's head that could be useful to the other side.'

'Well, I had another idea,' Peter ventured, not sure how Buxton would take it.

'Anderson's control is expecting him to deliver the complete Skydancer plans on Monday. Why don't we let him think he's doing that?'

'Go on,' Buxton frowned.

'Only it won't be the real papers that he hands over. Instead I'll provide him with a set that'll match the changes I made to the warheads; so when they are fired off in a few days' time, our deception will be complete. With any luck the Soviets'll think they have the real plans, with the warheads' performance confirmed before their own eyes, and no matter how much they spend on devising counter-measures, they'll all be totally irrelevant.'

'And the man who killed that wretched girl will get off scot-free?' Buxton spluttered.

Peter remembered what he had seen in Chiswick. Yes, he wanted revenge on the man who had done it.

'Perhaps he won't,' he replied noncommittally.

'It'll be a political decision,' the field-marshal said eventually. 'Have to be. Too much at stake. Too much that could go wrong. I'll have to talk to the PM.'

He looked at his watch. It was after midday.

'When are you due to contact Anderson again?'

'Sometime later today. I didn't fix a time.'

'Hmmmm. Best thing you can do, Peter, is to go for a walk. Let me sort things for a bit. Find a nice pub, have some lunch, and come back here at about half-past two. Perhaps I'll have an answer by then.'

To have two hours to kill was agonising for Peter, and left him feeling uncomfortably impotent.

Following the defence chief's suggestion, he took a walk along the Embankment to Westminster Bridge and crossed to the other side of the river. Heading east along the South Bank towards the City, he put the traffic behind him and felt invigorated by the brisk breeze and the sight of the thick, brown Thames water swirling seawards in a full ebb-tide. Pleasure boats, now unused in the winter months, strained at their moorings in the middle of the stream, and a police patrol launch nosed its way curiously amongst them.

Pulling up the collar of his fawn raincoat against the wind, he sat down on a bench overlooking the river. The South Bank walkway was deserted except for one solitary figure who had found a seat some fifty yards away. The man wearing a thick anorak pulled a folded newspaper from his pocket and began to read it.

Events had moved so rapidly in the past few days that Peter had had little chance to consider where they were leading. Now the idea of enacting a complete deception of the Soviet Union in the immediate future preoccupied him fully. But assuming the plan succeeded, what then? He assumed success would result in his suspension being rescinded, but it worried him that the Government was not committed to any nuclear weapons developments beyond the Skydancer project. Even if they wanted general research at Aldermaston to continue in the years ahead, how satisfying would his own job be without a specific advanced technology project to work on? For the first time he began to wonder whether Belinda's urging him to quit might be worth considering.

Peter breathed in deeply and stood up, his chin thrust forward. The wind blew his hair into his eyes and he pushed it back with his hand. The man in the anorak noted the gesture. He had seen him do the same several times in the last ten minutes.

Changing career at his age was risky, and surely even to think of it at that time was being defeatist, wasn't it? Peter turned towards Waterloo Bridge and set off down the pavement. The man in the anorak stood up casually, stuffed the newspaper back in his pocket, and ambled after him.

'Do sit down,' Field-Marshal Buxton gestured to a chair.

It was nearly four o'clock, and Peter had been waiting over an hour for the Chief of Defence Staff to return from Downing Street.

'They've agreed,' the old man declared conspiratorially. 'They want you to draw up some dummy plans, good enough to fool the Russians, but which don't reveal any sensitive information. Think you can do it?'

'Hmmm. There'll have to be *some* sensitive bits in it just to make it convincing. They must realise that, for heaven's sake!'

Buxton's intense grey eyes peered over his gold-framed half-moon glasses. He was wondering how frank to be.

'I've been discussing this business for the best part of an hour at Number 10. The Prime Minister called in the Defence Secretary and the heads of MI5 and MI6. Their initial reaction was far from favourable, I can tell you. Michael Hawke seemed to want you locked up in the Tower, along with Anderson and that East German fellow! He's very bitter about your disregard for security procedures; says he's going to ensure you are fully disciplined – thrown out of the Civil Service and all that!'

Peter groaned.

'Shouldn't worry. I don't suppose it will come to that,' Buxton soothed. 'Just trying to give you an idea of the atmosphere at this meeting! Well, I eventually managed to persuade them to give serious thought to your proposal, and interestingly enough it was the MI6 man who came to your aid. Liked the idea. Said it reminded him of the 1960s when they fed a doctored version of the plans for Concorde to the Russians – and you know what happened to Concordski!

'I, er, told them about your suspicion of a spy inside MI5. Dick Sproat said it was rubbish, of course! Couldn't really say anything else. He, er, he said that they knew about Anderson and Metzger. They've been keeping a watch on Anderson apparently. They suspected Metzger was an intelligence man, though they hadn't been able to confirm it yet.'

Peter's eyebrows arched with interest. If Anderson had been under observation, then presumably he must have been too!

'In the end they agreed, but they want strict safeguards. You're to have the plans ready for Monday morning, and then there will be a vetting committee here to check it out. Just a small select group; we've got to keep this utterly secret.'

'I hope Anderson will agree to all this,' Peter cautioned.

'He'll bloody well have to! He's got no alternative!' Buxton snorted.

'But what will happen to him when it's over? Does he get immunity from prosecution?'

Buxton's eyes twinkled for a moment.

'I'm sure the Ministry of Agriculture can be persuaded to find a job for him,' he mused.

It was six in the morning when Peter parked outside Anderson's house. This time he had telephoned in advance.

Alec opened the door within seconds of his ringing the bell – as if he had been waiting behind it. There was no sign of Janet or the children as Peter was ushered hurriedly into the library.

'What's happening? Who've you told?' Anderson demanded nervously.

He was dressed in bottle-green corduroy trousers and a navy-blue pullover. A small twist of cotton wool was stuck to the underside of his jaw where he had cut himself shaving. The corners of his mouth were tight with anxiety.

'Look, Alec, people are sympathetic, really they are,' Peter reassured him, hoping he sounded convincing. 'They'll do all they can to help you, and to ensure that Janet and the children are safe. But they want you to do something in return.'

'What exactly?' Alec asked tremulously. 'And who *are* these people?'

'People at the top. The *very* top. And they want you to help turn the tables on the Russians. To get our own back.'

He paused, noting the look of apprehension on Alec's face.

'On Monday morning I shall meet you in the Defence Ministry and give you a set of plans for the Skydancer warheads. They'll look convincing but they'll be deliberately misleading. Now, you are to pass these to Karl Metzger, insisting of course that they're the genuine ones. And in return you should demand from him the negatives of the photographs he's been using to blackmail you. It's that simple.'

Alec shook his head.

'Nothing is that simple, and you know it. Supposing he can tell they're false?'

'He won't,' Peter insisted. 'You'll have to trust me on that.'

Anderson stared at him silently for a moment.

'And if it all works like you say, what then? What

happens to me – at the Ministry?'

'They'll find something suitable for you,' Peter answered irritably. 'For God's sake, Alec! You're on the floor! You're being offered a hand up!' He suppressed an urge to take the man by the throat and shake him.

He glanced down at the desk, with its top rolled back. The photograph of Mary still lay there, half-wrapped in brown paper. He took it in his hand and held it under Anderson's nose.

'Yes. Yes, of course I'll do what you say,' Alec whispered. 'What else can I do?'

Peter stood up, the photo-frame still in his hand.

'I'll take this with me, if you don't mind,' he said.

Alec looked up questioningly.

'Sentimental reasons,' Peter explained.

On Sunday morning Oleg Kvitzinsky did not wake early. It had been a difficult night.

Saturday had been a relaxing day for him, immersing himself in the inconsequential issues that preoccupied the lives of Katrina's family.

Katrina herself had passed most of the day hovering around her little nieces, remarking to anyone who would listen that they were the most perfectly delightful children she had ever known. Oleg had cast the occasional anxious glance in her direction, knowing what this was leading to. His wife always became obsessive about her childlessness when they came to the dacha. The fecundity of the countryside and the ease with which her brother's wife produced babies made her reason inwardly that it must be possible for her to conceive here, at the dacha.

At supper she had frowned at Oleg and scolded him as glass after glass of vodka had passed his lips. Then, when her brother-in-law produced two bottles of Georgian wine for them to taste, she could feel tears of despair welling up in her eyes. Her husband would be no use to her drunk.

Before they finally fell into bed, Katrina had sprayed her body lightly with the Dior perfume carefully preserved from their last visit to the West. At first Oleg had shown all the signs of falling into instant slumber, but she had quickly unbuttoned his pyjamas and began to caress the soft, furry dome of his stomach. Slowly but surely she sensed his arousal.

Oleg himself had been surprised at the liveliness of his feelings after so much alcohol, and he had begun to believe that a rare degree of mutual satisfaction might be achievable that night. But then the noise had started in the next room. Katrina's brother and sister-in-law slept on the other side of the wall. The rhythmic creaking started softly and unevenly, but built up steadily to a persistent tempo.

'Oh, this is a farmyard!' Oleg groaned, feeling the vitality draining from him.

They had both lain awake after their failure, back to back, their bodies not quite touching. Oleg told himself he should have had more to drink, so not even the mirage of sexual potency could have arisen. On the other side of the bed Katrina let her tears of frustration soak into the pillow.

In the morning she had risen early to help her mother and busy herself around the house, trying to project an image of contentment. She found it impossible to discuss her personal difficulties with her family.

The intermittent sunshine of the previous day persisted, and Oleg took the children for a walk in the birch woods while the women prepared lunch. Katrina's brother spent the morning asleep. The freshness of the air, away from the pollution of Moscow, had a sweet taste to it which he savoured.

From a distant village the wind blew the sound of bells tolling the faithful to church. In this part of the atheist state the Orthodox Church was at its strongest. Congregations were growing as a result of the tentative liberalisation of the Gorbachev government.

But for Oleg the value of priests did not lie in their performance of ceremony and ritual for the masses, but in the unfettered communication of ideas which a select few were prepared to encourage.

It had been while walking in woods like these just outside Zagorsk that Oleg had first come across Father Yuri, one bitter winter about five years ago when twenty degrees of frost had given a crisp skin to the deep layer of snow. The priest's dog had fallen into a drift and the cleric had been struggling to free it.

Father Yuri had a small parish in Zagorsk, and led a necessarily simple life. The size of a parish was important to a priest, because his salary depended on donations made by his congregation. What Father Yuri lacked in funds, however, was compensated by gifts of food and drink from his parishioners. Whenever Oleg went to visit him, he would be pressed to help himself from the quantities of cakes and sweetmeats that seemed permanently to adorn the priest's table.

That Sunday, Oleg waited until four in the afternoon before making his visit. Lunch at the dacha was a necessarily lengthy affair, starting with borscht, and cucumbers in soured cream, followed by local wild duck and fried cheese cakes with plum jam. The side dishes alone had taken the women most of the morning to prepare.

Zagorsk was dominated by the onion domes of the Cathedral of the Assumption and the Trinity-Saint

Sergius monastery. Oleg parked his car just outside the fortress walls, and walked through the narrow streets with their doorways and pillars decorated in blue and gold until he came to the house which had almost become his confessional.

The door was opened by Yuri's wife, who beamed with pleasure to see Oleg again. It had been several months since his last visit.

She led him through the hallway with its faded green and gold wallpaper. On the floor the bare boards were covered by a threadbare length of carpet whose oriental pattern was scarcely discernible now. A single light-bulb, under a shade of etched glass, hung from the ceiling to illuminate their way.

She opened the door at the end of the passage.

'Look who it is who has come to visit you, Yuri,' she announced with delight.

'Oleg Ivanovich!' the priest bellowed, rising from a small wooden armchair in the corner of his study, and bustling towards the door with his arms outstretched. He was a large man, in his fifties, with a square face and widely-spaced eyes. The thick beard that completely concealed his chin had been jet-black in younger days, but was now flecked with grey. His strong, straight hair was brushed sharply backwards, revealing a baldness at the temples.

The two men embraced each other fondly, as the woman left them on their own together.

'Come, my friend! Sit down and be warm.' The priest beckoned him towards the two chairs on each side of the tiled stove. He opened its door and pushed inside small pieces of wood he had collected while out walking. His dog lay curled up in front of the heat, observing the arrival of the visitor with one eye.

'I expected to see you out walking this morning,'

Oleg exclaimed. 'The weather was so fine. But then when I heard the bells I remembered you had more pressing duties!'

The priest's bellow of laughter seemed to shake the brass chandelier whose electric candles cast a soft light into the room. They continued in flippant, jocular terms for several minutes while Yuri prepared the samovar. The priest did not touch alcohol but made an elegant ritual out of serving tea.

'And how are things at the centre?' he asked over his shoulder. 'It's so long since you visited that I imagine life must be very busy for you.'

The charcoal was well alight now and the water began to sing. Oleg stretched out his legs and hooked his hands behind his head.

'Things move in their own way,' he answered enigmatically, his eyebrows arched almost derisively. 'If what passes for life in Moscow is reality, Yuri, then this life of yours is pure fantasy,' he mocked. 'But on the other hand, if this is real, then . . .'

He didn't complete his sentence but his meaning was clear.

'Well, if you don't know which is the real life, it is too long since you last came to Zagorsk!' Yuri retorted, and bellowed with laughter again.

The samovar boiled, and the priest turned his attention to it.

'But, my friend,' he continued with concern. 'If you are serious, then you have a problem. For the truth is that it is all real. There – and here.'

There was a knock at the door and the priest's wife entered with two plates of cakes.

'Oleg Ivanovich must be hungry after his journey,' she fussed, placing the plates on the table by the window.

'Ravenous!' Kvitzinsky joked, reaching across to take a pastry.

She beamed at him and bustled out of the room again.

A silence fell between them for a moment.

'But you are troubled, my friend,' the priest prompted eventually. 'Troubled by doubts about the purpose and reality of your life? It's a common condition, you know.'

'Perhaps it is more a question of rightness than of reality,' Oleg explained. 'Morality even . . .' His voice tailed away.

'That's a subject I'm supposed to know something about,' the priest said gently, knowing for sure that Oleg had an overwhelming need to unburden his soul.

'You know I work for the military now?' Oleg looked up at his friend uncertainly. He was strictly forbidden to talk to anyone about his job, but in this house it was customary for such rules to be ignored.

Yuri handed Oleg an elegant porcelain cup and saucer. 'Is it still about computers?'

'Yes, it's still computers,' Oleg confirmed, sipping the pale green tea whose smoky perfume seemed to complement the scent of the charcoal in the samovar. 'Computer technology can free man from industrial slavery, so that his talents for craftsmanship can be liberated and developed. I really believe that.

'But it can do other things too, unfortunately. It can delude men into believing they can achieve almost anything . . . even total security against enemy attack. It's what the Russian people have dreamed of for centuries! Now there are those who believe it is a dream that can come true!'

'And that is why they moved you into military work, my friend?'

'Exactly,' Kvitzinsky whispered in reply. 'They believe that I . . . and my computers can achieve the ultimate for them. To build a shield which will be directed electronically and automatically to fend off every type of attack. It was an honour to be given this duty. I was deeply flattered. And a challenge – there is none greater. But . . .'

'But anything so perfect – it is of course impossible!' The priest completed his sentence for him.

'The funds are unlimited . . . everything can be sacrificed for this aim, it seems to me. The arthritis of Katrina's mother can go untreated . . . Katrina herself can remain childless – but nothing must hinder my work, so they say.'

The priest shivered. The window was not firmly latched, and he stood up to attend to it.

'You talked of morality. You know, of course,' he explained as he readjusted the curtains, 'that when it comes to morality, your masters and mine are in conflict. In my house, right and wrong are decided by a higher order than the Party. And it is for each and every man to decide for himself in whose house he is going to live. There is no other way, my friend.'

'Yes,' Oleg answered unhappily. 'I know. Sometimes, though, the circumstances make it too difficult to take a decision like that, don't they?'

For some time the priest let his hand rest on Oleg's shoulder. Then slowly he moved away and lowered himself back into the chair by the stove.

'I don't know,' he answered kindly. 'That's a question you will have to put to yourself.'

John Black lived alone in a three-roomed South London flat, surrounded by the few possessions he had accrued during his life. He had been married once, a long time ago, but it had been an unsatisfactory experience and he never talked about it.

He had felt certain that his Sunday at home would be disturbed before long. Indeed, he would have been worried if it had not. The plan to supply false versions of the Skydancer documents to the Russians was fraught with dangers, and he had ordered a tightening of the surveillance on all those involved.

After lunching on a frozen chicken pie hurriedly cooked in his microwave oven, he had settled down to watch an old Bette Davis film on television.

The interruption to his viewing came from a source he had not anticipated. Indeed he had not realised until then that the FBI worked on Sundays. The message from the signals analysis office in Miami had him kicking off his carpet-slippers and pulling on his thick-soled shoes within seconds.

His own office had rapidly found an address for the telephone number the Americans had supplied. It was the Berkshire area again. With a quick phone-call to Reading police station, so that they could alert his friend in the Special Branch that he was on his way, he slipped behind the wheel of his car and headed for the motorway.

On the passenger seat next to him he had placed a facsimile printer, and plugged it into a socket on the dashboard. Then he picked up the handset of his car-phone and dialled a number which would connect the printer directly with his office. While he sped on his way to Reading, the entire text of the intercepted telephone conversation between an unknown Englishman in Florida and a Miss Susan Parkinson in a Berkshire town would be transcribed for him to study.

It took him three-quarters of an hour to reach the

police station. Tom McQuade was waiting for him, still wearing the mud-caked shoes in which he had been doing his weekend gardening.

'Taking your disguise a bit seriously today, aren't you?' Black mocked, looking down at them.

The policeman scraped his shoes against the front wheel of the MI5 man's car. 'We know Susan Parkinson,' he announced as he slid on to the passenger seat from which he had removed the facsimile printer.

'She's in that same mob as the wife of the Aldermaston man; you know, Action to Stop Annihilation; the organisation our WPC got inside. Interestingly enough, our Jenny was at one of their committee meetings on Friday night. None of them seemed to know why the Venner woman had done a bunk. There was a lot of talk about it. Big mystery apparently.'

John Black handed him the facsimile sheet and lit up a cigarette. The policeman wound down the window to let the smoke out, and began to read the page.

'Who is he?' he asked when he had finished.

'We don't know, but he's obviously one of the officers on board HMS *Retribution*, and he shouldn't have been talking like that to *anyone*!'

'Too bloody right!' McQuade replied.

The address they had been given was in a street of small semi-detached houses on the outskirts of Newbury. The policeman had discovered that the woman was a schoolteacher.

Black stopped the car just short of the house so that they would not be seen too readily from the windows.

'There's a passageway at the side,' he murmured, stubbing out his cigarette. 'You pop round to the back while I do the front door, just in case any little bunny rabbits come running out of the stubble!'

The two men hoped they would be mistaken for

Jehovah's Witnesses if anyone saw them approaching the house. John Black waited until McQuade had slipped round the side, before pressing the doorbell. There was the faint sound of music from inside, which he recognised as Tchaikovsky, but it stopped abruptly.

After a minute with no response, he pressed the button again and held it pressed. He could hear the bell shrilling at the back of the house. Suddenly he saw through the patterned-glass door panel that someone was coming.

'What the hell are you doing with that doorbell?' a woman shouted at him as she wrenched open the door.

She was quite attractive, he thought to himself. Better than most of her type. The look in her eyes, though, reminded him suddenly of the woman to whom he had once been married, many years before. It set his teeth on edge.

'Ms Parkinson?' he enquired softly.

'Yes?' she answered nervously. 'What do you want?'

'I'm from the Ministry of Defence. I'm afraid I have some bad news about your boyfriend. May I . . . may I come in for a moment?'

For a split second her eyes registered shock, but she quickly hid it. Black put one foot on the sill. She pushed the door towards him to block his path. Suddenly Black saw a shadow move behind her at the far end of the hallway.

'I . . . I don't know what you're talking about!' she shouted. 'I don't have a boyfriend.'

'It's a security matter, Ms Parkinson. You'd be well advised to invite me in.'

He pushed hard on the door and she stumbled backwards. Then she began to scream. He hated this type; they were the worst, the screamers. His wife had screamed at him when she did not get her way. With these 'peace women', though, he knew it was a tactic to provoke arresting officers to resort to physical violence, which could then be held against them in court. In his case it often came close to succeeding.

Suddenly the screaming stopped. She had heard a noise behind her and turned to see Tom McQuade emerging from her kitchen with his large hands firmly clamped round the arms of another woman.

'Got someone here I think you'd like to meet, John,' he announced with a wry smile. 'This lady is Helene Venner!'

Chapter Seven

Shortly before midday on Monday an audio tape of the intercepted phone-call arrived in London. The flight from Miami had been delayed by a technical fault, and at Heathrow airport a police squad-car was waiting to rush the cassette to the Royal Naval headquarters at Northwood. There, a lieutenant-commander formerly with HMS *Retribution* had been briefed to listen to it carefully in an effort to identify the speaker. Ms Susan Parkinson had remained stubbornly silent about the name of her caller. Meanwhile preparations at the Ministry of Defence had been almost finalised.

Peter Joyce had spent his Sunday in the chief draughtsman's office at Aldermaston, doctoring the drawings and descriptions on the Skydancer blueprints so that a new version could be prepared to meet the criteria set by the security chiefs. At the front of his mind hung his mental picture of 'the Russian', to guide his thoughts.

At eight o'clock on Monday morning the documents were being pored over in Field-Marshal Buxton's office by intelligence experts and scientists. They had to be convincing without jeopardising national security.

Now that it seemed certain Karl Metzger had learned about the changes to the Skydancer warheads from a source on board the submarine, Peter's suspicions about the reliability of MI5 had diminished. He was not entirely satisfied however, still wanting to know why John Black had lied about the photograph in Mary's flat.

When the blueprints were finally approved, Peter was left on his own with the field-marshal and Sir Marcus Beckett.

'Is Anderson happy about what he's got to do?' Buxton inquired.

'*Happy* isn't the word for it,' Peter replied. 'But he realises he has no choice.'

'Shall we get him in, then?' Sir Marcus suggested, eager to start things moving.

Buxton pressed a key on the intercom.

'I wish to God I could be sure we're doing the right thing,' Sir Marcus mused uncomfortably. 'The Soviets have put a hell of an effort into getting hold of the Skydancer secrets. We may have found out about the East German and the spy on the boat . . . but I'm bloody sure they've got more tricks up their sleeves.'

'A spy on board one of our Polaris submarines!' Buxton exploded. 'How did the Navy let *that* happen? What on earth are they doing with their vetting procedures? I can tell you there are going to be some damned hard questions asked when we find out who the man is.'

There was a tap at the door, and Anderson came in.

'Good morning, Anderson. Sit down.'

Sir Marcus had taken charge. Anderson was a civil servant, answerable to him rather than the Chief of the Defence Staff.

'I think I should make it clear, Anderson,' Beckett began, 'that this is being seen as a salvage operation rather than an opportunity any of us would have sought. It would have been much better for the Skydancer project to remain under wraps instead of gaining such public exposure, and indeed the politicians look upon your activities with the deepest concern. Only by doing what you are about to do, will you earn *any* chance of favourable treatment. I'm not authorised to make promises about the likelihood or not of any prosecution against you. No decisions have been taken yet. Suffice to say, if what you are about to do proves successful, it can only count in your favour. Do I make myself clear?'

'Perfectly, Sir Marcus,' Anderson answered nervously.

'Now, what are your orders from the other side?'

Anderson cleared his throat.

'They haven't told me much yet. I . . . I have to be in a certain telephone-box at exactly twelve noon. Someone will ring me there and give me further instructions.'

'You will be under surveillance . . .'

'No!' Anderson almost shouted.

'For your own protection as much as anything else.'

'I don't want it! If they get the slightest inkling that this is a put-up job, I'm finished,' Anderson pleaded. 'Don't you see? It could ruin everything. Karl is already highly suspicious. He said he wouldn't hesitate. First sign of any trickery and he's going to send off those photographs.' Anderson coloured at this.

Buxton looked contemptuous and patted the envelope which contained the blueprints.

'No! I won't do it if you're going to have people tailing me!' Anderson insisted.

'Won't do it? I'm *ordering* you to!' Sir Marcus cut in.

'Perhaps . . .' Buxton intervened, 'perhaps the answer would be for you to discuss that little detail with John Black, since it's his department.'

Anderson cast a glance of alarm at Peter.

'It's all right,' Joyce nodded. 'They've found out who leaked the information about my visit to Florida – and it wasn't Black.'

Anderson seemed far from reassured. Nevertheless he took the envelope from the table and stood up.

'Then I'd better talk to him now. There's not much time.'

He looked at the carriage clock on Buxton's desk. He had just thirty minutes before his telephone rendezvous with the East German agent.

Peter decided to accompany Alec down to the security office where John Black had taken up residence for the day. Anderson led the way through the grid of corridors which Peter still found confusing, even after dozens of visits to the Ministry.

'They're pretty good, those plans,' Peter reassured him, when there was no one close to them. 'I don't think the comrades will guess.'

'Don't be too sure,' Anderson grunted. 'You're not dealing with children, you know.'

As they neared the security office, Peter took the other man by the arm.

'I'll leave you to talk to Black on your own,' he said. 'And . . . you'll ring us later? To tell us how things went with Metzger.'

Anderson's expression was blank.

'Yes, I'll call you.'

He turned and pushed open the door in front of him.

'Take a seat, Mr Anderson.' John Black was replacing the receiver of his telephone.

'Is there something that worries you about our arrangements?'

'Yes!' Alec almost shouted. 'It's imperative you don't have anybody following me today!'

'Could ruin things, you mean?'

'It might even be fatal if they get wind of this being a counter-intelligence operation,' Anderson insisted.

'Too much at stake, you think?'

'There certainly is! And if you have somebody tailing me, I'm not going through with it!'

John Black smiled benignly, and inhaled deeply from his half-smoked cigarette.

'I quite understand.'

Alec was startled by the other's conciliatory tone.

'You mean you agree?'

'Utterly. Nothing must be allowed to compromise the success of this operation.' Black oozed sincerity.

'But upstairs they were *insisting* . . .'

'Just a little misunderstanding. There'll be no surveillance, I promise you.'

John Black stood up and extended his hand.

'Good-bye Mr Anderson, and good luck!'

Reluctantly Alec shook the offered hand, but had no idea whether the security man had been telling the truth.

Black took a last lungful of smoke, crushed the cigarette on to the lid of his ashtray, and shredded the stub between his fingers.

Buxton and Beckett were waiting for Peter Joyce when he returned to the sixth floor. Both looked worried.

'Did Black manage to sort that out?' Sir Marcus asked.

'I didn't stay to see,' Peter responded.

'He'll let us know if he's got any problems, I'm sure,' the field-marshal soothed.

'Now, look here, Joyce,' Sir Marcus said hurriedly. 'I think we'd better clarify *your* position a bit. Officially, you're still suspended on full pay pending a security enquiry, but that's pretty impractical in the circumstances. You're right in the middle of this business and . . . well, your uncovering of Anderson was pretty sharp, let's face it.

'So, the Defence Secretary has authorised me to lift

your suspension as of this morning, and the fact that it occurred will be struck from the record. That's not the end of the matter, however. There will still be an enquiry into your disregard of security procedures, and your reinstatement today will not prejudice the outcome of that. But you can forget about the suspension.'

'Thank you,' Peter answered non-committally.

'Right. Well, I'll leave you to it.' Beckett rubbed his hands, and left the room.

Field-Marshal Buxton lowered himself into the large chair behind his desk.

'Now, Peter. About the missile test. I've decided it'll take place this afternoon,' he announced, '*if* they can get their act together down in the Atlantic. But they've got a spy to deal with first.'

Carrying a brown leather briefcase marked with his monogram, Alec Anderson walked along the Embankment until he came to the pair of telephone boxes described to him by Karl Metzger. The briefcase had been a rather ostentatious present from Janet several Christmasses ago. He did not normally take it to work, preferring the more anonymous black variety supplied by the MOD; but he had chosen the brown bag today because it did not immediately identify him as a civil servant.

He looked at his wristwatch again, even though he had already studied it just seconds ago. It was still only five to twelve.

The closest of the two kiosks was the one where he had been told to expect the midday call. He cursed silently: it was occupied. Of course, it would be! A large, fat black woman seemed in no hurry to finish her conversation.

Alec slackened his pace and tried to look relaxed. Pretending to have lost his way, he turned his head as if looking for street names. He was searching for faces, though, for any sign of anyone deliberately watching him. A shiver ran down his spine; he felt so exposed.

In the distance Big Ben began to chime the preamble to the hour. Still there was no sign of the black woman ending her chat. She saw him waiting and pointed to the other box.

'Doesn't work,' Alec mouthed.

What would they do? What would happen if they could not get through to him at noon? A harsh wind off the Thames chilled the sweat gathering under his armpits.

'Arl right now,' the black woman smiled at him, exposing broad gaps in her teeth. 'Sahry now to be so long.' She squeezed her way out of the phone-box, pulled her coat tight, and bustled away towards an underground station.

Alec hurried into the kiosk, recoiling from the smell of potato chips. A greasy paper bag lay on the floor. Opening the door again with his shoulder, he kicked it into the street. Almost immediately a man in an anorak occupied the booth next to him; a woman with a small child waited outside. He lifted the receiver, trying to conceal the fact that his fingers were holding down the rest.

His heart pounded and the sound of his anxious breathing seemed amplified by the confines of the booth.

At the first hint of a ring, he lifted his finger, and recited the number of the telephone.

The voice that answered him was not one he recognised.

'Is that the Stock Exchange?' a man asked. He had the hint of an accent.

'No. It's the Maid's Head public house and we're closed,' Alec answered, reciting the code that Metzger had instructed him to use.

'Listen carefully,' the voice continued. 'Walk to Charing Cross Station. Go in from the Strand. Just inside on the left is a row of phone booths. Use the third from the right. I'll call you there in ten minutes. Got that?'

'Yes. I . . .'

There was a click, then the dialling tone. Frantically Alec tried to remember exactly what he had been told.

He looked at his watch again. He had ten minutes.

It took less than five to walk to Charing Cross, but he stopped at several shop windows and looked round furtively to see if he was being followed.

He located the row of telephone boxes without difficulty. Third from the right – that was what the man had said. It was unoccupied. Lucky this time!

He quickly stepped into the booth and studied the directories while waiting for the call. At precisely twelve-fifteen the phone rang.

'Stock Exchange?' the voice asked again.

'Still the Maid's Head,' Alec replied.

'What's your name?'

'Anderson. What's yours?' he demanded with sudden boldness.

There was a snort of laughter at the other end.

'In front of you there is a shelf,' the voice continued. 'Put your hand under it. Do you feel something?'

'There's something stuck here. Something metal.'

'Correct. It's the key to a left-luggage locker. Do you have it now?'

Anderson peeled the sellotape from under the shelf and held the key in his hand.

'Yes. It's here.'

'Pick up a small suitcase from the locker. Take it to the gents' toilet. Go into a cubicle and look inside the case. There will be instructions to tell you what to do next.'

'But when do I . . .?'

The line went dead.

Anderson backed away from the phone. Sudden panic set his stomach churning. Perhaps the suitcase was a bomb? Were they trying to kill him?

Calm down, he told himself. Where were the left-luggage lockers anyway? Breathe slowly.

The station looked enormous. One or two people in the lunchtime crowd were staring at him – or was it his imagination? Suddenly he felt certain: someone *was* watching him.

The man on the phone, could he be here at the station? Was he being controlled by someone he could actually see?

Quiet, he told himself. Keep cool! Find that bloody luggage locker and get on to the next clue in this paper-chase!

It was twenty yards away, clearly marked with a sign. He started to walk, stifling an instinct to run.

The key slid stiffly into the lock, and the door sprang open. Inside was a maroon overnight bag.

Alec selected a cubicle at the far end of the row in the gents'. He flushed the lavatory in case anyone was listening, then sat on the seat.

The case had a zip-fastener which he undid slowly, covering the sound by clearing his throat.

Inside were a shirt, a pair of pyjamas, a washbag and shaving kit, and a large brown envelope. What the hell . . .?

With shaking hands he slit open the envelope and

emptied out a British passport in the name of W.J. Allenby. He opened it and saw that the photograph inside was of himself.

There was a British Airways ticket issued in the same name, for a flight to West Berlin leaving Heathrow at three-fifteen that afternoon.

Berlin! The handover was to be in Berlin! Oh God! He would be entirely at their mercy there! A sense of dread began to overwhelm him.

A typewritten list of instructions told him to travel to Heathrow airport on the underground immediately. He must make no attempt to inform anyone where he was going. When he reached Berlin he should take a taxi to Friedrichstrasse, and cross over into the East. He would be expected.

Oh God, oh God, oh God! Suppose they held him there until they checked the Skydancer plans? Suppose they decided the blueprints were fakes? They'd kill him, wouldn't they? Torture him first perhaps?

Anderson gulped. He had to control himself, get a grip!

He opened the passport again. It looked a perfect forgery. There was money in the envelope too, pounds sterling and West German marks. There was even an underground ticket to the airport. They had thought of everything.

The man in the anorak watched Anderson come out of the gents' toilets, and walk towards the underground station. He watched him pause by a tube-map to check his route. His own instructions had been very strict, to follow at a good distance at all times. Anderson must never guess that he was being watched. Any moment, though, things could get very tricky.

He flashed a pass, and followed Anderson through the barrier towards the escalators, keeping fifty yards behind. Right behind Anderson, he noticed a man in a dark blue overcoat glance over his shoulder and look around with professional thoroughness. Anderson had collected a minder, though he did not know it yet. The next part would be a matter of luck.

A thundering in the tunnel as he reached the bottom of the escalator told him that luck was on Anderson's side that day. He walked as fast as he dared, but was well behind the two men, who were already on the platform as the train came in.

The doors hissed open and shut again. Shit! He had blown it! From inside the carriage the figure in the blue coat looked out with ice-cold eyes. The edge of his mouth turned up slightly in a mocking smile.

The MI5 man cursed. John Black was not going to be happy.

When the signaller came hurrying to his cabin, clutching a sheet from his note-pad, Commander Carrington breathed a sigh of relief. They had spent the weekend idling in the depths, successfully avoiding their Soviet shadow, and waiting with growing impatience for orders to proceed with the missile launch.

The signal received on the VLF circuit from England consisted of just three words in code. Carrington dismissed the signaller, then spun the combination lock on the wall-safe and opened it to pull out his manual for codes of the day.

It took just a minute to translate the message, and he stared at it in surprise. This was *not* what he expected. What he had hoped for was a command giving the time and place of launch and the co-ordinates of the target area. Instead Northwood was instructing him to push his satellite terminal above the waves to receive a lengthy message from HQ. Carrington cursed. This could give away his position to the Russians.

By using burst-transmissions at predetermined times, large amounts of data could be transmitted in a few seconds, but even that could be long enough for a Soviet radar satellite over the Atlantic to pick up a minute reflection from their mast, and to report back the location of the sighting to Moscow and to any Soviet ships in the vicinity.

Carrington looked at his watch. They would have to close with the surface and push their antenna above it in just fifteen minutes.

In the control room, he checked with the navigator and the sonar operator to make sure the *Retribution* would be well away from other shipping when the satellite link-up took place. Then he ordered the long, trailing VLF aerial to be wound in, to prevent it fouling the propeller when they were just below the surface.

In the navigation centre next to the control room, he checked the time with the atomic clock whose accuracy ensured that the submarine and HQ could synchronise their actions perfectly. He made a small adjustment to his own watch.

'Right, officer of the watch! Bring her up to periscope depth,' he ordered when the moment came.

At the engineering control panel, hands reached up to open valves. Pumps began to hum and hiss as the buoyancy was adjusted to keep the boat just below the surface.

'Periscope depth, sir!' the coxswain reported.

'Up periscope!' Carrington called, and the shiny tube slid upwards from the floor of the control room.

He pressed his eyes to the rubber cups, gripped the

focusing handles, and carefully scanned the horizon.

There was a light swell, but not another vessel to be seen anywhere.

The periscope hissed back into the floor.

Carrington watched the second-hand.

'Up satcom!' he ordered. There were thirty seconds to go to their deadline.

Just two minutes later the antenna was lowered again and Carrington instructed the officer of the watch to return the submarine to the depths and to head away from the area, back towards the sector from where they expected to launch the missile.

The radio operator ripped the long sheet of paper from the teleprinter. The message was in full code.

'For your eyes only, sir.'

Back in his cabin, Carrington set to work again with his code books. This time he knew it would take him a good quarter of an hour.

But within minutes he realised he was translating the most staggering message he had ever received.

'Regret to inform you that enemy agent is aboard your boat. Lieutenant Robert Simpson must be put under close arrest immediately . . .'

So it began. Carrington stared in disbelief at the words and ripped a page of the code-book in his eagerness to translate the full signal.

At last it was done. It revealed that Simpson had telephoned England and talked about the secret visit to *Retribution* by the Aldermaston scientists, information which had subsequently found its way into the hands of Soviet intelligence. It was incredible!

'God almighty!' It felt like a personal blow. A member of *his* crew! It was like being told one of his family was a spy.

Also in the signal were included the orders for the test

firing. It was to be that afternoon, in three hours' time. They would have to get a move on to reach the firing zone by then.

Carrington returned to the control room grim-faced. He took the officer of the watch and the navigator to one side, and told them of the launch plans. He made them responsible for seeing that the submarine was in the right place at the right time. Then he asked his executive officer to come with him to his cabin.

With the door closed firmly behind him, Carrington gestured for his deputy to sit down.

'What I'm going to say will stun you!' he announced quietly.

Since the signal had been marked for his eyes only, he paraphrased its contents.

'I don't believe it!' Lt Commander Mike Smith exploded after listening open-mouthed. 'I could kill him, with my bare hands!'

'That's just the point, Mike. That's just what mustn't happen. But if it becomes known on board that Simpson is a spy, someone else might try to do that.'

'Unbelievable!' Smith exclaimed, shaking his head. 'Simpson? He's just a kid, hardly the stuff spies are made of. I suppose there can be no doubt? I assume they know what they're talking about in London?'

'We'll have to pull him in here and ask him. But it'd be better if you and I did it on our own. If we get the Chief to form an arrest squad, then word of it'll get round in no time. Let's try to keep it quiet. We'd better find out where Simpson is.'

That was not difficult. The supply officer was sitting in his cabin, checking his dry stores manifest.

'Lieutenant Simpson,' the executive officer began formally. 'The captain would like to see you immediately.'

Simpson frowned in surprise. He would normally expect to be addressed by his first name. Something was wrong.

'Right, sir,' he answered, rising to his feet. 'I'll come along then.'

He preceded Mike Smith down the short corridor to the captain's cabin. Carrington's face looked gaunt and drawn as Simpson walked in. Smith closed the door behind them and stood next to it.

'Lieutenant Simpson,' Carrington spoke softly, 'the Commander-in-Chief has instructed me to place you under arrest. You are to face charges under the Official Secrets Act and under Queen's Regulations, and I am to caution you that anything you say may be used in evidence against you.'

Simpson gasped. He shot a glance over his shoulder and saw that the executive officer was holding pen and notebook, ready to take notes.

'Wh . . . what do you mean, sir?' Simpson stammered. 'What's this all about?'

'Does the name Susan Parkinson mean something to you, perhaps?'

Any colour that was left in Bob Simpson's face drained away.

'Well . . . yes. Of course.' A look of pained confusion spread across his youthful features.

'You telephoned her from Miami, I believe.' Carrington's voice was cold.

'She . . . she's my girlfriend, sir. That's all,' he answered weakly.

'*All?* Just your girlfriend? That's not the impression they have back home.'

Simpson glanced around nervously and saw the hostility on the executive officer's face.

'Could you . . . could you explain to me, sir, just what

it is I am accused of?' he asked in a meek voice.

'I am informed by Northwood that you passed information to Miss Parkinson about work being done to the test missile on board this boat, and that the information subsequently arrived in the hands of an enemy power,' Carrington announced.

Simpson's face reddened. But then he frowned.

'Eh? Enemy power, sir? What enemy power?'

The thin lines to the left of Carrington's mouth began to twitch. He was fighting to control his anger.

'It's not my job to try you, Simpson,' his voice grated. 'You can fight your corner in court. But from what I've been told by Northwood they've got the evidence they need. My orders are simply to detain you until we hand you over to the authorities ashore. You will be locked in your cabin twenty-four hours a day. Meals will be brought to you, and you will be allowed to use the heads only under escort. Do you have anything to say?'

Simpson shook his head. He wanted to tell them that they had got it wrong: he'd not been passing secrets to an enemy. What he had told Susan would not have gone any further. But in view of the mission he *had* been planning, the less he said the better.

'Prisoner! Stand to attention!' ordered Lt Commander Smith.

Simpson was visibly shaking. The room seemed to be spinning in a blur.

'That will be all,' Carrington snapped.

The executive officer took him firmly by the arm and led him out. They stopped at an empty cabin and Simpson was guided inside.

'You'll stay in here for a while. You can go back to your own cabin, after I've searched it,' the Lt Commander told him, and locked the door.

Simpson's cabin was no more than eight feet square.

Smith looked around it, searching for anything out of the ordinary. The small desk was covered with routine paperwork. On the shelf above were two snapshots: one of a middle-aged couple, Simpson's parents he presumed; the other of an attractive dark-haired girl, warmly wrapped up in woolly scarf and gloves against the bright chill of an English winter's day. Written on it in ink were the words '*Love you. Sue*'

'So that's the girlfriend,' he thought to himself. 'Not bad! Quite a little Mata Hari!'

He then went through the lockers under the bunk. From Simpson's wash kit, he removed the razor and spare blades, but left an aerosol of shaving foam. Scissors and a pen-knife he put with the razor to take away for safe-keeping.

He could find nothing to connect Simpson with espionage, no diary or personal notebooks, and the volumes on the shelf were all standard textbooks or novels. Nothing subversive amongst them. He was disappointed.

'Right, Simpson, you can go back now,' he announced after unlocking the door to the spare cabin.

'Thanks very much!' Simpson grumbled. He was over the initial shock and had begun to resent this treatment. 'You're making a big mistake. I'm not a spy.'

'It's no good telling *me* that. Save it for the interrogators when you get back to England.'

Interrogators! The words struck a chill into Simpson's heart. Those sinister men with their black arts of mind-bending, what would they have done to his girlfriend?

'Do you know what's happened to her, sir?' he asked with sudden concern.

'No, I don't. Now sit here quietly and behave yourself. I'm going to lock you in. You'll get some food later.'

The sound of the lock turning seemed to echo inside

the small cabin. Left on his own, Simpson began to panic. 'Enemy power'? What were they talking about? If only he could talk to Susan!

Suddenly he began to fear she had told them everything, all about his real reasons for being on board HMS *Retribution*. That did not involve any enemy power. But what had the captain said? It was his words to Susan on the telephone that they were complaining about. Could she have passed the information to . . . He was wide-eyed with alarm. Surely not . . .

One thing seemed quite clear; the security men back home would treat him as a spy, a traitor. He had been incautious on the phone, and he *had* been planning sabotage on the boat. He could get thirty years, he realised – for trying to stop people being killed!

With dazzling clarity he suddenly knew that returning to the UK was something he could not afford to do.

Hanging from a hook on the wall was a dark blue canvas bag, standard equipment for every member of the submarine's crew. Its contents were going to be vital to him in the next few hours.

'Shouldn't we have someone on guard outside his cabin?' Smith suggested to the captain.

'It would have to be an officer if we're going to keep this business away from the crew,' Carrington answered thoughtfully, 'and with a missile-firing coming up we won't have anyone to spare. He can't get out, can he?'

'Not without breaking the door down.'

The two men returned to the control room. Preparations for the launch were well under way. The executive officer reverted to his normal duties and began to check that the submarine was on course and on time to meet its deadline. In the navigation centre he ascertained that the twin inertial navigation systems were performing perfectly. At the moment of firing, they would feed into the rocket the precise coordinates of the launch point so that the missile's computer could calculate the trajectory needed to reach the target with accuracy.

In the missile chamber he noted with satisfaction that the countdown procedure was moving ahead smoothly. Finally he descended the companionway to the missile control centre, where the Polaris systems officers were running test programmes on the electronic firing panel.

In due course all these men would have to be told about Robert Simpson, but now was not the moment. There should be no distraction from the work they had in hand.

Back in the control room he was told that the captain had returned to his cabin and wanted Smith to join him there. He set off immediately.

'Simpson's been hammering on his door. Says he's got the shits and needs to go to the heads,' Carrington explained. 'Bit difficult really; it was the chief steward who heard him. He was a bit puzzled to find the supply officer locked in. I had to explain, but swore him to secrecy. God knows how long we can keep this bottled up! The sooner we get Simpson off the boat the better. Anyway, would you deal with it, Mike? Take him to the heads?'

The executive officer grimaced at the prospect of having to watch the prisoner relieving himself.

'Of course, sir. I'll do it now.'

When he pushed open the door to the supply officer's cabin, Simpson had his back to him. There seemed to be something odd about his hair. It took Smith a split-second to realise what was wrong, but he was already too late to save himself. The prisoner spun round, his face encased in a gas-mask.

Simpson's arm reached out like a ramrod, clutching the aerosol of shaving foam Smith had left in his locker. He jammed his thumb down on the button, and the canister emitted a loud hiss.

Smith reeled back as the pain shot through his eyes! It was like needles piercing his eyeballs, from behind as well as in front. Instinctively he clawed at his eyes, thinking he could wipe away the foam, but there was none there!

He gasped at the pain, and the CN gas caught the back of his throat. He began to cough and choke. The muscles of his chest went into spasm. He felt he was going to die!

Beginning to twitch convulsively, he fought for clean air to sooth the burning of his nose and throat, but Simpson kept his finger firmly pressed on the aerosol button. Smith then tried to hold his breath, but an uncontrollable coughing overtook him. His head began to spin through lack of oxygen, and slowly blackness overtook him.

Simpson stepped over the body and went out into the corridor.

Startled by the noise, the chief steward came bustling out of the wardroom. He stopped dead in his tracks at the sight of the officer in the gas-mask, and within seconds he too was reeling backwards in pain and confusion.

The door to Carrington's cabin was at the end of the corridor and slightly ajar. Simpson ran for it, slamming the door open with his shoulder.

The captain's wall-safe was wide open, just as Simpson had hoped.

'What the hell . . .?'

The stream of gas hit Carrington right in the face. Eyes screwed up with pain, he reached out to try to close the safe, but Simpson lunged forward and punched him on the head with his free hand, knocking him off his chair and on to the floor.

Carrington had held his breath in an instinctive reaction to seeing the gas-mask on Simpson's face. So far the pain only burned his eyes. His own mask hung on the wall. Without breathing, he crawled across the floor and began to grope his way up towards it, expecting at any second to receive another blow on the head.

But Simpson was scrabbling amongst the papers in the open safe for the leather holster which he knew would be there. There it was!

Smiling grimly under the mask, he unbuttoned the retaining strap.

'That's enough, Captain!' his muffled voice threatened as he pressed the muzzle of the automatic pistol into the back of Carrington's neck. 'This is your gun, and I'm ready to use it! Now just get back to your chair and sit down.'

Simpson quickly closed the cabin door and locked it.

Carrington had staggered to the chair and was dabbing a handkerchief to his eyes and nose. His lungs were inflamed and burning though he had only received a small dose of CN.

Suddenly the tannoy on the ceiling crackled into life.

'Gas, gas, gas!' the voice of the officer of the watch bellowed from it. His message was being relayed throughout the submarine. 'Gas, gas, gas! This is no drill! Repeat, no drill! Gas-masks on immediately!'

The air-conditioning system of the boat had carried some of the tear-gas into the control room. Simpson heard heavy feet pounding the metal decks as men raced for their bunks to retrieve their masks. Outside the captain's door there were shouts as someone found the chief steward slumped against the wall, coughing uncontrollably – and then the feet of the executive officer poking out into the corridor from the supply officer's cabin.

There was a sharp rap on the door.

'Tell them to go away,' Simpson ordered in a whisper.

But Carrington could only cough.

'This is Lieutenant Simpson,' the supply officer shouted towards the door. 'I'm holding the captain prisoner. I've got his gun and I'll shoot him unless you do as I say!'

There was complete silence from outside. Then someone tried the doorknob and swore.

'Go back to your posts!' Simpson yelled.

After a moment, he heard footsteps moving away. So far, so good! But this was as far as he had planned. The next part would not be so easy.

'Captain, sir? Control room here!' A voice came from the intercom on the table.

Carrington was still wheezing and gasping for breath. Simpson leaned forward and pressed the key on the communications box.

'This is Lieutenant Simpson. The Captain is my prisoner. I have a gun. If you do what I say he won't be harmed.'

'What do you want, Simpson?' the voice answered angrily. At first he could not identify it; the man must be wearing a mask, too. Then he realised it was the PSO, Phil Dunkley. As a lieutenant-commander he would be the most senior man left, since the executive officer was out of action. For a moment he was fearful of what he had done to Mike Smith. He had given him a hell of a dose of gas; perhaps he'd killed him.

'The test launch is cancelled,' Simpson called back. 'There must be no missile firing, do you hear?'

There was a pause, with only static on the circuit.

'Anything else?' the PSO asked icily.

'Yes . . . there's a lot else. But I'm not going to tell you yet. I want you to send the surgeon in here, with some handcuffs for the captain. But no tricks! I don't trust any of you, and I'll use this gun if I have to!'

There was a longer pause this time.

'Very well,' Dunkley said eventually.

Five minutes passed before there was a tap at the door. Carrington's breathing had become easier.

Simpson tightened his grip on the pistol and trained it at the captain's head. Slowly he stood up and edged towards the door, turning back the bolt in the lock.

The surgeon-lieutenant stood outside nervously, wearing a gas-mask and carrying a set of nylon wrist-restraints. Simpson had selected him as the intermediary because of a vague feeling that a doctor should seem less of a threat than the other officers.

'Come in. Stand over there,' Simpson ordered, pointing towards the captain. He locked the door again.

'What do you want me to do, Bob?' the doctor asked in a quiet voice.

'Put those on the captain and loop them round the leg of his chair.'

The doctor fumbled with the restraints, unsure how they worked.

'Sorry about this, sir,' he whispered.

'Don't worry,' Carrington replied hoarsely. 'Just do as he says.'

The task completed, the doctor stood up again. Through the lenses of the mask, his eyes looked frightened.

Simpson stared, uncertain how much to trust him.

'Have they told you what I'm being accused of?' he began.

The doctor shook his head. 'Didn't know you were accused of anything.'

'They're saying I passed secrets to the Russians!'

'What?' The doctor turned towards Carrington. The captain nodded in confirmation.

'But it's not true! I just wanted to save millions of people from being killed . . . that's all,' Simpson insisted.

The doctor shifted uneasily. He still did not understand what this was about, but it looked as if Simpson had gone off his head.

'Well, we're all in the same boat there,' the doctor replied calmly. 'None of us want to see people killed, so why don't you just put that gun down, Bob?'

Simpson glared angrily at the surgeon-lieutenant, the pistol wavering between the doctor and the captain.

'Well, what exactly do you want?' the doctor pressed. 'It looks as if you're in command of the boat, at the moment. They want to know what to do.'

He gestured over his shoulder in the direction of the control room.

'I've got to get off,' Simpson explained, removing his mask. Carrington seemed to be recovering, which suggested the air had cleared. The doctor followed suit.

'I've got to get off this boat. Somewhere where I can be free,' he continued, holding the gun firmly in both hands. The gas canister was stuffed into his trouser pocket. 'I'm not going back to Britain!'

'But we're in the middle of the Atlantic, Bob,' the doctor explained reasonably, keeping his voice as smooth and even as he could.

'Yes, I know *that*!' Simpson snapped, 'but we're not too far from America, and there are islands. Cuba. What about Cuba? If we got near there, I'd get ashore in a Gemini. The captain'll come with me – as a hostage.'

'Well, what shall I do? Shall I tell the control room that you want to go to Cuba?' the doctor asked mildly.

Simpson hesitated. Cuba was some way away, and he was not sure what sort of reception he would get there.

'I want to see some charts. Bring me some charts so that I can see where there is that's closer.'

Simpson edged to the door, keeping the gun trained on the doctor.

'And no tricks!' he growled as he unlocked the door, and the doctor went out. He locked the door again and turned to look at the captain.

Carrington's breathing was easier now, though his eyes remained red and moist.

'What were you keeping that gas for, Simpson?' he rasped curiously. 'When were you planning to use it?'

Simpson laughed awkwardly.

'Well, sir, I'll tell you this. You'd never have launched the missiles if the order came. Somehow I'd have stopped you from genocide – that's what I planned.'

'On the orders of Moscow? So that the Russians would be free to commit genocide against the British people, when they had no means of retaliation?' Carrington snapped back.

'This has nothing to do with Moscow! It's to do with conscience, something you don't know anything about.' Simpson sneered.

There was a tap at the door. 'It's me,' came the doctor's voice.

Simpson turned the key, then strode back across the cabin and pressed the gun against the captain's head.

'Come in!'

The door opened gingerly, and the doctor entered, clutching a roll of charts under his left arm. His gas-mask was in his right hand.

'Lock the door!' Simpson ordered.

That done, the doctor stood waiting for the next instruction.

Reassured that the surgeon-lieutenant had returned alone, Simpson lowered the pistol.

'Bring them over here,' he said, indicating the captain's bed. 'We can sit here and spread them out.'

The doctor obliged, handing him the roll with a smile.

'They're all here, Bob. I'm sure we can sort something out.'

Simpson took the charts in his left hand, but still clutched the gun in his right. He paused for a moment, realising he would need both hands to study the charts properly.

He shot a glance at the captain to see that he was securely fastened to his chair. The doctor was still smiling benignly.

He hesitated, then slowly and carefully Simpson put the gun down on the bed beside him.

'Let me help you spread those out,' the doctor suggested.

He leaned forward as if to take hold of the first chart with his left hand. But suddenly his right arm lunged forward, jamming the gas-mask hard against Simpson's thigh! Bob felt the needle of the concealed hypodermic jab into him.

'You bastard!' he screamed, scrabbling frantically for the gun.

The doctor threw himself forward, punching with his left hand, and knocked the weapon to the floor. Carrington's foot reached out and kicked the gun into the far corner of the cabin.

Simpson struggled frenziedly, but the surgeon was a deadweight across his body.

'Five, six, seven, eight,' the doctor counted the seconds in his head, praying for the knockout drug to work. He had reached eleven before Simpson slumped across the bed.

Slowly, waiting to be sure the drug had taken full effect, the surgeon-lieutenant eased himself up, shaking from the shock of what he had just done. He carefully extracted the syringe from Simpson's leg, then pulled the lieutenant's head straight and checked his breathing. The man who had terrorised the submarine a moment ago was now his patient.

'Well done!' Carrington shouted hoarsely. 'Bloody brilliant!'

There was a hammering at the door and the doctor unlocked it. The chief petty officer burst in with two of the heaviest members of the crew, carrying clubs. He stared down at the supply officer, unconscious on the bed.

'Fuck me! You done it all on your own!' he exclaimed.

On the Caribbean island of Antigua, one thousand miles south of HMS *Retribution*'s position, the giant telemetry dishes of the US Navy Space Tracking Center rotated their bearings slowly and in unison, so that they were all pointing north, ready for the test firing of the British missile.

A further two thousand miles to the south-east, on the British island of Ascension, a further set of antennae lined up on the part of outer space where the Skydancer warheads would begin their dive into the atmosphere, obscured amongst clusters of decoys and behind a barrage of electronic deception techniques.

Both monitoring stations had been sent signals in

unbreakable code, giving the time and position of the Polaris launching.

Halfway between Antigua and Ascension, the 21,000 tons of the Soviet vessel *Akademik Sergey Korolev* wallowed in a long, slow, mid-Atlantic swell. The crew had been on stand-by for over forty-eight hours already. The Akula had signalled three days ago that it had lost the trail of the *Retribution*, and had warned that the missile test could take place at any time. The heat and the lack of sleep had made Kapitan Karpov extremely irritable.

On board HMS *Retribution* Simpson's abortive mutiny had jolted the entire crew and had created a greater than usual tension on board.

Carrington was again in command in the control room, his eyes red and swollen and his voice still hoarse. His executive officer was recovering in the sick bay.

Inside the missile control centre the dials on the launch control panel certified that the guidance gyros of the missiles were up to speed. The final countdown could begin.

They had had to sprint at nearly thirty knots to reach the launch position at the appointed time, but now they were in the right place, with a few minutes to spare. Carrington paced between the sonar operator's booth and the navigator's table. The signal from Northwood three hours earlier had predicted the ocean here would be empty, and the sonar equipment seemed to confirm it. If this had been war, he would have launched the missile without further checks, but in peacetime the demand for absolute safety was such that he needed to put up his periscope for a visual crosscheck.

'Better be sure there are no Atlantic oarsmen bobbing about above us!' he joked, as the officer of the watch peered through the eyepiece. After Simpson's attack Carrington did not trust his own eyes to be clear enough to see.

'Not a soul, sir,' the officer confirmed, sliding the scope down into its housing.

'Right! Descend to launch depth and zero knots!'

The rating at the helm pushed his control column gently forward, his eye fixed on the depth gauge.

On the engineering panel, the dial registering the rotation of the propeller shaft slipped back to zero.

The captain stood at the back of the control room and inserted a key into the switch with which he would give the final authority to launch the missile.

'Prepare to fire!' he called into the intercom.

On the deck below in the missile control centre, the Polaris Systems Officer opened the combination lock of a small safe on the floor below his control panel, and pulled out the pistol-grip with its red 'fire' button, which in war could execute millions of people at a single touch.

'Open missile hatch! Flood the tube!'

Dunkley dabbed on the buttons in the sequence prescribed in the control manual.

Behind him the computers had verified the co-ordinates of the target area, and had beamed the data into the missile itself.

'Ten, nine, eight . . .' he began.

In the control room above, Commander Carrington turned his key in the switch that activated the firing button below.

A green light appeared on the panel in the launch centre.

'One away!' the PSO yelled, clamping his finger round the pistol-grip.

With an explosive roar, the gas generator at the base

of the missile tube burst into life, pouring gas into the space below the rocket, propelling it upwards, out of the submarine and up to the surface in a cocoon of bubbles. As the tip of the missile appeared above the waves, the rocket motor ignited and with a brilliant flash the Polaris hurtled towards the sky.

'Up periscope!' the captain yelled.

The officer of the watch trained the lens upwards to see the missile arcing away towards the sun.

Carrington grabbed the microphone and pressed it to his lips.

'Your attention, please! This is the captain. I should like to inform you all that we have just enacted a perfect launch of one of our Polaris missiles. In the extraordinary circumstances of this day, to achieve our aim in any form would have been worthwhile; but to do it at the right time, in the right place, with such perfection, amounts to nothing less than brilliance on the part of everyone on board. Congratulations, and thank you very much.'

He hung the microphone back on its hook. There was an urgent radio signal to be sent but once he had completed that, he could at last get stuck into a long-delayed lunch.

The first inkling Kapitan Karpov had of the impending launch was the appearance of an aircraft on the *Korolev*'s radar. It soon became clear that the RAF Nimrod which had taken photographs of them a few days earlier was paying another visit. This time it was flying much higher.

Suddenly the giant radar dish that scanned the horizon over which the Polaris missile was due to rise detected its first blip. There was no mistaking the echo, rising fast into the sky overhead: it could only be a rocket.

At that very moment, six miles above the decks of the Soviet ship the RAF Nimrod began to scatter millions of tiny strips of aluminium foil which fanned out into an enormous reflective umbrella. Deep in the bowels of the *Korolev*, the radar screens suddenly became a blur of false echoes.

The operators knew instantly what had happened, and cursed the British. For days they had sat in sweltering darkness, waiting for the test launch, and now it looked as if they were going to be cheated of their ability to track it. Frantically they flicked switches and spun control knobs in an effort to filter out the unwanted echoes from the 'chaff' that had been scattered above them. The missile seemed to be aiming unerringly for the part of the sky that had now been obscured.

But their fury turned to delighted astonishment when they realised that the RAF had scattered its confusion in the wrong place. High-altitude winds were blowing the 'chaff' away from the line drawn by the trajectory of the rocket. The radar operators turned to one another and laughed at the incompetence of the British.

The missile's path had flattened out and they had seen the rocket section fall away from the 'space bus'. Suddenly the echo from it multiplied into a score of blips, as the decoys were released and the warheads ejected in that vital but indecipherable pattern which would dictate where they would strike the earth.

In the radar control room, giant data-recorders spun their spools to soak up everything that could be detected. The full analysis of the results would take weeks to accomplish, though preliminary data samples would be transmitted to Moscow that very day.

As the cloud of echoes from space began to descend towards the atmosphere, the aluminium-coated balloons used as decoys began to fall back and burst on contact with the air. Then a new pattern of blips began to confuse the screens as electronic jammers projected echoes forward, giving the Soviet observers the impression that the warheads were much closer to the ground than they were in reality.

On the foredeck of the *Korolev*, a robot-like structure studded with ruby lenses had been uncovered at the last minute. This was an infra-red scanner, whose capabilities were highly secret and which Kapitan Karpov had been instructed to keep hidden from Western eyes.

The scanner searched for tiny pinpoints of heat in the sky, heat generated by the friction of objects falling from space at great speed. It locked on to the first target detected, while continuing to search for others. Soon it was tracking a second and a third, and every few moments another, until thirty or forty 'targets' had been identified. The electronics specialists monitoring their computer screens sucked their teeth as they realised their equipment could not tell the difference between the warheads and the flares being released every few seconds to confuse them.

Two minutes later it was all over. The screens were blank; Skydancer had splashed into the sea.

Suddenly the Nimrod appeared from behind the stern of the Soviet ship, flying serenely at two hundred feet. It banked sharply across the bows of the *Korolev*, snapping a stream of pictures of the infra-red detector before the ship's crew had time to cover it up again.

Kapitan Karpov laughed as he watched the plane turn away and head back to Ascension Island. He nudged his first officer in the ribs.

'One crumb! One crumb of comfort for those

British, that's what their pictures will produce!' he sneered, pulling a Cuban cigar from his shirt pocket and clamping it between his teeth.

'They came here to stop us seeing what their missile could do, but they bungled it! What they've done – it's like losing the football match and then stealing the winner's champagne!'

The laughter that rang round the bridge was partly to humour the captain, but largely for a simpler reason: their work was over now and they could go home.

Chapter Eight

The telephone broke the edgy silence in the Defence Chief's office. The field-marshal snatched at the receiver. His eyebrows shot up as he listened to the message.

'Well, I'll be damned!' he exclaimed. 'At Heathrow Airport you say? Berlin! My God! Yes. Yes, he's here. I'll send him down right away.'

He slammed down the telephone.

'Well, that's buggered it. Absolute bloody disaster! You'll never guess where your sodding blueprints have turned up now!'

Peter's heart sank. 'Did you say Berlin?'

'Berlin be buggered! No! In another bloody rubbish bin, that's where!'

'What?'

'That was John Black. A Special Branch chap at Heathrow found an envelope with what looked like your doctored Skydancer plans, in a rubbish basket in one of the departure lounges. Straight after a load of passengers had departed for Berlin. Black wants you to go down to the security office to identify them.'

Peter snatched up his briefcase and hurried from the room. Heading down the corridors, he looked at his watch. It was seven in the evening. Anderson had promised to contact them long before this.

John Black's face expressed no emotion as he pushed a folder of papers across the table towards Peter.

'Recognise these?'

Sick with apprehension, Peter turned the pages. They were the same ones he had spent Sunday preparing.

'Yes. They're mine,' he sighed. 'But what does all this mean?'

'Don't know,' John Black answered flatly. 'But Anderson boarded a flight to Berlin four hours ago. We sent a picture of him to the airport and one of the British Airways check-in staff identified him. He must have crossed over to the East as soon as he got to his destination.

'We also know that he dumped these papers before he left. Now why? He must have been scared of something, scared that his people in East Berlin would recognise them as fakes, and carry out their threat to use the blackmail pictures. But he would hardly go off to Berlin empty-handed, would he now?'

'Christ! You don't mean . . .'

'Perhaps he didn't need your fake plans at all, Mr Joyce. Perhaps he still had a copy of the real ones . . .'

'Oh, no . . .' Peter groaned.

'Oh *yes*, Mr Joyce. Don't forget that because of this scheme of yours – a scheme which I never agreed with by the way – because of this scheme of using Anderson as a double agent, I was never authorised to set my boys on him. I never had the chance to do even something as basic as searching his house in case it alarmed his friend Metzger.

'So we have no idea if it was just one page of the real Skydancer plans that he originally photocopied, or the whole lot. My guess is that he had them all, and in the end the fear of those dirty pictures being seen by his wife made him decide to betray his country after all!'

Peter stared, horrified. 'I have to admit I can't think of any other explanation,' he answered. The strain of the past week suddenly began to crush him unbearably. 'It looks as if we've just given the Kremlin the complete secrets of Skydancer!'

John Black could not resist twisting the knife.

'The trouble is you lot just wouldn't leave security to the professionals! Insisted on plotting and planning all by yourselves, didn't you?'

His taunt stung Peter painfully.

'The security service hasn't exactly earned itself a reputation for loyalty and reliability in recent years, has it?' he snapped back. 'And if you *had* behaved like a professional, Mr Black, we might have had more confidence in you!'

The investigator's face hardened.

'I take exception to that remark,' he murmured ominously.

Peter reached down to his briefcase and pulled out the photograph of Mary Maclean which Karl Metzger had taken from her flat. He pushed it across the table.

'Remember this?' he asked sharply.

Black flicked the lid of his zippo lighter and took his time lighting a cigarette.

'Ah! Now where did that come from?'

'This was the picture you said never existed,' Peter pressed firmly. 'But you recognise it, don't you? Only a few days ago you assured me that it hadn't been in Mary's flat on the evening she was murdered. You knew perfectly well it had, though, and that the murderer had taken it. Lying about that wasn't very *professional*, was it?'

The investigator took hold of the photo-frame and turned it over in his hands.

'You'll have to put that down to foolish pride, Mr Joyce. Not very professional, I'll agree. To be honest, I hadn't noticed the photo was gone after she was found dead, and I should have done. When you remarked on it the other day, I just didn't feel like owning up. That's all there is to it.

'Tell me though,' he went on, skating over the awkwardness. 'How did you come by this?'

'Metzger gave it to Anderson as a warning of what he could expect if he didn't do as he was told,' Peter explained, 'and I got it from Anderson.'

Black fingered the photograph, pressing the glass against the backing to test the thickness. His forehead creased into a frown, and he placed the frame face-down on his desk.

'When did you say Metzger gave it to Anderson?'

'Last Friday evening,' Peter answered, irritated that his case against Black had been explained away so easily.

The investigator took out a razor-blade and carefully slit round the gummed brown paper holding the backing in place.

'And when did you get it from Anderson?'

'Saturday evening.'

'Ah,' Black murmured softly, lifting the rectangle of card from the frame. 'Look at this now!'

He tilted the frame towards Peter; a small electronic circuit had been sandwiched between the photograph and the backing.

'Good grief!'

Black touched a finger to his lips, and opened the desk drawer again to take out a soft leather pouch containing a radio mechanic's toolkit. He lifted the circuitry from the photo-frame, examined it cautiously, then snipped free the connections to a small flat battery.

'Microphone, transmitter, and battery. Standard issue East German bugging device,' he explained. 'Very clever.'

He slipped a miniature test meter from the pouch, and touched its probes to the wires still connected to the battery.

'Dead as a dodo now. Probably only lasted forty-eight hours, if that. But for two days or so this little device was listening in to everything within earshot. The transmitter's only short-range. Anderson's friend Karl probably had someone parked outside his house with a receiver.'

Peter was lost for words.

'Now let's see how good your memory is, Mr Joyce. See if you can remember everything you said to Anderson in the presence of this picture.'

Peter sighed, daunted by the prospect, but he realised the importance of what Black was asking him.

'Well, that first day, the Friday, he told me everything. It was like a confession! So Karl would have known immediately that Anderson had given him away.'

The MI5 man listened with pursed lips.

'Then on Saturday, I saw Anderson again, and told him he was to hand over the doctored blueprints to the East Germans; I told him he had to help us deceive the Soviets if he was going to save himself! I said all that while this bug was sitting on his desk.'

'So the Comrades were *expecting* to be given fake plans for Skydancer,' Black mused.

'But Anderson is giving them the real ones!'

'Now there's a turn-up for the books!' the MI5 man said facetiously. 'But will they believe him, that's the question?'

Peter's thoughts raced ahead. He closed his eyes to concentrate. Now more than ever he needed to think himself into the mind of 'the Russian', but it was like trying to break through an impenetrable wall.

'If only I knew exactly who was running the Soviet BMD improvement programme, it might make it easier to gauge their reaction.'

'Does the name Oleg Kvitzinsky mean anything to you?' the MI5 man enquired casually.

Peter was surprised.

'Oh, yes. He's pretty well known. A very clever man. He's been pushing the use of computers and robotics in their consumer industries. Making better washing-machines for the domestic market, that sort of thing.'

'He's not doing that any more. I had a note from MI6 this afternoon. Their men in Moscow have been doing a little overtime. Apparently Kvitzinsky switched to a secret military project over a year ago. They'd been having trouble integrating their radars with the new anti-missile missiles, and drafted him in to sort it out.'

'I met him once,' Peter said, his spirits reviving. 'At an international computer conference in Geneva. Can't say I got to know him well – we talked a couple of times, but at least I can put a face to him. Sadly it doesn't mean I can read his mind, though!'

The phone on the desk rang, and Black picked it up. Peter could hear Field-Marshal Buxton bellowing at the other end.

'Yes. Yes, he's confirmed it, sir. We'll come up right away, then,' Black replaced the receiver.

'CDS wants a conference – just the three of us – to put everything we know on the table. Looks as if we're all going to co-operate for once. Make a nice change, won't it?'

The field-marshal had set a cut-glass decanter on the table in his office, along with three glasses.

'Sorry there's no ice,' he said briskly, 'but I thought we could do with a drink while we sort out our differences. The past week has been marred by excessive secrecy between departments and even suspicion about each other's loyalty. Well, we now face a bigger crisis than ever before, so we've got to put our differences aside and pool information. All agreed?'

His bluntness took them both by surprise.

'Well, of course,' Peter acknowledged.

'Better late than never,' Black added, considering himself the aggrieved party.

'Right. Let's get on with it, then,' Buxton continued, pouring large measures of whisky into the glasses and nodding towards a low table.

'Now, what conclusions have you two drawn?'

Black raised his eyebrows questioningly, and Peter nodded that he should begin.

He explained how they believed Anderson had now delivered the real Skydancer documents to Berlin. Buxton looked unsurprised; he had already divined as much for himself. He seemed shaken, though, by the revelation of the bugging operation by Metzger's men. It added a new twist of uncertainty to their planning. John Black then also told him they had identified the scientist behind the Soviet plot.

'Kvitzinsky's going to be thoroughly confused, that's for sure,' Peter took over. 'The Russians will have two completely different concepts of how Skydancer works; one from observing the test firing this afternoon, and the other from the blueprints. He may choose to believe the test, or the plans, or neither.'

'Which is just the sort of confusion we set out to create when this whole business started a week ago,' Buxton chipped in. 'We seem to have come full-circle. Oh, you'll be glad to hear the test firing went well. I've just had a signal from Northwood confirming it. The RAF did their bit too, appearing to block the Soviet's view, but in fact dropping their "chaff" downwind to ensure the Russians had an unobstructed look.

'But they had trouble with that bloody traitor, Simpson. Tried to hijack the flaming submarine! The fellow definitely seems to be some kind of a nutter!'

'We've just started looking into his background,' Black replied. 'There seem to be some rather disturbing elements in it. Religious fanaticism, secret societies, that sort of thing. God knows how he ever passed the vetting.'

'Somebody should be shot for that!' Buxton growled.

'Well, we've got his girlfriend in custody,' Black continued. 'But so far we're not sure she was working for the Russians. It's just possible she was more into anti-nuclear campaigning and civil disobedience than espionage. The other woman we arrested, Helene Venner, she's a definite Soviet agent – photographed her last week meeting the KGB resident from the Russian Embassy. We think her real name is Ilena Petrova. But Susan Parkinson probably didn't know that. She may simply have been conned by Venner.

'And there's one more thing,' he went on. 'Karl Metzger left the country this afternoon on the Harwich-Hook of Holland ferry. We've been keeping a close eye on him since Friday night, when one of my men spotted him meeting Anderson.'

'What? You had someone in that pub?' Peter exclaimed.

'Oh, yes, we were there. We'd been tailing both Anderson and you for days. You were both suspects, you know.'

'I see.' He shifted uncomfortably. 'But Metzger's gone, has he?' he snapped suddenly. 'He's the man who murdered Mary Maclean, and you let him leave the country?'

'What else could he do, Peter,' the field-marshal interrupted. 'Deceiving the Soviets depended on Metzger thinking he still had the upper hand.'

Peter laughed bitterly.

'The trouble is, it turns out Karl knew all along that he was being tricked. God what a mess!' He turned to the MI5 man. 'Can you still get Metzger now he's left the country?'

John Black shrugged.

'Maybe. We've got our Dutch friends keeping a lookout for him, but we can't make any sort of move until we know what's happened in Berlin.'

The three men sat back in thoughtful silence and drank their whisky. It was clear to all of them that it all depended on Anderson now, and the mental machinations of Oleg Kvitzinsky.

'Right, that's it, gentlemen,' Buxton suddenly declared, rising to his feet. 'I don't think we can get any further this evening, and the Prime Minister is insisting on a report tonight. So I suggest we meet again in the morning. Peter, we'll need you here again, rather than at Aldermaston.'

Alec Anderson had been left on his own for over two hours. The walls of the small room were drab, and a single neon tube shed a harsh, dull pink light. Occasionally footsteps could be heard outside, approaching, stopping and moving away again.

Anderson was petrified, sweating profusely; his stomach churned remorselessly. The room was quite bare; just a scratched, unpolished wooden table and two chairs. There were no decorations on the wall except an old calendar from the previous year, which heightened his growing sense of having been forgotten and abandoned.

His mind kept returning to the departure lounge at Heathrow. He had had to leave it until the last minute to get rid of the dummy blueprints that Peter Joyce had given him. All the way out to the airport, he had been conscious of a man in a blue overcoat watching his every move. It was only when he had passed through into the departure zone of the terminal that the man had stopped tailing him, and he had felt free to get rid of the plans.

The warning on Sunday night had been specific; Karl Metzger had said that his 'source' in MI5 had tipped him off about the false documents. If there was the slightest hint that the Skydancer papers were not genuine, one of his children would be 'executed'. There had only been one choice: to deliver the real plans, while convincing his colleagues in Whitehall that he had handed over the false ones.

At the airport he had watched a cleaning woman shuffling around all the litter bins, emptying them into a large plastic sack. There had been no scrutiny, no interest in what the bins contained. It had seemed a sure and simple way of disposing of the blueprints without anyone knowing.

It was early evening when Anderson had landed at West Berlin's Tegel airport, and his taxi had had to struggle through rush-hour traffic to the Friedrichstrasse crossing-point, better known as Checkpoint Charlie.

He had been to Berlin once before, accompanying an army minister on a tour of the wall. He had hated the place for its atmosphere of threat and conflict, made permanent by the concrete monstrosity that divided the city.

That evening he had passed almost unnoticed through the American control point; tourists crossing into the East were two-a-penny these days. He had felt sick with fear on the walk to the Volkspolizei guard-house, with its dim lights and suspicious-eyed sentries.

Inside the immigration hall, he had looked around

for a sign of someone waiting to take him through, but there had been no one visible. He had carefully filled in his visa form and currency declaration, and changed his regulation twenty-five West German marks into twenty-five Eastern ones, an exchange designed specifically to benefit the economy of the communist half of Germany.

His passport had been taken from him by a border guard who displayed an overt loathing of Westerners. Anderson suspected it was his primary qualification for the job. The document had been slipped through a flap in the wall, and examined by unseen officials. A few moments later a small hatch had opened up and two pairs of eyes studied him carefully. Then the passport had been returned to him and he was through.

East Berlin. As he had looked back at the concrete wall, trying to imagine the desperation of those who had died trying to escape it, a man in a smart raincoat had tapped him on the arm. A car had been waiting to take him to the headquarters of the HVA, the East German Intelligence Service.

The Skydancer blueprints had been taken from him as soon as they arrived at the slab-sided grey building, and since then he had been alone in this bare room with nothing to look at but last year's calendar.

Why on earth had they bothered to put it there? It seemed a pointless decoration. Unless there was something behind it . . .

His heart began to pound and a shiver ran through him. He realised with horror that for the past two hours every bead of sweat, every flicker of his eyelids had been minutely studied from another room.

*

In Moscow, General Novikov had just returned to his GRU headquarters from a gruelling meeting with his KGB counterpart at the half-moon-shaped offices on the Moscow ring-road. Novikov's operation to get the Skydancer plans was beginning to cost the KGB dearly.

Already one of their key 'illegals' had been arrested, the woman responsible for co-ordinating the manipulation of the anti-nuclear militants in Britain. It had taken years to put Ilena Petrova into place, years of work that was now wasted.

Above all, there was now a threat to one of their longest-serving agents of all time, a man recruited at Oxford University in the 1940s. He had been the subtlest of the academic recruits, gently influencing young men to look kindly on the Soviet Union in their lives ahead.

But now, with the arrest of that young submariner, the British investigators would begin to probe, to delve into the past. It would only be a matter of time before they found the trail leading back to that small, select boarding-school attended by so many boys whose lives had later led them to positions of authority.

General Novikov had promised the KGB that his operation was nearing its end. Just a few more hours and it would all be over – successfully. The sacrifices would have been worth it; Kvitzinsky would have the blueprints he wanted, and Moscow's leaders could again feel that their future safety was as assured as was humanly possible.

Belinda Joyce had just finished watching the Nine O'Clock News when her husband arrived home. She was sitting on her own in the kitchen, looking at a small portable television. The children were watching another programme in the living-room.

After hanging his coat in the hall, Peter walked through to the kitchen and pulled a chair over beside her.

'I was watching the news,' she began nervously. 'They said two women were arrested at Newbury yesterday, and that a senior scientist at Aldermaston had been suspended!'

'They're a bit behind the times,' he replied. 'I was reinstated this morning and the suspension's been struck from the record. They didn't name me, did they? If they did, I'll sue them!'

Belinda saw that the lines around his mouth had deepened and his eyes had lost their brightness. He looked so defeated; she'd never seen him quite like that before. Standing up, she took down a glass from the dresser behind her.

'Would you like a drink?' she asked, indicating the wine bottle on the table.

'Love one.'

He sipped thoughtfully at the cheap burgundy before answering her unspoken question.

'Yes, one of those women they arrested was Helene, if that's what you're wondering,' he told her gently. 'Apparently her real name is Ilena Petrova. She's a Russian spy.'

The look on Belinda's face was one of pain rather than surprise, which made Peter think she had expected the news.

'Can they *really* be so sure?' she asked in the vain hope there might be some doubt.

'They're quite sure. They've photographed her with a KGB man.'

Belinda burst into tears.

'You don't know how hard she tried to persuade me to spy on your work – even steal some of your papers!' she sobbed. 'It all seemed . . . innocent at the time, like a – a game. But it wasn't. God, you must think me so stupid!'

Peter put his arms round her.

'We've both been pretty bloody foolish.'

For a few moments they were silent. They both sensed that the wounds caused by his love affair with Mary Maclean were healing. A permanent scar might remain, but it was one they would be able to live with.

Suddenly Belinda asked, 'Who was the other woman? The other one they arrested?'

'Someone called Susan Parkinson,' Peter replied. 'Know her? She's supposed to be a member of ATSA.'

'No. She must be from another branch. Are they saying she was a spy, too?'

'They think she may just have been a protester who went too far . . .'

'What'll happen next?' she asked anxiously. 'Perhaps they'll arrest me, too.'

'You shouldn't have anything to fear,' he smiled, and poured them some more wine.

'How much longer will this nightmare last?' she asked.

Her face creased with anxiety. Suddenly Peter felt a great fondness for her. He thought of Anderson and his frantic, disastrous efforts to preserve the happiness and integrity of his family. Love, affection, security, call it what you will – it was what they were all motivated by in one way or another.

'I don't know,' he replied eventually. 'But I think it's all about to come to a head.'

*

At eleven the following morning a dark-green saloon car drew up in the courtyard of the British Military Mission in Berlin. A small red and gold plaque on its bumper designated it as belonging to the Soviet Army. Officers from the forces of the four nations that had controlled the city since the death of Adolf Hitler had the right of access to each other's areas. Every day Soviet officers would drive into the West, and every day British, French and American officers would visit the East. However, for a Soviet officer to pay a call at the British headquarters was far from usual.

The Russian army captain walked into the building carrying a small brown envelope. The British major on duty looked surprised as the Soviet soldier slapped it down on his desk, stood back and saluted.

'Captain Borodin of the Military Mission of the Union of Soviet Socialist Republics,' he introduced himself. His voice was thin and nasal.

'Major Howlett,' the British officer replied coolly.

'You see, there is, mmmm . . . a British person in our section, who has been behaving unacceptably,' the Russian continued in a thick accent.

He tapped the envelope with his index finger.

'His papers,' he explained. 'You see . . . his passport has one name, but his driving licence has another.'

'I see,' the major answered non-committally, slitting open the envelope and tipping the contents on to the desk. He picked up the driving licence first, which was in the name of Alec Anderson.

'I *see*,' he said again. The name on the passport was Allenby.

'Tell me, Captain Borodin, do you have this man under arrest?'

The Russian officer shifted awkwardly. He was only a messenger, unable to answer such questions.

'He will be returned to you,' he began again, 'but there is someone special who must collect him.'

He pointed to a folded sheet of paper that had fallen from the envelope.

Puzzled, the major spread it open. It was a short letter.

'But . . . but this is addressed to the Chief of the Defence Staff!' he exclaimed. 'I'm not sure I should read it.'

'You must transmit it now!' Borodin insisted. 'It is very urgent.'

With increasing astonishment the major cast his eye down the page, scanning the conditions set for Anderson's release from the East.

'Well . . . I shall deal with it right away, Captain. We'll communicate with you in due course. Where, er . . . where should we address our reply?'

'I am at our mission. I shall wait for you to come.'

'Very well.'

The major stood up. The Russian saluted again, turned on his heel and strode out.

When Peter entered the field-marshal's office, following an urgent summons, he found the defence chief grim-faced.

'I've been talking with our security people,' Buxton began. 'We've had a message from Berlin about Anderson, to which we have to respond. Everything I say to you has been cleared with both MI5 and MI6, so there are no dissenters. We're all agreed as to the action we have to take.'

Alarmed, Peter said nothing.

Buxton took a deep breath.

'We want you to go to Berlin.'

'What?'

'The Soviets seem to be holding Anderson as some sort of prisoner, but say they will hand him over tonight, but only to you. Don't ask me why, I just don't know. We received a signal from our mission there this morning, relaying the contents of a letter signed by Oleg Kvitzinsky!'

'Good Lord!'

'Yes. It's all quite mystifying. He says the handover will be at a small crossing-point in the wall sometime after midnight, but it can only take place if you're there.'

'Why on earth would they insist on that?' Peter frowned. 'Do you think they're planning to grab me as well?'

'We thought of that, of course. They won't get the chance, though. You can be sure of that. You'll have an armed escort from our garrison, and there's no way the Soviets are going to start a shooting incident over this business. They're showing all the signs of wanting to keep it very quiet and discreet.'

'But what about the Skydancer plans?' Peter was thinking on his feet. 'Presumably this means that the Soviets think they are calling our bluff, that they believe the plans Anderson gave them are fakes and they want to rub our noses in it! Or does it?'

'God knows!' Buxton sighed. 'The big question is why Kvitzinsky should be involved? Presumably they got him to Berlin to cast his expert eye over the blueprints, but why he insists on seeing you is far from clear. My guess is that he is going to demand some further information as a final price for Anderson's release! You'll tell him nothing, of course – I hardly need say that. Our colleagues in the secret service have a different idea. They're quite excited! They seem to think he's going to defect!'

Peter whistled softly. That would be a remarkable bonus if it happened.

'Well, are you saying we've little to lose by doing what they want, and there's no real alternative anyway?'

'That's about it. You'll go, then?'

The same flight that had conveyed Alec Anderson to Berlin the previous day took Peter Joyce to the divided city. With him went a somewhat monosyllabic representative from MI6, to be present if Kvitzinsky did indeed defect, and who would also escort Anderson back to Britain. The two men sat in different sections of the aircraft; the intelligence man wanted to smoke, and Peter did not.

The sky was clear throughout the flight, but darkness had descended as they neared their destination. With twenty minutes to go before they landed, Peter looked out of the left-hand window and saw a line of lights stretching north as far as the eye could see. Suddenly he realised it was the inner-German border dividing East from West, capitalism from communism. He could imagine the lines of fencing and barbed wire that marked that border with its watchtowers and guard dogs, designed to keep the population of the East where it was.

The engine note changed and the Boeing began its descent towards West Berlin.

They were met at Tegel Airport by the major from the British military mission.

'Alan Howlett,' he introduced himself briskly. He had a pointed face with a receding chin, and looked both nervous and excited at the prospect of being involved in what looked like his first real spy drama.

'I've got my car here, so we'll go straight to my HQ for a briefing, and take it from there.'

The MI6 man snorted quietly to himself at the army's preoccupation with 'briefings'.

Peter had never been to Berlin before. It was raining; a steady downpour flowed off the car's windscreen like a river. The wipers made little impression on the blur of water; the garish neon lights of the city were magnified and distorted by the wet glass.

As they set off from the airport, Major Howlett tried to make conversation with the two men, but their lack of response discouraged him from further efforts.

Once inside the Military Mission they were taken straight to a conference room, where a young captain, introduced as 'the briefing officer', gave them an illustrated lecture on the divided city of Berlin. From time to time the MI6 man yawned loudly, to show his own familiarity with the subject, but to Peter much of what he was being told was new.

Then the major took over.

'So much for the general picture,' he began, looking down at his notes, 'which we thought we'd give you just in case you weren't too familiar with the city. But, now, on to tonight.

'The Soviets have named Kirchenallee as the place where Mr Anderson is to be released. It's not normally in use as a crossing-point. The boundary between the Russian and the British zones runs along the western edge of a railway track which is down in a sort of cutting. Because of lack of space on the western side, the Vopos built their wall on the east of the track at that point, even though the railway line is actually theirs. Here . . .'

Major Howlett clicked on the light of an epidiascope, which projected a vu-foil map on to the screen. He indicated the area involved with a billiard cue.

'As you can see, Kirchenallee crosses the railway line here over a narrow bridge. The wall is at the eastern end, with a solid iron gate across the road, and at our western end there is a chain-link fence, with another gate in it, padlocked from their side.

'Now, I've not done one of these before, but looking at the records of past handovers, the procedure seems to be this: we turn up and wait in our cars on our side of the bridge. They give us the once-over through their binoculars from one of the two watchtowers on the other side; then they open the iron gate in the wall, walk across the bridge and undo the padlock on the chain-link gate on the western side.

'They check our papers, then let us walk with them to the middle of the bridge. It's their territory officially, but for events like this the bridge is considered no-man's land. Then, in theory, they bring across the man in question and hand him over. Bob's your uncle!'

'What are your security plans tonight?' the MI6 man demanded suddenly.

'Ah, yes. There should be no problem there. We'll have a platoon with us who will take up firing positions just in case it turns nasty, and a couple of military policemen will escort you on to the bridge as well. We're not expecting any trouble, though.'

'Why are they going to such lengths?' Peter asked. 'Why all the cloak-and-dagger stuff? Why not just shove him across Checkpoint Charlie if they want to get rid of him?'

The major looked at him in surprise.

'I have no idea, sir. I rather assumed you knew the answer to that question.'

Peter felt the MI6 man was laughing at him inwardly. The bastard had seen it all before.

'Well, if there are no more questions,' Howlett continued, conscious of the awkward silence, 'then I'll take you to the mess. We've got rooms for you for the night, and after you've had a wash and so on, we could gather for a drink and some dinner. Our rendezvous with the Russians isn't until two o'clock in the morning, I'm afraid.'

Oleg Kvitzinsky hated Berlin. The Germans might be Soviet allies, but they despised the men from Moscow and did not mind showing it.

He had flown to the city, accompanied by two burly 'specialists' from the GRU, to examine the blueprints of the new British nuclear weapon system which the HVA claimed to have captured.

He had spent most of his time there sitting in the Soviet embassy, exhaustively examining the documents that Alec Anderson had delivered, and comparing them with the preliminary analysis of the Skydancer warhead test in the Atlantic, which had been telexed to him from Moscow.

From the top floor of the embassy building, he could see the endlessly-flashing neon lights on the other side of the wall, set up in prominent positions as a deliberate lure to those in the East. To Oleg it was a cheap capitalist trick – distasteful even – to try to tempt people with bright lights and baubles into a society that was attractive on the surface but which was rotten and crippled by unemployment underneath.

He had been shocked at what he had learned about Skydancer, shocked and dismayed. His decision to use Anderson as a bait to lure the designer of the weapon to Berlin had been an act of desperation. He was taking a considerable risk, but this was an opportunity he could not afford to ignore.

He dreaded that meeting, now; there had been a catastrophe that afternoon. It had made his goal virtually unattainable.

The door swung open. One of the GRU men stood there, pointing at his watch. It was after one o'clock in the morning, and time to go.

They had driven well clear of that section of the city that keeps humming throughout the night with its countless bars and brothels. Peter Joyce peered through the car window down the deserted side-streets, catching occasional glimpses of the wall, which was thrown into stark silhouette by the brightness of the observation lights on the other side. They seemed to be driving parallel with it, the side-streets cut short by its graffiti-covered bulk. The emptiness of the streets was almost eerie, as if no one lived so close to this frontier; as if the contrast between east and west was too painful to bear when seen so close.

'Not far now,' the major commented, trying to sound reassuring.

In front of them three Land-Rovers led the way, their thick tyres humming on the wet road. The red tail-lights of the last one sparkled in their rain-spattered windscreen.

'They could have chosen a better night for it,' Howlett muttered. 'It's ten to two now. We'll probably have a few minutes wait when we get there.'

'I shall stay in the car, out of sight,' the MI6 man growled. 'It'd have to be Gorbachev himself coming across to get me to stand outside on a night like this!'

The brake-lights of the Land-Rovers came on in

dazzling unison, and an orange flashing indicated a turn to the left.

'Kirchenallee,' Major Howlett announced as they rounded the corner.

Ahead of them stood the chain-link fence, with the wall a little way beyond it, just as it had been described in the briefing.

Peter swallowed hard. He felt suddenly unprepared. He had no idea what the Russian scientist would say to him, nor what he would say in reply.

'We're here,' the major said unnecessarily.

The car halted close to the wire gate. Its headlights briefly illuminated the road which ran beyond it, across the iron bridge, and the cold grey wall which finally blocked progress into the eastern half of the city. The drivers switched their headlamps off, plunging the road into blackness. Suddenly they became conscious of the two stark watchtowers on the other side, visible against the glow of the illuminations for the 'dead' zone behind. Shadowy figures looked down on them.

Soldiers were jumping out of the Land-Rovers and spreading out. Rifles in hand, some entered what looked like a derelict building at the end of the row of houses, others crouched in doorways, the rain glistening on their waterproof capes.

'Now we just have to wait,' Howlett explained quietly. The rain drummed on the roof of the car.

The major pulled out an electronic night-sight, and switched it on. After giving it a few seconds to warm up, he put it to his eyes.

'Nothing yet,' he reported, focusing on the edge of the iron gate through which the Soviets would have to emerge.

Peter imagined the unseen soldiers around them lining up the same view on the night-sights of their rifles, ready to kill with accuracy in the blackness, if ordered to do so.

There was a tap at the window, and the major wound it down a crack. 'All in position, sir.'

Peter recognised the voice of the young captain who had given the briefing earlier. Peering through the window he could make out the shapes of two men, one of them carrying a radio-set on his back.

'Right,' the major replied. 'Oh, standby! We've got some movement. Gate's opening!'

The captain hurried off to take up his command position, ready to direct his platoon, if action were needed.

'Vopo coming across the bridge. East German police. Better go and say hello. Stay here for the moment, if you don't mind, gentlemen.'

The major handed his night-glasses to the driver and cursed as he stepped out into the downpour.

A faint light from distant street-lamps made the wire-mesh gate just visible to the naked eye. Peter saw the German guard looming out of the darkness. With the aid of a small torch, he inserted a key into the padlock and struggled to turn it.

'Fookin' rusty, I reckon!' the driver exclaimed in a thick Birmingham accent.

The MI6 man sniffed.

'Last time they used this crossing was three years ago,' he commented disdainfully.

Half the gate swung open. Then the Vopo pulled at the bolt on the second one and opened that, too. The way on to the bridge was now clear.

The two officers stood in the middle of the road, talking. The British major seemed to be struggling to understand what he was being told. Repeatedly he appeared to be asking for clarification.

Eventually he hurried back to the car, his shoulders hunched against the rain.

Howlett threw himself inside, splashing water everywhere. He left the door half open. Peter noticed that he looked both shocked and puzzled.

'Well, I don't know . . . I think I understood him right, but they never mentioned this before. He said he wants us to back a Land-Rover on to the bridge. Something about a box. He kept saying "*eine Kiste, eine Kiste*". I don't know . . .'

'He means a coffin,' the MI6 man concluded sharply.

'Christ!' Peter breathed.

'Yes . . . I think you're right. I'd better get that organised,' the major stammered, and disappeared into the rain again.

'He couldn't have misunderstood, could he?' Peter hoped.

'Doubt it,' the MI6 man answered. 'Sounds bad.'

'Anderson?'

The man nodded.

Two minutes later the major was back. The engine of one of the Land-Rovers could be heard revving behind them.

'If you would come with me now, Mr Joyce . . .' said Howlett tensely, poking his head through the doorway.

Peter felt heavy with dread. He fumbled for the handle. The driver leaned back and opened the door for him.

The rain splattering on to his hair was ice-cold. He was glad of the umbrella that Howlett held ready for him to take.

'This way.'

A heavy gust of exhaust fumes swirled warmly around him, as the Land-Rover backed past and began to edge its way towards the middle of the bridge. An East German policeman waved it on with his torch, the sharply upturned brim of his cap standing out against the lights behind.

A pair of headlights began to approach from the far end of the bridge, the beams see-sawing up and down as the vehicle bumped across the uneven and seldom-used surface of the road.

The two vehicles stopped within ten feet of each other. Howlett grabbed Peter by the arm to prevent him going beyond the tail of their Land-Rover. The headlamps from the other side dazzled them. For a moment nothing seemed to be happening.

'Peter Joyce?'

The voice was high-pitched and tremulous.

Peter cleared his throat.

'Yes, that's me.'

'*Vorwärts bitte!* Please come forvords,' a different voice called this time, with a German accent.

'It's okay. Go ahead,' Major Howlett reassured him.

Peter stepped forward six paces, and stopped.

'Oleg Kvitzinsky?' he called. 'Your turn!'

The lights of the East German vehicle were off to one side now, and had ceased to dazzle him. He could see three men ahead. Hesitantly one of them began to move.

The man was tall and burly, wearing a heavy raincoat and a felt hat. He came right up to Peter and stopped. The spill of light reflecting off the wet tarmac gave a dull illumination to his face. It had been several years since they had met in Geneva, but Peter recollected the arched brows and the eyes that looked poised halfway between laughter and tears. They looked sadder than he had remembered.

'This was not what I planned,' Kvitzinsky stated,

only a slight accent tainting his words.

Beyond him Peter could see four men in uniform sliding something heavy from the back of the vehicle, which he could now see was a hearse.

'This afternoon your Mr Anderson was still alive,' Kvitzinsky continued slowly. 'It was intended that he would walk across here with me. But . . .'

Speechless with shock and anger, Peter watched as the policemen carried the coffin past. Two British soldiers helped them ease the plain wooden box into the back of the Land Rover.

'Who killed him?' Peter rasped.

'The *Polizei* have some papers. They will give them to your soldiers. It explains . . .' Kvitzinsky hesitated. His face was pained. 'It explains that there was an accident, that he was out looking at the city this afternoon when there was a traffic accident . . .'

Peter felt fury boiling up inside him. With his free hand he grasped the Russian by the lapels.

'You have the bloody nerve to just stand there and tell me . . .'

'Don't touch me, please,' Kvitzinsky whispered. 'They might shoot. Please. They are very nervous!'

Over the Russian's shoulder Peter could see that two of the guards had levelled their submachine-guns at him. Slowly he released his grip.

'You are right to be angry,' Kvitzinsky went on hurriedly. 'And of course it is not true about the traffic accident . . . but it was not our intention that he should die! You must believe . . .' he implored. 'He took his own life . . . from a window of the HVA, the police building. I don't know why. It was after he learned that he was to be handed back to you like this. It's the truth, Joyce, but the Germans didn't think you would believe . . . so they have written the other story.'

Peter stared blankly at the Russian, unable to decide whether Kvitzinsky himself believed what he was saying. Would Anderson have killed himself? It was not impossible.

'What do you want, Kvitzinsky? Why did you insist I came here to meet you?'

A gust of wind caught the underside of his umbrella and threatened to wrench it away. Kvitzinsky clutched at his hat to prevent it being blown off.

'I had a proposition to put,' he said, trying to keep his voice to a whisper. 'Now . . .' He shrugged and looked unhappily at the coffin. 'Now you would be right not even to listen to me, but I hope you will.'

His eyes were those of a man struggling under a terrible burden.

'You are a brilliant man, Peter Joyce, and you have a technology already which I am still dreaming of! Yes, I pay you a compliment! Your Skydancer is a very clever weapon. Of course,' he sighed, 'I now know how I can beat it. I know how to build a defence against it, but . . .'

His lips sealed into a thin line.

In the half-light of the car headlights Peter tried to read the Russian's face, to see what new vein of trickery was being mined.

Kvitzinsky had leaned forward so that his head was under the edge of Peter's umbrella. He spoke in a soft whisper, inaudible to anyone more than a few inches away.

'The people at the top in my country want it to be done. If I tell them it is possible, they will spend the money, buy me everything I need, steal me anything that money cannot buy. But if that money is spent on such military equipment, what will happen? Where will that money come from? You know the answer; it is the same in your country, the same everywhere. That money will come from the people. To pay for a defence against a weapon designed never to be used, hospitals will stay crowded and short of drugs; food supplies will run out and schools will close in the bitter days of winter because there is no fuel to heat them.'

Peter steeled himself against Kvitzinsky's outpourings. He smelled trickery. There had to be a catch, and he held himself in wait for it.

'Mr Peter Joyce,' the Russian began to plead with him, 'you and I, we are scientists, not gunsmiths. We are here on this planet to extend mankind's knowledge for his own benefit. For his protection, yes, but . . . if we build him an impregnable fortress and then keep him inside it with nothing to eat, what do we achieve?

'You . . . and me, I want us to try to reach an understanding. I know . . . I know from when we talked before in Geneva, in better times, I know that you are a serious and sensible man. If I build a defence against Skydancer, you will build a new weapon that can beat it, and then I . . . and so on and so on. There is no end to that. No security or peace for our families. Only fear. Joyce, listen to me. We must stop this, and now is the time to do it! No new defences, no new missiles!'

Peter stood back suddenly. He began to believe that Kvitzinsky was serious, that he was earnestly proposing a halt to one small part of the arms race, not a halt negotiated by politicians, but one unofficially agreed by scientists.

'You can't deliver that sort of deal,' Peter answered gently. 'Nor can I. You know that. We . . . people like us, we don't take decisions of that kind.'

The Russian's eyes narrowed.

'We can try.'

There was the sound of footsteps. Kvitzinsky shot a glance over his shoulder; the officers from the GRU were coming up one on each side of him.

He reached into the inside pocket of his coat, and pulled out a thick brown envelope.

'Useless!' he exclaimed in a loud voice, thrusting the envelope into Peter's hands. 'Your attempt to trick me into thinking these were the real plans – a waste of time! You do not fool us so easily, Mr Joyce! That is what I want to tell you. We have not been taken in!'

With that, he turned abruptly on his heel and walked back towards the wall, flanked by the Soviet security men.

For a moment Peter stood stunned and confused by what he had just heard. The hearse began to roll quietly backwards, its engine purring softly. The guards in their watchtowers seemed to relax now that the confrontation on the bridge was over.

'I think we should get moving,' Major Howlett muttered by his ear.

Peter stood for a moment longer, watching the vehicle that had delivered Anderson's corpse slip back behind the wall, Oleg Kvitzinsky walking beside it. The heavy iron gate began to close. For a few minutes there had been a contact on this bridge, a hope voiced, and then stifled.

He looked at the wall stretching away in each direction, with its wire and its searchlights, and the distant barking of its guard dogs. It was mistrust itself, cast in concrete.

Peter turned and walked beside the Land-Rover as it carried Alec Anderson's coffin slowly back into the West. Once they were off the bridge, the East German guard closed the wire-mesh gate behind them and secured the padlock.

'I think we have to assume it was all designed to trick us,' Field-Marshal Buxton stated. Sir Marcus Beckett nodded in agreement.

'It's a pretty standard Soviet ploy, disinformation and all that,' Beckett added.

They had gathered at the Defence Ministry the following afternoon.

'I think he meant it,' Peter answered, half to himself. 'I think he was genuinely trying to make a point. I wasn't sure at the time, but I believe it now. He's not a military man remember. Kvitzinsky got roped into the weapons business because of his achievements in the civilian sector. He's an idealist – still believes in communism as a force to benefit the masses. Naive perhaps, but I'm sure he was genuinely trying to stop one little piece of the arms race.

'He was scared to death of those security men, I'm sure of that. Covered his tracks in a hurry, in case they overheard him. That farce about giving back the plans that Alec had delivered, saying they were fakes. It wasn't for my benefit that he did that, but for the GRU men who were guarding him. It was his own goons he was trying to convince.'

Buxton and Beckett smiled knowingly at one another.

'You mustn't underestimate the deviousness of the Russians, Peter,' the CDS warned. 'We've accumulated quite a lot of experience of them over the years, you know. My guess is that at this very moment he's going through a copy of those plans of yours with a fine-toothed comb!'

Peter shook his head.

'I'm sure he was going to tell his own people that building a defence against Skydancer was impossible – that was the message I got,' he insisted.

'Well . . .' Buxton concluded, 'time will tell.'

'And what about Anderson?' Sir Marcus interjected. 'You don't seriously believe that story about suicide do you? The HVA bumped him off, just the same as they did poor Mary Maclean!'

Peter nodded. They could be right about that. He thought again of those bloodstains at Mary's flat and shuddered.

'And do they get away with it?' he asked bitterly. 'Two people murdered, and we can do nothing about it?'

The field-marshal frowned.

'If Metzger turns up in the West again, you can rest assured it won't be long before he's sent home in a box, too,' Buxton stated grimly.

'There's an emergency debate in the House tomorrow,' Sir Marcus cut in. 'The opposition have demanded it. The PM's going to say something about Alec. Berlin won't be mentioned – but he's going to say that Anderson died in a counter-intelligence operation, details of which can never be revealed, in the interests of national security.'

Peter thought of Janet Anderson. At least she could now believe that her husband died a hero. She would never know that he had been led into blackmail and into betraying his country.

It was the face of 'the Russian' which dominated his mind, a face which was no longer just imaginary. Kvitzinsky. *Was* he just another Soviet official, saying one thing and meaning another? Or had he been pleading with him from the heart?

Supposing Kvitzinsky did keep his word? Supposing

he made no effort to counter Skydancer? Could that be the end of it? The end of one small part of the arms race?

He shook his head. How could they ever be sure what Kvitzinsky would do, or whether some other Russian would soon take his place, some scientist with an altogether different view? Maybe Buxton was right; maybe the only way to predict the future was to remember the mistrust of the past.

The following afternoon, Peter Joyce returned home from Aldermaston soon after lunch, to listen to the radio broadcast of the emergency debate in the House of Commons.

The Prime Minister made a rousing statement about the wickedness of the foreign agents who had tried to steal British missile secrets, and declared that they had failed ignominiously, thanks to the heroic actions of a number of British personnel, including Mr Alec Anderson from the Ministry of Defence.

Pressed by the opposition to state categorically whether British defence interests had been damaged or not, he declared:

'This house may rest assured that Her Majesty's Government will preserve the effectiveness of the British independent nuclear deterrent, whatever measures the Soviet Union and her allies may take in an effort to undermine it. It is and will remain a weapon against which there is no effective defence, and whose guaranteed destructive power is the surest way we know to deter any nation in the world from waging war against us.'

Peter lay back at one end of the sofa in the living-room, staring at the ceiling.

'Does that mean you've just been promised a job for life?' Belinda asked warily.

Peter smoothed back the hair from his forehead. For a long time he just stared at nothing.

'I don't really know,' he answered eventually.

SHADOW HUNTER

Geoffrey Archer

arrow books

To Eva, Alison and James,
for their encouragement

CHAPTER ONE

Wednesday 16th October.

The restaurant was Greek. Kebabs and non-stick rice, washed down with retsina. Plymouth had a dozen like it; the evening trade was good in a navy town.

The watchers sat outside in a car, wishing they were inside so they could catch something of what the man and woman said to each other, but there'd been no spare table.

For a week, the two men from Special Branch had been shadowing the big blond man who claimed to be Swedish. The man had chatted up a young submariner in a pub, asking questions about nuclear propulsion that were too intelligent to be casual.

Up to now there'd been nothing; a dreary circuit of bars and dockside dives. Sometimes the man had drunk alone, just looking at faces. Sometimes he'd feigned drunkenness and joined in the raucous banter of the sailors, but there'd been nothing they could call a contact.

Clearly the man was searching. But for what? Information? Secrets? Or just companionship?

For most of the week the Swede had stayed in cheap lodgings. Then, that morning, he'd gone up-market – checked into the Holiday Inn. The receptionist had welcomed him as a regular client.

Now he'd met a women, a classy one at that, judging by the way she dressed. Someone else's wife, they'd guessed. She'd come separately to the restaurant, kissing him as she sat down. They'd been given a table by the window, easily visible from the watchers' car.

'If this job had been important, they'd have given us the gear and we could hear what Blondie's saying,' one of the watchers grumbled.

'Don't need to hear it,' the other replied. 'He's talking dirty. That's what the hotel room's for.'

Nearly ninety minutes passed. Concentration was flagging.

'Hey, look!' one of the policemen snapped. The woman was agitated. She was clutching her head in her hands, her shoulders shaking.

'She's blubbing.'

They saw the Swede grab her hand but she pulled it away.

'Talking too dirty, you reckon?'

'Hang on! She's moving.'

The woman stood up, then scrabbled on the floor for her bag. The man reached out, trying to pull her back. He glanced round, embarrassed.

The door opened and the woman ran into the street. Disoriented at first, she pulled a handkerchief from her bag and dabbed at her eyes. Then, darting a look over her shoulder, she turned right and ran down the street.

The Swede stayed inside and called hurriedly for the bill.

'She's got a car, look. A Golf. You follow her – I'll take Blondie.'

The watcher closed the passenger door and slipped into the darkened entrance of a newsagent's shop. His companion started the engine and moved off in pursuit of the woman.

Three minutes passed before the tall foreigner emerged into the street. He looked around briefly, pulled a cigarette from a pack, and lit it. For a split second his gaze rested on the doorway opposite. Hand and cigarette hovered for a moment.

Casually he turned and walked up the road, passing one pub, but pausing uncertainly outside another. The watcher was in the open now. He kept moving, knowing he'd been seen, but perhaps not yet recognized for what he was.

The Swede pushed open the door to the lounge bar. The watcher gave him a few seconds' start then crossed the road and followed him in.

The lounge was packed. No sign of him. The policemar eased through the crush to the bar, looking all around

He reached the counter and his eyes met the Swede's, inches away, grey-blue and hard as nails.

'Can you watch this for me? I must take a leak.'

The blond pointed to his pint of lager.

'Sure,' replied the watcher, unprepared.

The Swede elbowed his way to the gents'.

Did he know? Was his cover blown? The policeman dithered for just a moment too long.

He shoved through the crowd, drawing complaints and threats. Inside the toilet a cold wind blew through the wide-open window. Outside he heard a motorbike roar away.

'Sod it!' Blondie had been a professional after all, and he'd lost him.

* * *

Thursday 17th October.

It was weeks since Commander Andrew Tinker had worn a cap and the soft leather band felt like the steel hoop of a barrel. At sea submariners ignored naval formality, but heading back into harbour after six weeks on patrol, uniforms were brushed and smoothed, ready for the world of normal people.

'Funny smell.' Tinker sniffed, stepping clear of the hatch and stretching. He leaned his elbows on the edge of the tall, slim fin. The joke was an old one.

'It's called fresh air, sir . . . ,' the watch officer fed the expected line.

The early morning sky was grizzled, but there was no rain. Andrew gulped at the offshore breeze, rejoicing in its scent after weeks of confinement in conditioned air. As they rounded Penlee Point into Plymouth Sound, he could taste its sweetness; his senses peeled away the layers of smell – woodsmoke, wet grass, sea-weed.

It was like being released from sensory deprivation, every nerve newly sensitized. The gentle flapping of the bridge ensign was like a whip-crack to his ears, the light wind on his face seemed to tug like a gale.

He was pale; they all were after weeks without sunlight.

However, a few brisk walks on the moors would soon bring the colour back.

The conning tower stood thirty feet above the casing. Dark green water washed like liquid glass over the fat, blunt nose of the submarine and away to the sides. There was no sound, no vibration from the powerplant deep below the surface. The black shape probed and the smooth sea yielded effortlessly to its penetration. Brutal. Phallic.

Eyes fixed on the parting of the waters, his thoughts turned to sex. They could afford to now that he was going ashore. He'd learned to suppress such feelings at sea. Within hours he'd be home; Patsy would be waiting for him.

'About forty minutes 'til we're alongside?'

'That's right, sir. First line ashore at 08.00 – that's if *Truculent*'s cleared the berth in time. We should see her any minute.'

The lieutenant raised a heavy pair of binoculars and focused on the distant cranes of Devonport dockyard. The towering roof of the triple drydock dominated the view. At that range the black fin of their sister ship heading for sea would be difficult to spot against the vertical lines of the harbour side.

HMS Truculent was almost identical to Tinker's own *HMS Tribune*; a few pieces of equipment on board differed. Despite his eagerness to be home he envied *Truculent*'s captain. Commander Philip Hitchens was heading for the north Atlantic for biennial NATO exercises. This autumn the manoeuvres were being held closer to Soviet waters than ever before. Tinker enjoyed war games – stalking the massive American aircraft carriers and 'sinking' them with salvos of simulated torpedoes and missiles. It was a shame the patrol schedules had favoured Hitchens rather than himself. Hitchens would never admit to enjoying something as serious as war, even when it was just a game.

'Steer two-nine-zero. Revolutions for five knots!' Andrew ordered into the bridge microphone. They were passing north of Drake's Island, the Hoe to their right dominated by the disused lighthouse known as Smeaton's Tower.

'Got her, sir! She's just coming through the narrows.'

Andrew raised his own binoculars and followed the line set by the lieutenant. It was the *Truculent*, all right; and there was Phil on the bridge. The set of his head was unmistakable.

'Great sight,' Andrew whispered as the *Truculent* picked up speed towards them, bow-wave foaming.

'The best there is,' the young lieutenant concurred. 'A five-thousand-ton black mistress! That's what my girlfriend calls this beast.'

'Jealous, is she?'

'Hmmm. But they like to be jealous, don't they, women?'

Andrew didn't reply at first. He was very young, the lieutenant.

'Planning to tie the knot, are you?'

'No, not me. Not ready yet, sir.'

Truculent was less than half-a-mile ahead, aiming to pass a hundred yards to port. Tinker raised the binoculars again; the finely-chiselled face of Philip Hitchens stared straight ahead from the conning tower, cap pulled firmly down against the wind.

'Come on, Phil,' he breathed. 'Give us a wave. You're not making a movie!'

The two commanders had shared a 'cabin' at Britannia College, Dartmouth, and their careers had progressed in an undeclared spirit of competition.

It surprised Tinker they'd remained such good friends. Hitchens was so straitlaced he was a curiosity. He had breeding and style, yet often seemed overwhelmed by the responsibility of his work. His handsome features should have made him a 'ladies' man', yet Andrew had never known him make a pass at another woman, despite his own wife's questionable fidelity. Tinker found the mismatch of appearance and character intriguing.

Andrew saluted as the two black hulls passed one another silently.

'The bugger!' Tinker growled. 'He's not even acknowledging! Come on, Phil! What's the matter with you?'

To ignore the salute of a fellow warship was very bad form in navy protocol. Tinker sharpened the focus of his binoculars. His friend of twenty years was studiously ignoring him.

'Something we said, sir?' the lieutenant suggested blandly.

Within the hour they were alongside the jetty in Devonport submarine base, astern of the lustrous black hull of a sister boat just out of refit. Standing on the casing ready to welcome aboard the Captain of the Second Submarine Squadron, Tinker realized how tatty his own vessel had become. The black paint had lost its sheen and there were patches on the fin where sound-absorbent tiles had pulled away, the adhesive softened by weeks of immersion. *Tribune* would need a spell in the dockyard before her next patrol.

'Good morning, sir.' He saluted briefly.

'Morning, Andrew. Welcome home!'

Captain Norman Craig had eight nuclear-powered submarines in his squadron. He was responsible for the wellbeing of the boats and their crews.

'Lovely day. Let's get below for a chat. Won't keep you long.'

Tinker followed him down through the hatch and into the wardroom where the stewards were pouring coffee. De-briefing was routine at the end of a patrol. The weapons and mechanical engineers would hand over reports on defective equipment so the mechanics at the shore base, *HMS Defiance*, could put it right. Personnel problems would be raised, and gossip exchanged, but the session was always kept brief. The members of *Tribune*'s crew who were due to take shore leave would want to get home.

The briefing over, the two men crossed the quay towards *HMS Defiance*, the Captain hurrying to keep pace with Andrew's longer stride.

'Patsy picking you up?' Craig asked. Andrew looked at his watch.

'She'll be teaching. Home for lunch, I expect.'

'My car can take you back if you want.'

'You sure, sir? That'd be great.'

'The driver can't spend *all* day polishing it! It'll give her something to do. What time do you want to leave?'

'In about an hour? That'll give me time to complete my paperwork.'

The black Cavalier was driven by a WRNS, a plump girl with rosy cheeks and a warm Devon accent. As she swung the car expertly out of the suburbs of Plymouth and into the country lanes, they talked of the fortunes of Plymouth Argyll football club, of which both were fans. But the more she talked the slower she drove, which grated on his nerves, so he pulled a folder from his briefcase and pretended to read.

Coming home always made him anxious, gave him a fear that his domestic life might have changed radically while he'd been away.

The lanes grew narrower as they approached the village where he and Patsy had lived for the past four years. They'd had four different homes; appointments had moved him round the country, but they'd determined to settle in the West Country. Two limestone cottages knocked together had created a home large enough. The three children were away at boarding school; eight-year-old Anthony was just experiencing his first term of separation from his parents. School had started five weeks ago, so Patsy had handled the boy's last-minute tears on her own.

The red Devon soil glowed in the midday autumn sun. The car turned into a narrow lane and dived between banks and hedges. Soon it wound its way into the village of Yealmsford.

The vicar stepped out of the tiny post office carrying a newspaper, looked at the naval registration of the car, peered to see who it was, then waved in recognition.

He'll be getting me to read the lesson again before long,

Andrew thought. The vicar said he had a voice that made the congregation sit up and listen.

The Tinkers were well known in the village and Andrew was a celebrity. To command something 'nuclear' carried kudos in this part of the world.

Patsy was out. It irked him she wasn't there to greet him. She taught in the mornings at the village primary school, but should have been home by now. He carried his small grip into the house – a submariner takes few possessions to sea.

The emptiness of the cottage alarmed him. With all the children away at school now, there were no toys littering the hall. He put his bag down and called out. No answer. Where the hell was she?

Then he heard her car.

'Oh, you're back!' Patsy looked startled, as she came through the doorway. 'I wasn't sure when you were coming. Have you been here long?'

She dropped her briefcase in the hall and hugged him. Her copper-coloured hair brushed his cheek; it smelled of shampoo and the cigarette smoke from the school office. He squeezed her and lifted her feet off the ground.

'I missed you,' she purred, the way she always did.

'Missed you too!'

'You didn't! You had your boat to play with!'

'Not as much fun as playing with you!'

She pushed him away with a forced smile. It was stupid, but she always felt shy when Andrew came home. To cope with his long absences she'd made herself unnaturally self-sufficient. His homecomings were like the arrival of a stranger.

'Have you had lunch?'

'No, and I'm starving.'

'I'm not sure what there is. You can come shopping with me later!'

He followed her to the kitchen. He was used to this; whenever he returned from patrol, Patsy seemed to feel the need to 'house-train' him again.

'It'll have to be a sandwich for now. With the children away, I haven't been stocking up.'

'I was worried something had happened. It's so quiet in the house . . .'

'I know . . .'

She looked pained. She would never tell him how lonely she felt at times.

'How was Anthony when you took him to school?'

'He howled all the way there, and I howled all the way back! But he's fine now. I got a super letter from him this morning. We can have him home for a weekend soon. He's dying to see you.'

Andrew watched her work. With Patsy having her own job, her own friends, and being life's mainstay for their children, he sometimes felt himself an outsider.

'I saw Sara this morning. She looked dreadful,' Patsy said, slicing bread.

'Hitchens?'

She nodded.

'She's having problems with Simon. He's going to be thirteen soon and still hasn't got used to boarding school. His headmaster's accused him of vandalizing microscopes in the biology lab. Sara's worried he'll turn to arson next!'

'That's appalling! Philip sailed today. He ignored my salute! Not like him at all. Perhaps he was worrying about Simon. Last thing you need when you're going to sea.'

'Last thing a *mother* needs at any time,' she stressed pointedly. 'Particularly Sara. You know how unstable she is.'

'Over-emotional, that's all.'

'You fancy Sara, that's your trouble!'

'I just feel sorry for her. She's not so good at coping as you are. And I have to take an interest. Simon's my godson.'

'Ohh! Well remembered!' Patsy mocked. 'When did you last even see him? Last year? Year before?'

'Oh, come on . . .'

'Sorry. That wasn't fair. Here's your sandwich.'

She passed him a plate and they sat down at the kitchen table. 'I'm afraid we're out of beer.'

She smiled apologetically.

'Welcome home!'

* * *

HMS Truculent.

Commander Philip Hitchens had seldom experienced claustrophobia, but now the cabin felt as narrow as a coffin, as *HMS Truculent* hummed towards the Atlantic depths.

For eight hours after leaving Devonport, Philip had hardly left the control room. Inshore waters were the most dangerous, and avoiding collisions took maximum concentration. He didn't trust the watch; all young men, their minds wandered when he wasn't around.

They'd kept at periscope depth in the Channel; the sea was calm and visibility good. The sonar produced a jumble of tanker traffic, confused by echoes from the sea-bed, but he could see the ships clearly enough through the periscope up to five miles away.

Keeping busy had served another purpose, too; to distract his mind from the nightmare of the past three months, a personal nightmare of duplicity, the depth of which he had yet to fathom.

Now it was evening. South of Ireland, they were away from the shipping channels. Time to leave it to the watch. He withdrew to his cabin, to his solitary hell. Once there, he sat hunched at the foot of his bunk like a child. It was the furthest he could get from his work-table, from the framed photograph of Sara. Every time he looked at her picture, the shock, the misery, the pain engulfed him anew.

Betrayal! The word echoed in his mind like a slamming door; not just her – the bastard Russians, too!

He'd thought of putting the photograph in a drawer so as not to look at her, but ruled it out. Everything had to stay normal; no one must know. His cabin was also his office, visited by others. Family photographs were like icons in officers' quarters. Their absence would be quickly noticed.

He couldn't stop thinking of her. The night before they'd sailed he'd stayed on board, unable to sleep, knowing she was seeing that man again. She'd promised it was to say goodbye, to tell him they'd never meet again. But did he believe her? *Could* he believe anything she said, any more?

As for Simon – he couldn't imagine, didn't dare think, what his future would hold now. His son was the one restraint on what he planned. But he was at a good school; they'd see him right. Nothing must stand in his way.

There was a debt to be settled, vengeance for a past wrong, a terrible wrong which transcended all other considerations.

'*Captain, sir! Officer of the Watch!*'

The tannoy loudspeaker above his desk startled him.

He leapt up from the bunk and clicked the microphone switch.

'Captain!'

'*Sound room's got a sonar contact. They think it's a trawler, sir.*'

'I'm coming now.'

His cabin was just yards from the control room. He was there within seconds, glad of the distraction. Trawlers were the bane of submariners' lives in coastal waters. Fouling their nets could mean the early end of a patrol.

He headed for the navigation plot. The submarine's position was being provided by SINS, the Submarine Inertial Navigation System, a gyroscopic device that had proven remarkably accurate.

The navigator and officer of the watch was Lieutenant Nick Cavendish, a twenty-five-year-old on his first patrol with *Truculent*.

'Depth?'

'Seventy metres, sir. Thirty metres under the keel.'

'Should be okay at this depth. What's the contact's bearing?'

'Ten degrees on the starboard bow. Range unknown.'

He stared at the chart. They were approaching the edge of the continental shelf west of Ireland. A few more hours and the sea bed would drop thousands of metres, giving them all the water they could want to avoid hazards trailing from the surface. The chart showed no obstructions for miles.

'I need more sea room. They're bloody long, those trawl wires. Officer of the Watch, come round to 210.'

'Aye, aye, sir. Helm! Port thirty. Keep course two-one-zero.'

Best to take no chances; trawl nets were undetectable until their hawsers scrapped the acoustic tiles off the casing, by which time it was too late.

'Anything else on sonar?'

'One other surface contact up to the north-west, very distant. Sounds like a tanker. No submarines, sir. And none expected for the next twenty-four hours, according to the intelligence sitrep.'

Philip shot a glance round the control room. In the centre, the oiled steel periscope shafts glistened in their deck housings. About a dozen men, ratings in blue shirts, officers in white, were concentrating as the boat manoeuvred. The planesman at the one-man control console operated the stick that 'flew' the submarine through the water, marine engineers monitored gauges for the trim valves and propulsion system, and seamen, some of them not much more than eighteen, peered at the amber screens of the tactical systems.

Those who caught the captain's eye looked away quickly. They didn't like him much, the men of *Truculent*, but they respected him, and that was what mattered. He'd need that respect when the crunch came in a few days' time.

Across the room at the weapons control console, the weapon engineer officer, Lieutenant Commander Paul Spriggs was talking to a rating. Hitchens liked Spriggs; the man was crisp and concise in the way he handled his men, everything by the book. Spriggs would be vital to him at the end, a WEO who wouldn't question orders.

Philip hovered by the chart table, pulling out the sheet for the north of Scotland and the water between Iceland, the Faroes and the Shetlands. Known as the GIFUK (Greenland, Iceland, Faroes, UK) Gap, this was NATO's underwater front line, a strategic barrier through which Soviet submarines should not be able to pass undetected on their way to the central Atlantic.

A ridge of sand, mud and rock ran between the land masses, along which the US Navy had laid a string of hydrophones known as SOSUS, SOund SUrveillance System, able to detect the passing of almost any submarine. Sonar-equipped surface ships and aircraft patrolled above, to complete the barrier.

Truculent was taking part in Exercise Ocean Guardian, which involved over a hundred NATO ships and submarines, practising the reinforcement of Norway and control of the Norwegian Sea.

'Are we going tactical on the transit, sir?' asked the WEO. 'See how many Yank skimmers we can zap before they get a whiff of us?'

'Certainly not!'

Heads turned at the sharpness of Philip's reply.

'Sorry, sir,' Spriggs mumbled. 'Thought that was the plan.'

'No,' Philip repeated softly, conscious of his overreaction. 'We've got to avoid any risk of detection. We're blue at first, as you know. But then we go unlisted.'

Paul Spriggs frowned. He'd attended the pre-patrol briefing in the Northwood headquarters of Flag Officer Submarines, along with the captain and the first lieutenant; that briefing had certainly put them playing 'blue' (NATO) first, but by midweek they were due to switch to 'orange' (enemy). There'd been no mention of their going 'unlisted'. That meant some sort of secret mission, usually intelligence gathering deep inside Soviet waters.

'Will you be briefing us on that, sir?' he asked edgily.

Hitchens felt his face begin to flush. They were staring at him.

'Yes, WEO. In due course,' he answered curtly.

He stepped into the sound room adjoining the control room. Cordell, the tactics and sonar officer, was listening intently on headphones. Three ratings sat at panels controlling glowing green video displays. Here, the myriad sounds of the deep detected by hydrophones spread round the bulbous bows were translated into vertical patterns and gradations of light, unintelligible to the uninitiated. One of the ratings stood up from his seat and crossed to a cabinet to change the laser disc on which every sound detected was recorded in digital code.

'Got a hiccup with sonar 2026, sir.'

Lieutenant Sebastian Cordell had removed his headphones.

'Processor's gone barmy. The CPO's going to change a board, see if that cures it.'

The 2026 was the processor for the second sonar array, a yellow plastic tube over a hundred metres long, filled with hydrophones, towed a thousand metres behind the submarine. The computer for analysing the sounds it detected was highly sophisticated, and had developed a fault.

'How's that fisherman doing? Still tracking it?'

The possibility of the trawl net slipping like a sheath over the nose of the boat haunted Hitchens.

'We think she's passing clear astern, sir. Shouldn't be any risk of fouling now.'

'Thank God. You'll keep me informed on the 2026? I want a report on it.'

'Of course, sir.'

People seemed to be staring at him. He'd keep moving; didn't want them reading his face to see what he was thinking.

He passed back through the control room, heading aft, telling the officer of the watch he was making his rounds.

He sensed a conspiracy around him. Of silence. They knew about Sara!

They'd heard gossip ashore. Must've done. In the pubs. Perhaps some had even heard that sod of a chief petty officer boasting about how he'd screwed the captain's wife!

How would he have described it? Bonking? Poking?

Anger made his head swim. He put out a hand to steady himself as he made his way to the tunnel that crossed the top of the reactor to the machinery spaces beyond.

When the penny had dropped just a week ago, it was like a blow to the stomach. He'd taken Simon, home for the weekend, shopping in Plymouth for construction kits to take back to school.

Strolling down Market Avenue, Philip had vaguely

recognized CPO Terry from years before. He'd remembered the face, but not the name – until Simon called out, 'Hi Reg!' He'd sounded so pleased. The CPO had grinned at Simon, then glanced uncomfortably at Philip.

Surprised the boy should know Terry, it had been a minute or two before he'd asked about it.

'Just someone I know . . .' had been Simon's reply.

He'd felt panicky, suddenly aware how little he knew about his son's life. The boy was away at boarding school for most of the year, and when he was home for the holidays, Philip was more often than not away at sea. But why should he know Reg Terry?

He'd pressed him to say where they'd met.

'At home. He used to come and see us sometimes, me and Mummy.'

A door had suddenly opened into a world he knew nothing about.

Philip reached the airlock and turned the bar-bell handle that withdrew the heavy bolts securing the outer door. He was almost exactly in the middle of the submarine, forty metres from the dome of the bow-sonar, forty more from the end of the cowl that housed the silent propulsor at the stern.

He closed the outer door behind him and opened the inner one. He was now standing on top of the reactor. Beneath his feet the controlled uranium reaction generated enough power to serve a town of 50,000 people, the potential of the nuclear radiation to destroy his body cells held back by thick lead shielding.

There was no sound from the thousands of gallons of water being boiled into high-pressure steam below him. Millions of pounds had been spent on research into silencing the powerful pumps that circulated the cooling water through the reactor core, pumps whose reliability was essential to the life of the submarine.

He passed through into caverns packed with the machinery that drove his boat and generated the megawatts needed for its electrical systems.

Those who saw Philip greeted him smartly. The work of the men 'back aft', essential to the silent operation of the boat, was not considered as 'macho' as that of the weapon crews 'forrard'. Philip was conscious some COs tended to ignore the mechanical end of the boat, which was physically separated from the forward section by the reactor compartment. They may not like him, but he wouldn't be guilty of that.

Did these men know about Sara? What if they did? He must act normally, show no sign of weakness. His authority mustn't be questioned.

In the officers' quarters forward, Lieutenant Commander Paul Spriggs had returned to the cramped cabin he shared with the wiry first lieutenant, Lieutenant Commander Tim Pike. The first lieutenant was second in command – the executive officer and 'general manager' of the boat.

'Tim, at the ops briefing at Northwood . . . ,' Spriggs began.

'Mmmm?' Pike put down the nuclear propulsion manual he'd been studying for forthcoming promotion exams. 'What of it?'

'They said "free play", didn't they? Defined areas of sea, but we can do whatever we like within them?'

'Well, they didn't say we couldn't. But it's supposed to be a fast transit up to the Lofotens.'

'Yea, but if the opportunity's there, it's okay. That's what I said to the old man, but the silly sod jumped down my throat.'

'What? Our own dear warm-hearted Captain? You astonish me.'

'He was really narked. Then he went stomping off on an inspection.'

'Must be that time of the month. Mind you, they could have said something different to him afterwards. He had another session with FOSM later.'

'Did he? I didn't know. That fits what he said, that we're going unlisted.'

'Unlisted?' Pike frowned.

'You didn't know either?'

'He . . . er, hasn't seen fit to brief me yet.'

'Bloody hell, Tim! You're his second-in-command!'

Pike smoothed the ginger stubble he called a beard, his pale grey eyes betraying the wounded pride that came from being deputy to a man who trusted no one.

'I'm sure he'll tell us "in due course", Paul.'

' "At the right time", you mean.'

' "When we need to know".'

'You've been reading the rule book again!'

Pike shrugged. 'I've been through this before with Hitchens. Made an issue of it once. Wasn't worth it. He went out of his way to be bloody to me for weeks afterwards.'

'You don't surprise me. But tell me: you've worked with him longer than I have – how do you rate him as a skipper?'

'He knows his stuff. And he's the one with the most gold stripes. That's what matters when the chips are down. If I had a run-in with him, the men with scrambled egg on their hats would back him up to the hilt. They'd drop me like a lump of shit!'

* * *

Friday 18th October.

Vice-Admiral Feliks Astashenkov looked round cautiously as he entered the arrivals hall at Moscow's Sheremetyevo airport. He was not in uniform and had flown from Murmansk under a false name. The plane had developed an engine problem at the start of its taxi run; the passengers had had to wait on board for three hours while an Aeroflot mechanic repaired it.

As one of the *Vlasti*, the 'powerful ones', he was unused to such demeaning treatment. The Deputy-Commander of the Soviet Navy's Northern Fleet was entitled to better than that. But the message from the Soviet leader, delivered to his home by a courier, had insisted on maximum secrecy for their meeting.

At Murmansk Airport a KGB guard had recognized him. It was inevitable that someone would. He'd slipped the man ten roubles, told him he was Moscow-bound for a weekend with his mistress, but that his wife thought he was on a fishing trip. The policeman had passed the note across his mouth. His lips were sealed.

The silence he'd bought was to keep the journey secret from the Northern Fleet Commander, Admiral Andrei Belikov, rather than from his wife. Belikov was just a vassal of Admiral Grekov, Commander-in-Chief of the Soviet Navy, who'd been at odds with Nikolai Savkin, the new Soviet leader, from the moment he'd taken over.

They told Astashenkov he'd be met at Sheremetyevo and taken to the rendezvous. He elbowed his way through the crush, impatient at the willingness of his countrymen to accept such conditions. Astashenkov felt apprehensive. He'd been given no reason for this unorthodox summons to Moscow. He'd met the General Secretary on several occasions, admired his energy and reforming zeal. Nikolai Savkin was of his own generation, a man with the vision to press on with change even though the birth pains of the new, competitive Soviet Union had become intolerable to many of his countrymen.

Comrade Savkin was in need of friends, no doubt about that. Was that why he'd been summoned? But why him? It was in the factories and the Politburo that Savkin's support was waning. The armed forces had stood back from the arguments over the economy. And why call for him at this precise moment, when a massive fleet of NATO warships was assembling a few hundred kilometres from the Soviet coast for 'manoeuvres'? At a time like this he should be at his headquarters in Severomorsk, studying intelligence reports, ready to take action if the 'exercise' turned into something else.

'Comrade Vice-Admiral . . .'

The touch on his arm was casual, as if someone had merely brushed against him.

'Please follow me.'

It was the courier who'd delivered Savkin's message. Dressed in a brown parka with a fur-lined hood, he moved through the crowd slowly enough for Astashenkov to follow with ease. Not once did he turn his head to check; to anyone watching, the two men would appear unconnected.

They stepped outside. It was after eight in the evening and dark, and the October air had a nip of frost. The

Admiral spread the gap between himself and his escort. Ahead was the car park; Astashenkov fumbled for keys, as if he had a vehicle of his own to go to.

The messenger stopped by a battered yellow Volvo estate and opened the door on the driver's side. Astashenkov paused, placed his overnight bag on the ground and began to feel in his inside pockets, while looking around to see if he was being observed. The passenger door of the Volvo was pushed open. He climbed in.

They drove for nearly half-an-hour, the courier making it plain he had no wish to talk. Astashenkov had spent several years of his career in Moscow, but the part of the city through which they travelled was unknown to him. He suspected that the driver was making the route circuitous in order to confuse him.

They stopped in an old quarter. He followed the driver into what would once have been the townhouse of a prosperous merchant. Feliks was mystified; all this subterfuge for a meeting with the Soviet leader? What was going on?

Inside it smelled damp, as if seldom used. An oil heater burned in the hall. A guard emerged from the front reception room, carrying a sub-machine gun. The escort removed his parka and helped the Admiral off with his coat. Then he led the way upstairs.

Savkin seemed smaller than Astashenkov remembered, as if the burden of a national crisis had begun to crush him. At the sound of Astashenkov's entrance, the General Secretary of the Soviet Communist Party and President of the USSR stopped in mid-pace across the room.

'Ah, Feliks! A tired, impatient victim of air travel! And they always call it a "technical" fault, don't they?'

The smile looked forced. The pure white mane of hair looked as if it had not seen a comb all day.

'They wouldn't let us leave the plane! We were like pigs in a pen.'

'All the more reason for me to be grateful that you came.'

'It was my duty, Comrade General Secretary.'

Savkin's eyebrows arched momentarily. 'Duty' was

such a subjective concept. Where would the Admiral feel his 'duty' lay once he'd heard what Savkin had to say?

'Come and sit down. I must apologize for the room.'

He waved a hand dismissively. The walls were faded and peeling, marked with dusty rectangles where paintings had once hung. A heavy pedestal desk in one corner was half covered with files from an open briefcase. Savkin led the way to a green, leather chaise longue, and sat himself in the high-backed armchair opposite.

'The house belongs to the Pushkin. It's not used much, only for storing spare exhibits. My wife's cousin is curator of the gallery, so my link with the place is personal rather than official, which means it's clean – no bugs. And the guards here are my men. They'll bring us tea in a moment. Now, remind me. When was the last time . . . ?'

It was a gambit. Savkin would remember perfectly well. Such urbanity did nothing to calm Astashenkov's unease.

'It was June. At Polyarny. *Podvodnaya Lodka Atomnaya*. The nuclear patrol submarines – your inspection.'

'Of course.' Savkin nodded. 'It was a good turnout. Very impressive. Fine technology. The efficiency of your men was so vibrant you could almost touch it.'

'They were on their best behaviour. You must be used to that.'

'Yes, but you can tell when it's just show . . .'

There was a tap at the door, which had been left ajar. It was the guard bringing the tea. Conversation lapsed until he had left the room.

'Now. Why do you think you're here, like this?' His tone of voice was condescending, keeping the Admiral at a disadvantage. He would be asking a lot from Astashenkov, but did not want to appear to be a beggar.

The Admiral shrugged. There was no point in prevaricating.

'I really don't know. It might be that you require some service from me which would not win the approval of my Commanding Officer . . . ?'

Savkin smiled drily. He'd wanted a forthright reply. It saved time.

'And if that *were* the case . . . ? If neither Grekov not Belikov were to be involved?'

'Then it would be a difficult decision. I should need to understand why.'

'Of course.'

The grey eyes studied the sailor. Astashenkov recognized in them the flicker of uncertainty and weariness.

'Let me ask you something,' the General Secretary said. 'I've gained the impression, on the few occasions we've met, that your interests stretch wider than just naval matters. That *perestroika* has caused you some excitement; that you welcome it. Am I right?'

'It's my duty to be politically aware . . .' Feliks stalled.

'Yes, but you know I'm talking of more than awareness, Comrade. I'm talking of *commitment*.'

Astashenkov looked blank. Savkin would need to be more explicit.

'The changes on the farms and in the factories, and in the public services – making our people more responsible for their labour, and rewarding them individually – is a process I believe you support in principal, Feliks. But that process, as you know, is now at its nadir. People's lives have become harder, but not yet better. Faith in the policy has crumbled. It's no secret that the Zhiguli car factory has been on strike for two weeks because the enforcement of new quality standards has cut the workers' bonuses. What *is* still a secret, however, is how fast the strikes are spreading. Within two weeks, fifty per cent of our industrial production may be at a standstill.'

Astashenkov let out an involuntary low whistle.

'Yes. It's as bad as that,' Savkin was pleased he'd been able to startle the Admiral. 'And the strikers are supported by the majority of the Party. The *Nomenklatura* can hear the death-rattle of *perestroika*, and plan to finish it off!'

'But then what? A return to the old ways? They must know that's impossible now.'

'Is it? Are you sure?'

Astashenkov sensed he had been trapped.

'Well . . . , I'm only a submariner. I've no real understanding of economics . . .'

Savkin was not satisfied with that answer. He waited for Astashenkov to continue.

'It seems impossible to me. If we're not to be at an economic disadvantage for ever, we must produce at a price and to a standard that will enable us to compete worldwide. To return to a system of quotas without accountability . . .'

He knew he sounded if he were parrotting one of Savkin's own speeches. But it was what he believed.

'So you think we must continue with the policy? *Perestroika* at any price?'

Astashenkov breathed in deeply and let out a sigh. He sensed a noose tightening.

'It's what they accuse *me* of,' the General Secretary persisted. 'The *Nomenklatura*. They say it's my vanity, that I can't admit the policy is a failure.'

'Not all the *Nomenklatura*, Comrade General Secretary.' Feliks himself held one of those appointments which had to be approved by the Party.

Savkin frowned. Impatiently he pushed his fingers through the straggling white tufts at his temples.

'Feliks, I need to know how far you yourself will go, in supporting me?'

* * *

An hour later, Feliks Astashenkov stood outside one of those slab-sided apartment blocks that fill much of Moscow's suburbs. Savkin's courier had dropped him at the end of the road, as he'd asked, and he'd walked the last few hundred metres to Tatiana's flat. He was badly in need of the fresh air, which was cold enough to numb the end of his nose. What Savkin was planning had shaken him to the core.

He'd telephoned Tatiana the day before, to check she would be at home that evening. Opportunities to see her were so infrequent nowadays, he seized them whenever they arose. But now, as he stood looking up at the lighted windows, trying to remember which one was hers, he regretted making the rendezvous. Solitude was what he needed, not the distracting company of his mistress. He wanted time alone, to consider what Savkin had asked him to do. Not a word of his meeting would he be able to share with Tatiana. No one must ever learn from him what had been said that day.

She'd sounded edgy on the telephone, affecting indifference to his proposal to visit her. Feliks knew what that meant. His affair with her had started when he had been posted to Moscow three years earlier but since his transfer to the Kola Peninsula eighteen months ago, they'd not spent more than a dozen days together. He'd known it couldn't last. For the second time that day, he approached a rendezvous with trepidation.

* * *

Saturday 19th October.

Devon, England.

Andrew Tinker had been home for two days. He opened his eyes and looked at the bedside clock. It was just after seven a.m.; there was no hurry.

It was the birdsong that had woken him. At sea, he was accustomed to the dull roar of the ventilation system, to being awakened at any time by a call from the control-room and dropping off again easily. But here the persistent trill of a blackbird defeated him.

Patsy's naked body radiated warmth beside him. His first night home had been difficult. It usually was, with both of them tense from suppressing their feelings for so many weeks. Last night had been different, however.

He turned on his side; she had her back to him.

'Mmmm. Hello, stranger,' she mumbled.

'Hel-lo.'

'Are you the same stranger who did such lovely things to me last night?'

'That rings a bell . . . ' Andrew chuckled.

He kissed her neck. She smelled muskily of sweat and perfumed bath oil.

'Can you prove it?'

'Maybe. There's only one way to find out!'

* * *

'I'm going to do bacon and eggs,' he called to Patsy, who

was in the shower. 'Just to show you there's more than one thing I'm good at! Like some?'

'Put like that, how could I refuse . . . ?'

He was just dishing up when the telephone rang.

It was Norman Craig.

Andrew caught Patsy's eye across the kitchen and gave her a thumbs-down sign. Craig meant work.

'Hello, sir. Good morning to you.'

'I'm desperately sorry, Andrew. Pasty'll never speak to me again. But I'm about to ruin your weekend. If it's any consolation, I'm in the same boat, but I've been tied up since yesterday.'

'Sounds serious. What's the problem?'

'Look, I'm not being unreasonable, but I simply can't tell you anything over the phone. You understand. But if you could meet me in my office at about ten, earlier if you can make it, I'd be eternally grateful. It's bloody important. I wouldn't be disturbing your leave if it weren't.'

The captain's voice had developed an edge.

'No, of course not. I'll be on my way in a few minutes.'

Andrew replaced the receiver.

'What do you mean "you'll be on your way"? Where are you going?'

'To *Defiance*. To Craig's office,' he replied.

'Oh hell! When will you be back?'

'I don't know. He wouldn't say what it was about.'

'It's not fair. You've just got home, and now this . . .'

He poured them some coffee and began to eat fast. He would have to change into uniform if he was going to the naval base.

'Ring me, will you? When you know what he wants?'

'Sure. But I'm bound to be back by lunchtime.'

* * *

HMS Defiance was a building of concrete and brick. On the first floor Tinker pushed his security pass into a turnstile which let him into the administrative sector. The ground floor was packed with workshops; *Defiance* was primarily the maintainance base for the Squadron. As its

Captain, Norman Craig described himself as 'working from an office over a garage'.

'Oh, well done. You made it,' Craig remarked, ushering Tinker to the small sofa, while looking at his watch. 'Sorry I was cryptic on the blower, but this one really is a stinker. Bloody Sovs. Let me get you a coffee. NATO standard?'

'No sugar, thanks.'

'I've boiled the kettle. Shan't be a mo.'

Craig slipped into the clerk's office next door. None of the staff was in on Saturday. He returned, carrying the mugs.

'Now . . .' he began, dark eyes concentrating on Andrew. 'You're an old chum of Phil Hitchens, aren't you?'

Tinker nodded.

'You know his wife Sara?'

'Well, yes. We've been friends a long time. Their boy's my godson.'

'Of course. Well, she's in a spot of trouble.'

'Really?'

'In fact, I think we all are.'

Andrew frowned, wishing Craig would get to the point.

'Yesterday evening, I had a visitor. Chap from London. Security. Actually wore a trenchcoat, would you believe! There's someone they've been keeping an eye on, apparently. Claims to be Swedish, but they've discovered he's about as Scandinavian as Josef Stalin!

'Anyway, this man lives in London but does business in the West Country. That's *his* story, anyway. MI5 heard about him from the local Special Branch who'd been called in by our own security staff here at Devonport. They'd been tipped off by a young sailor, who met this so-called Swede in a pub and wasn't too happy about the sort of questions he was asking. The sailor's a marine engineer, on nuclear propulsion. He's a good lad. Did the right thing in reporting it.

'The Branch boys started tailing the man. On Wednesday night, something happened which made them call in MI5. They showed the London men a photo, but they had nothing on him.

'Then, by pure chance, MI5 got a tip-off in London. A couple of foreigners had done a bunk from their home in the middle of Wednesday night. They showed our local boys' picture to the neighbours and it all fell into place. They instantly reckoned the Swede was an illegal, a Russian undercover agent. Ten out of ten for sharp thinking!

'The fellow had quite a circle of naval friends in pubs around Plymouth, but it seems he was still building up confidence and hadn't asked too many clever questions yet.

'Anyway . . . , to cut a long story short – that incident on Wednesday. The watchers saw the Swede meet a woman in a kebab house in Plymouth. They seemed to know each other *intimately*. Lots of holding hands and whispering. But the woman got upset, and left without finishing her meal. One of the watchers followed her home. Can you guess who she was?'

Andrew's frown deepened.

'You don't mean Sara Hitchens?'

'The very same.'

'Bloody hell!'

'Exactly. And the reason MI5 decided to call on me yesterday is that when they raided the house in London they found the couple had left some bits and pieces behind. Including some of the little knick-knacks you get given free when you work for the KGB! The Swede *was* a Russian spy. Confirmed.'

'Shit!'

'Exactly. And we're in it. Up to our necks!'

'So, you're saying Sara was having an affair with a Soviet spy?'

'Correct. Not the first little dalliance, by all accounts. There'd been gossip about her among some of the wives, so I'm told.'

Andrew felt the back of his neck prickle, uncomfortably aware that the gossip was well-founded.

'But Sara can't know anything important,' he stated briskly. 'What would a KGB man hope to get from her?'

'Apart from a good time, you mean?'

'Yes, well . . . it doesn't quite make sense, does it?'

'I put the same point to MI5. They seem to think the man had only just started spying. Still feeling his way around, as it were, seizing any opportunity that presented itself. And one day, there was Sara. Do you know what she used to do when her old man was off on patrol? She used to go on her own to restaurants and pubs, sit at a table all by herself, and see who she could pick up.'

'I don't believe it!'

Poor Sara. Still desperate for affection, Andrew thought.

'It's true. She admitted it. Told MI5 that was the way she'd met the Russian. Said it usually worked a treat. Navy town – full of presentable young men, all a bit lonely, looking for female company . . .'

'What's happened? Has she been arrested?'

'No. Adultery's not a criminal offence. She denies utterly that she ever said anything to her lover. Anything secret, that is. There's nothing to charge her with.'

'But if she didn't know anything of any importance, and denies telling him anything anyway, why are you so concerned? Why . . .'

'Why have I dragged you in here on a Saturday morning? Quite simply because I'm far from sure that Sara told MI5 the truth. Normally, I'd agree, she wouldn't be much use to a spy, but in the last few days something may have happened to change that.'

'What do you mean?'

'She told the police that Philip had found out about her affairs and they'd had one hell of a fight.'

'Oh God!'

'In a situation like that, things get said. Things you wouldn't normally let on about, but in the heat of the moment . . .'

'When did you say you heard about this?'

'Yesterday.'

'Phil was at sea by then, so he wouldn't have known that the boyfriend was a spy?'

'Presumably not, since Sara claims she was convinced the man was a Swede.'

'So, you're worried that in the middle of a domestic

row he might have blurted out some state secret that she could later have passed to the Russians? Bit unlikely, isn't it, sir?'

'It's the timing that matters. The date when the row happened. As far as I can work out it must have been just after his ops briefing at Northwood.'

'But that sort of detail, he'd never bring it up in a screaming match with his wife!'

'It would only need *one* detail, Andrew . . .'

'Like?'

'Like exactly where he was going . . .'

The penny began to drop.

'They had something special on?'

'Precisely. *Truculent* wasn't just taking part in Exercise Ocean Guardian.'

'Can you say what it was?'

'I don't even know, Andrew. Just that it wasn't an ordinary mission.'

'I see . . . So, you want me to try to assess the likelihood of his having given something away? Because I know them both. Is that it?'

'I want you to go and see her. She may open up more to you than she did with the police.'

'Now, wait a minute . . .' Tinker cut in. 'In what capacity? Am I the Navy, or a friend?'

'Both. A special ambassador chosen because of your personal links with the Hitchens family,' Craig sounded unfortunately pompous. 'You're concerned for her welfare, and so is the Navy. And concerned for Philip, of course.'

The last point was the key consideration for Andrew. He pictured himself at the start of a two-month patrol, and wondered how he would cope if his own marriage had disintegrated days before he'd sailed.

CHAPTER TWO

He went home to change first, not wanting to look conspicuous by arriving at Sara's house in uniform.

Patsy was so consumed with curiosity he felt compelled to tell her something, but he'd been sworn to secrecy on the security angle.

'Look's like Sara's been a naughty girl. Picking up men in pubs. Philip found out, and did his nut,' he explained with forced levity.

'Doesn't surprise me,' she answered coolly.

'No? You knew about it?' He hoped the anxiety wasn't noticeable in his voice.

'The odd rumour, nothing more. Sara doesn't socialize much with other Navy wives; she's never come to terms with being wedded to one of you lot. And Philip's the last sort of man she should've married,' Patsy snorted.

'That's true.'

'He's an emotional cripple. Probably wears his uniform in bed!'

'Come on! He's not that bad.'

How often had he heard himself defending Philip?

'You watch out for Sara this afternoon. There's many a time she'd have got *you* into bed, given half the chance.'

'Rubbish!'

He thanked God she'd never guessed. It had happened just once – a mistake which had been safely buried until now.

'What does Norman Craig want you to do about it, anyway?'

'To find out what sort of mental state Philip was in when he left home. To make sure he's safe.'

'And a bit of marriage guidance, too?'

'Maybe. Might make a career of it when I leave the service,' he joked as he set off.

* * *

It was fifteen minutes' drive to where the Hitchens had their home, close by the river Yealm. The old, grey, limestone parsonage was a far larger house than they needed, but Sara had been determined they should buy it. With its large open fireplaces and an apple orchard, it was the English country home she'd never had as a child – the one she'd longed for as she accompanied her diplomat father from one strange place to another.

The village was pretty, with a river frontage and boats lying in the mud at low tide. The house was on the outskirts, and a little isolated. The Hitchens had few friends in the village; Sara was not good at the small talk of neighbourliness.

As he turned into her drive Andrew felt nervous, unsure how she would react to his visit. It was two years before that they'd had the briefest of affairs.

Philip had been at sea, and he at home on leave, just like now. Sara had rung him up one day when Patsy was at school and begged him to meet her, at a remote spot on the moors where they wouldn't be seen.

He was flattered and intrigued. Sara spelt danger, and it had excited him. Under normal circumstances, commonsense would have prevailed and he'd have said 'no', but her call had coincided with a blip in his own relationship with Patsy, a silly argument over money. She'd been furious with him because he'd bought a new car, instead of re-equipping their tatty kitchen. She'd hardly spoken to him for days.

Andrew had kept that rendezvous with Sara on the moors. Two days later they met again, on a warm afternoon in an Indian summer, and made love in the heather.

Sara was watching from a window as his car entered the drive.

'Andrew!' she greeted, as she opened the door. 'Surprise, surprise!'

Her pale lips smiled but her eyes were tense and suspicious.

'I was just passing . . .'

'No, you weren't! You end up in the river if you "just pass",' she retorted.

Suddenly she embraced him, and buried her face in his shoulder.

'I'm awfully glad you came,' she whispered. Her breath smelled of wine.

Then, just as suddenly, she broke away again and led him to the living room, where a south-facing French window looked across the orchard to the river.

'Why are you here? Is it official, this call? You know what's happened?'

'Yes. I'm sorry. It sounds a mess. Craig told me.'

'And he sent *you*?' She raised one eyebrow cynically. 'How thoughtful of him.'

'He knows I'm a friend. Of both of you,' Andrew hedged. 'He thought I might help. He's very concerned.'

She studied him for a moment and her waif-like face softened. Her thin mouth twisted mischievously.

'It's all your fault, you know. If you hadn't taken fright and we'd stayed lovers, I wouldn't have bothered with other men!'

'I'm not sure how to take that!'

'As a compliment, you oaf! Or a joke. I have to joke about it now and then. Otherwise, I just cry.'

Her face crumpled and she turned away.

She ran her fingers through her straight, chestnut hair.

'What're they saying about me?' she asked, turning to face him. 'Be honest!'

'I don't know who you mean by "they",' Andrew hedged again.

'Them. The Navy.'

'Well, if a sailor's wife runs around with other men while her old man's at sea – it's, er . . . it's frowned upon.'

She laughed at his restraint.

'And when one of the woman's lovers turns out to be a Russian spy,' she said, her voice rising in hysteria, 'then I guess the Navy shits itself!'

'You can say that again!'

'But . . . I didn't *know* he was a spy!'

She dropped onto a sofa and clamped her arms round her stomach as if it hurt her. She shook her head, her hazel eyes widening with disbelief.

'I can't believe all this.'

She reached for a packet of cigarettes.

'Inside, I don't feel I've done anything wrong. I can't accept that it's all *my* fault.'

She drew at the smoke as if it was oxygen, and coughed.

'Look, there's a bottle over there. Pour a glass and fill mine, would you?'

He handed her the drink and sank into a chair opposite.

'Why *did* Craig send you?'

'To try to find out exactly what's happened, I suppose.'

'*Why* it's happened. That's the question. Isn't anyone asking that? Some dreadful man from London – MI5 or something – came here reeking of cheap aftershave and B.O. Never even wondered *how* people get into this sort of mess. Don't *any* of you realize what it's like to have to share a husband with the fucking Navy?'

'Come on, Sara!' Andrew snapped. 'You knew what Philip did for a living when you married him.'

'I was only nineteen, Andrew! I'd only left school the year before!'

They both looked down at their drinks. Sara shivered.

'Sorry, there's no fire . . . It's chilly enough for one. We were hoping to put in central heating next year. But it's so expensive . . .'

'Don't worry. I'm not cold.'

There was an awkward pause. Andrew eased forward to the edge of the chair. There was one question he wanted answered above all others.

'Does Philip know? That you and I . . .'

Her eyes softened. She was remembering, as he was, the warm wind that had rustled the bracken around them as they'd lain on the moors that afternoon two years ago.

'No. He doesn't know,' she answered eventually.

She looked down at her hands. Was she lying? Andrew couldn't tell.

'How much do *you* know?' she asked suddenly. 'They told you about Gunnar, obviously?'

'Craig didn't say a name. Just that the man claimed to be Swedish.'

'That was feeble. I knew from the start he wasn't.'

'You knew? How?'

'I spent three years in Stockholm as a child, remember? I told you – I must've done. I told you *everything*,' she grimaced. 'No wonder you went off me so fast!'

Andrew laughed, but only for a moment. Sara pulled a crumpled handkerchief from her sleeve and blew her nose. Her voice had sounded bitter.

'Gunnar said he came from Stockholm. But he only knew the tourist places. He stopped talking about it once I said I'd actually lived there.'

'So, where *did* you think he was from?'

'I don't know. It didn't really matter at the time. We all pretend things. *I* told him I was divorced.'

'But didn't it occur to you that his interest in you might not be *entirely* romantic? A man with a false identity, you with a husband in the Navy?'

'Not at first, no. It did later . . .'

'Oh? Why was that?'

'Well, as we got to know each other, we kind of peeled away the layers of deception. It was a game, really. I told him I knew he wasn't what he said he was, and he told me he knew I had a husband in the Navy.'

'Did you ask him how he knew?'

'Just said he could tell. Knew the type. I'm not unique, you know,' she rounded on him. 'Navy towns are full of unhappy wives.'

'And what did you tell him?' Andrew prodded. 'Did you say, for example, that Philip drove a nuclear submarine?'

'Well, yes, I did. It's not actually secret, you know,' she retorted. 'But after that, Gunnar kept asking about Philip's work. So I began to think he could be spying for somebody.'

'What did you tell him about Philip?'

'Nothing, Andrew! Nothing of any significance, anyway,' she insisted, blowing a plume of smoke at him. 'I'm not stupid. At least, not in that way. Anyhow, I don't know anything about Philip's work, except that he spends six months of each year inside a black metal tube.'

'You *do* know things, Sara,' Andrew cautioned. 'Dates. When he goes away, when he comes back.'

'Anyone can stand on the Hoe and watch submarines go in and out of the dockyard.'

'But they can't tell one from another. They don't know if it's the same boat that goes out in the morning and comes back in the evening, or if it's two different boats.'

She shrugged and stubbed out the cigarette.

'But if you guessed he was some sort of spy, why didn't you tell someone? The police?'

She shook her head.

'How could I? What the hell would I have said? "Excuse me officer, but the man I'm having an affair with may be a Russian spy; could you investigate, but please don't tell my husband?" Don't be daft.'

She slipped off her shoes and pulled her knees up to her chin.

'I can see what you're thinking. And I don't blame you. You can't understand. You'll never be able to. But I'm going to try to explain it, just for my own sake.

'Being married to Philip – it's like doing something by halves. You know me; I always want everything, all at once, all the time,' she said ruefully. 'But Philip's only here half the year; when he is home, his thoughts are only half with me. I want him to pay *me* some attention!' she exploded. 'To do something with *me* that's exciting, or unpredictable. And when he doesn't, I find myself longing for him to go away again.

'And yet I do love him – sort of. He can't help the way he is, and he *is* reliable, honest. . . .

'But that's not enough. I'm left feeling so *empty*. And when Simon went away to boarding school, that was it. I couldn't cope with it any more. So I found a way. A way of staying married to Philip, keeping a home for Simon, and of filling the emptiness.

'There were . . . other men . . . after you, and before Gunnar. Most of them were nice, kind while it lasted, not interested in a long-term commitment. It was manageable, you see? Everything under control. Philip didn't know. I wasn't hurting anybody – except myself occasionally.

'So, you see, even though I had suspicions about Gunnar, I couldn't tell anybody. The whole thing would have come crashing down . . .'

'Which is exactly what's happened now,' Andrew said drily.

Sara took his words as a reproach. Her mouth turned down and her face hardened.

'But you can't accept it – the way I feel – because you've got a wife who *does* manage, who divides herself up, one bit for you when you're there, another for her job, and another for the children. Her life's like a time-share,' she concluded bitterly.

'Okay. Some women aren't cut out to be married to sailors,' he conceded. 'And you're one of them. But, for the moment, it's academic. You're in trouble; Philip's in trouble; the Navy's in trouble. So let's not think about the reasons why it's happened; let's just try and sort it out.'

She threw her head back, the sinews of her neck taut with despair.

'I've killed him, Andrew . . .' she whispered, eyes beginning to brim with tears.

He froze.

'If you'd seen his face . . .'

She clamped a hand over her mouth to prevent herself crying. Her bravado had suddenly evaporated.

'It was terrible when he found out. He went to pieces . . . I didn't know he could be like that . . . All that emotion – it'd been there all the time. And I never knew . . .'

'What d'you mean, you've killed him?' asked Andrew, shaken.

'Inside,' she sniffed, tears running down her face. She made no attempt to brush them away. 'He *trusted* me . . . ,' she whispered.

Andrew looked away awkwardly and ran his fingers through his hair. *He trusted me too*, he thought to himself.

Sara was a pitiful figure, her shoulders shaking with sobs. But it was Philip Andrew had most need to be concerned about. He pulled a clean handkerchief from his pocket and passed it to her.

'There are some details . . . , things I need to know,' he coaxed. She dried her eyes and blew her nose.

'When did all this happen, exactly? By the time the security people got wind of things, you'd already had the bust-up with Philip and he'd gone to sea. Is that right?'

'Yes,' she sighed. 'Everything fell apart about a week ago.'

She wiped her remaining tears with her fingers, leaving streaks on her face.

'Philip found out first about another man, someone called Reg Terry. I'd got very close to Reg and let him come here at weekends sometimes, when Simon was home from school. Stupid of me. Last weekend Philip and Simon went shopping in Plymouth, and they just bumped into Reg. Simon greeted him like a long-lost friend, and suddenly Philip began to click. Next day, he started asking questions. He just went on and on, until I got so angry I just told him everything and said it was all his fault.'

'You told him *everything*?'

'Almost everything,' she corrected herself, carefully.

Andrew's unease grew.

'What exactly did you tell him about Gunnar?'

'I told him my present lover was a Russian spy,' she whispered, stroking back some hair that had stuck to her moist cheek.

It had been at that point that Philip's temper had finally snapped.

He'd lashed blindly at her, punching her with his fists. The high-necked pullover she now wore concealed several purple and yellow bruises.

'For God's sake! You told him that? What did he say?'

'He went berserk. Knocked me round the bedroom. Then he stopped. For a time he didn't say anything. Just stared out of the window. Then he told me to try to remember everything I'd ever said to Gunnar about him, about the Navy, about our family. As I told you before, there wasn't much . . .'

Her voice tailed away.

Suddenly an alarming question occurred to Andrew. If Philip knew about the spy, why hadn't he said anything to the police, or to Captain Craig at the submarine base?

'Did Philip say anything to you about going to the police?'

'No. He didn't want anyone to know about *my shame*, as he called it. Kept asking me which of our friends knew. I said I hadn't told anyone. That was true.'

'But did he say he was going to do something about Gunnar? There must've been something. He wouldn't have left it. Not if he really believed Gunnar was a spy.'

Andrew put down his glass and leaned forward, hands clasped, elbows on his knees. Sara was holding back further tears. Her lip trembled. She was scared.

'I don't know what he was going to do. He made me swear I'd end it with Gunnar. That's what I was doing when the police saw us in the restaurant. But Philip hardly spoke to me again. He behaved like a robot. And on Wednesday morning he went to the boat.'

'Did he say anything to you about the patrol he was going on?'

'Nothing. He never did.'

'No mention of where he was going?'

'Heavens, no!'

Inwardly Andrew sighed with relief. Craig's prime security worry seemed to be unfounded.

'Why do you ask? Where *is* he going?'

Her voice sounded alarmed.

'I don't know,' he answered stonily.

She stared into his eyes, trying to read his thoughts.

He stared back, trying to imagine the hell Philip must've gone through, discovering what sort of wife Sara had been to him.

'He *had* decided to do something about Gunnar.'

Her voice cut through the silence that had descended on the room.

'What d'you mean?'

'I don't know, exactly.'

She rubbed her forehead, trying to order her thoughts.

'When he left, it was as if he'd taken some monumental

decision. He looked . . . ,' she fumbled for the words, 'grim, but in some way – satisfied. It's the only way I can describe it.'

'I'm not with you. What do you mean?'

'As if he'd decided on some sort of revenge, or thought of some way of getting even with Gunnar, or the KGB or whoever sent him here.'

'What sort of revenge?'

'I don't know. He'll find a way. Philip hates Russians, you know. He'll do something. I don't know what. Fire a missile at Moscow? Is that possible?'

She'd meant it as irony, but started when she saw the shock on Andrew's face.

'He couldn't! It's the wrong sort of boat, isn't it?' she gasped. 'What *could* he do to them, Andrew?'

'I shudder to think.'

Two minutes later Andrew drove away, his mind in turmoil. He hardly noticed the shabby Ford Escort parked in a gateway fifty yards up the road from the Hitchens' home.

Behind the wheel a dark-haired man in his twenties appeared to be taking a nap.

Andrew put his foot down and headed for the naval base. Philip Hitchens had to be got off the *Truculent*, and fast.

* * *

HMS Truculent was in her element. By Saturday afternoon her huge black hull was sliding silently through dark waters west of the Hebrides where the Atlantic is over two thousand metres deep.

Cruising north at eighteen knots, *Truculent* had stayed a hundred metres down for nearly twenty-four hours. Above and below, water layers of different temperature created acoustic barriers. The submarine moved in a 'shadow zone' where the risk of being detected by surface ships was minimal. That depth was also good for detecting other submarines. With her sensitive towed sonar restored to working order, *Truculent* could hear other boats over a hundred miles away if conditions were right.

The executive officer, Lieutenant Commander Tim Pike, had completed his rounds, looking for gripes to deal with before they became a problem or a danger. There'd been few. *Truculent* was a well-run submarine.

The control room watches lasted six hours, the tactics officer (TASO) and the navigator (NO) alternating as watch leaders.

Pike had little to do at that stage of the patrol, with the sea around them so deep and so empty.

He came into the zone for promotion in a month and was using his spare time for studying. He'd already passed the course to command a submarine, aptly named 'The Perisher'; if you fail it you have to leave the Submarine Service for good.

He'd commanded a diesel sub for two years after that, but was now lining himself up to take charge of an SSN.

'Day-dreaming again, Tim?'

The weapon engineer, Lieutenant Commander Paul Spriggs, nudged his arm.

'Yeah. Wondering what's in store for us.'

'This patrol, you mean? The captain's special orders. Hasn't he briefed you yet?'

'Nope. Not yet. I expect he will soon.'

'On the other hand . . .'

'He may not.'

'Exactly. Something's up with him. You've noticed how preoccupied he is. Hardly speaks at meals. Only smiles at my jokes out of politeness.'

'We all do that, Paul.'

'Oh, really? How extremely depressing.'

His chubby face looked genuinely perplexed. He pushed back the dark hair that fell across his forehead.

'But you're right,' Pike agreed. 'He doesn't seem to be with us on this trip. I might try to draw him out later. We've got a communications slot coming up in fifteen minutes. Perhaps he'll get a "family-gram" that'll cheer him up.'

'Be safer to write him one yourself!'

Tim Pike pulled a long face and crossed the cramped

control room to the navigation table. Three paces and he was there.

'Where are we, Nick?' he asked the navigator who was duty watch leader.

'Here, to be exact.'

The young lieutenant pointed to a cross on the continuous pencil line he'd drawn on the chart.

'The SINS puts us northeast of Rockall and west of the Vidal Bank. In about an hour we should alter course to zero-four-zero to keep us in the deep water east of Rosemary Bank.'

'We'll need a little dog-leg for a communications slot before that. Almost due east? What do you think?'

The navigator pulled out a chart with a different scale, showing their position in relation to the British Isles. To listen to the signals from CINCFLEET at Northwood, they used a long wire antenna that floated just below the surface so as not to reveal themselves to watching radar. To receive signals they had to align the antenna by pointing it towards the transmitter in the north of England.

'Almost exactly one-one-zero. Done this before, sir?'

'Once or twice. I expect you'd like an Omega fix, too?'

'Certainly would. What's the time of the comms slot?'

'18:00 to 18:30. We'll be at four knots and sixty metres.'

'Right.'

Cavendish plotted the details. The wire would also pick up low-frequency signals from Omega coastal navigation beacons. He'd get a position fix to within a mile, enough to confirm the inertial navigation system hadn't drifted. For a more accurate fix they'd need to poke a periscope or satellite receiver above the water, and risk revealing their presence.

Pike slipped out of the control room and rapped gently on the door frame of the captain's cabin. A curtain hung in the doorway, and Pike heard a hurried scuffling behind it.

'Yes?'

He pushed aside the curtain. Commander Hitchens was at his desk.

'Good evening, sir. We're proceeding as planned in

deep water at eighteen knots. We have a broadcast we're scheduled to monitor in about thirty minutes. With your permission, sir, I'd like to reduce speed to four knots, bring her up to sixty metres and deploy the floating wire.'

'Any other submarine activity?'

'Nothing at all, sir. We'll check the surface picture before we deploy the wire.'

'Very good. Carry on, Tim.'

'Er, one other thing, sir . . .'

'Yes, what is it?'

'I was wondering if sometime this evening might be an appropriate moment to discuss our mission profile.'

Hitchens fixed Pike with his unnervingly blue eyes.

'Sorry. Not yet. I'll brief when the time's right.

'From Wednesday we're dropping out of the exercise. Special op. I'll tell *you* that much, but it's not for general knowledge yet. This one really is very sensitive. You'll have to trust me.'

'Oh. Right. Okay then, sir; I'll carry on if I may.'

'Yes, please. And make the pipe to the ship's company, will you?'

'I will, sir.'

Pike returned thoughtfully to the control room. There was nothing he could put his finger on, but something wasn't right with his captain.

Philip closed his eyes and held his breath.

Damn it! Pike's request had caught him by surprise. He should've been ready for him, and he wasn't.

He ran through their brief conversation. It had been okay. He'd handled it. But he had to be prepared for next time, have an answer for their questions.

He expelled the air from his lungs.

Philip needed the men under his command. He was driving a nuclear-powered, hunter-killer submarine – one of the most deadly weapons-systems in the world. Those bastard Soviets would soon be finding out just how deadly, he told himself. But he couldn't operate it on his own. Co-operation and obedience from men like Pike and Spriggs would be vital if his mission was to succeed.

Philip knew what he had to do. That much was clear. How to manage it, however, was a different matter. There was still time to think the details through. Until Wednesday he'd follow the exercise brief. After that, he'd be his own master.

The loudspeaker clicked. Pike's voice boomed forth authoritatively.

The 'pipe' was heard on loudspeakers throughout the submarine. The broadcast to update the crew was made at least twice a day, a communication essential to team spirit on board.

The first lieutenant spoke for two minutes, telling the 130 men on board of the day's sonar contacts. They'd included a school of whales.

He talked of the upcoming communications slot, knowing some of the crew would be expecting the forty-word 'family-grams' that kept them in touch with their homes. He ended by reading the menu for the evening meal.

The next pipe – that'd be the time, Philip decided. Start to prepare them for what was to come. Little by little. Step by step.

His eyes strayed to the photograph he'd doggedly kept on his desk, to preserve his mask of normality.

He looked at her image and his guts turned inside out again. He closed his eyes tightly. Would he ever be able to look at Sara's picture without wanting to kill her?

She'd been everything he'd dreamed of when they'd met fifteen years earlier. He'd been serving on a *Swiftsure* class submarine at the time, circling the globe as part of a military sales drive. They'd gone ashore in Hong Kong, to a reception at the British High Commission. Their host had been accompanied by his stunningly pretty daughter – Sara. He'd fallen in love with her instantly.

Sara had glowed that evening; as they circulated socially, her eyes reached across the room to him like a lighthouse beam. Excitement had almost choked him. Until then, apart from brief relationships, the only woman in Philip's life had been his own straitlaced mother. Sara was vivacious, sensual and provocative; if his mother had ever had such qualities, she'd successfully repressed them after the trauma of her husband's disappearance. In Hong Kong he sensed he'd finally met a woman with the power to cut through his shell of inhibition, and free him from the dour restraint of his upbringing.

His mother had tried to prevent their marriage. Nineteen was far too young for a girl to marry, she'd declared. He'd ignored her, terrified that if he didn't bind Sara to him quickly he'd lose her to someone else.

Now he'd lost her anyway.

They'd been immensely happy together for their first two years. He'd had a shore-based job in Scotland, and the sense of personal liberation he'd hoped for became a reality.

Then he'd been given a commission at sea. Sara had been devastated by the separation and had applied intense emotional pressure on him to change his job. Philip had retreated into his shell, as he had learned to do as a youth when pressured by his mother.

Her face smiled at him from the frame. Deceptive, cruelly deceptive. Laughing eyes. Laughing at him? Mocking him?

In the control room, Pike hung the microphone back on its hook and bowed theatrically to the navigator.

'All yours, Pilot!'

Cavendish raised an eyebrow at the mock courtesy, then turned to the helm.

'Ten up, planesman. Keep sixty metres. Revolutions for four knots.'

The rating at the controls pulled back on the control-stick and watched the gauge. The deck began to tilt as the hydroplanes lifted the nose of the submarine. Pike grasped one of the overhead cable-ducts to steady himself.

'Sound room. I want a check for surface contacts!' Cavendish called.

'*Aye, aye, sir!*'

HMS Truculent came up fast from the depths, passing through the thermocline which had refracted their faint sound downwards, keeping them hidden from listeners on the surface. Her speed dropped from eighteen knots to four, at which it was safe to trail the wire antenna without breaking it.

'Level at sixty metres, sir,' the helmsman called.

'Deploy the wire.'

On the outside of the fin a small aperture appeared, and the VLF antenna began to unreel. Black plastic strips trailed from the wire to disguise it as seaweed.

In the sonar compartment the tattooed hands of the ratings tuned their acoustic processors to the new sounds of surface ships, or 'skimmers', as they were known.

Sensors outside the hull analysed water temperature and salinity and fed the data into a computer which predicted the refracted paths that the sounds would follow through the water.

'Cavitation on port bow, chief!' shouted one of the junior sonar ratings. Chief Petty Officer Hicks looked over his shoulder at the VDU, and confirmed it.

On the green 'waterfall' display, low frequency 'spikes' of sound detected by the bow sonar showed as overlapping vertical stripes. Hicks counted them.

'Two shafts. Six blades. That's *Illustrious*,' he announced with confidence. The last intelligence report had told them the British aircraft carrier was in the area.

'Range and bearing?'

The rating keyed in additional data from the towed array. Bearings from the two sonars were triangulated by computer.

'Range, 32.4 miles, bearing 039, Chief.'

The CPO pressed a button which transferred the data to the Action Information panel in the control room. There the carrier appeared on the tactical display as a triangle – a friendly target.

'*What about her escorts*?' demanded the officer-of-the-watch through the intercom.

Eyes scanned the screens and ears strained at headphones.

'Nothing else registered, sir,' came the eventual reply from the CPO.

Sound in water seldom travels in straight lines. *HMS Illustrious* had at least two frigates keeping her company, but *Truculent* couldn't hear them. The sound waves from the warships curved downwards away from the surface, then curved up again many miles distant, to a so-called 'convergence zone'. *Truculent* was in just such a zone for the carrier's noise signature to reach her, but not yet in one for the frigates.

Hicks stood up, desperate to stretch his legs. He stepped into the control room, leaving the sonar ratings to plot the remaining contacts – distant trawlers fishing the edge of the continental shelf around Scotland.

He crossed to the Action Information plot, and yawned as he watched it begin to fill with contacts from the sound room.

'Keeping you up, are we, Hicks?' Pike quipped.

'Off watch in an hour, sir. Boring day! Once we'd finally sorted out the 2026, there's been sod-all to do.'

'Did you report that to the captain? He wanted to know.'

'Yes, sir. Have no fear.'

Pike looked at his watch. Time for the broadcast. He stepped into the communications office as Cavendish ordered the final manœuvre to align the boat to receive signals.

'Planesman, steer one-one-zero, revolutions for four knots!'

At three sites inside Britain, enormous Very Low Frequency transmitter arrays, masquerading as civilian wireless stations, broadcast a constant stream of information for submerged submarines. Weather and intelligence reports are transmitted as routine, on an hourly cycle, backed up at fixed times with specific messages for individual submarines.

The communications room was tightly controlled. Only those with top security clearance could enter the tiny cabin next to the control room. From floor to ceiling, racks of equipment left little space for the signals officer and radio operator.

The young, black-haired sub-lieutenant in charge ran his own plastic security card through a slot on the cipher machine, then punched out a personal code number on a numeric key-pad. Nearly all signals traffic was in code, but the laborious task of enciphering and deciphering was done electronically.

The teleprinter began to chatter. The radio operator leaned over to check that the transmission wasn't garbled.

'Faroes, force ten,' he read. 'Grey-Funnel Line'll be chuckin' up!'

'You can feel it down here,' Pike pointed out as the submarine heaved gently with the surface swell sixty metres above them.

'Glad you volunteered for submarines?' Sub-Lieutenant Hugo Smallbone grinned, knowing full well the torrent of complaint his remark would release.

'Didn't fuckin' volunteer for *submarines*! Told to come here, wasn't I? The one soddin' boat in the Navy that's not supposed to communicate, and I get the job of radio operator!'

'At least you're not chucking up!'

'Prefer that to bein' down here. The money's what keeps me in this branch.'

The sub-lieutenant smiled patronizingly. He stood up to tear the first sheet from the printer.

ROUTINE 191800Z OCT
INT SITREP AT 1730Z
RO6 F229 F84 59.20N 008.50W
S 37 W HEBRIDES

'So that's where they think we are,' commented Smallbone at the reference to S 37 which was *HMS Truculent*.

R06 was *Illustrious*, the F numbers her frigate escorts. The position given was timed for half an hour earlier.

A string of chart references followed. They marked the last known positions of two Soviet *Victor* class nuclear attack submarines, and three AGIs – Soviet intelligence-gathering trawlers.

The teleprinter bell rang twice.

'Ah! Something for us,' remarked Pike.

He peered more closely at the dot matrix print tapping out across the page.

IMMEDIATE. S 37. SECRET. COMMANDING OFFI-

CER'S EYES ONLY.
CONFIRM RECEIPT BY SSIX AT 2000Z. FOSM.
INSERT COMMANDERS KEYCARD FOR MESSAGE.

'Here you are, Bennett. Got some work for you. Satcom at twenty hundred.'

'P'rhaps they've found me another job . . .'

'No chance!'

The sub-lieutenant tore the sheet from the teleprinter, placed the top copy on a clipboard and took the carbon. As he left the wireless room he added, 'Look smart. I'm getting the captain.'

'A satcom will *not* be popular,' Pike frowned. 'We're just about in range of the "*Bears*" here.'

'*Bear*' was NATO's code name for the big Soviet *TU–95* long-range maritime reconnaissance bombers which patrol the Norwegian Sea to track NATO warships. With Exercise Ocean Guardian underway, they'd be mounting extra missions. Raising a satcom mast above the surface could get *Truculent* spotted by the *Bear*'s radar.

Hugo Smallbone was in awe of Commander Hitchens. A rather immature twenty-one-year-old, he found almost anyone over the age of thirty intimidating. He nearly collided with Hitchens as the captain hurried from his cabin.

'That for me?' Hitchens asked, indicating the signal in Hugo's hand.

'Sir. It's just come in.'

He handed it over and watched Hitchens' face, expecting annoyance. But the expression in Hitchens' eyes was one he'd never seen there before. Panic.

'Thank you, Hugo,' Hitchens whispered, controlling himself quickly. Then he spun on his heel and went back into his cabin. 'Be right with you,' he muttered over his shoulder.

The sub-lieutenant hovered in the corridor. He could hear the soft clicks of the combination lock on the captain's safe, as Hitchens opened it to collect his security card.

'Still here?' Hitchens remarked, surprised to find Hugo hadn't moved.

'Let's get on with it,' he continued briskly, leading the way to the wireless room. 'Bloody nuisance, this need to transmit. Last thing we want.'

'That's what the first lieutenant said, sir . . .'

'What? You've told him about this signal? What the hell do you mean by it?'

'He was in the wireless room, sir . . .'

Hitchens thrust the sheet of signal paper under Smallbone's nose.

'Can't you read, boy? COMMANDING OFFICER'S EYES ONLY. Don't you know what that means? No one's to know about this signal except me!'

'Awfully sorry, sir . . .'

'You'd better watch your step, son.'

Smallbone flushed purple. He felt hurt and indignant. The captain was talking nonsense. The confidentiality applied to the message they had yet to decode, not to the preamble requesting confirmation of receipt.

In the wireless room, Hitchens slid his keycard into the deciphering machine, then tapped out his personal code on the numeric key-pad.

'I'd like you all outside,' he ordered as the teleprinter began its work.

Pike returned to the control room. Able Seaman Bennett glanced at the sub-lieutenant as they moved to the passageway; sensing the thunderous atmosphere, he said nothing.

The printer stopped. Philip ripped off the paper, including the self-carbonizing second sheet. He folded the pages into a small square that fitted his trouser pocket and pushed past the radio operators, heading back to his cabin.

'Whew!'

Hugo Smallbone spun back into the wireless room, before the control room watch could notice his beetroot face.

The teleprinter was chattering again. Messages for crew members. He busied himself with the intelligence reports.

When he calmed down he'd take them to the watchkeeper, so the charts could be updated.

Philip placed the signal on his desk.

COMMANDER HITCHENS.
DUE YOUR UNFORTUNATE DOMESTIC SITUATION, IMPERATIVE YOU TRANSFER TO SHORE. BRIEFING TEMPORARY REPLACEMENT COMMANDER TO CONTINUE
TRUCULENT'S PATROL.
SEA KING WILL RENDEZVOUS WITH YOU AT 1600Z. SUNDAY 20TH. POSITION N58.50 W06.30.
PLSE CONFIRM BY SSIX 2000Z TODAY.
FLAG OFFICER SUBMARINES.

They knew, despite Sara's promise to tell no one. The bitch! She'd betrayed him again!

What had she told them? He re-read the signal.

'Unfortunate domestic situation'. They weren't giving much away back at Northwood.

Had she told them about the Soviets or just the personal bits? In either case they all knew the worst part, knew how she'd humiliated him.

But why? Had she sensed what he intended to do? Were they trying to stop him?

Who would she have spoken to? Craig probably. There was no one else she knew. Craig would have passed it up the line to CINCFLEET.

The questions echoed in his head like prayers in a cathedral. There was one which came back from the recesses of his mind where he'd banished it. Why, *why* had she done what she'd done? What was it he'd failed to give her that she needed?

Lonely. She'd told him she felt lonely . . .

That wasn't enough. Other men's wives were lonely, but they didn't parade themselves like whores in public places? Didn't soil their bodies with other men's – stuff.

The trembling started again. An uncontrollable shaking that engulfed him whenever his mind re-ran those desperate shouting-matches with Sara, those moments of awful revelation.

He'd raged at her and she'd fought back with a taunt – the name of a man she claimed had been the first of her lovers. Someone he'd known closely for twenty years. A name that would hurt him more deeply than any other.

He'd laughed at her – called her a liar.

Andrew her lover? Not possible. They'd trained together, served together on their first commission as sub-lieutenants, stayed friends ever since. Andrew was Simon's godfather, for heaven's sake! The idea was ludicrous. Wasn't it?

There'd been times in the past week when Philip had wept like a child. One moment he longed for someone to confide in, the next that no one should ever know.

He stood up angrily now. He had to snap out of it, put those nagging questions out of his mind, concentrate on the matter in hand.

The signal – he had to respond to it.

Tim Pike gave orders for the VLF antenna to be recovered into the fin. Their time-slot for monitoring the broadcast was over.

'Steer course zero-two-five. Ten down, keep two-hundred metres,' Cavendish instructed. 'Keep revolutions for ten knots. Increase to eighteen when the antenna's wound in.'

That could take half-an-hour.

A leading seaman was doing duty at the chart table. Two strides and Pike stood beside him. Two strides could get you anywhere in the control room.

'Have you plotted the data from the int. brief?' Pike asked.

'Yessir. The closest *Victor* is here, sir.'

He pointed to a box drawn some seventy miles south of them.

'He'll be listening for the *Polaris* boats coming out of Faslane. Then there's another *Victor* 'bout four hundred miles northeast. On the other side of the Faroes-Shetland gap. A couple of AGIs fifty and seventy-five miles away, and that's about it.'

'I see. So we're well out of range of their radar. Aircraft

are the worry. And we don't know where *they* are. My guess is they'll be keeping track of the skimmers. The nearest to us is *Illustrious*, isn't it?'

''Sright, sir. Just about here.'

He pointed to a circle near the Faroes.

'He'll be down to ten knots with the gale up there,' Pike commented, checking the weather report. 'We'll start catching him up if we don't watch it.'

'He's still miles away, sir.'

'Yes, but I'm thinking of the Bears. They'll be searching a good hundred miles all round *Illustrious*, so we'll need to keep our distance. I'm going to slow down a bit.'

He spun on his heel to face the helm and found himself face to face with Cavendish.

'Nick, I'm worried about Bears . . .'

He explained the problem. The navigator nodded.

'Keep revolutions for ten knots!' he instructed.

'Why are we so slow?' Philip had entered the control room, his face betraying no sign of his private agony.

Pike took him to the chart table to explain his plan.

'I've been thinking about the satcom, sir. In an hour we'll be here.' He prodded the chart with a finger, pointing out the positions of the Soviet boats and their own. 'Should be the best place to avoid being spotted when we transmit.'

'What's the sea state?'

'Force six. Gusting seven . . .'

'Going to be uncomfortable. Have to get the mast high to avoid the waves breaking over it.'

'Gets worse further north.'

'Mmmm. We'll give it a try, then. I'm about to draft the signal. Send the wireless officer to my cabin to collect it in ten minutes, will you? The message will be brief. Very brief. And Tim –'

Hitchens pulled his first lieutenant to one side, out of earshot of the others.

'That signal that came in – we've got new orders. Top secret. The most sensitive operation I've ever known. I can hardly believe what they're telling us to do.'

'Oh?'

'I'll brief you as soon as I can, but it may be a few days yet. I'll have to tell the crew something soon; thought I'd do it tomorrow, on the pipe. Have to keep it vague, but they'll need to know we're on a special op.'

'Will you be giving new course instructions, sir?'

'Stays the same for the moment. As planned. Different tactics, though. CINCFLEET says the Yanks are not to know what we're doing. Got to get across the SOSUS array without them hearing us.'

That wouldn't be easy; the hydrophones on the seabed between the Faroes and Shetlands were remarkably sensitive. The American controllers of SOSUS would be expecting them too, and would listen out for them.

'One other thing, Tim. Listening to the signals traffic – it'll be a bit irregular from now on. We'll be going fast, so no trailing of the wire. We'll use the satcom mast when possible, but because of the sensitivity of the stuff coming in, I can't have anyone but myself seeing the signals traffic from now on. I'll have to clear the wireless room when the mast's up. Commanding officer's eyes only, you see.'

'Is that really necessary, sir?'

'Yes, it bloody well is! I wouldn't have said so otherwise! I'll distribute whatever I can, of course. Intelligence, met., news reports. But it may not be much. That's all.'

Hitchens turned on his heel and left the control room.

Pike's jaw dropped.

'Bloody hell!' he breathed.

CHAPTER THREE

Sunday 20th October.

Sunday morning brought relief to the small group of media personnel on board the US aircraft carrier *Dwight D. Eisenhower*. The gale had subsided in the small hours; they'd had no idea a ship of 90,000 tons could roll so much. The three members of the television crew pooling pictures for the four American networks had been seasick to a man.

The *Eisenhower* was about three hundred miles south of Iceland, heading northeast, the flagship for the eighteen American warships taking part in Exercise Ocean Guardian.

The six members of the media pool had been flown onto the ship from Reykjavik the previous evening, smacking down onto the carrier deck in a Grumman Greyhound Carrier-Onboard-Delivery (COD) aircraft. For all the journalists it was their first visit to a big carrier and the COD flight the most hair-raising journey they'd ever made.

Tightly strapped in to rearward-facing seats, the passengers had felt genuine terror as the almost windowless twin-turboprop aircraft was buffeted by gale force winds and manoeuvred sharply to line up with the bucking deck. Even the aircrew had looked scared; they knew what they were supposed to do if the 'controlled crash' of a landing went bad and the plane slipped from the deck into the sea, but they also knew the chances of surviving such an accident were slim.

One of the journalists had thrown up as soon as his feet touched the carrier deck, and the usual briefing on arrival had been postponed.

Now the six were seated in the half-darkness of the '3

deck' briefing room, listening to the public information officer, Commander Polk. Vu-foils illustrated his talk.

'Good-day, gentlemen. Hope you're feeling okay now. I just want to tell you something about Exercise Ocean Guardian, so's you get the big picture. The starting point for the game is this: a huge world power, which has no name but whose national language is Russian, is assumed to have threatened NATO – Norway in particular. Enemy surface ships and submarines are breaking out from their bases on the Kola peninsular. We have to do something about it. We've got eleven NATO navies with 122 vessels taking part, which makes it the biggest we've ever done.

'Now, we have two jobs to do. The first is to ensure we can control the sea line of communication – SLOC for short. The SLOC is the route across the Atlantic along which American reinforcements would be shipped if Europe were threatened by the Warsaw Pact.

'Right now, warships from the US and from European countries including Spain and Portugal are securing the SLOC for convoys – down here.'

Commander Polk pointed rapidly from the Southwest Approaches down to Gibraltar, and westwards across the Atlantic.

'What you are on board today, gentlemen, is the flagship of Striking Fleet Atlantic. The task for this group is to take control of the sea and the air, right up to the Arctic Circle. The *Eisenhower* is now here, just south of Iceland. And we're headed here.'

The journalists' gaze was directed at the most northerly tip of Norway.

'What we're doing this year is something new. We're taking this little tub, 90,000 tons of her, right up to longitude 24 degrees East. Now that's in the Barents Sea, and the Soviets like to think of those waters as their own.

'Gentlemen, the second main purpose of this exercise is to show the Russians and ourselves that we have the power and the motivation to get right up into the Arctic and stop them, if they try it on.

'We've got three jobs to do; to back up land-based airpower with our own combat planes in order to defend north Norway; to locate and destroy enemy surface ships and submarines trying to take over the Norwegian Sea; and to get their missile subs before they can scoot under the ice, and nuke our families back home.'

The correspondent for the TV networks raised his hand to interrupt.

'Aren't you gonna be a pretty big target for the Soviets to hit, if you go right into the Barents?'

'Sure. That's why in past exercises we've not gone further north than Westfjord.'

His pointer landed on the Lofoten Islands some four hundred miles south of the northern tip of Norway.

'And if this exercise was for real, we sure as hell wouldn't put a carrier up there until the air and sea threat had been minimized.

He turned back to the vu-foil map.

'There are two main threats. Aircraft we look after ourselves; submarines – we have a British Royal Navy Anti-Submarine-Warfare force ahead of us, moving north in the Norwegian Sea. The *HMS Illustrious* Task Group provides the first ASW screen; we provide the second.'

He looked at his watch. They had to get moving. He could give them more later. First he had to brief them for the photo-opportunity which had presented itself that morning.

Admiral Vernon Kritz was proud of his ship, and proud of the role it played in containing the Communist menace. He was glad to have the media on board, so they could tell the world just how good his ship was. But this morning something extraordinary had happened that had made him doubly pleased.

Without their realizing it, he would deploy the media like one of his own weapon systems. What they would show on breakfast television back home was going to make those soft-heads on Capitol Hill choke on their granola. 'It's time to trust the Russians' was their cry. The hell it was!

The Admiral had summoned his PIO, while the media group were being given their breakfast, and told him what the photo-reconnaissance aircraft had spotted at first light. When he'd seen the pictures of the Soviet freighter and its deck cargo, the commander had blasphemed in astonishment, then apologized hastily, conscious that the Admiral was a deeply religious man.

'Don't tell 'em exactly what they're gonna see,' Admiral Kritz had cautioned. 'Let 'em think they're getting the first close-ups *anyone's* seen. They'll get a kick outta that!'

All the print journalists and stills photographers were bundled aboard one SH-3 Sea King helicopter, the television team aboard another. The outing was described as a 'photo-opportunity' to get aerial shots of the *Eisenhower* and of a Soviet ship that was passing them in the opposite direction about ten miles away.

'It's a merchantman,' the PIO commander explained. 'But we treat all Soviet ships as hostile. Even if they're not warships, they're sure as hell spying on us.'

The helicopters took off and flew in tandem, one hundred yards apart.

The television correspondent wore an intercom headset so he could tell the pilot of his cameraman's requirements. Their first request was for a couple of circuits of the *Eisenhower*.

Satisfied they'd shot the carrier from every conceivable angle, the helicopter banked away to the south to fly low and fast towards the Soviet freighter's position, which had been radioed to the helicopter from a Hawkeye radar plane circling overhead.

'She's some sort of container ship, 'bout twenty thousand tons, called the *Rostov*. We believe she's headed for Cuba, but don't quote me . . .' the commander shouted above the grinding whine of the helicopter's machinery.

'How do you know that's where she's going?' the correspondent bellowed back.

The commander put his finger to his lips conspiratorially.

'Not allowed to tell!'

The cameraman had been sitting with his legs out of the open side-door while filming, a safety harness buckled round his chest attached at the other end to a hook on the helicopter's roof. But the wind was bitterly cold, and the crew-chief closed the door again for the transit to the next location.

There was little room inside. This was an anti-submarine machine, packed with sonar screens, control panels, and a massive winch for dunking the heavy sonar transducer in and out of the sea. There was a nauseating reek of hot oil.

'Okay . . . We got the Sov on the nose,' the pilot's voice drawled over the intercom. 'We're comin' up astern. We'll pass left of her then turn right across her bows, and come back the other side. Okay?'

'That'll be just great,' the correspondent answered, tapping his cameraman on the shoulder to be ready.

The crew chief slid back the big square door and the cold blast of air took their breath away. The tail of the Sea King sank as the pilot slowed to fifty knots. The grey-green sea surged a hundred feet below, the wind whipping white streams of spray from the wave caps.

To their left the black hull and cream superstructure of the freighter came into view. The correspondent pointed at it unnecessarily; the cameraman was already filming. On the funnel a red band bore the hammer and sickle. They'd need a close-up of that; the correspondent saw the cameraman's fingers press the zoom button. Good boy! He didn't need to be told.

Rusting red and orange containers were stacked on the outer edges of the deck, forming a corral with a space at the centre. There was something stored there. Fin-like objects, cocooned in pale fabric.

The helicopter reached the bows of the freighter and turned across them, giving the cameraman a long, continuous shot, showing the ship from 360 degrees.

'See that stuff in the middle there?' the correspondent's voice crackled in the throat microphone. 'Can't see what it is. Can you?'

'Look like wings to me,' the pilot answered.

'Like what?'

'Wings. Aircraft wings. Could be MiGs. With the rest of the planes in the boxes.'

'Shit man! We gotta get a closer look at that!'

'I can go round again if you want, but I can't get closer'n two hundred and fifty feet. Otherwise the big man has me against the wall for harassing the Russians!'

'Let's try it!'

The correspondent put his lips close to the cameraman's ear and told him to focus on the cargo in the middle of the deck. A raised thumb signalled he'd understood.

They repeated the circuit but came no closer; the shape of the cargo still could not be defined. The cameraman shook his head and shouted into the correspondent's ear, 'Get him over the top!'

The journalist nodded.

'Look, we got a problem,' he reasoned to the pilot. 'We have to be able to look right down on the deck from overhead . . .'

'No way, bud!'

'Look, that ship's going to Cuba! If she's carrying warplanes, that could threaten the US of A! That's something the American people should know about!'

'You want to get me thrown out the Navy?'

The correspondent turned to the PIO who was not wearing a communications set and was unaware of what had been said.

'Commander, you've got to help us . . .'

Shouting slowly, word by word, he explained their need to be certain of the Russian cargo. The commander pursed his lips and shrugged. He took the headset and began to talk to the pilot.

Looking through the open doorway they could see some of the *Rostov*'s officers gathered on the bridge wing looking up at them with binoculars. One had a camera and was taking photographs.

The commander grabbed the journalist's arm.

'Okay. You got your shot,' he shouted hoarsely into his ear.

The correspondent clamped the headset back on and clipped the microphone pads to his larynx.

'So, we're okay with that now, yeah?' he asked cautiously.

'I got new orders. It's his arse gets kicked now, not mine. But I still can't fly over that goddam Russian. But see here! I'm just gonna move up ahead and practise a hover. Now if that ship decides to steam right underneath my hover – that's his problem!'

'That's real neat!'

The helicopter banked to the left and the nose dipped to accelerate. Five hundred yards ahead the pilot pulled it sharply up into a hover, one hundred feet above the waves. He swung the nose round so that the side door looked directly back at the Soviet ship bearing down on them. The cameraman switched on and adjusted his focus.

The second SH-3 with the stills photographers on board flew parallel to the ship, but turned sharply away when it saw the first machine hovering in its path.

As the ship passed beneath them the correspondent's excitement mounted. The cocooned deck cargo revealed itself indisputably to be what the pilot had said; the wings of jet fighters. As the ship's bridge passed below, dark uniformed figures could be seen waving and gesticulating furiously.

Ten minutes later they landed back on the deck of the *Eisenhower*. The TV crew hurried below to prepare their tapes for transmission to New York by satellite. With help from aircraft recognition manuals provided by the PIO, they concluded the wings were for MiG-29 fighters, aircraft considerably superior to anything the Cubans had at present. They counted twelve individual wings; that meant six fighters.

Admiral Vernon Kritz appeared reluctant to jeopardize the secrecy of his ship's location by allowing the TV and newspaper men to transmit their reports, transmissions which could be detected by Russian satellites and spy planes. But eventually he allowed himself to be persuaded, and the media men set up a small gyro-stabilized satellite dish on the flight deck, in good time for the material to be turned round for the morning news programmes back home.

* * *

Andrew Tinker caught the early flight to London. Patsy had grudgingly driven him to Plymouth airport after an early breakfast.

She'd scowled for most of the previous evening, after he told her he'd been ordered to take command of *HMS Truculent* so that Philip could be brought home.

'It's not bloody fair!' she'd railed. 'Home for three days, and now you're off on patrol again! You'll be gone for weeks!'

She could well be right. He hadn't told her the real reason Philip was being brought back, simply that the Navy took domestic upsets pretty seriously.

'And so they should,' she'd answered. 'Damn Sara! If she couldn't have her affairs discreetly, she should've taken up pottery instead!'

At Heathrow, Andrew was met by the driver to Flag Officer Submarines. The black Granada slipped easily through the light Sunday morning traffic to Northwood. Forty-five minutes after touching down, he presented his identity card in the guardroom of the combined NATO and Royal Naval headquarters.

He was directed straight to 'the hole', the deep underground bunker that houses the operational command. Further identity checks, then he was through the heavy double doors, and down the steps to the Submarine Ops Room.

Flag Officer Submarines was Rear-Admiral Anthony Bourlet, a short, peppery man who had overall command of the Royal Navy's thirty nuclear and diesel-powered attack submarines.

'Very grateful to you for coming, Andrew,' he welcomed, grabbing him by the arm and leading him into his own small office next to the ops room. 'Alarming business, this.'

'We'll probably find when we get him back that it was all in Sara's imagination,' Andrew replied. 'I can't really believe Phil would do anything daft.'

'You're an old friend, aren't you?'

'Since Dartmouth.'

'Mmmm. Now look. This is what we've arranged. We've signalled Hitchens that he's to rendezvous with a helicopter off the Western Isles at 1600, and that he's to be replaced on board. He's acknowledged the signal, so with a bit of luck the scare'll be over by this evening.

'You'll leave Northolt in a 125 at 1300 hours for Stornoway. That's where you'll pick up the helicopter. The 125 will wait and bring Hitchens back here. When he's safely in our hands, we'll get the security boys in and find out what's at the bottom of all this. All right so far?'

Andrew looked at his watch. It gave him barely two hours to get briefed on *Truculent*'s mission.

'Fine, sir.'

'Now . . .'

Bourlet's voice sank lower.

'What you don't know is that Hitchens was given a special briefing before he left. A secret task for the exercise which is terrifyingly sensitive. The C-in-C shat himself when I told him the Russians had been sniffing round Philip.'

Andrew's eyebrows shot up. Craig had told him of a special mission, but not what it was.

'You'll know about the new "Moray" mines . . .'

'Of course. Remotely programmable microprocessors, incredibly clever target selectivity – laid in deep water they launch an underwater guided-missile that can penetrate even the heaviest Soviet double-hull.'

'Precisely. And at the first threat of war with Russia, and politicians willing, you lot would be told to lay them outside all the main Kola submarine bases.'

Andrew's jaw dropped.

'And that's Phil's mission?' he asked, stunned.

'To try it out. To try slipping through their ASW screen, get right up to the Kola Inlet and fire water-shots to simulate laying the mines.'

'Wheew!'

'Not the sort of job to give a man who's facing a personal crisis.'

'You can say that again! A hairy enough job for anybody!'

'The Yanks are in on it, too. They've tasked one of their *Los Angeles* boats to do the same thing further east, at Gremikha. As I'm sure you realize, the point of doing this in the middle of a big exercise is that the Russians'll probably be running a big ASW screen in the Barents. They'll be looking hard for our boats, and we need to know how good they'd be at finding us if we had to do it for real.'

Andrew nodded. It was almost routine for Allied submarines to probe Soviet waters on intelligence-gathering missions, but such operations were invariably conducted when the Soviets were known to be at a low state of alert. Going in when the Northern Fleet was mounting a full-scale anti-submarine sweep would be another matter.

'What's the time scale on all this, sir?'

'Well, there's a cover plan, obviously. He's scheduled to play "blue" in the exercise until Wednesday, and then switch sides. He then has five days supposedly acting on his own, playing "orange"; in reality he has that amount of time to get in to Polyarny and out again. I keep saying "he", but of course it's "you" now. Think you can do it?'

'I'll have a bloody good try, sir,' Andrew replied, trying to look more confident than he felt.

'The key thing is to be damned careful not to get caught. The last thing we want is an international incident with one of our SSNs trapped in a Russian fjord. At the first sign of your being detected – withdraw. Get well away from their territorial waters.'

'There's one problem, sir. I know about the Moray mines, but I don't know anything about the tactics for them.'

'No problem. *Truculent*'s the trials boat for the weapon system. Paul Spriggs is the WEO on board. Knows the mines inside out. And Tim Pike's the first lieutenant, so you couldn't ask for a better team.'

'And they know all about the mission?'

'Umm, well, probably not. Hitchens was alone at the

special session here, and he was told not to brief his crew until the last possible moment. "Need to know", and all that. There's still a good chance of CINCLANT getting cold feet and calling off the whole caboodle. And of course it's political, this one, too. Number Ten and the White House had to give the okay, in the same way they would in a real "time of tension". With President McGuire still feeling his way in foreign affairs, he might well pull out.'

Andrew looked at his watch again and gulped. In just a few hours he was due to take command of a boat full of strangers and head north for one of the trickiest patrols of his career. He felt desperately ill-prepared.

'I'd better look at some charts, and see what you've got in mind, sir.'

'You certainly had. Come along.'

Admiral Bourlet led Andrew along the subterranean corridor, their rubber-soled shoes squeaking on the polished floor, to the SSO room – Submarine Special Operations.

This was the most secret room at the Northwood headquarters. Only a handful of men and women ever entered it – even its very existence was known to only a handful more.

* * *

Washington DC.

Shortly after 10.00am in Washington, the Soviet Ambassador's car drew up outside the State Department at Foggy Bottom, escorted by police outriders, sirens wailing. All morning the television news programmes had been running and re-running the pictures of the Soviet freighter, the close-up shots of the fighter wings carefully cross-edited with file footage of MiG-29 aircraft in action.

The Ambassador was received by the Deputy-Secretary for US-Soviet Relations, the most senior official available at short notice on a Sunday, and ushered to a reception room on the sixth floor.

'My government has instructed me to protest in the strongest terms,' he began with grim solemnity. 'The incident in the North Atlantic this morning was outrageous.

A Soviet freighter called *Rostov*, on innocent passage on the high seas, was harassed without provocation by two helicopters from the American nuclear carrier *Dwight D. Eisenhower*. One helicopter passed directly over the ship at mast-top level. It was only by means of a sudden change of course that the captain of the cargo ship was able to avoid a collision. Look. Here, I shall show you . . .'

From his briefcase he pulled out two 10 × 8 black and white prints and placed them on the table. The photographs had been well taken; they showed the deck-derricks of the ship with the US Navy helicopter almost touching them and, in the foreground, crewmen on the bridge with arms above their heads as if protecting themselves from an expected collision.

'My government finds such aggressive behaviour by the United States Navy to be quite incompatible with the more relaxed relationship that has existed between Moscow and Washington in recent years, particularly since it has occurred at the start of Exercise Ocean Guardian, in which your warships will rehearse provocative NATO war plans almost within sight of the Soviet homeland. I am instructed to inform you that General Secretary Savkin is deeply disturbed by this event, and will not let the matter rest.'

The Deputy-Secretary feigned polite indifference to cover his embarrassment at being unbriefed on the affair.

'Thank you for your visit, Mr Ambassador. We shall look into this, and will give our answer to the matters raised in due course. May I express the hope that this incident doesn't prevent you enjoying the rest of this sunny Sunday, sir?'

He stood up and extended his hand. The Ambassador took it without a word, then gathered up his briefcase and turned for the door.

'Have a nice day, sir,' the Deputy-Secretary breathed to the Ambassador's back as he left the building.

Outside on the pavement, a handful of newsmen had gathered, including two TV crews. The Ambassador's press spokesman moved amongst them, handing out copies of the official protest and the photographs.

The Deputy-Secretary chewed at a thumb-nail. It was a set-up, he was sure of it. He'd watched the morning newscasts; the networks had done well to get their video on the air so fast. But the Soviets had matched that speed with their stills. To do that, the Russian ship must have been supplied with a professional photographer, a dark-room, a facsimile machine and a satellite terminal. Not the normal equipment of a Soviet merchantman, surely?

The Navy had walked into something. Goddam military and their club feet! And the Defence Intelligence Agency still hadn't answered the request for information that he'd lobbed in as soon as he saw the pictures. He had some 'phoning to do.

* * *

Moscow.

Dr Tatiana Gareyeva's apartment, in one of Moscow's anonymous residential areas, had a sad air about it and smelled stale. Ornaments on the shelves and tables had been collected over the years for sentimental reasons rather than for their intrinsic attractiveness. The furniture looked cheap; it had outlived its initial purpose to be used as a stop-gap until she could create a new home – with a husband.

Tatiana was over forty now, and time was running out. Standing by the window looking out on the bleak concrete landscape where thousands lived in similarly cramped homes, she turned to look at Vice-Admiral Feliks Astash-enkov, slumped in an armchair watching television.

He was no use to her any more. Any dream she may have had of making their relationship permanent had long since evaporated. He was a hindrance to her now; his sudden surprise visits a few times a year would be an embarrassment one day if she ever met a real suitor.

She caught a glimpse of herself in the mirror on the wall opposite. Her hair was flecked with grey; her eyes which once had sparkled blue now looked grey as well. Her face, once pretty, had filled to a dull squareness; her body was thickening towards an eventual shapelessness.

And Feliks? Age had not improved him either; he was

developing the heavy jowls and flabby waistline that came from the excess of good living since his promotion to Vice-Admiral.

When they'd first met, they'd loved each other with a passion. She'd almost convinced him to leave his iceberg of a wife and marry her instead. But the whiff of promotion had come his way – and his wife's brother was on the General Staff. . . .

And now? This weekend was the last they would see of each other. Both knew it but neither had said it. Feliks had tried to pretend nothing had changed, but his words had been hollow.

Tatiana turned away again to stare through the big square of glass. She had her work; a paediatrician would always be needed. But working in the Soviet health service had become no easier, despite the lipservice paid to reforms. Reductions in spending on military programmes had still not found their way through to the civil sector. Hospitals and clinics were still chronically short of drugs, dressings and equipment.

The medical problems were worsening, too. More babies were being born dependent on the heroin that had hooked their mothers, and the stringent tests being imposed on the profession meant hundreds of doctors had been sacked for incompetence. Good for the nation's health in the long run no doubt, but it created a shortage of doctors for the time being.

She'd have to make the best of her career; if she could find no love in her life, it would be all she had left.

The music for the opening of the evening news bulletin *Vremya* blared tinnily from the television. The sound was a relief to her. Feliks had said he would leave after the news, to catch the late flight back to Murmansk. She was going to drive him to the airport.

Feliks' eyes had been fixed on the screen for what felt like hours, but his mind had been focused elsewhere, on the real reason for his coming to Moscow that weekend, his meeting with the General Secretary. The more he thought back on it, the more his disquiet grew.

He'd made a promise to Nikolai Savkin, a promise to

help him, yet without any clear idea what it would involve. He understood Savkin's need for a foreign distraction to cool down the internal debate over *perestroika*, but what was his own role to be? The General Secretary had simply told him that sometime in the coming weeks he would call him, make a request for some special service, something undefined but which would be essential to the survival of the reform programme.

Feliks was afraid. He had to admit it to himself. He'd made an open-ended commitment. If things went wrong and Savkin went down like his predecessor had, then he, Feliks Astashenkov, would go down with him.

He glanced guiltily at Tatiana. He'd revealed nothing to her of his talk with Savkin, and because it had occupied his thoughts completely that weekend, he'd talked to her hardly at all. The fire of their affair had gone out anyway. It would soon be over; they'd say goodbye – he'd pretend it was *au revoir* but they'd both know it was *adieu*.

Suddenly he sat forward, startled. The television was reporting a speech made by Nikolai Savkin at a collective farm that afternoon. The video showed the General Secretary gesticulating angrily. Intercut with his words were the same photographs that had earlier been presented to the State Department in Washington, the *Rostov* being buzzed by American helicopters. The pictures showed the ship's crew ducking in terror before the American war machines. Library footage rolled, of US aircraft carriers catapulting bomb-laden fighter planes into the sky.

It was a disgraceful example of old-fashioned American imperialism and aggression, Savkin declaimed, which did not bode well for US–Soviet relations. It was a clear sign of the hostility intended by the NATO Exercise Ocean Guardian which had just begun – the largest and most provocative NATO exercise ever conducted right on the edge of Soviet waters.

Feliks was gripped by a sensation close to terror. It was beginning to dawn on him how far Savkin was preparing to go.

* * *

Scotland.

Andrew Tinker studied his watch with growing anxiety. It was already five in the afternoon. The helicopter should have found *HMS Truculent* an hour ago.

Strapped firmly into the canvas seat in the back of the Sea King, Andrew felt his legs going numb. The hard aluminium seat frame pressed against the underside of his thighs, stopping his circulation. Every few minutes he would shift his position, but what he needed was to get out of that infernal machine. They'd been airborne for one-and-a-half hours.

'Perhaps the rendezvous co-ordinates got scrambled in the signal from CINCFLEET,' he suggested, pressing the headset microphone against his lips.

'We're in the right place, I can assure you,' came back the tart voice in his earphones.

'Navaids are working perfectly. So's the VHF and UHF. If he'd surfaced anywhere within fifty miles of us he'd have heard us calling.'

They'd taken off from Stornoway in the Western Isles half an hour before the rendezvous. Despite the gale blowing and the turbulent seas, it should have been a smooth, routine manœuvre. Boat and aircraft would link by radio minutes before the deadline, and as soon as the submarine surfaced, down would go the winch-wire with Andrew on the end, to come up again a few minutes later with Philip.

But there'd been no sign, no hint that *HMS Truculent* intended to keep her appointment.

What did it mean? An accident? Highly improbable. A misunderstanding? Almost impossible – Philip had acknowledged the signal. Keeping out of the way to dodge a Russian submarine? None had been reported in the area.

Suddenly, Sara's words came back to him. *Philip hates the Russians – he'll have his revenge.*

A nightmare was beginning to unfold.

'Have you talked to Stornoway again?' Andrew demanded, his anxiety growing.

'Two minutes ago. They've told FOSM. Northwood

says there's been nothing from the boat. We've got fifteen minutes' fuel before we have to head for land.'

Andrew hated helicopters; the noise, the vibration, the smell of hydraulic fluid all gave him a feeling of claustrophobia he'd never experienced in a submarine. The Sea King they were using was an anti-submarine version, almost filled by tactical control panels, and a heavy, black winch for dunking sonar into the sea.

Clad in a dayglo red 'once-only' immersion suit, he was squeezed into a folding seat between the winch and the fuselage. Rubber seals gripped tightly round his wrists and his neck; the watertight suit would save his life if they ended up in the sea.

Andrew pressed the 'transmit' switch on his headset cable.

'Let's call it a day. He's not going to turn up,' he called above the gearbox whine.

'Bit worrying, isn't it? Will they start a search?' the pilot responded.

'Shouldn't think so. Submariners change their plans all the time. He'll turn up.'

He was trying to sound reassuring, without success. What the hell would they do now?

'Back to Stornoway?'

'Yep. Feet dry as fast as you can make it.'

He needed to get Admiral Bourlet on the line, fast.

* * *

HMS Truculent.

The invisible five-thousand-ton bulk of *HMS Truculent* was some two hundred miles northeast of the helicopter's position, her captain the only man on board who knew they'd missed a rendezvous.

For most of the past twelve hours Philip had stood in the control room, hovering nervously between the tactical displays and the chart table. He was desperate to get his boat into the deep waters of the Norwegian Basin, where a submarine could disappear with ease to run fast and free.

But their progress north had been halted by their need to cross the SOSUS barrier undetected. The chain of hydrophones stretching along underwater ridges from Greenland to the Shetlands would be sure to mark their passing unless they resorted to deception.

SOSUS was linked to a processing centre in South Wales, and the data could be presented within minutes as hard intelligence information at headquarters in Norfolk, USA and Northwood, UK.

Philip guessed the hounds would be rapidly unleashed once his masters knew he was out of their control. The Faroes-Shetland gap would be the obvious place they'd start looking for him; he didn't want to give them a head-start by revealing his position.

His first thought had been to hide amongst the noises generated by the aircraft-carrier *Illustrious* and her frigate escorts, but they were too far ahead, and would already have crossed the SOSUS barrier before *Truculent* could catch up.

So he'd decided to hug the continental shelf and pray for a merchantman to happen past. Throughout Saturday night they'd lurked, listening, west of the Orkneys. Philip had slept fitfully, leaving orders for the watch to wake him the moment a suitable decoy appeared.

Sunday morning came and went, with Philip finding it increasingly difficult to contain his fear of entrapment. He'd been on the point of making a run for it through the gap; to hell with the risk of being detected. If he was fast enough, he might slip away into the Norwegian Deep before the surface ships and the Nimrods could be marshalled onto his trail.

Then soon after lunch had come the breakthrough he was waiting for. A Russian fish-factory ship was heading back to Murmansk from the Scottish coast, laden with sprats and mackerel. The heavy thump of its diesel engine and the uneven beat of its imperfectly-milled propeller provided the screen of noise he needed.

To compound the deception, Philip ordered the trailing of a noise generator, a slim canister towed astern which transmitted a broad band of underwater noise, to swamp the discrete frequencies from the submarine which could identify it to the SOSUS system as a *Trafalgar* Class boat.

Philip crossed the control room to the chart table.

'How're we doing?'

Nick Cavendish was ready; the captain had asked him the same question every thirty minutes since lunch.

''Bout twenty miles northeast of SOSUS. Still at twelve knots, with the Soviet fisherman two miles to starboard.'

'Where's the *Victor*?'

'Last reported about one hundred miles north, but that was yesterday, sir. We're short of fresh intelligence.'

'Okay. Let's dump the noise generator, and head due north. Get down into the deep water and do some listening.'

'Aye, aye, sir.'

'Stretch our legs a bit. Once you're sure we're out of everyone's way, we'll stick a mast up and pick up an int. broadcast.'

'I'd like that, sir.'

Ahead lay the vast, empty waters of the Norwegian Basin, 3600 metres deep in places. Deep down, *Truculent*'s towed sonar array came into its own. If the Soviet *Victor* was anywhere within a hundred miles they'd have a good chance of finding her.

Cavendish gave the orders for the new course and depth. He set their speed at fifteen knots, fast enough until he had a better idea what other submarines might be sharing the waters with them.

He stepped into the sound room to look over the shoulders of the sonar ratings as they checked their waterfall displays. In the deep sound channel into which they'd descended they heard no trace of other submarines, just the squeaks and groans of countless krill. The *Victor* must have moved on.

Back in the control room he decided it was safe to put some distance behind them.

'Make revolutions for thirty knots!' he ordered. 'Maintain depth two-hundred-and-fifty metres.'

Their own sonar would be deaf at that speed, but he'd risk it for half an hour. He clicked the intercom to report the change of speed to the captain.

'Very good. Carry on,' Hitchens approved.

*

Thirty minutes later Cavendish ordered a return to fifteen knots. They were now over forty miles from the SOSUS barrier.

In the sound room the ratings scanned 360 degrees around the boat. Still no trace of man-made noise in the ocean depths.

The time was shortly before 1800 hrs. He'd checked with the wireless room; at 1814 there was a satellite transmission scheduled. Any submarine listening could take in the latest intelligence and news reports in a thirty-second burst of compressed data, together with signals directed at individual boats.

'Captain, sir! Officer-of-the-Watch,' Cavendish called into the intercom.

'*Captain!*'

'No contacts in the deep channel, sir. Propose to come up to sixty metres, and clear the surface picture. If nothing's around, I'd like, with your permission, sir, to return to periscope depth, raise a mast and take in the broadcast scheduled for 1814, sir.'

In the pause that followed, Cavendish imagined Hitchens studying his watch.

'*Sounds good. I'm coming to the control room, but carry on.*'

Cavendish swung round to the blue-shirted planesman. 'Bring her up to sixty metres, Jones.'

The rating pulled back on his control stick, keeping a careful eye on the angle-of-ascent gauge.

They came up fast and levelled out at a depth where they could hear the sounds of surface ships, hidden from them before by the temperature gradients which separate surface sounds from those of the deep.

Somewhere up here was the *Illustrious* task force, but Cavendish calculated the ships should be well north of *Truculent*, closer to Iceland, preparing to sweep the seas for submarines ahead of the *USS Eisenhower* battle group.

'*Control room! Sound Room,*' the loudspeaker crackled by Cavendish's ear.

'Go. Control Room.'

'*No contacts on sonar, sir. Surface clear.*'

Cavendish smiled with relief. Philip Hitchens joined him at the bandstand, behind the planesman.

'Did you hear that, sir?'

'Yes, I did.'

He looked at his watch. 1805.

'You can proceed to periscope depth. I'm going to the wireless room.'

Hitchens moved awkwardly across the control room, as if conscious the men were watching him. How many of them knew about the controls he'd imposed on the communications procedures?

He'd told sub-lieutenant Smallbone the previous evening that all future communications would be for his eyes only.

The burst transmission of digital data from the satellite would be recorded on magnetic disk, then fed through a processor to be printed out in real time.

'As soon as you've got the stuff printing, I need you out of the room, I'm afraid,' Philip reminded them briskly.

Smallbone and the operator Bennett nodded at him sullenly.

'I'm sorry. Not my idea. Orders from CINCFLEET,' Hitchens lied smoothly. 'Everything set now?'

'Sir,' Smallbone acknowledged.

Hitchens peered at his watch for the third time in a few seconds. He couldn't conceal his nervousness and spun back into the control room.

Cavendish was raising the forward search periscope.

'ESM?' Hitchens snapped.

'Negative, sir. No contacts.'

The Electronic Support Measures mast was the first to be raised whenever they closed with the surface. Its sensors were designed to detect radar transmissions from ships or aircraft, transmissions that could spot their periscope or radio mast.

Cavendish completed his all-round look.

'No visual contacts, sir. Sea-state five.'

Hitchens studied his watch again. 1814 precisely.

Philip stomped back to the wireless room. The disk-drive chattered as it filed the data.

'Transmission complete, sir,' Smallbone reported.
Philip turned on his heel and called into the control room.

'Officer of the Watch, down periscope, and take us deep again.'

Hugo Smallbone shuffled awkwardly out of the radio room, and stood outside the door, hands clasped behind his back as if at parade-ground ease.

'I'll press the tit for you then, sir?' Bennett growled.

'Yes, please.'

The rating did so, then scuttled from the room with exaggerated haste as the printer began to pour forth its data. Philip slipped inside and closed the door.

Lieutenant Commander Pike stepped into the control room having just completed his rounds. He spotted the wireless operators hovering awkwardly outside in the passageway.

'So, he's really doing it,' he murmured to the OOW.

'Didn't doubt the captain's word, did you, sir?' Cavendish retorted.

Pike raised one eyebrow in reply.

'Ten down. Keep two hundred metres,' ordered Cavendish. 'Steer oh four oh. Revolutions for eighteen knots.'

He looked at the control room clock. Just over half an hour until the end of his watch.

For Sunday's evening meal, the galley offered corned beef salad or 'oggies' – Cornish pasties – and chips.

Philip ate early, the steward bringing him a tray to his cabin. He wanted to be finished with his meal and with sifting the signals by the time the watch changed at 7 pm. It was the time he'd chosen to make the pipe; to give the men their first clue as to what he planned.

The signals were easy to sort. The intelligence reports he'd pass to the watch leader; the family messages and the summary of the world news he'd give to the first lieutenant for distribution. Those he placed to one side. He slid the messages for other submarines included in the burst transmission into the bin at his feet.

In front of him was the message he'd dreaded, the one he'd had to prevent the crew from seeing.

FLASH 201814Z OCT.
FOR: EXEC. OFF. HMS TRUCULENT.
FROM: FOSM NORTHWOOD.
RESTRICTED.
NEED IMMEDIATE EXPLANATION WHY YOU FAILED TO MAKE RENDEZVOUS 1600Z TODAY.
ESSENTIAL YOU COMMUNICATE HF/SSIX SOONEST.

They'd addressed it to Tim Pike, trying to by-pass him. Sent it without special code, so the whole fleet could see it. Clumsy. By making it so open they'd hoped to get the message through. They were wrong. It merely showed they had yet to realize what they were up against.

He smiled but with little satisfaction. He had no wish to take on his masters. Circumstances had forced him into it.

He carefully folded the signal and placed it inside the wall safe.

He waited until ten minutes past the hour, so the men would be settled in their mess decks or at their watch posts, then he stepped briskly into the control room, checked the navigation plot and the power settings, and unhooked the microphone that would broadcast his words throughout the boat.

'Do you hear there? Captain speaking. Just an update on our situation,' he began, hoping the tremble in his voice would not be noticeable. 'We're well clear of the Faroes-Shetland Gap now, and very shortly we're going to put on a bit of speed. Our destination is still somewhere in the north Norwegian Sea, but I can't be specific at this stage.'

He swallowed to moisten his throat, and turned away from the men in the control room so they couldn't see his face.

'I have to tell you that our orders have been changed since we left Devonport. It may well be that we no longer take any part in Exercise Ocean Guardian – that's not quite clear yet. The thing is, there's a bit of tension brewing between the Russians and NATO, and . . . er . . . we've been put on alert for a very special and very sensitive mission. Can't tell you anything about it at all at the moment; CINCFLEET has classified it Top Secret – Commanding Officer's eyes only. But, I *can* tell you what was on the BBC World Service news this evening – I've just had the summary through on the satellite.

'Earlier this morning there was an incident some way north of here, involving helicopters from the US aircraft carrier *Eisenhower* and a Soviet cargo ship called the *Rostov*, carrying MiG fighters. The Russians are apparently accusing the Yanks of threatening their ship. Mr Savkin, the . . . er . . . Russian leader, made a very provocative speech this afternoon, accusing NATO of all sorts of things, particularly slagging off this exercise that we're involved in.

'Now, it's not entirely clear what he's up to, but CINCFLEET isn't taking any chances. So, I've been given my orders. I hope to be able to give you some details in a day or two, but in the meantime please just take my word for it that whatever we do, there's a good reason for it. That's all.'

He made to hang up the microphone, but snatched it back again.

'Just one more thing. The video tonight, according to the first lieutenant's list, is *Gorky Park*. That's all.'

At the chief petty officers' table in the ratings' mess, CPO Hicks turned to Gostyn, the propulsion chief, knife held up in mid-air.

'What the fuck was that all about?'

'Not good news. Not good at all.'

In the wardroom six officers sat round the table, stunned into temporary silence. All eyes turned to Tim Pike.

'You heard the captain. I can't talk about it, can I?' he growled uncomfortably.

* * *

Northwood.

Rear-Admiral Anthony Bourlet paced like a caged rat up and down the floor of his office overlooking the main gates at Northwood Royal Naval Headquarters. Andrew watched him uncomfortably.

'This is bloody ridiculous! Something must have gone wrong with the boat. I can't believe a commander in Her Majesty's Navy would deliberately flout his orders and take off into the wide blue yonder on a personal vendetta! A man would have to be mad to do that.'

'That's just the point, sir. He may be. Some sort of breakdown.'

'They'd know. On the boat. The other officers would realize something was wrong, and sort him out, take command or whatever.'

'Eventually, yes. But how long would it take, sir? I'm no expert, but if Philip just appeared slightly odd, it wouldn't be enough reason for the executive officer to take over. If Pike misjudged it, he'd be on a charge of mutiny.'

'Mmmm,' the Admiral growled. 'What could you get away with on your own boat, Andrew?'

Bourlet stopped pacing. Fixing both hands on the desk, he leaned bulldog-like across it. The broad band of his Admiral's insignia glinted gold against the dark blue of his uniform sleeves. He'd commanded surface ships as a younger man, never a submarine.

'What d'you mean exactly, sir?'

'If you took it into your head to sink half the Soviet Navy, could you do it? Could you actually launch the torpedoes?'

Andrew smoothed down his thick, dark hair, and frowned, taken aback by the question.

'Well, that's the job of the weapon engineer.'

'Of course. But could you convince him to do it?'

Andrew reflected for a moment.

'It'd be bloody difficult. If we were firing a live round against a real target – there'd be a dozen men involved at least. It'd be war. Everyone on board would have to know.'

'Could you, as captain, convince them to do it?' Bourlet pressed. 'Tell them you'd received secret orders, a personal briefing, CO's eyes only? Something of that sort?'

Andrew expelled his breath through pursed lips, then shook his head.

'It'd be pretty impossible, sir, with the Harpoons or torpedoes. There'd have been signals, targeting data and so on. That stuff wouldn't be CO's eyes only.'

'Then we shouldn't have too much to worry about . . .'

'But if he's got mines on board. That could change things . . .'

Bourlet winced at the confirmation of his own fears.

The intercom on his desk buzzed twice. He pressed a key.

'Yes? What is it?'

'*Sub duty ops officer to see you, sir. Says it's very urgent.*'

Andrew got to his feet.

'Do you want me to wait outside, sir?'

Bourlet held up a hand.

'Send him in.' Then looking up at Andrew, he went on, 'Stay here. This may well be relevant.'

The duty operations watchkeeper entered, the same lieutenant who'd been directing Andrew's efforts at Stornoway earlier that afternoon.

'It's *Truculent*, sir. We think we may have had a trace of her.'

The young man's face was flushed – alarmed even.

'We've been comparing the SOSUS data with the radar surface picture from a Nimrod at about 1700 this afternoon. The SOSUS detected a Soviet fishing vessel heading for Murmansk, apparently in company with a trawler. Two surface vessels. But the Nimrod radar only saw one. The factory ship. No other trawler. We suspect the other noise was a submarine using a decoy, and *Truculent*'s the only one it can be, sir. Nothing else in the area.'

Bourlet shot a glance at the clock.

'God preserve us! That was four hours ago. You're absolutely certain?'

'Only explanation we can think of, sir.'

'Still no signals from her?'

''Fraid not, sir. And we're repeating our signal to her every hour on the broadcast and on the SSIX. She can't be listening.'

'Well, let me know instantly if there is anything.'

The operations officer left, and Admiral Bourlet turned to a large chart of the north Atlantic which covered one wall.

'Sod it! He could be anywhere within a hundred miles of the barrier by now. Even further by the time we get a Nimrod up to look for him. Sod Phil Hitchens! And sod bloody Sara Hitchens!'

Bourlet had been Flag Officer Submarines for two years, and had his eye on the promotion ladder. His tenure of office at Northwood had passed with remarkable smoothness. This sort of crisis was something he could do without.

The system was supposed to spot unstable personalities and weed them out before they could do harm. Hitchens had slipped through the net; ultimately that would be seen as *his* responsibility.

'What the hell's he up to, eh? What exactly did he say to that tart of a wife, before he sailed?'

'I don't think he *said* anything. She just sensed he was going to do something. I know what she means, sir. I've known Phil for longer than Sara – we joined the Navy at the same time, shared a cabin at Dartmouth. He – he can be pretty intense at times. Most of the time, in fact, when I think about it. I don't have many memories of him being really relaxed, having a good time, that sort of thing.'

'Bit of a bore, you mean?'

'He has been called that, sir. Some people find it difficult to tolerate his seriousness; he can be quite obsessive, particularly when it comes to the Soviets. Something of a cold warrior.'

'Nothing much wrong with that. Don't trust the bastards meself, despite the Gorbachev reforms and all Mr Savkin's charm. Still, holding views like that is one thing; planning to start your own war is quite another.'

He stared up at the chart again.

'Come over here and tell me what you think he's up to.'

Bourlet pointed to the Faroes-Shetland gap.

'From there to the Kola, what're we talking about? Twelve hundred miles?'

'Something like that, sir.'

'How long would it take him? A couple of days?'

'That'd be pushing it. He'd sprint a bit, but then probably want to drift so he could use his sonar. Doesn't want to go crashing into anything on the way.'

'Unless he's feeling suicidal.'

'Well, even if *he* is, the rest of the crew won't be, and they'll want to observe normal procedures. They'll stick to the water they were allocated at their briefing.'

'So that gives us *some* idea of where to look.'

'They're pretty big areas, but we can make a guess at it.'

'We'll have to. Now, what'll he do about communications?'

'My guess is he'll stick a mast up from time to time and take in a satellite. He'll want the intelligence data, if nothing else.'

'In that case our signal to the first lieutenant might have got through by now.'

'Unless . . .'

The same thought had just struck them both. If *Truculent*'s crew listened to just one transmission they would immediately know their captain was disregarding orders, and they'd be justified in seizing command. Hitchens must have thought of some way to prevent that.

'In this case . . .'

'Hitchens may have taken steps . . .' Bourlet completed the sentence. 'Pah! How on earth can we say that? We're assuming the man's behaving rationally and irrationally at the same time. God, this is ridiculous. It's like blind-man's-bluff in a lunatic asylum!'

A silence fell, and both men turned their eyes to the top of the chart, the Barents Sea and the Kola Peninsula. The Kola Inlet harboured one of the largest concentrations of warships anywhere in the world, including nearly fifty per cent of the Soviet Union's entire submarine fleet. If Philip Hitchens was bent on revenge, that was where *Truculent* would be heading.

'The special mission he had, sir? To simulate mine-laying. Can I get it absolutely clear? Did he have warshots on board? Live mines?'

'Mmmm. Four of them, I'm afraid. Just a normal weapons load.' Then, after a pause, 'You think he could persuade his WEO to lay them?'

'He might. The point about the Moray mine is that it's designed to be laid in an inert condition *before* a war starts, and wouldn't actually be activated until the start of the conflict. As you know, sir, it can be activated by a sonar transmission from a submarine, a surface ship, or an aircraft, anytime up to a year after being laid.

'He'd have to prepare his groundwork. But as long as no one suspected he'd lost his marbles, he might just convince his WEO they had orders to lay the mines in peacetime.'

'Believing the weapons wouldn't be activated until there was a crisis . . .'

'Exactly, sir.'

'Now the crunch question. Could Hitchens activate the mines?'

Andrew swallowed hard. He'd remembered a detail from Philip's career.

'I've a horrible feeling he could, sir. He trained as a sonar officer. Knows that sonar system inside out.'

Bourlet stared at him unblinking.

'Then he's got to be stopped.'

Suddenly the Admiral stood up and pulled his uniform straight.

'Come on. We're going down the Hole.'

With that he marched for the door; Andrew pulled himself to his feet and followed.

Outside, the night had become crisp and clear, with a half-moon high in the sky. As they hurried down the slope, two young WRNS coming towards them saluted smartly. Admiral Bourlet didn't give them a second glance. Unusual for him – he had a reputation as a bit of a lecher.

At the control post at the bottom of the entrance ramp, the Royal Marines security guards checked their identity badges and cleared them. The two men hurried through the heavy steel blast doors, and down to the first level airlock. The atmosphere in the bunker was kept at positive pressure to protect the occupants from chemical weapon attack, or nuclear fallout.

Four flights down, they entered the long corridor that led to the Operations Control room. The OPCON was dominated by a giant wall-screen; rows of computer terminals were manned by operators wearing headphones. This was the control centre for Exercise Ocean Guardian; all NATO naval operations in the Eastern Atlantic were directed from here.

Bourlet passed through it into the smaller Royal Naval control room beyond. The three men on duty scrambled to their feet.

'Relax,' he ordered. 'This is Commander Tinker, captain of the *Tribune*. He's here helping me with the *Truculent* problem. Now, what I'm about to say is Top Secret – UK Eyes Only. Not a word outside this room, understood? None of those NATO people must know.'

'Sir.' The three men nodded.

'We appear to have an SSN not responding to signals at the moment. Don't know why,' he lied. 'We've got to find that boat and discover what's up. Now what've we got in the *Truculent*'s area?'

The duty officer tapped at his keyboard and a map appeared on his screen.

'*Illustrious* is north of the Faroes, sir, with three escorts,' he announced, reading off the data. 'But *Truculent*'s probably 200 miles east of her. Bit too far for her helicopters to do anything useful. Two more ASW frigates are working a screen nearer to Iceland, so they'll not be much use either. Nor will the three "*O*" Class subs in the northern North Sea. The one boat that could help is the submarine *Tenby*; she's right up off North Cape.'

'What about maritime air?'

'One Nimrod MR2 from Kinloss is doing a search just inside the Arctic Circle. Currently tracking a *Victor 111* and a *Tango*. A second Nimrod is on barrier patrol between the Faroes and Shetlands. We could divert her, if we knew where to look.'

'Andrew, what do you think?'

'Anybody got a chart?' Tinker asked wrily. 'One of those paper things. I can't work from a screen!'

The duty officer pulled one from a drawer and handed him a pair of brass dividers.

Andrew calculated. It would be five hours after *Truculent* crossed the SOSUS barrier before the Nimrod could be on station. One hundred and fifty miles was the most the boat could have covered in that time.

He measured the dividers against the latitude marks on the side of the chart, then laid the points on the paper.

'If he's taking a straight line towards North Cape, the Nimrod'll have to lay a barrier a hundred miles wide to have a chance of finding him.'

'Get those co-ordinates and ask the Air Commander if we can divert his Nimrod,' Bourlet ordered. 'Now, what else is there on the ground?'

'The Americans' main force is still well to the west, sir, but they've got a *Los Angeles* boat way up north under the ice, keeping an ear open for the Russian BNs.'

'Mmmm.'

'The Norwegians might be able to help, sir. They've got a couple of *Oslo* frigates on anti-submarine duty off Trondheim Fjord.'

'No. The Norwegians couldn't keep a birthday party secret, let alone this sort of problem. No. *Tenby* looks our best bet. She's playing "orange", isn't she?'

Bourlet directed his question at the duty officer. The lieutenant commander nodded.

There had to be something he could do, Andrew thought. He knew Philip better than any of them. He might be able to talk sense into him if he could just get near enough.

'Just a thought, sir,' Andrew ventured, beckoning the Admiral to move out of earshot of the others. What he was about to suggest would commit him further than ever. He was glad Patsy couldn't hear him.

'Go on,' Bourlet growled.

'If I could get on board *Tenby*,' he whispered, 'and we managed to track *Truculent*, I could call them on the underwater telephone. Might be able to get Philip back on the rails. If not, at least I could alert the crew.'

'It'd also avoid our having to brief *Tenby* by signal, which wouldn't be bad. Mmmm. Got any other commitments at the moment?'

'Just shore leave. Patsy'll probably threaten divorce, but I think I can cope with that.'

'Won't be the first time, I'm sure. That's not a bad plan. How would we get you on board?'

They turned back to the duty officer.

'We want to get Commander Tinker on board *Tenby*. How do we do it?' Bourlet asked.

The lieutenant commander pointed to his computer screen, showing the northern tip of Norway.

'Tromso would probably be your best bet. We could order *Tenby* to approach the coast. There's a Norwegian Air Force base there with Search and Rescue helicopters.'

'How long to get to Tromso from here?'

'Depends what you're flying in, but about four hours in something like a 125, I'd say.'

'Mmmm. I'll need to clear this with the C-in-C, but it sounds the right plan. Get it started, will you? Alert *Tenby* that we may need to change her plans, and keep her close to Tromso. Don't give her any details or explanations at this stage. And check with the Norwegians, to make sure they can give Andrew a lift. Finally, book a 125 for tomorrow morning. I'll confirm everything later this evening, after I've talked to the boss.'

The duty men saluted as the Rear-Admiral and Andrew left.

'Got a cabin booked in the Wardroom?' Bourlet asked, after they'd stepped out into the crisp night air.

'Yes. I wasn't expecting to get back to Plymouth tonight, whatever happened.'

'Give my apologies to your wife. Feel free to blame me

for everything. I'm quite used to it. And, look: let the Wardroom hall-porter know where you are, 'cause I'll want another word. I'm just going down the road to Admiralty House. The C-in-C's having a dinner party, but he knows what's going on and is expecting me to call. I shouldn't be more than an hour.'

Andrew watched Bourlet's squat figure stomp up the ramp towards the main gates, then he turned left towards the accommodation blocks of the 'Wardroom' – the shipboard term the Navy used for the officers' mess, which at Northwood amounted to a good-sized hotel.

'You're much too late for dinner, sir, but they'll do you a sandwich if you're quick,' the hall porter greeted, looking at his watch.

Andrew realized suddenly how hungry he was. The only meal he'd had all day were the sandwiches the RAF had provided on the flight to Scotland.

He'd intended to ring Patsy right away; he took a step towards the coin-box telephone on the wall opposite, then hesitated. She'd have to wait, or he'd miss the only meal he was going to get; the way things were going, he couldn't be sure when he'd see the next one.

Rear-Admiral Bourlet had sent his driver home for the night, so took the wheel of the black Granada himself. Admiralty House was less than a quarter of a mile down the road, a substantial red-brick house at the end of a tarmac drive.

A white-jacketed steward emerged from the front door, and pointed to a parking space.

'If you'd care to wait in the study, sir, I'll tell the Admiral you're here. They're just finishing their coffee, so you've picked a good moment,' he chirped as he ushered Bourlet into the house.

The Commander-in-Chief of the Fleet was two ranks higher than he was, but as far as Bourlet was concerned, Stewart Waverley should never even have made Vice-Admiral. The man wasn't so much a sailor as a politician, with his eye on the First Sea Lord's job followed by a seat in the House of Lords.

He waited five minutes in the small study. Shelves lined with volumes of Who's Who, directories of key personnel in the media, and recent political biographies confirmed Bourlet in his prejudices about the man.

'Hello, Anthony,' Waverley greeted curtly. 'Hope this won't take long. I've got the editor of the Telegraph here this evening. What news of the *Truculent*?'

He was tall and elegant in a white dinner jacket, his straight, dark hair held in place by a sheen of oil. His breath smelled of claret and good brandy.

'The news is bad. For God's sake, don't give it to the Telegraph.'

Waverley scowled in irritation at the unnecessary piece of advice.

'There's been no word from her,' Bourlet continued, experiencing a perverse pleasure that what he was about to say would spoil the C-in-C's evening.

'But we think she's been detected. Crossing the SOSUS array between the Faroes and Shetland, about five hours ago. Pretending to be a trawler. I've diverted a Nimrod to look for her.'

Waverley blanched.

'What . . . what on earth's going on in that boat?'

Bourlet explained further, and watched the C-in-C's expression freeze as the implications sank in. When he'd finished, Waverley leaned back in his chair and stared at the ceiling.

'This is appalling!' he exploded, after what seemed like a full minute of silence.

'I'll have to brief the First Sea Lord; he'll need to tell the Secretary of State tonight. This thing's going to explode. The PM'll be horrified. I'm having lunch with her at Downing Street tomorrow. Wants me to tell her all about Ocean Guardian. The Russians have lodged a formal complaint, calling it "provocative". You'll have heard on the news all that business about the Americans buzzing a Soviet merchantman bound for Cuba with MiG-29s on her deck? And the furious speech Savkin made this afternoon?'

'I haven't heard any news – been a bit busy . . .'

Waverley didn't hear him, his mind running on what he would say to the Prime Minister.

'If we've got a rogue submarine heading into the middle of all this, it'll be like tossing a lighted match onto an oil spill. You will find her, won't you?'

'Sir, I don't know. If Hitchens doesn't want to be found, he'll make it bloody difficult for us. We've got to face it, unless we can divert every ship and plane involved in Ocean Guardian to help with the search, we may not be able to stop him doing whatever he intends to do.'

'Good God, man! We can't do that! The whole world would know what's happened. A *Royal Navy* nuclear submarine out of control? A *British* officer threatening a private war with the Soviets? This must never get out! You've *got* to stop him! I'm making you personally responsible for the operation. Set up a small command staff, give it a code name, and use your judgement. I'll look after the politicians – leave them to me. You just get Hitchens back in line!'

Waverley stood up. His hands were trembling.

'And now I've got to go back and entertain my guests without the editor of the Daily Telegraph suspecting anything!'

Andrew dropped three coins into the payphone, and dialled. He looked at his watch. It was nearly eleven o'clock.

'Hello?' Patsy sounded breathless when she eventually answered.

'Hullo, darling. It's me. Were you in the bath or something?' he asked.

'No, I've been out. Heard the phone when I switched off the car – came running in. Hence – breathless.'

'Been somewhere nice?'

'Hardly. Parents' Association meeting. Bleagh! Usual stuff; anxious fathers wondering why their eight-year-olds aren't being taught Shakespeare. Where are you? I thought you'd be at sea by now.'

'Plan's changed. I'm at Northwood. Can't talk much. Just to say things are getting complicated. I still expect to be away for a while, so I shan't be able to call you for a bit.'

'It's still this business with Philip?'

'Yes, but I'm on a public phone, so I can't go into details.'

'Well . . . , all right, but when are you likely to be back? Have you no idea? The children'll be home next weekend. You must be here then.'

Her voice sounded strained, angry even.

'I just don't know. A few days probably, that's all.'

'But it might be longer? Andrew, what *is* this?'

'Look, I'll ring you again when I can, but I may not be near a phone. Could you do something for me?'

'What?' she asked suspiciously.

'It's Sara. Could you keep an eye on her? Make an excuse to talk to her?'

'What about?'

'Well, you know – things. She'll be pretty worried. And she hasn't got anyone to talk to.'

'Hasn't she? I thought she had a knack of finding people . . .'

'Patsy!'

He cursed the constraints of talking on an open phone line.

'Darling, I can't explain any more. But please do it. Say hello to Sara, will you? It's *deadly* serious. And I chose that word carefully.'

There was silence from the other end, just the clicks and the hiss of the line.

'Oh,' she said, eventually. She sounded startled. 'Oh, all right. I'll look out for her.'

'Good girl. And if she says anything which you think is important, then go and see Craig and tell him to pass it on to FOSM.'

'How will I know what's important?'

It was a reasonable question, but on the open phone he couldn't explain.

'You'll have to use your loaf, love. Now I've got to go. I'll see you . . . sometime.'

He wanted to be reassuring, but knew he had failed.

'Be careful, won't you?'
'Don't worry. Bye now!'
'Bye. I love you, by the way.'
Andrew replaced the receiver, but left his hand resting on it. Could he have explained any better? Should he ring her back?
'Ah, there you are!' Admiral Bourlet's gravel voice boomed across the reception area. 'Let's go into the bar for a moment. Just time for a nightcap.'
He led the way in. Only a handful of officers were drinking, most of them young and unattached. They stiffened at the sight of an Admiral but Bourlet waved at them to relax.
'What's yours?'
'That's kind of you, sir. I'll have a horse's neck.'
'Make that two,' the Admiral told the barman.
They retreated with their drinks to a far corner of the bar, where two large, leather armchairs remained unoccupied.
'Right,' Bourlet began softly. 'The plan goes ahead as discussed this afternoon. I'm giving it the codename "Shadowhunt". Trying to find a "*T*" class boat that doesn't want to be found – it's pretty apt.
'Waverley's given me carte blanche. Ops have talked to the Norwegians and they're ready to help. *Tenby*'s been signalled and is on her way to a rendezvous with you. She's got no clue what it's about, of course. You'll have to use your discretion how much you tell her.
'The RAF'll be ready for you at ten-thirty at Northolt. They want you there fifteen minutes before that. You've got your passport with you, I hope.'
'Yes, sir. It's in my bag. Standard kit. There is one thing I thought of, though. My job as I see it, apart from finding *Truculent*, is to talk to Philip on the underwater telephone. The trouble is, I'm bloody worried about what to say. I mean, it's a bit like dealing with a gunman in a plane full of hostages.'
'Damned good point,' the Admiral growled. 'And I know just the person you need to talk to. Young friend of mine . . .'

He cleared his throat noisily and rippled his eyebrows to indicate he was about to be indiscreet.

'Surgeon-Commander Rush – Felicity Rush. Fleet psychiatrist. Based here at Northwood but travels all over the place dealing with mental problems. Delightful girl. Here . . .'

He reached into an inside pocket and pulled out an address book.

'Look, I happen to have her home number – can't imagine how.' Bourlet smirked with self-satisfaction. 'Why don't you ring her – see if she can spare you an hour tomorrow first thing? I'd ring myself, but . . . , well, her husband's around. Bit awkward, you know.'

His chuckle was like treacle.

'I see. Been needing a little therapy yourself, sir?' Andrew grinned.

'Mmmm. Not a good topic in the current circumstances.'

'Maybe not. I'll try the number now.'

Andrew felt in his pocket for change, then headed for the payphone.

He returned a few minutes later.

'Did you get her?'

Andrew nodded.

'She'll be here at eight in the morning.'

'Good. Then I'll bid you goodnight. Pop into my office for a word before you leave tomorrow, will you?'

* * *

HMS Truculent.

Lieutenant Commander Tim Pike ran a comb through his short, wavy hair. He always did that before going to bed, a hangover from his prep-school when Matron would inspect them all for neatness before lights-out.

It was after 0100 hrs. He'd stripped to his underpants for the night; there was no room on a submarine for luxuries like pyjamas. He looked at himself in the mirror, wondering if his skin still bore traces of the suntan acquired in Portugal four months earlier. His fiancée had insisted they go abroad to get rid of his undersea pallor.

Pike pulled at the elastic of his briefs to compare the untanned skin underneath with the rest.

'Checking your knob's still there?' Paul Spriggs jibed, lifting the curtain and entering the cabin.

'I don't do that by *looking* at it,' Pike quipped back, swinging himself up onto the top bunk. 'Sandra asked me to leave it behind, this trip. Said it was the only bit of me she'd miss!'

'So, instead you gave her a new battery for her vibrator.'

'Coarse at times, aren't you?'

Spriggs switched off the reading light, leaving the dim glow of the red lamp on the ceiling. The whole submarine was in red-light conditions in the hours of darkness. The men needed night-vision to use the periscope.

Spriggs didn't bother to undress – just took off his shoes and lay down on the lower bunk.

'Can I ask you a straightforward question?' the weapons engineer asked softly.

Pike braced himself to be interrogated on some aspect of his sex-life; he suspected his cabin mate had had little experience of women.

'If you must . . .'

'Well . . . have you *any* idea what the hell's going on. The captain won't let anyone in the wireless room when the signals come in. What's so secret about this change of plan, where the hell are we going, and why?'

Tim Pike lay staring at the ceiling. The answer he wanted to give was a bitter, anguished one, reflecting the offence he felt at not being taken into his captain's confidence. A first lieutenant on a submarine was meant to be the CO's right-hand man, but on this patrol Hitchens had been treating him like a mere sub-lieutenant.

'No.'

'No, what?'

'No, I don't have any idea what the hell's going on.'

They were silent again, the hum of the ventilation fans loud in the tiny cabin.

'Uh . . . , don't you think you *should* know?'

'There's nothing in the rule book that says a captain has to take his first lieutenant into his confidence, unless it's absolutely necessary for operational reasons. Our captain's doing it by the book. That's the *on-the-record* answer . . . Privately, and just within these walls – I'm as pissed-off as hell!'

'What has he told you?'

'Same as he told you and everyone else on the "pipe". Simply that the patrol task had been changed; we have to make all speed to the Barents Sea and he's been ordered to vet all communications personally until after the mission's completed.'

'Bloody odd, that – vetting *all* the comms. Ever happened to you before?'

'Once, maybe. For forty-eight hours or so.'

'But this is open-ended. Supposing World War Three breaks out up there – how'll we get to know about it? Can we rely on our captain to tell us?'

'Don't worry. The Russians'll let us know. They'll tap on the casing with a nuclear depth charge.'

'That's not funny, Tim.'

'Just put it down to experience. It's good training. Submariners are supposed to be lone wolves, operating in the dark. He's passing on the intelligence briefs telling us what else is in the area, so we won't hit anything, I promise you.'

Pike deemed it his duty to be reassuring, but it wasn't how he felt.

'You're sure he's all right, are you?' Spriggs asked with renewed earnestness. 'You don't think he's lost his marbles, or anything?'

'Why do you say that?' Pike snapped, alarmed that he was not alone in his suspicions.

'Well, Hitchens has always been a tight-arse, but he seems twitchier than ever this trip. He has domestic problems, doesn't he? Neurotic wife, or something?'

'Never confided in me . . .'

'Oh, come on, Tim! Stop being so fucking stiff-necked! You know bloody well what they say about him!'

Pike rolled over and looked down onto the bunk below.

'Tell you what, Paul – if you're really worried about

him, then so am I,' he confided finally. 'But we need to be bloody careful. I'm no mutineer.'

'Nor me, for God's sake. But what do we do about it?'

'We start making notes. Independently. Every time we notice something about his behaviour that's not normal, every time he does something that's not the usual procedure – we make a note of it. Just you and me. Nobody else. No conspiracies or he'll have us both by the neck!'

He rolled back, eyes fixed on the ceiling, hands behind his head.

'Okay,' Spriggs eventually acknowledged from below.

For a good ten minutes they lay there, staring at the red glow, disinclined to sleep, searching their memories for things Commander Hitchens had said and done since they'd left Devonport, things different from his normal behaviour. The more they thought, the more disturbed each became.

'The trouble with this game,' Spriggs moaned suddenly, 'is it leads to paranoia!'

'Mmmm. Let's rethink it in the morning.'

'OK. Goodnight.'

''Night.'

Less than a minute later, a sharp rap on the door frame brought them fully awake again.

'Sorry, sir.'

It was the young navigator. He was duty watch leader.

'Tried to raise the captain, sir, but he's out cold. Snoring his head off. Just can't wake him.'

Pike slipped feet-first from the upper bunk and reached for his shirt and trousers.

'What's the problem? What's happened?'

'Sodding great contact, sir. Sound room thinks it's a Russian *Victor* class sub, coming straight for us!'

CHAPTER FOUR

Monday 21st October. 0130 hrs. GMT.

HMS Truculent. The Norwegian Sea.

'Report!' Pike snapped at Cavendish, as he ran into the control room, still buttoning his shirt.

'Depth – two-hundred-and-fifty. Speed – fifteen knots. Course – zero-five-five,' called out the navigator.

'Water under the keel?'

'Plenty. Two-thousand-three-hundred metres.'

Pulling the back strap of his sandals over his heel, Pike hopped to the video displays of the action information consoles. The cross in the centre of the screen marked their own position, the small square box lower down and to the left that of the contact.

'We've been sprinting at thirty knots for three hours. Dropped our speed just five minutes ago for a listen, and then we heard him. We'd been deafening ourselves going fast.'

'Range?'

'Don't know. Could be ten miles.'

'Or more. At this depth and with the noise we were making, he could've heard us forty miles off easily. Another bloody triumph for NATO naval intelligence!'

The lanky figure of Lieutenant Cordell appeared between the periscope standards. He'd handed over the watch to Cavendish half an hour earlier, but had returned to the control room on hearing of the contact.

'Talk to me, Sebastian,' said Pike. 'What does our TAS officer think?'

'Definitely a *Victor*. The last intelligence sitrep mentioned one, but put it much further north. This must be another one. Could've picked up our track anytime during the past three hours. He's coming up astern on our port quarter. We detected him on the towed array when we dropped below eighteen knots.'

'We need to lose him. Where do we go?'

Pike knew the answer to his own question. But Cordell was new to *Truculent* and needed testing.

'He's chasing fast, so his sonar's deaf. When he slows down to listen, we should be invisible to him, now we've cut our own speed. He'll start guessing then, wondering whether we're keeping on the same course.'

'*Control room, sound room*!' The voice of the senior rating in the sound room came from the loudspeaker above the AIS console.

'Yes, Hicks,' Pike answered, keying the transmit switch.

'*Contact's fading, sir. Same bearing.*'

'There we are. *Victor*'s slowing down. When he finds out he's lost us, he'll guess we've detected him,' Cordell concluded. 'Now, will he expect us to keep the same course? If he starts searching left or right, he'll be stabbing in the dark. If he keeps to the same track he may think he's got a better chance of keeping on our tail.'

'So what do we do, brains?'

'I suggest we come left sixty degrees. That'll keep us in the deep Norwegian Basin, and put us at right-angles to him. We should pick him up on the bow sonar too, then – give us a better bearing and range.'

'Depth?' Pike pressured.

'He can go deeper than us, and faster. So why don't we go shallower, above the thermocline?'

The first sign of uncertainty flickered in his eyes. Pike was giving him no help.

'Disadvantages of going shallow?'

'Can't hear him any more. But still worthwhile, sir – I think.'

'What else was in that last intelligence report? Any other "hostiles"?'

'Nothing, sir – at least, not in the dope the captain handed out.'

Cordell's words were a reproach. Pike felt it directed at him. Glancing round, he sensed the attention of several pairs of eyes. They'd all been unsettled by the captain's 'pipe' the previous evening.

Pike wanted to round on them, saying he was as much in the dark about their mission as they were, but he kept silent; nothing should be done to undermine the authority of command at a time like this.

'Navigator, any hazards to the north?'

'None.'

'Right! Planesman, ten up. Keep fifty metres. Port ten, steer three-five-five. Revolutions for ten knots.'

Cordell smiled fleetingly; his advice was being followed to the letter.

Pike took Lieutenant Nick Cavendish to the chart table. Bending over it and pretending to study a detail, he spoke in a whisper.

'I'd better go and see Hitchens. You say you couldn't rouse him?'

'Yup. Knocked on the door, called loudly, shook him by the shoulder even, but he was out cold.'

'Wasn't dead, was he?'

'Don't be daft! I told you, he was snoring his head off. It's unlike him – he's usually a light sleeper. On his feet instantly if you call him.'

'Might've taken some sleeping pills. But he should have bloody told me if he was going to do that!' Pike hissed, resentful at yet another sign of his captain's disregard for him. 'Okay, Nick. You have the ship. And not a word about the captain. Understand?'

'Sebastian knows.'

'Well, keep it to the two of you then.'

Cavendish crossed to the ship control console to check his orders were being followed. Already the decks were tilting, as the submarine banked and climbed to its new depth and course. The planesman pulled back on the control stick, eyes locked onto the indicators.

Pike grabbed at pipework to steady himself as he headed aft. Beyond the control room the red-light glow of the night encouraged a stillness in the boat, even though half the crew was on watch.

Outside the captain's cabin he hesitated, listening for

any sound of Hitchens stirring. Hearing none, he rapped on the door frame and waited. No response. He pulled back the edge of the curtain and looked inside. It was exactly as the navigator had described.

Hitchens *could be* dead, for all he knew. The thin face was turned away from him, mouth open, cheeks hollow. Pike shook him by the shoulder. The body stirred at his touch, taking in a startled breath, and then with a grunt sank back into deep sleep.

Best to leave him, Pike thought. He wasn't needed in the control room, and would be little use if forced out of a drugged sleep.

He stood back from the bunk and looked around for a pill container. He found it inside a small, blue sponge bag on the table. The name on the label was unfamiliar, but the pharmacist's instructions read 'one to two at night when needed'. He pulled off the cap – it was one of those child-proof ones. Inside he counted about a dozen capsules. At least Hitchens hadn't taken the lot.

He looked at the wall-clock: 0200. Let him sleep it off.

Even asleep Hitchens' face looked stressed and unhappy. Enough stress to have unbalanced him? How could Pike tell? He was no medic, and they didn't have a doctor on board.

He pulled the curtain shut behind him and returned to the control room. The submarine was levelling off.

* * *

Over the Norwegian Sea.

The crew of RAF Nimrod call-sign Eight-Lima-Golf could hardly believe the drama unfolding below them. The four-engined jet criss-crossed the pitch-black Norwegian Sea at 220 knots, 300 feet up, monitoring and plotting every detail of the duel under the waves.

On routine patrol from its base at Kinloss, the Nimrod had been directed to the area by reports from the Norwegian Air Force, whose P-3 Orion maritime patrol planes had suddenly detected the Soviet submarine south of Vestfjord. Where it had come from, they didn't know.

Somehow it had escaped detection elsewhere in the Norwegian Sea.

The RAF were pleased to get in on the action; at first they'd suspected the target was one of the new ultra-quiet *Sierra* class boats. But then they picked up the characteristic noise signature of a *Victor*, albeit quieter than usual. Must've just come out of refit, they'd concluded.

It had taken time to find the *Victor*; the fix the Norwegians had given was over an hour old. The first line of sonobuoys they'd dropped into the sea had drawn a blank. Knowing the *Victor*'s ability to sprint at forty knots, the airborne electronics officer had gambled that the boat had turned north, to keep away from the shallows of the continental shelf.

He'd been right, but for the wrong reason.

Sixty miles north of the *Victor*'s last known position they'd dropped eight Jezebel sonobuoys two miles apart, in a chevron from east to west. Once in the water the buoys separated into two sections; one part, containing an omni-directional hydrophone, dropped 150 metres while the other section, linked to it by cable, containing a small radio and antenna, floated to the surface to transmit to the aircraft the sounds the hydrophone detected.

The noise of a speeding *Victor* can travel great distances. All eight Jezebel buoys detected it simultaneously. The two operators on the AQS.901 acoustic processor inside the cramped and tatty fuselage of the Nimrod grinned at each other at the strength of the signals they were hearing through their headphones.

To their left, on a large circular TV screen, the tactical navigator was constructing his plot of the water below. The line of sonobuoys was marked by eight small green squares, each identified with a radio channel.

'*Fifty and twenty-seven are top buoys!*'

The voice on the intercom indicated the Jezebels giving the strongest signals, the ones closest to the target.

Looking over the shoulder of the tactical navigator, the AEO saw that the top buoys were at each end of the chevron.

'Spot on! He's coming straight for us,' he shouted with satisfaction.

Suddenly one processor operator jabbed a finger at the top of his sonar display, the green 'waterfall' sound pattern detected by buoy '36' at the apex of the chevron. He was detecting something more than ripples in the pattern created by the distant *Victor*.

'Hey, I've got something!' he snapped into his boom-microphone.

He spun a roller-ball to move the cursor to the low-frequency noise that had caught his eye, a frequency too low to be audible to the human ear.

His fingers flicked switches to focus the narrow-band analyser onto it.

'I'm getting doppler effect on thirty-six,' he snapped again.

'Same on forty-two,' the second operator reported.

A minute reduction in the frequency detected told them something other than the *Victor* had just passed between two hydrophones and was heading away from the line.

The tactical navigator moved a cursor across his video map, to the position of the new target. He pressed a key to fix the co-ordinates in the navigation computer. The aircraft turned on its new heading.

'Prepare DIFARS seven-five and zero-nine,' the TacNav ordered.

In the rear of the plane aircrew selected directional buoys from a storage rack, set the radio channels, and loaded them into the ejection tubes.

A button on his control panel launched the first of the buoys. 'Seven-five, gone. Turn now,' sang out the TacNav. The plane banked sharply to reach the launch position for the second.

The AEO clutched the edge of the processor housing to steady himself. The 'G' force in the sharp turn threatened to buckle his knees.

'Zero-nine, away.'

He crouched in front of the processor screens. The DIFAR buoys, directional and highly sensitive, would give the speed and bearing of the target.

Ten buoys in the water was no problem for the AQS.901. Sixteen could be monitored simultaneously on the four displays.

'DIFAR seven-five gives bearing one-seven-zero, and decreasing.'

'Zero-nine gives two-five-seven, increasing.'

'Any classification yet?' the AEO asked.

The operators studied the pattern emerging on their screens. Listening didn't help; nothing but squeaks and crackles from shrimps and other marine life. It was down to the computer to analyse the low-frequency vibration of the target.

'Looks like a bloody *Trafalgar*! That's the noise signature!'

The second operator nodded in agreement.

So that was it. That was why the *Victor* had headed north.

'Bet he's never been that lucky before! A *Victor* tracking a *Trafalgar*? Impossible, according to the bloody Navy!'

'They're both doing nearly 30 knots!'

The bearings from the DIFARs changed rapidly as the target passed between them. The Russian boat was coming up fast through the Jezebel line.

'They'll both be deaf, going that fast,' the AEO remarked.

'Hang on!' called the TacNav. 'Our chap's slowing down.'

'She's sprinting and drifting. This is where he finds out he's picked up a tail. Could get interesting!'

While they waited to see what the *Victor* would do, the AEO grabbed the signaller's clip-board of intelligence signals. Very odd. Not a word about a RN boat being in the area.

The portly, middle-aged AEO chortled inwardly at the chance of embarrassing the Navy. He drafted a brief, sarcastic signal to the joint Maritime headquarters at Northwood, reporting their contact, and asking if they knew where all their own submarines were. The radio operator hunched over his keyboard, encrypting the message from a code card.

* * *

HMS Truculent.

Tim Pike was controlling the boat from the 'bandstand', a circular railing in the centre of the control room.

'Depth fifty metres,' yelled the helmsman.

'*Control Room, Sound Room!*' the communications box crackled.

Pike clicked the switch and acknowledged.

'*Contact's gone active, sir! The sod's pinging us!*'

Cordell threw himself at the AIS Console. Sonar data were transferred automatically from the sound room to the AIS.

The intercept sensor projecting like a stubby finger from the upper casing of *Truculent* had detected the faint 'ping' from below the thermocline. The computer gave them a bearing and range.

Cordell saw from the amber lines snaking across the screen that the 'ping' had been too weak to detect them. The sound-absorbing tiles coating their hull would have prevented an echo.

'Out of range,' he called over his shoulder. 'Contact bearing two-six-zero. Range five-thousand-three-hundred yards. Depth three-hundred metres.'

'Closer than we thought,' Pike breathed, leaning over the TAS officer's shoulder. 'Odd! The Soviets don't usually go active – don't want to give away their frequencies.'

The use of active sonar was a last resort for submariners; the signal inevitably revealed the position of the transmitting boat.

'He's just pinged again. Different angle. He's searching for us.'

'Time to show him our tail,' warned Pike. 'Steer zero-eight-zero. Revolutions for thirty knots. Clear the datum.'

'He's dead keen to keep tabs on us,' Cordell mused. 'Perhaps there's a promotion in it for him!'

The submarine banked to starboard; the men in the control room gripped fittings and grab-rails.

Truculent would make more noise going fast, and her

sonar would be deaf, but they needed the distance. Just a few minutes' sprint, then they'd slow down to listen.

'Give us room! Give us room!' Pike muttered to himself, his body spring-tight with tension. 'When he realizes we're not deep any more, he'll come up here looking for us.'

Silence fell in the control room, anxious eyes fixed on dials and screens.

'Still pinging?' Pike checked.

'No, he's stopped,' replied Cordell.

'Are we out of range if he pings again directly at us?'

'Probably not. Stern on, we're a small target, but he might get an echo off the propulsor.'

Truculent's propulsion system was like an aircraft's turbojet, a double row of compressor fans encased in a tube. Only from directly astern could the blades be detected on sonar.

'Another course change,' Pike ordered, swinging round to the planesman. 'Port five. Steer zero-six-zero, and be ready to go deep again.'

'How long now at this speed?' Pike asked.

'Six minutes, sir!' answered the navigator.

Three miles they'd covered; three miles further from the *Victor*, he hoped. Time to listen again.

'Reduce speed. Revs for fifteen knots,' he called.

The instruction was relayed aft to the manoeuvring room. The response from the propulsion plant was almost immediate.

'*Aircraft overhead!*' barked the tannoy.

Coming alive again, the sonar had picked up the roar of jet engines.

'Jesus! What *is* this? A plane too?'

'Because of the exercise?' Cordell guessed. 'The Sovs keeping tabs on Ocean Guardian?'

'Or something else. Something to do with what the captain was talking about. The East–West crisis!'

Pike hurled a silent curse at the sleeping Hitchens. Why hadn't the bastard told him what was going on?

Cordell's head turned, snake-like on his long, thin neck. There was a flicker of fear in his eyes.

'You mean the *Victor* was trying for a firing solution?' he asked aghast. 'Wants to torpedo us?'

'That's the usual reason for going active, isn't it?'

'You're joking!'

'Well, I *hope* I am!'

'Shit! The tubes are empty! We're defenceless!'

Pike thought hard. The intelligence reports had let them down. They were on their own. Better play it safe. He grabbed the microphone for the tannoy.

'Watch stand to!' he spoke, steadying his voice. 'We're being shadowed by a Soviet SSN, and will adopt defence watch conditions.'

'Taking it a bit personally, aren't you?' the weapon engineer chided as he entered the control room at a run.

'Taking no chances. Anyway, *you* were the one worrying about World War Three starting. Better bring the bloody tubes to the action state!'

Spriggs raised one eyebrow, but disappeared fast down the ladder to the torpedo stowage compartment below, where the ratings were already wrenching open the tube rear doors and loading the 1½ tonne *Tigerfish* torpedoes. Attached behind each propeller was the drum of guidance wire that would spool out after launch, keeping the weapons under the control of the submarine.

'Where's the target, TAS?' asked Pike.

'Moving away, sir. Bearing one-nine-three. Range ten-thousand yards. Heading one-seven-zero. Still pinging.'

'Good. Let's show him some more leg. Set course ten degrees. Revolutions for thirty knots.'

'Aye, aye, sir!'

* * *

In the sky above, the Nimrod banked and weaved. When the British boat slowed down she became desperately difficult to track.

They'd detected the start of her turn to port, but by the time they'd dropped a pair of buoys on what they thought was the new track, there was no sign of her.

Locating the Russian boat was easy. Its sonar 'pings' set the ink-pens quivering on the hard-copy printers of the acoustic processor.

'Noisy bastard!' growled the AEO. 'Doesn't want to lose our boy, does he?'

The pens quivered again and then a third time.

The AEO began to frown. It was doubly odd; a Soviet sub using active sonar, and a British boat being somewhere it wasn't meant to be.

'I don't know what's going on down there, but I'm not taking any chances,' he told the TacNav. 'Arm up a couple of Stingrays just in case that *Victor* decides to do something nasty.'

The navigator punched buttons to switch on the giros in two of the torpedoes in the bomb bay.

'Getting a reply to that signal, by the look of it,' remarked the radio operator, as the teleprinter began to buzz. He read the cipher as it was being printed and began to decrypt it from his code cards.

The AEO took the handwritten note when it was completed.

'Well, bugger me!' he exclaimed. 'They *didn't* know they had a boat here! They're ordering us to track her, and they're sending a tanker to refuel us so we can stay on task longer.'

'You mean we're not getting home today?' the TacNav groaned.

''Sright, sunshine.'

'My wife'll kill me. It's our anniversary! We'd got a dinner booked!'

* * *

0500 hrs. Soviet time. [0200 GMT]

Severomorsk.

The flight bringing Vice-Admiral Feliks Astashenkov back from Moscow was delayed again; then the taxi bringing him from Murmansk to the naval town of Severomorsk suffered a puncture, so it was four in the morning before he arrived at the comfortable villa that went with the job of Deputy Commander of the Northern Fleet.

He didn't go to bed. Apart from not wanting to wake

his wife, he'd come straight from the arms of another woman, and his conscience pricked him.

It had been a painful farewell with Tatiana. They'd both known they wouldn't meet again, but neither had said it.

He made himself some tea and slumped back in the red-velvet, wing-backed armchair that had belonged to his grandmother.

He felt afraid. Savkin had tricked him into making a personal commitment that could put him at odds with his own Commander-in-Chief, even the entire Stavka, the high command.

He knew what pressure the General Secretary was under from the Politburo. Savkin's survival was by no means certain, and if he lost his gamble to preserve *perestroika* Astashenkov could see himself being pulled down with him.

Why had he committed himself? Because he still believed in the complete restructuring of Soviet society that Gorbachev had begun, and Savkin was struggling to continue. But what if he could see that Savkin was going to fail, and still the call came to honour that commitment? Was he ready to destroy his own career for a lost cause? Better surely to hold his hand, to fight another day. All he could hope was that the call would never come.

His eyes focused on the canvas over the fireplace, an heroic oil painting of the destroyer *Sevastopol*, which his father had commanded in 1943 and in which he'd died. From childhood Feliks' ambition had been to honour his father by reaching the highest levels in the Soviet Navy, and having a warship named after him. At the age of fifty he was on track to achieve that goal – or would be if Nikolai Savkin didn't ask him to throw it all away.

In the dim light from the desk lamp, Astashenkov's eyelids began to droop. He dozed for about an hour.

He came to when the carriage clock on the mantelpiece chimed six. He stroked his chin and decided to begin the new day. Quietly he made his way upstairs to the bathroom.

After a shower and a shave he felt refreshed. His dressing room was separate from the bedroom, so he need not disturb his wife as he hung up his brown civilian suit and donned the dark-blue uniform of a Vice-Admiral with its two stars on the heavy gold shoulderboards, one broad band and two narrow ones on the sleeves.

The smell of coffee told him that his staff were awake and about their business. The house was managed by a middle-aged civilian couple from Leningrad; the woman cooked and cleaned, and her husband served at table, polished brass and silver and acted as valet to Feliks.

He also had a personal driver, who lived in the barracks in the main naval base area, a *starshina* who would arrive outside the house at 6.30 each morning, drunk or sober.

Feliks would take his breakfast in the kitchen, bread, sliced sausage, and coffee. His staff took pleasure in his passing the time of day with them; his wife treated them like serfs.

The kitchen window faced east, overlooking a distant creek where sailing boats lined the jetties of a small marina belonging to the officers' club. The sky was grey, but gold where the clouds broke to reveal the rising sun.

He would start early as soon as the driver arrived, tour the harbour and see who he could catch off-guard.

Severomorsk is a grey, granite naval town, ringed by greenhouse farms to provide fresh vegetables for the Navy. The town's only purpose is to serve as the headquarters of the Northern Fleet. Set on a bay on the east bank of the Kol'skiy Zaliv, the Kola inlet that leads to Murmansk, its piers stretch from the dockyard like outspread fingers. Heavy cranes tower black against the clouds.

They passed a guard post and the duty man hurried back into his hut to telephone ahead that the Deputy Commander was on the prowl.

To Feliks' right lay the sea, grey and choppy in the chill breeze that felt as if it came from the North Pole. The low hills on the far bank of the fjord five kilometres distant were discernible just as an outline in the mist.

Some of the finest warships in the Soviet fleet lined the piers. The twelve-thousand-ton cruiser *Slava* took up almost the whole length of No.3 jetty, some of her long-range missile tubes hoisted ashore for maintenance. Beyond her, at anchor in the bay, Feliks could see the distinctive outline of the aircraft-carrier *Minsk*.

He instructed the driver to stop the car, and wound down the window. The temperature felt below freezing, but he sniffed the air, savouring the odours of oil fumes and rotting fish. It was a smell of which he would never tire.

He was proud of his Navy, which had been expanded and modernized dramatically in the past decade. Yet he prayed it would never have to fight a war. He looked again at the *Minsk*. She carried a dozen vertical take-off jet fighters and a similar number of helicopters, but had none of the striking power of the Americans. The first of his own Navy's big carriers was still on sea trials and there'd be no more built.

Another pier, and a pair of *Sovremenny* class destroyers. They were due to sail any day now, to join the carrier *Kiev* and the cruiser *Kirov* maintaining the defensive barrier north of North Cape. Their departure depended on crew training; three-quarters of the men on board were conscripts. Autumn was the time for a new intake, and all the problems of moulding reluctant, ignorant young men into sailors.

His own submarine service was the worst affected. Greater skills were needed for the complex technology. With a rapid turnover of crews, harbour-time was high; most submarines in the fleet would spend all but a few weeks of the year alongside the jetty.

Feliks envied the professional, volunteer navies of other countries.

'Let's move on, Comrade,' he called to his driver.

They drove along the waterfront road that linked the heads of the piers. There were no submarines in harbour that morning; in fact, there were seldom any at Severomorsk, the main submarine bases being further north around Polyarny, at the mouth of the Kol'skiy Zaliv.

Looking out to the main navigation channel, he watched a fish-factory ship heading south for Murmansk, low in the water with the weight of its catch from around the shores of the British Isles.

Murmansk was an ugly sprawl of a city, whose population had grown to nearly four hundred thousand on the back of the Atlantic fishing fleet based there. The Gulf Stream kept the fjord to Murmansk open all year round with winter temperatures ten degrees higher than other Arctic zones on the same latitude.

To Feliks, however, the whole area was grim. He hated the bare rocks of the coastal zone, and pitied the puny shrubs and birch trees that struggled to survive inland. He longed for the gardened splendour of Leningrad.

The car turned left, past the storage sheds and maintenance workshops essential for keeping the complicated and costly warships operational. Men on bicycles weaved their way through dockyard clutter, as a night-shift finished and the day workers began.

Feliks decided against an unannounced visit to a ship. He'd bitterly resented such treatment from his own superiors when he'd been a submarine commander.

'Take me to the headquarters building,' he grunted. He'd put in an hour or so with the paperwork that threatened to take over his desk, before attending the morning command briefing.

* * *

0800 hrs. GMT.

Northwood, England.

Andrew Tinker searched the corridor of the Fleet headquarters for the office of the Fleet Psychiatrist. Finding the door, he tapped on it but there was no answer.

It was locked. He checked his watch – just past eight.

Behind him in the corridor he heard the click of high heels.

'Excessive punctuality's a sign of anxiety,' chided a confident female voice.

Andrew turned to see a short, red-haired WRN commander approaching.

'Tell that to those who trained me,' he countered.

She took his outstretched hand and held it loosely.

'It's a lost cause with me, I'm afraid,' she smiled.

Commander Felicity Rush was maturely attractive, but she looked weary.

'The thing is, I'm terrible at getting up in the mornings. Never normally see anyone before ten if I can help it. But when an Admiral orders. . . .'

She unlocked the door and led him in. Andrew was expecting it to be more like a consulting room than just another office.

'You *are* Commander Tinker?'

'Indeed I am.'

She placed her briefcase on the desk but left it unopened.

'Pull up a seat. There's nothing very comfortable, I'm afraid. I don't rate an armchair.'

Andrew dragged a typist's swivel seat over to the desk and sat down.

'Now, I've no idea what this is about,' she began, pulling a notepad from a drawer, 'except that it must be exceptionally urgent. Admiral Bourlet knows perfectly well how badly I function at this hour.'

Andrew raised an eyebrow at what he thought was innuendo, but there was no hint of embarrassment on her face.

'Are you the one with the problem?' she pressed, her eyes softening with professional sympathy.

'What? No, thank God! Not me. It's a friend of mine. He also drives a submarine, but the poor sod's just had a bust-up with his wife. We're worried he may have had some sort of breakdown.'

'Oh?'

'Yes. He's not responding to signals from headquarters and is now somewhere under the North Atlantic heading for the Arctic Circle at a rate of knots.'

For a moment her face didn't move. Then she frowned.

'Would you mind saying that again?'

Andrew began to explain. The Admiral had told him to tell her only what was necessary for her to form a medical opinion.

'This is utterly confidential. I can't give you all the details, but the blunt facts are these; the CO in question discovered his wife had been regularly unfaithful while he was away. That was bad enough, but then he found out one of her lovers was a Soviet agent.'

'Wow!'

'And it's beginning to look as if he's decided to get his own back on the Russians, using the weapons on his submarine.'

'Crikey!'

His words had shaken her out of her morning stupor.

'But that's appalling! Surely he'll be stopped by his crew.'

'Yes, but only if the other officers can see something's wrong and do something about it. That's why I'm here. I'm hoping you can give us some idea of how he'll be behaving down there.'

'I see.' She looked flustered. She'd never met a situation like this before. 'You'd better start again. Tell me what you know, from the beginning.'

As she listened, she took a note from time to time, usually just a single word to jog her memory.

'It's difficult without knowing the man himself. What you've described is a tragically common state of affairs. Infidelity is part of the human condition, and when the offended partner finds out about it, the effects can be devastating. It can tip someone over the edge into doing something wild, but that's usually a spur-of-the-moment thing. If I understand you correctly, you suspect that this man has planned some quite elaborate revenge. That implies a certain rationality – an irrational rationality, if you follow me.'

'Er . . , not altogether.'

'Let me explain. The initial reaction to marital breaks is the obvious one – anger and despair. That can lead to a depression which can become clinical – a sense of helplessness, loss of self-esteem, crying, physical disorders, thoughts of suicide. Now, if that's what your man is going through, it should be obvious to the other officers on board. He'll be unusually irritable, off his food, and above all indecisive. What sort of a CO is he, by the way? Easy-going or a stickler for discipline?'

'Definitely the latter, I would say. Not the most popular of captains. Gets the respect of his crew, but not their affection.'

'Pity. That'll make it more difficult for his first lieutenant. If he was a more relaxed type, his irritability would be more obvious. But it's odd. I'd expect a man like that to stick to the rules, whatever his personal problems. He might even find some comfort in the familiarity of discipline and order. Yet he's not doing that, you say. He's scrapped the rule book and taken matters into his own hands. He faces a court-martial for what he's doing, and if he does something nasty to the Russians, he's risking his own life and those of his crew and a great deal else besides. That suggests something much more serious than depression. He may be psychotic – unable to distinguish between reality and fantasy. But again, that should be pretty obvious to his junior officers . . .'

She was thinking aloud, tapping one end of her ballpoint on the pad, turning it over and tapping it again.

'Tell me more about him. I don't have a picture of the man yet. I'd get his file from the registry, but it's too early in the morning.'

'He's a year younger than me, and I'm forty. We trained at Dartmouth together – shared a cabin. He worries; always thought I had the edge on him because I'd spent a year in the big, wide world before joining up, even though I'd only driven a delivery van most of that time.

'Anyway, he'd come straight from school. A bit unworldly, I suppose; still is. Nervous of women, very few girlfriends before he met Sara. Certainly prefers the company of men, so he should be well suited stuck in a steel tube for months at a time!'

'Latent homosexual perhaps?' she asked casually.

'Oh, no. I don't think so. We slept in the same room for nearly a year; I just don't think he's very interested in sex.'

Commander Felicity Rush knew that no man was uninterested in sex and wrote down the words 'acute sexual repression' followed by a question mark.

'Are his parents still alive?'

'I seem to remember his father died when Philip was a kid. He was in the Navy, also a submariner. His boat disappeared up north, somewhere. I'm not sure they ever discovered what happened.'

'How old was Philip when that happened?'

'Don't know. Quite young, I think.'

'That's very interesting. A tragic loss in childhood can sensitize you; if you face something similar later you can react much more dramatically than normal. What about his mother?'

'I don't know anything about her. He never mentioned her. Funny, that. Used to talk of "going home", but never said who was there.'

'What about his work? He's respected as a commanding officer, you said; what's his attitude towards the Soviets?'

'Pretty sceptical, like most of us. Thinks they're a devious bunch of opportunists. Come to think of it, he's harder than most. Rants and raves in high glee when they get caught out.'

'So he hates the Russians?'

'Well, yes. He probably does.'

She arched her eyebrows and sat back, arms folded.

'All I can say is that you'd better stop him. And soon.'

'That may not be so easy. But that's why I want your advice. If we can get close enough to *Truculent* I'll try to talk to him – by underwater telephone. But if I say something wrong, I could make things worse.'

'Whatever you say may be wrong, as far as he's concerned. Look; if his mental disorder were just the result of a broken marriage, either he'd have had an emotional breakdown, which would be obvious to his crew, or he'd have come to his senses and given up any daft idea of revenge. Since neither of those things has happened, apparently, I can only assume he may have some sort of psychopathic condition, that's been dormant up to now.'

'Phil? A psychopath? That's ridiculous!'

'A psychopath isn't just someone going berserk with a

meat cleaver,' she explained. 'It's to do with attitudes. I'm sure Philip knows that launching an attack on the Russians is morally wrong, yet if he can't resist doing it, that's psychopathic. Such a person would be unaffected by anything you said to him. No. Your best bet is to talk to his first lieutenant. Tell him to relieve his captain of command.'

Andrew let out a deep sigh. The task ahead looked increasingly complicated.

Commander Rush suddenly leaned forward, elbows on the desk, her green eyes earnest.

'Suppose that doesn't work. What will you do then?' she asked.

Andrew looked away. He had always had an irrational fear of psychiatrists, that they could read his thoughts.

'That's something I haven't dared contemplate,' he lied.

* * *

0900 hrs. GMT.

Whitehall, London.

A black Mercedes turned into Horseguards Parade, and stopped at the rear entrance to the Foreign Office. The driver showed a pass to the policeman in the sentry box, who peered into the back of the car, recognized the passenger and waved the vehicle on.

The driver swung the wheel to the right and let the limousine roll easily up to the Ambassadors' entrance. The Soviet diplomat got out, glancing sideways towards Downing Street, conscious that it was there his message was directed.

A junior official received him on the steps and led him to the Foreign Secretary who had just returned from his monthly breakfast with the Diplomatic Press Corps.

Twenty minutes later the ambassador had delivered his protest about 'Ocean Guardian', and was back outside. He paused briefly for a news agency photographer to take his picture. Then the Mercedes sped him back to Kensington Palace Gardens.

* * *

12 Noon [0900 GMT].

The Kremlin, Moscow.

The news, that Monday morning, was not good. The Soviet leader could see the abyss opening before him. Strikes were spreading and he was in the throes of re-imposing full censorship on the media to prevent the situation snowballing out of control.

'*Perestroika* came too late for our people,' Nikolai Savkin muttered, half to himself, half to Foreign Minister Vasily Kalinin. The General Secretary had summoned Kalinin to his private office deep inside the Kremlin walls.

'Thirty years too late, maybe. Too many generations have been taught by the Party to believe the State will do everything, and that they, the people, need do nothing.'

'Such despair is not in your character, Nikolai,' Kalinin soothed. 'All is not lost; and don't allow yourself to think so.'

Savkin laughed self-deprecatingly. He knew he was the wrong man for the job. He silently cursed the Aeroflot mechanic whose carelessness allegedly caused the tragic and untimely death of his predecessor in a plane crash. Personally he'd always suspected the KGB had a hand in it.

Mikhail Sergeyevich Gorbachev had been in a different league from himself. He'd had the personality of a giant; if he were still alive the strikes would be short-lived. He'd have stormed onto the factory floors and argued the toss with the workers. If Savkin tried that tactic himself they'd spit on him.

Then there was the minority problem. Armenians, Latvians, Tartars; all were using the new freedom of expression under *glasnost* to voice the grievances of forty years. The KGB had played it cleverly; opposed to the new openness, they'd let the regional protests get out of control, so the politicians would be humiliated and have to turn to them to sort out the mess.

His control of the Politburo was on a knife edge; the

small majority still supporting his reformist views was being whittled away. He could only retain their support by buckling to pressure for the *perestroika* programme to be further diluted.

There were those in the Politburo who'd proclaimed their commitment to his predecessor's ideas, but without the man himself to hold the line now the going was tough, they'd begun to distance themselves from the policies. They had the rest of their lives to think of; if *perestroika* collapsed, and the old system of economic feather-bedding returned, Savkin thought, holding on to their jobs would be their number-one priority. Without the privileges that went with their status, life wouldn't be worth living in the chaos that followed.

He tugged at the bushy, white hair at his temples, then beat at his head with his knuckles, as if to drum sense into it.

'You're right, Vasily. I'm thinking like a defeated man. And if I think like one, soon I'll act like one. You must stop me.'

Kalinin was more than a foreign minister; he was also Savkin's oldest friend, an ally whose loyalty he believed he could count on for ever. A curious choice for a foreign minister, many thought; Kalinin had never travelled outside the Soviet Union before taking up his appointment. Yet he had an insight into the thinking of western leaders that Savkin found remarkably astute, all the more valuable because Savkin had little insight of his own.

It was Kalinin who had had the original idea of using the threat from the West as a goad to keep the Soviet economy on course for modernization. Previous regimes had used the fear of attack from abroad to tighten belts at home. What had been done before could be done again. The armada of Western warships currently on course for the Kola Peninsula provided just the threat that was needed.

'You know the irony of our plan, Nikolai?' Kalinin grimaced. '*Perestroika* is meant to curb the military budget and redirect funds to consumer goods. But if we make too much of the military threat from NATO, our beloved generals will be demanding the expansion of their arsenals again!'

'It's already happened. Admiral Grekov was here last night. Says he needs more ships to match the NATO navies.'

'I hope you told the Comrade Admiral he was pissing into the wind?'

'Yes . . . but not in those words. Something a little more refined. But tell me, what's the latest from Washington? Are they tugging at the bait?'

'It's too early to say. The predictable reactions have already occurred. Half a dozen Republican senators and the media have been raging about a new threat from Cuba. But McGuire hasn't commented yet. Our ambassador has been given a flat denial that the American helicopters posed any sort of threat to the *Rostov*, and the administration has had nothing at all to say about the MiGs.'

'And Castro?'

'He'll play ball. He's desperate for the aid we've promised him.'

'Is McGuire clever enough to know what's happening?'

'He knows little of life outside Middle America, so he takes advice. Tom Reynolds is the one he'll be listening to. And Tom's a cautious man. "Take no action until you have to" is his motto. They may be waiting to see what we do next.'

'And what will that be, I wonder,' Savkin ruminated. 'Every day that passes, the bigger the distraction needed to jolt our people back into line.'

'The Department of Naval Aviation is taking the television teams out this morning. Their film should be on *Vremya* tonight, and on the American networks. And Admiral Grekov is holding a press conference this afternoon for the foreign journalists.

'He'll condemn NATO strategy, call it provocative and dangerous. He can be pretty aggressive when provoked. And what he says is sure to get the American TV reporters on their hind legs baying at him. He'll call on NATO to abandon their exercise. By the end of the day the West'll be digging its heels in.

'Our own television will of course present the press conference in its true light: Grekov – the voice of reason; the American press – the hyenas of the West ready to bite into the soft and vulnerable throat of Russia. By the end of the day no one should be in any doubt there's a crisis.'

'We'll see,' the General Secretary answered doubtfully. 'It may not be enough.'

In his heart he knew it would take more than TV pictures and a press conference to jolt the Soviet citizenry out of their sloth. With sadness, resignation and fear, he realized it might take war.

* * *

1230 hrs. GMT.

Downing Street, London.

Every time he met the Prime Minister, Admiral Waverley was struck by her small stature and her femininity, which hid a steely determination. Both he and the Foreign Secretary were in a state of some trepidation about the meeting that lay ahead.

'Gentlemen, good day,' she greeted them in the hall. 'We'll go straight in and sit down, if you don't mind. I've got to be in the House at two-thirty.'

She led them into the dining room, where a small table was set with just three places, a large bottle of Malvern Water in its centre.

'You sit here, Admiral, and Nigel, there.'

The Prime Minister placed herself facing the door and nodded to the butler that he could begin serving.

'Now, Stewart, the Defence Secretary has told me about *HMS Truculent* and Commander Hitchens. It's appalling. And the Home Secretary's briefed me on what happened in Plymouth. This KGB officer – he's still on the loose. *Most* unsatisfactory!

'But it's the implications I'm concerned with. Lucky we had this little lunch arranged. Now, first of all, remind me about Ocean Guardian. As you know, the Russians are making the most extraordinary fuss. Heaven knows why; they've never bothered about it before.'

'That's right, Prime Minister,' Waverley answered. 'But the exercise has never been quite like this before. We hold them every two years; dozens of warships from several NATO countries deploying to the North Atlantic, but we've never taken the exercise right round the tip of Norway into the Barents Sea before, right to the doorstep of the Russian Navy's main harbours. That's why they're squealing. It's international waters of course, so they've no right to complain. And Norway *is* NATO's northern frontier.'

'So the Russians could conduct their manoeuvres off the coast of Scotland if they wanted to?' the Foreign Secretary queried. 'We wouldn't like that.'

'So long as they stayed in international waters, we could do nothing to stop them.'

'The idea is to be able to bottle up the Soviet fleet at the start of a conflict, correct?' the PM asked.

'That's right. The Americans took the initiative. They felt defending the Atlantic further south had become too difficult. The Soviets have so many new, quieter submarines.'

'Ambassador Bykov placed another protest on my desk this morning,' Sir Nigel remarked. 'Argued in most reasoned terms. Said this was a time of peace and improved east-west relations, and that such an "aggressive rehearsal for war", as he put it, was quite unacceptable.'

The PM waved him to silence.

'How big is our involvement? How many ships have we got up there?'

'About twenty. The Americans have eighteen, the Canadians, the Dutch, the Norwegians, Germans and French bring the total to over a hundred.'

Just then the door opened and a waitress brought in a tray of soup.

'Carrot soup,' the PM announced. 'My mother's recipe. I do hope you like it.'

The two men made polite, appreciative noises, and reached for their spoons. The waitress closed the door quietly behind her.

'Do continue, Admiral. You were interrupted.'

'Thank you, Prime Minister. Our main task is to provide an anti-submarine force centred on the carrier *HMS Illustrious*. With four escorts, she provides a screen ahead of the US strike fleet – the *Eisenhower* group. Our carrier will keep well away from the Russian coast, but two of her frigates will steam into the Barents, together with two of our submarines.'

'But *Truculent* had a special mission. Those new mines.'

'Exactly. She was due to break away from the exercise, to try to slip through the Soviet defences and get to the sort of position where the mines would have to be laid if war threatened.'

'Inside Soviet territorial waters?'

'Er . . , yes.'

'And the Americans are doing the same?'

'Further east, Prime Minister.'

'And the mines themselves? They're a great advance on anything we've had before?'

'Very much so. Anglo-American development. Launched from a torpedo tube in deep water. Very difficult for the enemy to detect. It's a two part device, with a sonar sensor – very clever – which can be programmed to look out for one particular type of ship or submarine, and the explosive bit which is really a high speed homing torpedo that gets launched once the target's been designated. And the whole thing can sit on the bottom for up to a year, doing nothing, then be activated or reprogrammed by sonar signal from up to forty miles away.'

'Right. We know what *Truculent* was *meant* to do – what is Commander Hitchens *really* going to do, Admiral?'

Waverley sighed uncomfortably.

'We just don't know, Prime Minister. We've had no response to any signals. He's ignoring orders, but appears still to be heading for the Kola Inlet. An RAF Nimrod picked up his track off Norway this morning, but lost it again. There was a Soviet submarine in the area, too.'

'But what about the rest of his crew? Are you telling me they're also ignoring orders?'

'Certainly not! But you see, Prime Minister, Hitchens could well say he's acting under secret orders issued to him personally. Often happens. Submarines operate in extreme secrecy. Frequently most of the crew haven't a clue where they are or why.'

The colour began to drain from the Prime Minister's face. She turned to Sir Nigel. Their looks met, each realizing for the first time the full implications of what Waverley had said.

'What . . . ah . . . what could he actually *do?*' Sir Nigel asked, clearing the frog from his throat.

'At worst, he could sink about a dozen Soviet warships . . .'

'Christ Almighty!'

'But that's improbable. To launch torpedoes and missiles he'd need the co-operation of his crew. He'd have to convince them war had broken out. Impossible, I'd say. But he has got those mines on board, four of them. It's just possible he could lay them . . .'

The Foreign Secretary put his hands up to his face.

'Just when Savkin's accusing us of undue aggression!' he groaned.

The Prime Minister tapped nervously on the table-cloth with her fingernails as she thought of what had to be done. She reached under the table and pressed a bell-push.

'Your soup's gone cold, Admiral. We'll go on to the next course.'

The waitress returned with her tray. While she cleared the plates and served them a main course of roast pork, the three remained silent.

'Now, Stewart. You obviously have a plan. What is it?'

'We've got about three days in which to find *Truculent* . . .'

'It's no good finding her if you lose her again,' the PM chided.

'Our submarines are designed to *avoid* being detected, Prime Minister. Twice he's passed through waters we were monitoring anyway, but keeping track of him when he doesn't want to be tracked is another matter.

'It's not going to be easy. The RAF are searching round the clock, but our best chance lies with *HMS Tenby*. Another SSN. A Commander Tinker, who knows Hitchens and is fully briefed on the problem, is flying to north Norway to join the *Tenby*. We have a good idea where Hitchens will go, and if Tinker can pick up his trail, he should be able to communicate with *Truculent* and stop him in good time.'

The Admiral had spoken in the most confident voice he could muster, but the Prime Minister had not been taken in.

'What if *Truculent*'s not listening?'

'Then we have a very difficult decision to take.'

'To do what?'

'Well, if we can find her, to stop her by force.'

'How would you do that?'

'Attack the *Truculent* with a torpedo. Try to cripple her without loss of life.'

'That's an appalling prospect. Is it possible?'

The Admiral shrugged.

'We've never tried it. Our weapons are designed to destroy boats, not wing them.'

'How many are there on board?'

''Bout a hundred.'

They fell silent again. None of them felt disposed to eat.

'There must be some alternative?' the PM suggested.

'We could tell the Russians what's happened,' the Foreign Secretary remarked. 'Warn them to keep clear of the mines until we can deal with them.'

'And give them a propaganda triumph of unimaginable proportions, Nigel. Just what they need to justify their claim that our manoeuvres are provocative. That's a ridiculous idea!'

'The earlier we pick up *Truculent*'s trail, the better,' Waverley pressed. 'And the more resources we put into the search, the sooner we're likely to find her. Sounds obvious, Prime Minister, but we've got precious few vessels in the right place. If we got some help from our allies – the Americans, the Norwegians, it could make all the difference.'

'No! I don't want any other nation to know about this. The name of the Royal Navy is held in the *highest* regard by friend and foe alike. What *would* people think if they learned that one of our submarine commanders could jeopardize the peace of the whole world? That our command structure has failed to prevent a madman going on the rampage in charge of one of Her Majesty's ships?'

Her eyes bored accusingly into the Admiral's.

'I assume you'll be examining your personnel selection procedures as a matter of urgency, Admiral?'

'That'll be our *second* priority, Prime Minister,' Waverley bristled. 'The first is to find the boat.'

'There'll come a time when our allies'll have to know,' Sir Nigel interjected gloomily. 'If you don't stop Hitchens in time, and he's about to blow up the Soviet Navy, it'd be better if our friends know before it happens rather than after.'

'That's a sound point, Nigel. President McGuire is difficult enough to handle as it is.'

She began to pick at her food and the two men followed suit. She frowned in concentration.

'*Do* you think you'll find him in time, Stewart?' she asked suddenly.

The Admiral swallowed some mineral water before replying.

'The chances are less than even, I'm afraid. Our best hope is that his officers twig what's going on.'

'What do you *think* he intends to do? What are we in for?'

'God knows! But if he lays the Moray mines outside Polyarny, and several Soviet submarines make a run for the open sea at the same time, he could take out four of them before they realize what's happening. Four nuclear reactors exploding underwater, pollution over a wide area, and at least four hundred dead! Not a happy scenario!'

'And all because his wife fooled around with some Russian? It's madness,' Sir Nigel exclaimed.

'A Russian who hasn't been caught,' the PM repeated.

'Perhaps he'll contact Mrs Hitchens again,' the Foreign Secretary mused, half to himself.

His thoughts were moving in a direction quite different from those of his leader. She'd dismissed his idea of warning the Russians, but it could be the only way to avoid catastrophe. It would have to be done with enormous care, and clearly without the knowledge of 'the boss'.

'If the worst does happen, Nigel, what's Savkin going to do about it?' the PM asked. 'He'll hardly declare war, surely?'

'I don't know,' Sir Nigel warned. 'He's making a lot of noise about "NATO aggression", much more than is justified. Got to ask ourselves why. Also this business of a ship-load of MiGs heading for Cuba; that has to have been done for a purpose. If Savkin's intention was simply to supply an ally with new planes, he'd have flown them to Cuba in transporter planes. No fuss that way.

'But to put them on the deck of a cargo ship and to sail it slap through the middle of the US fleet – I ask you! He *wanted* them to be seen! He *wanted* the Yanks to go screaming around in their helicopters and plastering pictures of his MiGs all over their television news bulletins. They're so bloody predictable, the Americans; they did exactly what he wanted! One more example of Western aggression to show to his own citizens on TV.'

'Yes, but come to the point, Nigel. What's Savkin up to?'

'Ah, now that's more difficult to say. The one thing we do know is that he's in big trouble with his economy. He's facing an unprecedented wave of strikes and civil unrest. He may be looking for a distraction, and banking on America, and us, supplying it. It's the oldest trick in the book, but it could be the only one he's got up his sleeve.'

The PM frowned with irritation; she'd foreseen her Foreign Secretary's conclusion, before he'd finished speaking.

'But I return to my point; he'll hardly declare war, will he?' she insisted.

'And I repeat *my* point; I simply don't know. The danger is he'll back himself into a corner; if he whips up enough anti-western feeling at home, and our Commander Hitchens then blows up some of his submarines, he may have no option but to declare war.'

The Prime Minister stared at him aghast. Then she turned to the Commander-in-Chief of the Fleet.

'Commander Hitchens must be stopped, Admiral. At *any* price!'

CHAPTER FIVE

Earlier that morning.

Severomorsk, USSR.

'Guard! Salute!'

The naval infantryman pinned his fingers to his forehead as the Zil limousine rolled to a halt outside the operations centre, its pristine black paint spattered with mud.

The Senior Lieutenant in charge of the guard opened the car door and saluted too, his eyes fixed on the horizon.

The Vice-Admiral ignored the young officer and strode briskly up the steps to the heavy, blast-proof, iron doors, eager to be out of the arctic wind. He heard the electromagnetic bolts click back, and the door swung open.

He entered the command centre of the Red Banner Northern Fleet. Built into a rocky hillside overlooking the town, the bunker was deep enough under the granite to withstand the megatons of nuclear destruction which the Americans had earmarked for it.

'Did you get a good catch at the weekend, Comrade Admiral?' fawned the Captain 2nd Rank staff officer. 'Some fine salmon for your dinner, perhaps?'

'No such luck,' Astashenkov growled, remembering the alibi for his weekend in Moscow. 'Nothing you could even feed to a cat! I shan't fish again until the spring.'

'The days are getting shorter.'

'I hate winter. It's at this time of year I wish I was commanding an *Eskadra* in the Mediterranean.'

Their footsteps echoed in the bare concrete tunnel. Ahead was the inner door, beyond which the air was filtered and recycled to exclude nuclear fallout or poison gas.

As they approached, there came again the click of opening bolts and the door swung towards them, driven by hydraulic rams powerful enough to push back rubble if the tunnel collapsed as the result of a direct hit.

Beyond lay another corridor lined with offices; then a corner, and the door to the operations room. The Captain 2nd Rank tapped his personal security code into a keypad, then opened the door for the Admiral to enter.

Two dozen uniformed men and women saluted. Astashenkov acknowledged them with a nod. He strode to the podium in the centre of the room. Admiral Belikov's staff officer hovered in wait.

'Good day, Comrade Vice-Admiral,' the young man bowed. 'The Commander-in-Chief is detained. An important telephone call from Admiral Grekov. He can't attend this briefing. He asks that you report to him in his office afterwards.'

Astashenkov nodded curtly, disguising his unease. Belikov talking on the phone to the Admiral of the Fleet? It must be urgent. Normally Grekov preferred to write.

Had they got wind of his meeting with Savkin?

He sat at the small desk. Another nod. The briefing could begin.

The wall was covered with a map of the northern hemisphere, the Pole at its centre. The Captain Lieutenant briefing officer was young, blond and enthusiastic. Astashenkov remembered himself being like that many years ago.

'This was the situation at 06.00 today,' the youth began, using a torch to project an arrow onto the map. '*Podvodnaya Lodka Atomnaya Raketnaya Ballisticheskaya*. We have eight PLARBs on patrol.'

These were nuclear-powered, ballistic-missile boats, their rockets targeted on the major cities in the United States. The newer ones were *Taifun* class, at twenty-five thousand tons the biggest submarines ever built. Each boat carried twenty missiles with a range of four thousand eight hundred miles, seven warheads per missile. Each boat could destroy one hundred and forty American towns or military bases.

This was the main reason for the Northern Fleet's existence; to keep operational forty submarines, carrying six hundred missiles with two thousand warheads.

So, eight were at sea. Not bad, Feliks thought, considering the maintenance they needed and the amount of shore leave for the crew.

'Four in the Barents Sea, four under the Arctic ice.'

The torch pointed to eight rings on the map. No precise positions, just the areas where the boats would patrol slowly, waiting for the orders they hoped would never come.

'*Podvodnaya Lodka Atomnaya,*' the briefing officer went on. PLAs were the nuclear-powered attack boats. 'Fifteen operational.'

Out of fifty? Not so good, thought Feliks.

'Three are in the Mediterranean, and two are currently returning from there. One is to the west of Scotland gathering intelligence on the British Navy, and one returning. Two more are on long-distance Atlantic patrol off the United States coast, and two transitting home. One of those is shadowing the US aircraft carrier *Eisenhower*. That leaves four on the barrier between North Cape and Greenland.'

'Four PLAs to try to stop the NATO SSNs from tracking our missile boats? It's not enough!' exploded Astashenkov in exasperation.

They all knew it wasn't enough; they also knew that the American *Los Angeles* class submarines and the British *Trafalgars* were so damned quiet, it would be difficult to detect them, however many PLAs they had on patrol.

'Permission to continue, Comrade Vice-Admiral?'

Feliks raised a hand.

'The surface fleet. In defensive positions facing the west, the *Kiev* and the *Moskva* are co-ordinating anti-submarine tactics, with five escorts.'

'What about the two *Sovremenys* in the harbour?'

'Due to sail tomorrow morning. Taking on final stores.'

The Captain Lieutenant rattled off a list of ships deployed further afield, then handed over to the intelligence briefer. Astashenkov concentrated his attention.

'The tactics in NATO's Exercise Ocean Guardian are

as predicted – what we'd expect them to be in the prelude to war.'

The boy had learned the jargon well, Astashenkov mused.

'The US carrier battle-groups have yet to threaten the *Rodina*. One is in mid-Atlantic, the other closer to the motherland, but still near Iceland. It's the British who are nearest our shores. Our radar satellite is tracking the *Illustrious* group in the Norwegian sea. And we have reports locating one or two of their submarines in the past twenty-four hours.'

Astashenkov's eyebrows arched in anticipation.

'The first came from a *Vishnya* intelligence vessel, north of Scotland. It heard a British helicopter trying to radio a submarine. There was no response and in desperation the pilot broke the code. He called "in clear" to *HMS Truculent*.

'The second may have been the same boat or another *Trafalgar*, west of Trondheim, travelling northeast at speed. A PLA tracked it for over an hour.'

'A PLA near Trondheim?' Astashenkov growled. 'I don't remember anything from last week's. . . .'

'Admiral Belikov, sir. The boat is under the personal orders of the Commander-in-Chief.'

'Ah, yes . . .' he nodded, pretending to know. 'And what do you conclude from these two – unusual – reports?'

'The communications security breach was carelessness,' the Captain Lieutenant answered a little too quickly.

'Or deliberate. . . .'

A silence hung in the air as they pondered the significance of the Admiral's remark.

'Indeed, sir.'

His eyes searched the chart. It was rare for NATO submarines to be detected so easily; he'd have liked to capitalize on the situation, and maintain the tracking, but the PLA near Trondheim had lost the target. He wasn't surprised.

Admiral Andrei Belikov, Commander-in-Chief of the Northern Fleet, had a square, lined face, with dark hair, thick at the sides but absent on top. He pushed his heavy-framed spectacles onto the bridge of his nose as Astashenkov entered his large, windowless office in the command centre.

Belikov gestured to a chair.

'Sit down, Feliks. Interesting briefing?'

'Nothing you don't know already, I imagine,' Astashenkov replied pointedly.

Belikov looked momentarily discomfited.

'Meaning?'

'I'm sure you know what's going on without having to attend a briefing, Andrei.'

'You're annoyed that you didn't know about that PLA in the Norwegian Sea. I'm not surprised; I would be too, in your place. But Grekov insisted on secrecy.'

He removed his spectacles and rubbed his eyes. He'd planned to involve his deputy in the KGB operation, but later rather than sooner. The chances of failure had always been high and if the plan came to nothing, the fewer who knew about it the better.

'Feliks, there's a little scheme underway, involving us and the intelligence departments which, if it's successful, could be the most significant since James Walker gave us US Navy submarine secrets.

'The British and Americans have developed a new mine which they believe is undetectable and unbeatable. If it came to war, they'd use them to close our harbours. They call them "Moray" mines, after that eel with the sharp teeth . . .'

'Yes. I know about them, of course.'

Belikov paused for effect.

'We think we're about to get our hands on one!'

'What? How?'

'The boat detected near Trondheim was *HMS Truculent*. We were expecting her. That PLA you hadn't been told about – it was there to pick up her trail, so we'd be ready to receive her and her little gift!'

'A British submarine? Coming here?' Astashenkov gasped. 'To *give* us a secret weapon?'

Belikov folded his spectacles.

'We *need* that mine, Feliks! They say it's undetectable by sonar. If the Americans and the British were to seed our coastline with those weapons, they could destroy the Northern Fleet before it fired a shot!

'Grekov himself ordered the KGB to give it top priority.'

'But how has this been done?'

Andrei Belikov savoured his reply.

'The key's in the hands of a very old man who lives near here – *exists* might be a better word. A prisoner of the State. He's close to death now, but he has a son. A son who'll do almost anything to see his father free before he dies.'

* * *

Murmansk, USSR.

The Moscow correspondent of the American Broadcasting Corporation couldn't stop the grin spreading across his fresh, Nordic face. *Glasnost* had opened countless doors for foreign journalists in the Soviet Union, but he'd never imagined the day would come when he'd be sitting inside the long, silver fuselage of a TU-95 maritime reconnaissance bomber, wearing the flying suit of a Soviet naval aviator.

Known as the *Bear-D* to NATO, the plane carried four giant turboprop engines, with double rows of contra-rotating propellers. The nose of the aircraft was glazed for observers to watch the sea below, and large bulges below the fuselage contained radar for locating shipping.

The pilot introduced himself simply as Valentin. He led the correspondent and his cameraman up a narrow, aluminium ladder into the cramped interior, followed by a technician from Gostelradio.

'When there's something to see, I'll tell you,' Valentin explained. 'Your camera can film through the glass.'

The compartment was crammed with radar scopes. There was nowhere to sit.

'Until then, you will be more comfortable in the back. There are seats there.'

He pointed to a narrow hatch.

'Jeez! Are we sure 'bout all this, Nick?' the American cameraman whispered from the side of his mouth.

'I guess we do as the man says,' the correspondent replied.

Passing the video camcorder ahead of them, they squeezed through the tunnel across the top of the bomb bay to the compartment behind the wing, which was equipped with seats as the pilot had promised.

It was going to be a long day. They'd left Moscow at 5 a.m., flying to Murmansk on a scheduled Aeroflot run. It was now 8.30 a.m. and they had to be back in time to catch the 3pm flight to Moscow, for a press conference with Admiral Grekov. Their material had to be on the satellite to New York soon after midnight if they were to make the evening news programmes on all four US networks.

It had never happened before – American journalists taking pictures of the US Navy from a Soviet spy plane. When offered it as a pool facility the networks had jumped at it.

They strapped themselves in as the first turboprop fired. The crewman thrust headsets into their hands, indicating that it was going to get noisy in there.

They were facing rearwards, and the seatbelts bit into their stomachs as the *Bear* accelerated down the long runway. Heavy with fuel for the long flight, it seemed to race ahead eternally before lifting sluggishly into the air.

There was no window in the rear compartment – just one dim, neon tube set into the roof. Claustrophobia gripped the two Americans, and from the expression on the face of the Russian cameraman, they knew he was similarly affected. It wasn't going to be fun, this assignment.

They slept a little. Two full hours passed before the pilot called them.

Forward of the crawlway, the radar operators turned from their screens to stare with unrestrained curiosity. Having Americans aboard their plane was an idea as alien to them as to the TV team.

'In five minutes you'll see something,' Valentin shouted through the intercom. He'd connected their headsets to the internal circuit.

'Where are we?' the correspondent called back.

'About five hundred kilometres east of Iceland.'

'There's a lot of water down there. Looks pretty empty to me.'

'Empty to you, but not to me,' the pilot boasted. 'We can *always* find your ships when we want to.'

'Oh, yeah?'

The two cameramen squeezed onto the single seat in the forward observation bubble and adjusted their lenses.

'You have a little microphone?' the pilot enquired.

'I've got a neck mike, if that's what you mean.'

'Put it inside your earphone. I'm switching to the frequency the Americans use. If they speak, you will hear.'

Nick fixed the microphone to his headset.

Suddenly the plane banked to the left and dived towards the sea.

'Sheeit!'

Nick grabbed for a hand-hold.

'Three ships in front!' called the pilot.

The journalists peered through the glass, seeing nothing but the grey sea flecked with foam.

Then both cameramen moved at once, eyepieces jammed to their faces. They'd seen the long lines of the wakes.

'Got them!'

The pilot dived and turned, skilfully keeping the American warships ahead of the plane's nose. Five hundred metres from the water, he levelled out, overshot and began a long slow bank round to make another pass.

Nick was no expert, but he knew a carrier when he saw one.

'Is that the *Eisenhower*?'

'No. The *Eisenhower*'s much bigger. That's the *Saipan*. Amphibious. For invasion. With her are one *Spruance* and one *Ticonderoga*.'

Nick felt uncomfortable at the ease with which his

nation's navy had been detected and identified by the Soviets.

'One more pass. Okay?'

'Yep.'

This time the Bear had slowed considerably. It banked over the *Ticonderoga* cruiser with its boxy superstructure housing the long-range, high-performance Aegis radar, and its deck covered with round hatches concealing Tomahawk and Standard missiles.

On the flight-deck of the *USS Saipan*, Nick counted six large helicopters. They flew low enough to see the deck crew gazing up at the circling plane.

'Those guys'd go ape if they knew a US TV team was up here,' he thought to himself.

'Enough?' Valentin's voice in the headphones.

'Well, I wouldn't mind . . .'

'But this is nothing. Don't you want to see your big ship?'

'Sure. Okay, we got enough here.'

The pressure was knee-buckling as the pilot pulled the TU-95 up steeply. A tighter, more intense vibration came from the engines as the propeller pitch sharpened, blades biting harder into the air to give them power for the climb.

Nick looked round. The radar operators ignored their screens, watching everything the Americans did.

'How d'you know where to look?' Nick asked into the microphone that pressed against his lips.

'National Technical Means.'

'What's that?'

'You don't know? You Americans invented the words.'

'Okay, but I didn't. I'm no expert.'

The pilot found that hard to believe. The Americans must surely have given special training to the man given the unique chance to fly in a Soviet warplane.

'Satellites. We have a radar satellite. Shows everything, even us.'

'So you don't need to use your own radar?'

'That's right. If we did, your sailors would know we were here.'

'They know now!'

The plane levelled from the climb. The pilot's fix for the *Eisenhower* was twenty minutes out of date. He'd guessed where she should have steamed to, but was wrong. There was no sign, not even a wake. He wouldn't get a new fix from the radarsat for another ten minutes. It would look bad not to be able to find the big ship before then.

The radar operators turned back to their scopes, hands reaching for the control knobs.

'*Soviet Naval Aviation TU-95!*'

The voice in the earphones was Texan. Nick's cameraman looked round at him and frowned.

'*This is US Navy Tomcat on your port wingtip. Please acknowledge! Over!*'

Heads whipped round to the left.

'Sheeit!'

Just beyond the end of the wing a dull-grey fighter floated upwards, US Navy markings emblazoned on the side. Inside its long perspex canopy, two sinister black visors and oxygen masks were turned towards them.

'*Soviet TU-95 – you're approaching a US Navy aircraft carrier. Please maintain a distance of five miles from the ship. Acknowledge. Over.*'

'US fighter plane,' Valentin's voice answered, high-pitched with tension. 'This is international airspace. Keep your distance! Over.'

'*Soviet aircraft –* ' The Texan voice sounded tired. '*The US carrier has a hot deck. For your safety, please make a left to maintain five miles from the ship. Acknowledge. Over.*'

Nick braced himself for a sudden change of course, but there was none. The Tomcat rose and banked away, ostentatiously showing off the racks of missiles under its wings.

Suddenly the *Bear* lurched to the left. From the right came another Tomcat, streaking past their nose, scarcely feet away.

'Christ! Somebody tell those guys there are US citizens in here!' the cameraman yelled in alarm.

The radio had gone silent. There was no point in posturing any more. Each side knew what the other was about.

The nose went down. The rush of air past the fuselage grew louder as they gathered speed.

'The *Eisenhower* is straight ahead. Soon you will have your pictures,' Valentin barked through the intercom. He sounded angry. 'They are very aggressive, your pilots. This is international airspace!'

Nick opted to say nothing.

Having failed to deflect the Tupolev from its course, the Tomcats settled one on each wingtip, indicating unmistakably that if the Russian showed the slightest sign of hostility towards the *Eisenhower*, they'd blow him out of the sky.

Ahead, the carrier came in view. The plane levelled off and dropped its speed. Nick guessed they were at about two thousand feet, but it was difficult to tell. The Tomcats dropped back to watch for the Tupolev's bomb-doors opening, ready to rip open the Russian plane with their 20mm Vulcan cannon.

'I will pass to the left of the ship, turn in front, and pass back on the other side,' the pilot told them, calmer now.

'She sure is big,' Nick whistled.

'Ninety-thousand tons. Eighty-five fighter planes on board. Nuclear weapons, too. Your navy has fifteen ships like that, our navy has none. They are a big threat to us.'

The microphone in Nick's headset was recording every word.

Fighters of different types were packed on the forward deck, wings folded, leaving the angled flight-deck clear for operations. Two machines were poised for launch on the steam catapults.

Past the ship, the two Tomcats closed in again, like guards pinioning a prisoner. The *Bear* attempted a turn but abandoned it just short of a collision.

'American Navy fighters! You are flying dangerously close! Please move away. This is international airspace. Acknowledge! Over.'

Neither fighter flinched from its wing-tip position. The radio was silent.

'American warplanes! You are violating the international rules of air safety. You have put my aircraft in danger!'

Silence. The cameraman grinned. The shots were terrific – big close-ups of the US markings. The foreshortening effect of the zoom made it look as if the wingtips were touching. In one of the Tomcats the navigator was taking pictures with a stills camera.

'Soviet aircraft!'

The Texan drawl was back.

'Okay, guys; this is where we say g'bye. We're five miles from our mother. Keep at least this distance, and we won't have to meet again. Have a good day now, y'hear. Over.'

The two Tomcats banked and accelerated away in perfect unison. From underneath came a third fighter, pulling up ahead to let them know he'd been sitting on their tail all the time, missiles armed.

'You have enough pictures now? Our time is up, I think.'

Nick looked at his watch. It was nearly noon. Time to head back to Kola.

* * *

Plymouth, England.

Patsy Tinker put an armful of carrier bags on the back seat of her car and closed the door. She was pleased with her purchases; it was high time she had some new things, and if Andrew complained about how much she'd spent, she'd say it was compensation for his disappearing again so soon after returning home.

She started the engine and crunched the gears, then looked over her shoulder as she eased out of the parking bay. She paused to let a silver-coloured Volkswagen Golf pass, then pulled out behind it.

Hang on, wasn't that Sara? She vaguely remembered the Hitchens had a silver VW.

'Keep an eye on Sara', Andrew had said. Okay, she'd follow; if Sara was going home, she'd drop in for a chat.

But the car turned up one of the Victorian terraces that led to the Hoe, then turned left, and left again into the close dominated by the modern tower of the Holiday Inn. There was one parking space free, which she took.

Patsy hesitated. She hadn't meant to follow Sara like a spy. Sara might be meeting a man.

She drove past the hotel and found a space. Sara was walking slowly up towards the Naval War Memorial on the Hoe.

Patsy got out, pressing herself against the car to avoid a dusty, red Ford Escort that pulled into the bay ahead.

Climbing the slope, Sara suddenly felt dizzy, her leaden limbs and dull headache the result of too little sleep for the past few nights.

Why had she come, she asked herself? Retracing her past? Trying to make sense of it? She'd walked here with Simon when he was younger.

She glanced back at the Holiday Inn, remembering the view from the sixth floor. She'd had a lot of fun with Gunnar in the hotel's big double beds, but now she was paying the price.

The weather was glorious, for a change – an autumn sun bathed the Portland stone of the monuments in mellow gold. As she reached the crest of the hill, she felt a breeze on her face, warm for October.

Ahead, the waters of the Sound sparkled in the sun. A white-sailed yacht made its way towards the marina, its wake stretching to the farthest shore.

Sara turned to look up at the weathered bronze statue of Sir Francis Drake, then bent her head to read the inscription. She'd been here so many times before, but had never read the words.

'Hello, Sara!' exclaimed Patsy, catching up with her. 'Fancy seeing you!'

Sara jumped.

'Patsy . . .' she gasped. 'You startled me.'

'Sorry. Didn't mean to. Such a lovely afternoon, I was passing and thought I'd stop to admire the view. You too?'

'I suppose so.'

Sara avoided Patsy's eyes. She found her self-confidence intimidating.

'Are you heading for the lighthouse? Perhaps we could walk together.'

'Why not,' Sara shrugged.

'Look, if you'd prefer to be on your own . . .'

'No . . . ,' she answered, puzzled at the sudden solicitude. 'Has Andrew told you?'

'You mean . . . , about you and Philip? A little. Just that there'd been a row.'

Sara gave a short, sharp laugh that caught in her throat.

'That could be an understatement,' she half-whispered.

They crossed the grass towards Smeaton's Lighthouse. A few couples had spread rugs on the turf to protect themselves from the moist ground while they enjoyed one of the last warm days of the year.

'D'you know, for years I thought that was a real lighthouse?' Sara remarked. 'I used to bring Simon here and tell him that at night the light shone right out to sea, to guide the sailors home – guide his daddy back to us. I never came here at night until recently . . .'

'It was real once.'

'Oh?'

'It was out on the Eddystone Rock for a hundred-and-twenty years. Then the rock began to crumble, so they brought it here and built a new Eddystone light on firmer ground.'

'Being a teacher, you'd know that sort of thing,' Sara sniped.

Patsy felt her scalp prickle. She and Sara had never liked each other much.

'Philip's gone to sea again, I gather.'

If Sara wasn't going to raise the subject, she would.

Sara stopped and eyed Patsy suspiciously, her face grey, her eyes red and ringed.

'This meeting's no accident,' she snapped. 'Who sent you?'

'No one sent me,' Patsy replied, edgily. 'Andrew said things were a mess – suggested I should say hello if I happened to see you. That's all.'

'How much of a mess, did he say?'

'Look, all he said was that you'd been seeing someone else, and that Philip had found out and was devastated. That's all.'

Sara looked away, embarrassed.

'He didn't say who?'

'Nothing like that, no.'

They began walking again, heading for a vacant bench by the lighthouse.

'I'm not really allowed to talk about it,' Sara said. 'I think it's an official secret.'

'What on earth do you mean?'

Sara chewed at her lower lip.

'I've been incredibly stupid,' she whispered. 'I can't believe how stupid I've been. You know, when I was nineteen, there was one sort of girl I used to really despise. Half drunk at a party – some boy with his tongue down her throat and his hand up her jumper. You knew that within the hour she'd be on her back and the next night it'd be with someone else. Well . . , they all think *I'm* like that now!'

'Nonsense! Who thinks that?'

'Philip. Andrew. The police.'

'The *police?*'

'Oh God, I shouldn't have said that. They're probably an official secret too.'

'You're not involved in anything . . . *criminal*, are you, Sara?' Patsy whispered anxiously.

'Criminal? I don't know. I hadn't thought of it as criminal.'

Sara looked round, checking no one was within earshot. Patsy found herself doing the same. They both ignored the nondescript, brown-haired man in a fawn windcheater sitting on another bench some twenty yards to their right.

'There were lots of men. I used to get so bloody *lonely* . . .' Sara's voice had become so soft as to be almost inaudible. 'One of those men worked for – a foreign government.'

'Oh. I see . . ,' Patsy answered, but didn't.

'Don't tell Andrew I told you.'

They stared in silence at the distant horizon. The aggressive outline of a frigate had come into view round the headland, making a sweeping turn towards the dockyard.

A foreign government? Patsy chewed at the words. God almighty! Sara meant a spy!

'Philip brought me here on our first afternoon in Plymouth, about ten years ago,' Sara digressed, half to herself. 'Wanted me to know where I could come to watch, when he set off in his submarine. We'd never been apart for more than a few days up to then. I had no idea what it was going to be like.'

Sara turned to Patsy, who found the digression aggravating.

'You're tougher than me, but it must upset you too, the separations?' Sara asked.

'Appalling. Particularly in the early days,' she answered briskly. 'But I learned to accept it, most of the time. There wasn't any alternative.'

She'd meant to sound matter-of-fact, but Sara took it as a reproach.

'The alternative's bloody obvious!' she snapped. 'Patsy, you're so *organized*, so bloody virtuous, I'm surprised you allow yourself to be seen in public with me! But surely, even in your well-ordered existence there must've been times, when Andrew was away, when you were desperate for . . . for *something?* I don't just mean sex; I mean emotionally?'

Patsy felt her neck and face begin to burn.

'You make me sound like a nun,' she laughed uncomfortably.

'Of course I get lonely, too. Of course . . .'

Patsy hesitated.

'I've never told anyone this. But I did have an affair, once. You must never, *never* repeat this. Andrew doesn't know, and he never will. It was a man I work with, a nice man. I shall always be fond of him. But one day I weighed what I was doing against my marriage and my children. And I ended it.'

'Blimey,' Sara whispered. 'So you *are* human!'

Patsy stiffened. A pair of gulls swooped screeching over their heads, one chasing the other.

'Is it our own fault, the way we end up? The sort of people we become?' Sara demanded. 'It can't be, can it? Our parents must take some of the blame.'

'I don't know. I suppose it's a bit of both . . .'

'My mother used to have one lover after another. Destroyed my father. I hated her, but now I'm just like her.'

Sara's eyes began to fill with tears.

Reminding herself why she'd engineered this meeting, Patsy decided she had to pull their conversation back on track.

'What did you mean just now? About your lover being from a foreign government?'

'I shouldn't have said that! You mustn't ask!'

But Patsy persevered, 'When politicians use that phrase, they mean a spy!'

Sara's face crumpled.

'A Russian?'

Sara nodded.

'Oh, God!'

Patsy felt chilled. This wasn't just a matter of infidelity; it was a betrayal of everything.

'Did you talk to him about Phil's work?'

'Of course not. At least, not in any way that mattered,' she insisted. 'Anyhow, I don't know anything about it, except what it does to me.'

'I see. But . . .' Patsy searched for something to say.

'Philip found out. And he flipped, literally. Something seemed to snap in his mind. Andrew was scared he might do something daft. I think they're trying to bring him back, but nobody's telling me anything. If *you* know what's happening. . . .'

'Not a thing. It's all news to me. But what did you mean about him doing something daft?'

'Blowing up the Russians? I don't know – some sort of revenge.'

'You can't be serious!'

'*I* don't know . . . !' Sara wailed, and burst into tears.

'It's not just because of what I did, though! I'm sure there's something else.'

'Like what?'

'I don't know. There's been something churning round in Phil's mind for months. Something to do with his work. He never said. Always denied there was anything wrong.'

Patsy felt deeply alarmed. She decided she'd better sound reassuring if she could.

'Well, let's hope they get Philip back soon. You'll have to talk the whole thing out with him, I suppose. But what about your marriage? Do you want to save it? You might still be able to.'

Sara shut her eyes and groaned. Patsy hadn't understood.

'It's too late for that! Don't you see?'

'Oh, I'm sure it's not. Andrew'll talk to him. Philip can get a job ashore, so he won't be away so much.'

'Patsy! *Listen!* He's not . . . coming . . . back! Ever!'

A shiver ran down Patsy's spine.

'It was in his eyes as he left. Philip is going to die!'

Patsy felt cold all over. The wind had got up.

* * *

Northwood, England.

'Are you there, Anthony?' the Commander-in-Chief shouted, pushing open the door to the room occupied by the Flag Officer Submarines.

Admiral Bourlet rose to his feet.

'We need to talk. About Hitchens. Can you come along to my office, and bring his file with you?'

'Of course.'

Bourlet had spent much of the morning studying the file. It had not made comfortable reading.

He closed the C-in-C's door and sat in the leather armchair to which Waverley directed him.

'Never seen the PM more alarmed. She's horrified at the very idea that world stability could be threatened by an officer in Her Majesty's Navy.'

'She's ahead of herself, in that case. It hasn't come to

that yet. We've still a good chance of stopping him, sir,' Bourlet announced, with contrived confidence.

'What I want to know is how such a lunatic managed to end up as the captain of an SSN. They're supposed to be our top talent, for God's sake!'

Sir Stewart perched a pair of half-moon spectacles on the bridge of his long, thin nose. He reached across for the file.

'To be frank, sir, he's been bloody lucky. Twice,' Bourlet explained as Waverley read. 'He scraped through his "Perisher" with the recommendation that his ability to command had yet to be proven. They said he should be given the chance to show his worth as an Executive Officer. Then one of the Gulf sultanates bought a fleet of small diesel submarines, remember? Offered enormous sums tax-free to our submariners to work five-year contracts training Arabs to drive them. We lost four COs in a month. Three from *Oberon* diesel boats, and one from an SSN.'

'And suddenly Lieutenant Commander Hitchens found himself in demand.'

'Exactly. Got an "O" boat to drive. Did all right for a couple of years. Not much flair, but no mishaps either. Then came his second lucky break. Look at his S206 dated a couple of years back – his Officer's Confidential Report, at the time he came up for promotion to Commander – Section 3, the General Report, says "A competent commanding officer of an 'O' boat, but a man obsessed by petty rules and regulations. Holds the respect of his men through firm discipline rather than any degree of affection. Not a team player. Could create unnecessary tension on board".

'Yet Section 5 recommends him for immediate promotion. The explanation comes in Section 6 – written by my predecessor. As you'll see, sir, he says that although Hitchens hadn't displayed the usual flair and leadership required for the command of a nuclear boat, the sudden shortage of SSN COs which occurred at that time made it essential Hitchens be considered for promotion.'

'Ah! It's coming back to me. There was some frightful accident. . . .'

'That's right, sir. Up at Faslane. Three SSN COs driving off base for a stag night. One of them was getting married the next day. Hit a petrol tanker. Went up in flames. All dead.'

'And suddenly we had three boats without skippers. Mmmm. That explains some of it. So, we've got an obsessive nit-picker on the loose, obsessed at the moment, it seems, with a personal grievance against the Russians. Anything else in the file, further back?'

Bourlet riffled through the pages.

'He came from a naval family. Father and grandfather. His father had a curious end to his career. Could be relevant. Remember the old *HMS Tenby*? A diesel submarine that disappeared in the Barents Sea in November 1962? All hands lost. No trace of her ever found.'

'Oh, yes. I remember vaguely.'

'Philip Hitchens' father was her second-in-command.'

'I remember it now; I was at Dartmouth at the time. But I can't remember the details. . . .'

'She was on an intelligence mission, monitoring Soviet torpedo trials. We believed some of them were nuclear-tipped. There was always a suspicion that the Soviets had sunk her, but never any evidence. Some boffin down at the naval architects' department in Bath came up with a theory that a fire on one of the mess decks could have flashed through into the torpedo room. Proved it on a test rig. The enquiry concluded that's what must have happened. Magazine explosion causing total loss. They changed the design of the class after that.'

'Hitchens the younger must've been still at school at the time. Traumatic for him.'

'Early teens. There's nothing in his file about his thoughts on the matter, except a curious line in his original application to join. He said he saw himself as "continuing the career which his father had been unable to complete".'

'That obsessive streak again. There, right at the start, and no one saw the danger in it.'

'To be fair, it's not an uncommon characteristic in the Navy, sir.'

'Hmmm. So what you're saying is that there's nothing in the man's record that could've led us to predict something like this.'

'Absolutely, sir. The file shows he's a weak link in the chain, slipped into the system out of temporary necessity. But there's nothing to suggest he'd ever defy orders. Just the opposite, if anything.'

'But how come he got chosen for this special mission with the Moray mines? We should've chosen a top operator for that job.'

'It's just the way the cards fell, sir. *Truculent* was already being fitted out as the trials boat for the mines when Hitchens took command. She's the only boat equipped to use the mines so far. It had to be him. There was no alternative.'

'Jesus! What a shambles! I don't think the PM'll swallow much of this. She's already looking for someone to blame,' Waverley concluded miserably. 'What's the latest on the search for *Truculent*?'

'Nothing new, sir. The Nimrods haven't made contact again, and at present *Tenby*'s not in the frame yet. Ironic that the name of the sub we're sending to look for Hitchens should be the same as the ship in which his father died.'

'God! If he ever finds out, it'll probably drive him clean round the bend!'

* * *

The Arctic Circle.

The mountainous spine of Norway turned a sinister grey as the RAF HS.125 executive jet flew steadily north. When the sun dipped below the horizon, the snow-covered tips of the peaks glowed pink. Directly below them the water in the fjords looked inky black.

Andrew felt restricted by the narrow cabin. They'd been flying for over three hours and he was desperate to stretch his legs. Even to stand up meant stooping to prevent his head striking the roof.

The landscape below had been dramatic to watch for a while, but the more he gazed down at the vast expanse of the Norwegian Sea stretching away to the left, the more pessimistic he became about the difficulties involved in finding the *Truculent*.

The captain eased his portly frame through the cockpit door. A surprisingly elderly man, Andrew thought, in his late fifties at least. A former fighter pilot, perhaps, who couldn't live without flying, but who'd grown too old for fast jets?

'More coffee, Commander?'

'No thanks,' Andrew answered. 'It just makes me need to pee, and the heads you have on board isn't the easiest to get in and out of!'

The RAF man grinned. 'We just call it "the can". Not a lot of room, I agree, but the plane's a delight to fly. Want to come up front?'

Andrew followed the pilot forward and ducked through the doorway. The second officer grinned a greeting. There was no room to enter the cockpit, so he just leaned in, supporting himself on the doorframe. The control panel was dominated by a multi-coloured radar screen in its centre.

'I've just spoken to Tromso. Should be there in about twenty-seven minutes,' the second officer announced. 'They said they were expecting you. Mentioned a Sea King.'

'That's right.'

'Going to join a ship, are you?'

'Yep. A submarine.'

'Rather you than me, on a night like this.'

'Heard a weather forecast, have you?'

'Force five, I'm afraid.'

Andrew grimaced. He disliked helicopter flights at the best of times, but to be lowered on a wire towards a conning tower, which was wobbling about like a wooden toy? Not pleasant.

'What does that radar screen show you?' Andrew asked.

'It's mainly for weather. Storm warning, but it maps the ground if you point it downwards.'

He indicated the green and yellow shapes interspersed with blue.

'That's the fjord where we sank the Tirpitz,' he pointed. 'Tromso's just on the shoreline. We'll start our descent in a couple of minutes.'

Andrew nodded, and studied the multitude of dials for a while. Then the radio crackled and the captain pulled earphones over his head. Andrew made a gesture of thanks and returned to the main cabin.

Cross-winds buffeted them as the main wheels touched the runway. Andrew peered towards the terminal building, where two helicopters were silhouetted against the lights of an open hangar. Then he strained to study another shape further away.

'Bloody hell, that's a Nimrod,' he muttered. 'What's the RAF doing here?'

The HS.125 jolted to a halt. Andrew unbuckled his belt and zipped up his holdall. The whine of the jets died as the pilot cut the engines. From the cockpit came the sound of switches being turned off, and the giros spinning to a standstill.

'Did you see that?' the pilot called over his shoulder. 'One of ours. Nimrod. Probably got a technical hitch.'

Andrew suspected its presence at Tromso was more significant than that. He stretched out his hand to shake the pilot's.

'Well, goodbye, and thanks for a nice flight.'

'Is that bag all you've got? No other luggage?' the RAF man asked.

'That's all.'

'Just staying overnight then, are you?'

'I've everything I need in here. S'long now.'

Andrew hurried off the plane, anxious to avoid further questions. On the tarmac was an officer in the grey-blue uniform of the Norwegian Air Force.

'Commander Tinker? I'm Major Mjell, the Station Commander. Welcome to Tromso.'

His Norwegian accent seemed to dip in and out of the words like a wading bird.

'Thank you. I'm glad to be here.'

'We should hurry. The weather will get worse. Even now the helicopter pilots are not sure they can land you on your submarine. We might have to try tomorrow.'

'I'm ready now. Let's get a move on. I must get aboard tonight. Is the helicopter ready?'

'Yes, but there is someone you must speak with first. Please to come to my office.'

He hurried across the tarmac to the far end of the terminal. The wind was icy and cut through the thick navy blue pullover Andrew was wearing.

'Ah, that's better. It's warm in here. Now I'll leave you three alone for five minutes. That should be enough?'

Andrew saw a whey-faced young man in a flying suit rise from a leather armchair to greet him. His shoulder insignia marked him as an RAF Flight Lieutenant.

'Five minutes should be fine,' the pilot acknowledged in a strong Scots accent, then introduced himself. 'Alex McCringle. I expect you saw the grey beast on the tarmac?'

'Nimrod MR2, unless I'm much mistaken.'

'Exactly. Just come off patrol. This is my AEO, Stan Mackintosh. He's the boss. Northwood told us to land here so we could report to you.'

'Picked up some curious activity which they said you'd want to know about,' Mackintosh explained.

'Oh? Did they say why I'd want to know?'

Andrew was curious to know how much the RAF had been told of the Navy's problems.

'Said it was to do with the exercise *Ocean Guardian*? You're involved in a special operation code-named *Shadowhunt*? Playing the part of the Soviets, trying to track one of our submarines?'

'Something like that, yes.'

He could tell they hadn't been convinced by the cover story.

'Odd sort of operation, when Northwood doesn't even know where its boats are,' the AEO needled. 'Anyway, let me tell you what we got.'

The flight lieutenant spread a chart on the office table.

His finger drew a square shape over the sea about two hundred miles west of Trondheim in southern Norway.

'We began a box search of this area at about one o'clock this morning. Beautiful clear night. Getting worse now, though. Anyway, we dropped a sonobuoy barrier looking for a *Victor* which the Norwegians had been tracking. Well, we found it but he wasn't on his own. He was chasing one of yours, a bloody *Trafalgar*.'

He pointed northeast on the chart.

'And what happened?'

'We tracked them for a bit, then suddenly your boy got wise and slowed right down. The *Victor* didn't realize what had happened at first, but then he slowed up too. We lost your boat at that point. They're bloody quiet when they're not rushing about, the *Trafalgars*. The *Victor* must have lost him too, because he suddenly went active! Practically deafened us!'

'Pinged him, did he? They don't often do that.'

'Exactly. Must have been pretty bloody eager to keep tabs on your boy, don't you think?'

'Well, they don't often get a chance like that. We're normally too careful for them. But this time. . . .'

Andrew searched for the right words, that would give nothing away.

'This time it's different tactics,' he added cautiously.

'Well, the sooner you get back to the old ones, the better, I reckon!'

'So what happened after that?'

'We never picked up the T-boat again. Nor did the Russian. He went pinging around in all directions, up and down, changing depths, but he never found him again. Northwood told us to try to track your man; we dropped buoys all over the place, but he'd gone. And that's it, Commander. Any use to you?'

'Very much so, thank you. Now show me again on the chart exactly where you lost her.'

The AEO pointed and Andrew made a note of the co-ordinates.

'So where are ye off to now, then?' McCringle asked,

making no effort to restrain his curiosity. '*Hunting the Shadow* underwater, are ye?'

'That's right. Trying out some new equipment . . .' Andrew lied.

'Hidden in that wee bag, is it?' he joked, pointing at Andrew's holdall.

''Sright. Don't need much space for a floppy disc . . .'

'Well, we'll see how good it is, then. We've been told to stick around here for a few more days. See if we can be of some help. My fiver says we'll find him again first!'

'If you do, I'll happily pay you ten times that.'

'You're on!'

They shook on it.

'When do you plan to fly again?'

'Tomorrow at eight,' said Mackintosh. 'They're flying in a Herc from Kinloss with a load of sonobuoys – we've almost run out.'

The door clicked open. Major Mjell poked his head round.

'You must go now to the briefing room, Commander. It's the last chance to get off tonight.'

'Good luck,' McCringle called as Andrew followed the major out.

He followed the Norwegian out onto the tarmac again. The wind was even stronger. They passed the HS.125, refuelling for the return journey, and walked on towards the big, brightly lit hangar with the two helicopters parked outside.

'This is the regional search and rescue headquarters,' Mjell explained. 'The Coastguard use it too.'

Warm air enveloped them as they stepped inside the flight office.

'Klaasen,' announced the pilot, introducing himself.

'Tinker.'

The three-man aircrew for the Sea King were dressed in drab green immersion suits that would keep them dry if they ended up in the sea.

The loadmaster took a quick look at Andrew, assessing his size, and took from a rack a larger rubber suit in day-glo red.

'You'll be familiar with this equipment, Commander?'

Andrew pulled down the heavy zip and stepped into the legs of the suit. Floppy black rubber boots encased his feet. He forced his arms into the sleeves, taking care not to rip the soft rubber at the end which made a water-tight seal with his wrists.

'We need the suit back,' Klaasen reminded him drily. Andrew knew how expensive they were. 'After you're safely on board the submarine, we'll lower a bag for you to put it in. And the life-jacket too.'

'Fine.'

Andrew slipped the life-preserver over his head and pulled up the strap under his groin.

'Now, if you're ready, I will start my briefing.'

The aircrew stood in a semicircle and checked their watches. Klaasen spoke in Norwegian for the first minute, outlining the flight plan. Then he broke into English.

'The rendezvous with the *Tenby* should be seventy kilometres west from here. It will take about half-an-hour to the area, and then we have to find her. She should be surfaced, but we have not been able to contact her on VHF. Some hills are in the way. We can try again in the air.

'The sea is high and the wind getting stronger, so we'll put you on the fin. We lower a guideline first, so that they can pull you to the right place as you go down. You use the same system, I think?'

'Yes. I've had the misfortune to go through this several times!'

'Then we'll waste no more time. We can go to the aircraft now, and the loadmaster will give you the safety brief. You have heard it all before, but we insist.'

'Fine by me.'

Major Mjell gripped him by the hand and wished him luck.

Andrew clambered into the helicopter, and felt his way into one of the aluminium-framed canvas seats that lined the fuselage. Klaasen flicked the power switch and a red light came on in the roof, just bright enough for Andrew to make out the layout of the interior.

'The door close while we fly. I open when the pilot finds the ship.' The loadmaster's English wasn't up to the standard of the pilot's. 'When I say, you unfix seat belt and sit on the floor. Very careful, it's a long way down. Then I put cable harness on you, you know?'

'Yes, I know,' Andrew answered patiently.

'Emergency exits.' The loadmaster pointed to the door itself and to two other panels in the fuselage sides. 'If we go in the water, you must wait until the rotor stops, otherwise . . .'

He made a sign of slitting his throat.

'Let in the water first. Then swim out as it sinks. Then pull life-jacket. Not to inflate before leaving aircraft.'

'Yes, yes. Fine.'

The pre-flight briefings made Andrew more nervous than the flight itself. It was all pointless anyway. Few people survived helicopter crashes – they all knew that.

With a muffled roar the twin jet engines lit and built up their revs to a high-pitched whine. The loadmaster gave him a thumbs-up sign, which Andrew returned. Then with a bowel-churning grind, the gearbox was engaged and the rotors began to turn.

It was almost pitch black inside the helicopter. From time to time as they flew, the loadmaster pulled out a flashlamp and shone it along the bare pipes of the hydraulic system, checking for leaks.

The two aircrew were bulky, anonymous shadows against the amber glow of their instruments; for the next thirty minutes his life lay in their hands.

He thought of home. Patsy. The children: Theresa, Mark, and Anthony struggling to cope with boarding school.

A change in the engine pitch; his heart beat faster.

He cursed himself for being so nervous. Eyes closed, he thought of the task ahead. The Nimrod could cover a greater area than a submarine, although its small sonobuoys lacked the sensitivity of the bigger, more powerful systems in the *Tenby*.

The tail of the machine dipped, slowing down, it banked right, then left, spreading the search. The loadmaster extended his hands forward and swayed from side to side, indicating the roughness of the water below.

For a good ten minutes they hovered or flew slowly backwards and forwards.

Suddenly the loadmaster touched Andrew on the knee and gave him the thumbs up. They'd found his boat.

The nose dipped, the machine banked and sped in a new direction. Three minutes later Klaasen eased it back into the hover. The loadmaster crouched by the door and wrenched it open, letting in an icy blast. Then he busied himself with the winch, unstrapping the harness, checking the cable and controls.

Klaasen manoeuvred the machine inch by inch. The loadmaster beckoned. Andrew unclipped his belt and slid forward onto the floor, clutching his holdall firmly. The loadmaster slipped the harness over his head. He tightened the strop under his arms and winched the cable taut.

Ahead and below was blackness. Then he saw green and red navigation lights, close together. A boat. A pencil of light from the helicopter pierced the dark, picking out white wave-crests in its search.

It found the smooth, shiny curves of the submarine. The beam followed the casing forward, a sparkle from the foam breaking across the steel, then the fin reaching up. On the top, the pale dots of faces looking up.

He had to land on that? Jesus, it looked so small! As he watched, the periscope and radio mast slid down into the fin so as not to obstruct his descent.

The loadmaster lowered a thin handline, weighted at the bottom. Through his microphone, he directed the pilot until the line was grabbed by a sailor on the bridge. Then he secured the line to Andrew's harness.

He was ready? Andrew nodded and pulled the rubber hood over his head. It was wet down there and bitterly cold.

A final thumbs up; Andrew felt the winch cable jerk the strop tight under his armpits. He sat on the ledge, legs over the edge. The downdraught from the rotor tugged at the loose folds of his survival suit. A firm push in the small of his back and he was in mid-air.

The cable jolted and jerked. The winchman lowered him a few metres at a time. Arms by the side; that's what they always tell you. Do nothing; just hang there; leave it to the other guys. It was an act of faith. It had to be.

The wind tugged at his feet; he felt salt spray on his face, or was it rain? Something pulled him sideways against the wind. He remembered the handline.

Suddenly his shins cracked hard against metal. He gasped at the sharp pain. Rough hands grasped his legs, then his waist. The edge of the bridge grazed his buttocks; he was down. The steel grating felt firm underfoot, and the chest-high rim of the conning tower supported his back.

He lurched against it. The submarine rolled like a plastic duck.

'Welcome to *Tenby*, sir,' the burly rating shouted in his ear.

'Thanks!' Andrew yelled, trying to beat the din of the machine overhead. 'There's a bag to come, and they want this kit of theirs back!'

He slipped the harness off and the rating held the strop to one side to show the winchman it was clear. Within seconds it was gone.

'Best take the gear off here, sir!'

He unstrapped the life-vest, then struggled with the zips of the survival suit; the rating helped him. In a few moments he was free from the gear and, ducking, began to make his way below. A young officer greeted him at the top of the ladder. As he climbed down inside the tower, a warm blast of air came up to greet him, carrying a familiar smell of machinery and cooking.

He emerged into the control room. A ring of faces greeted him.

'Hello, I'm Peter Biddle.'

The CO looked no more than a boy, smooth-skinned, fair-haired, waxy pale from the rolling of the boat. Andrew checked the gold bars on his epaulettes to be sure.

'Andrew Tinker. Glad to be aboard.'

'Ah, this looks like your kit.'

He glanced past Andrew at the sub-lieutenant carrying the holdall.

'Good. The sooner we get below in this weather, the better we'll all feel.'

Andrew heard the clunk of the upper hatch being closed.

'Upper lid shut and clipped,' the rating called.

'Officer of the Watch. Dive the submarine. Let's clear the datum!' Commander Biddle ordered.

Shortly afterwards, with the submarine at 180 metres, Biddle led the way to his cabin.

'Now take a seat,' he suggested to Andrew, 'and put me out of my misery. What the hell's this all about?'

* * *

Washington DC, USA.

President John McGuire entered the 'bunker', as he called it, and closed the door. He was a short man with wavy brown hair, blue eyes, and a nice smile. His National Security Adviser Tom Reynolds was already there, waiting for him.

The room was a new addition to the White House, just big enough to seat a dozen if necessary. Special wire mesh embedded in its walls, floor and ceiling prevented electronic eavesdropping.

'Okay, Tom. What've you got?'

McGuire was nervous. Newly elected, he was still feeling his way through the complexities of foreign policy. He hailed from a midwestern state where he'd built a reputation as a tough and efficient governor, but where Russians were still thought of as hostile aliens from another planet.

'It's thin, John. Real thin,' Reynolds drawled, stroking his long, angular chin.

A former US Air Force General, he'd spent much of his professional life studying the Soviet mind. The President relied on him to read the Russians, but this time he was unsure, and that made him nervous. He clasped and unclasped his hands.

'The Defense Intelligence Agency has confirmed they're MiG-29s on that ship, and that it's called the *Rostov* . . .'

'Goddammit, Tom! I knew that much yesterday! Where are they headed, that's what I need to know?'

'And that's what none of our agencies can tell us yet. It's weird. Real weird. We've not had a whisper out of Cuba or Central America to suggest they're expecting new fighters. There's been nothing on the satellites either. The latest pictures from the KH12 over Cuba, Nicaragua, and El Salvador yesterday – the sky was clear, the pix are great, but there's not the slightest sign they're getting ready for new planes.'

'So where are they going with those things? I got no feel for this, Tom. You've got to help me.'

'Could be just about anyplace. Angola, Mozambique, Libya – you name it.'

'Do those places matter to us? I mean, if they get the planes?'

Reynolds shrugged.

'We sure as hell would care if they went to Libya. But I don't think they will. Savkin and Gaddafy ain't speakin' much these days. No. I still think it's Cuba – if it's anywhere at all.'

'What the hell's that supposed to mean?'

'It's weird. Those planes are built just outside Moscow. The easiest way to get them anywhere is to fly 'em. So why take them all the way up to Murmansk to put them on a ship?'

'Maybe he hoped no one'd spot them that way.'

Reynolds shook his head.

'You don't steam right past a US Navy flat-top if you want to keep secret a deck-full of jet fighters.'

'So what're you saying? It was bait? And we took it?'

'Could be. We can't say for sure.'

'So, Savkin wants to wind us up, huh?'

'Could be. Maybe he thinks if he can make us look real mean, it'll strengthen his hand in the next arms talks. Don't forget, they want naval forces on the agenda this time. And we've got a lot more at sea than they have.'

McGuire stood up, spun round the chair so its back

was against the table. Then he straddled it, resting his arms on the top.

'Suppose you're wrong, and those planes go to Cuba. What do we have to do about it? What can this MiG do? Is it a threat?'

Tom Reynolds pursed his thin lips.

'Militarily? The MiG-29's like our own F-18. Good all-round fighter. But there's only six of 'em on the ship, so far as we know – peanuts.

'But politically? That's different. Any strengthening of communist forces so close to the US is bad news. You've seen what the media are doing with it. Watch the news-casts tonight and see how many congressmen have picked up the ball. I can name a handful who're guaranteed to be running with it.'

'Mmmm,' the President mused, calculating the political advantages in the various courses of action open to him.

'I guess the smart money's on not doing anything too fast,' he concluded, eyeing his National Security Adviser for his reaction. 'Just so long as the rednecks in Congress don't see it as weakness.'

He stood up and thrust his hands into his pockets.

'If Congress kicks up a fuss, I'll tell 'em the Soviets know damn well what to expect if they do anything that threatens the USA.'

'And if you're asked if the MiGs are a threat?'

'I'll tell 'em I don't know yet. Savkin hasn't told me where he's sending them!'

The President laughed, but was cut short.

'Then the media'll give us shit because the CIA and DIA haven't found out where they're goin'.'

'Okay! Then I'll be enigmatic. Say they're not a threat where they are right now!'

'Sure.'

Reynolds leaned back in his chair, hands clasped behind his head.

'You're right about keeping it cool, John. What I'm worried about is what *could* happen. Eighteen of our biggest and best warships are steaming into what the Soviets think of as their own home waters. Savkin means to use our exercise for his own ends. I can see some of what he's after, but not all of it. With those MiGs, we flew into a trap. We've got to look out for the next one and avoid it.'

'First thing is to muzzle the media on the *Eisenhower*,' McGuire growled. 'The only pictures of Russian ships I want to see from now on are the ones that come in from the Pentagon. Make sure the Navy knows that, will you, Tom?'

'You got it. And what do you want State to do about the protest from the Soviet Ambassador?'

'Throw it back at them. But do it diplomatically!'

The President stood up again, indicating their meeting was over, but Reynolds stayed seated.

'Anything else?' McGuire demanded, looking anxiously at his watch.

'Well . . . , I don't rightly know.'

'What's that supposed to mean?'

'Well, it may be nothing. Just something that's come from a US Navy Commander doing NATO duty at the east Atlantic headquarters at Northwood, England. He's talked about it to the Defense Intelligence Agency. Says the Brits have got big trouble with one of their submarines. Doesn't know what, but there's a lot of important people over there looking real worried. And they're not telling us about it, which is odd, since the sub's in the exercise.'

'Some kind of accident, you figure?'

'Nope. They'd be after our rescue vehicle if it was.'

'What then?'

'All the guy knows is, the boat ain't doing what it's supposed to. So there may be a joker in the pack, and if you're going to play poker with Savkin, you ought to know that.'

The President eyed Reynolds silently for what felt like a full half-minute.

'Thanks, Tom.'

* * *

At six that evening Washington time, the four main American television news channels went on the air with their world news bulletins. All of them led on the remarkable report from ABC Moscow correspondent Nick Hallberg, the first western journalist ever to fly on patrol in a Soviet warplane.

The sight of American jets flaunting their weaponry at the Russian plane made some viewers' hearts flutter with pride. It left others feeling apprehensive, however. Amongst the latter was Tom Reynolds.

By putting curbs on the US Navy's media facilities, he'd hoped to control US TV pictures from the North Atlantic. He kicked himself for his naïvety.

After the pooled Hallberg report, each network other than ABC switched to their own Moscow correspondent's despatch from the press conference given in Moscow that evening by Admiral Grekov, Supreme Commander of the Soviet Navy.

Grekov spoke no English. His words were relayed in the exaggeratedly American tones of the official Soviet interpreter.

The US Navy pilots had violated international law, he railed. They'd jeopardized the lives of the crew of the 'unarmed Soviet reconnaissance plane'. The aggression they'd displayed was symbolic of the whole tone of the NATO exercise about to be enacted close to the Soviet coast, he insisted.

The Admiral then stood up, resplendent in his uniform, and pointed with a stick to a chart comparing NATO and Warsaw Pact naval forces in Atlantic and European waters.

'Aircraft carriers: NATO has twenty-four, the Warsaw Pact just four small ones with no strike power. Submarines: about two hundred each. Frigates and destroyers: NATO has three times the number in our navies. With such odds in the West's favour, why does NATO need to mount aggressive manoeuvres in Soviet waters?' he demanded to know. 'It can hardly be for defence, so is it for war?'

Grekov directed his final query to the camera, his wrinkled face a picture of affronted innocence.

Tom Reynolds was watching four channels simultaneously in his room in the Old Executive Office Building next to the White House. Under his lean jaw, a nerve twitched.

The broadcasts finished with a brief commentary from the networks' Pentagon correspondents, confirming that the figures Grekov had quoted were fundamentally correct.

Reynolds snatched up the green telephone.

'Could you tell the President I need to see him again,' he barked. '*Right now!*'

CHAPTER SIX

Tuesday 22nd October. 0400 hrs GMT.

HMS Truculent.

Lieutenant Sebastian Cordell couldn't sleep. The night was nearly gone; three more hours and he'd be back on watch.

The bunk was too small; his head touched one bulkhead of the four-berth cabin, his feet another. He was alone; the three he shared with were on watch.

The cause of his insomnia wasn't the size of the bunk, however, but the turmoil in his mind.

In the past thirty-six hours, conversation amongst the officers had reduced to a single topic – speculation about their captain's highly irregular orders.

They'd all remarked on his heightened irritability, snapping at them one minute, icy calm the next.

The others could only guess what had got into the old man, but Sebastian – he reckoned he knew. And it had nothing to do with secret orders from CINCFLEET.

Whether to tell someone, that was the question churning round in his mind. He'd seen the first lieutenant and the WEO whispering secretly in corners. Had to be talking about Hitchens. Should he tell them their captain had flipped, and why?

He'd been dodging Hitchens' eyes, which seemed to burn with pain and anger. Sometimes he'd caught the captain looking at him across the control room; his expression seemed to say: 'I've got your number, you bastard!'

Sebastian cursed his luck for being posted to *Truculent* – for being brought face to face with the man he'd innocently cuckolded two years ago.

Sara Hitchens was the first woman he'd spent the night with – the first time he'd made love in a bed. Before that it had been fumbles in the back of his car – awkward, and hurried.

They'd not expected to strike lucky, that night in the restaurant two years ago. He and another midshipman had been celebrating his twentieth birthday, when two women had begun eyeing them from another table.

Bold as brass, one of the women had asked them to join them for coffee.

He'd suspected they were tarts; nice girls waited for men to make the first approach. But he'd soon realized he was wrong. These women had class.

They'd only used their first names – made it more mysterious. The women were ten or fifteen years older than them. Divorcees, the boys had reckoned.

'Come home and we'll have a little party!' the women had insisted, after a few liqueurs.

Back at Sara's old house out in the wilds, Sebastian had sensed she was still married. He didn't care, though; he'd drunk plenty by then.

It was the other woman who'd got things moving; she'd been all over Sebastian's chum, and dragged him off to a bedroom. Sara had been more hesitant, nervous even. Sebastian had liked her for it.

They'd had another drink, alone. Then, emboldened, they'd gone to her bedroom. It had smelt of perfume. He could still smell it when he closed his eyes.

She'd seen he was inexperienced, and took the lead; he could still picture the mischief on her urchin face as she began to unbutton his shirt. Her breasts had felt hot, so unbelievably soft. Skin as smooth as cream.

They'd made love, and for the first time for Sebastian the words had had meaning.

Then morning had come. A dry throat, a throbbing head – and the sight of her husband's photograph on the bedside table.

He'd not dared ask about him, not wanted to know Sara's surname. But on a pewter tankard next to the photograph, were engraved the words 'Congratulations to Lieutenant Commander Philip Hitchens'.

Two years later he'd been told to join *HMS Truculent*;

he'd thought of asking for a different appointment, but without a good reason, a man would damage his career that way. Anyway, TAS Officer was exactly the job he'd wanted.

When he'd first joined the boat, Hitchens had shown no sign of suspicion. Sebastian had relaxed, believing his secret was safe. Until the start of this patrol. On his return from shore leave this time, Commander Hitchens' attitude to him had changed radically.

Now the whole boat was in turmoil. Because of him, so he believed. Sebastian pressed his fists against the deck-head. The steel seemed to crush downwards.

How much had Sara told him? Everything they'd done that night?

He'd never seen her again – hadn't dared to. For months she'd haunted his thoughts. He'd never been so in love before.

He almost wished Hitchens would come out with it. Tell him what he thought of him and have done with it. But it was as if Hitchens had decided Cordell had ceased to exist. That look in his eye was of a man betrayed by his closest friends. A man whose mind had been turned by it.

He ought to warn them; tell them what he knew. But what if he were imagining it? Supposing there really were secret orders? He'd have made a fool of himself. It'd go on his file.

Best to hold his tongue for the time being. Just one more day. See what developed. But should he wait, when the whole ship's company might be heading for appalling danger?

He banged his fists against his head. He had to tell someone. He'd talk to Pike. That's what a first lieutenant was for.

Philip Hitchens checked in the small mirror that his hair was groomed. Doubt plagued him; he panicked even, at the thought of what he'd taken on.

The day ahead would be critical. No more wavering. He had to weigh his options – decide what to do.

He looked long and hard at his reflection. The strain was less noticeable now. Two nights of deep, drug-induced sleep had worked their beneficial effect.

He'd apologized to Pike for not telling him about the tablets. But he hadn't realized they'd put him so far under. He'd imagined he'd still be rouseable in an emergency.

His crew had done well handling that *Victor*, though he'd torn a strip off them for not waking him at the time. That was when Pike had rounded on him in the control room.

He'd realized then how close he was to wrecking everything. He'd taken stock rapidly, wrenching his emotions back under control. Now, after a second night of deep sleep, he felt ready.

Calm and consistent; that's how he must appear to his men if they weren't to doubt his authority. Whatever the outcome of his mission, he needed them to obey his orders without question.

Taking a deep breath to steady himself, he left his cabin and stepped into the wardroom for breakfast. Seated at the near end of the table was a short, stocky figure, shovelling bacon, egg and sausages through a small gap in his bushy black beard.

'Stoking up, Peter?'

'It's all fuel, sir,' answered the marine engineer officer, Lieutenant Commander Peter Claypole. 'Body's just like a machine.'

'Standard, sir?' asked the steward.

'Yes, please,' answered Philip. 'I can just about manage it this morning.'

'Standard' was egg, bacon, sausage, tomato and fried bread.

Further down the table sat Sub-Lieutenant Smallbone, the radio officer, and Lieutenant Cordell.

'Are you going on or just off watch, Sebastian?' Philip asked, pouring himself a cup of tea.

'Off – I mean, just going on, sir,' Cordell stammered.

There's something wrong with Cordell, Philip thought. The boy blushed whenever he spoke to him. He hoped he wasn't gay.

'This morning – and this affects both of you lads – we need a SSIXS. Scheduled at 1130, isn't it, Hugo?'
'That's right, sir.'
SSIXS stood for Ship to Shore Information Exchange Satellite.
'We'll need to take extra care this far north, Sebastian. The Russians are everywhere.'
'Yes, sir. I know that.'
The steward placed the greasy breakfast on the table. What would Sara say about all that cholesterol?
For a split second nothing happened.
Sara. Oh, Jesus!
The hurt hit him like a gloved fist. Eyes closed against the pain, he swayed and gripped the table.
'Everythin' okay, sir?'
The steward's voice sounded distant, as if deep in a tunnel.
From the far end of the table Sebastian and Hugo stared at Hitchens open-mouthed.
'Back to the stoke-hole,' muttered the marine engineer, noticing nothing and heading for the door.
'Yes . . . fine,' Philip managed to reply.
He forced down a sip of tea, and felt better for it.
He gripped the knife and fork and began to eat, forcing the food down. He mustn't give way like that again.
'If you'll excuse us, sir . . .'
Cordell and Smallbone were heading for the door.
'Of course.'

Lieutenant Commander Peter Claypole was brushing his teeth in his cabin, when the phone call came from the chief of the watch, aft. Trouble with a pump in the reactor's secondary cooling system.
Claypole looked like the popular idea of a submariner, stocky and bearded. He was a man of routine; three meals a day, regular as clockwork and never a problem with his health. Bodies were like machines; keep them fuelled and maintained and everything should run smoothly. He thought of submarines in much the same way.
But now a pump was playing up.

Passing through the control room, he glanced at the dials on the power panel. They were doing thirty-one knots.

'I may have to slow you down, Tim,' he warned.

Pike had been in command most of the night, and looked weary.

'Trouble?'

'Maybe.'

'Serious?'

'Let you know.'

With that he was on his way. Claypole never used two words where one would do.

He reached the tunnel over the reactor and pulled the lever on the airlock door. Before entering, he checked his radiation monitor card was clipped to his belt.

He hurried down the tunnel that led aft. Beneath his feet was the reactor compartment with its primary cooling circuits and steam generators.

Through the second door, and he was into the machine-spaces. He entered the manoeuvring room, the reactor control centre, where every aspect of the power plant and propulsion system was monitored. His eye went straight to the gauges showing the temperature in the pumps. The needle was high for pump three in the number two steam loop.

'Where's the chief of the watch?' Claypole asked.

'Three deck, sir.'

Logical. That's where the secondary circuit pumps were. He gripped the rails of the ladder and slid below.

The secondary circuit carried superheated steam from the reactor compartment through the turbines that drove the propulsor and the electrical generator. After the steam had released its energy it passed through a sea-water condenser; then, as water, was pumped back into the reactor heat-exchanger to start the process all over again.

Two deck. One more ladder, and he'd be there.

CPO Gostyn was crouched beside the silver-grey pump. He wore headphones connected to sensors built into the pump casing, listening to confirm his suspicion that the grinding noise from inside was getting steadily worse.

They were two of a kind, Claypole and Gostyn, yet separated by rank and status. Both men lived for their machines, knew the workings of them intimately. But Claypole, with his engineering degree ranked as an officer; Gostyn with his 'O' levels and an engineering diploma would probably never rise above warrant officer.

Gostyn removed his headphones and passed them across. 'Bearing, sir. Almost certain.' In a war, machine noise could be the death of them all. The smallest extra vibration or rumble could transmit itself to the water outside and pinpoint their position for an enemy.

Claypole pressed the phones to his ears.

'Not much doubt. Bloody dockyard was supposed to have checked that last time we were in!'

They both knew the fault probably lay with a microscopic flaw in the steel used in the bearing, but it helped to have someone to blame.

'We'll have to shut it down,' Claypole decided. 'If we leave it running, it'll seize. Captain'll go bananas.'

'Can't be helped, can it, sir? Not our fault.'

There were four pumps in each coolant loop, mounted on rubber rafts to absorb noise. Shutting down one pump meant the loss of about five knots.

'He's not going to like it. Wherever it is we're going, he's in one hell of a hurry to get there. What d'you think? If he won't play ball, how long can we keep it running before it seizes?'

Gostyn shrugged.

'Fuck knows! If the fucking bearing breaks up, he'll fucking *'ave* to slow down!'

Claypole smiled. He couldn't have put it better himself.

'Right. Wish me luck.'

In the control room Tim Pike was desperate to get his head down, but had hung on to hear what the marine engineer had to say.

'Don't baffle me with jargon, Peter,' he began. 'Words of one syllable please. Two at the most.'

'Got a duff bearing in a pump. Simple enough for you?'

'And you're proposing. . . . ?'

'Shut it down. Means you'll lose a few knots.'

'That'll knock us back on our schedule. Captain won't like it. Do you have to?'

'The bearing could go at any time. If it does you'll be down to twenty-five knots anyway. Shut it down now and you'll still have it in reserve – turn it on again if you really need it.'

'Sod it! We'll need to talk to the captain. This is his mission we're on. Only he knows our deadline. You'd better come with me.'

At that moment Philip entered the control room.

'Problem, Tim?'

'Trouble with a pump, sir. MEO wants to shut it down. We'd lose five knots.'

'We can't do that! We need the speed! And *why* is there trouble with a pump?' His voice began to rise. 'They're not supposed to need attention from one refit to the next. If one of your men's fouled it up, Mr Claypole, I'll have him on a charge!'

Philip's eyes blazed.

'Nobody's fouled anything up, sir,' Claypole bristled. 'Leastways, not any of *my* men. There's a bearing that's noisy and overheating. Ship's engineers don't have access to them. Dockyard job. But it must be shut down.'

'Don't tell me what *must* be done! You're being too bloody cautious, MEO. If we were at war you wouldn't be talking about stopping a pump.'

'I bloody would, sir!' Claypole growled.

Hitchens flinched. He could smell mutiny.

The men were staring. He suddenly realized he'd been shouting. Careful! He swallowed hard.

'All right, Peter. What's the percentage chance of that pump failing?'

'Oh, it'll fail. Hundred per cent. The only question is when. The bearing's got a rumble. Low-frequency. Probably not bad enough yet to be heard outside the hull. But it'll get worse. Could go very quick. If the bearing breaks up and bits of metal get into the lubricating system, then we could write the whole pump off.'

'What's the chance of failure in the next forty-eight hours?' Hitchens pressed.

'God knows!'

'Give me your considered judgement. You're an engineer, aren't you?'

Claypole frowned, as if deep in thought. Sod the bloody CO! Why couldn't he just accept that something was wrong and let them put it right? He tried to remember a previous incident that would give him a clue. He'd never heard of a bearing actually disintegrating on one of these pumps. Still, there was always a first time.

'Outright failure? I suppose the chance of that is low,' the MEO conceded. 'But deterioration, with the pump overheating and the noise level becoming detectable outside? The chance is higher. Much higher.'

'In forty-eight hours?'

'Can't guarantee anything, sir,' Claypole concluded sullenly.

'We'll risk it. We have to,' the commander decided. 'You can have a couple of knots if it'll help.'

'Every little bit . . .'

'Twenty-eight knots then, Tim.'

'Aye, aye, sir,' Pike acknowledged as Hitchens turned to the chart table.

'And I want reports every hour, MEO.'

Lieutenant Sebastian Cordell had just taken over the watch from Nick Cavendish, and was leaning over the chart. He eased to one side as Hitchens appeared next to him. Their course had brought them closer to the Norwegian coast, but they were still one hundred and fifty miles west of the nearest land. The Lofoten Islands were well to the south. Beneath them the ocean plunged two-thousand-five-hundred metres to total darkness, and a sea-bed of ooze and rock.

'ETA abeam North Cape?' Hitchens asked. 'At twenty-eight knots?'

Cordell picked up his brass-handled dividers, set them against the latitude scale and measured out the distance.

'About three-hundred-and-thirty miles to run . . .'

He pulled the calculator towards him and punched at the keys.

'2200 tonight, sir. And that allows for some slow running for comms.'

'Mmmm.' Hitchens looked reassured. He picked up the dividers and measured the distance for himself.

'We'll be crossing the edge of the continental shelf in about four hours. You'd better start plotting sea-bed soundings. When we get round the Cape there'll be Sovs everywhere. Won't be able to poke a mast up to get a satellite fix.'

'Yes, sir.'

Navigating by reading the topography of the ocean floor was a difficult art dependant on finding large features, like underwater mountains. There weren't too many of those in the shallow waters of the Barents Sea.

Hitchens pulled out the chart showing the northern tip of Norway and the western half of the Soviet Kola peninsula.

'Where are we heading after North Cape, sir?' Cordell queried nervously.

'You'll know when you need to,' Hitchens snapped. He slid the chart back into the drawer. 'Just make sure we get there.'

Unnerved by Cordell's question, he turned for the door.

'Call me when it's time for the satcom.'

'Sir.'

Philip felt panic rising. It was the tension in the control room that did it. They were all suspicious – all watching him. He had to have solitude to think things through, make decisions.

He slid shut the door to his cabin, and slumped into his chair. What was truth, what was lies?

Those KGB bastards! They'd led him by the nose. He'd believed their 'evidence', succumbed to their blackmail, agreed to their plan. But was it true, what they'd told him? How the hell could he tell, down there in the dark silence of the ocean.

And poor Sara. The way they'd used her – trickery,

lies. And all to make sure of him, as though the other thing weren't enough.

He remembered his stunned disbelief when a completely strange woman had stopped him on the cliff footpath, earlier that year, to tell him his father was still alive. The father whom he'd worshipped and whose disappearance thirty years ago he'd never been able to accept.

The letter and the photograph the Russian woman had produced as evidence – he could still picture them. The cheap paper covered with his father's still familiar scrawl had torn a little in the summer breeze.

It had poleaxed him, shattered him. At that moment, he'd become a boy again, a boy on the edge of his teens; a child who'd idolized a father all too often absent, a boy who craved paternal approval.

The words in his father's letter had cut into his heart, pleading, begging that he should do something to end his suffering. The handwriting had been uneven and shaky. They'd broken his father in the labour camp – the woman had admitted it. She'd even apologized; blamed it on the Stalinists.

She'd waited until their third meeting before revealing the price to be paid for freeing the sick old man. She was sure of Philip by then.

It was the second letter from his father that had sealed it; the handwriting strayed down the page and told of incurable heart disease. Did he have grandchildren, the old man asked; believing that one day he'd see them had kept him going all those years. He begged that before he died, Philip would make the dream come true.

Treason was the price to be paid for his father's freedom. Betrayal of his country's secrets to the KGB. Betrayal of the Navy which was his whole life.

Until that moment Philip had never questioned the meaning of 'loyalty'. It was absolute. Handing British naval secrets to the Russians was unthinkable. But now he faced a choice; loyalty to his country – or loyalty to his own flesh and blood.

It was only a small thing they asked, the woman had said. Just a small favour.

A small thing. To lay an inert Moray mine at a precise location off the Kola coast, so it could be retrieved by a Soviet submersible. Retrieved and dismantled, so that the most potent anti-submarine weapon ever devised by the West could be understood, and rendered impotent. A small thing.

His mind had rejected the treachery; but his heart hadn't.

Would it really do so much harm? The Soviets themselves must have similar technology. If they didn't learn the secret from him, they'd get it from someone else. They'd bribe some underpaid technician at the factory, perhaps. There'd never be a war anyway, so what did it matter?

It would be difficult, he'd warned her. There'd be no opportunity.

Yes, there would, she told him. They knew he commanded *Truculent*, the trials boat for the Moray mines. The thoroughness of the KGB's research had startled him.

A few months later, as she had predicted, he was ordered to the Kola, on the ideal mission to fulfil the KGB's plan. Although just a simulated mine-laying, he would be carrying war stocks, they told him.

Suddenly he had the means to free his father. It was fate; it had to be.

He met the KGB woman in Plymouth that night. She gave him the chart coordinates for the laying of the mine, and said his father would be moved immediately to a clinic in a neutral country, where he would be cared for until other arrangements could be made.

How he would explain the loss of a mine when he returned to Plymouth, he couldn't imagine. He'd think of something. The plan had to proceed.

Then suddenly, the whole thing had exploded in his face. He'd found out about Sara.

He'd been a puppet all the time. There wasn't just a KGB woman pulling his strings; there was a man too. A Russian who'd seduced Sara months before to make her talk. Talk about him, his obsession with his father, his vulnerability.

The bastards! They'd invented the whole thing! Faked the letter and the blurred photograph. They hadn't let him keep them, of course. Couldn't risk them falling into the hands of the British authorities, the woman had said.

It had been bloody clever. He cringed at the thought of how he'd fallen for it. *God*, how he hated them, and their evil masters in the Kremlin. Okay, he'd give them a bloody Moray mine. Right up the backside of an *Oscar* class submarine!

Thus he had begun the patrol blinded by anger and a thirst for revenge.

But now the doubts had come back. Supposing they *had* been telling the truth after all? Why shouldn't his father be alive? The writing had looked like his, the words and the expressions had been right. And the photograph – well, who could tell after so many years?

He sank his head in his hands. He must decide; go through it all again, all the evidence for and against. The reports he'd read of the catastrophic 'accident' nearly thirty years ago – think back through them. Remember what the Russian woman had told him about the survival of just two men, who'd escaped the destruction of the old *Tenby* because they'd been ashore on the Soviet coast when it had happened, taking photographs of a radar site.

He wanted the story to be true, wanted desperately to bring his father home to England, back to life. But he had to guard against self-deception.

Think. Think hard. Then decide. He mustn't have doubts when the time came.

The last time he'd seen his father had been in Guernsey in August 1962. Philip had been fourteen. That summer he'd felt closer to his father than ever before.

That's how he remembered it anyhow. Had it really been like that?

His father had been such a confident man, with firm views on everything – never a moment's doubt in his own judgement. Whenever he came home from sea, Philip would follow him round the house like a dog, he remembered, drawing strength from being close to him.

His father had been an aloof man, however, and in

truth there'd been few occasions when the two of them had been really close.

It had rained most of that summer. Much of the holiday had been spent indoors playing Monopoly, or even bridge whenever his father managed to bully a fellow holiday-maker into making up a four. Philip had no brothers or sisters; his mother had confided once that giving birth to him had been such a ghastly experience, she'd determined never to repeat it.

He'd sensed an unusual tension between his parents that summer. Perhaps his mother had known his father was about to embark on a spying mission; perhaps it was something personal. He would never know now.

When the news came that his father's boat was Missing Presumed Lost, his mother retreated into extended mourning, bitter at the world for taking away her husband.

Philip shuddered. Looking back on his unhappy boyhood would do nothing to answer the questions in his head.

What would Andrew do in his situation?

He often asked himself that – an old habit acquired soon after the two of them began their naval training together at Dartmouth. To Philip, every decision Andrew Tinker took seemed effortless; the man knew instinctively what to do, while he himself floundered in uncertainty and self-doubt.

He'd used Andrew as a life-raft when they were students; uncomfortably aware of it, he'd wondered that his room-mate tolerated him so gladly. One day in a flash of insight, he worked out why; for all Andrew's decisiveness and competence, there was one ingredient for a naval career which he lacked. Background.

And that was something Philip had plenty of. With a dead hero for a father, and a grandfather who'd been a Rear Admiral, it was 'background' that had brought him into the Navy and 'background' which he'd hoped might offset any lack of brilliance as an officer.

Coming from a family with no naval connections,

Andrew had hungered for the true taste of the Navy and its traditions. It was a knowledge Philip could provide.

The complementary nature of their original friendship had turned later into good-natured rivalry in everything they did – even marriage. Philip knew it had been Andrew's engagement to Patsy that had spurred him to find a wife for himself.

He and Sara had been wildly in love when they married. Dreams, all dreams. A nightmare now.

* * *

HMS Tenby.

Andrew Tinker sat huddled over the wardroom table of *HMS Tenby* and chewed his thumbnail. Spread before him were charts of the underwater landscape north of Norway and inside the Kola inlet.

'What we really need is a mind-reader,' Andrew sighed.

'He's been sitting in that boat for nearly a week,' Commander Biddle reminded him. 'Even if he were planning to blow up some Russians because a KGB man poked his wife, surely he'd have thought better of it by now?'

Andrew nodded. His own thoughts exactly.

'And if he hasn't, he must be really off his head. Somebody on board should have twigged.'

'But they haven't,' Biddle said. 'There's just been a signal in from FOSM. No news at all. No sign of the *Truc* since the "crabs" found and lost her yesterday.'

'The Nimrod should be airborne again by now.'

'That's confirmed. They're starting at twenty degrees east and working west.'

Andrew found the longitude line on the chart and nodded.

' 'S' about right. Couldn't have got any further than that if he'd gone flat out. Where are we?'

Biddle's finger traced a line northeast from where they'd picked up Andrew the previous evening.

'We're doing eighteen knots. Means we can listen on sonar and still end up in front of him. We'll sit tight off North Cape and wait for his signature as he comes steaming up behind us.'

'I can't for one moment believe it'll be that easy.'

Andrew pulled towards him the chart showing the Kol'-skiy Zaliv, the Kola Inlet where the Soviet Northern Fleet had its headquarters.

'We can't be sure that's where he's going,' Andrew continued.

'Best place if he's looking for Sovs to shoot.'

'Ah, but is that what he's planning? I've known Phil a long time. This picture we're painting of a man ready to risk war to avenge his wife's indiscretions – it just doesn't fit.'

'No? What about the mental breakdown theory?'

'I've thought a lot about that, and I don't buy it either. If Phil had a breakdown, he wouldn't be able to conceal it. He'd just go to pieces. Tim Pike's his first lieutenant; he's a good hand and he'd soon sort him out.'

'But he hasn't.'

'Exactly. Which is why I'm convinced there's something else behind it. Something much more complicated.'

'Such as?'

'Christ! If I knew that . . .' Andrew spread his arms wide and stretched.

'Would it be worth getting FOSM to look in his personnel file?'

'Maybe. I'll send a signal. Trouble is, I don't know what they should look for.'

They fell silent. *Tenby*'s wardroom began to fill up with officers finished with the night watch, but not yet ready to get their heads down. There were thirteen officers on board, but the dining table only had seats for ten. In a corner by the door was a small refrigerator containing beer and soft drinks. Andrew had been offered a beer the night before, but had noticed none of Biddle's officers drank when at sea, and had declined it.

'We've got a satcom slot at 12.20. But we can do an HF burst sooner than that, if you want.'

'Okay. I'll draft a signal.'

Instinctively Andrew made as if to return to his cabin, but checked himself in time. His sleeping quarter was a mattress pallet, clipped to the torpedo rack in the forward weapons compartment. Biddle had offered the use of his own quarters as an office, but it was desperately small, which was why they'd chosen to sit in the wardroom. He pulled out a small notebook and turned to a clean page.

'*Captain, sir!*' the loudspeaker crackled.

Biddle stood up and pressed the microphone key.

'Yes, Murray.' It was the executive officer.

'*Got a contact. At least, TAS says we have.*'

'On my way.'

They both headed for the sound room.

'The trouble with being the trials boat for a new sonar system,' Biddle explained, 'is the shortage of background data. Without more experience with the gear, we don't know whether we've really got a contact or whether the transputer analyser's imagined it!'

The green-glowing sonar displays in the big grey, shock-mounted cabinets looked the same as the ones on his own boat, but Andrew had been told that both the hydrophones trailed astern and the computer that analysed and categorized the different sounds had been developed a step beyond his own equipment.

'This is Algy Colqhoun. A very enthusiastic TAS. Says this new gear's so sensitive it can pick up the moaning ghosts from World War Two shipwrecks! Now then, TAS; what're you up to!'

The tactics and sonar officer pointed to the VDU at his shoulder. Vertical bands of green shading moved slowly up the screen. He pointed to a very narrow line running up the screen between two broader bands, and spun the screen cursor onto it, using the roller-ball control on the console.

'We've got a line at 370 Hz., sir,' he explained, grinning. 'Can't hear it on headphones, but it's definitely not part of the natural background.'

'Okay, so what is it?'

The TAS officer punched a few keys and displayed the frequency of the noise in a window at the right of the screen. Then the picture changed to a table of data, on the left a list of known sounds in that same frequency range. He pointed to a paragraph on the right.

'Closest thing in the classification guide is the main coolant pump in one of these.'

'A *Trafalgar?*'

'We don't often make that sort of racket, thank God, but if we had undetected pump trouble it'd be somewhere in that range. Must be going fast not to hear it on his own sonar.'

'Where do you think it is?' Andrew interjected.

'It's very faint, sir. Right on the edge of the capabilities of even this equipment.' He patted the console. 'We've got an ambiguous bearing of eighty degrees relative to the array. My guess is it's on our port bow, but I'd like to alter course twenty degrees to starboard to eliminate the ambiguity.'

The initial bearing from the towed array was always ambiguous; the hydrophones couldn't tell which side the sound was coming from. By altering course and taking new relative bearings, one fix would remain constant, the other would diverge further, clearing up the ambiguity.

'Well, hang on to it. It's all we've got,' Biddle ordered.

Andrew hurried to the chart table.

'There's nothing on the intelligence plot about any of our subs being in this area, so it could well be our man.'

'Starboard ten. Steer zero-two-five,' ordered Lieutenant Colqhoun. The blue-shirted rating switched off the auto-pilot and turned the steering column, glad of something to do.

It would be several minutes before the array steadied again behind them, after which they could get their new bearing.

'Exactly right,' Andrew breathed, laying the protractor on the chart. 'If it's confirmed as a portside contact, it puts him precisely where the Nimrod's searching! We may just have struck lucky!'

He took up the dividers and measured the distance between their present position and the track he imagined the *Truculent* was following.

'About three hours! That's all it would take!' he remarked.

Lieutenant Colqhoun called across from the Action Information Display.

'Got a confirmed bearing, sir. Two-eight-six degrees. Range – probably between fifty and a hundred miles.'

'Thanks.'

Biddle settled himself at the chart table. He would calculate an intercept course to close the range. They'd have to guess the speed of the target. Thirty knots probably, making that much noise.

He pulled the keypad of a small computer across the table and tapped in the figures. A split second later its narrow liquid-crystal screen displayed the course to follow.

'Steer three-five-six. Keep seventy metres, revolutions for fifteen knots!'

Andrew scribbled down his radio signal to FOSM. It was in two parts. The first gave their own position and the bearing and possible range of the suspected target, to be relayed to the Nimrod overhead; the second was to ask for a search of Philip's file for clues.

'We'll come to periscope depth for the transmission in ten minutes,' Biddle told him.

Then the commander leaned an elbow on the chart table. He didn't want the navigation rating to hear what he said next.

'If this *is* the right contact, Andrew . . .'

He didn't need to complete the sentence. Andrew beckoned and led the way out of the control room.

'Can we talk in your cabin?'

'Of course.'

Biddle pushed open the door for him. Andrew sat on the narrow bunk.

'My orders are to stop him,' he declared simply.

Carefully, he watched Biddle's face for his reaction.

'How we do that, I don't know yet. I hope to God it's easy and a few words on the underwater telephone will be enough to let Pike take over.'

'And if not?'

'Then I'll need fresh orders. But in the last resort – we're supposed to hit him. That's what they told me.'

He expelled a long breath.

'You can't do that!' Biddle almost shouted. 'There's a hundred guys in there, Andrew. I know most of them. You couldn't pull the plug on them.'

'Depends on the alternative, doesn't it,' Andrew countered sharply. 'If he's about to do something that'll make the Russians turn my children into nuclear cinders, then a hundred lives is a small price to pay. We let over twice that many die in the Falklands, for Christ's sake!'

'But how will you know what he's going to do?' Biddle persisted. 'Who's to be the judge of what effect his action'll have? We can't know down here, that's for sure. Will CINCFLEET decide? Or Downing Street?'

'You have a point . . . We're going to want to be in contact with base when the moment comes. But if we keep bobbing up to the surface to transmit, we'll risk losing him.'

'So in the end it may be down to you . . .'

Andrew's eye was drawn to the photograph on Biddle's desk. Two little girls aged about three. Twins, probably.

'I just hope to God it doesn't come to that.'

* * *

HMS Truculent.

Chief Petty Officer Gostyn was not a happy man. Not only did he have a defective pump in the number two steam system of *HMS Truculent*, and an unsympathetic Commanding Officer, he also had a bad apple among his mechanics.

He knew who it was. But could he prove it? Could he hell!

It was bloody Percy Harwood again, had to be. None of the other five sods whose job it was to check and maintain the steam system would have been so flaming stupid as to drop an eighteen-inch wrench down behind the defective pump and then pretend it hadn't happened.

Anybody else, any other bugger on the entire submarine, would have known what a disaster it was to do something like that and not report it.

Millions of pounds had been spent on inventing ways

to make all this machinery silent. Mounting individual pumps and piping on rubber, developing low-speed bearings, all of it to reduce the noise detectable outside the hull to a bare minimum. And all it took was Percy bloody Harwood to leave his spanner resting one end against the pump, the other on the deck, thus building a bridge across the sound insulation so that the rumble coming from the defective bearing could be transmitted straight out into the deep sound channel of the North Atlantic.

Gostyn had spotted it himself, while making his hourly rounds. Harwood had denied it was him, of course, but it couldn't have been anyone else. It was he who'd drawn the wrench from stores.

The question now was, should he report it? He was the chief down here; it might reflect on him. Lieutenant Commander Claypole might be sympathetic, but with this dodgy mission they were on, he'd probably report it to the captain. And Commander Hitchens could be bloody vindictive.

Something wrong with their captain, this patrol. The whole boat was talking about it. Some of the CPOs had even heard a rumour the other officers were plotting to relieve him of his command. Bloody riot that would cause, when they got back to Devonport. It'd never happen of course. They hadn't got the guts.

So he decided to say nothing about the wrench, nothing about the fact that their secret presence in the area had been revealed for a couple of hours to any passing ship or plane that had cared to listen. With any luck there hadn't been any.

All over with now. No more noises escaping to the outside world. And the pump bearing was holding up despite his fears.

* * *

Northwood, England.

Rear-Admiral Anthony Bourlet was on his third cup of coffee. At his insistence the WRNS who was his personal assistant had installed a filter machine when he took over the job of Flag Officer Submarines. He looked across his office to the brass ship's clock on the wall next to the barometer.

Nearly eleven. The 'crabs' should have been airborne for several hours already. The RAF hated the Navy's nickname for them, but Bourlet thought the tag apt. Airmen did seem to do everything sideways.

He downed a cup of Kenya blend and headed for the staircase.

'Going down the "hole",' he growled to his trim, smartly-uniformed PA as he passed the outer office.

'OPCON's on the line, sir. There's been a signal from *Tenby*.'

He swerved into her doorway and grabbed the outstretched phone.

'FOSM here,' he barked, then listened. 'Aha! Bloody good news!' He listened again.

'His file? Already been through that. Still, no harm in another look. On my way.'

He passed the phone back to his PA.

'Hitchens' file – we've still got it here, haven't we?'

'I think it's with Commander Rush, sir. She asked to look at it first thing this morning.'

'Ah. Get her to come and talk to me about it in an hour, would you? Or maybe a little later. Say twelve-thirty, and fix us some sandwiches – smoked salmon – and, er, a bottle of the Sauvignon, nicely chilled?'

He winked at her, which made her smile self-consciously. She knew he was a frightful lecher but she liked him anyway.

It took him three minutes to walk to the entrance of the bunker, and another three to descend to the computer-filled cavern of the OPCON centre. Thousands of signals a day were dealt with here, and stored for months on computer files.

'It's all happening, sir,' the duty operations officer saluted. 'We've just had the Nimrod on. They're in contact with a *Trafalgar* at this very minute. It has to be *Truculent*.'

'Bloody good news!'

'She's got a dodgy pump apparently; making a hell of

a racket. But she's doing twenty-eight knots and can't hear herself.'

'Where is she?'

The ops officer picked up an illuminated pointer and turned to the giant wall map.

'About two-fifty miles west of North Cape, heading northeast.'

A signals warrant officer tore a sheet from a printer and thrust it into the Ops officer's hand.

'Eight Lima Golf again, sir.'

'Thank you. Our Nimrod, sir,' the Ops officer explained to the Admiral.

'And . . . ?'

'They seem to have fixed the pump, sir. Noise signature's almost back to normal. She's slowed down to twenty knots. The Nimrod's asking if you want them to let the boat know they're there.'

'No! Absolutely not! They must stay with her – keep tracking until the *Tenby* can get close. She'll do the talking.'

'Right, sir. I'll send that off.'

'And fast, before the "crabs" bugger it up.'

* * *

HMS Truculent.

Philip stood in the 'bandstand'. They were getting close to Soviet waters. Time to go 'invisible'. He'd ordered a cut in speed to eighteen knots and told the MEO he could shut down the pump with the worn bearing. At their slower, quieter speed, Philip had ordered rapid changes of course to lose any hunters who might have tracked them while they'd been moving fast.

Philip looked at the control-room clock set on Zulu time – GMT. In ten minutes precisely, a communications satellite would beam down a stream of signals. The closer they came to Soviet waters, the more he needed the intelligence data it would include.

The sound room had reported nothing except the propeller cavitation of a couple of merchantmen butting their way round the craggy north Norwegian coast about forty miles away.

The information had not reassured him. Both his own Navy and the Soviets were bound to be looking for him. So, where were they?

At first the intelligence reports had listed the *Truculent*, but no more. *HMS Tenby* had received the same treatment. On Sunday she'd been west of Tromso, but on Monday there'd been no mention of her.

So was it the new *Tenby* they were sending after him? How ironic that it should be her, of all boats.

'Revolutions for six knots! Ten up. Keep periscope depth!' Cordell ordered.

Philip looked at the clock again, anxiously. Five minutes to their satcom slot.

* * *

RAF Nimrod, Eight-Lima-Golf.

Over the north Norwegian Sea.

Flight Lieutenant Stan Mackintosh was uncomfortably aware of his hangover. The night before, after discovering the price of Norwegian beer, he and his crew had retired to a hotel bedroom with some six-packs of lager and bottles of scotch, bought at NAAFI prices before leaving England.

'Tosh' had come to the conclusion that he was a bit too old for the heavy drinking the younger men could manage. His brain hurt and his stomach churned alarmingly as the Nimrod banked and turned, trying to keep track of the suddenly elusive submarine below.

He didn't know what had prompted the *Truculent* to take evasive action. They'd certainly not given away their presence. They'd dropped passive buoys only, and had kept above five-thousand feet so the boat wouldn't hear them through the water.

It had been easy at first; 'spearing fish in a barrel' was how he'd described it when they'd detected the boat's noisy pump over fifty miles away. But now the AQS.

901 acoustic processor was struggling to separate anything from the normal background noise.

He peered over the shoulders of the operators at the green screens. Even on the narrow band analyser none of the buoys they had in the water at the moment had kept a hold on the *Truculent*'s noise signature.

'We've lost the bastard,' yelled the Tactical Navigator in exasperation.

The big round screen showed the plot disintegrating. Bearing lines from the buoys, which had converged neatly to give the boat's position, now diverged wildly.

'Last seen heading north but believed to be turning west. We've got buoys still listening on that side, and there's nothing.'

'Perhaps the bugger's coming up to periscope depth,' the AEO suggested. They hadn't used their Searchwater radar so far. No need, and anyway its transmissions would give away their presence to any warship within a hundred and fifty miles.

Mackintosh swung his burly frame down the narrow tube of the aircraft to the radar operator's position. The bored flight sergeant was idly turning the pages of the Searchwater manual.

'All fired up?' the AEO asked.

'Red hot, sir!'

Tosh reflected for a moment. If *Truculent* stuck her periscope above the surface, she'd soon know the Nimrod was there. Northwood had told them to keep their presence secret. Yet if they didn't use the radar they might never find the boat again.

'Oh, what the hell! Give it a burst.'

The radar operator flicked the switch that brought his screen sparkling to life.

* * *

HMS Truculent.

Cordell checked the control room clock. Just minutes to go.

'Course zero-four-five. Reducing to three knots. Returning to periscope depth!'

The zig-zag they'd been following should have confused any trackers, in the unlikely event there were any. Their sensors had detected none. But you couldn't be too careful in these northerly waters; the Bears were everywhere.

'Periscope depth, sir!'

'Up ESM!'

The Electronic Support Measures mast, covered with radar detectors, slid upwards, its dome just breaking the surface. Shaped to reflect radar beams no more strongly than a wave-crest, it scanned the electromagnetic spectrum for emitters.

Cordell leaned over the shoulder of the CPO at the Action Information console.

Printed on the amber VDU screen was the data processed by the ESM computer.

'Four radars detected, but none of them a threat, sir.'

Cordell ran his eye down the list. The first trace was from the Soviet RORSAT ocean surveillance satellite, passing 180 kilometres above their heads. *Truculent*'s periscope wouldn't be large enough to register. Two other traces were the navigation radars of passing freighters, the fourth from a Soviet TU-95 *Bear-F* reconnaisance plane, too far away to matter.

'Raise the search periscope! Standby, wireless room!'

The search periscope came hissing up from the control room deck. Mounted atop its optical system was a conical satellite antenna.

Cordell pressed his face to the eyepiece and swung the viewfinder through 360 degrees.

'Nothing in sight!'

He looked away to the control room clock. It was time.

In the wireless room, Hitchens hovered behind the signaller, waiting for the burst of satellite data to be received and stored in the communications computer. At that point he would expel the others from the room, so that he could print out the signals unobserved.

The digital clock completed the hour. On the dot, a red l.e.d. on the satcom panel began to flicker. The signals were being sucked in. Within fifteen seconds the transmission would be over.

'*Aircraft overhead*!' bawled the Action Information rating.

'Searchwater, sir!'

'Bearing?'

'One-nine-two, sir.'

'One of ours. Thank God for that! What's he doing this far north?'

'What's happened?' Hitchens had heard the shout and came running from the wireless room.

'Nimrod, sir. South of us. Detected its radar.'

'What?' Hitchens screamed. 'Get the masts down, you stupid sod! Go deep! Go deep! Get this bloody boat out of the way!'

'But the aircraft's friendly, sir,' Cordell gaped.

Hitchens' eyes almost burst from their sockets. He looked ready to kill. Fists clenched, he advanced on Cordell.

Then he checked himself, Cordell's face, open-mouthed, inches from his own. All around him he sensed a stillness, the men watchful.

Unnoticed, Tim Pike had entered the control room. He saw the expression change on his captain's face. Rage became fear, then bewilderment; then the mask was back in place.

'Depth under the keel?' Hitchens demanded, breaking the silence.

'Two-sixty metres, sir!' called the navigator.

'Keep two hundred metres, come left, steer three-two-zero.'

Still struggling to control emotions which seemed not to belong to him, Hitchens took Cordell by the arm to one side of the control room. The boat heeled to port as the planesman responded to the orders.

'That aircraft. It's on the exercise. But we're not any more, see?'

Cordell didn't see, but nodded as if he did.

'Now, get us away from the datum. Evasion tactics. Lose the bloody Nimrod!'

Philip pushed past Lieutenant Smallbone and Radio Operator Bennett and closed the door firmly behind him.

Tim Pike caught the eye of the weapon engineer, Paul Spriggs. This was one more incident to add to the list.

Cordell took a grip on himself.

'Sound room! Call the best evasion depth when we reach it!' he barked into the intercom. 'Planesman! Call out the depth every thirty metres!'

'Sixty metres, sir!'

Built into the outer hull, a water sampler constantly measured the temperature and salinity of the sea, feeding a computer in the sound room which calculated the best conditions in which to hide and distort their underwater sounds.

'Ninety metres, sir!'

Pike joined Cordell at the chart table.

'The bastard was gonna hit me! Did you see?'

'Forget it. Sort yourself out. Concentrate on evading.'

'I'm not going to bloody forget it! There's more to this than you know about, sir.'

'One-hundred-twenty metres, sir!' the planesman yelled.

'What d'you mean?' asked Pike.

'The reason he's so bloody bolshie, sir. I know what's behind it.'

The two men leaned over the chart, so as not to be heard.

'What?'

'Well, it's er . . . , look it's dead personal, sir. Can we . . . ?'

'Okay. Tell me later. Now, let's think what the bloody "crabs" are going to do.'

* * *

Nimrod Eight-Lima-Golf.

'Riser, bearing zero-one-two!'

'Got it!'

The tactical navigator tapped the key which brought the radar data onto his display.

'Turned half a circle from his last position. No wonder we lost him.'

The flight navigator gave the new course to the pilot, and the plane banked sharply. They'd be overhead the submarine in two minutes.

'Prepare Barra 9 and Difar 20.'

In the rear of the aircraft the air electronics operator selected the directional buoys, set them and loaded them into the ejection tubes.

'Radar's cold! He's gone deep again!'

'Here we go,' Mackintosh groaned.

'I need a bathy-buoy, fast.'

'Bathy 34 ready in the multilauncher,' crackled the voice from the rear of the plane.

'Bathy away.'

'Barra 9 away.'

They'd just flown over the last known position of the submarine. The tacnav put one buoy to the west and south, told the pilot to turn hard right, and launched the other buoy to the north and east. It would take about a minute for the buoys to start transmitting their information.

'Difar 20 away.'

'Can't we go active?' the tacnav asked Mackintosh. 'Best chance of finding him.'

'Need clearance from Northwood for that, and there's no time. Just have to keep our fingers crossed.'

One of the processor operators called, 'Best evasion depth one-hundred-and-fifty metres, the bathy says.'

The bathythermographic buoy had measured the temperature and salinity of the water down to the sea bed. Up here the North Cape Current could produce sudden changes in water conditions that could affect drastically the passage of sound through the water.

'Touched bottom at three-hundred-and-fifty metres.'

'Thanks. Anything on the Barra yet?'

'Nope. Barra and Difar both cold.'

'Sod him! We'll have to put a circle round the area. Ten mile radius. And we'll be out of Lofars by the time we've finished.'

'Time to signal Northwood again,' Mackintosh sighed. None of this was making his hangover feel any better.

* * *

CINCFLEET, Northwood, England.

Rear-Admiral Bourlet cursed himself for having been so stupidly optimistic. When the earlier signals had come in saying *Truculent* had been detected, he'd called the Commander-in-Chief to tell him. Admiral Waverley said he'd ring Downing Street immediately with the good news.

Arse-licker! If it weren't for Waverley's bum-crawling he wouldn't now be facing the humiliation of having to tell the PM they'd lost the boat again.

There'd been no further signals from *Tenby*, but she was still over fifty miles from the search area, and if the Nimrod had lost track of *Truculent* while sitting almost on top of her, *Tenby* wouldn't stand a chance of hearing her at that range.

He finished scribbling a note.

'Store that signal for *Tenby* on the satellite, so she'll get it whenever she calls,' he ordered, and headed back along the tunnels and up the stairways to the surface.

It was always good to get into real air again. Underground the atmosphere smelled filtered and artificial.

He strode up the tarmac road to the office block by the entrance to the headquarters. The wind had got up and tugged at the White Ensign flying from a mast in front of the doorway.

He took the stairs at a run, and his heart felt surprisingly light considering the crisis he faced.

The reason for his headiness stood waiting outside his office, chatting to his PA, Hitchens' file tucked under her arm.

'Ah, Felicity, my dear. Thank you so much for coming,' he greeted her.

Commander Rush smiled saucily.

'I took it as an order, sir.'

As she followed him into his office, she turned to his PA and winked. The young WRNS raised an eyebrow.

* * *

HMS Truculent.

The long, black submarine passed undetected from the Norwegian Sea into the Barents. She'd zigged and zagged, alternating thirty knot bursts of speed with periods of near immobility. For the Nimrod to have kept up with her progress would have taken more than skill; the RAF would have needed extraordinary luck and an almost limitless supply of sonobuoys.

Without closing with the surface again, they'd never know for sure that they'd thrown off their shadow, but Sebastian Cordell was confident they were safe when he handed over the watch at lunchtime to Lieutenant Nick Cavendish.

'We got a satellite fix before the old man panicked,' Cordell confided to Cavendish. 'It showed the SINS is still spot on. We're here, at this moment.'

He pointed to a position half way between the shallows of the Fugley Bank and the pinnacle of rock thirty miles northwest of it which rose from the ocean floor like an aberration in the almost flat underwater landscape.

'Course-change due at 1315. New course zero-nine-eight. Next stop North Cape. All aboard for the mystery tour!'

Cavendish shook his head.

'He thinks we're a load of bloody schoolchildren,' he scoffed, 'not old enough to be told the facts of life! It's not on, you know. Bloody dangerous if we don't all know what we're up to. Did you get an intelligence summary on the satcom?'

'Yep.'

He pushed across the page of teletype.

'Still no mention of *Tenby*. Odd that. Nothing since Sunday, as if she'd disappeared.'

'Perhaps she's doing the same as us. Covert op,' Cavendish suggested. His eye ran further down the page to the Soviet deployments. 'Christ! That's quite a barrier for the Sovs. They don't usually get that many ships out for us.'

'Mmmm. I think we'll be looking for some little friend to help us through, don't you?'

Sebastian patted Cavendish on the shoulder and left him to it.

Lieutenant Commander Tim Pike was waiting for him in his cabin. The first lieutenant looked tense, and tugged at the short tufts of his ginger beard.

'Okay. Let's have it. What is it you wanted to say about the captain?'

Cordell felt a hot flush creeping up his neck.

'Oh, sit down, Sebastian, for heaven's sake.'

Pike pointed at the spare chair.

'As I said, sir, it's rather personal. But . . . , well . . . , about a couple of years ago I met a girl – a woman – in a restaurant, and we . . . , we went to bed together. I only knew her by her Christian name, you see. But it turned out she was Mrs Hitchens,' Sebastian concluded miserably.

'What? You've been knobbing the captain's missus? You rotten little sod!'

'I didn't know at the time, sir. She did all the picking up, not me!'

'I can believe that,' mocked Pike. 'Bloody hell! And you think the captain's found you out, is that it?'

'Yes, sir.'

'And that it accounts for his um . . . , overreaction this morning?'

'Exactly. And not just this morning. He's been pretty odd the whole patrol.'

'And you think it's all down to you?'

'Well, yes. I suppose I do.'

Tim Pike frowned. *Could* it be as simple as that? He doubted it. Rumours about Philip Hitchens' marital problems had been circulating for months, yet it hadn't affected his professional conduct before.

'Okay, Sebastian. Thanks for telling me about it. It's right that I should know. And I shan't tell anyone else, don't worry.'

'Thank you, sir.'

'Now, you'd better get along to the wardroom, or there'll be no lunch left.'

'Right, sir.'

Why would Sara Hitchens want to seduce a boy like Sebastian, Pike wondered? *Did* women fancy kids just out of school?

He spun the combination lock on the small wall-safe beneath his desk and took out a notebook. He looked through the list of things that had concerned him about Commander Hitchens on that patrol.

Each incident of jumpiness, aggression or secretiveness looked small and insignificant on its own, but a picture was beginning to emerge. But a picture of what?

Evidence of mental instability? Or just the tension of working under highly secret, highly sensitive orders?

But Hitchens had been on the point of strangling Cordell in the control room earlier; Pike had seen it with his own eyes. He'd lost his self-control, and that was dangerous. If he did it again when they were in contact with the Soviets he could put all their lives at risk.

The curtain across the doorway was brushed aside and Paul Spriggs came in. He spotted the notebook.

'Something new happened?'

'Could be.'

They'd each been making notes on Hitchens since the previous morning, keeping their writings separate. That way, if it came to anything, each man's evidence would have some claim to validity.

Suddenly the tannoy crackled.

'*Do you hear there! Captain speaking.*'

Both men looked at one another in surprise. Pike was expecting to make 'the pipe' himself in a few minutes' time.

'*Thought you'd like an update on our situation. We've just altered course to the east. Should be abeam North Cape sometime later tonight. We're heading on into the Barents Sea. Things are pretty tense up on the surface, so we'll all need to be very much on our toes from now on.*'

'Things are pretty tense down here too, old chap,' Pike muttered.

'According to the World Service News summary,' Hitchens' voice continued, *'there was a little confrontation yesterday between one of the American flat-tops and a Soviet Bear bomber that got too close. The Yanks came within an inch of shooting it out of the sky.'*

'Fucking Americans! Always overreact,' snarled Spriggs.

'The Soviet Northern Fleet has mustered a pretty strong ASW barrier to protect their bastions. We've got to get through it tomorrow, undetected, and close with the Kola Inlet before all their SSNs get loose. Can't say any more than that at the moment.

'Ahead of us we can expect up to two Victor IIIs and two Sierras, according to the intelligence report. With a bit of luck three of those will be well to the north of us, but we're sticking close to the coast – we have to because we're in a hurry – so there'll be a few SSKs around and a lot of aircraft.

'I'm sorry we didn't manage to take in any family-grams this morning. We had to put the mast down before we'd received them – for operational reasons.'

'Huh,' Pike mocked. 'In case our own side finds out what we're up to.'

'Do you mean that?'

'Shh!'

'In conclusion . . . '

Hitchens' voice sounded unsteady, almost emotional.

'I just want to say how terribly important this mission is. There's a lot depending on it, believe me. That is all.'

'So bloody important, he won't even tell me what it is!'

Pike pushed back his chair and stood up, bristling with anger.

'I've had enough! I'm going to have it out with him!'

Spriggs pushed Pike back down into his seat.

'Cool it Tim! If you go blazing in like that, you'll be up on a charge!'

'Fuck him! The bastard's got right up my nose!'

'Okay. But talk sense for a minute. That crash-dive this morning, to get away from one of our own planes? You think we're not *meant* to be here? The plane was looking for us, is that what you're saying?'

'Yes. That *is* what I'm saying, but I've no way of proving it.'

Spriggs was aghast.

'But why? Hitchens is a rule-book man. He'd never chance his arm . . .'

'Sure? Do you know what's going on in his mind? I don't. The man's a closed book to me.'

Paul thought of the explosive power stacked in the bow compartment of the submarine. Harpoon missiles that could devastate surface ships over fifty miles away; Tigerfish torpedoes that could rip through the double-hulls of Soviet submarines; and Moray mines that could lie dormant in the depths before darting from the dark to cripple the unsuspecting. He shivered.

'If you really believe he's acting against orders, Tim, then we've got to do something about it. And fast!'

'We need proof, Paul. And how the hell do we get it?'

CHAPTER SEVEN

Plymouth, England.

Tuesday 22nd October. A.M.

Two security men sat next to each other on a commuter flight to Plymouth. They spoke little.

Hillier was SIS, the Secret Intelligence Service or MI6, controlled by the Foreign Office. Black was MI5, a Home Office man. Hillier was tall and gaunt with a fine-boned nose, Black stocky with a tendency to sweat. The former styled himself a diplomat, the latter a policeman.

'Nearly there,' Hillier declared in a voice edged with boredom, glancing at his gold wrist-watch.

John Black pulled back his sleeve to reveal his own timepiece, digital and stainless-steel. It was a quarter-to-nine. They'd been served breakfast on the flight.

'The watchers'll have just changed shift,' Black mumbled. 'Boring bloody job, that is.'

'Did well yesterday, your man.' Hillier's voice was patronizing. 'Spotting Gunnar like that. Very timely.'

'Except that Gunnar spotted him at the same time. He'll get a reprimand.'

'Don't be too hard. He's probably given us an extra twenty-four hours. We needed that.'

The previous evening, Hillier had been halfway out of his office in the Soviet Department at Century House, when he'd received the summons to the Director's office. The instructions he'd been given were highly irregular. He didn't know where the orders came from, but it had to be the Foreign Secretary himself. And that meant the PM. He couldn't believe Sir Nigel would take a flyer on a thing like this.

The Director had been uneasy about the whole business. Doubted the wisdom of it. He refused to use their

Moscow agents to plant the information about *HMS Truculent*. The call from MI5 to say the Russian had been seen again, sniffing near Sara Hitchens' home, had been timely. Very timely.

Normally, feeding information to the Russians was an MI6 job, but handling Soviet spies on British soil was MI5. Hence the two of them were on the breakfast flight to the West Country. Their meeting with Mrs Hitchens was fixed for nine o'clock.

'Remind me what you've got on Gunnar,' Hillier asked wearily as they turned from the airport road onto the Plymouth by-pass. Black was driving the hired car.

'Not a lot,' Black grunted, braking sharply as a motorcyclist weaved in front of them. 'Knew nothing about him until all this blew up. Found out where he lived by accident. Sharp-eyed neighbour saw the man and his missus moving their stuff out of the house in the middle of the night. Called the police the next day.

'In too much of a hurry – they were. Got careless. Left some coding pads. We assumed they'd have got out of the country, but we kept a watch on Mrs Hitchens just in case. Yesterday he suddenly turned up. Drove straight past her house. It was us he was looking for. Saw us the same moment we saw him. Off like a rocket. Our man put out a call to the local police, but Gunnar disappeared.'

'Bit daring, isn't he, coming back to the house? She must've been giving him something special!' Hillier sneered.

'Probably wants to shut 'er up. Thinks she's the only one who can identify him. Do her in and he could slip back into the undergrowth for a year or two, then emerge with a new cover.'

'Well, she'll be safe enough with your brave boys parked at the end of her drive!'

Black felt the back of his neck prickle. Hillier was needling him because his watcher had failed to conceal himself properly.

'Have you met her?' Hillier asked.

'Mmm. Came down here when the case broke. Temperamental bitch.'

Hillier looked about him as they drove through the first of the grey stone villages to the southeast of the city. Some pretty properties here, he thought to himself.

'Will she play, d'you think?'

Black thought for a moment. He took out a cigarette and lit it. Hillier pointedly wound down his window.

'Tell her her old man's life could depend on it, and she might. Curious that; she says she still loves him despite all the stuff she got up to behind his back.'

'Ah, women! Where *would* we be without them!'

Black cast him a sideways glance.

'Some of us manage very well, thanks.'

Sara had been awake most of the night, worrying. The MI5 man had given no reason for needing to see her again. During the night she'd thought she could hear someone outside, prowling round the house.

She watched unseen from a window as the two men got out of their car, then waited for them to ring the bell before she let them in.

'Hello, Mrs Hitchens.'

Black tried to sound jovial.

Sara nodded a greeting, eyeing Hillier with suspicion.

'You'll have to make do with the kitchen, I'm afraid. That's where I live when I'm alone here,' she said, leading them in.

She switched on the kettle and pointed to the old pine table.

'I'm not sure why . . .'

'Let me introduce myself.' The SIS man extended his hand. 'Hillier from the Foreign Office . . .'

'I've already told Mr Black everything I can remember . . .'

'So you want to know why we're here? Naturally.'

Hillier spoke to her as if she had a mental age of five.

'Glad you've got the kettle on. I could do with a cuppa.'

Sara became increasingly nervous. She lit a cigarette and inhaled deeply.

'Tea or coffee?'

'Coffee, please.'

'Tea, if you don't mind,' added Black.

Sara reached for a cupboard.

'What a delightful kitchen.'

Hillier's comment annoyed her.

'Isn't it just?' she answered abruptly. 'But let's skip the polite conversation, shall we? Would you mind telling me what you want?'

Hillier's eyebrows arched upwards.

'Very well . . .'

Tread carefully with this one, he told himself.

'This man who called himself Gunnar . . ,' he paused. 'We're anxious to know if he's contacted you again?'

'Certainly not! He won't come back after what I said to him.'

She searched their faces for clues. Their blank expressions made her shiver.

'You think he will?'

The footsteps round the house last night . . .

'We think he might, yes.'

'He'll be in Moscow by now, surely?'

'We believe not, Mrs Hitchens,' Black chipped in. 'A man fitting his description was seen near here yesterday.'

'Oh . . .' Her voice caught in her throat.

'The fact is, we're keen that he should contact you,' Hillier added.

'Why?' she snapped defensively.

'We want you to tell him something; give him a specific piece of information.'

'What sort of information?'

'We'll come to that in a minute. But do you agree to help us?'

Hillier's face was friendly, Black's hard. In the familiar warmth of her kitchen the two men seemed enormous, threatening.

'I don't know. Why should I?'

Hillier folded his arms and sighed, like a schoolteacher whose patience was reaching its limits.

'I'm told you're an intelligent woman, Mrs Hitchens. I

don't need to spell *everything* out, do I? Suffice it to say, your husband is approaching the coast of Russia with a boatload of sophisticated weaponry. He's not behaving normally. Thousands of lives may be in danger, his being one of them.'

'Oh, God!'

Her worst fears were suddenly being confirmed.

'But what can *I* do about it?'

'Within forty-eight hours your husband may trigger off a spot of genocide. Now, of course all sorts of things are being done at official levels to ensure it doesn't happen. But it's just possible the Navy may not stop him in time. So, we – that's you and us – we're like an insurance policy. To give the Soviets an inkling that we've a problem we may not be able to handle. Have to do it indirectly, though. And that means you.'

Sara swallowed. Her heart was racing. Genocide? For God's sake!

'But . . . , how's that going to help, if the Russians know about the problem?' she demanded.

'It means they'll keep well out of the way, if they've any sense,' Black answered briskly. 'They don't want a war any more than we do.'

Sara felt sick. To think she'd started all this!

'Now, there are things we need to know,' Black continued. 'When you were seeing this man, how did you make contact?'

'He would ring when he came to Plymouth. If I wanted to contact him, I'd leave a message at the Holiday Inn. Even when he wasn't in Plymouth, they'd take calls for him.'

'I'll bet he's not using them any more,' Black growled. 'We think he'll contact you soon. A phone-call or a message of some sort.'

'But what does he want? I told him I'd never see him again.'

The two men shifted uncomfortably.

'He's obviously very fond of you, Mrs Hitchens,' Hillier said in an oily tone.

'There'll be no risk to you in all this,' Black explained. 'You've got protection. Twenty-four hour cover.'

Sara looked startled.

'Protection? From Gunnar?'

'Just a precaution,' Hillier soothed. 'One of John Black's men is keeping an eye on the house. You'll be quite safe.

'Now, this message you're going to give him. You mustn't say it's from us, of course. Pretend it's based on something your husband said to you, just before he sailed.'

'What?'

'That he intends to lay mines at the entrance to the main Soviet submarine base at Polyarny.'

'Poly . . . what?'

'Think of Polyanna. Tell him that, in fact. Mis-remembering the name will make it more convincing.'

'Is this true? How do you know what Philip's going to do?'

'We don't,' admitted Black. 'It's a guess. But if the Russians send submarines to sea from Polyarny, and they're blown up by your husband's mines – that'll be war, Mrs Hitchens.'

'What we need is time,' Hillier took over. 'If the Soviets keep their boats out of the way, it'll give our Navy more time to find your husband and bring him back.'

'But supposing Gunnar doesn't make contact, or I don't convince him?'

'Doesn't bear thinking about, does it?' answered John Black.

'I'm sure you'll do your very best. You must want to – after what's happened,' Hillier added pointedly.

Eventually they left. They gave Sara a card with two telephone numbers on it. One was Hillier's desk in London, the other a Plymouth number for the local watchers.

The silence in the house terrified her. She wandered from room to room trying to peer from windows without being seen. Somewhere out there were two men. One to protect her, the other . . . ? What did he want? Why had Gunnar come back?

It was unreal. Soon she would awake and the nightmare would fade.

And there was a third man, Philip. What wild obsession had gripped him? It wasn't just because of her – it *couldn't* be! The security men were blaming her for everything, but that was unfair!

There was much more behind it. If only she knew what.

Outside in the garden, a pigeon took flight with a clatter of wings. Somewhere upstairs an unfastened window banged shut in a sudden breeze. She shivered.

She was scared to be in the house alone, but they'd told her to wait.

Waiting for Gunnar. A title for a melodrama.

Suddenly there was the crunch of tyres on gravel. Her heart pounded. He wouldn't just arrive, would he?

She strained to see out.

Patsy Tinker. What did she want? If Gunnar came and saw the car he'd be put off.

She'd pretend not to be in.

Too late. Patsy saw her and waved.

'Thought I'd drop in,' Patsy explained. 'You seemed so down when we met on the Hoe yesterday . . .'

'Oh, I'm okay. I'm expecting someone, that's all.'

'Oh, I'm sorry.' Patsy looked embarrassed. 'Should I . . . ?'

'No, no. Come in. Have some coffee or something.'

They moved to the kitchen.

'Oh, you've had it done since I was last here,' Patsy exclaimed admiringly. 'New units. Very smart.'

'That was last year. Shows how long it's been.'

Sara busied herself with the kettle and mugs.

'That was pretty startling, what you told me yesterday,' Patsy ventured. 'All that security business. I'd be scared to death living out here on my own with all that going on.'

'Well, with kind neighbours like you dropping in to get all the juicy details, I don't have time to be scared, do I?'

'Sara, that's *not* why I came! I simply thought you might

want someone to talk to. It's bad for you, keeping it all bottled up. All those feelings locked up inside you. You'll burst.'

Sara was on the point of doing exactly that. She shook with anger at being lectured.

'Look, sod off! I didn't ask you here!'

And she burst into tears. It was what Patsy had hoped would happen. The tension was broken.

Patsy let her cry, saying nothing, until Sara's shoulders had stopped shaking.

The kettle began to whistle.

'I'll do that,' Patsy said. Coffee and tea had been left out, and there were unwashed cups and saucers in the sink. So, there'd been other visitors that morning.

Sara pulled a handkerchief from the handbag on the table.

'I'm sorry,' she sniffed. 'I know you mean to help. But really there's nothing you can do.'

Patsy placed a mug on the table next to Sara, and sat down.

'Thanks.'

'Is Simon all right? Have you been able to keep it away from him, all the problems?'

'Hardly,' Sara laughed bitterly. 'It was through Simon that Philip found out.

'I'd been very silly. A little while back, there was a man I . . . used to see. He came round here quite often. I let Simon meet him. Then, ten days ago, he and Philip bumped into the man in the city. Suddenly Philip had found the key to my little box of secrets.

'Simon was back at school when it all came out, so he missed the awful rows. I think he sensed it was coming, though; that's what's been behind the trouble at school this term.'

'Vandalizing microscopes?'

'That's it. I'm sure there's worse to come. Perhaps I'll bring him home for a while . . .'

'Why don't you? That could be good for both of you.'

'I think I will.'

They fell silent and sipped at their coffee. Patsy took a deep breath, and started the conversation again.

'This man you were seeing . . . The one you said worked for a foreign government . . . the Russian . . . did you . . . tell him anything at all that you shouldn't have?'

'I don't *think* so, but then I'm not sure what he wanted to know. Nothing really secret, that's for sure. I don't know anything secret. Do you? I mean, does Andrew talk about his work?'

'Never.'

'It's . . . , it's not my fault, Patsy,' Sara pleaded. 'Whatever Philip's doing – it's unfair to blame me for it. It's much more involved than people think.'

'How do you mean?'

'This "revenge" they think he's planning – they imagine it's just because of me and Gunnar, but it isn't. It's more than that. It has to be.'

Wishful thinking, Patsy wondered?

'They really think he's going to attack the Russians?'

'Yes. They told me this morning.'

'What? Who did?'

Sara scraped back her chair and stood up. She grabbed a transistor radio from the worktop next to the kettle, and turned it on at full volume.

'We may be bugged,' she explained in a whisper.

'Who by?'

'MI5. They were here this morning.'

The pop music was deafening. Patsy found it unbearable.

'Couldn't we walk in the garden? It's a nice morning,' she suggested. Sara led the way to the back of the house.

The garden was walled, sheltering it from the wind. Roses and honeysuckle clung to the old brickwork. The last of the season's apples weighed heavily on the branches of young trees which Andrew had helped Philip plant the previous year.

'We should be safe out here.'

'You must think I've gone mad.'

'I'd be the same, I assure you.'

Sara reached out and held one of the apples, giving it a tiny twist so that it parted from the branch. Perfectly ripe. She held it out for Patsy.

Patsy took a bite. 'Gorgeous.' Sticking her hands determinedly into her trouser pockets, Sara turned to face Patsy squarely.

'Do you know about Philip's father?'

'No. Should I?'

'Philip hero-worshipped him, but he died when Philip was just fourteen. *HMS Tenby*? Does that ring a bell?'

'Vaguely. One of the SSNs is called *Tenby*.'

'This was an earlier one. An old diesel sub. Disappeared on patrol in the Barents Sea in 1962. All a big mystery. Philip's dad was her first lieutenant.'

'Oh, yes. I remember something. An accidental explosion, was it?'

'Not according to Philip. He's convinced the Russians sank her.'

'What? I've never heard that said before!'

'It was an open verdict at the official inquiry. No wreckage was ever found. No survivors. Just theories. The one they settled for was that there'd been a fire on board and the torpedoes had gone up. They even made changes to the way the things were stored on board after that.'

'But Philip didn't buy that idea?'

'I suppose he may have done at the beginning; he was only a boy. But he overheard someone talking to his mother about it, a few years later, saying the *Tenby* had been in the Barents to keep an eye on Russian torpedo trials. Nuclear torpedoes.'

'Crikey! And was it true?'

'I don't know. But Philip thinks so. He became convinced the Russians tested a nuclear torpedo on the *Tenby* and vapourized his father along with the rest of the crew.'

'But that's madness! The Russians would never have done that. They'd have risked starting a nuclear war, wouldn't they?'

Sara shrugged. She'd never given much heed to Philip's theories before now.

'It was November 1962, the Cuban missile crisis,

remember? All very jumpy. The Americans and Russians on the brink of war – Philip reckoned the White House put pressure on Britain not to make an issue of the *Tenby*.'

'Oh.'

Patsy racked her brains to remember what that crisis had been about.

'What is it you're saying? That this revenge Philip's planning is to do with his father's death?'

'I don't know exactly. But I'm sure it's involved.'

'*Why* are you so sure?'

Sara hesitated over how much to say.

'This summer we went on holiday to Guernsey, all three of us. It was Philip's idea. He used to go there as a boy, but hadn't been back since. I didn't know before, but it was in Guernsey that he'd last seen his father. Straight after that holiday in 1962, the *Tenby* sailed north and never returned.'

'Oh, I see.'

'Something happened this summer, to Philip. We'd been there a few days, staying in an absolute dump of a hotel. He'd been a bit moody – memories and all that – then one afternoon he came back after a walk on his own, looking as if he'd seen a ghost. Simon and I were by the pool; I expected him to join us, and when he didn't I went up to our room to look for him. Well . . .'

She frowned.

'Go on . . .'

'He was – I didn't go into the room, because he seemed to be . . . crying. I could hear, through the door. I . . . I didn't know what to think. Philip's so – undemonstrative. So, I just stood there, listening to this awful croaking noise, sort of frozen. And then he said something, in a strangled voice. Out loud. He said "Dad, Dad, what have they done to you?" '

'Good Lord! But you still didn't go in?'

'I thought he'd be upset – embarrassed that I'd heard him. So I went down again and waited for him. He didn't appear for hours. Claimed he'd fallen asleep. I asked if anything was wrong, but he said no. So I just put it down to his being back in the place where he'd last seen his father. Something deeply buried coming to the surface.'

'And that was that?'

'Well, no. He didn't sleep at night, tossing and turning; always desperately short-tempered and wanting to be on his own. Then a couple of days later, some other mother I got talking to at the hotel was telling me about a beautiful walk she'd just been on, lonely clifftops and all that, when she mentioned having seen Philip up there, sitting on a bench – with a woman.'

'Oh, really?'

'I thought the obvious at first. That evening I asked him about it. It shook him that he'd been spotted, but he dismissed it; said the woman had just been another walker who'd stopped for a rest. He was lying; I can always tell – he does it very badly.'

'You think she had some connection with his father?'

'I don't know. We came home at the end of the holiday; life returned to normal, except that Philip had closed up. I couldn't get through to him at all. He was like a man facing a crucial decision, unable to make up his mind.'

'And he was still like that when . . .'

'When he found out about Gunnar. Yes. But that's just it. Afterwards – after all the screaming and recrimination – he was different. It was as if he *had* finally made up his mind, finally decided what to do about the problem that had dogged him since Guernsey.'

A blackbird began to sing shrilly from a heavily-laden pear tree further down the garden. They began to walk again, Sara bobbing down to pull a long tuft of rye-grass from a flower bed.

'Have you told anyone about this? The authorities?'

'Hardly! It's just the imaginings of a silly woman, isn't it?' she snorted scornfully.

'It could be rather more than that. I think you should tell someone.'

Suddenly Sara clutched at Patsy's arm. The noise of a car at the front of the house had startled her.

'Sounds like you've got another visitor. Shall I go and look for you?'

Sara shook her head.

'We can go round the side.'

A trail of paving stones led to the front of the house. A small green van was parked in the drive. Its driver stood outside the front door cradling a bouquet of roses.

'Ah,' the youth turned. 'One of you Mrs Hitchens?'

'Yes, me.' Sara advanced towards him.

'Could you sign here, please?'

She did, and took the flowers from him. As the van reversed down the drive, she stood quite still staring at the blooms, as if they were poisoned.

'Aren't they beautiful? No one ever sends me flowers,' Patsy complained.

Sara looked petrified, eyes fixed on the envelope pinned to the cellophane.

'Do you know who they're from?'

'I think so,' she answered in a whisper. 'I must find a vase.'

The front door was latched, so they walked the path back to the kitchen, Patsy feeling awkward. Greetings from a new lover or an old one, she wondered?

Sara gingerly unpinned the envelope and pulled open the flap.

Patsy tried to see. The card was almost covered with writing; Sara's hands trembled as she read it. The message continued on the back.

'Nothing wrong, I hope.'

'I'm sorry . . ,' was all she could say. She looked at her watch. She was plainly very scared.

'You want me to go?'

Sara nodded. Tears welled up again; she pulled a tissue from her sleeve and blew her nose.

'All right. But look. Ring me whenever you feel like it. D'you promise?'

'Yes, I will.'

Patsy clasped Sara by the shoulders and kissed her on the cheek. For the first time in her life she felt some kinship with her.

''Bye, now. I'll drop in again soon.'

Sara forced a smile.

'Thanks for coming. I mean that.'

Patsy turned her car into the road and headed for Plymouth. What Sara had just told her was immensely important. It was what Andrew must have had in mind when he'd asked her to get talking with Sara.

She decided to ring Norman Craig from a phone box, and arrange to see him at the Naval Base.

At the front of the old rectory, overlooking the road, was a small bedroom used to store junk. Sara unlatched a small window at the top of the frame and pushed it open. This was the signal she'd been told to make when Gunnar made contact. The room smelled stale; it could do with ventilation anyway.

She prayed the watcher was watching.

She still clutched the florist's card. The words, written in Gunnar's foreign script, had terrified but excited her.

He'd deceived her, taken advantage of her loneliness. He was an enemy of her country, who'd used her cynically. Yet he'd loved her with a passion she'd never known before, a passion which surely no man could fake.

The words seemed to smoulder on the card.

> My darling. I *have* to see you again. For me
> it is not over between us and can never be.
> My heart is broke, and you must mend it.
> Please!
> Big news! I'm leaving my employer, and need
> your help to make friends with the people
> you know. I depend on you. Please don't fail
> me!
> Cannot meet at old rendezvous, but you go
> there now. Don't delay. *Tell no one*. I'll
> know if you do. The H.I. desk will have a
> message for 'Mrs Mathews'. That will tell you
> where I am.
> Please do it! I long to kiss you again.
> G.

'Leaving his employer'? He wanted to defect?

Or was it another deception? Perhaps she should contact

Hillier first. If things were changing, would they still want her to tell Gunnar about Philip?

But she dared not delay. They'd told her to do nothing to make Gunnar suspicious. Was *he* bugging her phone? Would he be watching her from a distance as she drove into Plymouth to meet him? Possibly. She could take no risks.

She opened the wardrobe in her bedroom. She'd have to change. Couldn't drive into Plymouth in an old pair of jeans.

She'd wear the plum-coloured skirt and blouse, with the black jacket.

She looked at her watch; eleven-thirty. The traffic wouldn't be bad; she could be there by twelve. Her face was a mess. Anyone could tell she'd been crying. She splashed on some cold water, then applied some makeup.

Handbag, money, car keys, then she closed the front door and checked it was latched. She'd left the upstairs window open as instructed, but it made her uneasy. Burglaries were rife in the district.

A South West Electricity Board van was parked fifty yards from the Hitchens' house. The engineer sitting behind the wheel was eating a sandwich and drinking coffee from a flask.

The silver Volkswagen drove past him at speed, heading for Plymouth. The watcher picked up a microphone to report that Mrs Hitchens was on her way.

He finished his coffee. There was no great hurry; another car would pick her up at the next crossroads. His instructions were to follow at a distance, and hold himself ready for new orders.

At the junction with the Plymouth road Sara noticed the car behind her. A red Escort. Was it following her?

She turned left and the Escort followed, but two minutes later it turned off to the right. Unknown to her, the trail had been taken up by the green Vauxhall in front.

At the outskirts of the city she slowed down. The car she was following pulled into a filling station. Her heart raced as she neared the rendezvous. Fear gripped her, fear and excitement.

Left into a side street, up to the Hoe. She didn't notice the green Vauxhall following fifty yards behind. Left again into Citadel Road. She was in luck; a parking meter bay was just coming free.

The Vauxhall slid past her and disappeared. Sara locked her car and paused for a moment to compose herself. Her legs felt like jelly. Two deep breaths, then she started towards the Holiday Inn. She looked up to the sixth floor. It was where Gunnar had always stayed; a room with a view of the Hoe. Was he there now, watching her?

As she mounted the hotel steps, the red Escort drew up opposite. She was through the swing door and approaching the reception desk, when its driver began to cross the lawn to the hotel.

'Do you have a message for Mrs Mathews?' Sara asked the girl behind the desk, as calmly as she could.

'Oh, hullo!'

The receptionist had recognized her. Sara smiled; she was sure the girl had never known her name.

'Yes, here it is.'

'Thank you.'

Sara took it and walked towards the bar and the lifts.

My darling! We must be very careful! You are
being folowed.
Take the lift *alone* to the fifth floor. Make
sure you are alone in the lift. On the fifth
go strait to the fire stairs. Down to the
basement – the garage. Be sure no one
follows! In bay 16 is a Black VW. The door is
open, the keys inside. KEEP THE WINDOWS SHUT.
Drive out on the Exeter road. After 3 miles
take the left to Stumpton. On the edge of the
village is the Red Crown pub. Stop in the car
park and wait for me. If I'm not there after
twenty minutes, go inside and ask for the
phonebox. I'll ring you there.
I love you, rember.
G.

There was something endearing about Gunnar's spelling mistakes.

The lift came; the doors closed behind her. From the lobby, the man who had driven the red Ford Escort watched the lift indicator stop at number five.

They'd told him to protect her, but not to compromise her rendezvous with the target. Stupid bloody instructions! He couldn't do both.

He hurried to the payphone at the other end of the lobby and punched in a number. It answered instantly; he spoke for no more than five seconds and replaced the receiver.

Sara's heels clattered on the stone stairs. On every other flight she stopped to listen, but hers were the only feet she could hear.

The basement garage stank of petrol. It was dimly lit. At first she couldn't see the bay numbers, but recognized the car, a VW like her own but black.

The engine fired at the first turn of the key. She slipped it into first and drove up the ramp into daylight, realizing then that the windows were of dark-tinted glass. The Electricity Board van was parked opposite.

The watcher wasn't sure. It could've been her. Sod those blackened side windows! Better report it, just in case.

Sara found the pub with ease. It was lunchtime and the car park was already half-full. She swung the VW round to face the road. There was little traffic; just a green Vauxhall cruising past and up the hill to her left.

She re-read both his notes. She could almost hear him speaking the words in the fake Scandinavian accent he'd cultivated. She ought to hate him, yet she didn't. Evil? Dangerous? But he wanted her help to defect . . .

Doubts set in. Sara closed her eyes and prayed it wasn't a trick.

Behind the Red Crown a wooded hill rose steeply. From the car park a path led diagonally up it through beech and oak trees. A wooden railing lined the path.

Concealed amongst the beeches stood a man, himself built like a tree, training binoculars on the black VW below. This was Viktor Kovalenko, known to most of those he'd met in recent months as 'Gunnar'.

Kovalenko stood over six feet tall, his frame broad with muscle. His hair had been almost blond, but today it was dyed a dark chestnut. As a 'Swede' he'd let it grow long, but now it was neatly trimmed.

He worked for the First Chief Directorate of the KGB. His role was to establish an identity in Britain, to build an information network, and to identify targets to be assassinated if the Soviet Union went to war with the West.

Until a few weeks ago his mission had gone according to plan. He had lived with his 'wife' Elena in a London suburb; they'd blended well into the background. Now their cover had been broken, and he was to blame.

Elena had been picked to work with him by the First Chief Directorate, without thought to their personal compatibility. They'd experimented with a physical relationship, but it had only heightened their dislike for one another. The problem was a serious one for Viktor Kovalenko, a man with an inexhaustible sexual appetite.

He searched the road below for signs of watchers, but saw none; he'd give it another ten minutes to be sure.

He brought the binoculars to bear on the VW and cursed the black glass which prevented him from seeing Sara, the woman whose welcoming body and child-like hunger to be loved had given such a pleasurable edge to his duties. He and Elena had been activated in the summer. A naval attaché at the Soviet Embassy in London had learned the name of the commander of the trials boat for the new Moray mines. KGB headquarters in Moscow had then made the stunning discovery that a man with the same surname was a prisoner in a labour camp on the Kola. Checks at Somerset House confirmed they were father and son.

Keeping watch on Sara Hitchens' activities for a couple of weeks had been enough for Viktor to know she was a natural target. It had been easy.

At their second date, she'd talked of her unhappy marriage and mentioned the plan for a family holiday in Guernsey.

It was Elena who'd targeted Philip on the Channel Island clifftops. She'd handled it well, Viktor had to admit.

He knew he'd been careless. He'd made the unforgiveable mistake of letting a woman mean more to him than easy sex. A week ago, when Sara had told him Philip knew about their affair, and that she'd guessed he was a spy, it had shaken him. Years of training and preparation thrown away for allowing personal involvement to cloud his brain!

He'd told Elena by phone they'd have to leave the house before dawn, and driven fast back to London that night.

They'd moved to Bristol, a contingency plan ready prepared. The London house had been raided – they knew that – but how much of their scheme had been uncovered? Were their identities known? Had he been photographed? And above all, did the security services know what Hitchens had agreed to do for the KGB?

That was why he was here today; he had to find out even if it meant risking his neck.

She'd been waiting fifteen minutes. Time to say hello.

Sara glanced at the dashboard clock every minute while she sat there. Alone in the car, she felt conspicuous and vulnerable.

The sharp tap on the window made her jump in her seat. She didn't recognize him at first with his short, dark hair, but then came the familiar smile. Trembling, she unlocked the passenger door.

'I was afraid you wouldn't come,' he breathed, slipping into the seat beside her, and tossing his small rucksack into the back.

'I . . . I don't know why I did . . ,' she stuttered. 'You look so different with that hair.'

'The change is superficial, my darling,' he grinned, putting his arm round her. 'Underneath I'm the same!'

'Don't touch me!'

He pulled a face like a scolded child.

'Nothing's changed since last week,' she warned him.

'Except that you said you'd never see me again, and you're here now.' There was a twinkle of triumph in his eyes. 'But we can't talk here.'

'Why not?'

'Someone might come. Were you followed?'

'Not that I noticed. But then, I'm not trained to spot these things,' she goaded.

'One mile up the road. There's a parking place at the top of a hill. It'll be more private. Drive there please, my darling.'

She noticed his accent had changed. He'd dropped the Swedish lilt.

'All right.'

At the edge of the road she paused to allow a red Escort into the car park, then she sped off up the hill. Kovalenko kept his eye on the wing mirror, but there was no one following. The lay-by was signposted, and she pulled in behind a clump of bushes. The car park boasted public toilets.

'This isn't very nice,' Sara complained.

He was silent and didn't look at her.

'I want to know your real name,' she demanded.

'Don't you know it already? Haven't *they* told you?'

She realized he meant the security men.

'I don't think *they* know it.'

He smiled inwardly. She'd told him some good news.

'You can call me Viktor.'

It was okay to tell her now.

'I meant what I said in the letter,' he told her, then added eagerly, 'Did you like the flowers?'

'Yes.' She allowed herself a brief smile. 'They were lovely.'

'They were to say sorry for deceiving you.'

'You admit you're a spy. That's an advance; you were still denying it a week ago,' she answered tartly.

'What did you expect? But it's different now. You must listen to me, my darling.'

He edged closer to her, but without touching.

'When we first met it was for one reason only. Not because I'm a spy and your husband . . . I didn't know anything about that when we met,' he protested. 'Believe me. There was nothing in what you told me that was any use to Moscow.'

Sincerity blazed from his eyes.

'The reason . . , the reason we met was that we both wanted the same thing. Love. Why does a woman go to a restaurant alone? Because she wants a man. Why was I there alone? Because I needed a woman. We were looking for each other. And then you came back to my hotel, and we weren't just any man and any woman; we were *magic*!'

His face lit up and the grin spread from ear to ear. Sara laughed. It moved her when he looked like that; he was like a big child.

He took hold of her and this time she didn't resist. He kissed her mouth. Guiltily she sensed the arousal of her body.

'You are such a woman! So loving, so generous! What we have together is too good to lose!'

She pulled back and shook her head.

'No.'

This was dangerous. There was a purpose in meeting him again. A deadly purpose.

'I told you what I'm going to do,' he pressed. 'I hate my work. I want to stay in England, to prove to you that you can trust me.'

Sara shook her head again.

'Why did you come here if you don't believe me?' he snapped.

'Maybe I do believe you. I don't know. But the reason I had to see you is that I'm frightened.'

His eyes softened as if on cue.

'Not of you. Frightened of what's about to happen,' she blurted out.

Viktor slipped his arm round her shoulder. She accepted it.

'Philip – he knows what you are.'

'I know. You told me last week.'

'Yes. But I didn't tell you the way he reacted. He hates

you – he hates all Russians. For all sorts of reasons, good and bad. He wants revenge. He's on an exercise in the Norwegian Sea – I'm sure you know.'

'Of course.' He began to frown.

'Well, he's not doing what he should be doing. He's ignoring his orders. The Navy's got no control over him. His submarine's loaded with mines. They think he's going to blow up the Russian fleet!'

Viktor froze. His eyes turned cold; his jaw set like stone.

'How do you know this?'

'Philip said something before he sailed,' she blustered. 'He was so angry he just blurted it out about the mines. Then, I heard from someone else he's ignoring his orders.'

'How many mines?'

'I don't know.'

'Where do they think he's going exactly?'

'Philip said a name. Poly something, could it be?'

'Poly something?' He frowned. 'You came here today to tell me this? Why?'

'Because I'm so afraid of what might happen. Our Navy may not be able to stop him. Someone should be warned. Someone on your side. I don't want a war to start! If it did, it'd be partly because of you and me! Do you realize that?'

Viktor stared straight ahead through the windscreen. Instead of laying an inert mine for the Soviet Navy to recover, was Hitchens now going to use them in anger? He must signal Moscow urgently. But first he needed the rest of the information he'd come for.

'I'll make a deal. I'll warn Moscow. You must promise me something in return. To speak to your security people, on my behalf, so that I can defect.'

'I'll try.'

'Who d'you think could help? Who've you spoken to?' he asked innocently.

'There's a Mr Black . . .'

'Ah, MI5, I think.'

'And Mr Hillier. He's Foreign Office . . .'

Sara instantly knew she'd said too much. Viktor had gone very still.

'What have they said about me?' he asked softly.

'Well, nothing at all, not to me. They just ask questions all the time,' she stammered.

'Mr Hillier, too?'

'Yes.'

He could tell she was lying. What was this all about? Hillier was Secret Intelligence Service, not counter-espionage. Why should he be involved? This message about the mines. Was the SIS behind it? A false story? For what reason?

'Please find out more for me. Your Mr Hillier and Mr Black – I need to discover if they know who I am, and how valuable I could be to them. I need to know if they'll be sympathetic.'

'I'm not sure they'll tell . . .'

'Just try,' he insisted. 'We can meet again here tomorrow, or the day after. Listen carefully. I'll phone you each morning. I'll pretend to be arranging an appointment to mend your TV set. If *I* need to see you, I'll suggest a time; if *you* have news for me, you propose it.'

He smiled his broad smile at her. For the first time Sara realized he could do it to order. He leaned across to kiss her. Suddenly she felt frightened again.

'I want to go home now,' she told him.

'Yes, my darling. Return this car to the hotel car park and leave the keys.'

'How will you . . . ?'

He pointed to where a motorcycle was parked three spaces away. He reached to the back seat, pulled his rucksack onto his knee and extracted a crash helmet.

'I'll ring you in the morning. And remember – trust me.'

He pushed open the door and got out. Sara started the engine. A green Vauxhall parked near the toilets looked vaguely familiar, but she gave it no further thought.

Viktor Kovalenko pulled the chinstrap tight and swung his leg over the Kawasaki 750cc twin. He flicked the starter button and the twin cylinders burst into life.

Out on the road he headed back to the main route for Exeter and the north. He worried about the van that followed him to the junction, but relaxed when it turned right for Plymouth.

He turned left and settled down for the three hour ride to Bristol, checking constantly in his mirror to ensure he was not being shadowed.

He was oblivious of the helicopter flying two thousand feet above him.

CHAPTER EIGHT

Washington DC.

The briefing room at the White House simmered with suppressed excitement. The previous evening's TV news reports from Moscow had stung President John McGuire into calling an extraordinary press conference.

Over sixty reporters crowded the room; the walls were lined with TV cameras, their operators elbow to elbow. It was hot; already those in the front rows had begun to perspire under the lights.

President McGuire was a reluctant briefer of the press; he thought it better to say nothing than to risk saying too much. But the sight of the Soviet *Bear* pretending to be threatened by US F14s, followed by the injured innocence of Admiral Grekov had been too much for him. If America's own TV networks couldn't see when they were being manipulated, then it was time someone told them.

The press spokesman stepped up to the podium.

'Ladies and gentlemen, the President of the United States.'

There was a scraping of chairs as the reporters stood up; their chatter subsided expectantly.

'Please sit down. And thank you for coming here at such short notice. I have a statement to make, and then I shall be glad to take your questions.'

The podium in the briefing room had been lowered in height when McGuire took office. He stood just 5 feet 9 inches tall.

He smoothed the wave of hair on his forehead and took stock of the faces watching him.

'The Soviet Union has accused the United States Navy of aggression. I refute that. Soviet General Secretary and President, Nikolai Savkin, has described the NATO manoeuvres in the Norwegian Sea as provocative. They are not. The Commander-in-Chief of the Soviet Navy, Admiral Grekov, asks if the manoeuvres are a preparation for war. The answer is an emphatic NO. And Admiral Grekov. . . .'

McGuire pulled a sardonic smile. In front of him pens scribbled furiously.

'. . . is a distinguished naval commander, and knows better than to make such an asinine suggestion.

'Let me first deal with what happened yesterday, those pictures on TV last night, showing our fighters intercepting a Soviet warplane, which – it turned out – happened to be carrying an American camera team. The aircraft carrier *Eisenhower* – on a regular NATO exercise, notified in advance to the Russians – was in international waters, flying aircraft off of its deck. To comply with international safety rules any plane approaching a carrier with a hot deck is warned of the danger, and asked to keep a safe distance.

'The Soviet *Bear* reconnaissance bomber was asked that yesterday, but refused. In the interests, presumably, of producing the sort of TV pictures screened last night.

'Now, the question of the exercise itself. It's not provocative. It's defensive. It happens every two years, and the Soviets have not made a fuss about it before.

'How come it's defensive? First – and I've got to give you some figures here – first, because the Kola Peninsula is home to seventy-five per cent of the Soviets' submarine-launched nuclear missiles. Over two thousand nuclear warheads, capable of wiping out most of the USA, are installed in submarines operating from the Barents Sea. It is the right and duty of our navy to try to ensure those missiles could never be fired at us.

'Second – the Kola Peninsula provides bases for over eighty per cent of the submarines the Soviets would use to try to sink US ships reinforcing Europe in wartime. Ships that would be laden with US soldiers, airmen and their equipment needed to save Western Europe from a Soviet invasion. It is the right and duty of NATO navies to ensure those reinforcements would not end up at the bottom of the Atlantic Ocean. And the best way to do that is to stop those Soviet subs from ever getting into the Atlantic.

'Third – if the Soviets were ever to start a war, the north of Norway could be their first objective. The way to stop them invading is air power. That's why the carrier *Eisenhower* is in this exercise. To defend a NATO ally.

'Finally, ladies and gentlemen, let me give it to you straight. The United States will never be the one to start a war with the Soviet Union, but if *they* start one, we will be prepared.

'Now, if you have any questions. . . .'

Hands shot up in the front row. McGuire pointed to the dark-haired doyen of the White House press corps.

'Yes, Sam.'

'Mr President, is it true that NATO submarines are exercising closer to Soviet home waters than ever before? And if that's the case, isn't it open to interpretation as provocative at a time of greater East-West military détente?'

'Now, Sam. You know I can't talk about where our submarines patrol. I've just told you about the threat we face from nuclear missiles. The subs do what they have to do. But the Soviets can't see our subs – so how can they be provocative.'

A ripple of polite amusement swept the room. He pointed to another hand.

'Talking of provocation, Mr President, what about the *Rostov* and the MiGs headed for Cuba?'

'Is that where they're going?'

'What're you going to do about it, Mr President?'

'The Soviets haven't said where they're sending those fighters. They know our views about changing the military balance around the USA. The MiGs don't threaten us yet. If they become a threat, then I'll do something about it.'

'What . . . what'll you do, Mr Pres . . .'

McGuire cut him short and smiled at a woman from the Washington Post.

'Laura . . .'

'Why do you think Mr Savkin is so concerned about the naval exercise this year?'

'You'll have to ask him that.'

'He says we're being unneccessarily aggressive. Have you given instructions to the Navy to avoid doing anything which the Soviets might interpret as provocative, Mr President?'

'No. The Navy's doing what it does every two years or so. Normal manoeuvres. No special instructions.'

'But if Mr Savkin's out to make trouble, some people feel it'd do no harm to hold back a little, Mr President . . .'

'I don't accept your premise . . .'

'What about the other navies in the exercise? The British, for example. Can you be sure they won't do something to provoke the Russians?'

His blue eyes locked onto hers. What did she know? Reynolds had told him the Brits had a submarine gone AWOL. Had she heard it, too?

'Our NATO allies are at least as experienced as us in handling the Soviets,' was his non-committal reply.

'Last question, ladies and gentlemen,' the press spokesman called from behind the President's shoulder.

'Sir, d'you think President Savkin's trying to deflect attention from the problems he's having with *perestroika?*'

'I'm sorry. That's one for him to answer, not me. Thank you, folks. Have a good day.'

McGuire glanced at the cameras and turned to leave. He knew he'd disappointed them, but he'd had one simple message to put across, and he'd given it them.

'That was one goddam wasted morning!'

The bored male voice came from somewhere in the middle of the room, loud enough for McGuire to hear. But he didn't care.

* * *

'Press conference okay?' Reynolds asked anxiously, back in 'the bunker'. Presidents had a habit of being provoked into unwise statements by the media.

McGuire shaped his thumb and index finger into a bullseye.

'They got what I wanted, not what they wanted.'

Reynolds grinned, then pulled a folder from his brief-case and spread the contents on the maple-wood table.

'Intelligence agencies have been working nights,' Reynolds joked, flicking the pages of the files in front of him.

'First the easy bit,' he continued. 'Defense Intelligence Agency reports the *Rostov*'s going slow. Still headed for the Caribbean, but not in any hurry. Still nothing from the satellites that tells us it's Cuba, but humint sources in Havana say Castro's pretty happy about something, and he's not got much else to smile about right now.'

'They threw me a question on the MiGs. Some time I'm going to have to change my line. The question is, when *do* those fighters become a threat? That's when I'll have to say something different.'

'The Pentagon's working on an options brief. They'll have it for you tomorrow.'

Reynolds sounded impatient. He shoved the *Rostov* file to one side.

'Listen. The CIA's got something new out of Moscow. This stuff's hot!'

'Give it to me, Tom.'

'Savkin's just lost his majority on the Politburo. Only he doesn't know it yet. The faction that supports his reforms of the economy is now in a minority. Secretly the opposition to Savkin has decided to put the brakes on. They want to freeze prices, reintroduce subsidies on food, and break the link between pay and output. Strikes are spreading like crazy; they reckon it's the only way to stop them turning into riots.'

'Is that reliable information?'

'Copper-bottomed, the Company says.'

'And how come Savkin doesn't know what's going on?'

'It's one of his closest friends that has changed sides, and he's still choosing the moment to tell him. But the CIA thinks Savkin's seen it coming – that's why he's been sounding off about "American aggression". Wants a distraction. Needs one – at any price, John.'

His final words hung like a thundercloud. Their eyes met, unblinking.

'How far would he go, Tom?'

'That's the sixty-four-thousand dollar question. The Soviet section chief at Langley thinks Savkin wants a shooting-match – a little one – just so long as it's us that starts it.'

'He's not going to risk that!'

'I said "a little one". A small, contained conflict. A few shots fired, maybe one or two people killed – enough to make one hell of a big story back home to take the workers' minds off the bread queues, and to hold together any splits in the Politburo.'

'And how the hell do you arrange a "small, contained conflict" between the USA and the Soviet Union, for God's sake?'

'At sea. It already happened, a few years ago, in the Black Sea. One of our warships got rammed by one of theirs while we were exercising our right of innocent passage through Soviet territorial waters. If you take that scenario a step further, you'll get shots being fired.

'Right now Savkin doesn't reckon he has much to lose. He's just as committed to *perestroika* as Gorbachev was. If it fails, the Soviet Union heads back to the dark ages – that's his line.'

'For dark ages, read "cold war".'

Reynolds shrugged. It was a bleak picture. If the Politburo had its way, Russian relations with the West would take a dive. Yet for Savkin to hold on to power, he'd have to sacrifice all the east-west détente that had been built up in recent years.

'So, what's your advice, Tom?'

'Keep it cool. Like we've done with the *Rostov*. Don't give them the chance to pull us into a fight.'

'And the exercise?'

'You mustn't be seen to be changing any of it. But let's check the game plan. It won't be the surface ships that cause trouble; they'll keep west of North Cape, the way they always do. It's the subs that worry me. They got something different planned, but I don't remember what it is. You got the Chairman of the Joint Chiefs coming to see you in an hour. Just time for me to call him, to make sure he's briefed.'

'Okay. Do it, Tom.'

McGuire looked at his watch. He could grab a sandwich lunch before the Admiral arrived and have everything straightened out before he called the British Prime Minister at 4pm.

* * *

Northwood, England.

Rear-Admiral Anthony Bourlet was thunderstruck. He let the telephone receiver drop onto its rest. What Captain Norman Craig had just told him had given Operation Shadowhunt a ghastly new dimension.

Suddenly they faced the possibility that Hitchens wasn't suffering a breakdown after all, but was acting under some sort of duress, presumable from the KGB.

Bourlet checked his watch. 1700 hrs. There could still be someone at the registry. He jabbed a finger at the intercom button.

'Do something very urgently for me, will you?' he called his WRNS PA. 'Get onto the registry and see what you can dig up on *HMS Tenby*. Not the SSN. The old T-class with the same name, back in the early sixties. Disappeared in the Barents. I want to know when, where, and preferably the inquiry report, too. Hurry now. I'm just going along to the C-in-C.'

'He's just left his office, sir.'

'Well, see if you can catch him. Ring down to the security desk.'

The door to the C-in-C's outer office was open.

'Has he been gone long?'

''Bout half a minute, sir. Just missed him,' replied Waverley's staff officer. Just then the telephone rang.

'Oh, yes, sir. He's here now.'

The lieutenant commander passed the phone across.

'Is this really urgent, Anthony? I'm in a hurry,' came the irritated voice of Admiral Waverley.

'Vital, sir.'

There was a pause. Bourlet heard a sigh at the other end.

'Oh, all right. I'll come up again.'

Within two minutes Bourlet was explaining about the unknown woman who had met Philip secretly in Guernsey earlier that summer.

'Craig's been onto the security services. They're going to see Sara Hitchens again. Apparently the Russian who's been screwing her has a wife. MI5 suspects there was some sort of double-act going on.'

'I'm lost. What exactly do we suspect now?'

Waverley was hollow-eyed at the thought of having to break news of further horrors to the Prime Minister.

'Remember those words of Philip's that Sara overheard; "Dad, what have they done to you?" – something to that effect? Suggests Philip's father is still alive. If that's the case, the Soviets could be offering to free him – in exchange for something.'

Waverley swallowed hard.

'Like what?'

'Dunno. A *Trafalgar* class sub?' Bourlet joked grimly.

'Bollocks! His crew would never let him.'

'Well then, something else. . . .'

'A Moray mine?'

'Exactly!'

'Oh, Christ!'

Waverley pressed the flat of his hand against his brow, rubbing it back and forth as if to muffle the alarm bells ringing inside his head.

The implications were horrendous. The Moray was a British–American development. He could imagine the bad-mouthing that would pour from Washington if this nightmare came true.

'But, but even if Hitchens had been blackmailed into giving them a Moray, what about his wife's affair with the Russian? Are you saying he accepted that as just something else he had to put up with if his father was to be freed? Surely not.'

'According to Sara Hitchens, when Philip found out about her and the Russian, it seemed to make up his mind for him. Make of that what you will.'

'In other words, we haven't a clue what he's going to do.'

'That's about the size of it.'

Waverley stood up and smoothed his uniform jacket.

'I'll have to tell Downing Street. She's not going to like this, you know.'

Bourlet took a certain malicious pleasure in seeing the misery engraved on the face of his Commander-in-Chief.

'And you'd better signal Commander Tinker in *Tenby*, particularly as it's his own wife who's brought all this to light. . . .' Waverley frowned. 'What an extraordinary coincidence – the name of the SSN we've sent to find him. D'you think it means something?'

Back in his own office Bourlet opened Hitchens' file, and began to read. His own memories of the events of 1962 began to return. He'd been a sub-lieutenant then, on his first posting.

The official report had been a bland document for public consumption, making no reference to the spying mission that *Tenby* had been engaged in at the time. But a secret annexe to the report suggested the very real possibility that the Soviets had vaporized the boat with a nuclear torpedo.

But if Lieutenant Commander Hitchens, Philip's father, was still alive, that theory didn't fit any more.

* * *

Downing Street, London.

The Foreign Secretary, Sir Nigel Penfold, arrived at Number 10 at 8.30 p.m., half-an-hour before the call from Washington was due. In his briefcase were the notes from MI6, which offered an assessment of Soviet affairs almost identical to that provided by the CIA to President McGuire.

In the House of Commons that afternoon the Prime Minister had faced tough questions from MPs, suggesting the NATO manoeuvres were indeed provocative at a time when President Savkin needed all the help he could get. In reply she'd slammed into the 'blatant propaganda' emanating from Moscow, and trumpeted the right of NATO navies to exercise in the Norwegian Sea.

'I've had three calls from Admiral Waverley today,

Nigel,' she announced. 'The first to tell me they'd located the *Truculent*, the second to say they'd lost her again, and the third just this moment, to tell me that it now looks as if Commander Hitchens could be a Russian agent!'

'What?'

'The KGB may be blackmailing him. Something to do with his father. I've just launched a rocket at the security chiefs; I should have heard about it from them, not the wretched Navy!

'And Sir Stewart had the cheek to tell me that because the Royal Navy has the quietest submarines in the world, they may not be able to stop Commander Hitchens doing whatever he intends to do!

'Pour me another whisky, would you? It's been a long day.'

The Foreign Secretary obliged, but kept the measure small. He'd noticed the PM losing her concentration recently after too many whiskies.

'What's President McGuire going to say? Not a word to him about this business, Nigel.'

A buzzer sounded in the secure communications box. The PM picked up the receiver, and nodded to Penfold.

'We're ready. Put him through.'

She replaced the receiver and keyed the conference switch that operated a loudspeaker and microphone.

'Good afternoon, Prime Minister. John McGuire here.'

'Good *evening*, Mr President. How nice to hear your voice. I have Sir Nigel with me. Are you accompanied at your end?'

'Tom's here.'

'Good evening, ma'am, Sir Nigel,' came the voice of the National Security Adviser.

'Perhaps you'd let me make the opening shots,' McGuire's voice had an edge to it. 'Our intelligence assets think Savkin's on the way out. The conservatives on the Politburo are getting the upper hand and want to turn the clock back. Our assessment is that he's spoiling for a fight with the West as a distraction. Just a little fight, but something, nonetheless. Do you go along with that view?'

'We agree as to what's happening in the Politburo, and

your assessment of Savkin's actions is certainly a distinct possibility,' the PM answered.

'Our view is that Savkin's lost his hand anyhow. There's no way we can save him. All we can do is pray they don't turn the clock right back to Brezhnev's time.'

'You're more pessimistic than we are, John. But we agree in general with what you say.'

'So it's a time for the Western Alliance to keep its head down. Which isn't easy with about a hundred NATO warships steaming towards the Kola peninsula! Now, we've just discussed this with the Chairman of the Joint Chiefs of Staff. On his advice, we feel there's only one aspect of Exercise Ocean Guardian that needs to be modified to ensure we don't risk mixing it with the Russian Navy . . .'

'Mr President!' the PM interrupted. 'On no account must the Alliance be seen to be backing off in the face of blatant propaganda from the Soviet Union. At times like this we need to show strength, not weakness!'

'If I may continue . . . We won't be *seen* to be backing off at all! It's the submarine operations that should be changed. Their activities are secret anyway, so no one'll know we've given them new orders.'

This was dangerous ground. Penfold's concern grew as the PM reached for her glass.

'Go on, Mr President,' she said.

'I'm talking of two subs in particular, Prime Minister. One of ours and one of yours. Their exercise task, as you know, is to try to penetrate the Soviet surveillance barriers and simulate the planting of the new "smart" mines at the entrances to two major Russian submarine bases. Normally that sort of operation is fair game; we don't admit we're doing it, and the Russians don't admit it if they manage to detect us doing it. But with Savkin looking for a fight, they might just blow those boats out of the water.'

'Yes. I hear what you're saying. But that's an essential task for our submarines, in case a real war threatens. They've got to try it out, see what's possible and what isn't.'

'Let me put it this way. This afternoon I gave orders

that the *USS Baltimore* should turn back from her mission, and join the exercises with the Surface Fleet west of North Cape. There will be no United States submarines operating within a hundred miles of the Soviet coast for the immediate future. If your boat goes in there, she'll be on her own.'

The PM's expression froze.

'I earnestly recommend you to withdraw that boat, Prime Minister. We're all fully agreed on this side that it's the right thing to do. The operation can be set up again in six months when the Kremlin's settled down.'

'I hear what you say, John. We'll give it most urgent thought, I promise you.'

'Say, ah . . . there won't be any problem in recalling that boat, will there? No communications difficulties?'

'The Commander-in-Chief Fleet communicates regularly with all the ships under his command, Mr President. Now, if there's nothing further we need to discuss, I'd like to end this conversation so that I can pursue the points you've raised.'

'Fine by me. Glad to have talked with you. We'll stay in close touch.'

'That would be prudent. Goodnight, Mr President.'

The PM immediately picked up her internal telephone.

'Could you get me CINCFLEET on a secure line urgently, please?'

The Foreign Secretary suddenly thought of the orders he'd given the Secret Intelligence Service, to warn the Russians of the danger from *Truculent*. It now appeared the Soviets were expecting the boat anyway, and for some quite different reason. He hoped to God the PM never found out what he'd done.

* * *

Severomorsk, USSR.

Vice-Admiral Feliks Astashenkov found it impossible to sleep. His heart was racing from too much cognac, and his wife, who had a heavy cold, was snoring fitfully.

The green digits of his alarm clock told him it was just before one.

Despite his wakefulness, the knock at the door startled him.

'Admiral Belikov wishes to see you immediately at his home, Comrade Vice-Admiral,' came the grumpy voice of his valet who'd been woken out of a deep sleep. 'He's just telephoned.'

'All right. Order the car,' Astashenkov whispered, hoping his wife hadn't been woken. He could have walked it in five minutes, but the wind was bitter, and if he was to be deprived of sleep he didn't see why his driver shouldn't suffer, too.

The heavy smell of spirits in the car almost made him change his mind. But even if the *starshina* driver was drunk, he shouldn't come to much harm on the short drive.

'Left here, halfwit!' he yelled as they overshot the turning.

When they reached Belikov's house the driver slammed on the brakes, hurling Astashenkov against the seat in front.

'Right, you animal! Give me the bottle!'

The driver turned and shrugged, feigning bewilderment.

'That's an order!'

Grudgingly the *starshina* fished in the pocket of his heavy greatcoat and pulled out a flask. Astashenkov grabbed it from him, and emptied the contents onto the road.

'Wait here!'

He left the car door open and marched up to the portal of Belikov's villa. The guard had been watching for him and opened the door before he could knock.

The Commander of the Northern Fleet was waiting in his study, a large brandy bottle and two glasses on a tray on the desk.

'My apologies for this, Feliks. It can't be helped. No one's getting much sleep tonight. Grekov called me from Moscow an hour ago. He'd been woken by the KGB. Come and sit down. Brandy?'

'I'd prefer tea, if you don't mind.'

'Of course. So would I.'

Belikov signalled to the guard to arrange it.

'What's happened?'

'The operation we talked about yesterday – the British submarine that's bringing us a "Moray" mine . . .'

Astashenkov nodded expectantly.

'Damned KGB! Arrogant bastards! You know what they've done? Screwed up the whole plan! That's just the word for it, too; *screwed up!*

'Their man in Plymouth had to end up in bed with the wife of the British commander who's working for us! The commander found out and is so goddamned angry he's coming here to blow our Fleet to pieces!'

'What?' Astashenkov cried. 'I don't understand!'

The guard brought in the tea, giving Belikov time to cool down.

'All right, I'll explain the whole story,' he went on, when they were alone again.

Feliks listened with growing astonishment and anger. After five minutes he knew as much as Belikov.

'We must find that boat before it finds one of ours,' Belikov insisted. He was a surface-ship man, ill-versed in the details of undersea warfare.

'We must also face facts, Andrei. Our submarines make more noise than theirs. If we send out our boats to look for *Truculent*, it could amount to suicide. Do we want to risk that?'

'The *PLA* I sent south managed to intercept it. It could do so again.'

'The British boat was moving fast then. Now it'll be slow. Very slow and silent. We can hunt it from the air. It'll be safer that way.'

Belikov cursed and poured himself a cognac. He cocked an eyebrow at Astashenkov.

'All right. I'll join you after all.'

'Can we be certain he plans to attack us?' Feliks demanded. 'He might still be intending to give us the mine so his father can go free.'

'Nothing's certain. But we have to be prepared.'

Astashenkov's brow furrowed.

'If he wants to catch us with mines, he'll have to lay them at the choke points, where he knows we have to pass. That almost certainly means close to the mouth of this very inlet.'

'He could go further east, to the *Taifun* base at Gremikha . . .'

'Unlikely. The further east he goes, the greater the risk we'll catch him. No. He'll come here. I'm sure of it. What was the original plan, Andrei? Where was he going to deliver the mine? To the harbourmaster at Polyarny?'

The Commander-in-Chief glared. It was no time for jokes.

'He was to lay it about twenty kilometres off-shore, in less than one-hundred-and-fifty metres of water. The KGB promised to unite him with his father in Helsinki, after the mine had been recovered.'

'Hmmm. Not bad. A pity it may not happen now.'

Belikov swirled the brandy in his glass.

'Maybe it still will, but differently.'

'Meaning?'

The Commander-in-Chief leaned forward, clasping his glass globe between the palms of his hands. His words came as a hoarse whisper.

'If he comes into our territorial waters, we can sink him. The wreckage of *HMS Truculent* will give us a whole harvest of secrets – *and* a Moray mine.'

* * *

The north Norwegian Sea.

Midnight, Tuesday.

The Gulf Stream sweeps its warm water round the northern tip of Norway, keeping the fjords free of ice in the winter months, almost as far east as the entrance to the White Sea.

Off North Cape, Europe's most northerly outpost, the current flows eastwards at a steady half-a-knot carrying with it the smaller marine life like shrimps and krill that form the smallest components in the food chain, and create much of the background noise underwater.

HMS Tenby, 5,000 tons of steel packed with electronics, machinery and men, dipped in and out of that current deep below the surface, trailing her sonar array hundreds of metres astern. She was travelling at ten knots and heading east, hoping to hear *Truculent* coming up behind, but with no certainty the boat hadn't already passed her, further out to sea.

'I don't bloody well believe it!' growled Andrew Tinker, folding the signal in half and tossing it onto the wardroom table.

'May I?' inquired the commander, reaching across.

'Yes. See what you think of it. Sodding signal makes no sense to me at all.'

Biddle whistled softly.

'Shit! That's a bit strong! Phil Hitchens recruited by the KGB? Are we sure this isn't a joke?'

Andrew stuffed his hands in his pockets and waited for Biddle to finish reading.

'Huh! The cheek!' exploded Biddle. 'This bit at the end – "Decided you should know this, not because it materially affects your task, but to impress upon you the seriousness of the situation".'

'Bourlet's a pompous ass!' snapped Andrew. 'I can just hear him dictating this crap! Does he think we're treating it as a game?'

He dropped into a chair and took back the signal.

'You know, something I've realized in the last few days is that you can know someone for twenty years – think of them as a close friend, even – and yet not really know them at all. I'm stating the obvious, but it's sad, isn't it?'

Biddle nodded. It was approaching midnight and he was dog-tired.

They'd sped north and east after losing contact with *Truculent* earlier in the day. Every hour or so they'd risen to periscope depth, to receive messages from the satellite.

Two Nimrods were laying Jezebel barriers far to the north and east of North Cape. *Tenby*'s instructions were to stay close to the Norwegian coast, listening in Norwegian waters where the Nimrods couldn't search without prompting awkward questions.

'If you wanted to deliver a Moray mine to the Soviet Navy, how would you do it?' demanded Andrew.

'Explosively!'

'Seriously, how can Phil do it? Without the conscious support of his crew?'

'I'd say it's impossible. He can hardly go alongside in the Kola Inlet and hand one over. And if he's going to pop one out of a torpedo tube, his WEO would have to prepare it and take part in the firing. No. I just can't see it.'

'With the other plan we envisaged – to lay mines and activate them later – it's just possible he could convince his crew. But if he's trying to pass one of the mines to the Sovs, it'd have to be totally inert, otherwise the anti-handling devices would blow it up as soon as they tried to pick it up off the bottom. And to persuade a WEO to discharge a mine that hasn't been switched on? He'd never do it. Not in a month of Sundays.'

'It's mission impossible, isn't it? He'd have to place the mine with incredible precision, otherwise the Russians would never find it. It's supposed to be almost undetectable on sonar.'

The wardroom door opened. First Lieutenant Murray Watson stared at them in surprise.

'Sorry. Thought there'd be no one here. Just wanted a cuppa before turning in.'

'Pickles your liver, all that tea,' Biddle answered. He glanced at the wall clock. 'There's a watch change in a few minutes. Wardroom'll be busy. We'll continue this in my cabin.'

* * *

To the east of North Cape is Porsangen Fjord. Floating motionless in the middle of its ten-mile-wide mouth, 100 metres below the surface, was a *Kobben* class submarine of the Royal Norwegian Navy.

One of the midgets of the submarine world at just over 400 tons, the *Storm* was less than a tenth the size of *Tenby* and *Truculent*. Crouched inside were just eighteen crew, trained to say very little and to talk in whispers when they did.

Her task was to slowly criss-cross the North Cape current, silently and undetected, listening to the world go by. At this she was extremely effective. Powered by a 1,700 horse-power electric motor, she was completely noiseless when moving at a mere five knots.

Every twelve hours or so, within the shelter of the Norwegian coast, she'd raise a breathing tube for her oxygen-hungry diesels to recharge the batteries.

Tonight there was excitement on board, suppressed but still almost tangible. The young conscript crew had heard things they'd never heard before.

Sea creatures and passing tramp steamers were the normal acoustic diet of their bow-mounted sonar, but tonight there'd been submarines, friendly boats whose details should have appeared in the day's intelligence summary, and hadn't.

Norway's navy co-operated closely with Britain's, and expected to be informed when British boats passed through Norwegian waters.

The first contact had passed from west to east at about fifteen knots, two hours earlier. The noise signature had been that of a *Trafalgar* class submarine.

They'd guessed it passed within four miles for them to have heard it at all. *Trafalgars* were notoriously quiet.

The *Storm* had turned south again.

Then came the second surprise – an almost identical signature, moving more slowly this time, but on the same eastbound track.

The commander of the *Storm* smiled to herself and guessed they were heading for the Kola Inlet.

They must be on an intelligence operation, nothing to do with Exercise Ocean Guardian. That's why the British had said nothing.

This was the sort of thing her own navy would never indulge in. Living right next to 'the bear', caution and correctness were the catchwords for neighbourliness.

Another twelve hours and their patrol would be over. She'd report what they'd heard to her intelligence officer, but it would go no further. An ally's secret would be safe with them.

* * *

HMS Tenby.

Peter Biddle spread a chart on his bunk.

'Nothing from the sound room. Not a trace. Looks like we've missed him. Hope to God the Nimrod does better.'

Andrew sighed.

'Look, if the Russians are ever to find the mine, Phil's got to give it to them on a plate.'

'Eh?'

'So, let's look at the chart, and see if we can find a plate.'

Biddle frowned. 'I'm not with you.'

The sheet covered a fifty mile stretch of the Soviet coastline, with the Kola Inlet at its centre. The main Soviet naval bases were clearly marked in the bays around the fjord. A peninsula to the west curved north and east creating a natural shelter against the Arctic storms.

'That's the place!' Andrew exclaimed, pointing to a mark east of the Inlet. 'Has to be. That rock, ten miles off the coast, "Ostrov Chernyy". The chart shows a radar site on it, nothing else. But there's an underwater spit running north from it, covered with fine sand. Water's sixty or seventy metres deep, and the spit's not more than a hundred metres across. It's easy to find with bottom contour navigation; large enough for him to lay the mine safely; and small enough for the Russians to search with their bottom crawlers.'

Mission impossible? Not so impossible, after all.

He pushed the chart to one side and sat down on the bunk. Biddle dropped into his chair.

Andrew closed his eyes trying to remember exactly what had happened to the old *HMS Tenby* all those years ago, and to imagine the effect on a teenage boy of losing a father in such circumstances.

'It's an odd feeling, being on board an *HMS Tenby* in circumstances like these.'

'Bit spooky, really,' responded Biddle.

'Phil must've been shattered to lose his old man like that.'

'No corpse to grieve over.'

'What do you mean?'

'They say you can't complete the process of grieving unless you have the body to bury or burn. Makes it final. In Phil's case, perhaps the grieving process never finished.'

'And now he finds his father's alive. It's enough to send anyone nuts. Do you know the story of the old *Tenby?* You must have a potted history on board, Peter. Previous ships that've borne this glorious name, etcetera.'

'Sure, but it's all pretty bland. You won't learn much from that. Tell you what, though; Murray Watson's done some digging. I think he got a look at some secret files at Bath, once. Keeps threatening to write a book on it and tell the "real" story.'

'Pull him in here, can you? Before he gets his head down.'

Biddle stepped into the corridor and reappeared a few moments later with his first lieutenant, looking puzzled.

'I gather you're a historian, Murray,' Andrew explained.

'Far too grand a title, sir. But I know a bit about the old *Tenby*.'

'All I remember is that she disappeared in the Barents without trace, and they concluded her torpedo magazine had gone up.'

'Yes, well; that was a load of cobblers. But they were so mystified by the disappearance, they spent a fortune on analysing the design. A sharp engineer, keen to make a name for himself, calculated that there was a theoretical fire hazard. The scenario he dreamed up only had a 1 in 100,000 chance of happening, but it was the only conclusion the enquiry was able to reach. So, they spent millions refitting the boats.'

'But you don't reckon there was a fire?'

'No.'

'So what did happen to *Tenby?*'

A shutter seemed to close on Watson's face.

'I don't know, sir.'

'Listen, Murray. What happened in 1962 is connected with what's happening to us at this very moment.'

'Oh?'

'I'm not going to give you all the details; there's no need for you to know. But *Truculent*'s commander, Phil Hitchens: his father was first lieutenant on the old *Tenby*.'

'I knew that, sir.'

'Of course. You would if you've studied the case. Well, whatever Commander Hitchens is doing with *Truculent*, it seems directly connected with the death – or disappearance – of his father on *Tenby*.'

'Ah . . .'

Watson was intrigued.

'So, what I want to know is what the old *Tenby* was doing in the Barents Sea, and what you guess happened to her.'

'Well . . . she was spying. But the stories about watching Soviet nuclear torpedo trials are only half true. That was a cover for her real task.'

'Which was . . . ?'

Watson hesitated, as if he'd said too much.

'If I tell you, sir, you must never let on you heard it from me. I saw some documents once that I shouldn't have, see? And if the security people ever found out, they could trace it back to the bloke who showed me.'

'Agreed. We won't tell.'

'Well, then . . . *Tenby* was after a new Russian radar site. The intelligence bods suspected it was a long-range over-the-horizon type that could track NATO warships 1500 miles away. The installation was on a tiny island, no more than a rock really, about ten miles off the Kola coast.'

A little flag went up in Andrew's brain.

'The boat was to stay out of sight,' Watson continued, 'while a small reconnaissance team went by inflatable onto the island at night. It was to have been two marines from the Special Boat Squadron, but one of them got ill. Appendicitis. Lieutenant Commander Hitchens said he'd go in his place. We know that because the sub sent a signal just before the operation began. Last signal she ever sent –'

A second flag went up.

'The two of them were to get onto the island and hide. Then in daylight they'd take pictures of the radar, hide again, and escape the following night. Nobody knows if they ever made it.'

Andrew and Peter Biddle sat spellbound.

'What . . . what was the name of the island?'

'Ostrov Chernyy.'

The two commanders looked at one another.

'I can show it to you on the chart, if you like.'

'Thanks,' growled Andrew, 'but we've already found it.'

CHAPTER NINE

Wednesday 23rd October.

Moscow 0900 hrs.

The President and General Secretary of the Soviet Union Nikolai Savkin knew that the endgame was at hand.

His efforts to use the media to project a threat from the West had fallen flat. Ever since he'd re-imposed censorship, the Soviet people had treated everything in the newspapers or on television with deep suspicion.

In two days there was to be a full meeting of the Politburo. Without a genuine foreign relations crisis to rally its members, he knew he'd be outvoted and forced to end what was left of the economic and political reform programme.

The head of the KGB sat across the table from him.

Savkin mistrusted Medvedev; it was the Politburo who'd appointed him, demanding a new strong-man at the KGB after the organization's failure to control the secessionist riots in the Baltic republics earlier that year.

Savkin was only half-listening to Medvedev, who was reeling off a long list of arrests and deaths during the disturbances of the past week, expressing satisfaction that the figures were falling. That showed most of the ring-leaders had already been disposed of, he claimed.

Savkin gave Medvedev a watery smile when he eventually left, relieved at his departure.

Admiral of the Fleet Sergey Grekov was waiting outside. A stolid, non-political seaman, Grekov owed his promotion to Gorbachev's early efforts to separate the military from politics.

Their meeting had been hastily arranged that morning. The Admiral had insisted on seeing Savkin at the earliest opportunity.

'Please come in, Comrade Admiral,' Savkin welcomed him.

'It's good of you to see me at such short notice, Comrade President, I know how busy you are. I'm sure you'll understand the urgency when I . . .'

'Yes, yes, Sergey Ivanovich,' Savkin answered impatiently. 'Sit down, and get your breath back.'

The Admiral was sweating from the haste of his arrival at the Kremlin. Savkin had heard he'd been having heart trouble lately.

'It's an intelligence matter,' Grekov puffed. 'Disturbing information we received from London last night.'

The Admiral paused, trying to guess from Savkin's expression whether the KGB chief had already told him about the Englishman Hitchens.

'Oh?'

'Yes. Concerning a British nuclear submarine.'

'Really? Well, go on. I'm not telepathic . . .'

Grekov relaxed. Savkin's apparent ignorance meant he could simplify the details.

'A *Trafalgar* class submarine, according to information gathered by one of our agents in Plymouth – that's the home port for the boat – is heading towards our main submarine bases in Kola, intending to attack us.'

'What? That's ridiculous!'

'Her commanding officer is disobeying orders. He appears to have a personal grudge against the Soviet Union. It's possible some of his officers support him.'

'Are you sure? Has it been checked?'

'The British are searching for him. Their maritime aircraft are operating in the Barents Sea – that's almost unheard of, so far north. It means the submarine must be close.'

Nikolai Savkin's heart was racing. He struggled to control himself. If he believed in God, he'd have said his prayers had been answered. Grekov mustn't see his excitement.

'This is terrible! What are you doing about it?'

'We, too, are searching. Aircraft and helicopters are out at this moment, covering the widest possible area.'

'And what of your navy, Admiral? How many ships and submarines are also searching?'

'Comrade President, we have to take care. If the British commander wants our blood, we must not make it easy for him. The *Trafalgar* submarines are very advanced. Their technology makes them hard to find. In a contest with even our newest *PLA*s, the chances are the *Trafalgar* would win.'

'What are you saying, Sergey?' Savkin growled. 'That you dare not confront him?'

'Of course not, Comrade President. But when you know a trap's being set, but not where it is, you move cautiously. We must assume he's now close to the mouth of the Kol'skiy Zaliv. Nearby, there are six submarine bases; he could be lying in wait at any one of them.'

'Are you saying the Red Banner Fleet of the Soviet Navy is hiding in its harbours, for fear of one single British submarine?' Savkin bellowed in mounting fury.

'That's an insult, Comrade President!' Grekov hurled back, hauling himself to his feet. 'An insult to me and to the brave men under my command! It would be an act of the utmost foolishness to send out submarines which are now in harbour, without knowing whether the enemy has blockaded the ports. No military man of any experience would take such a decision.'

'All right. Simmer down, Sergey!'

Savkin drummed his fingers on his desk, his mind hyperactive.

Admiral Grekov felt his heart beating uncomfortably fast. The doctors had told him to avoid situations which excited him.

'What ships are already at sea?' the President continued.

'An anti-submarine barrier. Surface ships and submarines. They're to the west, facing the NATO fleets – the Ocean Guardian exercise. It's possible they'll find the British boat. He won't dare attack out there. Too many of us.

'The danger is inshore. He has mines of a new type. We know little about them . . .'

Grekov hesitated. Should he tell Savkin the KGB had bungled the operation to get hold of one? He decided not.

'If he lays the mines close to our submarine bases, it'd be suicide for any of our boats to leave harbour. We need time, Comrade. Just a few days, to find the *Trafalgar*, and neutralize the threat.'

'Has it occurred to you the British might be bluffing? That, far from disobeying orders, the submarine could be the spearhead for a NATO attack on our Northern Fleet? Under the guise of their manoeuvres?'

'We considered that, of course. It did seem possible; their naval strategy is very threatening. But all the intelligence information we have suggests the British are themselves close to panic. They're desperate to get their submarine back under control, but at the same time don't want their allies to know anything's wrong. The British claim to have the best trained, best disciplined Navy in the world. It could be damaging to their reputation.

'Also, our radar satellites show the NATO warships are no longer moving towards the Barents. They're manoeuvring off the coast of Norway, as in previous years. Perhaps our protests have had some effect.'

Savkin would have felt triumphant at the West backing down, if these had been normal times, but Grekov's words were like a body-punch. A diminishing threat from the West meant the crumbling of his last hope of using fear to bring the unruly Soviet people back to heel.

His last hope but one. There was still the submarine.

Savkin swung his chair round to face the window. The sky was a watery blue. He could see the top of the Spassky Tower on the Kremlin wall, crowned with its big red star.

'I want reports as soon as the submarine is traced,' he said, just loud enough for Grekov to hear. 'Whatever happens, keep me up to date. We may be on the brink of war.'

'It won't come to that, I can assure you, Comrade President.'

'No? We'll see. Thank you, Admiral.'

Grekov levered himself from his chair and saluted curtly, and left without another word.

Savkin sat almost motionless for a full two minutes. Then he pulled a diary from his jacket pocket, and opened it at a page of telephone numbers. A capital 'A' had been written beside one number. 'A' for Astashenkov, Vice-Admiral Feliks, Deputy Commander of the Northern Fleet at Severomorsk.

Looking at the number struck terror into his heart. Savkin was no natural gambler. Now he faced the most perilous decision of his entire life. If he chose to play the one card he had left, the odds on him winning or losing were impossible to calculate.

He faced two choices; he could yield his power to the forces of conservatism and accept that it was impossible to reform the monolith of the Soviet economy; or he could provoke a naval war in the North Atlantic, in the desperate hope that it would sober the Soviet workers into knuckling down to further hardship and belt-tightening.

The problem was how to provoke a conflict large enough to have the desired effect, but small enough to be contained without the risk of escalation.

The burden of making such a choice seemed to crush him. Alone, he found it impossible to decide, yet was it fair to entrust it to anyone else?

He picked up the telephone. His secretary answered.

'Would you call Foreign Minister Kalinin, and ask him to come to see me immediately?'

It was half an hour before Vasily Kalinin arrived from the Foreign Ministry, annoyed at having had to postpone a meeting with a delegation from Poland.

'Vasily!'

Savkin grasped his friend by the shoulders.

'The most powerful man in the Soviet Union is also the most lonely at times, my friend. It's an old saying, but truer than ever at this moment. I'm glad you're here.'

'They told me it was most urgent.'

'And so it is; so it is.'

They sat in a pair of high-backed, brocaded armchairs beside the window that overlooked the Kremlin courtyard.

'The Americans are holding back their fleet. Grekov says they won't come anywhere near our Kola bases.'

'Ah! That's unfortunate. President McGuire is showing

more maturity than we expected. The way he reacted to the *Rostov* affair has made it a dead issue in the American media. The "crisis" we'd anticipated hasn't materialized. I'm sorry.'

Kalinin had been joint architect of their plan.

'And at the Politburo meeting on Friday? I'll lose? The reformists will give up the struggle?'

'It's possible. I can't say.'

Kalinin was lying to his friend. He knew it was already decided.

'There are many who admire what the KGB has done in the Baltic,' he explained. 'They feel the old firm hand of authority at the centre is the only way to control our country. What the KGB has done to bring the dissidents into line, Gosplan must again do for the economy. That's what they think.'

'And you, Vasily? What do you think now?'

'Me? I'm with you, carrying high the banner of change and reform first lifted aloft by Mikhail Gorbachev.'

At the flowery words, Savkin looked hard into Kalinin's eyes. There was cynicism there and, he suspected, a hint of pity.

'But, Nikolai, my eyesight is good enough to see that the tide changed long ago, and we are going to be cut off.'

The President sensed he was about to be abandoned. There was a weariness in Kalinin's tone he'd not heard before.

'Don't give up just yet. There is one high rock that could save us from the tide. One you've not yet seen.'

Savkin's voice had sunk close to a whisper.

'Oh? Be sure it's not a mirage.'

'This came from Admiral Grekov. He's not a man to imagine things.'

'So, tell me about your rock.'

'A British submarine is approaching our Kola naval bases, intent on attacking us. The commanding officer has taken leave of his senses and is defying orders. The British are unable to control him.'

Kalinin's eyebrows arched.

'If this is a joke, it's a feeble one, Nikolai.'

'Grekov doesn't tell jokes.'

Kalinin whistled softly.

'Wheew! Then I'm beginning to see what you mean. And Grekov? What's he doing about it?'

'Nothing! Wants to wait to see what happens. But he's wrong. We must be ready to confront it.'

'That could be dangerous. Very dangerous.'

'Yes, but history shows it's a risk that can be justified. Remember 1982? Mrs Margaret Thatcher's regime was deeply unpopular. Heading for defeat. Then the British had their Falklands war. A small, limited war. Afterwards Mrs Thatcher and her reformist policies were transformed.'

Kalinin's eyes appeared to grow ever wider.

'You want a war? With the British? That would be most reckless.'

Savkin felt disappointment. He'd expected a more positive reaction.

'But the British would be shown to have started it. Think of the impact on our people. They'd rally behind us, as we justifiably fight off the aggressor and give him a bloody nose!'

'Possibly.'

'What's the alternative? To let our country turn its back on the chance to compete with the capitalists on equal terms? To lock our people away for another twenty years until someone else has the courage to look for change?'

Savkin paced back and forth, waving his fist to emphasize his point. Kalinin watched coolly. He admired his leader's devotion to the cause of reform, but recognized that whatever Savkin decided, it would be out of desperation, and that made him apprehensive.

'You may be right, Nikolai. It may be the answer. But openly to seek a war is not a gamble I'd have the courage to take. If the British commander is crazy enough to attack us, then we have every right to respond. But I suspect you have a different plan in mind – some way of provoking a fight. If that's the case, then it's better you don't tell me about it. I'd have to advise you against it.'

Savkin's pacing had brought him to the window.

So, he was on his own. He would have to take the decision alone, after all. He'd known it would be so. Supporting him in such a gamble was too much to ask of any friend, however close.

'Then I must ask one last favour of you, Vasily,' Savkin ventured, spinning round.

'Yes?'

'To forget that this conversation ever took place.'

* * *

Severomorsk 1000 hrs.

Inside the command bunker of the Red Banner Northern Fleet, Vice-Admiral Feliks Astashenkov listened to the briefing officer with close attention.

The lights were dimmed in the cavernous room, and a fine beam from the pointer in the briefer's hand highlighted the areas on the wall map where the search for the *Truculent* was being conducted.

From longitude 32 degrees, in a line north of the Soviet border with Norway, the anti-submarine surface force stretched its tentacles westwards. The carriers *Moskva* and *Kiev* were operating their helicopters round the clock, the Captain-Lieutenant told him, dunking sonar transducers into the sea.

Feliks doubted it was truly like that; few of the pilots were qualified for night flying from a deck.

Several possible contacts had been made, over a wide area, the briefer said. Feliks doubted that, too. Whales probably.

The British Nimrod aircraft were already operating east of the *Kiev/Moskva* group, almost due north of the Kol'-skiy Zaliv. That's where the *Truculent* would be now. Almost at the sanctuary gates of the Northern Fleet.

If they'd known her intentions earlier, Astashenkov would have ordered four submarines to sea immediately. He'd have given them each a sector in which to wait, drifting in total silence, listening intently for the faint, narrow-band sounds that could give away the approach of the British submarine.

But now it was too late for that; he agreed with Grekov

and Belikov that it would be foolhardy to send out submarines, now that mines could already have been laid outside their harbours. Aircraft would do the job almost as well.

On the wall map, blue boxes in an arc north of the mouth of the Kol'skiy Zaliv showed where the IL-38 patrol aircraft had sown a dense sonobuoy barrier. *Truculent* would have to pass through soon, unless she had already done so.

Inside the barrier the sea was further divided into sectors, each constantly searched by a rotation of helicopters, dipping their sonar transducers into the water.

So far there'd been dozens of possible sightings, but nothing that could be called a target.

Astashenkov was glad he was not Hitchens. The British submarine was entering waters of which it had limited experience, waters the Soviet Navy knew in intimate detail.

Soviet survey ships had charted every square metre of the sea-bed outside their harbours to find the best place to lay their own hydrophone intruder alarms. They kept their charts updated so the minehunters could tell when anything new appeared on the bottom.

If they'd not been warned a submarine was heading their way, *Truculent* would have a ninety per cent chance of getting in and out undetected. But with Soviet anti-submarine forces on full alert, Astashenkov rated the British boat's chances as less than even.

'Comrade Vice-Admiral?'

It was his acting secretary, a Captain 3rd Rank.

'There is an urgent telephone call for you. In your private office.'

His tone made it quite clear the call was from someone who should not be kept waiting.

'From Moscow. On the encrypto-phone. They won't identify the caller, but I think it's the Kremlin,' the secretary explained in a whisper, and then left Astashenkov on his own.

The phone had an electronic security device. Feliks inserted a magnetic card which controlled access. The calls were scrambled and de-scrambled at each end of the line which linked Severomorsk with Moscow. Both the Stavka (the Supreme Military Headquarters) and the Kremlin were linked to the system.

'Feliks?'

The voice was as clear as if in the next room.

'This is the President, Nikolai Savkin.'

'Good Morning, Comrade President.'

Feliks felt an uncomfortable dryness in his throat.

'I'm calling with reference to our conversation last week, Feliks.'

'Yes. I assumed that was it.'

'I warned you then that I might need to ask a service of you. If the future of *perestroika* was at stake.'

'You did, Comrade President.'

'I'm afraid that moment has come, Feliks. I'm sorry. I'm placing the future of the Soviet Union in your hands.'

* * *

Helsinki 1034 hrs.

The TU-134 jet, unmarked except for the Soviet red star on its tail, taxied to a halt. Immigration and customs officers boarded the aircraft to complete the brief formalities.

Within minutes an ambulance drew up beside it. The steps were pulled aside and an hydraulic platform positioned in their place. Two men in blue hospital overalls wheeled a stretcher out through the narrow aircraft doorway and opened umbrellas to shelter it from the driving rain.

Once on the ground, the stretcher was lifted from its trolley and eased into the ambulance. One of the Russian nurses accompanied it, the other stepped into an embassy limousine which had pulled up behind, joining two men in suits who'd also come off the plane.

Sedately, the small convoy drove from the airport, escorted by two Finnish police motorcyclists.

Inside the ambulance, the KGB nurse felt the pulse of the ashen-faced, withered, old man in his custody.

Still with us, just, he thought to himself.

Lieutenant Commander Alex Hitchens DSO (posthumous) Royal Navy, drifted in and out of consciousness. He had no idea where he was being taken. All he knew was that he had left the clinic in Leningrad which had been his home for the past few months, and that the pain in his chest was getting worse.

For the last four months peopie had been kind to him, and he was grateful. Grateful to have been taken away from the bleak and bitter prison camp on the Kola. Grateful to be given food that wasn't just broth and bread. Grateful to be allowed medicines that relieved the pain.

In his lucid moments he knew he was soon going to die. The last thirty years had been a living death, and he had often longed for the end.

But then they'd told him about Philip. Now he was desperate to live just a little longer.

'Is my son here?' he whispered in shaky Russian. He'd never perfected the language.

'Try not to talk. It'll tire you,' the nurse answered, not understanding what the old man had said.

Clouded eyes stared wildly from wrinkled hollows. His erratic memory suddenly recalled the photographs of Philip and his grandson they'd shown him in Leningrad. At the time, in his confusion, he'd thought he was looking at a thirty-year-old picture of himself with his own son. Once he had been a tall fair-haired good-looking man like that; and the boy, Simon, was the spitting image of Philip when he'd last seen him.

His eyelids closed again as the memory slipped away.

The ambulance turned off the main road and up a cobbled hill to the clinic. The tyres on the stones set up a drumming inside the vehicle.

Alex Hitchens turned his head fretfully. The drumming of the wheels was like the throbbing of the diesels in the submarine. The noise triggered memories, ones that had dogged him since 1962.

He'd been broken on the wheel of those memories, time and time again, broken by the guilt of knowing all the men on board had died because of him. He no longer remembered their faces or names. Time had been kind to him in that respect.

He'd gone ashore with one other man, a Royal Marine. They'd been captured together. The marine had been trained to resist interrogation, but Alex hadn't. He was only there because the second SBS man was ill. He remembered the marine – a short, stocky, silent figure, reduced to a bloodied corpse by the torture, preferring to die rather than talk.

Alex had not been so brave; the beatings had been relentless, the pain unbearable. He'd been terrified of death.

He'd confessed to spying; then, as they began to break his fingers, he'd told them the time and place for the offshore rendezvous with *Tenby*.

Later, they'd stood him on the cliff-top to listen to the explosions of the torpedoes and depth charges as they blew his submarine to pieces.

The resonant detonations had sounded like the slamming of the gates of hell. He'd imagined he could hear the screams of dying men borne on the wind. The noise haunted his sleep to this day.

The ambulance stopped. The rear doors opened, and different faces appeared – new men to carry out the stretcher.

'Where am I?'

His voice was barely audible. The KGB nurse heard it, but not the words.

'It'll be all right. Don't worry. You're safe.'

His enfeebled eyes saw a blur of lights and faces about him. A hand gripped his wrist for the pulse. Suddenly there were urgent words in a language he didn't understand. They began to hurry, along the corridor, into a small room. A nurse unbuttoned his pyjama shirt and placed suckers on his bony chest. Another rolled up his sleeve. He felt a pain as they tourniqueted his arm, raising his vein for the needle.

'Phil?' he called softly.

His mind spun like a catherine wheel, faster and faster.

His child, his boy. The men he'd betrayed; the men

who'd died because of him. Did Philip know what he'd done? Did they *all* know of his shame? How could he face them if they did?

The Finnish nurse taped the intravenous needle in place and connected the sedative drip. She looked up at the old man's face and noticed a tear roll down one cheek.

Poor old bugger, she thought to herself. Shouldn't have been moved in his condition. Why had they brought him? Nobody would say. All very odd.

* * *

HMS Truculent 0600 hrs GMT.

Philip Hitchens was summoned immediately the bow sonar on *HMS Truculent* detected the *Victor III*.

He'd not been able to sleep anyway. In the red-light glow of his cabin, panic had engulfed him in successive waves. This was the day when everything would be decided, one way or the other.

He cut their speed to three knots. The plot on the Action Information Console showed the Soviet hunter/killer crossing their path about five miles in front of them, heading south.

The towed array was picking up the heavy sounds of large surface ships belonging to the Soviet anti-submarine task force strung out along the unmarked western perimeter of the Barents Sea, well to their north. Intelligence reports had listed the *Moskva* and the *Kiev* as being in the task force, but identification was impossible; the sounds were being distorted by reflections from the uneven sea-bed.

This was the moment Philip had been dreading, the moment when the hunters began closing in from all sides.

They weren't going to find him, however; no one was going to stop him doing what he had to do.

Hatred for the Russians, and anger at the misery they'd inflicted on his family, surged inside him, but he suppressed it, forcing himself to concentrate on the immediate threat; the *Victor* might hear them if they got much closer.

Philip ordered a turn to port, taking them northeast,

and increased their speed to ten knots. It would give them sea-room.

Thirty minutes later their Paris sonar-intercept sonar detected distant 'pings' from transducers dipped by helicopters from the Russian carriers. Too far away to be any threat. Yet.

The *Victor* was well south by now, so they headed southeast again, back on course for the Kola Inlet.

At 0700 Sebastian Cordell took over the watch from Nick Cavendish, who looked relieved to be escaping the control room.

'Bugger's jumpier than ever this morning,' he confided.

Cordell glanced uncomfortably at Hitchens, who hovered by the AIO console, checking the display and the speed and depth gauges.

'Morning, TAS. Nick filled you in?'

The voice was strained, artificially brisk.

'Yes, sir. I'm just going to check on the sound room, with your permission, sir.'

'Yes, please.'

Sebastian scuttled forward, glad to be away from Hitchens.

'Morning, Chief. What's the equipment state?'

'Hundred per cent, sir. So far as I know,' CPO Hicks reported. 'I've just come on watch, sir.'

'How many contacts have we got?'

'About a dozen, sir. Most of 'em merchantmen. Three Sovfleet warships to the north, between fifty and a hundred miles. We lost the *Victor* on the LOFAR, but picked up a transient from the south about ten minutes ago. Could have been the *Victor*'s rudder moving. She was due to turn about then; have to, or she'd ground on the coast.'

'Well done. So she's probably coming back our way again?'

'If she does, she'll be nose-on this time. More difficult to hear.'

'Okay, Hicks. Anything else close to us I should know about?'

'Couple of freighters within twenty miles, sir. One's

heading west so we won't be tracking him much longer. The other's ahead of us. Big single diesel. One shaft. Four blades.'

Hicks pointed to the green waterfall display, and a ribbed smudge on the left of the screen.

'Fundamental frequency 4.7 Hz. Shaft revs 282 per minute. Could be one of their big supply ships heading back into Murmansk. Might find some useful broadband noise close up.'

'Mmmm. You're working well this morning, Hicks. How much of this is on the AIO?'

'Thirty mile radius, sir.'

Back from the sound room, Sebastian was studying the screens of the Action Information Organization. The senior rating aligned the display with the compass points to superimpose chart data on it.

'Depth's two-seventy metres here, sir. We're at two hundred. Oceanographics give an initial detection range of four miles, sir.'

Automatic analysis of the water conditions around them predicted the maximum distance at which they could be detected by the most sensitive sonar known. The nearest contact was well beyond that range, but Sebastian wasn't happy.

'Aircraft. That's what we've got to worry about.'

Hitchens was standing in the bandstand, watching him.

'I'm worried about the *Bears* and *Mays*, sir. This close to their coastline, the sky could be full of them.'

'What d'you suggest we do about it?'

Cordell was thrown. Hitchens sounded unsure, humble even.

'Well, sir, some sharp manoeuvring. Sprint and drift. To throw them off, just in case they've got a line on us.'

'Yes. Carry on. You have the ship. Call me if there are any new contacts.'

With that he stepped from the bandstand and abruptly left the control room.

Surprised to find himself so suddenly in charge, Sebastian hurriedly checked the chart and the AIO again.

'Steer zero-four-five. Revolutions for eighteen knots!'

The ratings at the engineering panel repeated the order back to him. He was going to put more distance between *Truculent* and the invisible *Victor* that could now be heading directly for them.

Just for a few minutes, then he'd alter course again. And again. Weaving and circling in a pattern so random no airborne tacnav would be able to follow him. He hoped.

Philip hurried to the officers' heads. His bowels were rumbling volcanically.

After relieving himself he returned to his cabin for the shave he'd not had time for earlier. His hands shook uncontrollably, and he nicked his neck with the razor.

He knew he should eat; there was a long day ahead. But the thought of food made him retch. He'd forgo breakfast. Drink some tea. That might help.

His brain felt paralysed by the conflict of his thoughts.

Revenge was the passion that had taken control of him again. To get back at the bastard Russians for seducing his wife, for murdering his father, and for forcing him to betray his country for a lie.

But was he right to believe his father dead? The KGB's efforts to prove him alive, had they *really* been a trick? After all he'd believed them at first, totally. The evidence – the letters, the photograph – *had* convinced him. Then he'd discovered how they'd used Sara and her knowledge of his vulnerability, his obsession with the fate of his father. An obsession powerful enough to blind him to reality.

Every piece of their evidence could have been fabricated. But he couldn't be certain.

What if his father really was in Helsinki waiting for him? If Philip set the Moray mines in the Kola Inlet, as he intended, several hundred Russians might die, but so would his father.

How the hell could he decide? Two hundred metres below the surface of the icy, grey-green waters of the Barents, isolated from his own people, isolated even from the bloody Russians, it was too late to ask for clarification. Too late for a lot of things. Too late to return to base and pretend there'd been a communications failure. Too late to save his career. No, he had to press on, give the Russians what was coming to them.

A sharp rap on the door frame made him jump.

'Yes?'

'May I speak to you, sir?' It was the first lieutenant.

'Yes. Yes, of course.'

Tim Pike slid the door shut behind him and stood awkwardly.

'I'm anxious that you should brief me on our mission, sir,' he blurted out. 'We're in hostile waters; I'm your deputy, sir. Not knowing why we're here or where we're going puts me in an impossible position.'

His short, ginger beard quivered as he spoke, his grey eyes staring at a point above the commander's head.

'I've told you, Tim, that the orders are top secret. For my eyes only. That's still the situation. Nothing's changed.'

'But there will come a point, sir, when a large sector of the ship's company will have to be told your orders. You can't operate the boat on your own, sir.'

'I'd caution you not to be impertinent, Lieutenant Commander.'

Their eyes met. Pike saw that behind the arrogance, Hitchens was afraid.

'May I sit down, sir?'

Philip gestured to the bunk, and turned away to fumble with a pen on the desk. Pike was right; he'd have to tell them something soon. But what?

'And there's another thing, sir. I hesitate to mention it. Don't want you to think I'm prying. But there's been some talk on board that you've been having some problems at home. Now, I don't know if that is the case, sir, but sometimes it helps to talk. . . .'

'How bloody dare you! Spreading malicious gossip about your Commanding Officer? That's an offence under Queen's Regulations. I'll put you on a bloody charge if you don't watch it!'

'Sir, I've not spread any gossip . . .'

'Well, who has? I want their names. Come on!'

He thrust the pen towards Pike.
'Write them down. All of them!'
'Sir, you're being unreasonable. You must understand – the men are uneasy. This patrol has been unorthodox, to say the least. The secrecy with the communications routines, the need to avoid contact with our own side as much as with the Soviets, the mystery about our ultimate mission – it doesn't make for a happy ship.'
'Are you challenging my authority?'
Philip's voice had risen in pitch. Pike looked at the redness in his eyes, the veins standing out from his neck. Was this rage? Or panic.
'Well?'
Now it was Pike's turn to be afraid. Was this the moment to take command?
He funked it.
'No, sir,' he muttered. 'I'm not challenging your authority.'
Philip subsided, relieved.
'Just as well,' he said drily.
'Just trying to help, sir. Do my job.'
'Mmmm,' Philip grunted, his temper now under control. 'Well . . . , don't think I haven't realized the difficulties you're all facing.'
He struggled to decide how much to say.
'You see, things are looking pretty bad, with the Russians. There may be some action. That's why I can't say much yet. Don't want to alarm the men. We're going in close . . . , that's all I can say. Very close to the Soviet submarine bases. You know what weapons we have on board. I hope it won't be necessary to use them. But I don't know how things'll turn out.'
'How will you get your final orders, sir. On the broadcast? The trailing wire antenna?'
'There'll be no more orders. I already have my rules of engagement.'
Pike was stunned. He could tell that Hitchens knew he'd said too much.
'That'll be all, Tim. What I've just said is in confidence. Just for you. Not to be passed on. Understood?'

'If you say so, sir.'

'I do. Now carry on.'

The conversation had disturbed Pike deeply. Already had his rules of engagement? Christ! That meant the decision to fight or not to fight was down to Hitchens, and Hitchens alone. Close contact with the Russians needed a CO with a cool head and a rational mind. The way Hitchens had just behaved had revealed no sign of either.

He headed for the wardroom and breakfast. Suddenly, the submarine banked sharply and Pike had to steady himself. Why the manoeuvre?

Breakfast could wait. He made for the control room. Sebastian Cordell stood in the bandstand, gripping the rail and calling out orders.

'Steer one-eight-zero! Keep 260 metres. Revolutions for twenty-five knots!'

'Why so deep? What's going on?' Pike demanded.

'Active sonobuoys. Someone's pinging us. I just called the captain. He said I should ask you. He didn't sound very well, sir. I think he was throwing up. He left the key down and I could hear him.'

'I see.'

Pike studied the Action Information screen. Depth of water 300 metres.

'I hope to God the inertial nav. system hasn't drifted. It can get pretty shallow around here.'

'We've a bearing on the buoy, sir!'

'Yes?'

'Zero-three-zero, sir! Range two-thousand-eight-hundred yards.'

'Steer two-one-zero! I'll shake the buggers off,' Cordell muttered. 'Take a depth sounding. The sods know we're here now. Making a bit of a noise won't matter much. Ident on the sonobuoy?'

'CAMBS, sir,' came a voice from the AIO.

Pike and Cordell stared at one another open-mouthed. CAMBS was one of their own.

'A Nimrod? Up here? Must be forward-basing on the sodding Kola Peninsula!' Cordell exploded. 'I don't get it. We're right inside a Soviet ASW area, and there's a bloody Nimrod operating. If things are as tense as the captain says, the crabs'll be shot down!'

Pike ran his hand over his beard. The boy had never spoken a truer word, if only he knew it.

'As the captain says'. That was the trouble. Everything they knew down there came from just one source; the captain. And God alone knew how reliable *he* was!

'And why's the Nimrod gone active? Does he *want* us to know he's there?' Cordell blustered.

'Maybe he does,' mused Pike under his breath.

'Thirty metres under the keel, sir!'

'I'd like to go deeper.' Sebastian's face glowed with excitement. 'The crabs' CAMBS may still be able to separate us from the echoes off the sea bed. Just a little bit closer to the mud and we'll be invisible.'

'Too risky at this speed,' Pike cautioned.

'Cut the speed to five knots?'

'Okay.'

'Keep two-seven-five metres. Revolutions for five knots!'

The helm responded and the deck tilted downwards.

'I'll change course back to the south again,' Cordell decided. 'Then ease round to the east so we get back on our original track. There's a big surface contact heading for Murmansk. If we can close with it, we can hide in her shadow.'

'Sounds good to me,' Pike agreed. The boy was doing all right for his first run as tactics officer.

Suddenly all heads turned towards the door. Ashen-faced, Philip Hitchens entered the control room.

'Everything all right, sir?' Pike asked softly.

'Fine. Cordell can brief me, then I'll take over,' he snapped.

'Right, sir. I'll leave you to it.'

Pike hurried to the wardroom. There were two men he needed to collar before they disappeared into the bowels of the submarine.

Claypole, the stocky, bushy-bearded marine engineer, was one of them. Pike stopped him as he was heading towards the tunnel over the reactor.

'We need to talk,' he whispered urgently. 'You, me and Paul. Confidential. In my cabin at 0900?'

Claypole shrugged, showing no curiosity.

'Sure. I'll have finished my rounds by then.'

Paul Spriggs was downing the last of his coffee. Pike dropped into the seat beside him and delivered the same message.

'Excuse me, sir. You 'avin' Standard, sir?' The voice came from behind his shoulder.

The steward looked at his watch to make the point that the first lieutenant was late for breakfast.

'Yes. Standard,' Pike glared.

When the rating was out of earshot again, Spriggs responded.

'You've spoken to him?'

'Yes. Just now. We need to get our act together. I think we're about to hit the shit!'

* * *

HMS Tenby.

'Active sonar, sir! Forty mile range. Bearing northwest.'

The call from the sound room brought Andrew Tinker, hard on the heels of Commander Peter Biddle, squeezing into the cramped sonar compartment.

'Frequency shows it's a buoy from the Nimrod, sir.'

'Could mean a change of plans, Peter,' Andrew breathed over Biddle's shoulder.

They'd been moving fast towards Ostrov Chernyy, hoping to reach the island ahead of *Truculent*, to head her off.

Andrew pulled Biddle out into the corridor, where they could talk privately.

'The Nimrod wouldn't want to go active with so many Sovs around,' he whispered. 'If he's pinging, he's trying to warn the guys on *Truculent* that something's up. And to tell us that he's found her.'

'So we close in?'

'We need more data. If the crabs are tracking her, they can vector us. We'll have to risk putting a mast up.'

'Mmmm. Don't like that much. We're only forty miles from the Russian coast.'

'Got a better idea?'

Again the rating called out from the sound room.

'Submarine contact astern, sir!'

Biddle poked his head back through the doorway.

'Classification?'

'Looks like a *Victor III*. It's suddenly come on quite strong. Must've turned up the power.'

'Going to investigate our pinger maybe,' Andrew suggested.

Biddle pushed back into the control room to order a change of course.

'Steer zero eight-five!'

The towed array was giving ambiguous bearings for the *Victor*. The change of course would clarify it in a few minutes.

'The sooner we try communicating with the Nimrod the better,' Andrew insisted. 'In a few hours we'll be smack in the middle of the main shipping lanes into Murmansk.'

He crossed to the wireless room to alert the operators and to prepare a signal for CINCFLEET.

Biddle checked in the sound room again. The CPO confirmed that the *Victor* was to the west and heading north. Safe to ignore for the time being.

'Keep 30 metres!' Biddle ordered. 'Sound room, plot all surface contacts on the AIO!'

Andrew joined Biddle at the chart table.

The navigator had their position plotted half-way across the thirty mile wide mouth of Varanger Fjord, east of the Norwegian/Soviet land border. Soon they'd be on their own; the Nimrod would go no further east, for fear of trespassing in Soviet airspace. It'd be one submarine against another.

Commander Biddle studied the Action Information plot. North of them in the main shipping lanes there were several contacts, the largest identified as a naval supply ship based in Murmansk. He needed to be further from them, for safety.

'Steer one-six-zero,' he ordered. 'Revolutions for fifteen knots.'

Then he turned to Andrew.

'Ten minutes, and we'll stick the mast up.'

* * *

Varangar Fjord.

The pilot of the Mil Mi-14 helicopter was not a happy man. He'd been scrambled, along with every other available aircraft, despite having a defective radar.

How the hell was he supposed to look for enemy submarines when only half his equipment was working? The squadron commander had given him the Varanger Fjord to patrol, assuring him no foreign submarines would enter the bay; there was nothing there worth spying on.

Operating from the Bolshaya Litsa naval base, the Mi-14 had an endurance of four hours; with a forty minute transit flight each way, the pilot could afford two hours on station and still have fuel in reserve for a diversion.

They'd been on station for an hour already, criss-crossing the bay, dipping the sonar transducer as they went, and hearing nothing but seals and porpoises for their trouble.

Soviet time was three hours ahead of GMT, so for the helicopter crew it was late morning. The *michman* loadmaster handed out ration packs.

Grey and showery at first, it had become a fine morning. The sun had broken through, casting silver-gold shafts onto the sparkling water. On the horizon was silhouetted the traffic of the shipping lanes. Closer to them, there was nothing but unbroken sea.

Suddenly the pilot did a double-take. Smack in the middle of a patch of light a thin mast protruded from the water. He nudged his navigator and pointed, flicking the intercom switch on the control stick.

The navigator nodded excitedly and pointed to the chart to show where they were. Deep water. No rocks nearby masked with warning posts. It had to be a periscope.

The two men in the cockpit laughed at their incredible

luck. It was difficult enough to spot a periscope with radar, but with the naked eye? Astonishing!

The pilot pulled the machine back into a hover. They were nearly a kilometre away from the target; if they got closer the submarine might see or hear them.

The Captain Lieutenant commanding the aircraft from the sonar suite in the rear cabin called his base by radio, and was startled to find his call being routed straight to the operational control centre at Severomorsk.

He was even more startled when, after a pause of a few minutes, his sighting report was answered by a very odd question. Did he speak English?

He could manage a few words, he replied.

Suddenly the pilot alerted him that the submarine had dived. The Captain Lieutenant reported the fact by radio. The orders he received a few minutes later left him stony-faced with astonishment.

The nose of the helicopter dipped. They began to race ahead of the spot where the periscope had been seen. They flew on for a kilometre, then hovered low over the water. The winchman released the safety lock on the cable and the bulky sonar transducer dropped through the hole in the helicopter floor, entering the water with a slight splash.

* * *

HMS Tenby.

The communications had worked well. The encrypted VHF call to the Nimrod revealed the plane had lost contact with the *Truculent* but the RAF gave them the last known position of the boat, less than fifteen minutes old.

In a burst transmission of the SSIX satellite, they'd passed back to CINCFLEET their theory about *Truculent*'s destination, and picked up a string of signals stored for them.

Andrew and Peter Biddle consulted the chart, trying to guess the direction *Truculent* would have taken to avoid the Nimrod.

Ping.

'Shit!'

The sonar transmission had been so loud they'd all heard it through the casing.

'Bloody hell, sound room! Where's the contact?' Biddle screamed.

Ping.

'Dead ahead, sir! Less than 500 yards.'

'Helm hard-a-port! Ten down. Keep one hundred metres. Revolutions for maximum speed!'

Biddle glared round at Andrew, as the submarine banked hard to the left.

'Told you this would happen!'

'We have no sonar contact, sir,' yelled the CPO in the sound room. 'Classified as active sonar from a *Haze* helicopter.'

Suddenly a high-pitched whistle issued from the loudspeaker at the back of the control room.

The underwater telephone!

The men froze.

The whistle stopped. A voice spoke, in a heavy Slav accent.

At first the words were terrifyingly incomprehensible, but then became mystifyingly clear.

'Helsinki is arranged. Helsinki is arranged.'

The voice repeated the words about ten times and then ceased.

'What the fuck's going on?' exploded Biddle.

'God knows!' Andrew answered, his mind racing.

Biddle stood over the Action Information console like a predator, pre-occupied with getting his boat away from the Russian aircraft that had so dangerously and embarrassingly found him.

Andrew felt himself in the way, and walked to the empty wardroom, where he slumped into an armchair.

The message from the Soviet helicopter could not have been meant for them. The Soviets wouldn't have known they were the *Tenby*. Yet it was intended for an English boat. The voice had spoken English.

Truculent. The Russians thought they were *Truculent*.

Suddenly the unbelievable possibility that Philip Hitchens had done a deal with the KGB seemed more real.

Helsinki. Was that where Phil was to see his father again, after leaving a Moray mine at Ostrov Chernyy?

The Russians had taken a hell of a risk with that underwater message, a risk of giving it to the wrong boat, or of arousing suspicion in the control room of *HMS Truculent*. Why would they do that?

Because they were scared. It had to be that. Scared that Phil intended to renege on their deal, because of the KGB's seduction of Sara.

Andrew looked up from his thoughts. The communications officer walked in to the wardroom.

'Signal for you, sir. Came in on SSIX. Just finished unscrambling it.'

'Thanks.'

He took the page of printout and the youth left.

FLASH 230630Z OCT

FROM CINCFLEET
TO HMS TENBY

TOP SECRET
PERSONAL FOR CDR TINKER
STILL CONSIDER IT MOST LIKELY CDR HITCHENS UNDER PRESSURE FROM KGB TO DELIVER NEW MINE.
ALTERNATELY HE MAY USE MINES TO ATTACK SOVIETS. UNCLEAR. CONSIDER ALL POSSIBILITIES. CANNOT ADVISE FURTHER.
INTERNATIONAL SITUATION VERY TENSE. ANY OFFENSIVE ACTION BY TRUCULENT WOULD BE SERIOUS THREAT TO WORLD PEACE. DOWNING STREET ORDERS YOU STOP HITCHENS. IMPOSSIBLE TO GIVE YOU OTHER SUBSURFACE ASSETS AS BACKUP.
ALL NOW UP TO YOU. USE WHATEVER RPT. WHATEVER MEANS NECESSARY TO STOP HIS ACTIONS. GOOD LUCK. GODSPEED.
FOSM.

Andrew swallowed hard. All up to him, now, the signal said. To stop an old friend from doing something unspeakably stupid.

'Phil! What have you got into?' he moaned. 'You crazy bastard!'

He strode back to the control room. Peter Biddle looked puzzled.

'That *Haze*. He's made no effort to track us, as far as we can tell.'

'Perhaps he doesn't need to. If the Sovs think we're the *Truc*, they may reckon they know where we're going.'

'Ahh. Got you.'

Biddle took him by the elbow across to the chart table.

'We're heading for a position thirty miles northeast of Nemetskiy Point.'

He indicated the tip of the Rybachiy Peninsula, the most northerly point on the Kola. South of them lay the densest concentration of military bases anywhere in the Soviet Union.

Andrew shivered as a wave of fear swept through him, from seeing on the chart just how close they were to the Russian bases.

'The *Truc* has to be west of us,' Biddle continued. 'She won't be doing more than eighteen knots, and taking a line from where the Nimrod lost contact puts her somewhere here.'

He indicated a wide arc of sea. Without the help of aircraft, it was a hopelessly large area to search. *Tenby* would need to be within five miles for her sister boat to have any chance of hearing her.

'We have to narrow the search area,' Andrew decided.

He moved his hand down the chart to the mouth of the Kola Inlet, which led to the Coastal Defence Headquarters and main submarine base at Polyarny, and the Soviet Northern Fleet HQ at Severomorsk.

To the west of the inlet the approach was narrowed by the protruding mass of the Rybachiy Peninsula. Twenty miles east of Rybachiy, beyond the main channel into the inlet and about ten miles north of the main Kola coast lay the island of Ostrov Chernyy.

'That's where Philip's going; into that gap. And that's where we've got to be, Peter. Looking straight up the nostrils of the Russian bear!'

Biddle chuckled, nervously.
'Bit heavy on the melodrama?'
'I'm not so sure. The Sovs are waiting for Philip. They don't know whether he's going to give them a mine, or try to sink some of their submarines. They're going to be using every asset they've got to keep track of him. We've got to find him before they do.'
'There's plenty of cover about. The AIO plot's filling up.'
They crossed the control room to the Action Information display.
'Talk us through it, Algy.'
The TAS officer pointed to the symbols on the screen.
'All surface contacts. We've lost touch with the *Victor III*. That's the main shipping lane into the inlet. Most of it's civil, freighters and fishing vessels probably going up river to Murmansk. But there's at least one military vessel identified. A naval supply ship. She'll be astern of us when we turn east. She's listed in the NISUMS.'
These were the Naval Intelligence Summaries carried on board every submarine.
'She's based at Severomorsk. Going home, I presume.'
'Mmm. If I was Phil Hitchens, I think I'd have found a comfy spot somewhere underneath that one. They'd never hear him with all that racket going on.'
Andrew agreed.
'And we need to keep ahead of her?'
Biddle nodded. When *Truculent* reached the target area, they had to be waiting.
Andrew pulled Biddle to one side, out of earshot of the others.
'Look, we've been ordered to stop him by any means possible. If we don't get close enough in time to use the underwater telephone, or if he takes no notice, then it'll have to be a torpedo.'
Biddle winced.
'You've got the new ones on board here, haven't you? The Hammerfish?' Andrew asked.
'That's right. We're still doing trials. They're supposed to be veıy clever, but their reliability's not proven yet.'

'Tell me what they can do.'

Biddle led him to the firing display next to the AI consoles.

'They're like Tigerfish, in that they're controlled from the submarine by wire. Guided either by the boat's sonar or by the torpedo's. But there are two big differences. First, they're much faster. Seventy-five knots they can do! And second they have a high-frequency, high-definition sonar that turns on two-hundred metres from the target.'

'What's the point of that?'

'Gives us a precise outline of the target, on this display here. It means the weapon operator has a couple of seconds to choose the precise spot where the torpedo will strike. Soviet subs are well protected, but if you can hit the right place on the hull . . .'

'Clever. Very clever. And that could be just what we need. Not to ensure we *destroy* the *Truculent*, but to ensure that we don't!'

Andrew's face brightened at the discovery.

Biddle looked at him doubtfully. It was the one aspect of the torpedo's performance they'd been unable to cover in training.

* * *

HMS Truculent 0900 hrs GMT.

There was hardly room for three men in the first lieutenant's cabin. Paul Spriggs hauled himself onto the top bunk to make room for the MEO Peter Claypole.

All Lieutenant Commanders, they were the three most senior men on board after the captain.

Tim Pike told them he no longer considered Commander Hitchens to be in a balanced or responsible state of mind. He listed his reasons; the secretiveness, the over-reactions to crises, and the unorthodox communications orders. There were now physical signs the captain was under abnormal stress; he was taking sleeping pills and there had been evidence that morning of vomiting and bowel problems.

'D'you think any of us is qualified to make a judgement?

We're engine drivers, not bloody doctors!' Claypole growled.

Pike was startled at encountering resistance from the engineer. After his brush with the captain the previous day, he'd expected support from him.

'If we suspect the captain's condition is a threat to safety, then we're bloody well entitled to our opinions,' insisted Spriggs.

'Oh yes. Opinions are all right. It's the next step that's the problem.'

'What're you proposing, Tim?'

Pike looked flustered as he answered.

'Since we left Devonport, there isn't a man on board who hasn't begun to wonder if the captain's gone off his head. You know that, Peter, as well as I do.'

'Aye. Wondering's one thing. Doing something about it's another.'

'Are you saying we should ignore these warning signs?' Spriggs interjected, his voiced tinged with exasperation.

'I'm saying we should be damned careful! There's precious little precedent for first lieutenants relieving their captains of command. It's not popular with the Admiralty Board. In a court-martial, even this little meeting could be seen as conspiracy to mutiny.'

'It might also be seen as senior officers using their brains to avoid a disaster!' Pike countered angrily.

'What disaster?' Claypole demanded.

Pike looked at his cabin-mate for support.

'Paul and I have been closer to it than you, Peter. You've only had the one row with him. For me, the friction's been there the whole trip. You ask "what disaster?" I don't know. *Why* don't I know? Because the bugger hasn't told me what his orders are. But . . .'

He hesitated. Hitchens had told him not to pass on what he'd said. Pike decided he had to.

'We're going close to the Soviet submarine bases, and Hitchens is saying there may be some action. What he means, Peter, is he may take us to war!'

Claypole scratched pensively at his bushy black beard.

Pike went on, 'He told me he's already got his rules of

engagement. He's not waiting for any more orders from CINCFLEET. It's for him to decide if we go in fighting. Now, if he orders the firing of a salvo of Harpoons, or the launch of a pair of Mk 24s, would you be happy to pull the trigger?'

'Well, put like that . . . But it's still only surmise,' Claypole cautioned. 'It's not enough if you're thinking of pushing him out of the bandstand now.'

'But if he orders weapons to be readied, then you'll back me?'

'In those circs you've got the right to see the orders, the rules of engagement and the target listings. Yes. If he won't show them to you, then I'm right behind you.'

'And you, Paul?'

'Oh, yes. I'll be with you.'

Pike expelled a deep sigh of relief.

'Let's hope we're imagining all this,' he concluded.

The three men went their separate ways, Claypole to the propulsion section aft, Spriggs forward to check the arsenal of missiles, mines and torpedoes, and Pike to the control room, where Lieutenant Cordell met him.

'We're heading for the Kola Inlet, sir. Captain's orders. Tucked ourselves under the *Boris Bubnov*, bound for Severomorsk. Plenty of broadband noise from her. Should make us invisible. I sodding well hope so.'

Tim Pike stepped past into the control room.

Hitchens stood in the bandstand; with his chiselled features and ramrod straight back, he looked like a figure from an heroic painting.

The image made Pike shudder; a captain clinging to the bridge of his ship – as it sank beneath him.

CHAPTER TEN

Bolshaya Litsa, Kola Peninsula.

1147 hrs.

The Kamov Ka-32 helicopter flew slowly along the line of jetties. Astashenkov, sitting beside the pilot, was struggling to differentiate one submarine from another. There were six of the broad-beamed 7000-tonners in harbour.

Then the pilot saw the orange armbands of the ground controller, on the fourth pier along. The machine circled once, feeling for the wind direction, before setting down gently, within a few metres of the companionway from the pier to the submarine.

The pilot saluted, and Astashenkov stepped down onto the concrete, clutching his cap to prevent it blowing away in the downdraught.

The Captain 2nd Rank who welcomed him on board the boat was well known to the Vice-Admiral. He'd been executive officer on Astashenkov's last command – a strategic missile submarine.

The commander of the newly commissioned *PLA* saluted, then offered his hand.

'You're most welcome, Comrade Vice-Admiral,' he shouted above the whine of the helicopter.

Astashenkov glanced admiringly at the rounded black hull with its coating of rubber to deaden sonar reflections. The submarine had a fat pod mounted atop the rudder, containing a towed sonar array, and was the newest in what NATO knew as the *Sierra* class.

'You're ready to sail?'

'We'll shut the hatches as we go below.'

Astashenkov took a last, quick look at the Bolshaya Litsa submarine base, his home port in younger days. He could be seeing it for the last time.

The piers for the big, nuclear-powered attack submarines were on the eastern shore of the fjord. Cut into the cliffs behind the quay that linked the piers were caverns for stores, spares and weapons.

To his right beyond the cliffs, the bleak granite rose two hundred metres in contours smoothed by the arctic ice of an earlier age.

A cutting wind came in off the sea, and Astashenkov shivered. Time to go, before the phones started buzzing between Bolshaya Litsa and the Severomorsk headquarters.

Astashenkov had been on board the *Ametyst* at her commissioning the previous year, but was again impressed by the size and comfort of her interior. Captain 2nd Rank Yury Makhov had a spacious day-cabin as well as his sleeping quarters. Fixed to the wall in the day-room was a photograph of President Nikolai Savkin. Feliks pointed to it.

'I'm acting on the direct instructions of the President,' he declared in answer to Makhov's unspoken question. 'But without the knowledge of the Commander-in-Chief, Admiral Belikov.'

'I see.'

The captain's pale face seemed to grow paler still.

'There is a British submarine attempting to penetrate the waters of the Rodina. We are to intercept and destroy it.'

'We've all been aware of the search going on. Never known so many aircraft operating at one time. I was beginning to wonder why we'd been left out,' Makhov answered.

Astashenkov decided not to tell him there was still a ban on submarines putting to sea. If Makhov knew of the risk that British mines had already been laid outside the harbour, he'd have the right to refuse to sail.

Nikolai Savkin's telephone call earlier that morning had almost caused Feliks to renege on the pledge he'd made him in Moscow the previous weekend. Savkin told him the nation needed a military confrontation with the West.

Sending a submarine to sea to confront the British intruder was the only way it could be made to happen.

He'd not been specific. He didn't need to be. They both knew of the danger from mines.

The implication of the President's request was clear; a Soviet submarine and the men on board were to be sacrificed, if need be, to secure the unity of the USSR.

Feliks knew he could never order one of his own commanders on a suicide mission. He could never live with his conscience.

There was only one way he could fulfil his pledge to Savkin – take the submarine to sea himself.

'Have you given the order to cast off?'

'It's being done at this moment, Comrade Vice-Admiral. Er . . , you said the Northern Fleet Commander Admiral Belikov doesn't know of our mission? He cannot fail to know within a very few minutes. Our departure from the dock will be reported.'

'I know. Do you trust me, Captain?'

'Of course, Admiral.'

'Then you mustn't ask political questions. I'm forbidden to tell you why we're acting alone. The situation in Moscow is tense; the Politburo threatens to tear itself apart. What we're doing is for Nikolai Savkin and may help save our country from chaos.'

His sombre words silenced Makhov.

'I understand. What are my instructions?'

'The *Truculent* was detected earlier this morning by a helicopter crew. The boat had a mast up, west of Nemetskiy Point. We believe, from our intelligence sources, that the captain of the British boat was receiving final orders to launch a provocative attack. To sink one of our major warships or submarines!

'The West wants to exploit the political crisis in Moscow, you see. A surprise attack from an unidentified aggressor. Something the West can deny responsibility for; they reckon it could shake the confidence of the Soviet people in their leaders and in us, their military protectors.'

Makhov's jaw gaped open. Astashenkov's bland delivery of the 'facts' had done nothing to conceal the impact of what he was saying.

'That's madness. It's unbelievable.'

'I'm not lying,' Astashenkov lied. 'If the *Truculent* is successful in her mission, it could be a disaster for the Soviet Union. We've got to stop her. And we have to do it alone. No communication with headquarters. Nothing that can ever be traced. We too must be totally "deniable".'

'I understand, I think. But where do we look? We need to know what the aircraft have found out. They may be tracking the boat by now.'

'Can you listen in to their radio transmissions? Before we dive?'

'Their stuff's all encrypted. We don't carry the right decoder.'

'Then it's up to us, isn't it?'

They both felt a slight jolt as the submarine nudged itself away from the pier. Normally tugs would assist a boat as large at the *Ametyst*, but not today. The 40,000 horsepower produced by her twin, pressurized-water nuclear reactors would need careful control to prevent damage as she eased her way out of the dock.

The Zapadnaya Litsa Fjord emerges into the sea twenty miles west of the main Kola Inlet. Within a mile of the shore, the waters of the Barents Sea plunge 250 metres to a sea-bed of black mud.

'We'll dive when we've passed Ostrov Kuvshin,' Makhov announced. This was an island at the mouth of the fjord. 'Then we can unreel the array. It's noisy when we do it, so let's hope the English boat isn't close already. D'you have any idea of her exact target?'

'No. It could be any of the naval bases. All we can do is patrol between here and Ostrov Chernyy. Sixty kilometres of sea. She has to cross our path if she's to complete her mission.

'The name of the boat, by the way – *Truculent* – I looked it up in a dictionary. It means "of merciless temper"!'

'How fitting. But if we are to destroy her, then we must be of even more merciless temper, mustn't we?'

* * *

Severomorsk 1254 hrs.

Admiral Belikov took off his heavy-framed spectacles and polished them with his pocket handkerchief. The waiting was dragging on his nerves. In the command bunker, the big screen was marked with dozens of triangles, denoting contacts detected by the maritime patrol aircraft and helicopters.

They couldn't all be *Truculent*, scattered widely over 4000 square kilometres of sea. The question was whether any of them were. None of the contacts had been confirmed, since the chance discovery of the vessel west of Nemetskiy Point. Infuriatingly the helicopter had had no spare fuel to give chase, so they'd had to start the search all over again. The Royal Navy was damnably good at silencing its boats.

It had been a gamble, ordering the message about Helsinki to be transmitted to the boat they'd discovered. He hoped it was clear enough to persuade Commander Hitchens to adhere to his arrangement with the KGB, but sufficiently mysterious for the rest of his crew to ignore it.

They'd know soon. Four helicopters were dunking transducers into the waters round Ostrov Chernyy. If Commander Hitchens delivered the Moray mine there, they'd be sure to hear the submarine's bow caps opening. If he didn't, they'd know he had a more sinister intent, and would concentrate the search closer inshore.

All aircraft had now been loaded with homing torpedoes or depth charges.

He replaced the spectacles and looked again at the screen. A fresh symbol had appeared, at the mouth of the Zapadnaya Litsa fjord – a circle this time, denoting one of his own submarines.

'Captain Lieutenant!' he spluttered. 'What the hell is that?'

The briefing officer hurriedly checked his computer terminal.

'The PLA *Ametyst*, Comrade Admiral. Sailed from Bolshaya Litsa an hour ago. Vice-Admiral Astashenkov is listed as being in command.'

Belikov stared at the small circle on the screen, transfixed. He dared not speak, knowing his voice would betray his horror; dared not reveal that his own deputy was acting without his knowledge!

A red flush spread upwards from his neck. He was conscious of a dozen pairs of eyes turned towards him. Every man and woman in that room knew the instructions that had been issued to all shipping in the Kol'skiy Zaliv, including their own submarines; to stay in harbour until the enemy boat had been located and neutralized.

What the hell was Astashenkov playing at? Trying to rid the Rodina of the submarine threat single-handed? Playing the glory seeker, at his age?

Suddenly he sensed the dabbling hand of Moscow. Someone was playing for power.

For his own deputy to risk everything, the orders must have come from the very top. From Sergey Grekov, Admiral of the Fleet of the Soviet Union, or Nikolai Savkin – the President himself.

But why? What was their plan? They knew the risks. It was Grekov himself who had ordered boats confined to port.

It had to be Savkin. If the *Ametyst* were destroyed by a Western mine, he'd have an international incident of mighty proportions to exploit for political ends. And if she found the *Truculent* and sank her, Savkin would also have a political feather for his threadbare cap.

He couldn't lose.

And himself? He needed an insurance policy.

His eyes focused on the screen again, looking north of the Rybachiy Peninsula.

'All the ships inbound to Kol'skiy Zaliv – have they hove to, as ordered?'

'Yes, Comrade Admiral,' answered the Captain Lieutenant. He pointed with a light pen to the northeast tip of the Ribachiy. 'The supply vessel *Boris Bubnov* is waiting off Voronkovskiy Point. She's the closest to harbour.'

'And the PLA *Ladny*? What's her position?'

This was the *Victor III*, detected by *Truculent* and *Tenby* earlier that morning.

'At last report she was following the *Boris Bubnov* in case the *Truculent* was using her as cover. She's due to report again in half an hour.'

'When she does, I have new orders for her,' Belikov intoned. 'Tell her that if she finds the *Truculent* within five kilometres of the Kol'skiy Zaliv, she's to sink her!'

* * *

Plymouth, England.

0900 hrs GMT.

John Black took a cigarette from the half-empty packet that had been new that morning, and offered one to Sara Hitchens.

She lit it and inhaled hungrily. Her face, ghostlike from sleeplessness and emotional stress, paled yet again when he told her what they wanted her to do.

They were closing the net. Orders from on high.

The day before, a police helicopter had followed Gunnar on his motorbike to Bristol, Black explained, but the Russian had abandoned it in a public car park there, and vanished on foot.

He wouldn't use the machine again, Black guessed. He'd be too careful for that, now he knew they were looking for him. The only chance they had of catching him was for Sara to lure him into a trap.

'You're sure he didn't say what time he'd ring you?' Black pressed for the third time.

'Quite sure,' Sara snapped, exhaling smoke. 'He just said it'd be this morning. But he's probably thought better of it. He could be on his way to Moscow by now.'

Privately she hoped he was.

For Sara, waiting was an agony. John Black would tell her nothing. She'd not recognized the MI5 man when he'd knocked at the door clad in blue overalls and clutching a tool bag. His Electricity Board van was parked out in the drive.

As she moved about the room, her right shoe felt heavy with the weight of the small radio transmitter fitted inside the heel. She was terrified it would show, despite Black's insistence that it didn't.

'You got your words sorted out?' he pestered. Women couldn't be trusted. 'You know what to say when he rings?'

'No, Mr Black. I've forgotten!' she answered sarcastically. 'I think *you'd* better talk to him!'

He turned away, embarrassed at the sharpness of her tone, then looked at his watch.

'I'll leave you to it, then. I've been here quite long enough to have fixed your cooker. Remember, we plan to grab him after your meeting's over, but we may need to move sooner than that, so if you hear me shout, do whatever I say and do it fast. Okay?'

'What are you going to do to him?'

Black picked up his toolbag, and stubbed out the remains of his cigarette.

'Ask him a few questions. If he doesn't co-operate, we'll throw the book at him.'

'He told me he wanted to defect.'

'We'll see, won't we?'

Sara watched as he climbed into the van and reversed it into the road.

With the MI5 man gone, the house became eerily silent. She could almost hear the walls breathe.

At night, during the past week, she had lain awake for hours, ears straining to catch the sounds of the darkness, imagining footfalls and twigs breaking. She could stand it no longer, being alone in the house. She would telephone Simon's school and persuade his housemaster to let him come home for a few days.

Philip would never return from his crazed voyage to the Arctic Circle, her certainty of that had grown stronger. It was time Simon knew what had happened, time for her to prepare him to understand that he'd never see his father again.

The shrill ring of the telephone had her leaping to her feet. She closed her eyes tightly, trying to stem the panic.

The phone rang four times before she picked it up, praying that her voice wouldn't fail her.

'Hello?'

'Mrs Hitchens?'

'Yes.'

'It's the TV man. The repair to your set? You wanted to fix a time for me to do it?'

Viktor Kovalenko had gone back to his Swedish accent.

'Oh, yes. That's right. This morning some time?'

The steadiness of her voice surprised her.

'Ten o'clock. As we discussed yesterday.' The voice was tense, clipped. 'Please make sure there are no other tradesmen with you. I like to work alone. Understood?'

Sara almost choked.

'Yes, of course,' she whispered, but the line was already dead.

He'd guessed it was a trap. He must have.

She ought to tell John Black, but there was no time. She had to get to the same car park they'd gone to yesterday, on the far side of Plymouth. It was already nearly half-past-nine. It would take nearly thirty minutes to get there. She'd have to leave immediately.

As she turned out of the drive, she was gripped by an urge to flee, to head away from Plymouth, anywhere to escape.

The MI5 man had bullied her mercilessly before she'd agreed to help, threatening her with prison if she didn't co-operate.

It was a ridiculous threat; she'd done nothing illegal. Nothing really wrong either, she decided. Whatever appalling plan Philip had conceived, the cause lay way back in his own past. Her infidelity couldn't have provoked that strong a reaction.

And Gunnar – Viktor, as he called himself now? She believed he really had loved her; maybe he still did. Perhaps she'd even loved him too. And now she was going to betray him.

She braked the car gently into a sharp bend, beyond which was a turning into a farmyard, disused since the farmer gave up milk production. She rounded the corner.

Suddenly, a figure leaped into the road waving. Sara braked hard and swerved.

The man had long, straggly hair and wore an old raincoat. He banged on the bonnet of the car and shouted as she tried to avoid him.

'Sara!'

The voice was Gunnar's; so was the face beneath the greasy wig. She stamped on the brake. He wrenched open the passenger door and threw himself inside.

'Drive on! Left into the farm!' he barked, twisting round to see if any car was following.

Sara obeyed, heart thudding.

A rutted track led to a group of farm buildings which had fallen into disrepair.

'In there,' he pointed to an open-sided barn. 'Next to the van.'

The car bumped over a broken brick floor; the van belonged to a firm of feed-merchants.

'Who knows you're meeting me?' he demanded, gripping her arm so tightly she thought he'd break it.

'No . . . no one,' she stammered. 'I came straight here after you rang.'

'You had a visitor this morning.'

She felt her lower lip trembling.

'The cooker. A man came to mend it. A hot plate had burnt out.'

He was frightening her. His eyes had never looked so cold. She squirmed.

'That wig. It's awful. Can't you take it off?'

'Not yet. Come. Get out. Into the van.'

He pulled open the rear doors and looked her up and down. She was wearing jeans and a dark blue guernsey.

'In those clothes you'll be all right in the back. There's some sacking to sit on.'

'Why? Where are we going?'

'Not far. Somewhere safe. Just a few minutes. Get in.'

She knew he'd accept no argument. The sacking smelled of fertilizer. He closed the door behind her. The only light came through a small window to the driving compartment.

He reversed backwards over the bumps. Where the track met the road, he turned right, back to the village.

She thought of the electronic bleeper in the heel of her shoe. The MI5 men were expecting a rendezvous miles away. Would they be able to track her here? Half of her hoped they wouldn't.

They passed her house. She strained to see it through the small pane, half expecting to see John Black's van parked in the drive. Nothing there.

Viktor turned right. She had to think for a moment where they were going. It was a narrow tarmaced road, little used, that ran round the back of the village, re-entering the main street beyond the church, and just short of the quay. Along the way they would pass a farm and three labourers' cottages, she remembered; one of them was for sale.

After less than a minute the van turned left off the road and jolted its way down a short track. Viktor swung right again and stopped. She heard him get out and walk round to the back.

'Okay. Out now,' he said softly, as he opened the door. He took her by the arm to help her to the ground.

She looked round. They were behind a cottage, hidden from the road.

'I was thinking of buying this house,' he smiled. 'To be near you.'

He led her round to the front. A large 'For sale' sign was fixed to the gatepost. From his pocket, he pulled a key attached to a label.

'Very trusting, the estate agent.'

The rooms were bare, and smelled of rot.

'Wait here.'

He climbed the steep, narrow stairs to the upper floor.

After a few moments he called to her to come up.

He was leaning against the wall, to one side of a window.

'You stand the other side and tell me if you see anyone coming. This way we look both ways at once.'

She did as he asked, conscious of wanting to calm her own breathing, but not being able to.

'Now we can talk.'

He pulled off his wig, folded it carefully, and pushed it into a pocket. He still looked strange to her with his hair, that had been long and blond, dyed brown and trimmed short.

'That's better,' she smiled.

'Have you heard anything more? About Philip?'

'They haven't managed to stop him; that's all.'

'And I risk this meeting, just for you to tell me that?'

His voice grated. His eyes flicked back to the window nervously.

'I was lonely. I wanted to see you again,' she heard herself say.

For a few moments he was silent, then he chuckled.

He pulled her away from the window. She felt limp, paralysed.

'You're a child,' he told her, putting his arms round her in a tender embrace. 'A beautiful, sensual woman. But also a child.'

Then he crushed his mouth to hers and, cupping his big hands round her behind, he pressed against her hungrily.

Sara struggled for breath. She wanted to stop him, warn him it was a trap, yet she felt powerless.

'Please, no,' she protested feebly.

'Please, yes. It's the last time I'll see you.'

His voice grated in his throat like gravel.

'I have to go away. It's dangerous for me here. But I can't go without feeling you again. Having you one more time.'

He pulled up her guernsey and tugged her blouse free of her jeans so he could slip his hands underneath to caress her.

'Gunnar . . . don't.'

He teased at her mouth with his lips, silencing her, and began to fumble with the zip of her jeans. He tore at it, breaking the button.

He unclasped the belt of his trousers.

Then he heard the helicopter.

He froze.

Sara whimpered. She'd heard it too.

Viktor seized her by the shoulders and held her so he could see her eyes. She looked away.

'You? You knew?' he whispered.

'I'm sorry . . .'

'Your police? Coming for me?' he hissed.

'I'm sorry.' She began to cry. 'They . . . made me.'

He let out a howl of rage. '*Bitch!*'

Drawing back his right hand, he balled it into a fist, and smashed it into her face.

Sara crashed to the floor, blood spurting from her mouth. Her midriff was bare, pullover pushed up, trousers on her hips.

Kovalenko darted to the window. The noise of the helicopter was deafening; it was landing in the meadow behind the house. They must not take him. Moscow's orders.

In terror and pain, Sara began to scream for help.

Kovalenko stared in shock at the woman whose sweet body had blinded him so fatally. Anger overwhelmed him. He calmly re-buckled his trousers and reached into the side pocket of his coat.

The first bullet ripped into Sara's groin, the second into her chest. The scream froze in her throat.

Wide-eyed and open-mouthed, she stared. She looked suddenly surprised.

Viktor aimed again and blasted a hole in the centre of her forehead.

He flung himself down the stairs. At the back of the house he could hear voices, and the helicopter turbines still whining.

The van started at first turn of the key. He slammed into reverse and swung the vehicle round to face the road. Left or right? It didn't matter.

He turned left, away from the village. He raced up through the gears, foot jammed hard down on the accelerator. There was a bend ahead. He rounded it, barely keeping the wheels on the road.

Just fifty yards ahead a South West Electricity Board van was slewed across the road.

His mind raced. Could he stop? No room! His foot

moved to the brake, touched it lightly, then swung back desperately to where it was before.

John Black crouched behind the van, an automatic pistol in his right hand. The expected drop in the engine note never came.

'Fucking hell!' he exploded, and hurled himself sideways into the ditch, as the van carrying Viktor Kovalenko smashed into the roadblock and exploded in flames.

* * *

HMS Tenby 1240 hrs GMT.

'Contact confirmed, sir. It's a *Trafalgar* ahead of us.'

'*Watch stand to!*' called Commander Biddle on the loudspeaker. Then he said to the weapons engineer, 'All tubes to the action state! Hammerfish torpedoes.'

'Aye, aye, sir!' The WEO looked startled, but scuttled down the companionway to the forward weapons compartment.

Biddle stood next to Tinker.

'At bloody last!' he hissed.

'We're only eight miles from the Rybachiy Peninsula. Well inside their twelve-mile limit,' Andrew warned. 'If we don't get it right, and we cripple him here, the Soviets'll have a whole *Trafalgar* class submarine to play with!'

'It's your decision, Andrew.'

'Don't I bloody know it!' he replied drily. 'We need to know the distance.'

'Steer zero-nine-five, revolutions for fifteen knots!'

The course change was to compute the range.

'*Aircraft overhead!*' squawked the communications box. '*Sounds like a MAD run!*'

MAD stood for Magnetic Anomaly Detector. A tail 'sting' on the Soviet IL-38 anti-submarine aircraft could pick out a large metal submarine from its interference with the earth's magnetic field.

'Steer zero-three-five!' Biddle called. 'Keep one-hundred-and-seventy-five metres!'

They'd need to go in for some fast evasive action.

'That's all we sodding well need!' Andrew cursed.

'*Stony ridge ahead, sir, rising to one-two-five metres!*' the navigator shouted. '*Distance on the new course, about three miles!*'

'Got that, thank you,' Biddle answered calmly.

They'd been navigating a deep-water trench some six miles wide, which led southeast into the Kola Inlet. Turning at a right-angle to evade the aircraft, they now risked smashing into the ridge at its northern edge.

The two commanders made the calculation simultaneously. Twelve minutes before they hit the rocks.

Andrew bit his tongue. He was in command of their overall mission, but Biddle was driving the boat.

'Revolutions for twenty-five knots!'

Biddle looked at the clock. He'd take no chances; just two minutes on this course and speed, before weaving east again.

Andrew stepped into the sound room to talk to the TAS, Algy Colqhoun.

'What's the maximum range of the underwater telephone here, d'you reckon?'

The lieutenant checked the Sound Path Predictor computer, linked to probes on the hull that analysed water samples.

'About three to four miles, sir. And at a guess, at least a dozen Soviet sonobuoys would hear it too, and get a nice fix on us!'

Andrew didn't need reminding. He went back to the control room.

'Revolutions for fifteen knots! Starboard twenty. Steer one-three-five!'

The deck lurched sideways with the violence of the new manoeuvre.

'Where's the range on the bloody target, TAS?' Biddle growled, knowing Colqhoun would be working on it without his telling him.

'*New contact, sir!*' the sound room announced. '*Astern. Submarine contact on the towed array.*'

'Classification?'

'*Working on it, sir. Looks like a Victor.*'

On the Action Information screen, contour lines marked the edges of the deep-water channel. Ahead of the symbol for their own boat, a small square representing *Truculent* changed to a diamond, signifying its range was now known.

The operator hit a key to open a window with the target data on the right of the screen.

'Range eight miles, heading one-four-zero, speed eight knots,' Andrew read. '*Eight* miles? Are we sure? That's beyond the normal detection range for a *Trafalgar*.'

'Told you the sonar fit on here's bloody brilliant,' Biddle answered. 'The *Truc*'s got the older set. Phil won't know we're here yet.'

'Eight more miles, and he'll be at Ostrov Chernyy,' Andrew grimaced. 'If he maintains that speed, he'll be there in an hour.'

'Target's changed course, sir,' the AIO rating called across.

'Dodging planes, like us, I guess,' Andrew commented.

'Steer one-eight-zero!' Biddle ordered, changing course again so the towed array could compute a bearing on the second contact, behind them.

'We've got to catch up with him, Peter,' Andrew insisted, 'before he gets there and lays a Moray mine on the shelf, like a bloody Easter Egg. Ten minutes at thirty knots might put us close enough to talk to him.'

'But we'd be deaf for those ten minutes. We're surrounded by Russians. And they've got sea-bed arrays somewhere around here. The noise we'd make could give them a firing solution.'

'Tow a decoy. Make them think we're one of their own.'

Biddle hesitated. The decoy would make even more noise – make them easier to track. Would it fool the Soviets if they tuned it to sound like a *Victor III*?

'*Second contact confirmed, sir!*' came the voice from the sound room box. '*Victor three astern. Heading one-two-seven degrees. Range ten miles, range decreasing. Estimated speed twenty knots!*'

'Okay, Andrew, you've got it,' Biddle decided. 'Time's running out. But hang on tight. It's going to be a bumpy ride.'

* * *

HMS Truculent 1310 hrs GMT.

Philip Hitchens gripped the padded rail of the bandstand, picking at its blue imitation leather cover with his fingernails.

'Steer zero-six-zero. Ten down. Keep two hundred and twenty metres,' he snapped.

The sound room kept reporting aircraft noise. The sky must be full of planes. What the hell were the Russians up to? If they wanted the damned mine, they'd do better to leave him in peace.

Had they decided he'd renege on the deal? Perhaps they were right. Doubt still paralysed him. He was acting on instinct now. Survival – that was all. Had to get away from those planes.

'Charted depth two-hundred-and-fifty metres, sir,' cautioned Lieutenant Nick Cavendish.

The chart was all they had to go on. They dared not use their echo-sounder, for fear it would be detected and give away their position.

Faces in the control room were tense and sombre. The day before, they'd found it hard to accept the Captain's warnings that the world above them was close to war. But today they were beginning to believe him.

A few hours earlier, Sebastian Cordell had summoned Tim Pike to the sound room, and clamped headphones on his ears so he could hear the sudden silence. The sonar had been tracking over fifteen surface contacts, from tankers to trawlers, but one by one they'd disappeared.

It was eerie. All around them, ships had cut their engines; propellers hung idle.

There was only one explanation; the Russians knew they were there. They'd ordered silence, to make it easier to find them.

Deprived of the *Boris Bubnov* as a noise shadow, they were now on their own in hostile waters, lacking the most important weapon a submarine can have – surprise.

The Action Information display was uncomfortably empty of contacts. Tim Pike felt like a goldfish in a bowl, surrounded by hungry Soviet cats.

Every post on the submarine was closed-up now, ready for action. Pike's task was to follow his captain's every move, ready to take over if ordered – or if he felt the time had come.

'It's almost as if they were expecting us, sir,' Pike murmured to the captain. 'They'll have sonobuoys everywhere.'

'Yes.'

'What're we going to do, sir?'

'Complete our mission,' Philip said icily, yet feeling as if someone else had spoken. He swung round to address Paul Spriggs.

'WEO. Bring all tubes to the action state. Load two tubes with Mark 24 torpedoes. Make ready three Moray mines.'

Spriggs shot a glance at Pike for support.

'What exactly are our orders for the mines, sir?'

There was a moment's silence, but Hitchens was ready for them.

'Very shortly, Paul, I shall be in a position to tell you. Tim? Take over. I shall be in my cabin.'

* * *

Severomorsk.

Admiral Andrei Belikov snapped his fingers for some more tea. He'd sat in the operations room in the underground bunker since the moment he'd learned of Astashenkov's 'freelance' mission on board the *Ametyst*, and his eyes were feeling gritty and tired.

Reports from the IL–38s had produced nothing but confusion; suspected contacts had been 'detected' in six different areas. Most of them were caused by malfunction in the equipment or by excessive optimism on the part of the crew, Belikov believed.

But there had been persistent traces of a submarine, northwest of Ostrov Chernyy. It was in the right place and on the right heading if Commander Philip Hitchens was intending to carry out his contract with the KGB. The trouble was that there had also been strong reports of another contact twelve kilometres further west.

The Captain Lieutenant seated in front of him turned from his communications panel.

'A request from one of the maritime aircraft, Comrade Admiral. The intermittent contact it was tracking now sounds to him like one of our own *PLAs*. He's asked if we can confirm it's the *Ladny*.'

'Which track is that?'

'Number four.'

The Captain Lieutenant shone his light pen at the more westerly of the two strongest contacts.

'Send *Ladny* a signal. Tell her to report her position.'

The submarine towed a communications buoy. The antenna could only receive, but she'd reply within minutes by raising a VHF mast above the waves.

Belikov drummed his fingers on his desk as they waited until the printer began to chatter. The Captain Lieutenant tore off the sheet, noted the contents and, with eyebrows raised, passed it to the Admiral. Then he tapped the keys on his computer terminal.

On the large wall-screen in front of them, a red circle appeared for the *Ladny*, well to the left of the triangle which was the contact reported by the aircraft.

'Hah! So the *Ladny* has a ghost!' Belikov exclaimed.

'I've asked the IL-38 to re-confirm the position of its contact, Comrade Admiral.'

'Where's the *Ametyst* got to? Could it be *her* the aircraft's tracking?' Belikov demanded.

'Not out there. She was detected close to the Kol'skiy Zaliv, half an hour ago.'

The printer spewed out more paper.

'Reconfirmed,' declared the Captain Lieutenant. 'The IL-38 reports the contact has headed east at speed, conducting evasive manoeuvres. They've lost it now. Should they try to track it?'

'Tell them, yes. And put out a general alert that the British submarine *Truculent* seems to be using a noise generator. She's pretending to be one of ours.'

* * *

Submarine *Ametyst*.

Feliks Astashenkov heaved a sigh of relief when he checked on the chart the position of the *Truculent* that the Severomorsk headquarters had just transmitted. If she was still that far out the chances were she'd not yet laid her mines.

The thought of the undetectable threat that might be sitting on the sea-bed anywhere in their path had terrified him since leaving port. Against another submarine they could fight, but a mine gave no warning, no possibility of retaliation.

Suddenly, he was filled with hope. There was a chance, after all, that they could complete their mission, that the British boat could be destroyed inside Soviet waters and the wreckage brought up so that the Soviet people could be shown how NATO threatened the security of the State.

'There you are, Yury. Those are the co-ordinates of the target,' he said, putting his arm round the younger man's shoulders. 'Let's go and look for it!'

* * *

Helsinki, Finland.

The young, white-coated doctor crashed through the swing doors with a trolley carrying a cardiac-arrest emergency kit.

Ahead of him he could see the Russian nurse holding open the door to the small, private room.

He swung the trolley inside; one of the clinic's own female nurses was pressing rhythmically on the breastbone of the old man on the bed.

They hadn't been told his name; they knew him simply as 'the patient in room 112'. But a nurse had heard him speaking English.

'He must be kept alive, doctor,' whispered the Soviet official who'd been guarding the room since their arrival earlier that day.

The Finnish doctor ignored the remark. Goddamned KGB! He could smell them a mile off.

He grabbed the old man's wrist. No pulse. The trace on the electrocardiograph screen was flat.

'How long?'

'Two, three minutes,' answered the nurse.

The doctor uncoiled cables and placed two electrodes either side of Alex Hitchens' immobile heart, removing the ones connected to the electrocardiograph.

'Stand back,' he instructed, and pressed the switch.

Four times he repeated the process, checking after each shock for some sign that the heart had restarted. There was none.

The ECG was reconnected. The trace stayed flat.

'He's dead,' he announced.

'Not possible,' hissed the Russian guard. 'He has to live!'

The doctor suppressed a desire to seize the Russian by the throat.

'He was half-dead when he arrived here this morning. You gave us no medical records for him. But he had clear signs of heart failure. You must've known that before you brought him here. You knew the risks. He should never have been moved in his condition.'

With that he began to pack up his equipment.

The Finnish nurse looked down at the wrinkled old man, his sunken eyes hidden beneath closed lids. No name. No past. No future. It was sad that anyone should end their days in such anonymity.

Then she noticed something that gave her a certain comfort – a trace of a smile on the old man's thin lips.

* * *

HMS Truculent.

Philip's mind was made up. The decision had come quite suddenly, as if placed in his brain by some outside agency.

His father was dead; he was suddenly certain of it. He'd been dead for years probably, though exactly when it had happened was irrelevant. The 'evidence' that he was alive, which the KGB woman had produced, was fake. The whole scheme was a trick. He knew he had been stupid, but it no longer mattered.

Now the Soviets would pay the price for destroying his father, destroying his marriage and eventually destroying him too. They were going to get what was coming to them.

'*Captain, Control Room!*'

'On my way,' Philip said into the communications box.

He hurried to the control room.

'Two submarine contacts, sir,' Pike told him. 'Both approaching from the west, both appear to be *Victor Threes*.'

On the chart he pointed to the island of Ostrov Chernyy with the underwater spit of sand extending from its northern shore.

'We're four miles from the island itself, two miles from the edge of the shallows. The first contact is five miles behind us on a bearing of three-one-zero. Coming straight at us. Fifteen knots. She may be tracking us, or else getting a steer from an aircraft.'

'Our speed?'

'Seven knots, sir.'

'And the second contact?'

'Less of a threat. Twelve miles distant.'

'Right. Spriggs, over here!' Philip ordered, suddenly sounding decisive and confident. 'We've got to be quick. They could be about to attack. Our task, gentlemen, is to lay three Moray mines close to their submarine lanes. Set the fuses for any submarine target, WEO, but with remote triggering. The mines won't be activated until later – by sonar burst. When, and who by, that'll be up to CINCFLEET. Is that clear?'

Pike hesitated. Spriggs was looking to him for a sign.

'The orders, sir . . . , they specify geographical co-ordinates for the mines? You'll give us the signal you received?'

Philip ground his teeth, determined to keep his nerve.

'The co-ordinates I was given no longer apply,' he snapped. 'It was supposed to be right in the mouth of the Kola Inlet. We'll never get there now. The fall back plan was to place them somewhere else. That's down to me.'

He prodded the chart.

'There. Just on the edge of the shelf, where it rises up towards Ostrov Chernyy. That's where we'll put them.'

In his mind's eye he imagined the spot; a slope of mud and fine sand, 150 metres down; protruding from it – the twisted metal of the old *T-class* boat, *HMS Tenby*. Soon, very soon, two Soviet *Victor* class submarines would be joining that pile of wreckage, if all went well.

'Right, gentlemen. Get on with it. We only have minutes to put those mines on the bottom and get the hell out of here!'

And Philip strode off to the sound room.

'Well?' asked Spriggs.

'Shit! I dunno! They won't be armed when we lay them. He says it'll need further orders.'

Spriggs raised an eyebrow.

'Look. I'm the one that'll get the chop if I'm wrong!' Pike reasoned. 'It's not the moment, Paul. We just haven't got enough evidence for me to relieve him. You'd better get the mines ready!'

* * *

HMS Tenby.

'Target's altered course, sir,' called Lieutenant Algy Colqhoun. 'He's heading for the shelf north of Ostrov Chernyy.'

'Christ!' breathed Andrew. 'The moment of truth! He's going to bloody give them the mine!'

'I'll proceed with the firing sequence?' Biddle suggested.

'Yes, but hold the final order,' Andrew told him.

'*Open bow caps!*' the WEO ordered the weapons compartment crew below.

Andrew looked hard at the AI plot. *Truculent* was five miles ahead. Too far for the underwater telephone.

'That *Victor*'s after us, Peter. Eight miles astern. We've not fooled her with our decoy. All we've done is given her something loud enough to track.'

'Dump the decoy!' Biddle shouted, swinging himself into the bandstand. 'Let it swim right here!'

He glanced rapidly at the plot.

'Starboard ten. Steer zero-nine-zero. Standby to fire!'

They were turning away from the decoy, weaving, almost certain the Soviet boat wouldn't detect them.

So, Philip was going to do it – betray his country – hand over technology that could be ten years ahead of anything the Soviets had.

A Hammerfish torpedo would take just four minutes to reach the *Truculent*. There was a chance, just a chance he could use it to stop the mine-laying and still let the hundred men on board survive.

'Get the bloody thing into the water!' he barked to Biddle.

The CO gave thc order.

'Fire!'

From the nose of the submarine the Hammerfish shot forward, propelled by its miniature gas turbine. Trailing behind, a thin wire linked it to the submarine.

The weapons controller had his eyes glued to his screen. The target was at the centre; a green symbol approaching it from below was the torpedo. Guidance was from the submarine's bow sonar to start with, but shortly the weapon's own sensors would begin to track the target.

Andrew hovered at his shoulder.

'When the range is down to two-hundred metres, and the high-definition sonar goes active, we're going to have to move bloody fast,' Andrew warned. 'If we get it wrong, all the men in that boat are dead.'

The operator swallowed hard, hand hovering over the joystick that would guide the torpedo on its last few metres of flight.

* * *

HMS Truculent.

'*Torpedo! Torpedo! Torpedo! Torpedo bearing red one-five-zero! True bearing two-nine-five!*'

'Shit!' Pike hissed.

'Starboard thirty! Steer two-nine-five! Ready the mines!' Philip bellowed.

'Only one mine ready in the tube, sir!' Spriggs called.

The control room heeled over as the submarine turned on its tail to face the threat.

'Fire a decoy!'

Forward of the control room a rating slipped a Bandfish decoy into a launch tube and tugged at the lever that propelled it into the sea. The cylinder of electronics hovered in the water emitting a high intensity signal to lure the torpedo.

'Course two-nine-five, sir,' Cavendish called as the boat settled onto the new heading.

'Are we tracking the bastard who's firing at us?'

'Bit confused, sir. Thought it was the *Victor Three*, but the transients of the bow caps and torpedo launch came from a different bearing.'

'Lay the mine!'

The forward weapons compartment reverberated to the thunder of compressed air, blasting the Moray mine out of the torpedo tube. It began to sink towards the sea-bed one hundred metres below.

'Torpedo's gone active, sir!'

'Give me a firing solution, sonar, for Christ's sake!' Philip screamed, clinging to the bandstand.

'Torpedo's sonar's classified as a fucking Hammerfish, sir!' came a yell of astonishment from the sound room.

Philip froze.

'Oh, my God! What have I done?'

* * *

HMS Tenby.

'Three hundred yards to the target, sir!' announced the weapons operator. 'The passive system's swamped by decoy noise, but the active's burning through it!'

'Just heard the target launch something from a tube, sir!' yelled the sound room.

'Two hundred yards! High-definition sonar now active, sir.'

'Make it look down! Below the bows,' Andrew hissed in the operator's ear. 'Track what's just come from the tube!'

'If it's a torpedo it'll be gone, sir,' the rating grumbled.

'It's a mine! Just try and track it,' Andrew ordered.

The weapon controller dived the Hammerfish towards the sea-bed. He'd never done this before.

'Got it, sir. Small object, dropping.'

'Spot on! Just one? Sound room! Anything from the other tubes?'

'Nothing detected, sir!'

'Fifty yards, sir. Do we hit the mine?'

'Yes. Blow the fucker to pieces!'

* * *

HMS Truculent.

Inside *Truculent*, the double explosion boomed with a terrifying resonance. The blast wave lifted the bows and tossed the boat sideways.

In the control room ratings and officers crashed to the deck. Paul Spriggs gashed his forehead as he fell, blood trickling into his eye.

Tim Pike grabbed the edge of the bandstand and pulled himself to his feet.

'Oh, God! Oh, God!'

Eyes closed, the captain was gibbering meaninglessly, his mind a tortured jumble.

The moment had come.

'I have command!' Pike shouted. 'Damage reports!'

Peter Claypole pressed the key on the ship control panel that linked him with the manoeuvring room, aft. He listened, then reassured the first lieutenant.

'No problems with propulsion.'

'Casualties in the weapons compartment!' called Spriggs, pressing a handkerchief to his forehead. 'I'm going down there.'

'Starboard twenty. Steer zero-one-zero! Revolutions for maximum speed,' Pike ordered. 'Nick, give me a safe depth.'

'Two hundred metres for five miles. Then come up to one twenty.'

'Ten down. Keep two hundred metres. TAS, what are the contacts doing?'

'Closing,' Cordell replied. 'Nearest at four miles, now

classified as *Trafalgar* class. Closest *Victor*'s disappeared. Guess it must've been a decoy. Lost track of the other *Victor*. We've a firing solution on the *Trafalgar*.'

'You must be joking! What the hell was he doing firing at us, anyway? And where the fuck's the C.O.?'

The bandstand was empty. Hitchens had gone.

'Hugo,' Pike shouted, spotting the radio officer. 'Find the captain. He's not well. Get him back to his cabin and stay with him. Get a steward to help if you need to.'

* * *

HMS Tenby.

Even four miles away the double detonation of the torpedo and the mine was heard through the hull.

'Bloody well done!' Andrew clapped the weapons operator on the shoulder.

He turned to a grinning Peter Biddle.

'Let's hope Pike's got the message by now. What's the *Truc* doing, TAS?'

'Moving. Fast. Heading north, thirty knots.'

'We do the same? Right?' Biddle checked.

'Right. And keep close. When we're clear of danger I'm going to have a few words with Phil Hitchens on the underwater telephone.'

* * *

Severomorsk.

The operations room of the Soviet Northern Fleet was electrified.

The four helicopters hovering over the waters round Ostrov Chernyy reported the explosions within seconds of each other. Using passive sonar transducers, only one had been close enough to the *Truculent* to hear her bow caps open and the mine being expelled.

Admiral Belikov frowned. They didn't match. The contact discovered by the helicopter and the one the *Ladny* had been following – they were too far apart to be one and the same.

Two foreign submarines? Had the second boat come to

try to stop Commander Hitchens betraying his country? Had the *Truculent* been sunk?

'Tell them to go active. Search the area thoroughly. Put out a general signal to look for foreign submarines. There may be several boats, with the ability to make themselves sound like our own.'

The Captain Lieutenant hastened to relay the order. Using active sonar in the shallow water round Ostov Chernyy would not be easy; reflections from the uneven seabed could make the readings unintelligible.

Decoys. Of course! Belikov snapped his pudgy fingers. The explosions could be a decoy too. To make them concentrate their search round Ostrov Chernyy, while the submarines headed elsewhere! Inshore? To the mouth of the Kol'skiy Zaliv? To lay the new mines where they could do most damage, just outside the main submarine bases? It made sense.

And who would be waiting for them? Felix Astashenkov – ready to claim the military and political glory of destroying the foreign intruder.

Belikov fumed at the thought.

'Send a coded signal to the *Ladny*,' he ordered the Captain Lieutenant. 'Tell her to head inshore fast. I believe the British boats are making for Polyarny.'

* * *

Ametyst.

'The sonar computer puts the explosions at fifteen kilometres northeast of here, Comrade Vice-Admiral,' announced Captain 2nd Rank Yury Makhov.

Mines. And they'd found a target. Feliks had misjudged it. He'd thought the only place the *Truculent* would lay them would be the mouth of the Kol'skiy Zaliv. He'd been fatally wrong.

'The sonar has no submarine contacts yet?'

'Regrettably not, Vice-Admiral. We'll need to be close to a *Trafalgar* to hear her.'

'Then we must close the gap, Yury. Ten minutes at maximum speed will bring us near.'

Makhov disliked driving his vessel fast in inshore

waters, making his sonar deaf. But he could see the anxiety on Astashenkov's face.

'I share your determination. We'll have our revenge on the Englishman!'

He ordered the reactors to maximum power. Imperceptibly the 7,600 ton leviathan began to accelerate to 45 knots.

* * *

HMS Tenby.

'Ten up. Keep one-hundred-and-twenty-five metres, revolutions for fifteen knots!' Biddle directed. They were slowing down to listen, desperate to know what had happened on the *Truculent*.

'Contact bearing zero-four-five. *Trafalgar* class, sir!' the sonar CPO announced. 'Range. . . .'

He waited the few seconds it took the computer to calculate it.

'Two-point-seven nautical miles, sir. No other surface or sub-surface contacts registered.'

'Right. This is it.'

Andrew lifted the handset of the underwater telephone.

'British submarine, British submarine! This is your sister vessel speaking. I am Commander Andrew Tinker. Do you hear me, over?'

HMS Truculent.

Tim Pike spun round, thunderstruck by the voice that suddenly crackled from the loudspeaker. He grabbed the handset.

'I hear you clearly, sir. This is the first lieutenant speaking, Lieutenant Commander Pike. Over.'

There was a lapse of a few seconds before the reply reached through the water.

'Listen carefully, Tim. Commander Hitchens is unwell. You must take command of the boat immediately. I repeat. You must assume command. That is an order from CINCFLEET. Understood? Over.'

Pike felt his shoulders sag with relief.

'I've already taken command, sir. Repeat. I am now in command. Commander Hitchens is being attended to in his cabin. Over.'

Again, a pause for the reply.

'Good news. Give him a message from me, will you? Tell him not to worry. His problems can be sorted out. Tell him I'll help him when we get back home. Now. Get well clear, and when it's safe call CINCFLEET. Over.'

'We have an emergency on board, sir,' Pike continued. 'Two men badly injured. Legs crushed by a torpedo dis-loged by the explosion. Over.'

'Sorry about that. Better try to get them ashore in Norway. Tell CINCFLEET to organize it. See you in Devonport. Out.'

Tim Pike replaced the handset.

'Clear the datum!' he called. They had to move fast. The Soviets were bound to have heard their conversation.

'TAS. Take control. I'm going to see the captain.'

So, they'd been right about Hitchens all along. The man had thrown a loop. CINCFLEET must have known it soon after they'd left port. Had to send a bloody submar-ine to get the message through!

He shuddered to think what Tinker had intended when he'd launched that torpedo at them. Had he meant to hit the Moray mine, or had *Truculent* herself been the target?

In the flush of relief that they'd survived, the anger he'd suppressed for days began to boil over.

Hitchens had been happy to risk all their lives in pursuit of some crazy plan of his own. The bastard!

Sub. Lieutenant Hugo Smallbone stood at ease outside the captain's cabin.

'He told me to get out,' Hugo whispered, tapping the tip of a finger against his temple.

Pike pushed into the cabin. The captain's face was like a cast, devoid of emotion.

'There's a message for you, sir. From Commander Tinker.'

Suddenly Pike saw the mask crack. At the mention of the name, Philip's lips began to tremble; a tic set his eyes blinking.

'Said you weren't to worry, sir. He'll help you sort things out when we get home.'

Philip clenched his eyelids to stop their movement. Pike's voice echoed inside his head.

Andrew? Out here? *Andrew* had come after him? The man Sara had named as the first of her string of lovers? *Andrew*, who'd betrayed nearly twenty years of friendship by seducing his wife and setting her on the path to ruin? How could this be the man they'd sent?

'*He'll help you sort things out when we get home.*' What a mockery! *God*, how patronizing!

'Sir? Sir, are you all right?'

Pike's voice was agitated.

'You're suffering from shock, sir. I'll get the medical assistant to give you something. Just hang on, sir.'

Alarmed at Philip's uncontrollable shaking, Pike hurried to find the steward who'd done a first-aid course. He remembered where he was; he would be attending to the two men with crushed legs in the torpedo compartment.

He clattered down the ladder to the deck below.

'Where's the MA? Quick, get up here with your bag of goodies. Something to sedate the Captain.'

Suddenly Pike heard Hugo Smallbone bellowing for him.

'The captain's gone! Just rushed past me. I thought he was going to the heads. . . .'

Suddenly an alarm bell sounded.

'The forward escape hatch!' Pike yelled and hurled himself along the corridor.

In the escape chamber, the lower hatch was closed, a red light flashing to warn that the chamber was flooding.

Pike wrenched at the hatch. It crashed open, icy sea water drenching down onto the deck. Pike fought his way up through the torrent, gasping for breath. He seized Philip's legs and both men crashed down onto the deck, choking.

The medical assistant and Hugo Smallbone dragged Hitchens to one side so that Pike could get back into the tower. Water streaming past him, he reached up, and fumbled for the flood valve to shut it off.

Soaked and shivering he collapsed onto the deck, water swilling away into the drains that led to the bilges.

'Jesus!' he panted. 'Jesus Christ!'

* * *

Neither the *Ametyst* nor the *Ladny* was aware of the other's presence, both deafened by the speed at which they were moving. Their two captains had a single aim; to find the British submarine before it could lay more mines.

The *Ladny* had been ordered to head inshore, the *Ametyst* was bound for the open sea.

The collision came at a combined underwater speed of 72 knots.

The *Ladny* struck the *Ametyst* aft of the forward planes. The protective outer casings of the two vessels crumpled like paper, until the pressure hulls struck with a terrible wrenching of steel and an explosion of escaping air.

The forward weapon compartment of the *Ladny* telescoped, then split open like an egg dropped on concrete, spewing men and oil into the black water. The section of the *Ametyst* ahead of the fin was torn away by the impact. Exploding electrical circuitry jolted the foreshortened hull nose-up, allowing air to escape in a seething column to the surface.

Water surged down through the control and accommodation spaces, stopping only at the watertight hatches through the reactor compartment. Battered and disorientated by the violent movement, the men had no time to don escape masks. Within minutes, more than half the crew had drowned – amongst them Vice-Admiral Feliks Astashenkov.

Devoid of buoyancy, the forward section fell towards the sea-bed fifty metres below, propelled by the still-rotating screw. The aft section of her hull lifted up by the air trapped in it, the *Ametyst* began to somersault.

The safety systems in the two reactors tripped as the hull passed through the critical angle, but it was too late. The hull inverted. Steam percolated back into the reactor pressure vessel, replacing the water which moderated the nuclear reaction. Deprived of coolant, the temperature in the core began to rise. By the time the broken nose of the hull buried itself in the mud of the sea-bed the core was melting.

On the *Ladny*, too, there were no survivors forward of the reactor section. The boat sank to the sea-bed, nose-down, but upright. The engineering crew aft succeeded in scramming the reactors; control rods dropped into the core to absorb the neutron flow and damp down the reaction. Then panic set in.

One hundred metres separated the two wrecks on the bottom. The heat in *Ametyst*'s reactors climbed fast. The molten core burned through the steel of the reactor compartment, then through the hull itself. Ice-cold water surged in and exploded into steam.

The detonation of the reactor compartment released a tidal wave of energy, scattering the shreds of the *Ametyst* like sea-weed, and knocking the *Ladny* onto its side.

* * *

HMS Tenby.

The sounds of the collision, the ripping of metal, and the explosions that followed were heard by the two British submarines twenty miles to the north.

Andrew took the headphones from the sonar rating in the sound room and listened to the brain-curdling racket.

'Where's it coming from, for God's sake?' he asked, suddenly scared that Philip could have laid other mines earlier.

'Bearing one-nine-five, sir. Range twenty miles.'

Andrew hurried to the navigation plot, and picked up the dividers. He measured the distance onto the chart.

'Five miles north of the inlet. Not guilty. *Truculent* never got that far south.'

'It's that *Victor III*,' announced Colqhoun. 'She was sprinting. We tracked her all the way in. Look, it's on disc.'

'Play it back, CPO.'

The sonar chief cued the disc and directed Andrew to the VDU. The phosphor-green wave pattern began to spread up the screen.

'That's the *Victor III*, sir,' explained the chief, pointing to a ridge on the waterfall pattern at the frequency generated by vibration from the Soviet submarine's pumps.

'And what's that next to it?' Andrew asked.

'Just an echo, sir. Shallow water.'

'Couldn't it be another boat?' Andrew pressed.

The CPO keyed the target information into a window on the screen.

'Same bearing, sir. Just an echo.'

'But if there were two boats, and they collided. . . .'

'See what you mean, sir.'

'Spin back five minutes on the disc.'

It took a few seconds.

The chief keyed instructions for the computer to analyse the tracks.

'You're dead right, sir. They were on different bearings.'

Andrew folded his arms. For two Soviet vessels, the submariners' nightmare had come true. A collision at speed.

Peter Biddle appeared at his shoulder.

'We've got to get a signal off fast,' Andrew announced. 'Before the Russians accuse *us* of sinking their boats.'

CHAPTER ELEVEN

Wednesday late.

Journalists in London and Washington were invited at short notice to special briefings at Downing Street and the White House respectively.

They were told the British and US governments had received irrefutable intelligence information that two Soviet submarines had collided accidentally earlier that day, with heavy loss of life. American spy satellites had picked up extensive radio traffic emanating from the major rescue operation the Soviet Navy was mounting.

When asked why they were releasing the information in such an unprecedented manner, the press were told that it was to forestall any attempt the Soviets might make to blame the incident on the West, and more particularly on the NATO exercise Ocean Guardian.

The story made the lead on late-night television news bulletins and would form the splash headline in the newspapers the following morning.

* * *

Moscow. Midnight.

The telephoned report from Admiral Grekov was not the one Nikolai Savkin had expected. The disaster stunned him.

Couldn't it have been NATO mines that had been responsible, he'd asked? Grekov had been adamant. A collision. They'd used the word on open communications. They'd had to; most of the rescue and pollution control vessels had no encrypted communications systems.

Incompetence was the cause, Grekov had insisted. The real culprit was whoever had instructed Feliks Astashenkov to defy orders and take the *Ametyst* to sea.

From the bitter note of recrimination in Grekov's voice, Savkin knew that he knew.

He sat slumped in his chair, in the dimly-lit sitting-room of his Kremlin apartment. Who would they send, he wondered?

An hour had passed since Grekov's call. Then there came a gentle tap on the door.

'Ah, it's you, Vasily,' Savkin sighed with relief at the sight of his Foreign Minister and friend. 'Thank . . .'

His voice caught in his throat as KGB chief Medvedev followed Kalinin into the room.

'There was a meeting earlier this evening,' Kalinin began, unsmiling. 'The vote went against you. You no longer have a majority in the Politburo.'

'Who was it? Which one changed his mind?'

Kalinin dropped his eyes.

'You?' Savkin whispered incredulously.

'It's been too much for you, Nikolai,' Kalinin explained. 'Your sense of judgement . . .' He shook his head sadly. 'And when we learned what happened tonight . . .'

Medvedev stepped forward.

'Comrade Savkin, I must ask you to come with me . . .'

The President of the Soviet Union stared wildly at the two men.

'You could resign on grounds of ill health, Nikolai.' Kalinin added, softly, 'It would be best.'

'Out of the question. We'll meet tomorrow. There'll be another vote.'

'Too late. Your successor's been chosen.'

Savkin gasped.

'What? Who?'

This time Kalinin held his gaze steady.

'It was unanimous. They all insisted it should be me.'

Savkin gripped his shoulders.

'How long have you been planning this, Vasily?'

'The experiment has failed. Our people cannot handle "freedom". We must put the shackles back on. It's the only way if the Union is not to disintegrate. Control from the centre. It'll be better this time. No corruption. More efficiency. We've learnt lessons from *perestròika*, lessons that can never be unlearned.'

Nikolai Savkin turned away, his heart heavy with guilt and sadness.

It had all been in vain. Admiral Astashenkov and the other men who'd died in the submarines had perished to no purpose. If anything, their deaths had now compounded the nation's troubles.

It was over. The collective leadership of the Soviet Union had decided to turn its back on the future.

* * *

Thursday 24th October.

Helsinki.

A small van with Soviet plates drew up to the rear entrance of the clinic, so that the plain wooden box could be slid inside.

The staff at the hospital never knew the name of the man who'd died there the previous day. He'd just been a case number. Now the body was being taken away; the file could be closed.

The van left the city, heading east. It was nearly two hundred kilometres to the Soviet border.

The KGB driver looked at his watch, then pressed his foot to the floor. He'd have to hurry.

Once over the border, there were still another fifty kilometres to drive to deliver the wooden box to the incineration plant.

* * *

Friday 25th October.

The Norwegian Sea.

A two-man Medevac team from the *USS Eisenhower* was lowered by wire from an SH-3 Sea King onto the forward casing of *HMS Truculent*.

They were led down through the forward hatch to the sick bay. The two men whose legs had been crushed in the torpedo compartment were in a bad way. The Royal

Navy medical assistant had done well, but the men needed urgent surgery and intensive care.

Gently they strapped the casualties into stretchers, then organized a team of ratings to lift them through the hatch onto the casing.

Hitchens was groggy from continuous heavy sedation. Tim Pike took his arm and helped him out into the open air.

Anxiously Tim watched him lifted off the casing, the strop held tightly under his arm-pits, arms limply at his sides, until the helicopter crew-chief pulled him backwards into the airframe next to the two stretchers.

They'd feared the commander would try another suicide attempt, and had thought it too risky to lift him off by helicopter, but he'd reassured them. He no longer wanted to die. It was time to get home, to try to sort out the mess.

Andrew was already on the windswept deck of the *Eisenhower* when the helicopter landed. He dreaded Philip's arrival. Pike had sent a signal from *Truculent* warning that after his attempt to kill himself, Philip had raved incoherently, naming Andrew as the man responsible for his troubles.

Andrew could guess what that was all about. Sara. She must have told Philip about their brief affair. Could he explain it to him? Hardly. Probably better to try to convince him it was untrue.

He'd also have to break the news to him that Sara was dead.

* * *

Late Afternoon.

RAF Northolt.

The US Navy Grumman Greyhound approached the runway from the west, skimming low over the dense line of commuter traffic heading home from London at the end of the day.

Philip had made no attempt at conversation during the flight. He'd been glad of the deafening noise that made communication almost impossible. Also, it meant Andrew hadn't been able to hear him when he wept.

When the machine had come to a halt, they removed their survival suits, and walked down the loading ramp into the mild, autumn air.

'Ah. I can see Patsy,' said Andrew raising his arm to acknowledge her wave. She was waiting in front of the old pre-fabricated terminal building. Behind her stood two broad-shouldered men; Andrew assumed they were from Security, waiting for Philip. He could also see the squat figure of Admiral Bourlet and, with Patsy's arm round him, a schoolboy, rather small for his thirteen years.

'Isn't that Simon?'

'Yes,' Philip gulped. 'What am I going to say . . . ?'

'We'll help. Don't worry.'

Patsy rushed forward and flung her arms round Andrew's neck.

'Thank God!' she breathed in his ear. 'The Admiral's told me what you've been up to. Promise me you'll never do it again?'

'Congratulations, Andrew,' Bourlet rumbled. 'Bloody well done!'

Then, uncomfortably, they all turned to the lone figure of Philip.

He was staring at his son, spellbound. Just for a fleeting moment he'd seen himself, thirty years earlier.

In the boy's eyes he recognized the same fear he'd felt whenever his own father had gone away, the fear of being left alone to face the world, unprepared.

Suddenly Simon ran forwards, face crumpling as emotion overwhelmed him.

'Dad . . .' the boy sobbed.

Philip hugged him into silence.

'Hullo, son,' he whispered. 'I'm home.'

[illegible]

[illegible]

[illegible]

"[illegible] What are you going to say."

"Well, Dad, what?"

[illegible]

"Thank God, [illegible]"

[illegible]

[illegible] of Jane.

[illegible]

[illegible]

[illegible]

Suddenly [illegible]

"Dad [illegible]"

[illegible]

"He [illegible]"